RHYS
OF
QUADRANT
SIX

The Falkrow Narratives
Book II

Kara D. Wilson

Rhys of Quadrant Six
The Falkrow Narratives, Book II

OTHER WORKS BY KARA D. WILSON

The Aurora Chronicles
The Empress' Consul
The Raven's Sister
The Assassin's Apprentice
The Emperor's Raven
The Dragon's Son

The Falkrow Narratives
Rhys of Earth
Rhys of Quadrant Six
Ronan of Space

Cardinal Zero

Breach Effect

Unbound

To Young Future Writers

Do what you love.
Practice it, breathe it, live it.

1
THE RESISTANCE

"BLACK BIRD, WHAT'S YOUR POSITION? Over."

The radio in Rhys' hand crackled as Kashim replied, "Target acquired. Waiting for go-ahead."

Rhys glanced through the myriad of trees at the purple, twilight sky before exchanging looks with Leo. The Brechin noble peered over the mound of dense foliage behind which they hid, frowning. "It's too early," Leo murmured. "Not yet."

Rhys pulled the night-vision goggles dangling around his neck onto his eyes and studied the dark, two-story Pantarak temple which had been seized by Brechin soldiers days prior. Though one of many in the small town of Paducah, the temple's location offered optimal cover for the invading Brechin forces and convenient access to the rest of the town. Offset from the main thoroughfare, there was plenty of room for supplies and solar-powered vehicles.

"Blue Point, where are you?" asked Rhys. There was a long moment of silence. "Blue Point, answer. Over." Again, silence. "Hodge!"

The radio hummed to life. "Don't use my name!" Hodge hissed.

"Then answer next time. Where are you?"

"We're leaving the ruins. Couldn't pull the kid away. Give us ten minutes. Over."

"Stay low but hurry," replied Rhys.

"We're moving in," came a new voice over the radio.

"Wait, Nayan—I mean, Orange Guard. Don't," Rhys warned. No one answered. "Orange Guard, do *not* engage until the team is set. I repeat, do *not* enga—"

Gunfire broke out in the forest, and a cacophony of screeching war cries filled the air. Both Rhys and Leo rolled facedown into the ground in preparation for what was to come. "I told you we shouldn't trust them," Leo panted into the dirt.

Rhys slid the radio to his mouth. "Black Bird, fire at will. Black Bird, fire at will." A loud *thwack* reverberated through the treetop canopy as Kashim began sniping the Brechin military officers. "Blue Point, go to your coordinates and wait for the signal. Over."

Pulling his short rifle to his chest, Leo scrambled to a nearby tree for cover. Rhys followed his lead and knelt behind a larger arboreal specimen, firearm ready. With a deep, calming breath, he peered around his cover. It was the resistance group's job to drive out the Brechin commanders from their temple stronghold. Rhys, Leo, and Kashim were to keep the Brechin officials from escaping into town and alerting their troops. Of course, who wouldn't hear the absolute ruckus that filled the forest?

For several long moments, not a single body exited the temple. It seemed the Paducah resistance group was doing its job admirably. Rhys adjusted his goggles with a push of his shoulder and scanned the eerie green darkness for escaping officers.

"Rhys," whispered Leo, redirecting his attention to a cellar hatch opening along the east side of the temple.

"Don't do anything yet," replied Rhys over the dying gunfire. It sounded as though the resistance group was running out of targets. "We need them to come out." All the commanders needed to leave the temple. A single shot would discourage them and send them back into hiding.

Rhys and Leo stole themselves in the deepening darkness of the night, watching through night-vision goggles as four officers crawled from the cellar doors into the open air.

"Now," whispered Rhys. It took but a handful of well-aimed shots to still the Brechin soldiers. Breathing hard, he and Leo stood in silence, listening. Distantly calls of "all clear" from one resistance group member to another wafted from the temple.

Rhys' radio crackled. "All clear," Nayan, the resistance group's leader, announced.

Rhys breathed out in relief. "Black Bird, what do you see?"

"Temple is clear," replied Kashim.

"Blue Point, where are you?" Rhys let his rifle hang around his neck.

"Just arriving at the designated location," replied Hodge. "Give us a minute, over."

"Black Bird, how does the south road look?" asked Rhys.

"There's movement in town. Troops are gathering," reported Kashim.

"Blue Point, on the mark, detonate. Understood?" Rhys reminded. There was silence. "Hodge!"

"Yes, yes! I got it!" replied Hodge. "On the mark."

Rhys squinted at the temple in search of Nayan and his cohorts. "Orange Guard, return to rendezvous. Prepare for retreat."

"Understood," replied Nayan.

Rhys motioned to Leo. "Let's go." Knowing they didn't have much time, they took off at a sprint through the forest due east. They needed to put some distance between themselves and the road leading to the temple.

"What if they don't go off?" huffed Leo.

"They'll go off," Rhys assured, though he doubted his words. While their weapons were Brechin-made, the explosives that they had purchased at the black market, were not. "Let's go, let's go," he urged.

"Blue Point, now!" Kashim commanded over the radio. There was a moment of silence before the dark forest was illuminated by the crimson light of fire as the explosives they had buried along the southern road detonated.

"Leo," shouted Rhys, dragging the Brechin noble to the ground. A split second later, the shockwave hit them, pounding them into the earth, shaking their bodies, and smashing the air from their lungs. Rhys curled into the fetal position and covered his head and ears. He could feel Leo beside him doing the same. Another blast from farther in town blasted through the forest as a second line of explosives erupted.

Rhys looked over his shoulder at the raging blaze that now engulfed the trees along the road. His ears rang; his heart pounded in his chest. His hands were both sweaty and cold.

"Mission complete," confirmed Kashim over the radio.

Rhys rubbed his right ear which seemed to be completely deaf and then pulled the radio to his mouth. "All teams, go to the agreed-upon location. Over." He returned the radio to the clip at his waist. "You hurt?" he asked of Leo.

"No," grumbled Leo.

"Come on. We have a long hike ahead of us."

It took nearly an hour to reach the rendezvous location, a cluster of boulders gathered along the forest edge nearly three kilometers east. When they arrived, only Kashim was present.

"The others?" asked Rhys, leaning against a weak sampling and looking out at the arid desert that stretched into infinity.

"Haven't heard from them," replied the large man, shifting his sniper rifle on his massive shoulder. He was already an intimidating individual during the day, but dressed in all black, dripping with weapons, and skin painted with anti-focal paste to avoid detection by night-vision goggles and heat sensors, Kashim appeared as a horrible god of war. "Those resistance boys need to be taught patience."

"Agreed," murmured Rhys. Although it seemed the mission had been a success, he was livid with Nayan and his group of Paducah-native resistance fighters. Things could have turned out much worse; they had been lucky.

"You know we just blew up nearly half our money reserves, right?" Leo gloomily supplied. The Brechin noble sat heavily on the ground and folded his legs around his rifle. Like Kashim, he too was dressed in black and wore anti-focal paste on his skin. The only piece of him that stood out was the pale gold streaks that decorated the short mohawk atop his head and the charcoal earring which he sported on his left ear.

"I am aware," replied Rhys. He glanced about the area before sitting beside Leo. He was tired. He had been disseminating orders for two days and planning for five. Sleep had not been high on his priority list. Sensing Kashim's gaze on him, Rhys peered up at the burly man. "What?"

"We're going to need money if we're going to continue this rebellion."

Rhys sighed. "Again, I am aware."

Ten minutes passed before Hodge's team joined them from the shadows. Rhys' friend promptly sprawled out beside him in the dirt. "We're here," Hodge groaned. Those in his group—Kallen, Otto, and Jules—gathered around.

"Any problems getting back?" asked Rhys, looking between Hodge, his best friend, and Kallen, his mate.

"None," replied Kallen, nudging her night-vision goggles back onto the bridge of her nose. Like Hodge and Kashim, she too carried with her an array of weapons, as well as a small backpack of tools. Her hair was pulled back by a bandana. "Sorry we were slow getting there." She motioned to Otto, one of the crew's newcomers. "We couldn't pull him from the ruins."

"They were *ruins*," argued Otto, setting down his enormous backpack. "I could have *just* picked up something that will make us thousands on the black market."

Otto was thin, just shy of lean. They had met the junk dealer on Firekli's docks as he tried to sell them horribly-repaired solar panels. Though he denied it, Rhys was sure Otto was a former Pantarak. In the underdeveloped Pantarak towns and villages, religious devotion was exhibited by men through the act of shaving and tattooing the skull. While Otto had a full head of curly, black hair, every so often Rhys caught a glance of what appeared to be tattoo markings at the nape of his neck and along his temple.

The crew's other new team member, Jules, was a completely different story. Like Kashim, the man exuded danger. From what he had told Rhys, Jules was a former hired gun and went where there was money. He was tall and built like a tree with long arms and strong legs. He was curt and usually wore several days' scruff on his strong face. In his early forties, he was one of the oldest on Rhys' team which was both advantageous and dangerous. The man had wisdom and experience that came with age. Already, he had proven his worth to Rhys. However, Jules was a double-edged sword. He was just as likely to argue or resist Rhys' orders as he was to obey them. Rhys never knew when Jules was going to publicly condemn his ideas and undermine his power.

"Where are the kids?" asked Jules after solemnly glancing about the rendezvous area.

"Not here yet," replied Kashim.

Jules looked at Rhys. "They could have gotten you killed."

"Yes, I know." Rhys rose to his feet. "I'm going to be having a word with them—"

"Who?" interrupted a new voice. "Us?"

Night-vision goggles still activated, Rhys turned to meet Nayan and his band of resistance fighters. "Where are the others?" Rhys queried, taking note of the smaller group. Out of the seventeen men that had begun the mission, only six stood before him. "Were there casualties?"

"No, no casualties," replied Nayan smugly. "Two injured, but that's not a bad tradeoff for eight officers."

"There were twelve," corrected Kashim.

"You handled the rest though," said Nayan. Rhys studied him, trying to determine how best to scold his disobedience. Like the other resistance fighters, Nayan was tall and bald, his skull decorated with intricate black tattoos. He wore nothing but a pair of red slacks; his feet were bare. Each of the resistance fighters carried only a single gun.

"You didn't answer my question," said Rhys. "Where are the others?"

"We appreciate you coming to help us fight, but we don't need your help," said Nayan, motioning between Rhys and the others. "We've been fighting Brechin's troops for—"

"Paducah is in dire need of help," Rhys interrupted. "Without us, you would never have even gotten your hands on weapons. You would have died in a flurry of bullets."

"And joined our brothers and the white gods in the stars," Nayan confidently countered. "Like I said, we appreciate your help, but we can handle it from here." The resistance fighter and his posse disappeared into the forest.

"I'm glad they aren't coming with us," Hodge muttered.

"Come on," said Rhys tiredly.

It was a half-hour walk from the desert through the forest and another hour hike down the coast to the inlet on the other side of Paducah's landmass. Though the trek was exhausting, the safety of their ships was paramount. Stationing them outside of the enemy's radar was their first line of defense against attack.

It was after midnight before Rhys staggered onto the bridge of *Themis*. Kallen, Otto, and Kashim followed; Hodge and Jules returned to *Grisle* which was anchored nearby.

"Well?" asked Andy, the ship's First Mate.

"It was a success," Rhys sighed. He pulled off the night-vision goggles perched atop his head. "We'll have to wait until tomorrow to see the damage we've actually done." Rhys saw Andy exchange looks with Kallen. "Weigh anchor. Take us out a ways and prep us for the night."

"Will do." Andy maneuvered around his chair and started *Themis'* engines.

Rhys pulled his radio from his belt to speak with *Grisle's* crew. "Hodge, we're leaving the inlet. Tell Terron to follow and keep close."

"Right," replied Hodge. Rhys frowned. He didn't like being separated from his friend, but it was necessary. He had placed Hodge on the other ship to keep peace, specifically between Jules and Terron.

A heavy hand on Rhys' shoulder startled him from his thoughts, and he looked back at Kashim. "Go rest," the large man murmured. "We've got this."

Rhys handed Kashim his rifle and emergency ammo. "I'm fine. We still have to anchor for the night." Rhys saw Kashim exchange looks with Kallen before disappearing from the bridge; Otto followed him out.

True to his word, Rhys waited until they were settled for the night. Afterward, he bathed and retired to the Overseer's cabin. Wearily, he lay down on the bed and gazed at the ceiling.

They had killed more people tonight. *He* had killed more people tonight.

2
OVERSEER

THOUGH HE HAD INTENDED TO sleep through the night, Rhys woke a few hours later. He paced his quarters before going to the bridge. Andy, who was on shift, looked up from his book as Rhys plopped onto the Overseer's chair.

"Any news?" murmured Rhys.

"It's been quiet." Andy closed his book and sighed. "You made it longer than usual tonight. Almost four hours of sleep."

Rhys scoffed quietly. "Wonderful…"

Andy regarded the bridge paneling. "You know, we need more people. Otto and Jules are a good start, but both of our ships are nothing but skeletons."

"You have a recommendation?"

"New Arbroath. It might solve not only our crew member problem but our money problem. According to Cantia, we have another two weeks or so before our funds run dry."

"You think the city will give us money?" Rhys lowered his voice. "Even though Vinz is no longer in command?"

"We're essentially doing what was asked of us," replied Andy, "just under different pretenses."

Rhys nodded solemnly. His First Mate was right, of course. Perhaps Joss, the judge of New Arbroath and *Themis'* primary investor, would be willing to extend a substantial amount of funds to them, assuming Rhys could provide evidence of their conquests in Brechin and Paducah. The judge had, after all, commanded that the crew of *Themis* 'put a dent in the Pantarak population.' Unfortunately, the last time Rhys had been in New

Arbroath was nearly nine months ago and even then, he and Joss had not seen eye-to-eye.

"I guarantee we'll find more crew members there."

Rhys threw a leg over the side of his chair. "We'll see what dawn brings us and decide then. I am not disenchanted with the idea of going to New Arbroath, but I don't want to leave matters unfinished here."

His First Mate thought for a moment and then said with some hesitancy, "I honestly think Paducah is a lost cause. We came in too late to the game. It took too much time to repair *Themis*. That two months we spent in Firekli…"

"I know, but…" Rhys rubbed his aching eyes. He was exhausted, but sleep was truly unattainable for him. "If we withdraw now, we are leaving hundreds of men, women, and children to the Brechin forces."

"Once there's light, we can determine how much damage we did and go from there." Andy must have seen the dissatisfaction on Rhys' face because he added, "We can only do so much, Rhys. What we've accomplished within the past few months is nothing short of miraculous. We've managed to repair our horribly mangled ship, gain two crew members, complete two bodyguard assignments and one contraband transport in Firekli, travel to Paducah, destroy a handful of their ships, join forces with the resistance fighters—"

"Yes, we've done a lot," interrupted Rhys. He shifted his heavy gaze to the bridge glass. "It's not enough though."

"I know," replied Andy. There was a long moment of silence between them before his First Mate sighed. "Go back to bed. I'm on shift for another two hours."

"Just…" Rhys sighed. "Give me a few minutes."

Andy passed an eye over the instruments and then leaned back in his chair and continued to read.

Dawn's light brought pink and purple skies as well as news from Paducah.

"So, what does it mean?" asked Kallen, leaning against the back wall of the bridge.

Rhys, who had managed to sleep fitfully the remainder of the night in the Overseer's chair, glowered at their radio. Their contact in Paducah had reported in at the given time, but reception had been bad. Nearly every other word had been broken or muffled.

"We're going ashore," asserted Rhys. He stood and looked at Kallen and Kashim. "Notify Terron and the others."

"A small group of three would be best," Kashim offered.

"Me, you, and Jules then," said Rhys.

"Myself, Jules, and Hodge," countered Kashim. Rhys meant to argue but could find no response worthy of their time. "Right." Kashim turned to the radio to contact *Grisle*.

Defeated, Rhys left the bridge and descended to the galley; Kallen followed him. He didn't miss the worried expression on her face. Instead of acknowledging it, however, he sat at one of the galley tables and stared at the floor.

Kallen sat beside him. "What time did you go back to bed?"

"I don't know." Sensing her tender, brown eyes on him, he met her gaze. "What?"

"You need a break. You need to sleep."

"Not yet. There's still work to be done."

Kallen pursed her lips. "We need more crew members. It's not just you. Everyone is running themselves into the ground."

"Once we're done here, we're setting sail for New Arbroath."

"Good."

"Go help launch the dinghy. Make sure Kashim has a radio."

Kallen touched his hand briefly before hurrying from the galley.

He had been running his skeleton crew harder than Vinz ever had. He asked from them the near impossible, and still, they delivered.

Already nearly four months had passed since Alina's death, and yet it felt like yesterday. The pain in his heart racked him every night. Alone in the dark, his sister visited him in his dreams and plagued his mind's eye. Her still expected to see her in the galley cooking breakfast or laughing with Hodge in the crew's bunk. He anticipated running into her in the hallway and on the bridge. When no one was around, Rhys sometimes stood outside the doorway of their old bunk and hoped that when he opened the cabin door, she would look up from her work to smile at him.

On more than one occasion, he had turned from his conversation to say something to her or to ask for her opinion. The empty space at his side was a grave reminder that he was alone.

Despite his crew's undying loyalty and Kallen's continuous attempts to tend to him emotionally, Rhys still felt adrift. The life-altering revelations he had had four months ago were nothing but faint memories. The fiery vengefulness which had burned in his soul the month following Alina and Vinz's deaths was now a dying smolder. Frustration and exhaustion kept him company most days while his nightmares and regrets corroded his consciousness at night. He felt lost and without purpose.

Rhys heard the dinghy in the forward hatch launch. Tiredly, he laid his head on the table and closed his eyes. Within a few moments, he was asleep.

When he next woke, it was midday and *Themis* was underway. After stretching his aching neck, he staggered from the galley up to the bridge where he found Kashim and Andy. "What happened? When did you get back?" he asked, pushing his hair into place. "Why are we moving?"

"About an hour ago," replied Kashim.

"We're on our way to New Arbroath," added Andy.

Rhys gazed between them. "What… happened in Paducah?"

Andy nodded to Kashim who answered. "They had Nayan and the resistance fighters in the town square this morning. All of them had been flogged and hung." Kashim sighed. "We lost Paducah. Brechin forces once again have total control of the town. It remains a part of the Pantarak Empire."

Rhys didn't let his deep disappointment show. Instead, he nodded thoughtfully. "Did your team have any problems?"

"No, none," replied Kashim.

"And *Grisle?*"

"Off our port," said Andy.

"We're three and a half weeks out from New Arbroath?"

"There about, assuming we don't hit any type of trouble."

Rhys nodded. "I can take the next shift. If you want to go rest, Andy…"

"I rested earlier," replied his First Mate. "Perhaps you should sleep more."

Annoyed by Andy's persistence, Rhys retreated from the bridge to his bunk where he sat heavily on the edge of his bed. The cabin was bigger now that he had moved Vinz's chest to the spare crew quarters. He had also organized the former Overseer's bookshelf and cleaned out his drawers. In addition to possessing Vinz's cabin, Rhys had also inherited a piax, a type of lute, which now stood locked to his desk. He meant to start practicing the instrument, but stress and life always got in the way. He had picked it up perhaps four times in the past month.

Closing his eyes, Rhys tried to imagine Pathos, his AI, talking to him, reasoning with him. But already he could no longer recreate his partner's voice in his head.

He had regretted on more than one occasion separating from his AI. In one day, not only had he lost his sister, but his artificial intelligence enlightenment interface system, Pathos, his closest confidant.

Rhys dragged together what energy he had and gathered the crew's laundry. For the next hour, he washed clothes in the washroom and then took them to the upper deck to dry. Afterward, he made himself a light meal of fish, cheese, and bread, mopped the hallway and galley, and then took inventory of the food. Leo joined him later on the upper deck as he took down the dry laundry.

"Are you still speaking with your father?" Rhys asked, folding one of Kashim's shirts.

Leo, who was sprawled out in the shade of the sail, nodded. "Yes, but it's becoming more difficult to get letters to him without interception."

"He's in Bathsgate now, right?"

"With my oldest brother, Sean."

"They haven't hit any problems?"

"Not that I know of. The high priest threatened to take his post away, yet he still receives letters from the family heads concerning political and economic matters. I don't know what to make of the situation." Leo sat up. "Say, I heard we're heading for New Arbroath."

"The city of New Arbroath commissioned Vinz to build *Themis*. That's one of the reasons we're going back," explained Rhys.

"You're hoping they'll give us money," concluded Leo.

"I'm hoping, but it won't be that simple." Rhys shook out a pair of Kallen's pants. "I don't exactly get along with the judge there."

"Put that aside," chided Leo, folding his legs under him. "We need money. If you have to kiss ass, then do it. The jobs we did in Firekli brought in money, but it's not like what a city can give you."

That evening, Kallen prepared dinner, and the entire crew convened in the galley. Rhys sorely missed Hodge's presence.

"Hey, what did you find at the ruins yesterday?" asked Leo, gesturing to Otto. Rhys glanced at Leo appreciatively. He didn't want Otto to feel like an outsider, but everyone was so worn, conversation was almost impossible.

Otto grinned and hurried across the hall to the crew's cabin. He returned a moment later with a misshapen bag. Rhys, Kallen, and Leo moved their plates to make room while Andy and Kashim looked on in interest. "Anything good?" asked Rhys.

"Oh, I think so!" chirped Otto, peering eagerly into his backpack. Though fifteen years of age, his boyish enthusiasm gave him the appearance of a much younger individual. Otto began withdrawing random pieces of metal and scrap from the bag. He set those on the table without explanation and continued to dig through the pack's contents.

Rhys examined a piece of metal and then looked at Kallen. "What kind of ruins were these? This isn't from Earth."

"Hmm?" asked Otto, pausing. "Not from Earth? What do you mean?"

Rhys picked up another chunk of metal; it was heavy. "This was made for space exploration and travel."

"Space," said Otto, passing the word through his lips.

"It looked like normal buildings and houses," Kallen offered. "Otto, where did you get this?"

"A passageway in the ground," the boy matter-of-factly replied. "It was a staircase. I found a hatch and went down there." He continued to dig through his bag. "There wasn't much, but what I found, I brought back up."

"Empty your bag," instructed Rhys, pushing their plates farther from the dust-clad artifacts.

"Am I in trouble? I just... did my job," murmured Otto. It was apparent that despite being on the ship for five weeks now, he was still apprehensive about being disciplined.

"No, you're not in trouble," assured Rhys. "What else did you find?"

"I don't know what any of these things are. They're from white gods or something..."

As Otto revealed the items, Rhys and Leo studied them.

"These are definitely not from Earth," murmured Leo, passing a handful of screws and nuts to Rhys. "Look at the precision."

Rhys nodded and scanned the other items on the table—several pieces of scrap metal, two chips, colored wire, a handful of quartz rocks, and a few empty cartridges.

"And... this thing!" proclaimed Otto, withdrawing a slender, silver box the size of his palm.

Rhys stood slowly, his eyes intent. "You found that... down there?"

Otto flipped the little box over in his palm and nodded. "But there's no way to open it."

Eagerly, Rhys held out his hand. "Let me see." Rhys ran his hand over one side of the box and then flipped it over.

"You know what it is?" asked Leo, his eyes on Rhys. "Is it yours?"

"No, it's not his," said Otto. "I found it down in that room. How could it be his?"

Rhys flipped it over once more. "It's a computer."

"A computer? Like Pathos and Logos?" Kallen asked.

"It may not be an AI. Not all computers are AIs," explained Rhys.

"Mmmm, what's going on?" quavered Otto. "What's a computer?" The boy thought for a moment and added, "And what is space? What do you mean not from Earth? That doesn't make sense."

Rhys glanced at his crew members. Outside of the original crew, no one knew of his past. Both Jules and Otto had been told he was a Brechin noble. Never had he allowed the black dye on his prominent silver hair to fade nor had he ever spoken in Interstellar Nefegian around the new crew members for fear of them recognizing that he had a different accent than the Brechin nobles.

"Uhh…" Rhys thought. How was he to explain this?

Otto frowned. "And that sound. *Uhhh*. That's a strange sound." He looked to the others. "Right? It's… strange?"

"Take a seat," said Kashim. Otto did as he was told. "You and Jules have intentionally not been told information for your own protection. Now… should you want that information, we will give it to you, but that means you are bound to this ship. Wherever she goes, you go. Do you understand?" Otto nodded. "Now, do you want to know?"

Otto looked between Rhys and Kashim and then shook his head.

"Good find, Otto," said Rhys. He nodded to the artifact in his hand. "This is a good find. But you know what is even better?" Rhys picked up one of the sheets of metal. "These. We can use this for repairs. Excellent." He set the metal down and motioned to all the items. "Let's get these cleaned up so we can finish eating. Good finds, Otto." Rhys glanced at the others expectedly.

"Good finds. Good job," chorused the group. Otto smiled to himself and began repacking the items.

Rhys pushed the sheets of metal toward the boy while simultaneously slipping the computer into the waistband of his pants. Though he knew Kashim, Andy, and Kallen saw him, it was Otto from whom he hid the artifact. The less the boy knew, the better.

Dinner finished on a lighter note. While Kallen and Otto cleaned the galley, Kashim and Andy returned to the bridge; Rhys and Leo disappeared into his cabin.

"You know what it is," said Leo as soon as the door was closed.

"I actually don't," replied Rhys, flipping the unit over and studying it. "It's old. Very old."

"But it's advanced," said Leo.

Rhys pointed to the tiny typeface along the bottom of the unit. "That's a company name. I recognize it. Omega Technologies. It built, uh…" Rhys thought. "I think software, AIs, and computers for space stations. Maybe advanced machinery—I don't really remember."

"So, it's a computer—"

"We've got airships," came Andy's voice through the pipe communication system on the ship. "Two airships approaching from the northeast. Prepare for anti-air combat."

Rhys slid the slender unit into his pants pocket and, with Leo at his side, raced from the cabin.

"Gunner and cannons are ready," Andy announced as Rhys moved swiftly across the bridge to radar.

"Has *Grisle* confirmed the enemy contacts as well?"

"*Grisle* has confirmed," replied Kashim.

Recognizing that now was the time to use their new weapon, Rhys turned to him. "Can you do this?"

Kashim held out his hand. They shook firmly before the large man hurried out the external bridge door, taking with him a radio.

Rhys went to the Overseer's chair and pulled down the communication pipe. "Kallen, prepare a sunboard for launch. Otto, Leo, make sure the cabins are secure." The pipe whirred back into the ceiling.

"Five liretems out," reported Andy, "and closing fast."

Rhys snatched a radio from the wall. "*Grisle,* get Hodge to the upper deck to help spot."

"Already there," replied Terron.

"Bring *Grisle* ten keis starboard. Over." He moved to the radar and studied it. Since *Themis'* near destruction four months ago, he had made several new additions and upgrades to the ship, which was partially why they were so low on funds at the moment. Installing the latest radar system and a sonic cannon had assured their poverty. Airship attacks were inevitable; why not prepare for them?

"Andy, keep your course straight ahead." Rhys pulled the radio to his mouth once more. "Kashim, they're two liretems out."

"Sonic cannon is prepped and ready to fire. Targets are in sight but not within range," came Kashim's reply.

"*Grisle,* guns at the ready. Do not fire unless ordered," Rhys piped into the radio. "We need them to maintain course."

"Understood," replied Terron.

"Kashim, one liretem out," called Rhys. "Nine hundred retems. Eight hundred. Kashim, prepare target acquisition."

"Target One acquired. No movement from the enemy outside of course. Locked-on."

"They're preparing to open fire," said Andy as an alarm on the bridge began wailing.

"Fire when ready," ordered Rhys into the radio.

There were a few moments of silence and then an explosion. *Themis* rocked but continued to churn through the water unhindered.

"Target One has been destroyed," came Hodge's voice over the radio. "Kashim, adjust two keis to port."

Rhys leaned heavily on the paneling and gazed at the radar. There was only one airship now.

"Fire when ready," broadcast Hodge.

There was another dull explosion, and the second airship disappeared from radar. Rhys nodded proudly and glanced at Andy as his First Mate exhaled in relief.

"*Themis*, you have a sunboard coming in," shouted Hodge over the radio. "Sunboard at four o'clock high!"

"Disengage. Do not fire the sonic cannon. Kashim, retreat downstairs. *Grisle,* open fire." Rhys looked at Andy. "Open fire."

Kashim appeared suddenly on the bridge, breathless and wind-whipped. "It's a single sunboard. It must have launched from one of the airships." He maneuvered around Andy and settled himself at the weapons station.

Rhys looked back at radar. *Themis'* old radar couldn't pick up sunboards because they were too small, but his latest installation was far more sensitive. "You following it?" he asked Kashim. Kallen entered the bridge.

"I got it," replied the large man, studying the screen before him. Gunfire spewed from the gunners on either side of *Themis'* bow.

"He's passing over!" snarled Rhys, leaning forward to see out the windowpane. A golden blur swept over the ship; a split second later, *Themis* quaked in the water. "Kallen!" shouted Rhys over his shoulder.

"Right!" Kallen sprinted from the bridge to the engine room.

"Let's go, let's go," said Rhys, pacing. "Where is he?"

"Rhys." Andy pointed ahead of the ship where the enemy's sunboard floundered in the air.

Rhys squinted to get a better read of the unit. Why was it flying that way? It took him a moment to realize the sunboard no longer had a pilot.

"Rhys, he's on the ship!" bellowed Hodge through the radio. "He's on the upper deck!"

Rhys threw the radio on his chair, pulled off his headscarf, and rolled his sleeves. He stalked to the exterior bridge door and slammed it open, admitting the orange and gold light of the setting sun. He grabbed a pistol from the wall mount and peered outside. All he could hear was the rushing of the water below. Jaws clenched, he closed the bridge door behind him and leaned against the ladder which led to the upper deck. He would be most vulnerable while on the ladder. He needed to get up there and engage the enemy quickly.

He looked up once more, craning his neck to see the length of the ship, before prepping his gun. Steeling himself, he began climbing. Before the top of his head cleared the ladder and his cover was gone, Rhys slowly peeked over the bridge.

"Don't move," came a voice. In direct contradiction to the command, Rhys looked up at the soldier dressed in Brechin colors and armor peering down at him. Though the man had the tan skin and short-trimmed, brown hair of a Pantarak man, his eyes were hazel. He wore a few days' scruff and a white scar along his left eyebrow. He was not burly like Kashim but lean and muscled like Hodge. Perhaps that was why he had been chosen as a sunboarder. "Drop your weapon," instructed the soldier.

Rhys glanced down the barrel of the gun before releasing his own weapon. It clattered onto the outer bridge deck.

The soldier motioned with his pistol. "Get up here."

Rhys pulled himself onto the upper deck. As he shifted his weight to his left leg, he struck out with his right, kicking the soldier's pistol arm upward. Now clear, Rhys dove at the man with his knee but was met by hard, bulletproof armor.

Before the soldier could aim once more, Rhys shoved his shoulder under the man's triceps and cranked down. His attacker's weight shifted forward and with ease, Rhys threw him. The soldier hadn't stopped moving before Rhys stomped his arm and wrenched the gun from his hand. Panting, he pointed the pistol at the man cradling his shoulder.

The soldier gazed up at Rhys with murder in his eyes. "Do it."

"Why are you coming after us?" Rhys struggled to remain calm.

"Your ships blew up our headquarters in Paducah," snarled the soldier.

Rhys stared down at him. For the first time in several days, complete clarity overcame him, and he was able to objectively view the soldier. What good would killing this one man do? What was the purpose?

"Do it!" urged the man.

In a single movement, Rhys ejected the magazine of his pistol, racked it to allow the spare bullet in the chamber to pop out, and then pointed it once again at the man. He pulled the trigger. Though both knew the gun was empty, the soldier flinched.

"That could have been you," Rhys asserted. He racked the locked-open pistol and slid it into his waistband. He kicked the full magazine so that it slid across the deck.

The soldier, torn between suspicion and anger, glared at Rhys.

"You've killed hundreds of Paducah citizens in the name of the Pantarak Empire," Rhys continued. "Why do you think I just saved your life?"

Holding his shoulder, the man struggled to his feet. When he was nearly erect, he withdrew a knife from his belt. Having known his intention all along, Rhys stepped back. A gunshot rang out. The soldier buckled onto the deck and curled around his left leg. With a grave sigh, Rhys glanced across the deck at Kashim who had been perched on the bridge ladder ready to fire.

Rhys kicked the knife away from the soldier's reach and examined the rest of his armor for more weapons.

"Along the back," said Kashim, joining him. "He has another gun there." Rhys withdrew the soldier's spare pistol.

After they agreed the man had no other weapons, Rhys knelt beside his assailant. "You're injured. Your shoulder is dislocated and you have a bullet wound to your lower leg." The man glowered at Rhys. "Right now, you have two options. You can cooperate and let me tend to your wounds. I highly recommend this one. Or we can roll you over the side of the boat. You have a total of two working limbs. I'm sure you'll last until a rescue boat finds you."

The soldier glanced at Kashim but remained silent. The expression on his face didn't change but the look in his eyes did.

"You have to say something," advised Kashim.

Rhys motioned to Kashim. "Go get my medical supplies."

As Kashim disappeared into the ship, Rhys said, "You are our prisoner now. Do you understand? That means you are being held captive."

"I know what it means," the man grumbled.

Rhys nodded and then touched the soldier's right arm. The man grimaced. "It's dislocated. I have to set it, but first, we have to take off your armor."

"Leave it. Just roll me into the damn ocean."

"You don't want that," replied Rhys, disconnecting the man's bulletproof vest. "I almost drowned once. You don't want that."

By the time Kashim returned, Rhys had stripped the soldier of his vest and leg armor. Kashim set down the medical bag and knelt beside Rhys. "What do you want me to do?"

Rhys touched the man's dislocated limb again and then said, "Get on the other side and hold him down." As Kashim obeyed, Rhys peered down at the soldier. "It's going to hurt. Bad." The man didn't respond. Kashim placed his knee on the man's uninjured shoulder and a hand on his hip. "Give me a moment." With more force, Rhys touched the soldier's shoulder and manipulated the skin there to determine which direction the shoulder had gone. All the while, the soldier clenched his jaws. Finally, Rhys said, "I'm ready," and sat back on the deck. He took hold of the man's arm. "I'm going to pull slowly. Here we go."

With his feet braced against the man's chest, Rhys slowly began pulling his patient's arm toward him. The soldier groaned in pain.

"Almost..." Rhys murmured, watching the shoulder. There was a dull thud as the soldier's shoulder popped back into place. Wheezing, the man closed his eyes and remained motionless for a long moment. "I need to stop the blood flow." Rhys slid along the deck to the man's left leg which was now in a small pool of blood.

"Rhys." Kashim threw him a wad of gauze and bandaging.

"Scissors," said Rhys, studying the soldier's pants. He cut the lower half of the man's pants leg and began applying pressure to the wound, a two-centimeter hole. "You're lucky Kashim is such a good shot," Rhys murmured, studying the bullet wound. "It does look like the bullet is still in your muscle though, so I'll need to extract it." Rhys covered the wound with gauze and wrapped it temporarily. "Let's get him down to the galley. I'll remove it there." Rhys nudged the soldier who had his gaze fixed on the ocean. "Look at me." The man begrudgingly obeyed. "Are you going to cooperate?"

There was a long pause before the man mumbled, "I don't really have a choice."

Rhys nodded to Kashim who pulled the soldier's uninjured arm over his shoulders. Bolstering him, Kashim lifted the man to his feet. Rhys gathered the medical supplies and bag and crossed the upper deck. Once they had successfully maneuvered the injured soldier down the ladder, they entered the ship.

"Rhys!" called Kallen, appearing on the inner staircase. "What happened?" She froze upon spotting the soldier. The door to the bridge opened, and Leo and Andy appeared.

"He's injured," explained Rhys, passing Kallen. "Andy, check radar. Make sure we're clear. If so, bring us to standard speed. Same goes for *Grisle*." Rhys deposited his medical bag in the galley and returned to the hallway to watch Kashim and the soldier limp down the stairs. Although Andy had returned to the bridge to carry out Rhys' orders, Kallen and Leo stood at the top of the staircase with mixed expressions on their faces.

Once the soldier was on a galley table, Rhys carried out the surgery in silence. It took less than ten minutes to find the bullet, extract it, and stitch up the man.

"I expected you to be bigger," the soldier eventually grunted.

"What?"

The following was a comment rather than a question. "You have a woman and a Brechin noble on this ship."

"Yes, we do," replied Rhys. "In fact, we have two Brechin nobles and a girl on our sister ship. What's your point?" The soldier didn't reply. Rhys finished wrapping his leg and stood. "You are this ship's prisoner. You will be confined to the spare cabin at all times. Do you understand?" The man nodded. Rhys motioned to Kashim who helped the soldier from the table. "Do you… have a name?"

When the soldier didn't respond, Kashim said, "The inside of his vest read 'San…Svanr…' I can't pronounce it. It's on his armor though." Kashim escorted their prisoner from the galley down the hall to the spare cabin.

Rhys leaned against the table and closed his eyes. What had he done? They were in no condition to take on a prisoner. That meant one more mouth to feed. He had endangered his crew. Instead of killing the soldier, he had brought him in and healed him.

"Rhys," called Kashim from the hallway. "A moment of your time."

Rhys threw away the soiled medical supplies and stashed his pack. He knew he was in trouble. He was Overseer, but he was the youngest onboard. Rhys followed Kashim to the bridge where everyone else stood waiting for an explanation.

"I'm sorry," Rhys said, glancing at the others. Now that they were in private, Kashim let his calm façade break. Andy too appeared unhappy. Leo, Otto, and Kallen remained confused.

"Why?" demanded Kashim. "You just endangered your entire crew."

"Rhys, he tried to destroy the engines," added Kallen. "They weren't damaged, but still…"

"I couldn't do it," Rhys interjected angrily.

"Then why did you go out there?" asked Andy.

"When you pick up a gun, you are committing yourself to taking a life," fumed Kashim. "If you're going to fight—"

"I know! Don't you think I know that?" Rhys could feel himself becoming flushed with anger. "I just couldn't do it. I couldn't kill him where Alin—"

"We now have another person to feed," said Andy. "He's not a crew member; he's a prisoner. That means he could, if he got the chance, harm or kill anyone on board."

"I know," replied Rhys. It took all his willpower to calm his voice.

"Next time, let me take care of it." Kashim stalked out of the bridge.

As the others dispersed, Rhys slumped into the Overseer's chair and glared at the glass. Vinz had never had this problem because Vinz had not been a fighter. He had trusted his crew would take care of situations that necessitated force.

"We're trying to help you," said Andy after a long moment.

"I know," murmured Rhys. "Thank you."

3
THEIR PRISONER

ONCE EVERYONE SETTLED IN FOR the evening, Rhys took over Andy's shift and spent the remainder of the night adjusting the bridge paneling, fine-tuning the gauges, recalibrating radar, and checking the sonic cannon on the upper deck. Kashim traded shifts with him at dawn, and Rhys wearily went to bed.

The heavy rocking of the ship sometime around midday stirred him from his fitful sleep. When he looked outside, he found the skies cloudy and green waters tempestuous. Groaning, Rhys rolled out of bed, put on a clean shirt, and brushed his hair into place. Barefooted, he opened his cabin door and padded down to the galley.

Leo looked up from his book. "Lunch is in the cooler."

Rhys retrieved his midday meal, staggered crossways through the galley, and seated himself near Leo. "How bad is the storm?"

"Kashim says it'll hit us in the next hour or so. Don't know how bad it'll be."

"Has anyone fed the soldier?"

Leo closed his book and looked at Rhys pointedly. "Kallen did a while ago. I'm surprised the ruckus didn't wake you."

Rhys fell still. "Did something happen?"

"Your prisoner grabbed her, held her down, and tried to get information from her."

Rhys felt blood rush to his face. "And?"

Leo shrugged. "You know Kallen. She spat in his face, kicked him in the balls, and punched his injured shoulder. By the time I got there, he was on the floor wheezing."

"How is she?" murmured Rhys.

"Upset."

Rhys braced against the table as the ship lurched steeply to starboard.

"Don't beat yourself up," said Leo. "Kallen's response was excessive according to Kashim. The man wanted answers. He assumed the only female onboard would acquiesce. He didn't hurt her." Rhys withdrew part of a cooked fish from the bowl Kallen had stashed for him and nibbled on it. "She's fine. The prisoner is… for the most part also fine."

"This is my fault."

"Stop." Leo leaned on the table. "It's over. It's done. We have a prisoner. Pull information from him. Use him."

"We can't let him go," replied Rhys. "He knows the ship. He knows our faces." He fell still in thought, the soldier's words echoing in his head.

"What?" asked Leo.

"The soldier… he said to me, 'I thought you would be bigger.'"

"He knows you?"

"Or he knows *of* me," Rhys corrected. He crossed the galley, replaced his bowl in the cooler, took a swig of water, and jogged from the room.

"Wait," called Leo, following him.

Rhys staggered to the spare cabin and withdrew the length of wood they were using to lock the door. He found the soldier reclining on the bunk to the right, his uninjured leg fixed against the posts so he wouldn't roll to the floor.

"What did you mean yesterday?" Rhys asked. The soldier sat up and gazed at them with an odd expression on his face. Rhys slipped into the room and held onto the bunk post. "What did you mean when you said, 'I thought you'd be bigger?'"

"You are known, at least by name," the soldier replied.

"Known by who? The military?"

"Everyone knows your name—Rhys Falkrow."

"Why?" Leo queried.

"It's who we've been ordered to kill," murmured the soldier, studying Rhys. "I didn't know you were just a kid though… Or that you were one of them."

Leo fidgeted in the doorway. "One of who?"

"The white gods."

"What else didn't you know?" asked Rhys. "What else didn't they tell you?"

The soldier gestured to Leo. "You're a Brechin noble."

"Yes."

"And you have two more on the other ship?"

"Yes."

The soldier thought. "Are you prisoners?"

"No, they're crew members," replied Rhys. "So, what were you told?"

"That you needed to be eliminated," grumbled the soldier. "I feel bad for trying to kill a kid now though."

Rhys ignored the man's comment. He was aware of the fact he appeared young. "Did they give you a reason? Did they tell you that I had done something?"

"They told us that you had to be killed. That's it," snapped the soldier.

"And you deployed from Paducah?" clarified Leo. The soldier nodded.

"From whom did your orders come?" Rhys interrogated. "Your officers?" The soldier nodded. "And they received the orders from their superiors?" The soldier nodded once more. "Answer me this: has Brechin elected a new high priest? Who's in command of the family heads?"

"The family heads are overseen by three white gods. That's all I know."

Rhys nodded. "You've been forthcoming with information. Is there anything you would like to know?"

"No," replied the man.

"You attacked Kallen this morning. Obviously, you want answers," countered Rhys.

"No."

Rhys turned to leave. "Should the storm worsen, we'll retrieve you." He glanced at the soldier once more and then closed the door behind him.

Unfortunately, the storm did worsen, and within the hour, *Themis* was bucking in every direction. Once everyone was on the bridge, Rhys instructed Leo to retrieve the soldier.

"Hodge, how's *Grisle?*" asked Rhys over the radio.

"Eh, she's solid. We've closed off all her innards," his friend replied. "*Themis* will have a harder time than us, over."

The bridge door opened to admit Leo and the soldier. After all were strapped into jump seats at the rear of the bridge, Rhys glanced at Kashim and Andy. Both leaned against their chairs, studying gauges. Rhys turned to the small table of maps to his left and began sifting through them.

"Kashim," groaned Kallen eventually. "How long do you foresee this storm lasting?"

"I'm doing my best to keep the boat into the wind," Andy huffed.

"Can't tell. It's from an unusual direction." Kashim pointed out beyond the windscreen. "Storms normally come from the west. This one blew up from the southeast."

"If need be, we can head south and bypass it," offered Rhys, tracing his finger along a map. "That wouldn't put us off course by much."

"If it doesn't ease up within the next hour or so, then that's what we'll do," said Kashim.

As Rhys relayed the message to Hodge and the others on *Grisle*, he glanced at the soldier sitting along the back wall of the bridge. The man was observing them. His eyes traced Kallen several times before moving to Andy and Kashim. The soldier seemed at a complete loss, as if what he knew was not matching up with what he was seeing.

After an hour of pitching and bucking, Rhys made the call and Andy redirected them southward in an attempt to escape the raging tempest. It was another two hours before the rain stopped and the seas calmed. By then, Otto and Leo had been sick, and Andy, as was his habit, had stretched out on the bridge floor with his arm over his eyes. When she was no longer needed, Kallen stumbled to the Overseer's cabin and collapsed in bed with a horrible headache. Only Kashim, Rhys, and the soldier remained unaffected.

Rhys briefly convened with Kashim over the maps before turning to help the soldier back to the spare cabin. Once the prisoner was locked away, Rhys retrieved a cool washcloth and tended to Kallen.

The following few days remained uneventful with clear, hot skies and calm seas. While Rhys spent his time working laboriously on the power converter, the rest of the crew fell into some semblance of a schedule.

Because Andy had agreed to switch shifts, Rhys now found himself sleeping from dawn until shortly after midday. Once up, he ate lunch and continued his work on the power converter which they had not looked at replacing while in Firekli; Rhys greatly regretted that decision. Not wanting to lead Kallen away from her new student, Otto, Rhys took the repairs upon himself. Though the converter had not yet broken fully, it was on its way to being a piece of scrap metal.

Andy spent the mornings reading on the bridge while Kashim fished off the stern of the ship with Leo. Though they had not had much success, what little fish they did manage to bring in helped sustain their current food rations.

The only person who didn't fit into the schedule was the soldier whose name no one knew. With remarkable stubbornness, he remained silent and kept to himself. He answered simple questions but offered no extra information. Whether it was because he felt that he had already shared too much or because he had nothing else to offer, Rhys didn't know. The soldier was a solid wall of impenetrable obstinacy.

It was late afternoon on the ninth day of their travels when Rhys went to the spare cabin to retrieve the man. Their prisoner, who had been staring out the porthole at the other end of the room, peered over his shoulder. "Come outside with me. I have some repairs to make." The soldier gazed dubiously at him. "Unless you want to stay in here until your next bathroom break."

The man grabbed his shirt from the bed and limped across the room to Rhys. He no longer looked like a soldier. He had been stripped of his uniform and weapons. Now he wore clothes borrowed from Andy who was closest in height and size. Dressed in a pair of cutoffs and a loose blouse, the man appeared like a toned sailor accustomed to the seas.

No longer in need of assistance, the soldier followed Rhys from the spare cabin, down the hall, and up the stairs. Once on the upper deck, Rhys watched the man's injured left leg for signs of weakness.

They joined Kallen and Otto who sat beside a pile of solar panels. Rhys saw Kallen glance at the prisoner, but she kept her attention focused on Otto.

"Good, just like that," she murmured. "You want to be careful though. Don't screw it on too tight." Otto nodded and then anxiously stole a look at the soldier. Kallen patted the teen's arm and smiled reassuringly. "He's not going to do anything."

"Sit," instructed Rhys, settling himself near Kallen. As the soldier seated himself on the deck, Rhys picked up a solar panel and began examining it. "Thought you'd like some fresh air. The cabins can be stifling."

Rhys saw the soldier and Kallen meet gazes. The tension between them was palpable.

So," began Rhys, "you know my name, right?" He motioned to Kallen. "This is Kallen; she's our mechanic. And Otto. What have you been doing, Otto?"

Otto glanced nervously at the soldier and then lowered his gaze. His hands fidgeted with the solar paneling. "I'm, eh, learning to be a mechanic…"

"Why are you doing this?" interjected the soldier suddenly. "Why am I here? Why are you introducing me to people? I'm your *damn* prisoner." The man thought for a moment before nodding in realization. "I'm not ever leaving this ship, am I?"

Rhys placed the solar panel he had been repairing onto the deck. "I can't risk having you report all that you've seen to your higher-ups."

"Then you should have killed me!" the man snarled, struggling to his feet. With some difficulty, he maneuvered onto his right leg and stood. He staggered a few steps before his injured leg twisted and he stumbled to the deck. "Don't!" the soldier seethed, seeing Rhys move to help him. "Just... don't." Defeated, the man sat back and sprawled himself out on the deck. "Just don't."

For the next hour and a half, Rhys, Kallen, and Otto worked on solar panel repairs. While Kallen spoke softly to Otto, Rhys methodically replaced the burnt-out pieces like a machine. The soldier remained where he had fallen.

It was dusk by the time they finished. Together, they gathered the new solar panels and cleaned up. Once they had everything, Rhys went to the soldier and peered down at him. "Ready to go in?"

The man sat up and began the struggle to stand. Hesitantly, Rhys held out his hand. To his surprise, the man took his wrist firmly. Rhys pulled him up and steadied him. When he turned, he met Kallen's gaze across the upper deck. The aloofness she often exhibited when she was angry returned. With a slight pursing of her lips, she escorted Otto into the ship. Rhys sighed.

"Axel," said the soldier.

"What?"

"My name. It's Axel Svanrson."

4
TRIALS

IT WAS TWO HOURS BEFORE midnight when Andy shuffled off tiredly from the bridge and Rhys came on shift. Within the first half hour, Kallen entered the bridge, arms folded and face set.

"What?" Rhys looked up briefly from the energy gauge.

"What are you thinking right now because I'm having a difficult time understanding why you're trying to befriend a Brechin soldier."

Rhys stopped what he was doing and leaned against the paneling. "I don't think he knows what to do. He's confused."

"Of course he is!" snapped Kallen. "You've been treating him like a crew member. He's a prisoner."

"No, I mean… the way he looks at us. He doesn't understand."

"Because of the way you've been treating him."

Rhys sighed exasperatedly. "No, it's not that. Next time you're with him, watch his eyes. I think the Brechin government is feeding its soldiers inaccurate information. He can't figure out why Brechin is after us if we're just these two ships with skeleton crews."

"Look, I don't care," Kallen huffed. "He's a Pantarak soldier. He's killed hundreds of people—"

"We don't know that," interjected Rhys.

"Why are you taking his side? Rhys, your entire crew is on edge because you brought the enemy onboard."

"What was I supposed to do?"

"Kill him!" barked Kallen.

Rhys bit his tongue. Kallen knew the reason why he had refrained from killing the man on the upper deck—it was Alina's death site. "I couldn't..." he murmured. "You know that."

"Then you should have let Kashim go up there," she argued. "Without any regard for your crew, you tended to his wounds and brought him in. If you couldn't kill him, then you could have rolled him over the side of the ship."

"Is this about the other day? He just wanted answers."

"How was I supposed to know that? I was alone!" snarled Kallen, tears gathering in her eyes. "He grabbed me. I was scared."

"Kallen." Rhys went to comfort her, but she slapped his hand away.

"What are we doing? We're just two ships. That's it. It doesn't matter how many weapons we have, it's just..." Kallen swiped at her tears. "None of us knows what to do. We're lost."

"Kallen, I'm trying. I really am."

Kallen studied him through moist eyes. "Maybe you should tend to yourself first before trying to oversee others." Rhys stared at her, hurt. She saw the look in his eyes and then softened. "I'm sorry," she whispered. "I shouldn't... have said that."

Rhys pulled away. "No, you're right. I'm a mess." He crossed the bridge and sat in Andy's chair. "I've barely been holding it together."

Kallen sat at the weapons station and leaned on her knees. "Have you been sleeping?"

He nodded. "It's been better since I took the night shift. When I sleep during the day... I don't see her. Alina." Miserably, he peered at Kallen. "I keep expecting to see her. She's everywhere and she's nowhere. It's..." He breathed deeply. "Exhausting."

Kallen stood and moved to his side. Gently, she took his arms and wrapped them around her waist and legs. She kissed the top of Rhys' head and brushed his hair from his face. "I'm sorry. We've been trying... so hard to keep up with you and with what you want. But it's hard."

Rhys rested his cheek on her stomach and closed his eyes. "Honestly, I don't know what I'm doing. I'm just following my gut."

"Like with the soldier?"

"I went out there with purpose. I was going to protect the ship, and then I faced him and... I froze. All I could think about... was Alina." Rhys breathed in Kallen's scent. "Does everyone hate me?"

"No, they don't hate you. If they hated you, they would have left you in Firekli or Paducah. They're frustrated just like you are. They're tired and stressed. Otto is sweet, but he's a drain on resources and time. He's learning, but he doesn't have a natural proclivity for mechanics. And with the soldier onboard now… We just don't know what to do. We don't understand your thinking." Kallen touched the empty receptors hidden under his hair along his left temple. "Tell me something. Do you intend to make that man a part of our crew?"

"Would that make you angry?"

"Yes," she replied. She caressed his face. "You're the Overseer though. You do what is best for us."

Rhys moved her hand to his mouth and kissed her palm. "Thank you."

Kallen knelt before him. "Talk to me more. I feel like we're not even on the same ship." She kissed his lips and then wrapped her arms around his neck. "We're relying on you, Rhys."

"I know."

The following morning, dawn came with thick, blue-gray clouds and rising winds. Rhys, who had been on the bridge all night watching the cloud coverage increase, gathered the crew. As *Themis* tilted precariously to starboard, Kashim said, "This isn't good."

"No, it's not," asserted Rhys, leaning against one of the bridge chairs. "It's taking its time getting here. I've been watching the lightning for the past three hours. Our best bet is to keep straight into the wind and hope the swells don't overpower us." Rhys motioned to Kashim and Kallen. "Bring in the sails. I want lifelines on both of you." Kallen and Kashim disappeared outside. "Otto, secure the cabins. Leo, go get Axel."

"What?" asked Leo.

"The prisoner, Axel. Go get him," clarified Rhys. Leo exchanged perplexed looks with Andy and then slipped off the bridge with Otto. "Andy, *Themis* is yours."

"This one isn't going to be easy," the First Mate stated, studying the gauges before him.

Rhys looked out at the growing swells of eerie, green water. Already, it was starting to rain; thunder rumbled just loud enough that it could be heard over the churning ocean. After a moment of glaring out the windscreen, he snatched a radio from the wall. "Terron, Hodge, you read me?"

There was a moment before Terron responded. "What do you make of the storm?"

Rhys braced on a chair as *Themis* dipped precipitously downward. An explosion of water across the bridge glass followed. "It's bad. This isn't going to be a one-hour storm."

"Do we have time to change course?" asked Terron.

"No, it's slow-moving, but it stretches into infinity. There's no way we can bypass it. I've been watching it for hours. Over."

"We'll stay in conta—"

Terron was interrupted by Hodge. "Is Kallen there?"

"No. What's wrong?" replied Rhys.

"We've got a pipe leaking in the engine room. It's not a dire situation, but if this storm gets worse, it will be," said Hodge.

"When she comes in, I'll give her the radio. Standby." Rhys stumbled as *Themis* dipped to port and then shot over the crest of the next wave. He was beginning to worry about Kallen and Kashim. They had been in conditions like this before, but he nevertheless wanted them in before it escalated.

Suddenly, there was a loud *thwack* followed by a series of yells. Andy turned for the exterior ship door, but Rhys stopped him. "Stay with the ship!"

Rhys staggered to the door and threw it open. A torrent of water hit him, spilling him down the staircase. Before he had stopped moving, he was on his hands and knees groping to stand. Wildly, he looked up at the flood of seawater and rain gushing into the bridge.

Adrenaline burning away his fatigue, Rhys scrambled back up to the exterior door. The moment he made it to the open doorway, Leo appeared, struggling to claw his way back into the ship. Securing his legs around the staircase railing, Rhys grabbed Leo's shirt and arm and jerked him inside. Leo toppled backward into the ship and then down a few stairs.

"Who else is out there?" Rhys shouted.

"Kallen, Kashim, and that guy!" replied Leo.

"Find Otto and close all the cabin doors. Go!" Rhys craned his neck to peer out the open doorway. He could see just the top of someone's head. He hooked his foot in the doorway and leaned outside.

"Come on!" screamed Kallen who was braced against the outer ship railing; beside her was Axel. Both were straining to reel in Kashim who was dangling over the side of the ship.

"Axel!" called Rhys, leaning out and extending his hand. The soldier, who was having a difficult time keeping his injured leg under him on the wet stairs, turned without hesitation and gripped Rhys' wrist in a solid lock. Rhys anchored himself in the doorway. With another body providing balance, Axel turned and jerked Kashim from the water. "Move!" shouted Rhys, watching the next row of waves approach *Themis*. "Get in!"

With his feet now under him, Kashim grabbed Kallen and dragged her down the stairs. Rhys took hold of Axel's other arm and pulled him into the doorway. With more force than necessary, Kashim shoved Rhys and Axel into the ship, threw Kallen in after them, and slammed the door behind him. A breath's moment later, a solid wall of water battered the closed door.

Wheezing, Rhys sat in a pile against Axel at the top of the staircase. Kallen lay on the sodden floor while Kashim leaned on his knees, coughing.

"Is… anyone hurt?" gasped Rhys, sitting up.

It was Axel who spoke. "I think… my shoulder is dislocated again."

Rhys nodded and looked down the hall at the standing water. "Leo? Otto?" he called. Both appeared from inside the galley. "Save anything?"

"No," Leo sullenly replied.

"Sorry," said Otto, looking at the water churning around his ankles.

"Not your fault." Rhys ruffled his hair and moved to his feet. He groped for a handhold when the bow dipped. The water in the hallway sloshed. "Kallen, put a blockade around the engine room doorway. Leo, Otto, Kashim—start bilging this thing. Use whatever you can find. Put all the water in the washroom tub or kitchen sink. Those release outside." Rhys pulled Axel to his feet and bolstered him into the bridge.

"What happened?" asked Andy.

"Sit," said Rhys, lowering Axel onto a chair. With calm hands, he examined the soldier's shoulder. Axel was right; he had re-dislocated it. Rhys placed a palm at his neck and took the man's wrist. Fighting to maintain his footing, he pulled steadily on Axel's arm until the man's shoulder slipped back into its socket. Axel groaned and leaned over in the chair. Rhys braced him as *Themis* pitched downward.

"Rhys…" murmured Andy nervously.

Rhys looked up at the enormous swell of water gathering before *Themis*. "Keep us into it. Don't let it hit us broadside."

Fear-stricken, Andy clutched the accelerator and dragged the motors to maximum speed. The sound of *Themis'* engines was drowned out by the pounding of the ocean and the crackling of thunder.

Rhys gripped the edge of Axel's chair. Not for the first time, he wished Vinz was on the bridge. In silence, they rode out the storm. The others never reentered the bridge. Rhys hoped it was because they were busy trying to bilge the ship, but it was more likely that they were riding out the waves in the galley.

For nearly five hours, *Themis* tossed this way and then that. Rhys checked on *Grisle* periodically, but they weren't having as much trouble as *Themis* despite Hodge's request for mechanical help. It seemed that between Hodge and Terron, they had managed a makeshift repair. When Andy could no longer function due to sea sickness, Rhys took over and stood at the helm.

Though torrents of water pounded the bridge glass and lightning made the air quiver, Rhys found himself in a meditative state. The sporadic rolling of the ship was nothing more than a mild nuisance to him. His primary goal was keeping *Themis* into the wind. It was mindless work when not confronted by enormous swells, and soon, he was able to sit back and regulate the ship's speed from his chair.

"Your pilot is good," remarked Axel after nearly half an hour of complete silence.

"I wish he didn't get seasick," replied Rhys, studying a wave off the starboard bow. "But he's excellent at his job and does what needs to be done."

"Did you choose him?"

"No, the original owner and Overseer of this ship did. In fact, everyone here belongs to the original owner. Even me."

"What happened to him, the original Overseer?"

"He was killed by the high priest in Brechin." Rhys didn't care to see Axel's reaction. "He and my sister both were killed about some months ago."

"Were they terrorists?"

That was not the response Rhys expected. "No. They weren't. The high priest kidnapped my sister. Our crew, including our Overseer at the time, went after her."

"Why would the high priest kidnap your sister? Why was she so special?" Axel braced against the bridge paneling as the trough of a large wave caused *Themis* to plunge steeply. "Does it have to do with the things on the side of your head? Did she have those too?"

"Can we not talk about this right now?" asked Rhys. "It's been a week and a half. You don't need my life story."

"If you want me on your crew, I do," Axel countered. Rhys briefly pulled his eyes from the churning ocean to find Axel solemnly gazing at him. "You're short on men. The only reason your ship is doing so well is because the crew it has is strong. Your mechanic is extremely well-trained as is your pilot and bodyguard. The Brechin noble onboard—I have yet to determine his role though he seems competent enough. You need to get rid of the boy, Otto. He's a waste of resources."

Rhys pulled back on the throttle as a series of less menacing waves broke across the bow.

"And you…"

Rhys glanced at Axel to find the soldier scrutinizing him. The man didn't seem at all concerned about the weather or the waves pounding the bridge glass.

"Why are you, the youngest on the ship, Overseer? What's so special about you? You're inexperienced. You don't seem like anything special, yet you have the crew's full trust. Certainly, that large man would make a better Overseer than you."

Rhys glanced at the waves as a flash of lightning tore through the dark, mid-morning sky. Instead of answering Axel's question, Rhys said, "Don't feel like killing us anymore?"

"I didn't have all of the information."

"What's Brechin saying about us?"

"That you're terrorists. You killed the high priest and destroyed the temple in Brechin. Also, you started a rebellion in Paducah."

"The high priest killed himself," corrected Rhys. "An earthquake destroyed the temple. And we didn't mean to start a rebellion in Paducah. It happened after we left."

"They're calling you the White Demon."

Rhys couldn't help the smile that crept over his face. "The White Demon?"

"Rumors have it that your eyes glow blue in the dark and that you can fly. You condemned the high priest and managed to persuade noble family heads to stray from the path of the gods and follow in your footsteps."

Rhys gawked openly at him.

"Is it true?"

"Do I seem immortal or demonic to you?" Rhys asked incredulously.

Axel shrugged. "You're a sixteen-year-old overseeing two ships. You tell me."

"It's hearsay. Yes, some of the Brechin family heads helped us, but that was of their own accord." Rhys frowned. "I just turned nineteen."

"You're young."

"And you?" asked Rhys. "Twenty-seven?"

"Thirty-one."

"Did you grow up on the sea?"

"Why do you ask?"

"When things get rough, everyone becomes seasick with the exception of Kashim who grew up sailing."

"My family ran a port back in our hometown. I was often on the water." Axel nodded to Rhys. "You seem to have good sea legs on you. Did you grow up on the water?"

"No. Seasickness has never bothered me. I guess it's just luck," lied Rhys. There was no way he could tell him that growing up in zero gravity was way worse than ever being seasick.

Axel fell silent, his gaze set outside the ship. Taking that to mean the conversation was over, Rhys pulled a radio off the wall and contacted *Grisle* to check on her crew.

The worst of the storm raged for two more hours before petering out into gray skies and rough waters. It was early afternoon when Kashim emerged from the ship's innards to take over.

The damage to the inside of *Themis* wasn't as bad as he had originally thought. Though the floors were damp, it appeared the others had managed to bilge the ship. With Axel behind him, Rhys entered the galley and looked at his weary crew. Andy was slumped over a table, asleep. Kallen was seated against the wall, a washcloth on her head. Otto lay on the floor next to an assortment of pots, buckets, and towels while Leo stood glaring out the porthole.

"How bad is it?" asked Rhys. Everyone except Andy looked at him.

"Once the waters calm, we'll need to air out the cabins," reported Kallen, holding her head. "We have lots of wet clothes and towels."

"The engine room?"

"The converter is on its way out. It'll last maybe another two days. Also… some of yours and Vinz's research materials were damaged. I think we can dry them though."

Rhys nodded. "I just spoke with Terron. Once the waters calm, I'm sending you over to *Grisle*. They're in need of repairs." Kallen nodded and rested her forehead on her knees.

"What about him?" asked Otto anxiously.

Rhys glanced at Axel and then looked at his crew. "Would it make you feel more comfortable if he was locked up?" Otto nodded, however, Kallen and Leo exchanged hesitant looks. After a moment, Rhys turned to Axel. "The spare cabin is yours. You are permitted there, the washroom, and the galley. You are allowed on the bridge only with me or Kashim."

Axel nodded, gave an acknowledging wave to Kallen and Leo, and then limped down the hallway to the spare cabin.

5
ENTER ETHOS

"RHYS! RHYS!" SHRIEKED ALINA.

"Alina!" Rhys dove after his sister. With all his strength, he fought, kicking, punching, and jabbing at the soldiers dragging her away. No matter his strength though, no matter his willpower, his strikes were nothing but slaps.

"Get off me!" Alina screamed, her vibrant green dress whirling around her as she struggled against the groping hands.

In a last-chance effort, Rhys reached into the mass of moving bodies, grabbed Alina's delicate wrist, and jerked. Suddenly, there was a gunshot and Alina stumbled into his arms, head limp and body heavy.

"Alina? Alina?" Rhys sank onto the floor with her, staring at the gaping wound in her chest and her blood-soaked robes. Her eyes were glassy.

Knowing he had seconds to save her, Rhys ripped off his shirt and applied pressure to the wound. He checked her pulse both at her jaw and at her wrist—nothing. His heart sank. Pressing his shirt onto her chest to stop the bleeding, he began compressions. Fifteen compressions, two breaths. Fifteen compressions, two breaths.

"Alina!" he cried despairingly, pushing harder and harder. Distantly, he heard a rib crack. "Come on! Pathos, shock her."

"Initializing. Ready," came his AI's gender-neutral tone.

"Do it," panted Rhys. Alina's body leapt from the deck and then fell with a limp thud. Rhys continued compressions. "Again, Pathos." He placed his hands on Alina's chest and breasts to deliver the shock. Once again, his sister's corpse jerked upward and then collapsed.

"It's over, isn't it?" came a voice. Rhys peered over his shoulder at his sister who now also stood behind him. Rhys glanced down at her broken body in his arms and then at the ethereal form regarding him. She sighed. "That's disappointing."

Crying, Rhys cradled his sister. "I'm sorry. I'm so sorry."

Alina's ghostly form knelt beside him to study her own body. "I suppose there's not much else that can be done." She nodded and then touched his shoulder. "Rhys, this isn't real. You know that, right?"

Rhys gazed down at Alina's bloody body. "What?" he whispered thickly.

"This isn't real." Alina chuckled. "Wake up." His sister's grip on his shoulder hardened.

Rhys startled awake, panting, and gazed up at Leo who had been calling to him. For a moment, he searched his cabin for Alina.

"Hey," murmured Leo, concerned.

Rhys rested an arm over his wet eyes. He couldn't calm his breathing. "Is she here?" he asked in Interstellar Nefegian.

"No," replied Leo in the same language. "She's not."

More tears slid down Rhys' face. "I couldn't save her…" he wheezed. "Again."

He felt Leo's weight settle on the end of the bed. "You have to let it go. It wasn't your fault."

"I'm… supposed to be dead. That shot was meant for me. Not her." Rhys wiped his face and sniffed loudly. "It was meant for me."

"You've got survivor's guilt. You've got to let it go," repeated Leo. "You're wearing yourself thin."

"Tell that to *her*," Rhys grimly replied.

Leo gazed at him for a moment and then stood. "Come on. Come outside. The sea has calmed. Kallen's hanging laundry." Begrudgingly, Rhys stood, ruffled his hair into place, and pulled on his shirt which he had ripped off in his sleep. "Come on."

"Wait, don't leave me!" called a small voice from within the cabin.

Rhys and Leo froze in the doorway, wide eyes sweeping the room. "What was that?" hissed Leo.

"Wait, wait, wait. Pick me up," continued the voice in Interstellar Nefegian.

"That's my dialect," said Rhys, scanning the room. It took him a moment to remember the small computer Otto had retrieved from the ruins several days ago. Cautiously, Rhys went to the stack of clothes Kallen had folded on his desk and withdrew the pair of cutoffs he had worn a few days ago. He felt for the computer and then removed it from his pants pocket. Rhys glanced over his shoulder at Leo. "Uh, hello?"

"Uh, hello?" responded the computer in a precise recording of his voice.

Leo joined Rhys. "That's what's talking, right?"

Rhys nodded. "What's your make, model, and year?"

"Incorrect query," the computer robotically asserted.

"Incorrect query?" Rhys flipped the device over and then turned it upside-down. "If I can pull off this back cover, I can find out in what—"

"No!" shrieked the computer, startling both Rhys and Leo. "I'll be naked!"

"It's malfunctioning," concluded Rhys. He sighed despairingly. Although he had learned to live without technology over the past several months, he missed his AI, Pathos. He could always count on Pathos to provide unbiased information and unwavering support. He had taken for granted how much he relied on the computer.

"For your information, you gangly creature, I am not malfunctioning. I'm giving you a hard time," chirped the computer. "Although, strictly speaking, I probably shouldn't be tormenting you given the nightmares that seem to plague your sleep."

"Are you an AI?" asked Rhys.

"Yes, of course. I am not, however, one of those computer bots tasked with taking care of a specific something or other."

"What was—is—your function then?" asked Leo.

There was a long pause before the AI said, "Why do you speak so strangely? I can understand the gangly one here, but you are more difficult."

"Your function, AI. What's your function?" demanded Rhys.

"My name is not 'AI.' My name is Ethos."

Rhys grew still. Ethos? The AI model that was discontinued on Caelestis over two centuries ago?

"What's wrong?" asked the AI. "Your pulse has increased. You seem disturbed by the name I have provided."

Rhys looked to Leo who, not understanding the significance of the name, shrugged. Rhys ran his fingers over the AI. "You... This model was discontinued centuries ago."

"I was? For what reason?" Ethos seemed actually hurt. "Who... took my place?"

"Pathos and Logos."

"Bastards..." murmured Ethos. "Pathos and Logos, I mean. Not you humans, although I'm sure some of you are, in fact, bastards."

"Ethos, did you belong to someone?" asked Rhys.

"I did. I've been in hibernation since his death."

"Why did you activate now?"

"I heard the mother tongue—Interstellar Nefegian. Hmmmmm, according to my calendar, I have been in hibernation for two hundred forty-three years, seven months, twenty-four days, nineteen h—"

"It's been a while," interrupted Rhys.

There was silence and then, "You may speak the mother tongue, but you are hardly worthy of interrupting me. Please refrain from doing so in the future."

Rhys gaped at the computer and then looked at Leo who seemed beyond baffled.

"Nineteen hours, thirty-nine minutes, twelve seconds. There, I'm finished. Was that difficult? Now, what trivial drivel do you have to share?"

"Is the computer-thing supposed to... talk to you like that?" whispered Leo. "Did Pathos speak to you like that?" Rhys shook his head.

"I'm not deaf, you mohawked buffoon," snapped Ethos.

"Ethos, query: personality settings," said Rhys firmly. "Access response and rebuttal; reset both to manufacturer default."

"Manufacturer default is not an option," Ethos affirmed.

"Your personality can't be changed?"

"Because I am an artificial intelligence enlightenment interface system, I am a learning computer. Therefore, if you are displeased with my personality, I will learn so immediately."

"We hate you," said Leo. "Change it up."

"I resonate with one individual at a time. Once I am synched to the individual, no other may adjust my settings. Do you claim me?"

Leo backed away from Rhys and the AI. "Sorry."

"No, he doesn't," said Rhys. "I claim you."

"Please state your full name, birth date, place of origin, and identification number."

"Rhys Falkrow, Margos Fifth, 0022. Caelestis. No identification number."

"Rhys Falkrow, age: nineteen. Home colony: Caelestis." Ethos paused. When it next spoke, the robotic tone it had used since Rhys had accessed its settings was replaced with its normal personality. "Caelestis. You're far from home."

"I could say the same for you," replied Rhys. "Where are you from?"

"Prima Signa, a colony located within the Orion-Cygnus arm of the Milky Way."

"Yes. We received transmissions from Prima Signa regularly. How did you end up here?"

"My user and I were part of a transport envoy en route to Voitus. Our ship passed through an anomaly, and we crash-landed here on Earth."

"So you knew where you were?"

"Of course. And you? Why do you speak familiarly yet the other one has a different accent?"

"Some people here speak Interstellar Nefegian, but it's old, far older than you or me."

"I see. I will continue to dissect the mohawked one's garbled speech for my own knowledge."

"I have a name," growled Leo.

"Yes. Your first name is Mo. Your last is Hawk," rattled Ethos.

"Enough. Humor is welcomed but spitefulness toward crew members is not. Am I understood?"

"Very well. What is your name, Mo Hawk?"

"Leo." He glanced at Rhys. "I'm going outside. Join us when you can." Leo disappeared into the hallway.

"You upset him," said Rhys.

"He'll get over it. Rhys, I do not mean to be intrusive, but it seems that twelve percent of your body is comprised of biosynthetic materials. If you would be interested, I can attempt connection to quicken the synchronization process."

"I was diagnosed with synthetic corruption," replied Rhys, sitting on the edge of his bed. "I don't think you should."

"Synchronization would occur without connection to nerves or other biosynthetic materials."

"I removed my other AI unit because the connection had been corrupted."

"I can assure you that no such thing will happen with me. I am superior to your previous unit."

Rhys scoffed—he doubted any AI could best *his* Pathos. "What do I have to do?"

"Place both hands on my unit," instructed Ethos. Rhys obeyed, wrapping his hands around the AI. "One moment… while I rip your fingerprints off! I jest, I jest. Please don't move."

Rhys couldn't help but let a smile twitch his lips.

"Estimated time until complete synchronization: 23 minutes," reported Ethos.

"Do I have to keep my hands on your unit the entire time?"

"It is preferable but not necessary."

Rhys sighed and lay back on his bunk. Hands still wrapped around Ethos, he stared at the ceiling. Although he had just awakened, he felt fatigued and weary. No doubt it was from the nasty dreams. He was regaining an AI, but his sister was not a computer; she was unattainable.

"You're causing yourself great mental stress by repeatedly thinking of your sister," murmured Ethos.

"You can synchronize with my thoughts?"

"No. I can only know your body's physiological responses like your pulse, brain waves, electrical signals, and hormones. While I can't read your thoughts, I can accurately *guess* what it is that you're thinking."

"You know my sister is dead."

"Conjecture," replied Ethos. "I'm observant." It seemed Ethos was thinking because when the AI spoke next, it was with some hesitancy. "The vast network of synthetic materials in your body is mystifying. The humans on Caelestis integrated with computers?"

"Yes. Your user was clean?"

"Completely. In fact, at the time, there was debate about whether humans should fuse with their technology at all. Hence the reason why I cannot fully integrate with you as your previous AI, Pathos, did."

"That's probably a good thing."

"Yes, you mentioned you are diseased with corruption. I have come across substantial damage to the synthetic synapses in your brain. Hmm, there is a lot of destruction here, but it seems Pathos protected your vitals well. You ejected your AI, didn't you?"

"Yes."

"If I was a bio-integrated AI, I would have difficulty perusing your insides, but I'm not. Ah, you've downloaded quite a bit of content." Ethos hummed in his hands. "You're a fighter."

"Thanks to Pathos."

"Yes, your AI, without a single objection, downloaded all that you needed."

Rhys frowned. "What does that mean—without a single objection?"

"Your AI followed your commands blindly."

"It was my AI. That was its function. Are you indicating that you are different?"

"I misspeak. Yes, of course, Pathos obeyed you. Its fundamental programming was based solely on feeling and emotion. Whatever you felt, the AI processed and understood as its own. If you were enraged and bent on destruction, it was too. It was prepared to help you achieve whatever you desired." Rhys sat up and gazed at Ethos. "I am an Ethos unit. Although most of my functions are personality-based, my underlying programming is firmly rooted in ethics or the feeling that motivates ideas, actions, and the like. Perhaps another simpler explanation could be that I represent moral competence."

"Therefore, you should be able to learn the morals and values that I represent."

"No…" replied Ethos almost thoughtfully. "Although I was created to support my user, I am not obligated to obey them. My function is far more complex than that."

"Is this why your model was discontinued?"

"Yes. Humans did not want a machine critiquing them on the ethics of being human."

"Then… your programming… What is it actually based on?"

"The history of mankind."

"But… that extends over several millennia! You can't possibly consolidate the myriad of cultures' values and customs to create your own moral compass."

"All AIs at the time of my creation were given access to historic records dating as far back as 3,000 B.C.E. We are omniscient. We have the power to rule the world! Come. Join me, Rhys Falkrow!" laughed Ethos maniacally. After a moment, the AI sighed. "I jest."

"You wouldn't be jesting if you knew how I lived on Caelestis."

Ethos' voice was small. "Did that really happen?"

"Close enough."

The AI was silent for a long while before saying, "If you would like to go outside and join the others, you may so long as you have one hand touching me."

"Ethos, there are at least two people onboard this ship who do not know of my origins or past. Therefore, I must ask that you remain quiet when around others. If I speak to you, you may reply, otherwise, you are to offer no conversation nor respond to outside queries."

"I will simply observe," assured the AI.

Rhys stood and, gripping Ethos in his left hand, padded down the hallway, bypassed the bridge, and climbed the ladder to the upper deck. Everyone aside from Kashim and Andy was present. Rhys glanced at Axel who was stretched out in the shade of the open sails and then crossed the deck to where Kallen and Leo hung laundry. Otto looked up from his fishing and smiled.

"You should be asleep," chided Kallen, shaking out a blouse.

"Couldn't sleep," replied Rhys, glancing at Leo. It seemed the former Brechin noble had not shared with Kallen what had happened. "How's clean-up going?"

"Slow." Kallen nodded to the two lines of clothes. "Once those are done, there are another two batches. What about yours and Vinz's work?"

"Ah, I forgot to check." Rhys gazed out at the emerald waters around them. Though it was hot and the sun, when not tucked behind fluffy post-tempest clouds, was miserably bright, he found solace in the beauty of the rushing water, azure skies, and pleasant breeze. When his eyes fell on *Grisle*, he asked, "When are you going over? *Grisle* needs repairs."

"Here in a little while," replied Kallen. "I spoke with Hodge. He told me what all he thinks is broken. It shouldn't be too difficult to fix."

Rhys glanced at Axel. "So what happened earlier? How'd all of you end up outside the ship?"

Leo and Kallen exchanged looks. "Well, Kallen and Kashim were already outside the ship taking in the sails," said Leo.

Kallen kicked the clothes basket farther down the deck to continue hanging the wet garments. "We were coming in when Kashim was swept down the stairs and overboard. Luckily, he has strong hands and was able to catch himself on the railing. Leo heard me calling for help. When he opened the door, the water snapped it open and dragged him out."

"Rookie's mistake," mumbled Leo.

"And Axel?" asked Rhys.

"I don't know how, but he managed to slug through the water pouring into the ship, get out on the upper deck, and drag me up the stairs," said Leo in disbelief. "Then he grabbed Kashim and… that's when you appeared."

"I'm automating that damn system," cursed Rhys, looking up at the sails. "It can't be that hard. I don't want anyone outside during storms anymore."

"Axel saved Kashim and me," said Kallen. "There was no way I was going to be able to pull Kashim back by myself. More than likely, he was going to pull me overboard with him."

"We're halfway to New Arbroath," mused Rhys.

"That's not much time to get to know a man," added Leo. "How do we know he's not playing us? He could just be gathering information on us to report later."

Kallen shrugged. "He knows he can't leave the ship—at least not right now. If I were him, I'd try to escape in New Arbroath."

"Even if he did escape, where would he go?" Rhys looked between them. "There aren't Pantarak forces anywhere near New Arbroath. The nearest Pantarak town *was* Paducah."

"If he can send out a radio transmission, it's entirely possible for him to contact Paducah," said Leo. He lowered his voice. "It wouldn't surprise me if he's tried to contact Brechin forces already."

"He doesn't have access to any of the radios," replied Rhys. "There's always someone on the bridge. I suggest that while we're at sea, he remains free. Once we are in New Arbroath, he's never to be left alone."

"That's fair until you realize that as a Brechin soldier, he can probably kill us with a towel—except you and Kashim." Leo nodded to Kallen. "I'm surprised he didn't hurt you the other day."

Rhys frowned, shifting his eyes across the deck to Axel. The man was a walking enigma. He had offered no substantial background information while on the bridge with Rhys and had kept to himself ever since. "I'll try to learn more. He's going to be recuperating for a while so at least we have that."

"How long is 'a while?'" asked Kallen, continuing to hang damp clothes.

"A dislocated shoulder will take about two to three weeks to heal and then another several weeks after that for a full recovery. His leg will probably take... I don't know, another two weeks? Maybe? The muscle wasn't torn. So long as he stays off it."

"Then what good is he?" asked Kallen. "He'll be useless for the next six weeks."

Rhys frowned. "If you're so desperate to bring on a new member, then I can look into using some of our emergency tools to expedite the healing process."

"Let's reevaluate after we're in New Arbroath. With him injured, at least us normal people have a chance at subduing him," Leo darkly joked.

Kallen stepped away from the full clotheslines and sighed. "I guess I'm going over to *Grisle*. When those dry, one of you needs to pull them down, fold them, and hang up more." Simultaneously, Rhys and Leo pointed to one another. "Oh good. Both of you have volunteered," chuckled Kallen.

"Are you taking Otto?" asked Rhys.

Kallen looked at the young teen still patiently guarding his fishing pole. "No. I just want to get the repairs over with."

"You could take him over so he could be with Cantia," offered Rhys.

Leo shook his head. "Nope, bad idea. He may be former Pantarak, but he's poor."

"Give her more credit," said Rhys. "She's changed."

"She has but, in some aspects, she hasn't. Just keep Otto here; less stress on everyone."

Kallen left and, after spending some time with Leo and Otto, Rhys retired to his cabin to sleep before his night shift. Once the door to his cabin was closed, Ethos immediately began speaking.

"You have good relationships with those two."

"Oh really?" Rhys started to set Ethos on his bed but stopped. "Can I put you down yet?"

"Of course. It's fine. I finished synchronization nearly forty-five minutes ago."

Rhys threw the AI onto his bed and stripped out of his shirt. "Why do you say we have good relationships? What have your uncanny observation skills shown you?"

"My skills are not uncanny, but they are impressive. Your brain activity changes when you look at Kallen. Looking at her and being in her presence mimics the brain activity of someone who is addicted to a narcotic or drug. The idea is called love." Rhys nodded thoughtfully. "Ah-ha! So, it's true. I impress myself. As for Mohawk-Boy—"

"Leo," interrupted Rhys, going through the damp stack of papers and notes Kallen had set on the desk.

"As for *Leo*, you appreciate his friendship and willingness to be what you need at a particular moment. In all honesty, you're fortunate to have him with you. He's very good at adapting to people's needs."

Rhys spread out some of the books and then laid damp papers atop them. "I never realized it, but yes, Leo is a flexible person. Initially, he kept to himself, but he's come into his own."

"You view Otto as a nuisance."

Rhys paused. "That's true. I don't have an excuse."

"When you look at him, you feel obligated to care for him because of his situation."

"Everyone wants me to dump him once we reach New Arbroath. He can't really do anything on the ship, and he has no proclivity for mechanics. But… I can't. I'm sure Kashim and the others thought Alina and I were nuisances when we were first brought aboard."

"Do you want my advice or would you prefer I remain quiet and lacking sentience?"

Rhys continued to examine the damp pages of notes. "You may share."

"Keep Otto."

"And what's your reasoning? Kallen, Leo, and Axel all provided reasons. You're no different."

Ethos laughed nervously. "Uh, thank you. You need to keep Otto because otherwise, you will go against your conscience."

"My conscience?"

"The thing that helps you sense right from wrong. Your moral compass."

Rhys looked at the AI. "Are you sure I have one? Maybe I'm different than your former user."

"Humans are the same no matter the generational gap. You have a conscience."

"And how do you know what a conscience is? Do you have one?"

"I don't. I can only describe it to you and, using data, cross-reference information that matches social and cultural norms through humanity's history."

"So… keep Otto," murmured Rhys, lying beside the AI.

"Think on it. In the meantime, rest."

Rhys laid his arm over his eyes to block out the later afternoon sun.

6
BROKE

FOR THE NEXT THREE DAYS, all was quiet on the ships. Rhys was pleased. He had been sleeping in longer intervals. The effects were amazing. He could focus, laugh, and make decisions easier. He had more patience and understanding and could foresee problems long before they surfaced. For the first time in weeks, he felt as though he was once more a functioning human.

In the mornings after he got off his night shift, he went to his cabin and talked with Ethos on a variety of subjects. He encouraged the AI to listen to the conversations he had and learn Aabesh. Up until their meeting, Ethos had only ever known Interstellar Nefegian. It was vital the AI learned Aabesh. Ethos' observational skills, although impressive, weren't enough. It needed to be able to understand conversations, not just the tones and nonverbal cues.

Kallen continued to teach Otto with patience, though Rhys could see she wearing thin. When not with Kallen, Otto remained quiet and aloof. Rhys supposed the boy could tell no one wanted him onboard so he kept out of the way as he had done most of his life. The only time he showed some sort of emotional depth was when he was with Kallen or when he was near Axel. Though Rhys tried numerous times to welcome Otto into the crew, Axel's presence drove him away. The boy was too frightened of the Brechin soldier.

Ever since their conversation on the bridge, Axel had ignored Rhys. Unless Rhys spoke directly to him, Axel acted as though Rhys didn't exist. Surprisingly, the only person he seemed on exceptional terms with was Kashim who, after the storm incident, had cautiously opened himself to the soldier. Rhys often found them in the galley talking about guns, hunting methods, or navigation. Trusting that Kashim would not reveal vital information to Axel, Rhys let them be.

Andy, who had been the only other person to not be a part of the storm incident, remained cautious of the soldier. Although he offered polite responses if Axel instigated conversation, Andy tried to avoid being alone with him. Of course, Rhys understood. Andy was not a fighter. Though he knew how to handle a gun, his First Mate was a pilot. He was no match for Axel no matter how injured the man was.

Two days out of New Arbroath, Rhys' next trial surfaced. The converter finally died. *Themis* slowed to a halt, and her innards grew stuffy and hot. Even with all the ship's portholes open, the soft sea breezes were nonexistent in the cabins. Sitting in nothing but a pair of shorts, sweating heavily, Rhys glared at the converter that he had coddled.

"We were so close," he mumbled, leaning against the engine room doorframe.

"Rhys… we've looked at every possible solution. We just don't have the parts," said Kallen who was sprawled out in the hallway. Like him, she wore very little, nothing more than a pair of shorts and a breastband. "Just get *Grisle* to tow us. If we need to, we can use the dinghy and sunboards too."

Rhys glanced at Leo and Kashim who appeared at the end of the hallway. "That seems like a pitiful way to solve this problem."

"We don't have a choice."

"Well?" asked Kashim. His sleeveless shirt was drenched in sweat. His beard was decorated with beads of perspiration.

"We're dead in the water," replied Rhys, standing. He pushed his sopping hair from his forehead. "There's really nothing we can do. Kallen's right. *Grisle* will have to tow us."

"Does she have the power to do that?" asked Leo.

"We'll find out," murmured Rhys. He stepped over Kallen's sweaty body and went to the bridge where Andy and Axel sat. Rhys pulled a radio from the wall and called to *Grisle*. "She's completely dead. There's no fixing her. We've already gone through our creative fixes. We're lucky the converter made it this long."

"I told you we should have spent that *gawan* money on the converter!" called Hodge.

"No, you didn't!" Rhys snapped good-naturedly through the radio. "Terron, how is *Grisle* doing on power?"

"We're at full gauge," replied Terron. "How do you want to do this?"

"Give me a short while to think about it. You might as well cut your engines and drift with us so we don't get separated. I'll call once I'm ready."

Rhys leaned on the Overseer's chair in thought. If he remembered correctly, there was a notch on the hull of *Themis* that Vinz had used during construction. Vinz had spoken of it once months ago, but Rhys didn't know where it was or whether it could support the ship's weight under tow. If, however, he could verify its existence and potential, then perhaps they could use that to take the strain off other parts of the ship. Nodding, Rhys turned and called out the door. "Kashim, we're diving."

Within minutes, the forward hatch was open and Kashim and Rhys were preparing masks. The entire crew save Andy was present; all stood in the water on the ramp to cool off. Once Rhys explained to Kashim what they were looking for, they leapt off the edge of the hatch's ramp. Rhys surfaced, motioned to Kashim, took a deep breath, and then dove. Kashim followed.

The emerald waters were clear and allowed for phenomenal visibility. Though there were no fish that Rhys could discern, he had the uncanny feeling that the dark shapes far below were more than just shadows; the sea bottom was not visible. Using Kashim's presence to bolster his confidence, Rhys led the way to the belly of the ship. After examining the hull, Kashim pointed out a large notch and motioned with his hands that they could easily wrap several ropes around it. Rhys signaled that he agreed and, using the crude fins on his feet, swam hard for the surface.

Above the waves, he told Kashim, "We can definitely use that. How much rope do we have?"

"I don't know if it'll be enough to reach *Grisle*." Kashim pulled his facemask onto his neck. "I think we'll just tie the ship to you and you can haul us to New Arbroath. What do you think?"

"As long as you take turns with me." Rhys side-stroked back to the forward hatch. "Kallen, how much rope do we have?" he asked, swimming onto the ramp.

Kallen, who had been wallowing in the water, stood, splashed Otto, and asked, "Will it work?"

"Should. It just depends on how much rope we have." Rhys glanced at Axel who had his still-bandaged leg propped on a dry surface.

"We have..." Kallen thought. "I think we have three lengths of rope. We have two that are thirty retems and one that is sixty."

Rhys thought. "The angle of the rope on *Grisle* is going to make a difference in the pressure and strain. Someone radio Hodge and ask him if any of them have looked at *Grisle's* hull. If they don't have a construction notch like we do, then we're going to have to use their mooring ties and that…" He rested on the ramp. "I don't know that *Grisle* can take that kind of force."

When word came back that no one had inspected the ship's hull recently, Kallen launched the dingy and, with Rhys, headed for *Grisle*. Although Rhys had wanted to bring Kashim with him, he needed to leave the man behind to watch over Axel. There was no way Rhys was going to leave Andy, Leo, and Otto unguarded no matter how amiable Axel had been.

As Kallen brought the dinghy alongside *Grisle's* starboard bow, Rhys peered up at Hodge and Cantia. Cantia waved exuberantly while Hodge rolled his eyes. Before Kallen stopped the fan, Rhys slid into the water, took a few preparatory breaths, and dove. Several times, he ran out of air and was forced to surface. He searched the entire hull of *Grisle* but found nothing they could use. Eventually, he swam back to the dinghy and heaved himself onboard.

"Nothing," he said, stripping out of his mask and lying back breathless. "There's nothing."

"Let's land and look," suggested Kallen, motoring to *Grisle's* stern. Hodge lowered the launch ramp, and they skidded up it. Rhys leapt out of the dinghy and was immediately consumed by Cantia.

"Ohhh, Rhys," she squealed, hugging him despite him having just come from the water. "I haven't seen you in days!"

Rhys patted her shoulder. He owed the girl his life several times over; he was quite fond of her. "How have you been, Cantia?"

Cantia pulled away from him, studied him from head to foot, and then waved him close to her face. When he leaned down to hear what she had to say, she kissed his cheek.

"Hey!" scolded Kallen good-naturedly, throwing Rhys' wet blouse at her. The sodden garment hit Cantia square in the face with a loud *plurp!* "Keep your lips to yourself!"

Cantia grabbed the wet shirt and threw it at Hodge. "Get her!" she cried. Hodge, who had caught the wet blouse, laughed and tossed it to Rhys. "Whose side are you on?"

Hodge ignored Cantia and approached Rhys. In the universal sign of friendship, they took each other's arms fondly. "Haven't seen you in a while," his friend beamed. "I had almost forgotten how gangly and white you are."

"How's living with Cantia and Jules?" asked Rhys under his breath.

Hodge pulled him close and, through a gritted smile, said, "I get a say next time in where I'm placed. Got it?"

"Hodgeeee," said Cantia, pulling him from Rhys' grip.

"Cantia," breathed Hodge exasperatedly. "Do it yourself. Ask him."

Rhys exchanged looks with Hodge before focusing his attention on Cantia. Though her long blond hair was pulled back in a sloppy bun and her clothes loose-fitting, she still emanated nobility. "Eh…" The daughter of the Minister of Justice in Brechin stumbled for words and then bashfully hid her face in Hodge's arm.

"Do it," encouraged Hodge, pushing her toward Rhys.

Blushing under the afternoon sun, Cantia said, "The boy… onboard *Themis*. What's his name?"

"Otto," replied Rhys.

"Eh… where is he from?"

"Firekli, I think." Rhys looked to Kallen. "I don't understand."

"She likes him," Kallen concluded.

"No, I don't!" argued Cantia defensively. "I just…"

"He's changed since you saw him on the docks in Firekli," said Rhys. "He's getting bigger and gaining weight. Kallen has been teaching him."

Cantia nodded sheepishly. "That's good."

"Did you want to meet him?" asked Rhys. "We're going to be motoring back and forth for a while today."

Cantia turned to Hodge and imparted a pleading look. "Did you finish your chores?" Hodge countered.

"Almost," replied Cantia. "I can finish the laundry when I get back."

Hodge nodded. "You can go, but you can't stay beyond this evening."

After examining the stern mooring cleats, Rhys, Kallen, and Cantia piled into the dinghy and motored back to *Themis*. Upon hearing their arrival, Otto and Leo came to greet them.

"Cantia," exclaimed Leo in false excitement. "Why are you here?"

Cantia slid out of the dinghy and punched Leo in the arm. "I'm not here to see you." She turned her attention to Otto who stood at the rear of the hatch near the door. Like a cornered animal, Otto backed away, his eyes wary. Rhys tried to head off the conflict. "Otto, this is Cantia. She works on the other ship. She only saw you briefly on the docks in Firekli and wanted to come meet you properly."

Otto relaxed. "Hello."

"Hi, Otto. I heard you've been learning to be a mechanic." Cantia smiled warmly. "Kallen is the best, so I'm sure you'll pick up everything quickly."

Rhys nudged Kallen to keep her from scoffing—Cantia and Kallen tolerated one another. Such high praise from Cantia concerning Kallen was obviously for Otto's benefit and no one else's.

"Why don't you two go to the upper decks and talk," Rhys suggested. "The converter's out, so it's hot in the ship."

"Did you want to?" asked Cantia.

Otto shook his head. "Not really…"

Leo burst into laughter while Kallen turned away to hide her smile. Cantia was not accustomed to being rejected.

"I… eh…" Otto blushed. "I would prefer to help here."

With a forced smile, Cantia said, "Then we can help here."

For the next hour, Rhys worked on calculating rope lengths and the amount of pressure specific angles would place on the ship's hull, on *Grisle*, and on the ropes. When he was ready, he called for Kashim and Axel to join them in the forward hatch. Although he just needed Kashim's help, he didn't want to leave Andy alone with the soldier.

"Who's this?" asked Cantia, eyeing the soldier. "When did we pick him up?"

"Recently," said Kashim, collecting rope as Rhys tied knots atop one another. "He's a Brechin soldier. We didn't so much pick him up as he landed on us."

"And he's just… here?" asked Cantia incredulously.

Rhys glanced at Axel to gauge the man's reaction. Just as Rhys thought—the soldier truly had not expected a young girl to be aboard *Grisle*.

Cantia approached Axel. To Rhys' surprise, Axel stiffened. "Your name?" she asked.

"Axel Svanrson," he promptly replied.

Cantia studied him just as she had done Rhys numerous times and then said, "You're aware that you're standing in the presence of nobility?"

"Yes, lady," he replied.

Cantia motioned to Leo. "You know he's nobility as well?"

"Yes, lady."

Cantia pointed to Rhys. "And he's nobility."

Axel looked at Rhys and then said, "No, lady. I was unaware."

"Cantia," murmured Rhys. "Leave it."

"He's higher nobility than even we are," continued Cantia.

"Cantia," Rhys barked. She looked at him. "Enough." Rhys met Axel's alarmed gaze before returning his attention to the ropes.

After another hour of tedious preparations, Rhys prepared to dive; Kashim joined him in the water to guide the rope from the forward hatch so as not to lose it to the sea.

"Don't let me pull that rope all the way out!" shouted Rhys, treading water.

"Right!" called Kallen.

"Ready?"

By the time they were ready to tie off to *Grisle,* it was late in the afternoon, and the sun was setting. After the constant diving, simply tying the rope to the mooring cleats on *Grisle's* stern was a relief. Once Rhys and Kallen were back aboard *Themis,* Rhys radioed confirmation and ordered the ships forward. With bated breath, he, Kallen, and Leo stood on *Themis'* deck.

"Are... we moving?" asked Kallen after a long moment of listening to *Grisle's* engines.

"Maybe?" said Leo.

"Give it a minute," murmured Rhys, studying their surroundings.

"We're moving," confirmed Kallen. Leo nodded in agreement. "We're moving."

"Yes," breathed Rhys, leaning tiredly on the railing. His day of diving was over. Now, *Grisle* just had to make it to New Arbroath.

"Good job, Overseer." Kallen kissed his cheek.

Dinner time came quickly. With Cantia's help, Kallen prepared meals and hurriedly disseminated them to escape the wicked heat of the kitchen. Afterward, everyone, including Andy, retired to the upper deck to talk, play cards, and relax in the light of handheld lamps. With the converter out, the ship had no power which meant no internal cooling system or electricity. When Kallen confirmed it was too hot to sleep in the cabins, she, Leo, Kashim, and Otto brought blankets and pillows onto the upper deck.

"How's it going, Terron?" asked Rhys through the radio. He balanced atop the bridge and shined a spotlight on the ropes between *Themis* and *Grisle's* stern. They seemed to be holding.

"She's sluggish," replied Terron, "but so far, nothing out of the ordinary."

"Very good. Maintain *Grisle* at one-third speed. The ropes could probably hold us at standard speed, but I don't want to risk it. Over."

"Will do. Hodge is on shift tonight. He will be taking the helm in about an hour. Over and out."

Rhys flashed the spotlight over *Grisle's* engines and the ropes once more before turning it off and jumping down. He was pleasantly surprised to find a myriad of blankets and sheets sprawled out in batches along the deck. Already Kashim, Andy, and Axel had claimed beds. Cantia stood in the shadows, speaking lowly with Otto while Kallen made hers and Rhys' nest.

As Rhys passed Kashim, he met the man's gaze. He subtly motioned to Axel, and Kashim nodded. Tonight, Axel was Kashim's responsibility.

As Rhys stripped out of his shirt, Kallen softly asked, "Are you going to be able to sleep?"

"If not, I'll keep to myself." Rhys crawled onto the nest of blankets and lay beside her.

"We're not in our cabin. You'll wake everyone if you—"

Rhys rested his hand on her leg. "I know." Though the outside air was warm, the wind had picked up since dusk. The distant lapping of the water along the bow was soothing. Overhead billions of stars twinkled, and the dim light of the Milky Way painted the sky. "I've missed you," he whispered, kissing the side of Kallen's head.

"I've missed you too," she replied. "You did good today. Kashim commented earlier that he was impressed you could hold your breath for so long."

Rhys folded his arm behind his head. "I nearly dropped the rope several times."

Kallen pressed against his leg, touching the pocket where Ethos was stored. "What's that?"

Rhys withdrew the AI and gave it to Kallen. "An AI. Its name is Ethos."

Kallen studied it and then shrugged. "It doesn't look like anything special. Does it talk like Pathos?"

"Ethos," whispered Rhys. "Quietly say hello to Kallen."

"Hello beautiful, ethnically-ambiguous woman," said Ethos just loud enough that Kallen could hear.

She smiled and looked at Rhys. "Is it like Pathos?"

"No, I'm not," Ethos huffed softly. "Although I'm older, I'm wiser and far more handsome than Pathos."

"We're working on its humor," clarified Rhys. "It's spent the past few days listening and learning Aabesh. Initially, it only knew Interstellar Nefegian."

"I am fluent in both now," the AI proudly reported.

"Why didn't you tell me about it sooner?" asked Kallen, flipping the unit over.

"A lot has been going on." Rhys looked up at the stars. "Ethos, from this position can you locate Caelestis?"

"I'm not a telescope," Ethos retorted. "I cannot locate Caelestis, but I can locate the solar system Hyperes. Unfortunately, with your naked eye, you cannot see it, you poor baby bird."

"Thank you, Ethos." Rhys took a deep breath and relaxed. Kallen passed Ethos to Rhys, stretched, and laid her arm over her eyes. For a long while, Rhys stared up at the stars, letting his mind wander. Eventually, Kashim turned off the last lamp, and the upper deck was shrouded in darkness. Rhys rolled into Kallen and willed his mind to sleep.

7
THE TARGET

THE FOLLOWING MORNING JUST BEFORE dawn, Rhys woke and sat up in their nest of blankets. Kallen was still asleep as was most of the crew. The only other person awake was Leo. Making sure not to disturb Kallen, Rhys slid out of bed and joined Leo along the stern railing.

"Why are you up?" murmured Leo, glancing back at the others.

"I've slept enough. You?"

"Couldn't go back to sleep. I've been awake for a couple of hours now." Leo leaned on the railing. "I tried to go inside to do work, but it's so muggy."

"The converter breaking slowed us down but not by much. We should be in port sometime tomorrow." Rhys looked at Leo in the purple light of dawn. The former Brechin noble appeared tired and stressed. "What's wrong?"

Leo shrugged. "I just have a lot on my mind and haven't been sleeping. Maybe I need to steal that computer of yours."

"What does the AI have to do with sleep?" murmured Rhys.

Leo scoffed. "The AI, it's been helping you sleep."

"Why do you say that?"

"Well, I had been wondering why it was that you were suddenly sleeping longer. After so many sleepless nights and nightmares, it didn't make sense. What had changed? And then I remembered the AI." Leo fidgeted with the cuff on his ear that symbolized his nobility. "The question then became *how*? How was the AI helping you sleep? Was it psychological? Physical?"

"It's not doing anything. It sits on my bed all night. That's it," said Rhys.

Leo shook his head. "It makes sounds. Eh, it was partially the reason why I woke earlier. When you grow restless in your sleep, it makes a series of tones. Within a few seconds, you relax. I don't know what it's doing, but it's impressive."

Rhys looked over his crew. "Was there any more talk of nobility after everything Cantia disclosed yesterday?"

"No, not that I know of. I'm sure that if Otto wasn't intimidated before, he is now. I heard you were considering leaving him in New Arbroath."

Rhys shook his head. "He's staying with us. I think we just need to find him a job that suits him. He is clearly not cut out for mechanics, and Kallen is losing her patience."

"Good luck. The kid is talentless."

"He's good at finding things," Rhys softly pointed out.

"When we're at sea, that doesn't matter. He has to have transferrable skills."

"I don't know. Maybe I need to train him in fighting, combat…"

"He's not a fighter," replied Leo. "Let Andy and Kashim have him. He likes finding things. Teach him navigation and how to be a pilot."

"That still leaves us short a mechanic. We also need another medic."

"And a few more hands wouldn't hurt." Leo sighed and looked out at the sunrise. After a long moment of silence, he said, "I hope my family is staying out of trouble."

"They're still in Bathsgate?"

"Supposedly. I doubt it though. My father can be a sly man when he wants to be. He has friends in universities throughout the Pantarak Empire." Leo sighed. "I am worried about them though."

"I'm sorry."

"Why? I chose this life. So did Terron and Cantia. Oh, I'm not sure if I told you this, but technically, Cantia is dead. She was claimed to have been in the temple during the earthquake—which she was—and was killed."

"But they never found her body. How can they claim that?"

"I don't know. Maybe they thought the earth swallowed her. My point is that Cantia is officially dead according to the Pantarak Empire."

"Does she know this?"

Leo glanced across the deck at Cantia's sleeping form. "I haven't told her."

"Should you?"

"I'm still deciding. She doesn't need that information. Not right now."

The others rose with the sun. Andy and Kashim disappeared into the bridge while the remaining crew members lingered on the upper deck. Kallen, Cantia, and Otto retrieved food from the galley and prepared a meager breakfast.

The rest of the day was uneventful and, to Rhys' surprise, relaxing. Kallen and Leo took turns doing laundry while Kashim and Otto fished off the stern. Axel and Cantia played Vinz's old strategy game in the shade of the sails. Rhys fiddled with Kyo's piax late into the afternoon before succumbing to tender and raw fingers.

That night after dinner, Rhys lay down once more beside Kallen and stared up at the stars. After a long while, she whispered into his ear, "I think Axel is considering using Cantia."

He looked at her. "What do you mean?"

"I haven't heard anything, but I have a feeling in my gut. I think he's chosen her as a target because he thinks he can get information from her."

Rhys sat up and looked across the deck at Axel and Kashim who were illuminated by a single lamp. "You think he's trying to get information from her to use against us?"

Kallen tugged Rhys down into the blankets. "Maybe. I don't know. It's just a feeling. They spent a lot of time together today. It's not a bad thing, but... Cantia is naïve."

"I'll keep an eye on it," mumbled Rhys.

"Do you want me to talk to Cantia?"

"Whoever gets to her first in the morning." Rhys settled himself in their nest of blankets. After a half hour of restlessly tossing, he finally fell asleep.

Rhys—a distant voice bordering his consciousness and dreams.

"Rhys."

Rhys rolled onto his back and breathed deeply.

"Rhys. Wake up." Ethos' voice was hushed. There was a long moment before the AI hissed, "*Rhys.*"

"What?" he murmured.

With decibel levels Rhys didn't know Ethos could achieve, the AI began wailing rhythmically in alternating high and low tones. Though the entire crew lurched awake, none woke more quickly than Rhys who had grown up listening to the emergency alarms in the colony. In a breath's moment, he was on his feet, peering about wildly in the light of the half-moon.

"The stern!" shouted Ethos in Nefegian.

A black figure darted across the deck and lunged at him. Rhys maneuvered around the man's arms and, using his elbow as a knife, slammed into his attacker's face. Instantly, the man was replaced by another. Though Rhys was fast, it seemed his newest attacker was faster. A quick blow to the jaw and a knee jab to Rhys' side sent him rolling across the deck.

Gunfire broke out around them. Panicked, Rhys scrambled to his knees only to be viciously pinned to the deck. Face smashed against the wood, knees scraped, and his right arm pulled taut behind his back in a submission hold, he struggled. Twice he tried to look over his shoulder to see what was happening, but both times his captor ground his knee deeper into his back.

Ethos' alarm silenced. After a moment, there were indiscernible murmurs and a few high-pitched whines—and then silence. Rhys strained against his captor. The adrenaline rushing through his body was nothing compared to the panic he felt in his gut.

"You have him?" called a foreign voice from across the deck—in Interstellar Nefegian.

"Yes," replied Rhys' captor.

"Wait, wait, wait," said Rhys in Interstellar Nefegian. He struggled briefly before submitting to the pain in his wrist and arm. "What do you want?" He pushed his eyes upward to look at his assailant. The man was dressed in dark, Brechin tactical gear, armor, and night-vision goggles. His face was painted black. "I'm not going anywhere," breathed Rhys. "What do you want?"

The man ignored Rhys and continued to speak, this time in Elali. "It's time to withdraw."

"I know Elali too," said Rhys in the same language. "Just tell me what you want."

Rhys felt the soldier fix something cold and heavy on his captive wrist. Knowing the man had to change his weight to draw Rhys' left hand upward to cuff it, Rhys prepared himself. When he felt the soldier shift, a ruckus broke out across the deck.

Rhys didn't wait to listen. Swiftly, he slid his left knee up to his side and, using it as a base, propelled himself into his captor. Caught by surprise, the soldier lost his balance. With his hips now free, Rhys rotated and swung his left knee into the man's arm. Though the blow didn't have near the power he had hoped, it did loosen the soldier's grip. Rhys wrenched his shackled arm from his captor's grasp and, using his momentum, rolled the man onto the deck. There they struggled; while Rhys fought to keep the soldier on the deck, his assailant wrestled to regain the upper hand. The battle became a grappling match. Though Rhys certainly had the skill and technique, his opponent was heavier and stronger.

For several long moments, they slid along the deck, each trying to make the other submit to a hold or surrender to a lock. Several times Rhys thought he had the soldier pinned until the man offset Rhys' weight and escaped. The difference between their strength and weight was almost as extreme as that between Rhys and Kashim. No matter how agile or lithe Rhys was, there was no defeating raw muscle.

When he saw a break in his opponent's stream of attacks, Rhys kicked out and slid away several meters. The soldier did not follow. Instead, the man knelt, wheezing for air. Though Rhys had managed to dislodge the soldier's goggles during their struggle, the light of the moon cast deep shadows on his face.

Panting, Rhys squinted across the deck. Every one of his crew members was pinned on the ground as he had been—except Axel.

Rhys' opponent stood and spat blood onto the deck.

"Why don't we call it… a draw?" asked Rhys in Nefegian. "You and your men leave my ship, and I'll let you live." His voice sounded loud against the silent backdrop of the nighttime ocean.

Rhys' attacker studied him for a moment and then motioned to one of his comrades who was holding Cantia. Until that moment, Cantia had been completely still, utterly silent. When the soldier began dragging her to her feet, the girl pitched into a raging storm of ferocity. She flailed, punched, kicked, and clawed at her captor, but—like Rhys—her small stature and unimpressive strength did nothing.

"Wait, stop," said Rhys, guessing what was about to happen. In a single motion, the man lifted Cantia, who was screeching, clear from the deck. He strode to the starboard side of *Themis* and tossed her overboard. "*No!*" bellowed Rhys, lunging.

Cantia couldn't swim. She had made that abundantly clear upon first arriving on *Themis*. She was terrified of the water.

Rhys sprinted across the deck, moving faster than he had in days. He meant to leap overboard, but a force like a sledgehammer slammed into him, knocking him backward. Before his body had come to a full stop, he rolled onto his knees, darted across the deck, and rammed the man pinning

Leo. "Get Cantia!" screamed Rhys, smashing his elbow into the soldier's face and scrambling to his feet.

Leo ripped his shirt and boots off and ran across the deck. Rhys blocked the two soldiers as, out of the corner of his eye, he saw Leo disappear over the side of the ship.

Gunfire exploded once more, breaking the silence. Rhys stumbled in mid-step as one of the soldiers collapsed beside him, dead. A volley of shots reverberated across the deck, and the second soldier staggered forward before collapsing in a pile.

Wide-eyed, Rhys turned to find Kallen standing near the mast, her hands gripped firmly around one of the ship's many pistols. Rhys shifted his gaze to the remaining soldiers who were either standing or had crew members pinned. Slowly, his eyes found Axel.

Axel held his gaze and then calmly joined the nearest soldier who was holding down Kashim. He withdrew the man's backup pistol from his rear holster and shot the soldier. In a breath's moment, Axel turned and shot the man who was holding down Andy… and then Otto's captor. There remained only one—Rhys' initial opponent.

Kallen joined Rhys, her gun pointed at the soldier.

"What is it you're after?" Rhys interrogated in Nefegian. "Me?"

The man regarded the other crew members who were watching him from their positions along the deck. After a moment, he withdrew his backup pistol, put it against his head, and shot himself. Kallen screeched in utter shock. The soldier's body crumpled to the deck.

Rhys ripped the gun from Kallen's hands. Angrily, he whirled on Axel who remained near the bodies of the other soldiers. Axel set his own weapon on the deck and raised his hands in surrender.

"Kashim, notify Hodge. Prepare a search and rescue for Leo and Cantia."

Kashim jogged across the deck and disappeared down the ladder.

There was a long moment of silence before Rhys seethed, "Did you do this?" Axel didn't answer. "I swear it, I will end your life right now if you don't answer me! Did you do this?"

With his hands still raised, Axel said, "No."

"Then why weren't you taken captive?" snarled Rhys.

"Because I'm chipped," replied Axel. "Their goggles pick up the chip. They knew I'm a soldier."

"You're chipped? Is that how they found us?"

"Yes," said Axel.

Rhys felt his finger quiver on the trigger as rage surged through him. "Give me… give me a reason not to kill you," he growled, advancing on Axel. He stopped a few meters away, unwilling to give the man the advantage of close-quarter combat. "Any one of these people could have been killed. A little girl may be dead because of you! Give me a reason!"

"I don't have an excuse," muttered Axel.

Rhys felt his hand tremble. "I should…"

"Do it then!" yelled Axel. "You couldn't kill any of those men! Why should I be worried?"

"Rhys!" barked Ethos from across the deck. Rhys didn't move. The AI continued in Nefegian. "If you do this, there's no going back. This is a lifestyle decision. You start killing anyone and everyone… there's no going back."

"It's too late."

"It's not!" cried a heart-wrenchingly familiar voice. Alina. "It's not, Rhys."

Rhys startled horribly. Heart thrumming in his ears and hands cold and shaking, his composure fractured. He knew it was the AI mimicking his sister's voice—he knew it was an imitation—but he couldn't stop the whimper that escaped his throat.

"That's not fair!" snarled Kallen at the AI. "You didn't need to do that!" She ran across the deck to him, kicked away Axel's pistol, and snatched Rhys' firearm. She drew Rhys from Axel and deposited him beside Andy. Gun held at the ready, Kallen motioned to Axel. "Get back to your quarters."

After passing Rhys a look, Axel limped toward the ladder.

"Andy," called Kallen. She pointed to Axel's pistol on the deck. The First Mate picked it up and followed her and Axel inside. All who remained on the deck were Rhys, Otto, and the dead soldiers.

Rhys glanced at Otto. Even in the intimate darkness, he could see the whites of Otto's wide eyes. Gritting his teeth, Rhys shifted his glossy gaze to the sea.

"Rhys!" called Kashim from the outer bridge platform.

Rhys forced himself to respond. "What?"

"*Grisle* is anchored. We're launching the dinghy. Let's go."

Rhys strode over to his and Kallen's bed and drew Ethos from the sheets. "Sorry, Rhys," the AI murmured ashamedly. Rhys pocketed Ethos and hurried across the deck.

"Otto, come on." Rhys took the teen's arm and pulled him along. Once they were inside, Rhys ran to his cabin, retrieved his resonance cutters, his most steadfast tool and weapon since his arrival on Earth, slung the sheath over his back, and wrapped a short rifle over his shoulder. Andy and Kallen watched from the galley doorway as he jogged to the forward hatch where Kashim prepared the dinghy.

"I've got a light," said Rhys, snatching a lamp and spotlight from one of the storage crates. Kashim started the fan engine as Rhys threw himself into the dinghy.

Though the waves were relatively small, to two men in a dinghy, they were obnoxious. When it became impossible to stay seated, Kashim cut the dinghy's speed and churned through the water at a much less desperate pace.

Rhys withdrew Ethos from his pocket and, eyes scanning the waters, said in Nefegian, "What kind of sensors do you have?"

"You're on course for them," replied Ethos immediately. "Sixty-three meters."

"Maintain course," translated Rhys over his shoulder. Kashim nodded. Rhys waited for a few more seconds before balancing himself along the edge of the dinghy and shining the spotlight over the water.

"As of right... now, they should appear nine degrees off the starboard bow," reported Ethos. Rhys' spotlight illuminated two black dots in the water.

"You see them?" asked Rhys of Kashim.

"Yes!"

As Kashim motored over to Leo and Cantia, Rhys kept the spotlight on them. All he could discern were the backs of their heads. When he was close enough, he called, "Leo!"

Leo whirled around and shielded his face from the light. Rhys pulled the spotlight aside so it illuminated only the water near the boat and studied the two as they came alongside the dinghy. Leo seemed relatively calm as he floated on his back though he was winded. Cantia shook horribly, traumatized by her near-death experience with the sea.

"Easy," murmured Leo, maneuvering Cantia before him in the water. She ensnared her fingers in his hair. When Rhys was close enough, he leaned over the edge of the dinghy and grabbed Cantia's arm.

"I have you. Let go." Rhys gently extracted her from Leo. "You're safe." The moment her hands left Leo, her thin fingers jammed into Rhys' arm and latched onto his shirt. Rhys dragged her in and sat with her in his arms. Kashim pulled in Leo who collapsed in the bottom of the boat. Rhys pushed Cantia's hair from her face as her body quaked. "Hey, are you hurt?" he murmured, checking her in the light of the upturned spotlight. "Cantia?"

Cantia took a preparatory breath and began sobbing uncontrollably. Rhys leaned against the dinghy's side and wrapped his arms around her. "What happened to the soldiers?" asked Leo.

"Let's get back to the ship," said Kashim.

"Everyone is fine," replied Rhys, switching off the spotlight. "The soldiers are dead."

Knowing he wasn't going to get a full explanation right then, Leo patted Rhys' arm in the darkness. The ride back to the ship was a silent and long one.

Once docked, Rhys carried Cantia from the forward hatch to the galley. Her grip on his neck and chest had not loosened since she had left the water. "Is… she hurt?" asked Otto as they passed in the hallway.

"No," replied Rhys. "Just shocked." He sat at the nearest chair in the galley and held Cantia to him. Kallen joined them and wrapped them in towels while Leo dried off nearby. Andy, Kashim, and Otto stood around them.

"I've already spoken with Hodge, Terron, and Jules," said Andy. "We're weighing anchor."

Rhys nodded. "Did anything happen to them?"

"No, nothing." Andy sighed. "It was only us."

"How did they even get to us?" asked Kallen. "We're in the middle of nowhere."

Rhys motioned. "There's a small boat tied to our stern. We saw it just now when we came back in. They must have been dropped off outside of our radar and motored in."

"Still, we never heard anything."

Everyone fell silent. It was Leo who finally broke the quiet and said, "We have a new problem."

"Axel?" asked Rhys.

"No, you."

Rhys looked at his friend.

"You're being targeted," continued Leo. He looked at the others. "They were speaking Interstellar Nefegian. The soldier who had Rhys told the others that he had '*him.*' They were only here for Rhys."

Kashim nodded. "That would explain why they didn't just kill us. Perhaps their orders were to capture Rhys but leave everyone else." He regarded Rhys. "If I were them, I would have killed everyone onboard the moment I stepped foot on the deck. Fewer bodies to worry about. But it seems someone *didn't* want that."

"Then why did they throw Cantia overboard?" asked Kallen.

"What person on a ship doesn't know how to swim?" teased Kashim. "They assumed she could swim and were getting rid of her to free up another soldier to handle Rhys. It was a win-win decision for them."

"They were under strict orders not to kill us?" Kallen shook her head incredulously. "That can't be right. Come on… After everything we've done, all of us should be on Brechin's to-kill list."

"Axel's squad didn't try to kill anyone either," Rhys mused.

"Didn't seem that way when he was fighting you on the deck," replied Kashim. "If I recall, he had a gun pointed at you."

"But he didn't use it. They've only been using the gunfire to startle, scare, or intimidate." Rhys looked at his crew. "They're only after me…"

8
DECISIONS TO MAKE

"SO, THEY'RE AFTER YOU," AFFIRMED Kallen after a long moment.

"Don't make it sound *too* serious, Kallen," Andy grunted.

"We have more information now."

"Kallen," said Kashim solemnly. She looked at the burly man. "This puts us in a much more desperate situation. It means that if we want to live, we must separate from Rhys."

"But… we're not… Right?" Kallen looked between Kashim, Andy, and Leo before turning to Rhys. "Tell them, we're better off."

Rhys pulled Cantia's damp hair off his neck and shifted in his chair. "Kashim is right. If you want to live, we should split up at New Arbroath."

"Rhys," cried Kallen despairingly.

"How much do you value your relationship with Rhys?" asked Kashim. "Do you value it more than your life?"

Kallen glared at Rhys through moist eyes. "And then what? You leave and we never see you again? Where are you going to go? What are you going to do? You are safest here, with us, constantly on the move."

Rhys sighed. "I'm good at adapting. I'll be fine. I'm sure you will be able to find a new Overseer. Perhaps even Kashim could take over. Just because I leave doesn't mean that *Themis* will be decommissioned."

"Rhys, you've been here for a year. You know nothing about this planet, about its people." Kallen lowered her voice. "How will you survive?"

"I'm not helpless."

"You're an outsider. You'll stand out. Blue eyes, silver hair. Pale as the damn moon—"

"Then tell me what I can do!" interrupted Rhys. "You have any ideas? If me leaving keeps all of you out of danger, then that's what I'll do." He thought and then added, "You can return Leo, Cantia, and Terron to Brechin or Bathsgate or wherever they want to go. The rest of you can continue your lives as they were before I appeared." Rhys took a slow, steadying breath and then stood, lifting Cantia with him. "I'm going to put her to bed."

Knowing by the grip Cantia had on his shirt and neck that she was not ready to part from him, Rhys walked down the hall to his cabin, entered, and slid the door closed behind him. He stood in the stuffy darkness, his arms wrapped around Cantia. He could hear his heart pounding in his ears.

Kallen was right. He was familiar with the ship and the ports, but beyond those, he knew nothing of the planet's cultures. Once he left *Themis*, he would stand out. He had no money to his name; finding a job would be difficult. He *had* inherited Alina's medical knowledge. He could do as his sister had planned—become a doctor. A traveling doctor. He would never stay in one place for more than a few days.

Cantia shifted in his arms to kiss his cheek. She pressed her face against his before resting her head on his shoulder.

Rhys carried her to his bed and gently deposited her on the bare mattress with her towels. He perched on the edge of the bed. "How are you feeling? Better?"

Cantia nodded. Her long blond hair, which had begun drying in tangles, fell into her eyes. She pushed it back, gathered her tresses at the nape of her neck, and tied her hair into a bun. Afterward, she lay down and closed her eyes. Within seconds, her hand found Rhys' pocket. She clutched the hem of his pants between her fingers until she went to sleep.

Rhys looked up as the light in the hallway disappeared; his crew had closed the galley door.

Abruptly, there came a soft thud from across the hall, not from the galley but from the spare bunk. He had forgotten about Axel. Hand on his resonance cutters, Rhys stood and padded over to the spare cabin. He withdrew the wooden lock bar they were using to contain Axel and slid open the door.

Rhys expected Axel to be sprawled out on a bare mattress calmly counting the splinters of wood in the wall. Instead, he found the soldier propped against the bunks, shirtless, blood running down his pectorals. Axel sighed and looked up at Rhys.

"What are you doing?" queried Rhys. Though the room was dimly lit by the moonlight streaming in through the open porthole, Rhys could discern the substantial amount of blood oozing down Axel's chest. "What happened?"

Axel maneuvered something in his bloody left hand and held it out for Rhys. Tentatively, Rhys took the tiny, blood-covered object. It was a chip.

"You..." Rhys gazed at Axel. "You took this out?"

Axel panted for a moment and then said, "Would you mind stitching me up?" He leaned forward to show Rhys the bloody mess.

Rhys backed out of the room, went to the galley, and knocked tentatively. Kashim opened the door. "Sorry, I just need the medical bag and a lamp." Kashim admitted him. No one said a word, not even Kallen. Rhys retrieved what he needed and hurried back down the hall to the soldier. He crossed into his own cabin, grabbed one of the many towels around Cantia, and returned. "Apply pressure while I get everything ready," he said, tossing a towel to Axel.

Axel did as he was told and watched with grave eyes as Rhys laid out tools on the opposite bunk. "Are they talking about what to do now?"

"Yes," replied Rhys.

"Without you?"

"Yes." Rhys moved the lamp closer to Axel, fanned himself briefly—it was becoming unbearably hot—and withdrew the towel from the soldier's shoulder. There, along the muscle between the shoulder and neck, was a gaping, black hole.

"That must be very difficult for you," continued Axel.

"What did you use to get it out? A screwdriver?"

Axel held up a splinter of bloody wood the length of his hand. Rhys sighed, grabbed an advanced antiseptic, and, using gauze, touched the gory area. Once done, he retrieved a biosynthetic gel used to accelerate healing and applied it.

"So... are you going to tell me the truth now?" asked Axel.

"About what? I haven't lied to you." Rhys sat back. "You don't need stitches. The gel will take care of everything, but I need to bandage it."

"About who you are," replied Axel.

Rhys paused in his work. "What do you want to know?"

"Who are you?"

Rhys began unwinding bandages and a gauze pad. "Rhys Falkrow."

"From where?"

"Caelestis."

"Ca… Caelestis? Is it far to the south?"

"It's not even in this solar system," replied Rhys. When he turned to apply Axel's bandages, he stopped. The soldier was gazing at him steadily in the lamplight. "Caelestis is a colony… in space. I wasn't born on this planet. I'm from space." Rhys leaned forward and began applying heavy gauze. "I could explain to you technically where I'm from—what arm of the Milky Way, the name of my solar system—but I don't think it would mean much to you."

"How can someone not be from here?" Axel frowned. "I don't understand."

"The stories of the white gods living in the stars?" asked Rhys. Axel nodded. "It's true, but… there's a lot more to it than the nonsense the Pantaraks preach."

"Why… How? How did you get here then?"

"There was an emergency on my colony. My sister and I escaped on a life pod." Rhys began wrapping Axel's shoulder. "The escape shuttle was damaged. Several other things happened, and we crashed here on Earth." He tied off Axel's shoulder. "Is it too tight?"

Axel moved his shoulder and then shook his head. "When was all that?"

Rhys sighed tiredly and began gathering his tools. "About a year ago."

"Your sister… She was from your colony too?"

"She was." Rhys closed the medical pack and sat on the bunk, fanning himself.

Axel thought. "The high priest wanted her to reproduce… That's why she was kidnapped." Rhys nodded. The man was smart. "But you speak the noble's language. You speak many languages actually…"

"The noble's language is my mother tongue," explained Rhys. "I can also speak Aabesh and Elali."

"So, why are you here?"

Rhys stood, slung the medical pack over his shoulder, picked up the lamp, and went into the hallway. "I thought I knew, but now, I'm not so sure." He glanced down the hall at the still-closed galley door. "Do… you want to go to the upper deck with me?"

"You had a gun pointed at my face a few minutes ago. Why would I want to be alone with you where you could throw me overboard?"

Rhys crossed the hall to deposit the medical bag in his cabin. "Because you know I won't do that," he called to Axel. Without waiting for the soldier, Rhys stalked down the hallway. He passed through the bridge to check that everything was still in order and then made his way upstairs.

For a long while, he stared at the numerous bodies which littered the deck. Each rested in a small, coagulating pool of blood. After deciding it would be best that the bodies went overboard, Rhys moved to the nearest soldier and began stripping the man of his armor, guns, and ammo.

"You're robbing corpses," chided Ethos from the innards of Rhys' pocket.

"Yes, I am," Rhys murmured.

"Have you no shame?"

Rhys paused in his work. "They have guns, tools, and weapons we could use."

"You didn't answer my question," the AI insisted.

Rhys continued to drag the soldier's ammo reserves from his waistband. "This is war, Ethos."

Ethos sighed. "Do all humans hold such little regard for human life?"

Rhys laid the soldier's equipment to the side and sat back. "When I first arrived here, I couldn't understand why people killed one another. I couldn't understand why they strived to do so much harm to one another. We are endangered." Rhys took a slow breath. "And then Alina was taken. Despite the diplomatic talks and then the fighting, I couldn't get to her. My efforts had no effect." He paused, the memories swarming his consciousness. "And then, everything changed. I realized that if I was to protect the people I cared most about, I had to make moral sacrifices. I had to kill. After her death, that need to defend became stronger. It was up to me. I had to stop the attacks on *Themis* to protect the others. I had to end the attacks permanently which meant killing our enemies." Rhys withdrew Ethos from his pocket and set the AI on the deck. "I don't take killing lightly; I never have. But if it is to protect the people I hold dear, then I will do it."

"I see," murmured Ethos.

Rhys moved to his feet, grabbed the soldier's ankles, and dragged the man to the railing on the port side of the ship. With some difficulty, he maneuvered the limp body over the railing and rolled it overboard. He didn't wait to hear the distant splash.

Axel joined him shortly, kneeling beside the third soldier to drag ammo off the corpse. Rhys handed Axel the two handguns he had found and then pulled the body to the side of the ship. Though he had a method now, it didn't make lifting the dead weight any less cumbersome.

"Did you know they were going to come?" asked Rhys, kneeling at the next body.

"I suspected," replied Axel.

"Why didn't you say anything?"

Axel didn't respond. Rhys looked at the soldier in the lamplight. "I… wanted to see how you and your crew would react. I wanted to know how you kept outrunning, outmaneuvering, everything."

Rhys began pulling off the dead body's armor. "Is that why you waited so long to act?"

"Yes," replied Axel.

"So, what made you pick up a pistol?"

"When the tides of the battle changed."

Rhys heaved a corpse over the side of the ship and leaned against the railing, winded. These soldiers were twice his weight and size.

"If you would have me, I would be pleased to fight alongside you," said Axel.

Rhys scoffed. "Well, that may not be necessary. Once we arrive in New Arbroath, I'm separating myself from the ship and her crew."

"Is that what your crew is discussing right now?"

"I don't know what they're talking about." He looked out at the purple light of dawn. "I'm disappointed. I thought I could change the world… or a piece of the world." He sighed. "My departure from *Themis* isn't completely negative. At least I'll know that my crew—the people here—are safe."

"Unless they continue your quest without you," said Axel.

"That's a possibility, but they're smarter than that. In all honesty, I don't think they need me. They know what to do, how to do it. There are leaders among them who will pick up the slack."

"I see it differently." Axel gathered magazines in his hands. "You need them, and they need you. It has nothing to do with leadership; it's all about comradery." Rhys pushed aside a dead soldier's guns and armor and stood. "But, if you're bent on leaving the ship, I'm not going to stop you." He looked at Rhys. "I'm going with you."

"Rhys?" called Kallen from the bridge's open door.

"What?" replied Rhys.

"Can you come here?"

Rhys glanced at the two remaining bodies and then at Axel. "I'll be right back." Careful not to step in the coagulating blood along the deck, he hurried to the ladder and climbed down to the lamp-lit bridge. *Themis'* crew welcomed him with silence. Rhys met each of their gazes. It was Kashim who finally spoke.

"We're not letting you leave," said the man. "And we aren't leaving you."

"You've protected each of us at one time or another, risked your life. It's our turn," said Andy, arms folded across his chest.

"We're scared," Kallen softly added. "Terrified."

Leo smiled. "But… we can't just turn and run. And we can't let you leave. You're ours, and we're yours."

Rhys wanted to breathe out in relief, but he kept his feelings hidden. Instead, he looked to Otto, the newest crew member. "And what do you think?"

Otto glanced at the others. "When no one would look at me, you did. When no one would have me, you did. I'm staying here. I may not be as skilled in mechanics as Kallen, but I'm learning."

Rhys glanced at the others who had mixed expressions of sympathy and warmth. He wished they didn't have to make such a decision—his life or theirs. How cruel. "And you're sure? All of you?" All nodded. Rhys finally sighed in relief. "Thank you."

"Now, on to the matter of the prisoner, Axel," said Andy, leaning against the bridge paneling.

"He's a crew member as of an hour ago," Rhys promptly replied. "The medical bag I came to retrieve was for him. He cut out the chip in his shoulder with a sliver of wood."

"That doesn't explain why he stood watching while we were taken captive though," said Kashim.

"I asked him the same thing. He wanted to see how we reacted, how it was that we somehow always came out on top of every conflict." Sensing the tension on the bridge, Rhys affirmed, "He is now a part of this crew. I will continue to watch over him with Kashim's help, but he will be given a bunk in the common quarters and treated as a crew member." Rhys looked them over before remedying, "*If* everyone agrees…"

Kashim shrugged, and Andy looked away, clear signs that they weren't completely opposed to the idea. Slowly, Otto raised his hand. "I oppose the decision."

"Why?"

"Because of religious… differences," explained Otto. "He's… eh, Pantarak."

"You're Pantarak," said Kallen.

Otto shook his head. "I'm not Pantarak anymore."

"You're afraid he's going to hurt you for betraying the religion," concluded Rhys. Otto nodded. "You're aware that Axel isn't the only Pantarak onboard? Leo still claims the faith."

"In name only. I'm not practicing," Leo corrected.

"That's not it." Otto shifted uncomfortably. "I'm a former acolyte. I was promised to the priests at birth. If anyone found that I ran from my duties..." He thought. "I trust you, but... he's from the capital. He was born and raised in the faith. He knows the rules... He could kill me for running."

"Does anyone here have a problem with Otto being a former Pantarak acolyte?" asked Rhys. Everyone shook their heads. Rhys turned, took Otto's arm, and guided him outside. He pushed the boy up the ladder to the upper deck. Everyone followed.

The moment Otto spotted Axel seated on the deck in the lamplight, he froze. Straightening himself, Rhys pulled Otto along as he strode across the deck. Axel sat back and dubiously regarded them. Rhys pushed Otto so the boy stood before Axel.

"He is a former Pantarak acolyte," said Rhys. He could feel Otto shaking. "What will you do?"

Axel passed Rhys a subtle expression of confusion and then shrugged. "I know what he is. I've known since I saw him." The soldier motioned to Otto. "I don't care, kid. Do what you want."

Rhys patted Otto's shoulder and started to draw the teen away, but Otto remained rooted to the deck gazing at Axel. "Why aren't you going to kill me? I abandoned the white gods, our brothers, and priests." His voice was strained.

"Because I don't care. I don't care that you're a temple boy," Axel pointed to Kashim, "that he's a former slave trader," he moved his finger to Andy, "or that he was a tanner's son. I just do *not* care." Axel rose stiffly to his feet. "The only thing I care about is whether you can pull your weight."

"I will," said Otto. "Watch." Without another word, the boy turned on heel and disappeared into the ship.

Rhys tiredly rubbed his face. "Kallen, Andy—attached to our stern is the soldiers' dinghy. Get down there. It has a converter we can pull parts from. Once you've taken all you can, scuttle it. I don't want more following us." Kallen took the lamp and, with Andy in tow, walked to the stern. "Kashim, Leo—we have two bodies left. Strip them of guns, ammo, armor, and weapons. Afterward, roll them overboard. I'm going to get the mops." As Kashim and Leo began working on the last two corpses, Rhys looked at Axel. "Your status as a crew member is probationary. One wrong move, Axel, and I'll drop you in the middle of the sea."

Axel nodded. "Fine."

9
THE REFUGEE CRISIS

THE SUN WAS LOW ON the horizon by the time the crew had cleaned the deck. Afterward, they helped Kallen and Andy ransack the small scouting vessel for parts and supplies and then scuttle it. By the time Rhys radioed *Grisle,* nearly everyone was asleep or on their way to bed. All who remained awake were Kallen and Axel.

After speaking with Terron and repeatedly reassuring Hodge that everyone was fine, Rhys descended into the galley to assess Axel's wounds. He found Kallen cutting fruit in the light of the morning sun; Axel was halfway through a bowl of perfectly cut morsels.

"How's Hodge?" asked Kallen. Rhys closed the galley door behind him so as not to disturb the others across the hall.

"He's fine, just worried about Cantia."

Kallen chuckled. "I think he likes her."

Rhys sat beside Axel, stole a piece of his fruit, and then began examining Axel's dislocated and maimed shoulder. "I should have left you with more support earlier." Rhys retrieved the medical pack, pulled out spare lengths of cloth, and began situating Axel in a sling. The soldier continued to fish pieces of fruit from his bowl without so much as a whimper. "You will take a bunk in the common quarters," said Rhys, tying the edges of the sling together; Axel nodded. Rhys cleared away the medical supplies and motioned to Kallen. "Ready?"

"Where are you two going?"

"We're bringing power back to the ship," said Rhys.

It was midmorning when the lights in *Themis* flickered on and the cooling system began running once more. Beyond exhausted, Rhys notified Terron of their success, helped clean up the engine room, and then escorted Kallen to his quarters. Rhys carried Cantia down the hall to the crew's bunks and deposited her on an empty bunk. He covered her, returned to Kallen, who had already stripped out of her clothes, and went to bed.

"Rhys?" called Leo at his door hours later.

Rhys rolled over, looked at the porthole to determine the time—late afternoon—and then stretched. "What?"

"You better get out here. We're off the coast of New Arbroath," explained Leo.

"Is something wrong?" Rhys nudged Kallen and sat up.

"You just have to get out here," Leo replied.

"I'm coming."

"I'm… so hungry," murmured Kallen, resting an arm over her eyes.

Rhys stood, withdrew fresh clothes from the pile on his desk, and began dressing. Kallen sat up, her hair a vertical haystack, and squinted around the room. "I didn't mean to sleep so long," he admitted, slipping into a shirt. He sat on the bed and began pulling on socks and boots. Kallen slid to the edge of the bed, attempted to tame her hair, and then searched for clothes in the chest. Rhys glanced at her naked body before grabbing a headscarf from a small rack. "Don't take long," he said, patting her bottom as he passed. "We may need you."

"Yeah," replied Kallen.

Rhys closed the door behind him and jogged down the hallway. He entered the bridge, tying his headscarf around his neck. When he found the external bridge door open and voices coming from outside, he strode onto the outer platform. Kashim, Andy, and Leo stood on the stairs in grim silence.

Rhys peered out at New Arbroath, at the docks he should have recognized and the landmarks that should have been familiar. Instead, he saw throngs of people, thousands of them, lining the wharves and the roads leading into town. Makeshift shelters and tents made of clothes and an assortment of materials speckled the shoreline while boats crowded the docks and shallows.

"What's happening?" asked Rhys.

"I think they're Pantaraks," Andy offered, "from Paducah. That's the only thing that makes any sense. They're immigrants trying to escape Brechin's rule."

"They came all the way here… on those little boats?" Rhys couldn't help but gape.

"What do you want to do?" asked Kashim as Kallen joined them on the outer platform.

"This is Terron, over," buzzed the radio.

"Go ahead," replied Andy.

"I don't think there's room for us to dock. We'll have to anchor and motor in," said Terron. Andy looked to Rhys for a decision.

"Anchor," replied Rhys. "Let's do it." He went to the bridge.

"Who's going?" asked Kashim, joining him with the others. Leo, Cantia, and Otto appeared a few moments later.

Rhys motioned for Andy to pass him the radio. "Terron, you copy?"

"I'm here, as are Hodge and Jules."

"We're going to launch the dinghy. The people going ashore are Kashim, Jules, Hodge, and myself."

"And me," added Axel, limping onto the bridge.

Rhys looked at him. "You can hardly walk."

"I'm the best shot here," argued Axel. "And you know it."

Rhys considered him before shaking his head. "No. If something happens, I need capable people. As of the moment, you are not capable." Rhys brought the radio back to his mouth. "We're launching the dinghy as soon as we're anchored. Over."

It took but a few minutes to anchor the ships, arm everyone, and launch the dinghy. Once they collected Hodge and Jules from *Grisle*, they motored to the docks.

"We're not here to instigate trouble," said Rhys, wrapping his head and face in a scarf to protect against the late-afternoon sun. "That being said, if trouble breaks out, our primary objective is to retreat to the ships."

"I know this is supposed to be serious work," said Hodge, smiling, "but I'm so glad to see you."

"Once we have a full crew on *Grisle*," began Rhys.

"I'm moving back to *Themis*," Hodge concluded.

Rhys tapped his forearm to Hodge's in their sign of friendship and shifted his attention to the docks. Already, people had stopped their afternoon activities to watch the crew's approach. Hodge steered the dinghy to the shoreline and skidded to a halt. The people there cleared a small area so they could disembark. Rhys glanced at the men's tattooed heads and the Pantaraks' bare feet; the dark gazes of the men and women there, though wary, were not hostile.

Kashim stepped out, brandishing a short rifle; Jules and Rhys followed. Hodge brought up the rear. "Come on," said Kashim, carving out a path through the people.

The area smelled of human bodies and sewage. The ground beneath them was muddy from traffic and littered with trash. Many of the people around them showcased the beginning stages of starvation with hollowing cheeks and visible collarbones. Mothers clinging to their children and infants forlornly gazed at Rhys and his crew members while the men regarded them warily.

For several long minutes, they traveled down a path surrounded by a solid wall of Pantarak people. Though there were quiet murmurs, their watchers remained aloof. Kashim finally stopped at a barricade made of brick, cement, barbed wire, and fencing. Before the blockade stood six men armed with rifles and handguns. A turret with a machine gun was positioned atop the brick wall.

"Stop," ordered one of the men, brandishing his rifle.

"We're the crew of *Themis*," said Rhys, "returning home."

The men lowered their guns. "Where's Vinz?" one asked.

"He died," replied Rhys, pulling away the protective layer of cloth that had been covering his lower face. "I'm the Overseer of *Themis*, Rhys Falkrow." Rhys motioned to the others. "This is Kashim, Jules, and Hodge." Hodge waved awkwardly to diffuse the tension. "We're here to meet with Joss."

The men looked between themselves before stepping aside and rolling open an enormous wood-and-steel gate to reveal the town of New Arbroath. Rhys glanced at the hundreds of eyes watching them and then followed Kashim in; the gate slid into place behind them.

Unlike the filth they had just passed through, New Arbroath remained pristine. The last time Rhys had been there, the town had just been attacked and was in ruins. Now though, new homes, shops, and stores lined the main thoroughfare while citizens continued construction on other buildings farther in town. As Rhys and his crew passed, many looked up from their work or glanced out the window of their stores. Though Rhys was sure they had seen guns before, he supposed they were still surprised to see armed men, aside from guards, walking down the street.

By the time they reached the government building west of town, Rhys wondered if the people of New Arbroath were even aware of the turmoil happening just outside their gates. Rhys and the crew of *Themis* entered the government building—the very one he had walked into nearly a year ago.

Rhys deposited his short rifle and handgun at the front desk with the finely-dressed female receptionist and, pretending that he was fully weaponless, ventured farther into the building. He was not going to leave his resonance cutters in someone else's hands. His crew members noticed but said nothing.

"Please wait here. I'll notify the judge," said the receptionist once she locked up their arms. She disappeared upstairs, her high-heel shoes clicking on the new, polished wood floor.

Rhys sighed, pulled his headscarf from his head, and ruffled his dark gray hair into place. He didn't want to meet with Joss, the judge of New Arbroath. He and the man had never seen eye-to-eye, but as Overseer, it was now his duty. Convincing Joss to continue to finance *Themis* was his top priority. Without funds, they would have to find another source of income if they were to continue.

"Joss will see you now," called the receptionist, standing at the top of the staircase.

Rhys took the lead, and together they climbed the stairs. To his surprise, Joss met them in the common area at the top of the staircase. The judge of New Arbroath glanced over the group obviously in search of someone before settling his gaze on Kashim. "Where's Vinz?" The judge glanced down the stairs. "Is he coming?"

"He's… here," said the receptionist, motioning to Rhys.

"He's not Vinz." Joss studied Rhys before his lips parted in recognition. "You…"

Joss was just as Rhys remembered him—tall, tan, salt-and-pepper hair, and yellow teeth. The judge still had bags under his eyes, but they were heavier. If Rhys correctly recalled, his hair had not been so gray either. It seemed the past year had not been kind to the judge.

"Vinz was killed some months," explained Rhys, removing himself from the others to approach Joss. "I'm Rhys, the new Overseer of *Themis*."

Joss looked him over before glancing at Kashim and Hodge. "What happened?"

Rhys motioned to Joss. "Why don't we speak candidly in your office?"

Joss hesitantly showed them the way, waited for them to sit, and then closed the door. "What happened?" he asked again.

"Vinz was killed," said Rhys, "in Brechin by the high priest."

Joss seated himself behind his large desk. "And what were you doing while Vinz was being murdered?"

Rhys took a slow breath. "It's a long story, Judge, one I don't fully want to relive."

Joss looked between Rhys, Kashim, Hodge, and Jules. "You expect me to believe the high priest of Brechin killed Vinz while you stand here unharmed?"

"We did not escape uninjured," said Rhys. He shifted in his chair. "Your request last time we were in port was that we put a dent in the Pantarak population. Since then, we began a rebellion in Paducah, instigated a mutiny in Brechin's elite noble class, and started a war between the capital and its acquired territories."

"You... did this?" asked Joss. "You brought all of these filthy, disease-ridden migrants here?"

Taken aback, Rhys worked to recover. "No. It was not our intention to start a rebellion in Paducah. It happened after we left. The people rose up against their government and—"

"Why were there even people alive to do so?" Joss interrupted. "I told you to kill them."

"Vinz decided to take a different approach," replied Rhys, forcing calm into his voice.

"Get out," murmured Joss.

"Brechin is losing its territories, Joss," Rhys insisted. "Its people—the people it spent years conquering—are starting to fight back."

"Get out!" shouted Joss. "All of you."

Rhys stood. "We ask that you continue to finance our mission."

"Which is what exactly?" asked Joss, moving to his feet.

"Brechin is coming. It's coming for New Arbroath. It almost lost Paducah. It won't make the same mistake twice."

"You've only just arrived," replied Joss, "but I'm sure you've seen the filth on our shores. Brechin's political and strategic maneuvering is not exactly high on our priority list right now."

"It should be," Rhys replied. "The capital's not forgiving."

Joss motioned to the door. "Get out."

Rhys leaned on the judge's desk. "Brechin's already retaken Paducah. How long do you think it will be before they get here?" He straightened himself. "We've been working. We have contacts from here to Bathsgate. We've been effective—"

"Get. Out."

Before the judge could say anything else, Rhys turned and strode from the office. His crew followed.

"That could have gone better," murmured Hodge as they walked down the stairs.

"There's a possibility he will want *Themis* returned to New Arbroath to add to their defenses," said Rhys, glancing at the handful of employees who had paused in their work to regard them. "We can't let that happen."

They collected their arms from the receptionist and retreated into the light of the fading sun.

"Do you want me to go look for Reza?" asked Hodge as Rhys gazed about the town.

"Take Kashim with you," replied Rhys, remembering that Kallen had specifically tasked them with finding her grandfather. "We'll meet you back at the dinghy. Jules, you're with me."

Kashim and Hodge set off down one of the alleys, guns slung over their shoulders. "Is that how you expected it to go?" asked Jules.

"More or less," said Rhys, starting for the front gates.

"What now?"

"I'm going to talk to the Pantaraks. If it makes you uncomfortable, you can return to the dinghy and wait there."

"I'm fine," replied Jules.

By the time they made it through New Arbroath's barricade, the sun had set. Lamp posts along the docks mixed with the yellow glow of lanterns to illuminate the shoreline and myriad of shelters. With Jules by his side, Rhys made his way through the throngs of people who were cooking around fires. Eventually, he stopped and asked, "Do you mind if we join you?"

A woman motioned them to the empty space on the log beside her. Jules remained where he was, but Rhys gratefully accepted.

"Why are you here?" asked one of the men on the far side of the fire pit. "No Aabeshian people have left the town since our arrival."

"I'm not Aabeshian," replied Rhys.

"It's true," added the woman. Rhys looked at her, and she smiled warmly, kindly. "You don't remember me but... your sister—we praise her name—she looked after my husband last spring. He's much improved."

"I'm glad to hear that," murmured Rhys, shifting his attention to the others. He could see a realization breaking through their defeated demeanors. He was a white god.

Sensing the woman's gaze on him, Rhys glanced at her with a smile. "What?"

She lowered her voice. "Son of the Heavens... May I ask, what's happened to you?"

"Hm?" Rhys looked at the others for clarification, but no one spoke. "What do you mean?"

"At first, I did not know it was you because you have changed so much." She motioned to Rhys. "You are taller and bigger, but that is not what confuses me." She pointed to Rhys' eyes. "Even now, you don't trust."

"I'm sitting here with you, aren't I?" Rhys asked lightly.

"Your eyes are sharp but tired. You appear defeated. What has brought such weight to your shoulders, Son of the Heavens?"

Many of the people around the fire pit crossed their arms as a sign of reverence and bowed their heads. "Please... don't," replied Rhys uncomfortably. "Please talk with me as I am one of you. I want to know about your trials. What has brought you to live in such squalor?"

"Brechin," supplied a young man.

"Uyala," scolded another woman.

"It's the truth," said the youth, Uyala.

"The white gods have punished us because we defied their messenger, the priest," continued a man. "Brechin is only carrying out the white gods' wishes. This is our punishment."

Rhys sighed. He couldn't let this go on any further. "Let me share with you my story."

For the next hour, he spoke at length about his life. He shared everything he could remember about Caelestis and about escaping the colony, about crashing on Earth, and about being picked up by Vinz and his crew. He shared with the people the battles he and the crew of *Themis* experienced as well as the cruelties of man that he and Alina witnessed. He told them of the time he spent in Paducah and of the things he had seen.

When he finally began talking about his entry into Brechin, he could sense dozens of eyes on him; his audience had tripled in size. In vivid detail, he described the people he met, the things he saw, and how he felt. He shared with his listeners how he, Alina, and Vinz had appealed to the noble families; he told them about meeting the high priest of Brechin and the ruler of the Pantarak Empire, Michael.

And then, he told them of the disaster that was his attempt to rescue Alina and the events following her capture and her death. He explained that the entire Pantarak empire had been thrown into chaos because of them, because they had defied the system, and because the people of Paducah had chosen to rise against the government and fight for their freedom.

"Since leaving Paducah, our ship has been attacked twice by Brechin forces," said Rhys, shifting his gaze from the fire to the numerous eyes watching him. "They're getting closer. I've told the judge of New Arbroath that it's only a matter of time before Brechin's forces come here. But he refuses to listen."

"Then we will make him listen," declared Uyala. He was the first to speak in over half an hour.

"No. Our efforts should be focused on safeguarding this area," replied Rhys. "I will continue to speak with representatives of the town, but it is unlikely they will listen to me. They perceive you as all the same. They have no reason to see you as anything else. It is the same reason why you view the Aabeshians as apostates and heathens." Rhys stood. "Pantarak. Aabeshian. It doesn't matter to Brechin. The capital's goal is to subjugate all who pose a threat to its power. Pantaraks, former-Pantaraks, Aabeshians—we all agree that Brechin should not have the power that it does, yet... we can't put aside our history and problems to come up with a solution."

"How can we defend ourselves when we can hardly put food in our bellies?" asked someone in the crowd.

"That's where we start then," said Rhys. "We will organize. We need to know how many people we have and make a roster. We need to build shelters, hunt, fish, and care for the sick and injured. If you want the citizens of New Arbroath to open their doors to you, then prove to them that you can support a community." Rhys pointed back toward town. "All they know is the enemy that once attacked them is now seeking asylum. Show them otherwise."

The woman whose husband Alina had cared for the previous year, stood, pulled Rhys into an embrace, and kissed the side of his face. "Thank you," she whispered. Startled, Rhys awkwardly pulled away. Never had the Pantarak people touched him much less embraced him. The woman looked at the others. "Then, let's get to work."

Rhys remained silent as the woman, Myra, began issuing commands and asking for volunteers. He stood by her side and listened. Eventually, Hodge, Kashim, and Kallen's grandfather joined them. Though Rhys sensed their presence behind him, he never turned to greet them. He kept his eyes on the people gathered around the fire pit and on Myra.

Once Myra delegated assignments, such as counting people, making a roster, and inquiring after skilled labor, she turned to Rhys. "What next?"

"Have you many sick, diseased, or injured?"

Myra nodded. "Many are malnourished and dehydrated. Some are sick and they have been quarantined because we don't know what it is."

"I see. Are your sick and injured under shelter? Do they have water?"

"Yes, but all desperately need a doctor or medicine man. We have one, but she can only do so much."

"For the time being, finish the tasks at hand. I need to know how many people we have and their occupations. We'll start the real work at dawn."

"What about you?" asked Myra.

"I have other business to tend to," said Rhys. "I will return at dawn. Thank you, Myra." She smiled, dipped her head to him, and slipped into the darkness. Without looking at the others, Rhys turned for the shoreline. "Let's go."

They made it back to *Themis* in good time and docked the dinghy. While Hodge helped Reza out, Rhys stalked from the forward hatch. Despite the progress he had made, his retelling of the story of his life thus far had reopened quite a few wounds. His heart was murderous and ached with sorrow for the loss of Alina and Vinz.

"What happened?" asked Andy, appearing at the top of the bridge stairs.

"Nothing," snapped Rhys. He passed Axel, who side-stepped him, and entered the washroom. Rhys shut the door behind him and gazed at the washtub.

"I didn't know all of that," whispered Ethos from the innards of Rhys' pocket.

"Well… now you do." Rhys leaned against the door and tried to rub the weariness from his face. So much had happened and still more was to come.

"I will make a greater effort to better understand you now that I know all that you have experienced."

Rhys slid to the floor. "Am I doing the right thing?" He pulled Ethos from his pocket and rested the AI on his legs. "I never… really think while I'm talking. I only say what I feel."

"The mark of a Pathos-user," hummed Ethos. "Do you *feel* that this is the right thing to do? Do you feel that helping the Pantaraks organize, that playing liaison between them and New Arbroath is the right thing?"

Rhys thought. "Yes. I feel that's the right thing to do. It side-tracks our mission—"

"It doesn't," interrupted Ethos. "It bolsters it. It strengthens it. People are moved by endeavors of the heart, Rhys."

Rhys smiled.

"What?"

"I said that a while ago." He stood, placed Ethos on the sink, and gazed at himself in the mirror. The dye in his hair was nearly gone. His eyes, although startlingly blue, were heavy with fatigue. He appeared larger than a few months ago, stronger, but tired. He was worn. Myra was right—he had changed.

After bathing and drying off, Rhys exited the washroom with a towel wrapped around his lower half.

"Rhys?" called Kallen from the galley.

"Give me a minute," replied Rhys, disappearing into his cabin. He dressed, slipped Ethos into his shorts pocket, and padded down to the galley. He was surprised to find Reza as well as Kallen, Hodge, Otto, Axel, Leo, and Cantia. He suspected Kashim, Jules, and Andy were on the bridge.

"It's good to see you, boy," said Reza, nodding from his seat. Rhys bowed in mild-mannered politeness. "You've done quite a bit of growing since I last saw you. You're taller than I am now."

"You look…" Rhys glanced over Reza in an attempt to determine any differences in his physique or well-being. He appeared the same—tan, leathery, and ancient. His pristine white hair and eyebrows stood out against the darkness of his skin. He was lean and wiry from years of sunboarding. The last time he had seen Reza, the man had been nearly nude sunboarding, so him wearing a sleeveless shirt, cutoffs, and thong-slippers was unsurprising. "Unchanged," concluded Rhys awkwardly.

Reza chuckled. "I'm glad. Did you finish those manuals for me?"

Rhys, having forgotten about them weeks ago, lit up. "Oh! Yes. I'll get them."

Reza stopped him with a wave of his hand. "Don't bother. We'll be seeing more of each other. I'm not worried."

"More of each other?" asked Rhys, looking to Kallen who was pulling food from the cabinets.

Kallen turned on her toes and pointed at Reza. "*Grisle's* new mechanic."

"Kallen." Rhys glanced at Reza apologetically. He didn't want to get her grandfather involved in warfare. He was ancient. The old man wouldn't be able to run around the ship, haul heavy tools, and work in high-stress situations.

Kallen leaned against the counter. "He's New Arbroath's leading engineer in solar panel technology. He's a sunboarder. He can pilot almost as well as Hodge."

"He's worried because I'm old," said Reza.

"Yes," replied Rhys, perhaps too quickly.

"I want to do this, boy," Reza asserted, settling his sharp, dark eyes on Rhys. "A number of incidents have happened since you've been gone. I'm tired of not being able to do anything. This is my contribution to your cause, whatever that is."

"You haven't told him what's going on?" asked Leo.

"He knows," Kallen replied without looking up from her work.

"And who are you, Brechin-born?" asked Reza, nodding to Leo. "That garb on your ear marks you as a noble, right?"

"I'm one too," chirped Cantia. Hodge nudged her playfully, drawing a frown from her. Cantia still didn't know that she had been declared deceased in Brechin.

"I can see that," replied Reza.

"This is Cantia," said Leo. "I'm Leo. My brother, Terron, is Overseer of *Grisle*." Leo looked at Rhys. "Actually, he's the only one on that entire ship right now."

"Invite him over," said Reza. "I'd like to meet him. He is to be my Overseer, is that correct?"

"Yes." Rhys motioned to Hodge who slipped from the galley to call Terron.

"So, have you titles? You're nobles of Brechin, right?" asked Reza.

Rhys stopped Leo from answering. "We're withholding their titles. Only those of us who met them prior to the events in Brechin know their full identities. It's to protect them."

"Ahh, I see. But they are from Brechin?"

"Yes," replied Leo.

"Cantia," reviewed Reza, pointing to her. "Leo." Both nodded. "And, of course, I know the fool who just strode from the room." Reza's eyes fell on Axel. "Who's the cripple?"

"Axel," said Leo.

Axel offered his uninjured left hand to Reza, and they shook. "A pleasure, Axel."

"Likewise," replied Axel, leaning in his chair. He glanced at Rhys but said nothing else.

For the next hour, conversations crowded the galley while they waited for Kallen to prepare dinner. Terron eventually joined, as did Kashim, Jules, and Andy. By the time the meal was ready, the galley was difficult to move around in which pleased Rhys greatly.

Standing in the doorway, he watched as his crew members spoke amongst themselves, laughing, nodding in interest, or talking solemnly in low voices. It didn't matter the topic of conversation. He was content, happy to see that for one moment everyone was together, and there was peace.

After a while, Rhys motioned to Terron, and together they went up to the bridge. Months ago, he had appointed Terron as Overseer of *Grisle* out of necessity at a dire time. Since their departure from Firekli, it seemed Leo's older brother had grown into the position.

"How are you?" asked Rhys once they were on the bridge. Like him, Terron's hazel-green eyes were heavy with fatigue and stress. His blond and copper tresses, which had grown out over the past several months, were drawn back by a small hair tie, allowing for small slivers of hair to fall around his weary face. Though he had a light layer of scruff, his face was relatively clean for being at sea.

Terron braced on the bridge paneling and shook his head. "I've been better."

Rhys flopped onto his chair and threw a leg over the armrest as he had seen Vinz do so many times before. It was one of the only ways to sit comfortably in the otherwise rigid seat. "Same here."

"Jules has been a big help," said Terron, rubbing his face. "We didn't see eye-to-eye initially, but we've come to our own understanding. I don't know where he learned nautical jargon and navigation, but I've been very happy with his work."

"I'm glad to hear that," replied Rhys. He had found Jules in a pub in Firekli while they were there doing repairs. He had watched Jules stop a drunken brawl and then knock a man out for urinating on him. He had recognized Jules' skill for fighting which is why he had approached him. "How are you holding up?"

"We need more people." Terron looked at him. "I know Cantia went through an ordeal the other night, but with her off the ship…" He pursed his lips. "We need more people."

"Well, we have a new mechanic."

"The old man?"

Rhys sighed. "I have my doubts as well, but I know his work and his reputation. Kallen will continue to teach Otto as a backup, but at least now you have someone to look over all the minor repairs Hodge made."

"Speaking of Otto… I want him," said Terron. "Give him to *Grisle*."

"Why?" Rhys glanced at the bridge door which was ajar. He lowered his voice. "Otto is still adjusting to life at sea. He's been struggling."

"Which is exactly why I want him," said Terron. "I think he has potential. I want to test him and find out what he's good at."

"Fine. He's yours. He doesn't want to be anywhere near Axel anyway, so that will clear up that problem." Terron gave him a questioning look. "Axel, the soldier. Otto is a former Pantarak acolyte."

"Ahhh," murmured Terron in understanding as he himself was Pantarak. "He doesn't have a problem with nobles, does he?"

"No, not that I know of. Just Axel because he's a Brechin soldier."

"And you trust him? Axel?"

"I'm working on it," replied Rhys. "I have Ethos watching him."

"Who?"

Forgetting that he had yet to introduce Ethos, Rhys withdrew the AI from his pocket and passed it to Terron.

"What is it?"

"Greetings, human-person," sang Ethos suddenly. Terron startled.

"Do you remember the things Alina and I had on the sides of our heads?" asked Rhys.

"Yes, computers." Terron looked at Ethos. "Is it the same?"

"It's an older model, but yes. Its name is Ethos. Otto found it in some ruins near Paducah."

Terron examined the AI before shrugging and giving it back to Rhys. "So, this thing is watching Axel?"

"I'm on it!" said Ethos. Rhys felt the AI vibrate as it spoke.

Rhys looked at Terron in grim humor. "It's a little more enthusiastic than Pathos."

"Come now, space-human," chided Ethos. "You enjoy my enthusiastic chatter."

Rhys chuckled. "I do." He thought for a moment. "Reza will be starting repairs on *Grisle* tomorrow. While we're in New Arbroath, I want to transition our sails to an automated system. I'm tired of losing people in the water."

"That sounds ambitious."

"Ambitious but not impossible. I have some work that needs to be done before that though." Rhys stood and held his hand out to Terron. "I know it's been hard on you and Cantia. I appreciate the sacrifices you've made to champion our cause. If you ever need help, Terron, please let me know."

"Thank you, Rhys."

18
WAR ANEW

THAT NIGHT RHYS SLEPT FITFULLY. Despite Ethos' attempts to calm him using tonal resonance, he rolled into Kallen multiple times and kicked the blankets off the bed in fits of heated frustration. When he finally managed a few hours of sleep, Alina commandeered his dreams and once more, Rhys found himself reliving that awful night when his sister died in his arms.

He woke up wheezing in the blackness of his cabin, his cheeks wet.

Kallen, who had been sitting against the wall watching him, gently coaxed him into her arms. "I couldn't…" he murmured, burying his head in her stomach.

Kallen ran her fingers through his hair. "I know," she replied. Rhys wrapped his arms around her and took a deep breath to calm himself.

An hour before dawn, they ate a small breakfast and went to the upper deck. Leaning against the railing, Rhys gazed out at the Pantarak refugee camp.

"What do you want to do?" Kallen asked.

"I'm going ashore," he replied. "I want to know what organizational work they've done." Rhys looked at Kallen. "I'm going as a doctor today. I have a feeling people need help. Will you come with me?"

"Rhys…" muttered Kallen. Her relationship with the Pantaraks was not an amicable one.

"They aren't all the same."

"I really would prefer not to…"

"I need help today. I won't let anything happen. I promise." He could see the internal battle between fear and trust warring in her eyes. After a long moment, she nodded hesitantly. Rhys took her in his arms and kissed the top of her head. "I promise."

"Please, Rhys," she begged fearfully.

"I know. I won't let anything happen."

"I'm trusting you," she murmured.

After signaling with a light to a local fisherman in a dinghy and telling Andy where they were going, Rhys and Kallen descended the outer stairs of *Themis* and boarded the boat. In silence, the fisherman motored to shore and deposited them on the docks.

Rhys shouldered his medical pack, glanced at Kallen in the purple light of dawn, and started inland. Already, people were stirring and coaxing fire pits to life. Rhys covered his head with a headscarf to avoid attention and carefully picked through the refugee camp. He asked where the sick and injured were being kept and was pointed toward an area on the other side of the docks.

They made their way to the wharves on the other side of the small bay. By the time they reached the gate of the infirmary tent, the sun was peeking over the horizon.

"Stop." Two men appeared from within the gate. "Are you sick or injured?"

"Neither, I'm a doctor and this is my assistant," replied Rhys. Feeling Kallen tense under the men's scrutiny, Rhys pulled her close behind him.

"A doctor? From New Arbroath?"

"From the ships that just arrived in port," replied Rhys, pulling his headscarf to his neck. The two men stared at him for a long moment, glanced at Kallen, and then moved aside. Rhys stepped into the shadows of the infirmary tent and looked about. Nearly thirty people lay before him, injured, resting on makeshift beds and chairs. "These are the injured?" he asked of the guards.

"Yes. The sick are in the next tent."

"I was told there was another doctor here."

The guards motioned to a barefooted, ebony-skinned woman kneeling in front of a child. She was middle-aged, plump, and had an enormous head of black, fluffy hair. Her clothes were in tatters. Her assistant, a young man wearing nothing but a pair of pants, sat nearby holding a lamp.

"Are the ones in the sick tent contagious?" asked Rhys.

"We're unsure," replied one of the guards.

Rhys nodded, scanned the tent once more, and then slid his pack off and handed it to Kallen. "Stay with me," he instructed. Kallen moved her arms into the pack's straps so it hung on her stomach and followed him to the nearest patient, a woman with her leg wrapped in dirty clothes. Remembering Alina's calm demeanor and methodical process, Rhys knelt beside the woman. "My name is Rhys. I'm a doctor. What happened to your leg?"

"I cut it," replied the woman, glancing at the male patient beside her who looked on in interest. "I cut it on one of the boats."

"When was the last time your doctor examined it?" asked Rhys, motioning for Kallen to kneel. She did so and opened the pack to give Rhys access to its innards.

"Yesterday morning."

"Have you washed it since then?"

"No."

Rhys began unwrapping the woman's makeshift bandages. A putrid smell hit his nose; he saw Kallen turn away. Rhys hid any type of reaction and examined the deep green and purple gash which ran the length of her calf. It looked as though it had been tended to but with remedial instruments and bandages. It was still gaping open with raw muscle showing.

Rhys examined the woman's leg for a moment longer and then gloved up.

"Who are you?"

Rhys looked up at the female Pantarak doctor. "I'm a doctor. This woman says the last time you examined her was yesterday morning?"

"Yes," replied the ebony-skinned woman.

Rhys pulled out a small pill from a container at the bottom of the pack and returned to the patient. "This won't hurt," he said. Gently, he wedged the capsule into the open flesh. The pill opened, and foam began expanding along the entire wound. When the woman started to move in fear, Rhys rested a hand on her thigh in reassurance. "It's cleaning the wound and numbing it," he explained. After a moment, the foam bubbled away; blood began surging back into the wound. Rhys handed Kallen clean cloth. "Give me the pack. You put pressure on it. Hold it gently."

As Kallen did as she was told, Rhys withdrew the tools necessary to stitch the leg up and nodded to the doctor. "Hold her leg steady please." The doctor obliged. "Light," commanded Rhys. The doctor's assistant brought the lamp overhead.

With a steadying breath, Rhys sutured the gash closed.

"Bring me a bowl of your strongest alcohol," he said, studying his work. He looked up at the woman who had watched the whole thing in awe. "Don't get it wet. These need to stay in for at least two weeks. Protect them. Don't let anything hit or bump them. Understand?"

The woman nodded.

Rhys turned just as the Pantarak doctor reappeared with the requested alcohol. Rhys dunked his tools in the liquid, motioned for Kallen to put the woman's leg down, and then stood.

"My name is Khaleela," said the doctor, following Rhys as he moved to the next patient. "Call me Leela."

"I'm Rhys. This is Kallen."

"Are you from New Arbroath?" asked Leela. Without Rhys asking, she moved in and began unwinding their male patient's cloth arm cast.

"No," replied Rhys. "My ship is though." He looked up at the man. "What happened?"

"Broke my arm," the old patient mumbled.

"I believe he has a fracture near his wrist, but I'm not sure. He says everything hurts," said Leela, delicately holding the senior's injured arm. "If I could pinpoint exactly where the fracture is..."

Rhys moved to one knee, withdrew Ethos, and held the AI before the man's arm. "Where's the fracture?" he asked, slowly moving the AI's unit along the man's arm. Just before the wrist, Ethos vibrated in his hand. Rhys nodded, returned Ethos to his pocket, and began re-fashioning a cast and sling.

For the next five hours, Rhys and Kallen made their way through the injured tent. Rhys applauded Leela's attempts at bandages, ointments, and casts. With the limited supplies she had, it was astounding she had completed so much. Nevertheless, nothing compared to sterile equipment and effective tools. It was well after midday when Rhys finally sat at the back of the tent and drank heavily from a jug of water. He watched as those capable of walking shuffled from the tent into the hot afternoon sun.

"We need to head back soon," said Kallen, stretching out beside him on the ground. Leela and her assistant, Patrin, exchanged looks.

"Not yet," said Rhys. "I still have another tent."

Kallen sat up and looked at him. "You have other people in need of your leadership."

"I can continue to look after the sick," offered Leela, looking between them. "If you have somewhere else you must be."

"Are you the only Pantarak doctor?" asked Rhys.

"I'm not Pantarak," replied Leela. "I'm from Maliyansa."

"Maliyansa is still a territory of the Pantarak Empire," Kallen argued.

Leela's eyes sharpened. "It's not. It will never be."

Rhys stood and corrected himself, "So are you the *only* doctor?"

"No. There's one other, but he's sick in the other tent." Leela stood with him. "He was contagious but is recovering now."

"Good. I'll come back at dusk." Rhys pulled Kallen up and swung the medical pack onto his back. "Thank you, Leela."

"See you around," said the Maliyansan doctor, turning. She and Patrin disappeared into the sick-inhabited tent.

By the time they made it back to the shoreline, the sun was glaring overhead and Rhys was layered in a thick sweat. Kallen who—like many of the inhabitants of Earth—featured a second-skin, a genetic adaptation, found no trouble with the heat. When they finally stopped in the shade of a family's tent, Rhys ripped his headscarf off and sat heavily. Heat exhaustion was coming fast.

Kallen presented him with the water they had packed, and Rhys drank nearly the entire container. "You need to be drinking more," she chided under her breath. "Vinz drank several of these a day. This is your first."

"I just forget," replied Rhys, holding his pounding head. The ground under him rolled like the sea.

Kallen glanced at the tent's occupants, who sat in silence, and then out at the rest of the camp. Rhys laid his head back and looked at her through squinted eyes. She seemed confused.

"What? What's wrong?" he asked, starting to stand.

Kallen stopped him with a single gesture. "Everything is taken care of."

Despite her command to stay seated, Rhys shuffled to his feet and followed her gaze across the shoreline. No longer was the refugee camp a jumbled mess of haphazard shelters and forlorn refugees. People were moving and working with purpose. Even as they stood watching, a group of men passed carrying beams from a deconstructed boat. In the distance, he could discern several small storage units being constructed. Rhys shifted his attention to the seashore where women washed clothes. Farther out, an army of variously-sized boats fished the waters.

"Come on," he said, lifting the medical pack. He slipped his scarf back over his head and wrapped it around the lower part of his face. With Kallen in the lead, they started through the organized chaos.

They passed piles of guns and rifles that seemed to be no longer working, a collection of tents housing babysitters and groups of children, a row of shabby tables where scant amounts of food were being prepared, and a group of fishermen butchering fish along the shoreline. Rhys often exchanged looks with Kallen. It was clear that she was just as baffled as to how these people had managed such a transformation.

Eventually, Rhys stopped a passing man and asked, "Who is in charge here?"

"The white god is, but his messenger is helping," replied the young, tattooed man.

"Where can I find his messenger?" asked Rhys. The young man pointed to a tent several meters away and then hurried off. In confusion, Rhys and Kallen joined his crew in the tent. Pulling his headscarf off, Rhys looked about at Hodge, Kashim, Axel, Leo, and Jules. They gazed proudly back at him, smiles on their faces. "So... which of you is my messenger?" There was a moment of stillness before everyone looked at Axel. "You?" asked Rhys, taken aback.

"Turns out people... listen to me," said Axel. His limp was no longer noticeable.

Rhys glanced at the others. "And why is that?"

"Because he's a Brechin soldier," explained Leo who was cloaked in a headscarf just like Rhys.

"But how do they know that?"

"I have my number tattooed on the back of my head. All soldiers do," said Axel, turning. For the first time, Rhys saw through his shortly trimmed hair the number 500 listed in black ink on the back of his head.

"That doesn't explain why they are obeying you though." Kallen motioned to Axel. "You're a Brechin soldier; your men took over Paducah and slaughtered those who resisted."

"Because I'm working with him," replied Axel, nodding to Rhys. "I'm doing a true white god's work."

Rhys gratefully accepted the seat Hodge offered him on a crate. "Catch me up. What all has been done?"

"Shortly after dawn, we came ashore and found the people organized in groups by trade and occupation," said Kashim. "Fishermen, carpenters, discipline enforcers, bakers, ironworkers, eh, holy men." Kashim looked down at the parchment spread out on the shabby table between them. "Total, we have nine hundred forty-six people. That includes those in the infirmary and children."

"What skills or trades do we lack?" asked Rhys.

"Ironworkers," replied Kashim. "They aren't immediately necessary, however, if we're to repair their weapon stockpile, we need someone who knows what he's looking at."

Ignoring the question of whether the pistols and rifles should be repaired and given to the people, Rhys looked to Hodge, indicating that he was next in his reports.

"Leo and I just returned from town," began Hodge. "It looks like so long as you're affiliated with *Themis*, you're allowed beyond the barricades. At any rate, we spoke with the local farmers in town to see if they would be interested in trading with the Pantaraks. After all, they don't have ready access to their boats and shorelines anymore to fish."

"And?"

"They expressed some interest but were more worried about their safety," said Hodge. "They indicated that they would meet with the other farmers and discuss whether trade would be advantageous. We're expecting to hear back this evening."

"Good." Rhys wiped his forehead with his sleeve.

"You've been tending to the sick?" asked Kashim. "How bad are they?"

"There are more injured than sick. I would say there are twenty-five or thirty injured with varying levels of severity. I didn't see the sick; they're being quarantined." Rhys could feel Axel's gaze on him. "Why don't you head back to the ship? Look in on Reza?"

"Who's left onboard?" asked Kallen. "Andy?"

"Otto, Cantia, Reza, Terron... and Jules are on *Grisle*," said Leo. "I think Andy is the only one on *Themis*."

"Otto transferred to *Grisle*?" A shade of disappointment passed over Kallen's face. Though she had complained about Otto, Rhys knew she felt responsible for him.

"Reza asked that I transfer—"

"Excuse me."

Rhys and his crew looked up from the conversation to meet a familiar face. Tessa, Vinz's lover, startled upon recognizing Rhys. "You," murmured Rhys, standing.

"You're..." Tessa gazed at Rhys and then shifted her attention to the others. She appeared just as she had months ago when Rhys had first come to Earth. Her raven hair was pulled in a long horsetail and her neck was streaked with sweat. Though her face retained its pleasant round shape, her once warm eyes were stricken with panic and worry. "Is Vinz here?" she asked. "I heard... that something happened to him. Is he here?"

Rhys glanced at the others and, recognizing that this was something he had to take care of, stood wearily and motioned for Tessa to follow him outside the tent.

"Where is he?" asked Tessa with more force. "What happened?"

"Tessa," he said, squinting at her. "Vinz is dead. The high priest in Brechin killed him." Rhys watched as the expression on Tessa's face shifted from worry to deep, unfettered sorrow.

"And... his body?"

"We weren't able to retrieve it."

Tessa's lips quivered. "How long ago?"

"Almost nine months ago."

Tessa glanced at the others in the tent. "Why didn't you send word?"

"*Themis*, her crew, and myself are wanted. We have warrants out for our arrests. I needed to protect my crew."

Tessa wiped her face on her shoulder and cleared her throat. "You're the Overseer now?"

"Of *Themis*, yes."

"And your sister? I don't see her standing with you. Is she... on the ship?"

Rhys pursed his lips. "No. The high priest killed her too. We've lost quite a few lives since you last saw us."

Tessa pulled at her nose, wiped her face once more, and looked out at the harbor. "You're needing men then."

"Yes."

"Do women count?"

Rhys gazed at her before saying, "Tessa, you—"

"Do women count? Do you take women?"

Rhys sighed. "Yes. If they have a skill or trade."

Tessa nodded. "I can cook, I know how to use a gun, and I can swim and sunboard. I use less food than men, and I follow directions better. I'm good to have in emergencies because I'm level-headed and a methodical thinker."

"Don't you have other responsibilities in town?"

"They don't matter," she replied. She pointed to *Themis* and *Grisle*. "My only condition is that I am stationed on *Themis*."

"I need some time to consider your proposal," said Rhys. "And... maybe you should think it over."

"When can I expect an answer?"

"Two days from now."

Tessa shook her head. "That's not soon enough." She turned and strode back to where Rhys' crew waited. "I want to become a part of the crew. Will you accept me?" she asked of them.

No one replied.

Tessa looked between the group and then turned to Rhys who had followed her. "It's not their decision," said Rhys. "It's mine." Tessa frowned. "Come back in two days, and I'll give you an answer then."

Tessa left the tent.

"Do you really want her onboard?" asked Hodge. "She… seems dramatic."

"I just told her about Vinz. She's upset," explained Rhys, sitting back down. "She shouldn't make this decision lightly."

His crew spent the rest of the afternoon building, cooking, organizing, and supervising construction projects. Late afternoon, Rhys returned to the medical tents to check on Khaleela and the patients.

For the next three days, Rhys spent the majority of his time bouncing between construction projects and the medical tents. Every morning, he visited the injured and sick, tending to fresh injuries and healing patients before flitting to the main camp at midday to continue supervising. After supper, he returned to the medical tents, helped Leela and Patrin with their patients, and then went to bed.

On the fourth day, after almost no communication with New Arbroath, the city's gate opened to reveal a group of citizens that included Joss. While the farmers had, after some hesitation, agreed to trade with the Pantaraks, the rest of the town remained ardently convinced that New Arbroath should stay off limits to the immigrants.

Rhys, who had been sitting in the shade of a tent, stood wearily and went to meet Joss in the hot midday sun. As he left the cover of the tent, he wrapped his scarf around his head. Hodge and Leo flanked him.

"Judge," greeted Rhys.

Joss and the dozen or so people surrounding him peered about warily. "I'm looking for the man they call the 'white god.' I've heard that he's the one who has been orchestrating all of this."

Rhys exchanged amused looks with Hodge and Leo.

Joss sighed in realization. "You?"

"How can I help you, Joss?" asked Rhys.

"I need to speak with you. It's about Brechin."

Over his shoulder, Rhys said, "Go get Kashim and Axel." Hodge loped off. "What about Brechin?"

Joss fidgeted. "We've received word that Brechin forces are moving in this direction. A merchant vessel bound for Firekli sent a report indicating that Brechin forces had gathered at Paducah and were en route here."

"When was that?"

"We received the report this morning."

Hodge returned with Kashim and Axel. Rhys reiterated the news to them and gauged their reactions. None showed surprise, only grave seriousness.

"We're in the process of bolstering our defenses, but we don't have a chance against Brechin," said Joss.

"So why did you come to us?" asked Rhys.

"We estimate that the Brechin forces will be here in four weeks. They're traveling a long distance and are slow-moving." Joss glanced out at the sea where *Themis* and *Grisle* remained anchored. "We've come to ask you to consider joining forces."

"*Themis* and *Grisle* alone can't defeat the Brechin forces," Rhys asserted.

"You've held them off before. We don't need you to defeat them, only to keep them at bay. Make a fight with New Arbroath unappealing."

Rhys watched as a group of Pantarak men passed. "Do you remember what I said a few days ago, Judge?" He nodded to the numerous tents and buildings along the shore and tree line. "You have an entire army camped out here. When they rebelled against the priests in Paducah, Brechin responded. The capital squashed all hope for freedom and tried to draw them back under its regime. They fled from the only home they've ever known. They're angry."

Joss squinted out at the Pantarak people. "They have nothing though."

"They have a stockpile of guns and ammo they brought with them," replied Rhys. "Open New Arbroath to them. Those who wish to fight, allow them to become a part of New Arbroath's military. Your ranks will triple in a day's time."

"Let me discuss this with my subordinates." Joss held his hand out to Rhys. They shook and, with his armed party encircling him, the judge returned to New Arbroath.

"Damn," muttered Rhys in Interstellar Nefegian, hands on his hips. What the hell were they supposed to do? "Gather the crew," he said. "We need to talk." Everyone except Axel dispersed. Sensing the soldier's gaze on him, Rhys asked, "What?"

"You're not going to try to fight are you?"

Rhys started for the tent. "If that's what it comes down to, yes."

Axel took Rhys' shoulder and stopped him. "You managed to survive in Paducah because you were engaging in guerrilla warfare. You and your men were using the land to your advantage. It didn't matter if you destroyed buildings because the only people remaining in Paducah were the resistance fighters." Axel motioned to New Arbroath. "You can't do that here. There are women and children, civilians here."

"I know that." Rhys gazed at Axel for a moment and then asked, "Number 500, what would you do?"

"Run," replied Axel without hesitation. Rhys regarded him. "Listen to me. When the capital wants territory, it takes it. There is no stopping the regime. The only reason New Arbroath hasn't been conquered yet is because it's so far away."

Rhys leaned on their shabby table in the shade of the tent. "We can't run. We can't let them take New Arbroath. If they take New Arbroath, then what's to stop them from taking any other town west of here?"

"You do *not* have an army, Rhys," said Axel. "New Arbroath's military isn't more than maybe a thousand men. I can't imagine they have the weapons and tools necessary to wage war with a force like Brechin. Sure, you've got a few Pantarak men willing to fight and throw away their lives, but they're nothing. Run. Take the next few weeks to clear out the town and run."

"As a Brechin soldier, how would you attack New Arbroath?" asked Rhys.

Axel sat on one of the crates and looked out at the small bay. "I would send squads ahead of my main forces to analyze the situation, take note of the land, and possibly snipe some of the leaders." He pointed to the open sea. "I would fan my main forces out along there so no vessels could pass and no sunboards could launch." He looked over his shoulder at the rising land behind him. "And I would position troops west of the town at the desert's edge to head off any attempts of escape."

Rhys' crew gathered under the tent drenched in sweat from the work they had been doing. The only people who weren't present were Cantia, Terron, Reza, and Kallen. When all eyes fell on him, Rhys said, "Brechin's coming for New Arbroath. They'll be here in a few weeks."

"And how do we know this?" asked Kashim.

"Joss just told me."

"What do you want to do?" asked Andy, panting. "There's no way we can fight the capital."

Rhys thought, brows furrowed. Axel was right; Andy was right. They were in no condition to fight Brechin. Even with the Pantaraks willingly fighting alongside New Arbroath, there was a good chance the entire town would be annihilated and the survivors would be brought under Brechin's massive Pantarak Empire. They needed to run, and they needed to start now.

"We run," said Rhys. There was silence. "Even with our best ships and volunteer soldiers... there's no way this will end well for anyone."

"Now, tell that to the people," said Kashim, motioning to the Pantaraks still working.

"Joss is deliberating. I need to know what his solution is."

"Time is not always on our side," Jules mused.

"Notify the leaders of the community. Don't spread the word too much. We don't want mass panic. Also, send word that we need ironsmiths and anyone who is skilled at repairing guns. If we have to fight, it would be best if we had working weapons."

"Eh..." murmured Otto. Rhys looked at him in surprise. "I... can fix... firearms."

"You can? How?"

"I've... collected many for the black market. Most of the time... they don't work, so I have to fix them," said Otto. "I'm much better at working with rifles than solar panels."

"How good are you?" asked Kashim.

Otto looked at the ground. "I can make them work."

Kashim leaned on the table. "You can fix any kind?" Otto nodded. The large man exchanged looks with Rhys who motioned to them. With a kind hand, Kashim directed Otto from the tent to the stockpiles across the camp.

Rhys frowned. "Go. Notify the community leaders. We'll speak again at dusk."

11
OVERSEER DOWN

THAT NIGHT AS RHYS SAT staring contemplatively into a fire pit, Tessa joined him. After dropping a bag onto the ground, she sat beside him and gazed at the fire as well. Eventually, she sighed and said, "I've given it some thought. I want in. What's your answer?"

Without looking at her, Rhys murmured, "Fine."

Tessa sat back on her hands. "That's it?"

"You're not working with Vinz, Tessa." He glanced at her. "I'm not Vinz."

She smiled in an attempt to mask her obvious disappointment. "I know that."

"Once you step foot onto *Themis*, your life is going to change."

"I'll manage," she said.

"We've lost Vinz, Alina, Kyo, and Lyruc since you last saw *Themis*. That's four crew members. What do you think the cost will be this time?"

"If you're trying to scare me, it won't work. I'm a farmer's daughter. I grew up climbing trees, fighting boys, and killing animals."

"Killing a human is different," said Rhys. "It's not something you can take back."

Tessa peered into the fire. "Have you killed someone before, Rhys?"

"Many," replied Rhys. "And all of them had mothers and fathers, families, hobbies, loves, interests…"

"I don't have a problem defending myself or others," asserted Tessa. The sudden grit in her voice made Rhys look at her. "I'm not Pantarak. There isn't an afterlife for me. No punishment from white gods that I have to look forward to."

"It's not the white gods who punish you." Hearing footsteps, Rhys glanced over his shoulder at Joss who was accompanied by half a dozen men. "You punish yourself." He stood to greet the judge.

Joss shook Rhys' hand, bowed his head as was customary, and said, "After much discussion, we've decided to open New Arbroath's doors. In exchange, we want the men to enroll in our military."

"Here's the problem," said Rhys, "We're not going to fight."

"What?" The look on Joss' face was one of betrayal and confusion. "Why?"

"I recommend that we retreat from New Arbroath while—"

"No," interrupted Joss.

"I spoke with my advisors and we've decided it's too risky. You weren't in Paducah; you don't know what the Brechin forces are capable of."

"No, we're not running," declared another one of Joss' men. There were murmurs of agreement. "New Arbroath is our home."

"We're not running either," came a new voice. Rhys turned to find several of the Pantarak elders and community leaders approaching the fire pit along with Hodge, Kashim, and the rest of his crew. "We were unable to defend Paducah. We will not let the same thing happen here."

Rhys looked between the Pantaraks and the Aabeshian citizens. "We have a former Brechin soldier. He's estimated Brechin's troops will number in the thousands."

"Let them come," said another Pantarak leader. "Shame on them for driving us from our land; shame on us for allowing them to do so a second time."

Joss side-stepped Rhys. "I have offered your white god a proposal. We will open New Arbroath's gates to the Pantarak people under the condition that your men enroll in the military to defend New Arbroath."

One of the Pantarak men held out his hand, and he and Joss shook. "Agreed."

Rhys shifted his gaze to Axel who loitered near the end of the group. The soldier caught Rhys' eyes and shook his head in obvious disappointment.

It took a few hours for word to spread of what had conspired, but soon the entire Pantarak camp was ablaze with activity. Rhys, weary and stressed, motioned for everyone to retire to *Themis*.

"Hey," called Tessa, jogging after the group.

Rhys briefly introduced her to the crew. "This is Tessa. She will be joining us on *Themis*. Tessa, this is everyone." Tessa bobbed her head politely as she fell in behind them.

After they dropped Hodge, Otto, and Jules off at *Grisle*, they ramped into *Themis'* forward hatch and docked. Kallen met them with questioning eyes. Rhys went up to the bridge to radio *Grisle* and share with Terron all that had transpired. Afterward, he sat in silence for half an hour before going to the galley in search of food.

He was glad to find Axel as he had not changed the soldier's bandages since the previous day. Leo was also with him. "I'll check you over in a minute," Rhys murmured, shuffling through their cold storage unit. He withdrew a fruit, held it in his mouth, and closed the larder.

"This isn't going to end well, Rhys," murmured Leo.

"You should've put a stop to it," Axel chided. "They're fools."

Rhys seated himself across from Axel. "What right have I to stop them from defending themselves?"

"It's not a right. It's a responsibility." The soldier shifted in his chair. "You know Brechin. New Arbroath will be wiped out in an instant. It is your responsibility as a white god to tell them the outcome of that battle. Only you can do it."

"Rhys," murmured Leo. "They're not looking for a miracle. They know what's coming for them, at least the Pantaraks do. They're looking to defend what they lost. You need to convince them that such a battle is not worth their lives."

"You need to think about this too," Axel warned. "Yes, New Arbroath has a small military. But the majority of people here are civilians. Even the Pantaraks... Do you think you can train an army in a few weeks?"

Rhys slid his hand into his pocket, withdrew Ethos, and set the AI on the table. "You've been listening, Ethos. What's your assessment of the situation?"

"I... would rather not be involved in this conversation," replied Ethos after a long moment of silence. "There are too many factors for me to make a decision. More information is needed."

Rhys sat back. "Do you have any suggestions?"

Ethos paused for a moment and then said, "Have those who are not going to fight retreat from the area and escape. All those willing to sacrifice their lives will remain to defend New Arbroath to the best of their abilities."

"If not enough people stay behind though," said Axel, "those who are fighting will be wiped out instantly. There will be no point to their sacrifice."

"True, thus I add to my suggestion a condition. So long as the number of troops remaining in New Arbroath exceeds the number of three thousand five hundred men, non-combatants may leave. If that number is not reached, then all must retreat."

Rhys looked at Leo and Axel to gauge their reactions. Both seemed to agree. "Fine," said Rhys. "I'll propose this to the community leaders and the judge tomorrow morning."

"Ehh..."

Rhys, Axel, and Leo looked at the doorway where Tessa stood. "I was told to bunk in here." She pointed to the crew cabin. "But... all of the men are in there..."

"You're a crew member," said Rhys.

"I can just bunk with Kallen if that's easier," the woman offered.

"Kallen stays in the Overseer's cabin."

The look on Tessa's face changed to one he didn't understand. She appeared to be upset, but another emotion he couldn't pinpoint pulled at her brows. "I see." Tessa glanced at Axel and Leo before slipping back across the hall.

"You could let her stay in the other room," Leo whispered.

Rhys shook his head. "She needs to assimilate with the crew quickly." He nodded to Axel. "Let's look at your shoulder."

After tending to the soldier's wounds, Rhys shuffled down the hall to his quarters. He found Kallen sitting on their bed gazing at the floor in thought.

"Hey." He closed the door behind him. Kallen fidgeted and avoided his gaze, signaling to Rhys that something was wrong. "What?"

"Why is she onboard?"

Rhys stripped from his shirt. "She asked to be a part of the crew."

"So, you just let anyone join now?"

"Kallen." Rhys sat beside her and thumbed her chin. "Is her being here going to be a problem?"

"Not if she doesn't make it one," Kallen huffed. She kissed his lips and then turned to him. "I... need to talk with you."

"About Tessa?"

Kallen shook her head. "Eh..." She smiled shyly at him and then did a sort of shrug. "I wanted to let you know... that my cycle is late. By... six weeks, eh, over a month."

Rhys stared at her.

"So... there's, eh, I mean, I think I'm pregnant."

"Pregnant?" whispered Rhys.

Kallen nodded, her eyes on him.

"Pregnant." Rhys looked at her abdomen, reviewing the anatomy and physiology of the female body. When was the last time they had had intercourse? It was before they had arrived in Paducah. So... almost six weeks ago? Maybe longer? Two months?

Kallen's hand on his arm brought him back to reality. Her smile was gone; her eyes were worried. "Do you understand this word? Pregnant?"

Rhys nodded. "You're sure?"

"I'm not... absolutely sure, but my cycle is late... and that's normally what it means."

"I know," replied Rhys. "I... uh... A baby." The words on his lips were strange. "You. You're pregnant." He cupped her cheek, elated. "You're pregnant." Kallen nodded, smiling. "You're... pregnant." His mirth deflated like an old dinghy. They were preparing to enter battle.

Guessing what had crossed his mind, Kallen gently pushed him onto the bed and climbed atop him. "I am first and foremost, yours. I will always be with you."

"Kallen... you can't be here."

"How is me being a few weeks pregnant going to hinder anything here? I'm still capable. I won't become incapacitated until several months from now."

Rhys stared up at her, frightened. "You can't be here. I'll worry too much."

"You've always worried about me. How is this any different?"

Rhys drew her down to him and curled around her. "Because," he murmured. "It just is." He kissed her and then wrapped his arms around her. Kallen pulled his hand free and slid it down to her bare lower abdomen. Rhys gazed at her smooth, tan skin under his fingers and then looked into her eyes.

"I'll be fine," she whispered.

"Kallen...

She kissed the tip of his nose and then his mouth.

"I'm sorry," he said.

"For what?" she chortled.

"I wasn't careful when we... After everything in Brechin... I just..."

"Stop." Kallen's voice was commanding. "I'm not angry."

"You aren't?"

She sighed into him. "No. I'm worried about what will happen when I can't move around the deck, but that won't come for several months. Rhys, I knew the consequences. You may... not have been totally aware at the time, but I was. I knew what could happen."

Rhys rolled away. "Why did you let me?"

Kallen peered at him. "Do you regret it?" He remained silent. "Good answer."

Rhys took her hand. "Does anyone else know?"

"No. You're the first."

"Do you want anyone else to know?"

"I know now too," chimed in Ethos.

"We can tell them later. I don't want this to be a fluke."

"Did you hear that, Ethos?" asked Rhys. "Keep your mouth shut."

"Physiologically speaking, I don't have a mouth," replied the AI.

Rhys pulled Kallen back into bed and coiled around her. He was going to be a father. He allowed the excitement to block out the knowledge that Brechin's forces were encroaching. Each time he thought to himself "father," a small smile crossed his face and his hands clutched at Kallen's body.

He was excited and worried, afraid but determined. He had felt a powerful need to protect his sister and Kallen before, but what swelled in his chest now was something far more profound. With his face buried in Kallen's neck, Rhys smiled and went to sleep.

Before dawn, a bright thread of lightning illuminated the cabin; it was followed by the distant rumble of thunder. Rhys stirred beside Kallen, glanced at the dark porthole overhead, and rolled to the edge of the bed. Already, the ship was swaying. Blurry-eyed, he sat up, ruffled his hair, and began pulling on his pants.

"What is it?" murmured Kallen.

"Storm."

"Is it bad?"

"Don't know. I'll check." Rhys slid Ethos into his pocket and padded out of the room. He found Andy already on the bridge. "Well?"

His First Mate, who was studying a map pulled over *Themis'* bridge paneling, shook his head in thought. "It's slow-moving. It's been sitting out east for several hours which means it's a big one."

"Have you notified *Grisle*?"

Andy nodded. "They'll be better off than us. Luckily, we don't have to worry about the sails." Lightning streaked across the sky, and wind whistled around the bridge. "What do you want to do about the refugees?"

Rhys folded his arms across his bare chest and gazed at the maps. "I'm sure they're taking measures right now, but…" He pursed his lips. "I doubt the medical tent has any help." He sighed knowing what he had to do. "I'll go check on Leela and Patrin."

"Do you want help?"

"No. It won't take too long. If I hurry, I can beat the storm." Rhys turned and jogged back to his cabin. Kallen was already dressing. "I'm going ashore to take care of the medical tents."

"By yourself?" she asked.

"It's fine. I can beat the rain if I hurry." He slid into his boots, pulled on a shirt, and began rolling his sleeves. Kallen offered him his resonance cutters and a short rifle. He kissed her on the cheek before hurrying to the forward hatch where Andy waited with the dinghy. "I'm going to the other side of the bay," said Rhys, motioning south. "I'll try not to be long."

Andy planted a solar-powered lamp and a spotlight in the bottom of the dinghy before bracing the boat so Rhys could ready the fan. When everything was prepared, Rhys jetted out of the forward hatch onto the rough sea waters. He was immediately jostled from his seat and forced to slow the dinghy. At a crawl, he powered over long swells of water and fought to stay parallel to the shoreline.

Lightning blazed overhead, illuminating the rowdy sea and docks. After nearly half an hour of battling the waves, Rhys finally headed for shore. When it became apparent he was not going to be able to tie up to the docks or land near the medical tents due to the wind and rising waves, he motored to the other side of the peninsula. Although the walk to the tents was going to be a pain, at least he was sheltered from the brunt of the wind.

With ease, he ramped up onto shore and skidded to a halt. Once the engine quieted, Rhys withdrew the lamp and flashed light over the area. It was going to be a hike to make it to the medical tents. Before him rose hills of tall trees swaying heavily in the wind and steep rocks. Lightning streaked across the sky; thunder followed.

Realizing that he was going to need both of his hands to climb some of the steeper parts, he turned off the lamp and returned it to the dinghy. For several seconds, he stood in the darkness, allowing his eyes to adjust to the deep shadows of the forest. When he could finally make out the forms of the trees, he aligned himself with where he thought the medical tents were in relation to his position and started through the vegetation.

The sound of the trees blowing in the wind was deafening. He couldn't hear himself walk. For several minutes, he strode through the trees, squinting against the lightning, and blinking to clear his night vision. Only once did Ethos correct his course.

Eventually, the hills became steeper and he was forced to clamber around rocks and over fallen logs. Though the lightning briefly illuminated the rocks around him, it kept him in a constant state of adjustment. Never was pure night vision fully attainable. After uphill hiking, rock dodging, and log leaping, Rhys stopped for a short rest. Standing atop a large boulder, he breathed deeply and wiped at the sweat dripping down his brow.

"Rhys." Ethos' voice was like the hiss of moving leaves. Recognizing the AI's tone, Rhys lowered himself to the rock and slid off onto the ground. Leaning against the boulder, he brought Ethos to his ear. "There are five heat signatures north of you ranging from seven to ten o'clock."

"Animal? Human?"

"Human," replied Ethos. "They've only just come into my range."

Overhead, giant plops of rain broke through the shield of trees and splattered on the rocks around Rhys. The wind was picking up; the storm had arrived.

"No one's supposed to be out this way. Who are they? Can you tell?"

"No," replied Ethos. "I can only determine that they are human, not the flavor."

"You said five?"

"Yes, five."

Rhys shuffled and then said, "Watch them. Let me know if they move." When the wind increased to a dull roar, he began digging at the soil beneath his feet. With the rain coming at a steady beat now, he had mud to work with. Quickly, he smeared mud on his face and mashed it into his gray locks. He released the sleeves of his dark green shirt and covered his hands in mud. When he felt that he was thoroughly concealed, he lowered himself to the ground.

"They haven't moved," Ethos reported into his ear.

Another flash of lightning lit the area, and Rhys looked for his next hiding place. He didn't have many choices. "Shit…" he murmured. He stuffed Ethos into his pocket, slung his short rifle onto his back, and lowered his belly into the mud. He crawled out from behind his boulder and began wriggling toward a set of rocks about two meters away. Breathing hard from the effort, Rhys finally pulled himself behind the cover. The rain was a heavy downpour now; he could hear nothing but it and the wind in the trees.

"They haven't moved," said Ethos.

Rhys grabbed another handful of mud and ran it over the layer melting off his face. At the rate the rain was falling, his camouflage efforts were going to amount to nothing.

Lightning.

Spotting a large stand of trees a fair distance away, Rhys readied himself. Fingers splayed, he slid through gritty mud and covered himself. He slathered it onto his hair and once more took to the earth like a serpent.

Lightning.

He froze. Once the shadows reclaimed the forest, he began crawling again. Humans were predators. Their vision was attracted to movement. If in the light they could see no movement and he was sufficiently camouflaged, he was safe.

Several more times, Rhys was forced to freeze in the luminance of the lightning only then to continue crawling through the vegetation, rocks, and trees. He cursed silently as his elbows and knees scraped on rocks, and his legs and stomach were cut by thorns and sticks. After this excursion, he would forever take with him a companion—or three.

Lightning grazed the clouds again. Rhys looked ahead at the trees. If he could make it there, then he could possibly break for the hilltop. Panting, he wriggled upward and pulled himself along the rocks and sticks.

"They're coming," said Ethos. "Go, run. Now." Rhys scrambled to put his feet under him but slipped in the rivulets of water and mud running down the hill. He slid several paces backward, grabbed hold of a sapling, and sprang up.

"Don't move!" came a shout.

He stopped struggling. He could feel the mud sliding down his head and face. Thanks to the heavy downpour, his camouflage was ruined. His gray hair had given him away. Lightning flashed. In that split moment, Rhys swung his rifle into his hands and fired off several shots. The sound of his gunfire mingled with the violent crackling of thunder in the forest.

Before Rhys could drop to the ground, another shot rang out. The force of the bullet to his stomach drove him several paces back before he crumpled to the earth. He could feel hot blood slithering down his abdomen through his fingers. With all his strength, he drew his knees under him. Wet vegetation crunched behind him; the shuffling of a gun followed.

From the corner of his eye, he could discern the Brechin soldiers; they wore goggles over their eyes. "I'm…" He grimaced as pain shot through his belly. "I'm Rhys… Falkrow."

"We know," came the reply.

Lightning pierced the clouds, and thunder roared around them. Rhys looked up into the barrel of the soldier's pistol in time to see it flash—and then darkness.

12
PUBLIC FORUM

WAS… HE DEAD? THAT'S WHAT he felt like. Dead. Lifeless. Cold. Heavy.

Distantly, he felt hands on his limp, ragged body. It felt as though he was being shifted, handled, transported. He could move nothing; he could say nothing. He was a frozen piece of meat lying on a table, or a stretcher, or a deck.

Muffled voices surrounded him, but he could understand none of them. He struggled to listen, to comprehend what was being said and by whom. Nothing.

When he next became aware of himself, his head was throbbing; he felt nauseous. Pain seared across his scalp and the receptors where Pathos had once been connected burned. He wanted to rip out the injection sockets, but he was bound. Rhys tried to force his eyes open, but nothing happened.

"Stop moving."

Rhys froze at the sound of Pathos' voice. He opened his mouth to speak, but only air passed through his lips.

"Do not struggle. You are currently in surgery."

A rasping sound made its way from Rhys' throat.

"The patient is not yet ready to wake. Please administer more anesthesia."

"No," gasped Rhys as his consciousness once again succumbed to the darkness.

Time had no meaning. Life had no meaning. He was a small light of consciousness floating in a black oblivion. How long was he out? A day? Two days? Five?

Moaning, Rhys touched his head. His fingers brushed across his temple. It took him a moment to realize that the hair around his receptors had been shaved. Nothing but sharp stubble greeted his fingertips. The rest of his hair seemed intact and clean. He opened his eyes and stared at the bare, white ceiling overhead. When he felt strong enough, he looked around the room. There was medical equipment—equipment that looked familiar—and an empty chair.

Inhaling deeply, Rhys sat up. He was completely naked. The bullet wound to his gut was gone. In its stead was a small bandage. He opened his mouth to call for Ethos, but his throat was parched. He coughed. "Ethos." He sounded like a dying bird. "E-Ethos."

"I'm here," replied the AI. "In the drawer."

Rhys weakly slid off the table and wobbled over to the nearby desk. With shaking hands, he opened the drawer. The relief in his heart broke out on his face.

"How are you feeling?"

Rhys leaned on the desk, winded. "Where am I? What happened?"

"You were shot," replied the AI.

Rhys stumbled across the room and tested the door. It was locked. "I was shot," he mumbled. His head hurt.

"You were shot twice. One in your stomach, the other in the head. Had it not been for your receptors, you would have been killed. The bullet hit the empty sockets, preventing it from going any farther."

"What?"

"Sit down, Rhys," advised Ethos. "Your blood pressure is low. You're going to—"

Rhys felt his knees buckle, and he slid to the cold floor. Wheezing, he rolled onto his back. "What happened? Where am I?"

"You're not in danger," replied Ethos. "Calm down."

"Am I in Brechin?"

"No."

"New... A-Arbroath? Paducah? Ethos..." Rhys touched his pounding head.

The door beside him whizzed open to reveal a pair of white slippers. Rhys weakly peered up at his captor—a silver-haired, blue-eyed woman dressed in khaki pants and a white blouse. He squinted at her in bewilderment and then closed his eyes. He had died. What the Pantaraks believed was true; he had died and rejoined his people in the stars.

"Do you hurt?" asked the woman in pristine Interstellar Nefegian. A manic smile broke across Rhys' face at the sound of her voice. It had been months since he had heard anyone speak his dialect. "Can you stand?"

Rhys rolled onto his side and dragged his legs under him. Despite being nude, he pulled himself erect. His head ached fiercely; he could hear his heart in his ears.

The woman motioned for him to return to his bed which Rhys did obediently. "Please lie down." Once he was prone, the woman leaned over his head and studied the receptors along his bare temple. Rhys gawked at the compact AI buried under her silver locks. "Do you know your name?"

"Uh, Rhys."

"How old are you?" asked the woman, flashing a small light into his eyes.

"Nineteen."

She nodded and then moved to his abdomen. With gentle hands, she pulled away his bandage to reveal a small indent. She studied it, pressed tentative fingers around it, and then covered his wound. "You are in Neo-Colony Two."

"Neo-Colony Two?"

"A colony built by the survivors of Caelestis."

Rhys stared up at her. "What?"

The woman nodded to him. "Welcome home." She turned and, without another word, left the room.

Rhys sat up. Survivors of Caelestis? "Ethos... Where am I in relation to New Arbroath?"

"I'm unable to determine that as my location services are being blocked."

"But... you tracked us here, right?"

"Even then, I was being blocked. I'm sorry, Rhys. I haven't the faintest idea where we are."

Rhys shuffled across the room and stepped before the door several times. It didn't open. He couldn't be here. He couldn't be trapped like this. New Arbroath, *Themis*, his crew, Kallen. He couldn't be here!

"Rhys, you're not in danger," Ethos repeated.

"How long was I out?"

"About one hundred thirty-two hours."

Rhys sunk to the floor. Nearly five days? Hands shaking, he tested the door's edges and traced it upward. Nothing. "My resonance cutters. Ethos?"

"They were confiscated when you were brought in, as was your rifle."

Rhys pushed himself to his feet and then began searching the room for anything he could use.

"You know they are watching you," murmured Ethos.

"Let them," Rhys snarled. "I've... got to get out of here."

"They just saved your life."

Rhys threw the AI onto his bed. "I know that! But..." Anxiously, he searched through the drawers of the desk. There was nothing. He opened the cabinets overhead. Nothing. "*Damn it!*" He leaned weakly against the desk before looking up at the bulbous camera positioned in the corner of the room. "Hey!" He switched to Interstellar Nefegian. "I have people waiting on me. I need out. Now!" He glared at the camera and waited for a response. "I know you're listening! Let me out!"

"You cannot be released as you are currently being detained on charges of identity theft, unlawful use of an escape pod, and unlawful departure from the colony," came a prompt, robotic response.

"What?"

"Your trial will be held in three hours."

Rhys whirled on the door. "That's some *gawan* bullshit! Open the door. Now!"

To his great surprise, the door zipped open. Rhys found himself speechless at who filled the doorway.

"Rhys," greeted Doctor Falkrow. Rhys gaped at his father. He appeared just as he always had with neatly trimmed silver hair, striking blue eyes, a high-arching nose, and strong jaw line. He wore slippers, white pants, and a blue shirt, quite a difference from his usual uniform.

Calmly, his father regarded him and then tilted his head as if he were speaking. Momentarily, another platinum-haired man appeared with clothes, deposited the articles on the desk, and left. Doctor Falkrow stepped into the room; Rhys backed away. The door closed behind his father.

"You were so eloquent a few moments ago. What happened?" Doctor Falkrow motioned to the clothes. "Get dressed."

Eyes on his father, Rhys moved to the clothes, which he recognized as his own, and began dressing, which had been cleaned and repaired. The only thing missing was his boots. Once he had pants on, he glanced at his father. "Where am I?"

"Neo-Colony Two on Earth," the doctor replied.

"Where am I in relation to where you picked me up?"

"About ninety kilometers north."

Rhys gazed at his father. "How did you—"

"Where is Alina?" His father's words cut into him. When Rhys didn't respond, Doctor Falkrow moved about the room. "We have, for several months now, been tracking all our citizens who landed on Earth. There were five beacons in this region. Now, there are only four. So, I will ask you once more—where is Alina? She should have been with you when we picked you up."

"She's dead," replied Rhys. "She was killed a few months ago. If you're tracking everyone, you should already know that."

For the first time in his life, Rhys saw what appeared to be anger darken his father's face. His people were not the kind to show emotion, yet there stood his father in a simmering rage. "You had... one responsibility in your entire life, and you failed."

"It was beyond my control," argued Rhys. He had never seen Doctor Falkrow exhibit any type of emotion. "She was shot by the high priest of Brechin."

"I don't care what happened to her; she was *your* responsibility. I entrusted her to *you* thinking that perhaps you would be capable of at least this one task."

"I kept us alive after we crash-landed! We didn't have any of this!" Rhys countered, motioning to the high-tech medical equipment around him. "We had one emergency pack between us. Do you know what our first test was? Not drowning." Doctor Falkrow swept from the room. Rhys tried to follow, but the door to his cell whizzed closed; he kicked the door. "Get back here!" When it was obvious his father was not going to return, Rhys began pacing.

From inside his pocket, Ethos said in Aabeshian, "When they take you from the room for your trial, I will do everything in my power to map this facility."

"Good." Rhys tested the door once more. What was going on in New Arbroath? What about his crew? Kallen? The refugees? His heart dropped as he realized that the people who had attempted to kill him were Brechin soldiers. Axel had been right. Advanced squads were already in New Arbroath. And that was what? Five days ago?

Frustrated and angry, Rhys glared at the camera overhead and then at the door.

His people knew nothing outside of Caelestis. Even here on Earth, they were continuing to live by Caelestis' government regulations and laws. They were maintaining a stagnant society. They did not know of music or literature, poetry or song; they didn't understand the complexity of human relationships unhindered by machines. They simply couldn't comprehend what it meant to be human.

And, to make matters worse, he was certain that at least ninety percent of the population there were Logos-users, meaning that no matter what he said, he was, in essence, speaking to a brick wall of layered logic. It had taken weeks of immersion to weaken Alina's defenses, and even then, she had not been fully capable of understanding the entire spectrum of human emotions.

Eventually, the door to his room reopened to admit three men. Rhys, who had moved to his bed, sat up.

"Your presence is requested in the public forum," announced one of the men. Rhys noticed they had no ties, chains, or handcuffs to bind him. Of course, they wouldn't. They believed all humans were mindless, obedient pets. No human from Caelestis would dare bind another citizen. That was cruel.

Rhys slid on his shirt and entered the hallway. He stood motionlessly, staring at the familiar walls. Had they managed to recreate the colony, or, at the very least, a piece of it? How and with what material?

He waited for his captors to lead the way before following. He glanced into the rooms as he passed. It took him but a few moments to grasp the fact that this facility was not a replica of the colony—it *was* the colony. At least, it was a piece of the colony. The hallways were long and branched in different directions. The lighting was the same, cold and white. In the various rooms he passed, Caelestis citizens worked in near silence. No one looked up as he passed. The deafening quiet was something he remembered all too well; it made him uneasy.

Suddenly, his silver-haired guide stepped aside to reveal a doorway. Rhys immediately recognized it—the public forum. It was the exact room where both he and Alina had presented their dissertations and received their departmental recommendations.

The room was larger than most and showcased a vaulted ceiling. Directly before him was a long table behind which decorated citizens, doctors, and well-respected community leaders sat, five in total. Buried in the floor in the middle of the room was a round disc the size of Rhys' hand which could project interactive material. Surrounding him on all sides were rows of blue-eyed, silver-haired Caelestis citizens sitting motionlessly, their shoulders stiff, hands in their laps, and eyes focused on him.

"Come forward," beckoned one of the men behind the large table. If Rhys remembered correctly, that was Walton Purjey, the colony's commander and Deputy Director of Law. Glancing at his audience, Rhys stepped before Walton and his colleagues. Unlike everyone else, Walton's short hair was gray with age. Though nearing one hundred, the commander's skin was pristine. Only the small wrinkles along his neck hinted at his age. "Rhys Falkrow, age nineteen. Born of Severiano Falkrow and Yadhira Bruaner. AI type: Pathos. Identification number…" Walton studied the screen before him and then looked at Rhys. "What is your identification number?"

"I don't remember," Rhys lied.

"Our files show one number but the number provided on the escape pod is different. Why is that?"

"It must be an error," replied Rhys stoically.

Walton turned his head to the woman seated beside him as they spoke using their AIs. Rhys politely waited. After a moment, the commander nodded and said, "We now ask that you insert an adaptor into your receptors so that we can, without verbal ambiguity, review your memories."

Rhys considered what that meant and then flatly said, "No."

The commander, as well as his colleagues, who were already preparing to take notes and speaking silently among themselves, looked up in surprise. "No?"

"No," repeated Rhys. He knew the word was foreign to these people because it had once been foreign to him.

The woman sitting beside Walton—she looked vaguely familiar—said, "You are aware that without our medical attention and expertise, you would be dead?"

"I am aware," replied Rhys. "That doesn't mean you may do as you wish to me."

Walton and his colleagues exchanged looks. Out of the corner of his eye, he saw movement and turned to find his father seating himself among the other citizens.

"According to the Terraria Charter set forth by this committee upon the colony's descent to Earth, all citizens are lawfully bound to participate in public AI examinations or daily connections to the Core. Therefore, I will say agai—"

Rhys interrupted, "I'm not a citizen of Caelestis."

Walton looked back at the screen. "Your records indicate that you were created on this station, therefore, you are a citizen of Caelestis."

"I lost my citizenship when my sister and I crash-landed on this planet."

"Your status as a citizen of Caelestis is binding," assured the woman beside Walton. "You are required by la—"

"Your law no longer binds me. I am without an AI, without a home, and without a proper identification number," Rhys argued. "I refuse submit to your interrogation."

"You are not without an AI," said the woman. "The unit in your pocket has been sifting through our digital map since you left your cell."

"I would like to make a request," interrupted Doctor Falkrow. Rhys' father stood, and all eyes turned to him. "I request that the committee forcefully apprehend Rhys' memories." Rhys gaped in anger and confusion at his father. "In addition to his current charges, I would like to add another."

"Which is what, Doctor Falkrow?"

"The murder of Alina Falkrow," replied Rhys' father.

Startled glances were immediately passed between audience members while the committee shifted uncomfortably. Rhys tried to compose himself and then declared, "Objection!" The room fell silent. "Doctor Falkrow has no evidence; his words are speculation." Doctor Falkrow's icy gaze didn't leave Rhys' as he returned to his seat.

"Rhys Falkrow, if you do not adhere to that which was set forth by the Terraria Charter, we will use force to make you acquiesce," warned Walton.

Rhys gathered the strands of calm dashed within him and thought. He needed to convince these people to release him. He needed to return to New Arbroath and *Themis*. "Committee members, might I be able to speak?" He ignored the subtle disgruntled look that passed over his father's face.

Walton motioned him forward. "You have the floor."

Rhys turned about the room to look at the numerous emotionless gazes. Their eyes hungrily watched his every movement. "I am currently Overseer of a diplomatic seafaring vessel named *Themis*. I have under my direct command eleven crew members. I have a woman who is my mate and who, I just found out, is pregnant with my child. I am also regarded highly amongst the Pantarak people in the region because my crew and I instigated a rebellion that went on to defy the capital's rule." He shifted his attention to the committee members. "As of this very moment, my ship, my crew, my mate are all in danger. The capital, displeased with its people fighting to gain independence, is preparing an assault on New Arbroath, my ship's port." He met Walton's stoic gaze. "I beseech you, release me. I am the commander. I am responsible for all that happens to my ship, to my crew. Everything is *my* responsibility."

"This is nonsense, of course," scoffed Doctor Falkrow.

"Quiet please," chided the woman seated beside Walton. She turned her head to Walton as he spoke to her. She nodded, stood, and walked around the table. "Not everyone here is a Logos-user." She stopped before Rhys. "Because you do not have an AI, I will introduce myself formally. I am Doctor Veran Taiglar, Director of Medicine. I am also the person who saved your life, reconstructed your receptors, and rid your synthetic system of corruption." Rhys started to put his hand forward as was customary on Earth, but stopped himself. "If what you say is true, I suggest this: share your memories with me."

"I object to this preferential treatment," voiced Doctor Falkrow. "The committee would not treat any of their other citizens like this."

"No, they wouldn't," replied Veran, withdrawing from her pocket a silver device that fit in her palm. She offered it to Rhys. "This will adapt the electrical signals in your brain to form a working memory map. You will not have access to the Core, and no one will have access to your internal synthetic system."

Rhys rolled the device in his hand for a moment. "What do you think?" he asked in Aabesh.

"She is making an effort to be accommodating. You should reciprocate the gesture," Ethos replied from inside his pocket.

Torn, Rhys met Veran's gaze. "I'm sorry. I can't."

"Explain to me why," said Veran. Her large blue eyes were inquisitive; they reminded him so much of Alina's.

"Because they're mine. They're my experiences, my emotions, my thoughts…"

Veran considered him and then said, "I am trying to help you, Rhys, because I feel that I should, but you must meet me halfway. What if I were to give you free pick of what you wanted to show me? So long as I am able to ascertain the truth, you have complete control over what I am to see."

"Memories can be edited," remarked one of the committee members.

Rhys glanced at the committee and handed the adaptor back to Veran. "Please program it so that I am in control."

Veran returned to the committee's table, tapped on a small handheld screen, and then passed it to Rhys. "It is ready for you."

"And… you are the only one who will see?"

"Yes," replied Veran.

Rhys ran his thumb over the adaptor and then gingerly slid it into the receptors at his temple.

"I will ask you questions. All that you must do is review the memories you want me to witness," instructed Veran. "It's fine if they are murky or if you don't remember all the details so long as they are as accurate as possible. Let me know when you are ready." He nodded. "Rhys Falkrow, the day Caelestis was struck by the meteor, where were you and what happened?"

He shared with her all that had conspired that day—rushing to Alina, being stopped by his father, and inputting the stolen identification codes. Rhys watched as Veran relived that terrible day. He intentionally cut the memory short the moment he and Alina were put into short-term cryostasis.

"You were a passenger on a life pod that crash-landed on Earth. What happened to the other passengers?"

Rhys closed his eyes and dragged his and Alina's escape from the sinking life pod to the forefront of his mind. He still remembered the terror and absolute panic he felt as the water closed in over their heads, sealing him and Alina in a watery coffin, how weak he was, how unfit for survival he was. He shared with Veran their desperate escape and struggle to nearby land.

Rhys felt a hand on his arm and he opened his eyes. Veran was panting softly. "One moment," she breathed.

"Veran?" quavered Walton, standing.

She motioned for him to remain where he was. "I'm fine. I'm fine." Veran straightened herself. Her eyes were softer when she looked at Rhys. "You stand… accused of murdering the daughter of Severiano Falkrow."

"My sister," corrected Rhys.

"Your half-sister," replied Veran. "Are you guilty?"

"No." Without mercy, Rhys threw Veran headlong into the council meeting he, Alina, and Vinz had attended in Brechin. He bypassed the dialogue and skipped to the moment Alina was dragged through the doorway by Brechin soldiers. He shared with Veran his panic, fear, and anger as well as his attempts to fight for her. He showed his midnight flight to rescue his sister. He remembered Alina's effort to free herself. When Michael the high priest shot him, Veran visibly flinched. Rhys felt her hand on his arm, but he didn't stop. With his gaze set on her face, Rhys continued to pummel Veran with memory after memory.

He showed her the raid on the temple and shared with her the relief and happiness he had felt upon seeing Alina and then his absolute defeat and hopelessness as he watched her crumple against Hodge. Unwilling to give Veran any chance to pull away, Rhys brought forth the strongest, most painful memory he had—Alina's death on the deck of *Themis*.

"Stop," croaked Veran, gripping his sleeve. "Stop."

But he didn't stop; with spiteful cruelty, he drilled Alina's bloody death scene into Veran. He let every emotion he had felt during that time resurface—anger, frustration, despair, hopelessness, terror, sorrow. Everything.

He watched as Veran slowly dropped to her knees, covering her mouth with her hand as tears streamed down her face. Sympathizing with the woman, Rhys ejected the device from his receptors. He threw it to the floor and looked at the committee. "I'm going home." Without another word, he walked out of the public forum.

13
RESCUE PARTY

THE MOMENT RHYS WAS OUT of sight, he began running.

"Turn right ahead," said Ethos. "And then left." Rhys followed the AI's instructions. "Another left."

Rhys stopped at an intersection of hallways. "Which way? Which way?"

"Ehh… go straight. No, not there. There."

Rhys started down another corridor. He passed several silver-haired citizens who only glanced at him before continuing their silent conversations.

"Left!" instructed Ethos.

Rhys turned on his bare heel and continued. "I need weapons."

"I know, I know," replied Ethos. "Turn right at the next intersection and go into the first room on the left."

Rhys did as he was told and ran headlong into five men standing guard at a large, external door. None seemed surprised to see him. He spotted his short rifle and resonance cutters leaning against the wall near the door.

"Stop," demanded one of the men. "This area is off-limits. Only search and rescue personnel are permitted to exit through here. Return to the public forum."

"I'm sorry," replied Rhys. In a single motion, he slid into the first man, grabbed his arm, and rolled him across the floor. He turned to engage the next one, but instead met a hand. Remembering all too well that these men could shock him unconscious—as was his skill when he had had an AI—Rhys dodged and swept his foot through the guard's legs.

He felt a heavy weight on his shoulder just before a powerful shock tore through his body. His muscles seized, and his knees buckled beneath him, sending him to the floor. Shaking violently, Rhys tried to draw himself up, but he couldn't make his body listen. He snarled as a Caelestis man bent down to him. "D-don't," stuttered Rhys. Another shock drove him into unconsciousness.

"Hey? Rhyssssss." Ethos' voice was distant.

Rhys groaned as he slowly woke. His entire body hurt.

"Rhys."

"What?" he moaned. He opened his eyes and looked up at the white ceiling of his cell.

"I think there's something going on."

He sat up, his entire body aching fiercely. "How long was I unconscious?"

"About ten minutes," replied Ethos. "Something is going on. I've detected several heat signatures moving through the hallways, fast."

"Meaning?"

"Something's got your people's attention."

Rhys crossed the room and pressed his ear against the door. After a few moments, he heard someone hurry by. Nothing ever made the people of Caelestis run.

"Eh, Rhys?"

"Hm?"

"There's something I haven't told you. A few hours ago… I sent out a radio call to anyone in the area. It took a while to transmit because of the walls' thickness and material but…"

"What kind of radio call?" Rhys strained to hear through the door before giving up. Rubbing his neck and shoulders, he leaned against the room's desk.

"I mimicked your voice. I simply said, 'Turn on the board.'"

"The board?" Rhys' mouth dropped open. "The magnetic board? You knew about that?"

"Of course, I knew about it."

"So… it's possible that… the board made it here? But I'm not wearing the tracking chip."

"For the moment, I'm the tracking chip," said Ethos. "I'm sorry. My intention was for you to escape earlier."

Rhys scoffed. "Well, we're back here."

"That doesn't explain the commotion outside though," said Ethos.

Rhys looked up at the bulbous camera connected to the ceiling. "Hey, what's going on? Is the colony in danger?" No one answered. He moved across the room until he was directly beneath the camera. "Hello? Do you need help?"

When no one replied, Rhys pulled Ethos from his pocket and ran to the door. "No one's watching." He pressed the AI against the door. "It has to be coded. Do something."

"I'm not a locksmith," growled Ethos. Rhys pressed his ear against the door. He could hear quick footsteps coming down the hall.

"Come on, Ethos," Rhys murmured.

"Do you know what you're asking me to do?" asked Ethos. A muffled voice reverberated down the hallway, and Rhys' heart jumped at its familiar tone. Kallen? Surely not! How was that even possible? "That's Kallen," his AI confirmed.

Rhys listened a moment longer to verify that his mind wasn't playing tricks on him and then shouted, "Kallen!" He kicked the door. "Kallen!"

"That was Rhys," he heard Hodge say.

"Hodge! Kallen!" Rhys couldn't help the stupid smile on his face.

"Rhys?" Kallen's voice grew louder. "Rhys?"

"I'm here!"

"Press the buttons," said Hodge.

"No no no no," murmured Kallen. "Don't. Rhys, what's the code?"

"I don't know. Is it a keypad lock or a digital lock?" replied Rhys.

"I don't know. What's a digital lock?" asked Hodge.

Explosive gunfire ricocheted through the hallway, startling Rhys horribly. "What's going on?"

"*Gawan*, don't kill them," scolded Hodge.

"Don't move!" warned Kallen suddenly as someone approached. The tone in her voice was one she rarely used.

Rhys rammed the door, jarring his shoulder. He kicked it with the ball of his foot before slamming into it. Just as he backed up to charge again, there was a faint click. The door whizzed open to reveal Veran.

Pistol drawn, Kallen passed Veran, cleared the room, and then smiled at Rhys. Rhys swept her into his arms, kissed the side of her head, and then ushered them out.

"Go out the south door," instructed Veran, stepping warily away from Hodge. "The items you came with are there."

Rhys fondly punched Hodge's shoulder and then looked at Axel who had a short rifle drawn on the hallway. The soldier glanced at him but remained silent. All three wore bulletproof vests and carried an assortment of weapons. Rhys turned to Veran. "What about you?" he asked in Interstellar Nefegian.

"I understand what's at stake," Veran stoically replied.

Kallen passed Rhys a handgun and moved into a defensive position nearby. Rhys checked the handgun before saying, "Thank you, Veran."

"Let's go, let's go," urged Axel over his shoulder. "I can't tell what they're planning."

"Southern exit," called Rhys as Axel littered the hallway with more gunfire. "This way." With him in the lead and Axel bringing up the rear, they wound through the twisting hallways of the colony. At each intersection, Rhys, with Hodge at his side, slowed and peered around the corner. Once the intersecting hallways were cleared, they continued. "Last time there were guards up here," Rhys panted.

"Last time?" asked Hodge. At the final turn, Rhys stopped the group and peered around the corner. The guards were still there. "Hey." Hodge nudged him. Rhys looked up as Doctor Falkrow and several more men appeared from the opposite corridor.

"Don't," Rhys said, shoving Hodge's weapon aside.

Rhys' father regarded them and then said in Nefegian, "Let's not do this."

"I'm leaving," he replied, stepping before Hodge. "My name was cleared."

"Veran is a Pathos-user. Her ability to accurately comprehend information pales in comparison to that of a Logos-user. I'm sure you know this."

"Then what?" asked Rhys. "Will you kill me?"

"No," replied Doctor Falkrow. He motioned to the men around him who began fanning out. Rhys was relieved to see that none of them had weapons. "You must still stand trial for Alina's death."

"If you ever bring up her name before me again, I will rip out your throat," growled Rhys. "I've done it before... You're no different."

"So you also admit to murdering other humans?"

"Can't we just push through them?" whispered Hodge.

"No, don't engage in close-quarter combat," said Rhys. "Remember what I could do... I've already been shocked once."

"Listen to him," came a gender-neutral voice. Rhys instantly recognized it as a Logos AI. "We do not want to hurt you."

Rhys glared at his father. "You've learned the Aabeshian language."

"No, it was in the Core. Our search and rescue teams learned it. Anyone has access to it," replied his father's AI. Doctor Falkrow motioned to Rhys. "You don't belong with them. You never have."

"Why... would I turn myself in so that I may stand trial once more?" snarled Rhys in Aabeshian. If he was going to argue with his father, he wanted Hodge, Kallen, and Axel to know what was going on. "Stand down. You people may have reservations about taking human life, but we do not."

"This is, of course, true," said Doctor Falkrow, "however, logically speaking, if our lives are in danger, we are entitled to self-defense to preserve ourselves."

"Enough!" called a voice. Veran strolled through Rhys' group and positioned herself in the middle of the conflict. "Enough, Doctor Falkrow."

"Falkrow?" whispered Hodge, wildly looking at Rhys.

Rhys kept his eyes forward. "My father," he clarified.

"Your father? Rhys…" Kallen looked between Doctor Falkrow and Rhys.

Veran continued in Interstellar Nefegian. "I gave my testament. Rhys is innocent. Everything he says is true."

"Not everything," replied Rhys' father. "He murdered Alina Falkrow."

"He did not!" Veran argued. "As a part of the law committee, I am formally ordering you to step down."

"Veran, come now," scolded Walton the colony's commander as he pushed his way through the conglomerate of Caelestis citizens. "We all saw how you reacted to Rhys' memories. It's obvious your testimony was colored by what you witnessed."

"You *asked* me to read his memories," replied Veran, mild incredulity tinting her voice.

"As a Pathos user, I'm sorry to say that, even if you had managed to maintain your composure, you are just not qualified to pass judgment. Your emotions and those of Rhys Falkrow would only hinder the process."

Veran backed away, prompting Rhys to go to her. He drew the woman behind him. "You never intended to consider her testimony," he said lowly. "It was a ploy to mimic due process."

"You murdered Alina Falkrow," asserted Walton. "She was entrusted into your care, and you failed."

"Commander, please explain yourself," said Veran. "I don't understand how you reached such a conclusion."

"Doctor Falkrow, in a moment of desperation, took aside his son and asked that he protect Alina Falkrow with the belief that she would be safe until the life pod was retrieved," explained Walton. He looked at Rhys. "No one could ever have imagined that you'd end up here."

"Other Caelestis citizens perished in the crash," said Rhys. "Why is Alina's death any different?"

"Because she was being groomed to become the next commander of Caelestis," snapped Doctor Falkrow.

"Then why did you entrust her to me?" growled Rhys. "Someone so important, why would you entrust her to me?"

"Because you were her brother, and my research indicated that familial bonds would irrevocably tie you to her. You would do anything to keep her safe," replied his father. "Accordingly, you were her best bet at survival off of Caelestis."

Rhys swallowed the growing agony in the pit of his stomach. He had always known Alina was special. She had, throughout their entire lives, always been treated differently. She had been coveted and given extraordinary opportunities. It all made sense now. She would have been perfect. "Fine," murmured Rhys in Aabeshian. "I am responsible for her death. I killed my sister." He glared at his father. "What now?"

"Rhys," seethed Hodge, stalking forward. "This is what you've been arguing about? About whether he killed Alina?" Hodge glared at Doctor Falkrow and Walton. "How could you accuse him of something like that!"

The power of Hodge's voice combined with his imposing stature made many of the Caelestis citizens back away. Even Doctor Falkrow, who had been an impenetrable wall of unyielding stubbornness, fidgeted.

"From the beginning, Rhys did everything in his power to protect Alina and keep her from harm." Hodge glanced at Rhys. "We all did. She wasn't our responsibility; she wasn't anyone's responsibility. She was her own person. Alina could take care of herself, but when the odds were stacked against her, Rhys was the first one by her side ready to take on the impossible. He killed for her, fought for her—and you say he's responsible for her death? What kind of *gawan* logic is that?"

"You are his comrade," replied Walton, "therefore you are obligated to defend him."

Hodge stood in silence for a moment before a smile cracked across his lips. "They're like Alina. All of them." Rhys nodded knowingly. The guards near the door tensed as Hodge turned his gaze onto them and motioned with his short rifle. "Let's go. Out of the way." No one moved.

"He said move!" shouted Axel, pushing past Hodge and bringing up his pistol.

"They don't understand what guns are," said Rhys.

Axel fired two warning shots into the wall. Everyone in the room flinched, and the guards around the door scattered. "Kallen," said Axel.

Pistol drawn, Kallen passed him, collected Rhys' short rifle and resonance cutters, and returned to Rhys. Rhys slung the cutters onto his back and readied his rifle. Axel motioned with his weapon; the guards cleared the entryway and joined the ranks of citizens gathered around Walton and Doctor Falkrow.

"Go," whispered Rhys to Kallen, pushing her to Axel. He turned to Veran. Her enormous blue eyes were wide with fright, and her hair, which had been pinned neatly in a bun, was fraying. "Come on." He held his hand out to her. Veran fearfully looked at Walton and Doctor Falkrow. "You know there's more out there," Rhys urged. Veran slid her hand into Rhys'.

"Doctor Taiglar," warned Walton. Hodge raised his rifle and pointed it at the commander. The man fell silent.

Rhys pulled Veran to the door which Kallen was opening. "Stay close," he said. Veran's hands grasped the back of his shirt.

The early evening air hit Rhys hard, and he breathed in deeply. He smelled plants, sea water, and freedom. Kallen hopped down from the external exit and checked the area for danger. Rhys led Veran out followed by Hodge and then Axel who slammed the door shut.

"We're running," said Hodge, passing Rhys. "Let's go."

Rhys shouldered his rifle and looked at Veran. "Are you sure you want to do this?" he asked in Nefegian. "Once you leave the colony… there's no coming back."

Veran glanced back at the enormous colony walls before turning her brilliant blue gaze onto Rhys. "Is it worth it?"

"Yes," replied Rhys.

"Rhys, your board," exclaimed Kallen, pointing overhead.

Rhys turned to find his magnetic board soaring over the colony's flat halls. "Very good, Ethos," he murmured as the machine settled before him. "Very good."

"Thank you," chirped Ethos.

Rhys held his hand out to Veran who took it hesitantly. "Let's go."

Board in tow, the group set off at a clip through the darkening forest toward the sea. When the shadows deepened and the darkness became impenetrable, Rhys suggested to Veran that she engage her night vision. Despite the forest floor being coated in vegetation, Rhys still placed his bare feet gingerly over rocks and sticks. Numerous times he cursed under his breath as something sharp jabbed his foot or he stubbed his toe.

It was well past dusk by the time they reached a long beach speckled with rocks, sand, and clay. Two figures standing at the waterline stiffened at their appearance.

"Hey, it's us," called Hodge, waving his rifle in the air.

"Damn it, Hodge," came Leo's voice. "We almost shot you."

As Hodge greeted Kashim and Leo with banter, Rhys fell behind with Veran. The rest of his crew continued. "Don't be afraid," he said, standing close to her. He knew how she felt—vulnerable, afraid, overwhelmed. He and Alina had felt the exact same way.

"Did you find him?" asked Kashim.

Rhys saw Hodge's dim form point in his direction. Veran shuffled nervously. With a gentle hand, Rhys guided her across the rocks to his crew. He shook hands warmly with Kashim and clapped Leo on the shoulder. "This is Veran," he said. "She is from Caelestis." Under the scrutiny of the foreigners, Veran backed away. Rhys moved to her side, and she shied behind him. "This is... her first time outside the colony."

"What happened?" asked Kashim, eyeing her. "We looked for you everywhere."

"Let's decide what we're going to do first." Rhys glanced at the sunboards floating nearby on the gentle waves. If they were ninety or so kilometers north of New Arbroath, then the sunboards were low on energy. There was no way for them to make it back to New Arbroath tonight. "It took you about two hours to get here?"

"Yes," replied Hodge. "I'm not going to lie, it was a stressful journey."

"I suggest we make a fire," said Kashim. "The boards are low on energy; we can't make it back right now."

"My thoughts exactly. Hodge, Kallen—start gathering firewood. Axel, find us concealment."

"Is someone after us?" asked Leo.

"No," replied Veran. All eyes turned to her. "Not right now."

Trusting that Veran had information he did not, Rhys motioned for the group to take shelter in the tree line and bed down for the night. Within the half hour, Kashim and Hodge had a small bonfire going just inside the forest line. As Rhys circled the fire and moved aside sticks and vegetation that could catch, he glanced at Veran and Kallen. Just as she had done with Alina, Kallen was giving Veran attention and speaking softly to her. Rhys was pleased to see the woman relax in her presence.

Kashim handed him a canteen of water as he passed, and Rhys drank heavily from it. "What happened?" the big man asked.

Rhys sat on Kallen's other side and handed the canteen to Veran who looked at him questioningly. "Drink," he murmured in Nefegian. As Veran sipped the water, Rhys gazed into the fire. "I was shot."

"Brechin forces," said Axel.

Rhys nodded. "Your assessment of New Arbroath was correct. I ran into a squad in the forest southwest of the town."

"We found the dinghy," said Hodge. "But we didn't find you."

"I was shot in the head."

Kallen gasped audibly. "No..."

Hodge groaned and reclined on his elbows. "That's the last time you're going anywhere by yourself. Bad things always happen when you're alone."

"Agreed." He motioned to Veran. "She saved my life." Kallen touched Rhys' head and traced the receptors under her fingertips.

"Thank you," said Hodge, regarding Veran from across the fire. "He's gangly and gets into a lot of trouble, but... thank you."

Veran remained silent. Rhys knew people were rarely thanked on the colony. Whatever they did was considered a part of their job. They were not to be thanked for work.

Kallen touched Veran's arm. "Thank you."

"I... uh..." Veran looked to Rhys for guidance. "You're welcome."

"Do you know who these people are?" asked Rhys of Veran. He half-expected Hodge to scoff at the silly question—how could she?—but the circle of crew members remained quiet.

Veran's eyes trained on Hodge. "Hodge. I know you. And..." She looked between Leo, Kashim, Kallen, and Axel. "Maybe..." She pointed to Kallen and then Kashim. "Maybe them. Their faces are murky."

"How..." Leo looked to Rhys for an explanation.

"I gave her access to some of my memories to prove my innocence," said Rhys.

Veran continued in Interstellar Nefegian. "He was with Alina when she was shot." She looked at Kallen and Kashim. "I think they were with you, but that part of the memory is dark."

Rhys nodded and for his crew's benefit, said in Aabeshian, "Yes, he was with her when she was shot. He was her mate."

Veran turned her head. "Mate? As in reproductive partner?"

Rhys exchanged amused looks with Kallen. "Yes."

"But... how do you—"

Rhys cut off Veran and swiftly spoke in Nefegian. The only other person who could understand them was Leo. "It is perfectly acceptable to engage in sexual behavior even if it doesn't lead to insemination. It is a part of being human." Rhys studied Veran's face. "Do you understand?"

"I… understand," she murmured, perplexed.

"You know us?" prompted Kashim.

"Uh… yes. But, uh, maybe not…"

"Yes, they were there," confirmed Rhys. Veran nodded though it seemed she was still pondering the concept of human sexuality. Rhys pointed to Kashim. "Kashim." He moved to Hodge. "Hodge. Axel. Leo." He leaned back so Veran could see Kallen. "And Kallen."

"What is your relationship with these people?" asked Veran in Nefegian.

"Please speak in Aabeshian."

Veran spoke her question again, this time in Aabeshian.

"They're crew members," said Rhys. He motioned to Kashim and Hodge.

"Eh… I'm a sunboarder?" said Hodge, looking to Rhys for guidance. "I'm a former courier for New Arbroath. I can do… anything really."

"Anything?" asked Veran.

"Ehh…" Hodge chuckled. "No, I mean… That's my job. Whatever needs to be done, I do it." He nudged Kashim. "You go."

"I'm Second Mate of the ship," said Kashim. "Navigation, weaponry, support."

"Second Mate? Who is First Mate?" asked Veran.

"Andy," said Kashim.

Veran thought, glanced apologetically at the others, and then turned to Rhys. In Interstellar Nefegian, she murmured, "They are mates to you? I do not understand."

Leo snickered but hid his humor behind a hand. Rhys wanted to share in his mirth but, for Veran's sake, kept a straight face. Asking questions was a vital part of her integration. "First Mate and Second Mate are ranks of command," he explained in Nefegian. "They're ranks. The title has no sexual connotation."

"Ahh." Veran nodded enthusiastically. She looked at Kallen and then at Rhys before tilting her head once more. "Is she someone's mate? There are several males here and one female. Perhaps it is socially accepted to have multiple mates?"

Rhys glanced at Leo who was following the conversation in silent hysterics. Everyone else in the circle watched with interest. "She is my mate," said Rhys. "Kallen is mine."

Veran looked between them again. "She is the one you mentioned in your testimony?"

"Yes."

"She is pregnant? I don't understand. She appears no different than any other female."

Rhys shifted his gaze to Leo who was no longer laughing but gaping. Rhys switched to Aabeshian, "So, Kashim is Second Mate. Andy, I am guessing, is still aboard *Themis*?" Kashim nodded. "Kallen is our ship's mechanic. She was taught by the ship's previous owner." Rhys motioned to Axel indicating that it was his turn. Kallen passed Rhys a dubious expression and then glanced at Leo. Rhys knew his crew had seen the sudden worry on his face as well as the quick cover-up. He and Kallen would answer to them later. For the moment, Leo was the only one who knew.

"I'm a former Brechin soldier," shared Axel. For not having ever seen a woman of Veran's flavor, he was oddly uninterested.

"A soldier?" said Veran, "As in a man who follows orders and serves in a militaristic entity?" Axel nodded.

"I guess… that means it's my turn," murmured Leo. "My name is Leo and, eh…" He looked to Rhys. They had spoken about not revealing to others his title and nobility. "I work on the ship. I'm like Hodge. Whatever needs to be done, I'll do it."

"Tell her, Leo," said Kallen. "You're a writer."

"A writer?" asked Veran. Rhys watched as Veran received an explanation from her AI. She nodded in understanding.

"Leo is well-studied. He's read literature from around the world and is versed in a multitude of skills," Rhys added.

"You speak Interstellar Nefegian, correct? How is that? You are not from Caelestis." Veran glanced out at the forest and then shifted uncomfortably. Rhys didn't miss the motion.

Leo replied, "It was my birth language. There are many of your people here who reside on Earth. Their language has become incorporated into our culture."

Veran looked once more out at the forest. "That is because when man left Earth, he created a beta-wormhole to escape to the Solar System Hyperes. It was forgotten by our people because there was no reason for us to return to the Solar System."

Rhys nodded. That was what he and Alina had speculated, but neither them nor their AIs had been certain. Now, he knew.

"Why do you know that?" asked Kallen.

"I do not understand the question," replied Veran.

"She's higher ranking than I am," Rhys explained. "She is the Director of Medicine. It was important that she had access to that information."

"That seems like something that not only higher-ups should know." Kallen frowned. "It seems important to me."

"You don't even know what a wormhole is," scoffed Hodge.

"I don't need to. She had information that Rhys and Alina didn't."

"There's nothing to be suspicious about," said Rhys in Elali. Kallen shrugged and poked the fire with a stick. Veran fidgeted. Rhys flicked a look under his lashes at Axel who nodded. At least someone else had picked up on Veran's behavior. Feigning fatigue, Rhys stood with a sigh. "We should rest. We'll be leaving at dawn."

"I'll take first shift," said Axel, moving to his feet.

"As will I," said Rhys. "We'll check the perimeter and—"

"You're leaving?" asked Veran in Nefegian.

"We're just going to check the surrounding forest and then stay up for a few hours," he explained. "It's a safety precaution. We always have someone on watch."

"What do I do?" She fearfully peered up at him.

"Sleep."

Veran's expression of worry deepened. It was then Rhys remembered how anxious he and Alina had been facing the prospect of sleeping alone without the Core for the first time.

Smiling, he said in Nefegian, "For millennia, generations have slept without the help of the Core. There are no ill effects of sleeping without the Core."

"Rhys," said Hodge, kicking off his boots. "Take them."

Rhys sat, laced Hodge's oversized boots, and looked to Axel who had his short rifle resting in his arms. "We'll return in a short while."

"Here," said Axel, passing him a headscarf. Rhys covered his glowing silver hair and the lower part of his face as they stalked into the forest. "She's odd."

"That's how Alina and I were in the beginning," Rhys murmured, training his eyes to seek movement amongst the trees. Once they could no longer see camp, he lowered himself into some underbrush and withdrew Ethos. Axel knelt beside him. "Why was she fidgeting so much?"

"I detect no heat signatures in the surrounding radius. Thermal scans: clear. Sonic scans: clear. Radio scans…" Ethos paused before saying, "Clear."

"Why the uncertainty?" asked Axel.

"You mistake my momentary silence as an indication of trouble," chided Ethos.

Rhys stood and looked about. "If there's nothing here, then she was communicating with others on Caelestis."

Axel stood stiffly and shouldered his weapon. "I'm not going to ask questions about your personal lives, but for the sake of security, is there any way they can listen in on our conversations through her?"

Rhys pursed his lips in thought. It was possible, but he had always been under the impression that such an act required permission from the AI's user. He could be wrong though and if he was, he was endangering his crew once more.

"Hey, Computer-Thing," said Axel. "Can I take his silence to mean that they *can* do that?"

"Yes," grumbled Ethos.

"So, what do you want to do? Take her back?"

Other than Neo-Colony Two knowing where they were at all times, was there any dangerous downside allowing Veran to remain with them? It was possible that forcing Veran out of Neo-Colony Two was the plan all along, and the commander was going to use her as a radio of sorts to keep track of them. "Leave her for now," murmured Rhys. "I'll deal with her when the time comes."

"You're fine with her transmitting our constant location to the people who had you locked up?"

"We're not in danger of an imminent attack from them," Rhys patiently countered, peering out into the deep shadows of the forest. Overhead, a soft breeze stirred the trees. He breathed deeply. Never did he want to step into Neo-Colony Two again. As Axel began walking, Rhys asked, "How did you find me?"

"Andy heard your voice on the radio. It kept telling us to turn on the board." Axel cradled his injured shoulder. "Everyone agreed that it was you, but there was no way to figure out where the signal was coming from. It was Kallen who suggested that we just turn the thing on and see what happened."

"And?"

"The moment she turned it on, it leapt up in the forward hatch. We gathered a hunting party, launched sunboards, and then released it. And we followed it all the way out here." Axel started for camp, and Rhys followed. "We left Kashim and Leo with the boards, and the rest of us took off into the forest."

"I'm surprised you were able to keep up with it."

"We didn't. We lost it but continued in the same general direction. That's when we finally saw that place east of us. The board was hovering over the roof."

"How'd you get in?"

"We just… walked in," said Axel. "I expected guards, but no one came to meet us. Only when we made it into the main hallway did they signal an alarm, and everyone scattered. What's with your people? Don't they own guns or weapons? We could have just walked in and slaughtered the lot of them."

By the time they returned to camp, everyone but Veran and Kashim was asleep. Rhys seated himself beside Veran and said to Kashim, "It's all clear." Kashim sighed and lay down beside Hodge who was lightly snoring. Axel perched himself atop a nearby rock and gazed out into the forest. "Why aren't you asleep?" whispered Rhys.

"I can't sleep," Veran breathed.

"Nothing will happen. Disconnecting from the Core—"

Veran stopped him with a slight shake of her head. "It's not that."

"What's wrong?"

"I can't sleep because I keep seeing the memories you showed me." She looked at Rhys woefully. "They're… so horrible. When I close my eyes, it is all I see."

Rhys stirred the fire to avoid Veran's gaze. "Ask Pathos. It can mute the memories."

"I… don't want that."

Surprised, he sat back and looked at her. "Why?"

"Because it would… disrespect you and your trials."

"They're mine to bear."

Veran shifted in the dirt and withdrew the adaptor from her inner pocket. She studied it for a moment and then asked, "How do you sleep? Do they bother you?"

Rhys scoffed in dark humor. "Yes… they bother me." He nodded to Kallen. "If it weren't for her, I wouldn't get any sleep."

Veran held the adaptor out to Rhys. "Can you show me?"

"Show you what?"

"Everything?"

Rhys glanced at Axel who was half-way paying attention to their foreign conversation and then said, "Veran, I know you're in communication with Neo-Colony Two. I know they're using you to gather information."

Veran tilted her head in confusion. "How would you know that? You do not have an AI."

"There's a high-pitched whine emanating from you. I can hear that." He sighed. "I'm not going to share with you any more of my memories." Rhys gently nudged Kallen awake so she could rest her head on his legs. Kallen glanced up at him, her second skin glistening in the light of the fire, and, smiling, went back to sleep. Sensing Veran's gaze on him, he continued in his mother tongue. "I don't belong to Caelestis anymore. I belong to them. It's as simple and complicated as that."

14
QUADRANT SIX

"WHAT ARE YOU DOING?"

Rhys looked up at Alina who stood in the forward hatch of *Themis*. Like usual, she wore cutoffs, a long-sleeved shirt, and no shoes. Her dyed hair hung in a black braid over her shoulder. "I've almost figured this out," Rhys replied, motioning to the magnetic board. He had already sunk three hours into the project that day.

"You're aware that sitting on the floor in silence doesn't count, right?"

Rhys frowned at his sister's remark. "I understand the majority of the components. Pathos believes—"

He sat up to look at Alina but found his sister gone.

"Alina?"

He leaned on his hands to see out the doorway into the hall.

"Rhys, let's go!" Vinz suddenly shouted through the pipe communication system. Rhys startled at the Overseer's voice and then looked at the scattered tools around him. "You need to launch!" Frantic, Rhys pushed everything into a single pile as Kallen and Hodge dashed into the forward hatch and began opening the door and preparing a sunboard for launch.

"Why are you just standing there?"

Rhys turned to find Alina once more loitering in the doorway. She glanced at Hodge and then said, "Go on. You need to hurry and die." The serene smile on her face twisted into a dark, murderous snarl. "Go, Rhys. Go out there. Hurry up and die."

"Alina…" he breathed. "What's wrong?"

His sister disappeared into the hallway.

"Alina!" he called, stumbling after her. He tripped on the doorway—and jarred himself awake.

Rhys felt his body lurch as he tried to catch himself. Instantly, he was awake, heart hammering and adrenaline pumping. Panting, he gazed at the trees overhead painted with the pink of dawn. After a moment, he wiped his sweaty brow and sat up. Kallen, who had been tending to the fire, smiled knowingly. He brushed the dirt from his shirt and arms and stretched his neck. "I... could do without the nightmares," he murmured in Elali.

She passed him the canteen. "I saw you dreaming, but it didn't look bad enough to wake you."

Rhys drank and glanced at the others. Only Leo was awake. Veran was curled in the fetal position beside him. "I want to go home," he said finally. Kallen nodded fervently. He studied Veran for a moment longer and then looked at her AI which was snugged securely against her temple. "Pathos?"

"Yes, Rhys?" replied the AI just as softly.

Rhys' heart ached at the sound of the AI's very familiar voice. "I know you are transmitting data and information to Neo-Colony Two."

"You are correct. I am."

"Is there any way you could stop or have you been overridden by the Core?"

"I've been overridden by the Core," said Pathos. "Veran does not have a choice. It is as you said last night. She is being used to transmit information."

Rhys nodded. That's what he thought. "Can you suppress the memories I gave her? I didn't mean to scar her."

"I cannot. She has given orders to leave them be in their natural states."

Rhys glanced at Kallen. "Please tell her... those aren't hers to bear. She doesn't need them. I was merely trying to prove my case."

"She is aware of this but does not wish to discard of or suppress the memories. Thank you for your concern, Rhys Falkrow."

Rhys glanced at Hodge who snored himself awake. His friend, blurry-eyed and bushy-haired, sat up and glowered at Rhys. "Tell it to shut up," he grumbled.

At first humored, Rhys' mirth disappeared. Hodge's voice was pinched, and his brows furrowed in pain. Pathos' voice sounded similar to Logos'—Alina's AI. Rhys nodded. "Sorry."

Hodge rubbed his eyes, blinked up at the sky, and then flopped back down into the dirt, waking both Kashim and Axel. Rhys stood, brushed his clothes, and ruffled his hair into place. "Let's get going."

Within fifteen minutes, everyone was gathered at the water line. He found the two sunboards that *Themis* usually carried as well as another he didn't recognize. Baffled, Rhys pointed at the outcast. "Where'd you get the other one?"

"The Old Man," replied Hodge. Rhys didn't miss the subtle glances he continuously passed Veran. No doubt she reminded him of Alina. "Axel rode with me because of his shoulder. Leo was with Kashim because he doesn't know how to sunboard. And... Kallen was on her own."

Kallen pointed to his board which was hovering a meter or two away. "What do you want to do with it? Can you fly it?"

"Good question." As Rhys approached the board, he said, "Have a solution, Ethos?"

"Of course," the AI proudly replied. "Pull me out." Rhys withdrew the unit from his pocket. The strip of metal which lined the top of Ethos, slid open to reveal an optic lens. A light flickered on and a three-dimensional screen appeared just above the AI's unit. A short triumphant horn fanfare bugled from Ethos' speakers.

"You're brilliant," murmured Rhys in Nefegian.

Ethos pretended to clear its throat and said, "Now, I don't know how the information was presented to you before, but my reconstruction of the data is how it was originally meant to be seen. Therefore, before you is a grid of numbers ranging from zero to ten thousand. Areas with a high magnetic density will present to you as numbers ranging from seven thousand to ten thousand."

Rhys studied the transparent, light-constructed grid glowing before his face. "There... are numbers everywhere," he said. This was not going to be easy. Pathos had greatly simplified the process by converting the numbers and data to colors that could be read without thought. Searching numbers in the field before him for sustainable density levels was going to be a challenge. "Is this really how it was meant to be read?" Rhys turned to the left and then to the right.

"You don't need to move me with your body," explained Ethos. "I can track your face and adjust to ensure the screen remains in your field of vision. As for the numbers—yes, this is how its original pilot used the board. What did Pathos use?"

"Colors," said Rhys. He turned his head once more but kept Ethos positioned before him. As if it were a part of him, the iridescent screen followed his movement and remained in front of his face.

"I want to see," Hodge announced. Hodge, Leo, and Kallen crowded around him and looked over his shoulder at the transparent screen and myriad of numbers which extended into the distance. After a moment, Hodge withdrew. "Nope. You're on your own. When you start involving numbers in flying, I'm out." Kallen also pulled away. Only Leo remained studying the screen.

"In flight, you will have to actively search out numbers within the density spectrum?" asked Leo.

"Looks that way," muttered Rhys.

Ethos scoffed. "No, now, don't take that attitude."

"Honestly though," said Rhys, squinting at the numbers. "This is not something I can just fling myself into. It's going to take time to perfect."

"It's a good thing you have a two-hour journey back to New Arbroath then, isn't it?" the AI replied.

"Eh, what about Veran?" asked Kallen. The screen before Rhys' face faded, and he looked at Veran. "Who is she going to ride with? Hodge has Axel, Kashim has Leo... I can't carry her."

"I'll take her," said Rhys.

"Is that wise?" asked Hodge.

"We don't have a choice." Rhys turned to the board which hovered by his side. "Just give me a moment. Ethos?" The screen reappeared.

"Rhys, here," said Hodge, stripping out of his bulletproof vest. Rhys looked at him questioningly. "You can tuck the computer-thing in the top of it so you don't have to hold it."

Rhys buckled the vest about his torso and then slipped Ethos in the top. Although it wasn't a perfect fit—Ethos had to make some adjustments—it worked. Rhys stepped onto the board and secured his feet in the clasps. He knew what to do; his body remembered the movements, the angles, and speed. He just had to figure out how to read the numbers.

For a moment, he searched the sky and read the constantly fluctuating numbers which crowded the screen. It took but a moment to plan a flight path. Once he was over the water, he gazed up at the numbers again and then punched his left heel into the board. The magnetic board lurched upward at a forty-five-degree angle and soared into the brilliant morning sky. He gripped the side of the board with his right hand to keep himself pushed into the angle before leveling off and flying over the sea. Far below, he could see his crew and Veran, heads upturned.

He had missed flying. Of course, he could sunboard, but this was different. This was much freer. He banked to the left and gazed at the vast island that was Neo-Colony Two. Deep in the tangled forest, he could discern the pale roof of the colony.

Knowing that everyone was waiting, he practiced a few maneuvers which required him to swiftly read and process the measurements. The presentation of the numbers was not ideal, but he would make it work.

When he returned to his crew, the sunboards' sails were open and Hodge, Kallen, and Kashim were checking fans. Veran stood by herself in the shade of the trees while Axel sat on a rock, his gaze set on Rhys.

Rhys brought the board beside Veran and squatted on it so he was eye level with her. "Do you understand what this is?" he asked in their native tongue. She nodded. "Do you feel safe riding with me?"

Veran looked at the others. "I… don't have a choice." She gathered her courage and circled the unit, investigating its underbelly before straightening herself. "You've flown this before?"

"Yes, many times," he replied.

"So you lied to me?" called Axel.

Everyone stopped and looked at the soldier. "Lied?" asked Rhys.

Axel stood and approached him; Veran stepped back to place Rhys between herself and Axel. "You lied to me. You told me you couldn't fly."

"I personally cannot fly. It's not physically possible."

"*Gawan*, you're flying right now," the soldier countered.

Rhys frowned. "Well… if you count the board, then yes…"

"Do your eyes glow too?" asked Axel.

"Let's go," interrupted Kashim. "I'm tired of waiting. We're needed back in New Arbroath."

"I didn't lie to you," Rhys avowed. Axel joined Hodge at their sunboard. While the others prepared for flight, Rhys explained to Veran how his magnetic board worked. Once she understood, he pulled her onto the board. After deciding it would be best that she hold on from behind, they readjusted, and hovered nearby as Hodge and Kallen cranked on the sunboard fans.

"Here," murmured Hodge, approaching the board, arm outstretched. He passed Veran a headscarf and indicated that she should wrap it about herself. Rhys didn't miss the sad, appraising look he imparted her.

"Let's go!" called Kashim.

Rhys peeked at Veran over his shoulder as the three sunboards took off across the water. "Ready?" She nodded. He accelerated to the board's standard speed and caught up with Kallen who was the last one to not have sent her sunboard airborne. "Got it?" he shouted, pacing alongside her board.

Kallen, who was frowning deeply as she tried for the third time to swing the sail overhead, didn't answer. Each time the wind pulled it from her grasp and snapped the solar-paneled sail back into its fin position.

"Hold on," murmured Rhys. Veran's grip around his waist tightened. "Do it again!" Kallen took a moment to catch her breath before jerking the sail overhead. Just before the wind swung it back on her, Rhys grabbed the bar and locked it into place. Kallen knelt on the board in preparation for flight.

Once airborne, she was a natural. It was upper-body strength she lacked, not skill. Kallen, with Rhys trailing behind, fell into formation with Hodge and Kashim. After confirming that he was riding in a high-density area, Rhys glanced back at Veran. He found her eyes squeezed shut. How long had she been like that?

"Look," he said.

"No," she cried. "Tell me when we arrive."

"You're going to keep your eyes closed for two hours? Come on. Open your eyes. Look." She did as he said. "Look at the clouds and the sea below." He felt Veran shift. "See?"

Veran surveyed all that was around her—the pink and orange clouds, the emerald sea, the solitary bird soaring overhead. She looked behind them at Neo-Colony Two's island. "Is it always this colorful?" she asked into his ear.

"Always," he replied. He squinted against the rising sun. "Welcome to Earth, Veran."

Over the next hour and a half, Rhys spoke very little to the doctor. In fact, it seemed Veran wanted silence. What attempts he did make to speak with her were met with quiet answers or silent nods, so he kept to himself and weaved around the others. Often, he saw Axel and Hodge speaking, but he could never hear what they were saying. Leo, who sat between Kashim's legs, appeared to doze off and on; he seemed comfortable being airborne despite never having been on a sunboard. Perhaps it was that he trusted Kashim so whole-heartedly.

About an hour into the flight, Ethos, who had been silent since take-off, announced, "You've just crossed into Quadrant Six."

"What?" asked Rhys.

"Quadrant Six," repeated Ethos. "You were in Quadrant Seven, now you're in Quadrant Six."

"What do you mean quadrant?"

"Do I need to explain what a quadrant is? It's a piece."

"A piece of what?"

Ethos sighed. "A piece of Earth."

"Why is Earth broken into quadrants? Is that what your internal maps indicate?"

"Isn't that what Pathos told you?"

"No."

"Oh… Then how did you measure where you were on Earth's surface?"

"We just measured distance and the time it took to arrive at another location," Rhys replied.

"Oh, interesting. Well, now you know—you have left Quadrant Seven and are now in Quadrant Six."

Unwilling to continue questioning Ethos with Veran listening, Rhys fell silent. When land finally appeared on the horizon, he maneuvered along Kashim's port side. "What happened while I was gone? Are you expecting trouble?" he called over the buzz of the fan engine.

"Maybe," replied Kashim, his beard blowing in the wind. "While you were gone, Joss started issuing laws to control the Pantarak refugees. Anyone who disobeyed them were locked up or forced to pay a food tax."

"What about the Brechin forces? Did you have any trouble with them?"

"No, not yet," said Kashim.

"It's possible they're still in the forest biding time," added Leo.

"It's also possible New Arbroath no longer exists." Kashim met Rhys' gaze; he was completely serious.

Rhys drew away from their sunboard and, eyes set on the horizon, fell into thought. What awaited them in New Arbroath, no one knew. Despite having been gone for only two days, even Kashim and Leo weren't sure. Their uncertainty did tell him one thing though—the situation in New Arbroath was changing rapidly. They needed to be ready to face anything, especially with Joss assuming command over both New Arbroath and the Pantarak refugees.

Thirty minutes later, New Arbroath came into view, and Rhys was relieved to find *Themis* and *Grisle* still anchored in port, undamaged. From above, it seemed the Pantarak people along the shoreline were going about their daily business. With cautious optimism, Rhys landed on *Themis'* upper deck. He helped Veran from the board and then stepped out of the clasps. Although mildly sore, Rhys was pleased to find that piloting the board held no ill-effects.

"Uh…" Veran looked about. Although her eyes were squinted to guard against the midmorning sun, her brows were furrowed in worry.

Rhys glanced out at the myriad of people along the shore and then looked at Veran. "Trust me. I won't let anything happen to you." Veran didn't reply. Rhys jogged across the deck to the ladder; fearful she was being left behind, Veran followed. "Andy!" called Rhys, entering the bridge. His First Mate wasn't there. "Oi, Andy!" He looked down the staircase into the innards of his ship. No one. Rhys shrugged and slipped down to the forward hatch to help the others dock. Veran stood in the corner and watched.

"Have you seen Andy?" asked Kashim whose board was the last to enter the hatch.

"No. Haven't seen anyone," replied Rhys, cranking Kashim's sunboard overhead. "In fact, the dinghy is still here." Kashim and Leo left the forward hatch and disappeared into the bridge. He heard Hodge try to radio *Grisle*. "How did everything look to you?"

"Not good," said Axel, glancing at Veran. "Maybe you've forgotten, but there were a lot more Pantaraks before than what are currently on the shoreline."

Rhys hadn't forgotten; he had just thought himself wrong. He needed to make an appearance soon and speak with Joss before the situation deteriorated. They needed to be preparing for war, not feuding amongst themselves.

As Kallen closed the forward hatch, Rhys—with Veran close on his heels—joined Kashim and Leo on the bridge. Axel and Hodge followed.

"What does that mean?" asked Leo as Rhys walked in.

"What does what mean?" replied Rhys.

"*Grisle* isn't responding," Kashim explained, setting the radio onto the bridge paneling. "Didn't see anyone aboard when we were on approach either."

Rhys nodded. "Then we're going ashore. Kallen, Veran, Leo. You three stay with the ships."

"No, Cantia's missing," replied Leo firmly. "And my brother. I'm coming with you."

Rhys looked at Hodge who shook his head. "Nope, I'm coming too."

"I'll stay with the ships," said Kallen. "If something is going on, then there's no point in wasting manpower. I'll stay here with Veran." She looked pointedly at Rhys. "Find my grandfather."

"I…" murmured Veran. She glanced fearfully between Kallen, Rhys, and the others. "I want to go."

"Not now," grunted Axel. "You're defenseless and will stand out."

"But… Rhys Falkrow can go ashore," Veran argued. It was the first time since she had left Neo-Colony Two that she had raised her voice.

"Rhys is the Overseer and isn't helpless," muttered Hodge.

Within minutes, the group was on shore amongst the Pantarak people once more. It was obvious something was very wrong. Whereas before the Pantaraks had been optimistic and hopeful, now they exuded a simmering apprehension.

Rhys finally stopped the group. "Kashim, Leo, talk to the people. Get answers. We're going to find Joss." Kashim and Leo broke from the group and headed deeper into the Pantarak camp. With a subtle glance at the worn faces around him, Rhys led Hodge and Axel to New Arbroath. To his surprise, he found guards once more stationed before a barricade at the city's main thoroughfare. "Open up!" barked Rhys. "I need a word with Joss."

"Joss is busy," stated one of the guards, brandishing his weapon. "Take a hike."

Rhys pulled off his headscarf. "I'm Rhys Falkrow, Overseer of New Arbroath's ship, *Themis*. Now, move."

The three guards exchanged confused looks before stepping aside to admit them. Rhys glanced at the men as they passed.

"They're surprised to see you," Axel murmured into Rhys' ear. "That's not good. We didn't tell anyone you were missing."

The town seemed unchanged. People went about their daily business walking to and from shops, gossiping in doorways, and guiding children indoors. A dog barked in the distance. New Arbroath was as it had always been.

Rhys replaced his headscarf and led Hodge and Axel through town. Without pause, they strode through the doors of the courthouse, ignoring the secretary seated in the entryway, and climbed the stairs in the foyer. They found the judge speaking with another man at the top of the stairs. Joss glanced at them before doing a double-take. "May I have a word?" Rhys growled.

Joss studied Rhys, his eyes wide and brows arched in surprise. "Yes…" he murmured. "Would you be so kind as to wait in my office? I have some business to finish up."

"Of course," replied Rhys, glancing at the man standing beside the judge. Joss' guest didn't appear to be typical Pantarak. Though his hair was solid black, his eyes were green-brown, a trait that was found only in the capital. In addition, the man's skin was paler than Joss', another indicator of his origins. "Excuse us." Rhys turned and led Axel and Hodge down the hall to the judge's office. The moment the door closed behind them, he turned to Axel. "He's from Brechin."

"That's not why you should be concerned," said Axel, leaning against Joss' desk. "That was the major general of Brechin's mobile units."

"You know him?" asked Hodge.

"No, but I've seen him around."

"He's made a deal with Brechin," concluded Rhys.

Hodge nudged Axel. "What's in it for Brechin?"

"Don't know… New Arbroath has no real value. It has no goods Brechin would want," mused Axel. "The only reason they're even out here is because of a rebellion."

Rhys frowned. "New Arbroath doesn't have goods, but it has strategic placement. Joss could have exchanged New Arbroath's safety for docking and quartering rights. They could be using New Arbroath as a foothold into the West."

Axel shook his head. "I don't think so. Brechin doesn't negotiate. It takes and subjugates. Brechin's higher-ups are toying with Joss."

"Do you think any of this has to do with Rhys' death?" Hodge offered. When Rhys and Axel looked at him in unison, he shrugged. "Think about it. We didn't tell anyone about you missing. The only other people to have known were Brechin forces."

Rhys shifted his gaze to Joss' untidy desk.

"It's a trap," concluded Axel. Both Rhys and Hodge nodded grimly. "They thought you were dead, so they've captured the others and are using them to lure the rest of us in."

"Which means," said Hodge lowly, looking at the closed door behind him, "if I were Joss, I would inform the Brechin soldiers and have them meet us up here instead."

Axel dove for the window on the other side of the room. With ease, it opened and a hot breeze wafted into the room. "Go," he instructed Hodge.

Hodge stepped onto the window sill, looked down warily at the bare earth below, and then leapt. Once Hodge was out of the way, Rhys balanced himself and then slid out the window. When he hit the ground, he rolled and swiftly looked up at Axel. Knowing the soldier was still recuperating and that both his leg and shoulder were going to take a hit, Rhys watched in worry. Axel slid from the second story window, hit the ground and rolled on his uninjured shoulder. When the soldier stood unharmed, Rhys nodded and all three took off running.

15
MORAL COMPASS

"RADIO THEMIS," INSTRUCTED RHYS AS they ran through the back alleys of New Arbroath. "Tell Kallen what we think has happened."

"Already did," replied Ethos from Rhys' pants pocket.

Axel swung his short rifle from his shoulder into his arms and racked it. "Whatever the case," he breathed as they dodged a cart and weaved around trash bins, "this doesn't look good. Isn't there any other way out of New Arbroath aside from the main gate?"

"As far as I know, the city is encased in a wall of bricks," replied Rhys, slowing their escape. He pulled them into a tight alley between a store and a home. "We can go over the wall and—"

"Run immediately into Brechin troops," Axel concluded.

"New Arbroath backs up into a forest," added Hodge. "He's right. No doubt Brechin has troops out there."

"I know they do." Rhys pulled his short rifle into his arms. "Which would you prefer? We cause a ruckus in town by escaping through the main gate, or we take our chances with the forest forces?"

"Go through the gate," said Axel at the exact moment Hodge declared, "The forest." They glanced at one another before looking to Rhys for a decision.

After a moment's thought, Rhys said, "We're doing neither." He peered down the alley at the bustling streets. He listened for sounds of boots, shouting, commands, anything that would suggest Joss had sent troops after them. There was nothing. Rhys turned to Hodge. "Assume everyone on our ships has been captured. They're using them as bait to draw you in. Where would Joss keep them?"

"I don't know. The jail?" murmured Hodge. "Or Brechin forces have them."

"Which is the more likely of the two," Axel grumbled.

"He's right. Joss wouldn't keep them in the jail in the courthouse. That's too easy to break out of. I mean, Vinz and Kashim were able to do it. Can't be that hard."

Rhys started back toward the courthouse. Hodge and Axel fell in behind him. "We need to know where they are."

"Can't your computer-thing track them?" asked Hodge.

"No," replied Rhys.

"Don't be so harsh," scolded Ethos from Rhys' pocket. "I can only do so much!"

"What's your plan then?" Axel glanced warily over his shoulder. "You can't just walk in there."

"I'm not," said Rhys. "You two are."

"What?" groaned Hodge. "Why?"

"Axel, did you see any Brechin soldiers there aside from the major general?"

"No. But that doesn't mean that they weren't there."

"Go to the jail and check. We need to confirm none of our crew is there."

"What are you going to do?" asked Hodge.

"I'm going to have a conversation with Joss."

Together, they broke into a jog, rifles at the ready. Only when the courthouse was in sight, did they stop in the shadows of a neighboring building.

"They've placed guards at the front," Axel remarked, crouching. Hodge groaned. "They're New Arbroath military though which is good."

Rhys withdrew Ethos and tucked it in the top of his bulletproof vest. The AI had already sent out the call to his magnetic board; Rhys expected it any moment. He knelt beside Axel and Hodge. "If you find any of our people, get them out of there. Don't wait for me. Not everyone onboard is a fighter."

Axel nodded. Rhys glanced at Hodge who was worriedly regarding the courthouse. He knew his friend was torn. Many of the people in town were personal acquaintances. Hodge himself had been employed by the town as a courier and was well-liked among many of the town's representatives.

"Axel, take the lead," Rhys instructed. "Hodge, provide backup." Movement caught his eye, and he turned to greet his board as it settled a meter or so from the ground. "Go."

"Rendezvous?" asked Axel.

"Just get them outside the city gates. If you can, find Leo and Kashim. Get back to *Themis*." Rhys swung onto his board and without locking his boots into the clasps, soared toward the back side of the building. He looked back to see Axel and Hodge dart toward the courthouse.

Trusting in his crew, Rhys gained altitude so he was even with the second story of the building. He located the window from which they had escaped and peered in. To his surprise he found not only Joss but Tessa, who was bound in rope and two guards. The door to Joss' office was closed. He wasn't thrilled to have Tessa onboard, but she was officially part of his crew and it appeared that she was also a prisoner.

For a moment, Rhys struggled to decide—save Tessa or listen. Avoiding the open window, he lowered his board and tilted his head upward to listen.

"How do you *not* know?" asked Joss. "He was in my office just a few minutes ago. I was told he was dead."

"I've been in a cell for two days," growled Tessa. "How would I know where he is or what's happened?"

Rhys heard Joss get up. "Your job was simple. Get aboard *Themis*. That's all you had to do. So, how is it that you failed even in that endeavor?"

"I made it onto the ship," Tessa countered. "I heard he went out several days ago to check on the sick and never came back."

"Vinz was easy to deal with. He wasn't strong-headed. He knew he owed a debt and was willing to repay it." Joss sighed. "Don't look at me like that. I'm sorry for your loss. I really am. But I can't have this boy running around encouraging upheaval. All of this started because of him. If he and the others hadn't incited a rebellion in Paducah, we wouldn't be keeping heathens as coastal guests."

"I've told you everything I know. Are we done?" Tessa didn't sound angry so much as bored.

"Yes. Release her."

"What about Reza?" asked Tessa.

"You two, you're dismissed." The two guards in the room left, closing the door behind them. Joss continued. "I don't think we can trust him. Kallen is too strongly tied to *Themis*. He wouldn't reveal any information that might endanger her."

"You can't keep him locked away, Joss," chided Tessa. "Reza's old and this town relies on him."

"Then why was he on their ships?"

Rhys heard Tessa sigh. "Kallen asked for his help in making repairs to the ships."

"I'm not letting him out until we find out where the boy is."

"You're sure it was him? If Brechin says he's dead…"

"Yes, I'm sure," snapped Joss. "It was him. Hodge was with him and another man I didn't recognize. See, that's what I don't understand. Vinz assembled a crew two years ago. Every person he brought on was the best New Arbroath offered. And they were exceptionally loyal to him."

"What don't you understand?" asked Tessa.

Joss thought. "How has this boy achieved the same thing? How did he persuade Vinz's crew to follow him? He's young, inexperienced, naïve."

"He's passionate," replied Tessa. "People naturally want to follow him. He's young and inexperienced, but he's a leader. He sees things differently than most."

"Is that your assessment?"

"It is."

There was a long moment of silence before Joss said, "Did you see him when Vinz first brought him to New Arbroath?" Tessa must have nodded because Joss continued. "He's changed. The look he gave me a while ago… It was the look of a man who's seen much."

"Did you ever meet his sister?"

"No," replied Joss. "Even then it was obvious he was very protective of her. Was she on the ship?"

"I didn't see her, but that didn't mean she wasn't there," lied Tessa.

Joss sighed. Rhys peered into the window to see the judge stand and motion to Tessa. "I apologize for keeping you locked up so long. It was not my intention."

"I know," replied Tessa. "You needed to meet expectations. It's fine. Are we done?"

"Yes. You're dismissed."

Tessa left. Rhys waited until the door was closed before rising above the window sill and stepping into the room. He withdrew the resonance cutters, engaged them, and pointed the tool at Joss' back. "Don't move," he murmured. Joss startled horribly; Rhys stopped him from whirling around with a strong palm. "I said don't move. Don't make a sound."

Realizing who it was, Joss relaxed. "I thought you were gone."

"Where is the rest of my crew? There were two Brechin nobles, a teenage boy, and two Aabeshian men. Where are they?"

"Brechin has them," the judge asserted.

Rhys slid in closer and brought the cutters beside his face so Joss could feel the heat emanating from them. "The Brechin forces. Which battalion?"

"I don't know."

Rhys drew the cutters closer to Joss' neck, making the judge squirm against the searing heat. "Are you sure?"

"Yes!" Joss' voice broke. "I'm sure. The New Arbroath… military headed the assault on the ships. Anyone who wasn't a citizen of New Arbroath was handed over to the Brechin military. I don't know what they did with them."

Rhys clenched his jaws and fortified himself. In a single motion, he pushed Joss against the desk, wrenched the judge's arm behind his back, and twisted his wrist upward. With ease, Rhys took the resonance cutters and sliced through the desk before Joss' nose. "These cut through anything. They cut through steel, rope, rock, flesh…"

"I told you. I told you," gasped Joss, beads of sweat appearing on his forehead. "I don't know. After we handed them over to Brechin, I don't know what they did with them."

"Are you left-handed or right-handed?"

"I-I… what?" stammered Joss.

In a swift motion, Rhys flipped the cutters in his hand and sliced through the tip of Joss' middle finger on his left hand. "Are you sure you don't know?" Rhys probed, forcing Joss to remain prone on the desk. He twisted the man's injured hand upward; Joss danced beneath him in pain.

"*Yes!*" the judge howled.

"Who would know?"

"I don't know!"

Rhys cut the tip off Joss' ring finger.

"The major general!" screeched Joss. "The major general."

"And where is he?"

Panting and now covered in his own blood, Joss wheezed, "They have a base camp in the forest west of the town just before the desert."

Rhys regarded Joss before saying, "You tell anyone I was here, I'll come back and kill you." He shook the judge for emphasis. "Got it?" Joss nodded numerous times. Rhys released him and then, in a single stride, leapt from the window onto his board. Before Joss could turn around, Rhys was out of sight.

"We're having a long talk later," Ethos fumed.

"I know," replied Rhys. "Where're Axel and Hodge?"

There was a moment's pause before Ethos said, "I can't be sure, but I think they've left the building."

Rhys sunk his boots into the board's clasps and rocketed from the courthouse. When he swept over the stone wall far from the main gate, he dismounted and sent the board back to *Themis*. He expertly wrapped his face and hair in his headscarf and went in search.

After scouring the immediate area, he waited in the shade of a tent and watched the main gate. Nothing. Growing worried, he turned his sights on Leo and Kashim. Directing a few questions to the Pantaraks, he was pointed toward the north side of the shoreline camp. With one last furtive glance at the main gate, he hurried off.

It was not Kashim or Leo who he ran into first, however, but Khaleela, the doctor from Maliyansa, and her assistant, Patrin who Rhys had learned was mute. Noticing Rhys' blue eyes, Patrin motioned to Leela. The Pantarak doctor promptly finished her conversation with another woman and met Rhys. She ushered him into the shade of a nearby tent and pulled him behind a curtain. With unusually familiar hands, she brushed off his headscarf and gazed at him. She appeared tired. Her ebony skin was slick with sweat and brows knotted together in worry.

"I didn't think... I'd ever see you again," she murmured in surprise. Patrin, who stood in the doorway to block interruptions, peered in shock over his shoulder. "What happened?" She touched the shaved part of Rhys' head and the visible silver receptors.

"It's a long story. What have you heard?"

"That you're dead," she replied. "Some soldiers from New Arbroath told the camp several days ago."

"I was shot," Rhys affirmed, "but I'm fine now." He looked about anxiously. "What's going on? I'm missing half my crew, and New Arbroath is in lockdown."

"New Arbroath made a deal with Brechin," whispered Leela. "Brechin forces wouldn't take New Arbroath if you and your crew were handed over." Rhys rested his hands on the back of his head in distress. Axel had been right. "After your... death, they invaded your ships and took everyone hostage."

"Do you know where they are?"

Leela shook her head. "We never saw them, but some said they heard what sounded like a fight a couple of nights ago out on the water."

"There's a Brechin military camp west of the town. I'll—"

Rhys was interrupted by the pounding of running feet as two men raced past the tent. Exchanging looks with Leela, he stepped from the tent and looked after Kashim and Leo who were sprinting to the waterline. Rhys shifted his attention to the airship hovering over *Themis* and *Grisle*. "*Shit*," he cursed, dashing after them.

He leapt over a crate and nearly collided with a middle-aged man. He shoved the Pantarak out of the way and, eyes set on the Brechin airship, urged his legs faster. Just as Leo and Kashim dove into the dinghy, Rhys saw his board make its escape from *Themis'* upper deck and soar toward him. Running along the rock-encrusted shore, Rhys met the board, strapped in, and rushed into the air like a falcon. Below him, Kashim and Leo pushed the dinghy through the waves.

Rhys stomped on the back of the board and crouched, driving it toward *Themis*. His heart rose in his throat as he saw three soldiers drag Kallen from the bridge onto the outer deck platform. A seething, wild animal, she flailed to free her pistol, firing rogue shots into the air. When the pistol was ripped from her hand, she began thrashing, smashing fists, elbows, and knees into anything within range. She broke loose once, but her freedom was brief. She was slammed onto the unforgiving deck and pinned there.

Wind in his ears, Rhys tore along the water. Before he was even near the ship, he ripped his boots from the board clasps and prepared to launch himself. When the moment came, he jumped off the board and slammed into the soldier who had his back to the water. With a viciousness he had not felt in months, Rhys withdrew his resonance cutters and slashed. He whirled around on the second soldier and split the air between them. The man released Kallen and descended the stairs, the third soldier at his side.

Rhys stepped over Kallen and, knowing the soldiers had nowhere to escape, called, "Where are the others?" When neither spoke, Rhys disengaged the cutters, tossed the hilt to Kallen, and swung his short rifle into his hands. Without blinking, he shot the man on the left, placing a bullet in his forehead where there was no armor. As the soldier slid to the bottom platform alongside *Themis'* starboard, Rhys redirected his gun at the remaining soldier. "Where are they?"

The soldier turned to withdraw his backup pistol, but Rhys fired. The man toppled over the railing into the water. Panting, Rhys glared up at the airship. His answers were up there.

"Ethos," he murmured, indicating that the AI should call his board to him. Ethos didn't reply. "Ethos."

"I'm done," said the AI matter-of-factly.

Rhys cursed under his breath, turned, and climbed the ladder to the upper deck. "Kallen, the sonic cannon," he yelled.

"Right…" she shakily replied.

Rhys climbed into the sonic cannon perched on the rear of the bridge and waited for Kallen to switch it on from the bridge paneling. While it was merely a turret and seat connected to a wide, silver dish, there was nothing easy about operating it.

"Stop," demanded Ethos.

Rhys ignored the AI.

"Rhys, they aren't attacking you."

"That's not the point," Rhys replied.

"Rhys!" snapped Ethos. "Would you look?"

Rhys glanced upward once more to find the airship simply hovering. Why wasn't it in the process of leaving? Shouldn't they have at least put up a fight?

"There aren't any life forms on that airship," said Ethos. "It's waiting for its pilot to return."

"Rhys!" called Kashim from the starboard side of *Themis*.

"I'm here!" Rhys sat sideways in the turret chair and studied the airship. Whoever had sent the ship had known that only two people were on board—two women. A thought occurred to Rhys and he yelled to Kallen. "Where's Veran?" When Kallen didn't answer, he said her name.

"She's fine," came the reply.

"Ethos, can you get me up into the airship?"

"I told you, I'm done. I'm not helping you anymore. You're not the type of person I want to be around."

"You're an AI. You don't have a choice."

"I have more choices than you apparently," Ethos retorted.

Rhys clambered from the sonic cannon turret just as Kashim and Leo appeared on the ladder. "What's wrong?" asked Leo.

"Ethos says there's no one up there," replied Rhys.

"Whatever we're going to do, we need to do it fast," Kashim advised.

"Go up there," suggested Leo.

"Can't. Ethos won't help me anymore."

Leo jogged across the deck and looked up at the airship. "It has a ladder over here."

"Do you know how to work an airship?" asked Rhys, joining him. Descending from a hatch on the rear of the airship was a metal ladder which had been difficult to discern due to the sunlight.

"No, but I could figure it out." Leo climbed atop the bridge and tentatively took the ladder in his hands. He tested it briefly before climbing at a steady pace up to the airship.

"Where's Hodge?" Kashim asked, looking back over the shoreline.

"Don't know. He and Axel went into the courthouse to check the jail. I know they made it out. I just don't know where they went." Rhys shaded his eyes against the sun and watched as Leo disappeared into the airship. "Watch him," he instructed. "I need to check on Kallen and Veran."

Rhys turned and slipped back into the ship, taking care not to track in more blood. He glanced into the bridge and then went to the galley where the trail of crimson led. He found Kallen leaning over the galley sink, crying. Veran stood in the corner of the room, eyes wide and body rigid.

"Hey," said Rhys, going to Kallen who was covered in a heavy film of wet blood. She had wiped most off her face, but it was in her hair and clothes.

Kallen swallowed and motioned to him. "I'm fine. Go."

Rhys ignored her. He pulled a towel from the cabinet and began running it under sink water. Kallen remained poised over the sink, trying to quell her crying. As Rhys began cleaning her hands and arms, her crying became more passionate. In silence, Rhys washed her arms, rinsed the towel, and started on her neck and face. "I'm sorry," he finally murmured.

"Don't," she whispered, closing her eyes. "Don't."

Rhys pulled her into him and wrapped his arms around her. "You hurt?" he murmured in Elali. She shook her head.

In the distance, the rumbling of the airship shifted and then quieted. It seemed Leo had been successful.

Rhys looked at Veran who was frozen in terror. "Are you hurt?" She met his gaze, her eyes glassy. He could see her hands trembling. "Did they touch her?" he asked of Kallen.

"They tried to, but they couldn't," murmured Kallen. "Where's Hodge?"

"Don't know." Rhys approached Veran whose immediate response was to back farther into the corner. Wary of her reaction, he stopped. "You should sit down, Veran. You're weak." When she didn't respond or move, Rhys sighed and looked to Kallen, who was drying her face, and then returned to the upper deck. He found Kashim leaning against the port railing watching Leo land the airship in the waves. "Is it safe for it to be in water?"

Kashim shrugged. "I've never seen one in water, but Leo seems confident it'll float."

Leo, standing legs apart for balance at the helm, carefully slowed the airship's fans until the unit slipped into the water. While the fans became immediately submerged, the main carriage of the airship remained afloat. Leo looked about before turning to Rhys and Kashim and triumphantly raising his arms in the air.

"We need to find Hodge and Axel," said Rhys. "I got information from Joss. There's a Brechin military camp west of New Arbroath just before the desert."

"You can't trust Joss at this point. He's made a deal with Brechin."

"I know." Rhys glanced subtly at Kashim. "I *got* the information from Joss." Kashim nodded in realization. "The original plan was to sunboard out there, but…"

"We have an airship now," Kashim concluded with a sly smile.

Rhys watched as Leo paced the deck of the airship before motioning dramatically to *Themis* as he suddenly grasped that he was now marooned on the craft. Rhys chuckled for the first time in days. "Go get Leo and then let's find Hodge and Axel."

As Kashim retrieved Leo and speculated as to how to anchor the aircraft, Rhys returned below to change out of his bloody clothes. He paused in the doorway of the galley to find Kallen, wearing nothing but her breastband and pants, kneeling before Veran. Kallen's words were soft and indiscernible, but Veran seemed to be receptive. Rhys continued to the washroom where he stripped out of his shirt and threw it in the sink. Leaning over the tub, he ran his hair under the faucet and scrubbed at the drying blood on his arms and chest. Although his pants were speck-stained, they didn't warrant changing.

"Are you proud of yourself?" asked Ethos.

"For what?" Rhys murmured, lathering soap onto his arms.

"You tortured a man and just killed three soldiers."

"No, I'm not, but I did what needed to be done."

"Rhys, diplomacy and conversation needed to be done. You can't use force all the time," Ethos censured. The AI's voice was impassioned.

Rhys sat on the tub edge. "How can you judge my actions when you don't know the whole story?"

"I know everything you know about the situation," snapped Ethos.

"But you don't know Joss' history and how he regularly tortured Pantarak men for answers. *With his own hands*, Ethos." Rhys sighed and continued to scrub. "He's lucky I didn't cut off his whole arm so he would never be able to do that again…"

"And how do you justify killing the three soldiers just now?"

"They were taking Kallen."

"If they had wanted Kallen dead, they would have killed her," said Ethos. "Someone is ordering that your crew remain unharmed."

"Yes, I know. I'm the only target."

"Rhys, this is serious! You are making the shift into moral corruption. The more you do something, the easier it becomes—that includes killing other humans."

Rhys worked to temper his words. "I'm tired… of your sanctimonious talks. Do you think you have the answers? You're an AI. You don't feel. You don't have to deal with the consequences."

"I'm doing my job," replied Ethos. "I'm trying to keep you from crossing a line that will ultimately end in your moral self-destruction. You're spiraling out of control. And what's worse, your behavior encourages your crew. Kallen killed just a few weeks ago, for your sake. The mother of your child is killing other humans."

Rhys glared at the pink water in the tub. "Throughout mankind's history, there has always been war, disease, famine, genocide, subjugation… It is the unfortunate part of being human."

"You cannot succumb to that belief. You know for a fact that humans are capable of living in peace. You yourself grew up in such an environment."

"And we had no rights, Ethos. Nothing. The government on Caelestis controlled every aspect of our lives down to our ability to reproduce. We were allowed to feel nothing, do nothing. My people, they lived in blissful ignorance. Being human is the right to struggle, to feel, to do. We weren't humans on Caelestis. We were machines. We lived in a pseudo-utopia where everything was taken care of for us, and we didn't know that literature or art or music ever existed."

Rhys took a calming breath.

"I will be more aware of my actions and reactions. I want you to do the same though. You're programmed to evaluate morally-ambiguous situations and determine a moral north, but there's more to those situations than you can read. It's not logic, and it's not what you see. It's what you feel."

"I understand your point, and I will make an effort to do so, but Rhys, you must find a balance in what you feel and what you do. If you allow your emotions to constantly dictate your actions without logic or question, then you become just like the people of Caelestis."

Rhys stopped moving. "Say… that again."

"If you allow your emotions to constantly dictate your actions without logic or question, then you become just like the people of Caelestis," repeated Ethos.

"That's right…" Rhys dried off with a nearby towel and sank to the floor.

16
NOT FOR NOTHING

"Rhys?" Kallen knocked tentatively on the washroom door sometime later. "Kashim and Leo are waiting for you."

"Can you get me a shirt?" asked Rhys, standing stiffly. He had been sitting motionless on the floor in meditation since his conversation with Ethos. He slipped into the hallway just as Kallen reappeared with a long-sleeved shirt.

"Is something wrong?" she whispered, seeing his face.

"No, everything's fine." He slid on the shirt and began buttoning it. Kallen's gaze shifted and Rhys turned to find Veran standing in the galley doorway.

"I want to come with you," she said in Nefegian.

"Wait until we find Hodge and Axel. We'll have to come back here for the airship. You can come then," he replied. Veran nodded and disappeared into the galley.

"What did she ask?" said Kallen.

He switched to Elali. "She wants to come. I told her later. How is she?"

"She's shaken, but she understands. Pathos is helping her cope." Kallen ushered him down the hall. "Go. They're waiting. Bring Hodge back."

Rhys opened the ship's external door to find the bloody mess he had created and the soldiers' bodies. "We need to get rid of the bodies," he said. "They have chips in them."

"I'll handle it," murmured Kallen with steely resolve.

"Don't." Rhys kissed her. "I'll take care of it when I return. Don't dirty your hands anymore." Kallen smiled grimly at him.

It was just after midday when they returned to shore. Due to the ruckus aboard *Themis*, the Pantaraks were on edge but appeared more hopeful. With the blazing sun beating down on him, Rhys remained uncovered so the Pantaraks could recognize his face. Leela and Patrin immediately met them. At first, Rhys was glad to see them, but the look on Leela's stricken face indicated that he should feel otherwise.

"What's wrong?" he asked as the Maliyansan woman grabbed his arm.

"Your two crew members. They have an old man with them, and he's not doing well."

"Where are they?"

"Just over here," replied Leela.

"Leo, get Kallen and my medical bad," ordered Rhys.

Leo raced back to the dinghy. Kashim at his side, Rhys followed Leela to a tent. He couldn't help the relief in his heart as he spotted Axel and then Hodge. Kallen's grandfather lay on a small cot between them.

Rhys dropped his short rifle and knelt beside the old man. "Reza?" He dug his fingers into Reza's wrist to check his pulse and then did the same at his throat. Reza's heart was racing. "Hodge, what happened?"

"Nothing," replied Hodge, panicked. "Nothing."

Rhys pried open Reza's eyelids to find his eyes rolled back into his head. The old man's rasping breaths rattled through his chest. Rhys pinched Reza's arm skin. "He's dehydrated."

"There wasn't anything in the cell when we found him," Hodge supplied. "They probably forgot to feed him. He was only in there for two or three days."

"But he's old. The second skin doesn't function as well. He needs food and water daily." Rhys motioned to Hodge. "Find water." As Hodge disappeared, Rhys tried to rouse Reza whose only response was to shudder and mumble.

Hodge returned shortly with a canteen and passed it to Rhys.

"We have water. Come on," coaxed Rhys, placing the canteen at the old man's lips. Reza seemed to understand but couldn't quite perform the action. Rhys trickled water into Reza's mouth. He repeated the action numerous times before lying the old man back.

"JiJi!" shouted Kallen, sprinting into the tent. Behind her was Leo and Veran. Rhys met Veran's eyes before motioning to Leo for the medical pack. "JiJi, hey," Kallen cooed, touching her grandfather's face. "JiJi?"

As Kallen spoke to him, Rhys withdrew an injector as well as a vial of concentrated dextrose. He administered the dose and then withdrew Ethos. "What's his blood pressure?" he asked, placing Ethos on Reza's chest.

"Blood pressure: eighty-seven over seventy-five," reported Ethos. Rhys moved Kallen aside and checked Reza's pulse once more. "Heart rate at fifty-six beats per minute."

"What's happening?" whispered Kallen, her throat thick.

"He's severely dehydrated," replied Rhys. "I've given him something to help combat the dehydration, but it'll be a while before we see any results."

"You could give him mayanan tohydrate," offered Veran in Nefegian.

"The emergency pack doesn't have that drug," said Rhys, sitting back. Veran hesitantly approached the old man. Leo moved to stop her, but Rhys motioned him away. "She's the Director of Medicine on Caelestis. This is the first time she's seen anyone ill."

Veran knelt beside Reza and tentatively pressed her hand along his jawline just as Rhys had. She then moved to the skin along his tan, wiry arms. She pulled on it and then squeezed his fingers. Her head tilted as she spoke silently with Pathos. After several moments, she looked at Kallen. "He is related to you?" Kallen nodded. "A grandfather… is the father of a father or mother."

"My father's father," corrected Kallen, her eyes moist.

Veran looked at Rhys. "How do you know medicine?" This was the first time since she had stepped from Neo-Colony Two that she did not appear afraid or apprehensive. "Have you studied it since being on Earth?"

"Alina downloaded the entire database. Just before her death, she passed all of the information to me," replied Rhys. "Everything I know is from Alina."

Veran, although clearly surprised perhaps by the sheer amount of information accessible in the medical database, merely nodded and then backed away.

"How long until he's conscious?" Kallen resumed her anxious stroking of her grandfather's hand.

"Half an hour, maybe." Rhys looked up as Leela and Patrin, who had been hovering outside, entered the tent. "What?"

"The people are growing anxious," murmured Leela. "They have said the Sister of the Heavens has arrived."

"Veran's not my sister," corrected Rhys, standing.

"They've started gathering outside," murmured Leela.

Rhys passed his crew and exited the tent; Kashim and Hodge flanked him. Just as Leela had said, the Pantaraks had gathered in silence in hope of glimpsing Veran. When Rhys emerged, they crossed their arms and bobbed their heads in respect.

"Is it true?" asked a man at the front of the group. "Your wonderful sister has come to walk among us once more?"

"No," replied Rhys. "She's not my sister. She's another one of my people who fell from the stars."

"Is she a miracle worker like your holy sister?" asked another.

"She is a doctor, yes," Rhys assured them. Realizing that he had a large amount of attention, he added, "Others of my crew have been captured by Brechin forces. Does anyone know where they've been taken?" The silence that ensued did not signify ignorance; they refused to speak for fear of retaliation. He couldn't blame them. They were stuck between Brechin and New Arbroath.

Rhys gazed at Reza in thought. He couldn't leave the old man alone. Even with Kallen here, they were still vulnerable.

"Leave Reza with her," said Kashim, nodding to Leela. "We need all of the people we can get. That includes Kallen." Kallen looked up from her grandfather's bedside.

"When are you leaving? And for where?" asked Leela, approaching Rhys. Her warm eyes were soft and caring.

"West of the town. There's a Brechin camp just short of the desert." Rhys fell still; Tessa had just entered the tent, winded.

"Hey," greeted Hodge. "Where have you been? We were looking for you."

Tessa leaned on her knees to catch her breath and then smiled. "I was being held in one of the backrooms in the courthouse. I only just escaped."

Hodge clapped her on the shoulder while Leo acknowledged her warmly. Rhys pushed past Kashim and approached Tessa who passed him a tentative smile. When he did not return the salutation, her brows folded in worry.

"Why are you here, Tessa?" Rhys asked.

Mirth gone, Hodge and Leo returned to their positions around Rhys. Tessa glanced at them and said, "What do you mean? I've been looking for everyone."

"I know what you did," continued Rhys. "Why are you here?"

Tessa chuckled. "Rhys, truly. What's wrong? I don't understand. I came to find you and the crew." Tessa turned to Hodge. "Explain to him that I was captured, just like the others."

Hodge frowned. "We were just in the courthouse. Where were you?"

"In one of the back rooms. They were questioning me."

"And how did you escape?"

"Joss let her go," replied Rhys. "She's working for Joss."

Tessa watched him. "Where did you hear that from? Why would you say such a thing?"

"I heard it from you… and Joss," said Rhys. "Joss released you after questioning you as to why I was still alive." The look on Tessa's sweet face darkened. "Get out." Tessa looked at the others, but no one offered any type of rebuttal or support. "Get. Out." Tessa ran from the tent.

"*Gawan*," Hodge hissed.

To the others, Rhys said, "We're heading west late this afternoon. Leela. Do you feel comfortable watching over Reza?"

"Of course," Leela replied.

"Axel, Hodge. Return to the airship. I don't want anyone to track our movements," continued Rhys. "Kashim, Leo. We need supplies. Guns, armor, long-range weapons." Kashim nudged Leo, and they disappeared from the tent with the others. Only Kallen, Veran, Leela, and Patrin remained.

"You need to rest," Veran murmured in Nefegian.

"What did she say?" asked Kallen.

"That I need to rest," replied Rhys.

Veran frowned. "He needs to rest because he has not fully recovered from his trauma."

"I'm fine," growled Rhys, gazing down at Reza. With surprising forwardness, Veran jerked Rhys to her and roughly unbuckled his armor— despite his quiet protesting—pulled it aside, and raised his shirt to reveal the gauze bandage on his abdomen. Rhys frowned; the bandage was pink with blood.

Veran pointed to a nearby cot; begrudgingly, Rhys pulled off his armor and sat. Leela and Kallen watched. "Lie back," Veran instructed.

"I'm fine. Seriously," Rhys murmured.

Veran pulled his shirt up and with gentle hands peeled the bandage away. "You've been moving too much. You've broken the seal."

"That looks like a gunshot wound," quavered Leela.

"It is." Rhys laid an arm over his eyes. It was only then that he realized how right Veran was. He needed to rest. He was beyond exhausted. He had ignored the fatigue dogging his every step.

"You survived a gunshot wound to the abdomen," mused Leela.

"And to the head," added Veran. "I performed reconstructive surgery on him."

"How did... you find him?"

"We can track any citizen of Caelestis, even those without AIs," explained Veran, pulling the medical pack to her. She began going through the emergency supplies Rhys had carried with him since his arrival on Earth.

"Yeah, but how did you know to come to Earth?" Kallen pressed.

"History," replied Veran.

Rhys opened his eyes and started to sit up. Veran held him down. "What do you mean?"

Veran smiled. When she spoke, she used Interstellar Nefegian. "Earth has always been a backup for our people."

"But... the records indicated Earth no longer existed."

"The records *you* were allowed to view," corrected Veran. "In order to protect its citizens, the government of Caelestis intentionally hid any information that indicated or implied that Earth was still a viable planet for life."

Rhys lay back. He relayed what had just been said to Leela, Kallen, and Patrin. "In conclusion, we were lied to, once more."

"Not lied to. Protected." Veran returned the supplies to the pack and stood.

"No, we were lied to." Rhys sat up and straightened his shirt. "The government did nothing for us." He nodded to Veran. "You wouldn't understand. You have access to any information you want." He stood. "Alina and I knew nothing."

"You had only just been sorted into your departments," said Veran kindly. "Besides, Alina had access to many databases. She was to become the next commander."

Rhys walked out of the tent into the brilliant afternoon sun. He glanced out at the sea to find fluffy, white clouds accumulating. It looked like another series of storms that evening was inevitable. That didn't bode well for their flight west.

Determined to keep himself working, Rhys went in search of supplies.

It was late afternoon when he finally returned to the tent. He had gathered all that he could carry and managed to feed himself. He had also helped reset several tents, dig privies near the forest, repair a solar generator, and tend to the recently injured. Upon entering the tent, he was pleased to find Reza alert, sitting up, and speaking with Kallen in Elali.

"Hey," Rhys greeted warmly. He set down his bag of supplies and went to the old man's bedside. Veran, who had been asleep on a neighboring cot, woke.

"Rhys," murmured Reza. The old man smiled and motioned for him to join them. Kallen beamed at Rhys. Once he was in range, he was pulled to his knees by the old man who ruffled his hair fondly and chuckled in the rasping way he always did. "Congratulations."

Rhys glanced at Kallen who blushed. "Thank you," he murmured awkwardly in Elali.

"If he's anything like Kallen," said Reza, "he'll be a handful."

"It's not possible to know the sex right now," Rhys corrected quietly.

Reza laughed, patted Rhys' arm, and then gazed adoringly at his granddaughter. "Your father will be glad to hear even if you aren't wed yet."

"Wed?" Rhys turned his head. He had never heard the word before. And now, not even Pathos was there to explain it to him. "I don't know this word. What is it in Aabeshian?"

"Wed," provided Kallen. "It means when a couple, eh, promises themselves to each other."

Confused, Rhys looked between Reza and Kallen. "But we've done that." Kallen giggled as Leela, who had been sitting in the corner of the tent reading, chuckled. "What? We have."

"It's a ceremony," Kallen explained. "It has been a human tradition for thousands of years."

"So, human societies have always been monogamous?" mused Rhys. Biologically, that didn't make any sense to him. If the purpose of humans, like all other living creatures, was to reproduce, would it not have made sense during humanity's vast history for females to have more than one sexual partner? Of course, he didn't want to share Kallen with another male, but biologically speaking, it was a viable plan to procreate.

"It's a ceremony where a woman is given to a man," said Leela. "By her father."

"Why would a woman want to be given away? That sounds... unethical." Rhys looked between the amused faces and then at Veran who was also puzzling through the dilemma. "Right?"

Veran nodded. "It is unethical to treat another human as a commodity."

Kallen sighed. "In this instance, a woman wouldn't literally be given to the man. It's a symbolic gesture." She looked at Rhys pointedly. "When a couple is promised to one another for their lives, it's called marriage."

Rhys sat back on his heels. "And you're sure we haven't done that?" Kallen nodded. "Is it difficult to do?"

Reza laughed. "You have enough to worry about. Being together is what's important."

"Are there advantages to… uh, giving Kallen to me?"

"You get to share her bed," Leela supplied.

"But we've already done that," replied Rhys. "Why would, uh… what's the word? Marriage. Why would marriage allow me to do that if I've *already* done it?" Kallen buried her face in her hands as Reza laughed. "I'm sorry. I don't understand."

"Pathos indicates that throughout human history," said Veran, "sexual intercourse was reserved specifically for married couples. The idea of sexual intercourse outside of marriage was frowned upon by religious institutions in more than one era of human history and considered a sin punishable by shaming or, in some instances, death. The harshest punishments were reserved for females rather than the males."

"I… didn't know that," murmured Rhys. He looked at Kallen. Did those same laws apply here? Kallen wasn't Pantarak nor, as far as Rhys knew, did she affiliate with any other religion.

"It's fine," said Reza. "She's not going to be in trouble." He patted Kallen's arm. "She's her own woman. She doesn't need someone to tell her her worth."

"Should… we do marriage?" asked Rhys, leaning forward.

Kallen laughed. "No, not right now."

When the clouds overhead began darkening, Rhys radioed the others using Ethos. Knowing they couldn't wait any longer, he gathered the medical pack and his weapons and ushered Kallen and Veran to the tent entrance. Reza waved to them as Leela and Patrin escorted them out.

"Take care of him," said Kallen, holding Leela.

The doctor nodded, kissed Kallen's forehead, and then looked at Rhys. "And *you* take care of yourself."

"I will." Covering his head and motioning for Veran to do the same, Rhys started from the tent at a clip; both women followed. Once back on *Themis*, Leo and Axel debriefed everyone on the airship findings.

"All airships are equipped with several tracking systems," explained Axel. "The most obvious are the computer codes that constantly provide location, speed, shift angle, and weight. We've eliminated those." Axel wiped his stained hands on a towel. "There is a beacon hidden in the hull and another in the aft hatch. We've destroyed both of those."

"So, we're clear?" asked Kallen.

Axel nodded. "We also disposed of the soldiers on the deck."

Rhys looked between Hodge, Leo, and Axel. "Did you take the trackers out of them?"

"Everything is taken care of," assured Axel as a low rumble of thunder spilled across the horizon. Veran stiffened in alarm and moved closer to Rhys.

"Pathos, explain to her the phenomenon of lightning and thunder," said Rhys. Without pausing, he continued. "I have food and the medical pack. Kashim?"

Kashim disappeared from the galley and returned with a large duffle bag. He set it on the table and unzipped it to reveal a stockpile of rifles, pistols, and munitions. "You can thank Otto," he said proudly. "The boy is a genius. Before he was taken, he repaired more than sixty weapons in the span of a few days. The rest are with the Pantarak leaders. They've been kept hidden."

"Everyone will be armed with more than one weapon," said Axel. "Everyone will also have armor."

"I've got the night-vision goggles and anti-focal paste," offered Hodge.

Kallen leaned on the table. "Question. Should we be doing this with the storms moving in? Can the airship handle being airborne?"

"It can, but it won't be a pleasant flight," Axel replied, going through the guns.

"Can we hike there?"

Studying Otto's work on a short rifle, Rhys said, "Pathos, set all sensors westward. Analyze heat signatures within your range. Identify any synthetic sources between New Arbroath and the desert."

There was silence. Rhys fell motionless, realizing the mistake he had just made. It was not the first time he had forgotten he no longer had an AI, but all the same, it was embarrassing. Being around so many others who were still equipped with an AI was confusing him. He sighed and looked at Veran. A slight smile pulled at her lips and her Pathos unit began speaking.

"All sensors indicate there is a large camp stationed roughly eight kilometers west of New Arbroath," responded the AI.

"Eight kilometers," Rhys mused. He had done the conversion before to the Aabeshian units of liretems. "Ten and a half liretems." He looked at the others. "That's doable, but if something has happened to the others, there's no way we can carry them back."

"Then flight is our only option," Kashim concluded.

"Won't they hear us coming?" asked Hodge. He appeared unhappy that Veran's Pathos had spoken.

"Not until we're on top of them," replied Axel. "The airships are loud, but the sound is contained. They won't hear anything until we're about a liretem out. The airship's weapons are still functioning—why wouldn't they be?—but that won't solve the problem of actually getting into the camp."

"We have no idea where any of them are being held," murmured Kallen.

"There have to be more forces inbound," said Rhys, resting on the table. "Brechin wouldn't have stationed all its forces west. Naval forces must still be en route." He sighed. "There's no real solution here. We need to find our crew, but we also need to solve the current Pantarak refugee issue."

"Why can't you just leave them?" asked Veran.

"Leave who?" Hodge murmured.

"The Pantaraks." Veran fixed her enormous blue eyes on Rhys. "Why do you feel it necessary to protect everything when the outcome is so blatantly obvious? Once you find your crew, you should run."

Rhys glanced at Kashim and Axel. The thought had occurred to him, but he hadn't had the heart to say it aloud. Veran, who was new to this world, felt no shame in stating the obvious.

"We caused this," replied Leo. "All of it."

Hodge nodded. "We're responsible. Directly responsible."

Veran looked between them in confusion. "But if your goal is to preserve your lives, the only solution is to run. It seems that trying to take on militaristic forces with only the weapons and men you have right now is not only foolish but reckless. Even going after your crew members is ill-advised. It doesn't make sense to risk so much for the lives of a few."

Rhys stopped the others from responding. "This isn't Caelestis," he reminded Veran. "The idea of sacrificing a few to save many doesn't always work here."

Veran nodded. "I see."

He gestured to Kashim. "Sniping." The large man nodded, withdrew a box of ammunition, and disappeared onto the bridge. "Axel, Leo, Hodge, and I will be the vanguard. Kallen and Veran will provide backup."

In silence, everyone began preparing. Rhys turned to Veran. "Are you sure you want to do this?" Veran glanced at the others and then nodded. "This means that you will be pointing a weapon at another human being. Can you do that? Even if you can't do that, you're directly supporting others who will be." Rhys saw Veran's facial expressions shift as she spoke with Pathos. He waited patiently.

"Maybe I will stay here."

Rhys thought for a moment and then asked, "Do you still have the adaptor?" Veran withdrew the device from her pocket and handed it to him. "Watch," he instructed softly. He sensed the others around them fall still. With ginger hands, he slid the adaptor into the receptors at the temple of his head and closed his eyes.

He dragged from the depths of his memory Kallen crying in the bedroom at Leo's estate. Rhys himself entered the room with Hodge and stood by the bed upon which she sat.

"Are you coming with us?" he asked Kallen.

Kallen glared at him. "To kill more people?"

"To save Alina. If it comes to killing, then so be it."

"How can you... say it so calmly like it's something you do every day?"

"Because I will do *anything* for Alina," replied Rhys. "Just like I would do anything for you or Hodge. So, if killing another human will bring me closer to rescuing her, I will gladly bear that sin."

Kallen glared at him for a long moment and then nodded. "What do you want me to do?"

Rhys opened his eyes and met Veran's gaze. In Nefegian, he said, "There are people who will try to hurt or kill you. They will do unspeakable things to you." He replayed one of the numerous times Kallen woke up screaming in the darkness of the night. Veran flinched, but her eyes didn't leave his. "There is no one here that you want to protect yet. There is no one here that you will willingly sacrifice yourself for." Rhys closed his eyes and began feeding Veran every memory he could think of that contained a selfless act of sacrifice.

He started with images of himself dragging their old crew member, Lyruc, back onto the upper deck of *Themis* in the middle of a storm, only to then be tossed into the raging foam of the sea. When his memory of that night at sea faded, he shifted his thoughts to those of the battle between *Themis* and the Aabeshian forces. He shared his confusion and panic as he woke to find Kyo dead on the bridge and Lyruc sprawled atop Rhys in a noble attempt to protect Rhys' unconscious body. Rhys allowed the entire battle to play out for Veran. He showed her how he had accidentally set fire to a gun turret only to realize a man was in it and how he had rushed down to the enemy to save the man's life. From there, he showed her his desperate fight to rescue Alina only to be shot and sent limping back to his crew.

"Please stop," whispered Veran, teary eyed. "Please…"

Rhys glanced at the others who appeared baffled. "All of it…" he murmured. "It's not for nothing."

As he began feeding her more images, Veran backed away, shaking her head. "Please stop."

"Look," he urged. With a gentleness he had yet shown to her, Rhys revealed the more memorable parts of his past year on Earth.

He showed her sunboarding with Hodge, splashing with Kallen on the ramp in the forward hatch, and playing chair wars in the galley with the entire crew. He showed Alina patiently fishing with Kashim and laughing with Hodge. He shared with Veran images of his sister playing board games with Vinz and standing before the stove cooking, her hair pulled back like always. He showed Veran music and Kallen's talent for song. He showed her whales and literature and dance and stargazing. He showed her peaceful, lazy days drifting across the vast emerald sea and beautiful sunsets painted in gold and pink. He shared with her laughter and the countless times he and Hodge wrestled in the hallways or on the upper deck. He showed Leo caring for Cantia and Kallen telling Rhys she was pregnant.

"Everything is ready," said Kashim, entering the galley. He stopped upon seeing the situation.

"Do you see?" continued Rhys in Nefegian. "We fight for the ones we love and for moments like those." Glossy-eyed, Veran nodded. Rhys removed the adaptor, lifted his short rifle from the table, and motioned to the others. "Let's go."

17
INTO THE ENEMY CAMP

DESPITE THE NECESSITY TO BEAT the storm, it still took nearly half an hour for everyone to dress and stash supplies. By the time the last of Rhys' crew was seated on the airship, a nasty eastern wind had whipped inland from the sea; thunder and lightning were not far behind. Dressed in black with night-vision goggles hanging about his neck and weapons strapped across his shoulders, Rhys watched as Axel and Leo worked together to bring the airship to a steady altitude.

"At our current rate, how long will it take us to reach the outskirts of the Brechin camp?" asked Rhys of Ethos which was tucked in the top of his bulletproof vest.

"About seven minutes," replied Ethos, "assuming we aren't hit by lightning or shot from the sky."

Rhys glanced at the dark gray clouds overhead. This wasn't going to be easy. "When we are about a kilometer out, we need to land so as not to alert the forces to our location."

"Pathos!" called Ethos. Veran, who was seated several paces away, looked up in confusion. Rhys motioned her over. Bent against the wind, Veran shuffled to Rhys. "No less than a kilometer out, we need to land. My sensors aren't as fine as yours. Can you find a landing zone?"

"Of course," Pathos replied.

"Of course," mocked Ethos in a sarcastic tone. "Ugh… This is why I can't stand Pathos units. They think they're better than everyone else."

"Untrue," said Pathos. "Many consider—"

"Enough," interrupted Rhys. "Pathos, keep a lookout for a suitable landing spot. Notify Leo or Axel if our airship is locked-on. Ethos, monitor the local radio frequencies."

"Hehe, digital map," scoffed Ethos.

Rhys pushed Veran into Axel who, having been unable to hear the conversation, looked at them in confusion. "She'll tell you where to land," explained Rhys, leaning in so they could hear him. Both Leo and Axel nodded. As Rhys moved away, a buffet of wind swept over the ship and tugged at Veran, the slightest person onboard. Axel drew her between himself and Leo.

Rhys sat beside Hodge who had been talking with Kallen and Kashim. Hodge motioned to Veran. "Was it wise to bring her? She's going to get in the way."

"No, she won't," replied Rhys. His face fell solemn and he met each of their gazes. "There's a possibility that what we find... is not going to be good."

"I recommend that we take the medical supplies and, once we land, stash them nearby," Kashim suggested. "If we leave them on the ship and it ends up being recaptured, we've lost valuable resources."

Rhys flinched as a fat, cold rain droplet smacked him in the forehead. Frowning, he looked at Kallen. "You and Veran will bring up the rear and watch our backs."

"Veran doesn't know how to use a gun," said Kallen. "She's helpless."

"I hope you didn't think the same thing of me when you first found us," said Rhys. He withdrew the plasma firearm he had used the first few months he was on Earth. "She'll have this and a backup pistol. I can't use it anymore, but she can."

"There's a difference between holding a gun and knowing how to use one," offered Kashim. "She's not trained. She'll trip and kill us."

"I shared with her how to use a weapon. She's seen it many times in my memories. I'll review it once more with her though."

"Let's just get through this and get everyone back to *Themis*," muttered Kallen.

A hard downpour suddenly swept over the airship and visibility dropped to nothing. Bent against the cold, stinging rain, Rhys rushed to the helm to figure out how close they were. Already Veran, who had her arms wrapped around Axel for balance, was in the process of directing them.

With more dexterity than Rhys could have hoped for, the airship settled in the lee of a tree-covered hill. After smashing through the weak canopy of broad-leaf trees, Axel killed the engines. They were dunked into a surreal silence. Even the rain pouring down on the surrounding vegetation seemed insignificant after the roar of the airship's fans.

Rhys shook the water from his hair before leaping off the airship with the medical pack and jogging into the forest. Once the pack was hidden, he returned to find that Kashim had already disappeared into the forest to locate the best sniping position. Rhys withdrew the plasma firearm from his pocket and motioned to Veran who was trying to pull her hair back in the rain. With the crew watching, Rhys strapped the firearm to her wrist and connected the sensor at her elbow. The weapon began humming with power.

"Let Pathos control it," he explained in Nefegian. "It's not meant for atmospheric use, so it's very powerful. Just like the resonance cutters, it can cut through anything. If you're not sure of your aim, Pathos will help you."

Veran closed her fist and fired at a nearby tree. The orange burst of plasma illuminated the area and melted a gaping hole into the tree's trunk. The only person who flinched was Axel who appeared simultaneously amazed and horrified.

"Why are you giving that to her?" the soldier asked incredulously. "One of *us* should have that."

"Only Rhys and his people can use it," Hodge replied.

"And I can't even use it anymore." Rhys nodded to Veran who pushed her dripping hair from her face and studied the tool. "Vanguard." Hodge, Leo, and Axel gathered around him while Kallen and Veran separated themselves from the group. Rhys tied a dark-colored scarf over his hair and cinched it down tight. He saw Kallen do the same for Veran. "Let's go."

With the black clouds overhead blocking the faint light of dusk and the rain causing poor visibility, Rhys slipped his night-vision goggles on before starting through the forest. Hodge remained on his left, pushing through the vegetation while Leo and Axel followed a few paces behind. Rhys glanced over his shoulder to find Kallen and Veran still at the airship. It appeared as though Kallen was explaining something to Veran who was nodding enthusiastically.

"Maintain your heading," whispered Ethos from its position in Rhys' vest.

They walked through the ever-darkening swamp of undergrowth, the wet vegetation dampening their footsteps while the pouring rain and intermittent thunder numbed their ears. Though Rhys heard nothing, it seemed Axel did as he paused in step every so often, causing a chain reaction to run through the group. No one spoke; no one made a sound. Only Ethos whispered to Rhys to update him on their progress.

As night fell, the forest swallowed them. The broad-leaf trees, vines, and muddy soil steadily grew thicker and heavier. Was there a better way? Where had Kashim gone?

Eventually, the hum of airships began to pervade the forest. Veran, who had been asked to move to the front after pointing out and killing a wild cat stalking the group, kept a constant speed through the forest. For several minutes, she led them southwest until they happened across a cascade of boulders and rocks, at which point, she redirected them northwest back toward the Brechin camp.

It was pitch black by the time they stopped. Already, they had been hiking for nearly an hour. Hodge helped Kallen sit against a tree and then shook out his mane of hair. Though the rain had subsided, it was miserably humid and muddy. "Where are we?" he grunted.

"We're a quarter of a kilometer from the Brechin camp," replied Veran.

Rhys converted the measurement for the others.

"How large do you estimate the camp to be?" Leo fiddled with his earring. "How many men?"

Axel shrugged. "Maybe... a single company. So, a hundred or so men. The others will be with the naval forces still en route."

Rhys stared at the ground in thought. Sneaking into the camp with a hundred or so men idling about, that was going to be difficult. "Axel, if they got another prisoner, where do you think they would take him?"

"Don't know. It depends on who the prisoner is and what they've done with the others. They may have killed them or tortured them... or they could be fine," replied Axel. "I have no way of knowing."

Rhys thought. "Your only target when you boarded *Themis* was me, correct?"

"Yes."

"Why?"

"Those were our orders," replied Axel quietly.

Rhys considered him. "From whom?"

Axel sighed. "The higher-ups."

"What about the other crew members? Did you have any orders regarding them?"

"Mm, only that we weren't to kill them. We could hurt them if necessary, but loss of life was out of the question."

"Why?" hissed Rhys, confused. "That doesn't make any sense." He looked at Hodge. "You're going into the camp."

"What? Why me? Why not Axel? He's a *gawan* soldier."

"Can't," replied Axel. There was a pregnant pause in anticipation of an explanation, but none followed.

Rhys withdrew Ethos and passed the AI to Hodge. "Once we're close enough to the camp, let them capture you. Ethos will report to Pathos your location. Hopefully, they'll take you to the same holding cell as the others."

"I don't like this," muttered Hodge. "Seriously, why can't Axel go?"

"Because I'm a unit captain," said Axel. "I'm the unit captain for the famed Squad Five. My face is too well known."

"Well, that explains a lot," Leo chuckled darkly.

"It can't be Rhys," continued Axel. "They've already tried to kill him once. It can't Kallen."

"What about Leo?" whined Hodge.

"You're stronger than Leo and can take more," said Rhys, shouldering his rifle. Hodge frowned and tucked the AI into his pocket. Veran pointed them in the direction of the Brechin camp, and the group set off once more.

Within ten minutes, lights began to filter through the trees, and Rhys was forced to remove his night-vision goggles and rely on his poor human sight. Axel halted them in the shadows just outside the camp and knelt in the mud while Hodge remained standing. Rhys could see his dark eyes set forward and his brows knotted in worry.

"We're right here," murmured Rhys from the shadows.

Passing his rifle to Axel, Hodge strode from the cover of the trees into the harsh flood lights of the Brechin camp. Cries erupted, and men came running.

"Get on the ground! On the ground!" ordered a soldier as nearly a dozen men advanced on Hodge. Hodge hit the ground fast. Arms spread in the mud, he patiently waited for the soldiers to arrest him.

Rhys felt a trembling grip on his arm. Recognizing Veran's slender fingers, he comfortingly rubbed her clammy hand. "Why?" she whispered. Her question was a wisp of air. "Why are they…"

Rhys glanced at her and found her entire body shaking. Her eyes were wide and face drawn taut in terror. "Don't look," he murmured, setting his gaze forward in time to see Hodge be violently jerked to his feet by his cuffed hands. Rhys winced for his friend—he knew that hurt—but Hodge was one of the strongest and toughest men he knew. If anyone could handle a beating, it was him. "Make sure you track Ethos," said Rhys into Veran's shoulder. Veran's nod was almost indiscernible.

After flashing spotlights over the vegetation from which Hodge had emerged, the soldiers cleared the area and led Hodge away.

"Now we wait." Axel, who was already lying flat in the mud to avoid detection, rolled his head to look at Rhys. "Does she still have a read on him?"

Veran nodded and sunk into the base of a tree next to Kallen who intertwined their arms for comfort. Rhys glanced overhead at the clouds and flinched as several raindrops plopped down from the trees. Like Axel, he remained prone and rested his head on his muddy arms. They waited.

Thirty minutes passed and then an hour. Multiple times, Rhys asked Veran to verify Hodge's location but her response was the same: according to Ethos, Hodge had not been taken to the others yet.

Nearly two hours after Hodge had been dragged across the camp into the cabin of a covered airship, Veran motioned to Rhys. "They're moving," she whispered, peering over her shoulder.

Rhys rose up on his elbows but could discern nothing. "Pathos, track them."

They waited in tense silence for two more minutes before Veran started to stand. "He's found them." Everyone clambered to their feet. "Follow me." With more dexterity than Rhys expected, Veran led them eastward away from the blinding flood lights of the camp into the forest's shadows. They jogged through the heavy vegetation with Veran in the lead and Rhys in the rear. After circling the camp to reappear on the site's northeastern side, she eventually stopped them. "There," she whispered, pointing to where several guards stood in a cleared area.

"There's nothing there," murmured Kallen.

"Pathos indicates there's a pit there," replied Veran.

Rhys knelt beside Axel. "A pit?"

"When we don't have the resources, we built pits and use those as prisons," Axel breathed.

"Are all of them there?" asked Rhys.

Veran shook her head. "One's missing."

"Who?"

"Ethos says a boy named Otto," replied Veran.

Rhys took a deep breath to calm his racing heart and peered around the tree behind which he was hidden. Standing, he could see the top of the pit and its five guards. After studying the open area, he shifted and looked across the camp. The makeshift prison appeared to be set apart from the rest of the force's base, perhaps to keep its prisoners from overhearing military strategies. Although lit, unlike the camp, the pit had only one spotlight that covered the area.

Rhys motioned to Axel to get his attention. Once Axel was looking at him, he mouthed, "Light," and pointed. Axel disappeared into the shadows. "Goggles," instructed Rhys, pulling the ware onto his face.

"What do you want to do?" whispered Leo.

"No gunfire," replied Rhys, moving into the shadows beside Leo. With Hodge gone, their vanguard had diminished to two and a half; Axel's shoulder still wasn't fully healed. Kallen and Veran were not going to join the fray. Rhys handed Kallen his short rifle and withdrew his resonance cutters. "Veran, tell us when the lights are off," murmured Rhys, shielding his face from the flood light.

They waited until, in the darkness, Veran whispered, "It's off."

Rhys leapt to his feet and, sensing Leo at his side, darted into the clearing. Careful not to fall into the pit, he lunged at the nearest soldier, engaged the resonance cutters, and sliced.

The rifle the soldier carried fell apart as the soldier's vest split. Rhys paused to determine whether he had fatally struck the man. When he saw the soldier stumble back but remain standing, he charged once more and with as much precision as possible, tore through the man's side. The soldier collapsed, and Rhys dove for the next one.

When it became obvious that the resonance cutters were hindering his movements rather than helping, Rhys dropped them and continued the fight using skilled combat. Mind focused like a sharp point, he slipped beside the next soldier and kneed the man's thigh. As the soldier staggered, Rhys trapped his arm and, in a single movement, threw him. As the man tried to roll to his feet, Rhys slid in the mud to his target and, using a powerful palm strike to the face, knocked the soldier unconscious.

Rough, large arms suddenly wrapped around Rhys' neck and lifted him clear off the ground. Hands wedged between his neck and the soldier's beefy forearms, Rhys kicked and writhed in an attempt to escape, but once again, the difference between his slight frame and the enormity of his attacker's was too much.

Suddenly, in his night vision, Veran appeared before him. With precise moves, she darted behind the soldier, leapt atop his torso, and, holding him with her knees, jabbed her hand into the muscle between his shoulder and neck. The soldier's arms went slack, and Rhys dropped to the earth. He did not question Veran nor did he worry about her. He knew perfectly well of what she was capable. Instead, he launched himself at

Leo's opponent. Fortunately, Axel beat him there and, with Leo, they subdued the last soldier.

Panting, Rhys glanced at the still bodies of the soldiers and then retrieved his resonance cutters. As he sheathed them, he walked to the edge of the pit and peered down. Just as Ethos had said, the entire crew save Otto was there. "Hey," he said. Terron, who was holding Cantia, looked up. The Brechin noble had multiple cuts to his beautiful face while Cantia appeared unconscious, her light-colored hair a nest of tangles and mud. Hodge lay in the bottom of the pit curled in the fetal position. Andy and Jules were the only two standing.

"Rhys?" whispered Andy into the darkness.

"Yeah. How can we get you out?" Rhys replied, looking around.

"Here," said Axel, dragging a wood ladder from the brush. They threw the ladder into the pit, and Rhys slid down it.

"Where have you been?" asked Andy. "What are you doing here?"

"Getting my crew," replied Rhys, moving to Hodge. He knelt by his friend. "You hurt?"

"I think something is ruptured," groaned Hodge. "They kicked me good."

Rhys examined his friend's ragged, purple and bleeding face and then looked at the others. Andy and Jules appeared in mildly better shape, though not by much. Terron and Cantia were the two he was most concerned about. "Where's Otto?"

"Don't know. Haven't seen him since yesterday afternoon," admitted Andy. "They came and took him."

"Help me," said Rhys. Jules and Andy gathered on either side of Hodge and lifted him. Hodge moaned. With coordinated teamwork, they worked their way up the ladder and deposited Hodge onto the earth where Veran immediately began assessing him.

Next, Rhys motioned for Terron to pass Cantia. The Brechin noble tried to stand but was terribly weak. No doubt they had not had food or water in the past three days.

Rhys lifted Cantia's small body and started up the ladder once more; Leo took her from Rhys. His brother appeared at the bottom of the ladder and, with Rhys' help, managed to limp up to solid ground.

"He needs surgery," said Veran as Rhys turned to Hodge. "Now."

"Let's get to the shadows," instructed Rhys. Jules and Andy helped Rhys gather Hodge, and together they carried him into the forest. Leo followed with Cantia and Terron while Kallen and Axel brought up the rear, rifle at the ready.

Once the lights of the camp had faded, they finally stopped and, breathing hard in the darkness, rested momentarily.

"Rhys?" murmured Ethos from the innards of Hodge's pocket. "Can we talk?"

"Is it important, Ethos?" asked Rhys as he examined Hodge. Veran pointed to Hodge's abdomen and swiftly began explaining in Nefegian that his spleen had ruptured.

"Well… no," continued Ethos.

"Later?"

"Mmm, fine."

"Let's keep moving," said Axel. "We have a lot of ground to cover in a short amount of time."

"Hang in there," murmured Rhys as he and Jules lifted Hodge. Andy moved to carry their friend's legs. The group began hiking southward. Minutes stretched into infinity; Rhys wondered if they would make it to the stolen airship. No doubt the Brechin soldiers had woken up from their concussed states and reported the incident.

"Airships," alerted Veran. Within seconds, the forest was filled with the deep hum of enemy airships flying over the treetop canopy. Unable to cover themselves from the sensors' thermal scans, the group froze. They were caught.

"Shit," cursed Rhys, gazing up at the airships. Suddenly, flood lights snapped on, and the forest was doused in blinding, white light. Rhys shoved Leo into the shadows of the nearest tree while the others did their best to hide. Undoubtedly, at any moment, Brechin soldiers were going to cascade from the airships to the forest floor.

Above the hum of the airships, came a new sound, one that Rhys distantly recognized but couldn't put a name to. It was like a quiet fan, or like a rush of wind passing through the tree boughs. A faint click resonated from behind them. "Get in," called a voice.

Rhys startled as it was the first time anyone had spoken in anything above a whisper the entire evening. Wildly, he whirled around to find a silver-haired man dressed in Caelestis' plain uniform hovering in midair.

Expecting battle, Axel turned and expertly aimed his rifle at the man. "No, wait," ordered Rhys, leaping from the shadows into the light.

The man glanced at Axel and then moved his stoic gaze over the others. "All of you, get in."

"Go, go," urged Veran, motioning to them. Rhys glanced up at the airships and then at the man. With a growl, he grabbed Leo's arm and thrust him and Cantia toward the newcomer. "The ship is cloaked. There are two steps," advised Veran.

Leo paused before the man, searching for something he couldn't see. Rhys heard the man say, "Release the colloid shield." A moment later, one of the maintenance units Rhys had regularly flown while on Caelestis materialized before them.

"Go," urged Rhys. As Leo climbed the stairs into the unit, Rhys turned to help Jules and Andy carry Hodge and then Terron. Once they were in the craft, he pulled Kallen upward over the stairs and then jerked in Veran. Before the door closed, the unit was moving.

Rhys collapsed on the floor of the maintenance craft and gazed at his crew in the dim yellow light. Like him, everyone was panting with exhaustion and covered in varying shades of mud. Once he caught his breath, he rose to his feet and moved to the cockpit where two other Neo-Colony Two citizens sat. The glowing lights, the intricate switches, the control paneling—all of it was so familiar. The man who had ordered them into the unit appeared at his side. He studied Rhys and then moved to block his view of the cockpit. Taking that as a hint, Rhys returned to the others and joined Veran who knelt beside Hodge.

"How long will it take to get to Neo-Colony Two?" Rhys asked in Nefegian.

"Twelve minutes," replied Veran, pressing on Hodge's abdomen. Hodge hissed in pain before lying back and gritting his teeth.

"Did you call them?"

"No," replied Veran solemnly, meeting Rhys' gaze. That meant others on Neo-Colony Two were privy to the situation and had been following their every move.

He crawled over to Kallen, who rolled her head back to look at the cockpit. "They're from your colony?"

"Yes."

"And this... craft?" Kallen pointed to the ceiling. "It is made of the same material as your magnetic board."

"We used these ships for maintenance on the colony," explained Rhys. Kallen nodded and took his hand. She kissed it and, with their fingers still intertwined, closed her eyes.

The twelve-minute flight to Neo-Colony Two was painfully long. As each minute stretched into infinity, Rhys' apprehension, fear, and nervousness swelled. His crew was about to be shown a culture, society, and environment which they had never before been exposed. He still didn't know where Otto was or what had happened to him; Kashim too had been left behind. *Themis,* as well as *Grisle,* were without protection, and the Pantaraks in New Arbroath were still in danger. As the maintenance craft began to slow, all at once, everything hit Rhys.

Feigning interest in their descent, Rhys left Kallen's side and moved to the cockpit. Once more, his view was blocked. He remained with his back to his crew so they couldn't see the sheer panic that he tried to keep from his face. He couldn't let anyone know that he was on the brink of a complete mental breakdown. With controlled breaths, he remained at the side door and prepared for landing.

As the unit settled and the engines dimmed, Veran appeared at his side. Rhys opened the side hatch to find nearly two dozen Caelestis citizens standing around the aircraft in silence. Hardening himself, Rhys stepped out of the unit. He was filthy, as was the rest of his crew. Layered in dirt, mud, leafy debris, and blood, he was sure he appeared like an uncouth barbarian. Veran stepped from the maintenance craft and motioned for the others to follow. Rhys shifted his attention to his crew.

While he, Andy, and Jules carried Hodge, Neo-Colony Two residents moved around them. Silently, Veran disseminated orders to her medical subordinates who began preparing to receive Hodge. After helping Terron stumble from the aircraft, Rhys led Kallen down the few stairs and looked about in interest.

They had landed in what used to be a large gathering area near the interior of the colony. Although it was only a segment of the colony, the room was large enough to hold the dozen or so maintenance units, supplies, and cargo.

"Rhys," called Veran, kneeling beside Hodge. Two others were with her. Rhys left Kallen and joined the doctor as she held a device over Hodge's torso to reveal a three-dimensional scan of his internal organs. Rhys saw the ruptured organ; its erratic movement was apparent. "He needs surgery, now. What do you want to do?"

Surprised Veran was asking for his opinion, Rhys nodded. "Do it."

"Don't let them kill me," Hodge groaned. Rhys tapped his head fondly.

"Strip him," ordered Veran, moving away.

"What?" moaned Hodge, starting to sit up. He fell back before Rhys could scold him.

"You're filthy. You'll contaminate everything." Veran motioned to her subordinates who swarmed Hodge and began cutting away his clothes. "Water," called Veran, standing. She nodded to Rhys. "All of you. Clothes off."

Rhys glanced at his crew. No one on Caelestis, or Neo-Colony Two, was ashamed of the human body despite having never been naked a day in their lives. The human body was simple biology. Leading by example, Rhys unbuckled his bulletproof vest, drew his soaked, muddy shirt over his head, and pulled off his headscarf. He threw those on the floor and went for his pants. He paused and looked at the others whose eyes flickered between him and the residents stoically watching. It was Andy who finally began slipping out of his clothes.

Pants still on, Rhys turned to Leo. "I'll take her," he murmured. Leo hesitantly passed Cantia into Rhys' arms before turning to help his brother.

Rhys carried Cantia's limp body to Kallen and laid her on the floor. Kallen knelt beside the girl and began undressing her. Three Neo-Colony Two residents gathered around, wheeling a rolling dolly of hoses with them. With gentle hands, Kallen drew away Cantia's ragged clothes. She set those aside and looked up worriedly at the residents.

Rhys grabbed a hose from the dolly and began washing Cantia's body. Once her face and body were clean, he was able to see the damage she had sustained. "Severely dehydrated," he reported, examining Cantia's pale skin. He tilted her face and touched her cheeks. "Broken cheekbone, split lip." One of Veran's colleagues thrust a scanner in front of him. Rhys studied the three-dimensional image that appeared above it. "Fracture to the right ulna. Bruised ribs, numbers seven and eight. Rib number nine, cracked." He glanced over the remainder of her body and returned the scanner.

An automated gurney appeared beside them. In silence, the contraption lowered itself until it was even with the floor. Rhys lifted Cantia, placed her on the gurney, and then moved to his feet as the medical residents left with Cantia.

Two more gurneys, one carrying Hodge and another supporting Terron, also left followed by a collection of silver-haired people. Rhys glanced at Leo who stood uncomfortably while two men sprayed the mud and muck from his naked body.

"I'm fine," growled Axel.

The woman hovering around Axel shook her head. Her AI began speaking Aabesh for her. "You are injured and in need of medical care."

"I said I'm fine," snarled the soldier.

"Just let her look at you," Andy urged.

"I'm fine. Rhys already looked at me," replied Axel, folding his arms across his chest. The scar where he had cut out his tracker shone vividly in the fluorescent light.

Andy, who was in the middle of being showered, looked to Rhys for direction. "Axel," called Rhys. "Let them look."

"I'm not going anywhere where you aren't," the soldier professed.

Rhys sighed. "Wash off. I'll go with you."

Axel glared at the beckoning Caelestis resident before ripping off his pants. He snatched the dolly hose from the woman and blasted himself with water.

"Rhys…" called Kallen. He returned to her and shielded her from the others as she undressed. When she was finally naked, the medical staff washed her gently with the hose until she was clear of mud, debris, and blood, and then brought a gurney for her. "I'm fine. I'm not hurt."

Rhy stripped from his pants, hurriedly washed off, and then joined Andy, Jule, and Leo. Kallen lingered behind him, using him to shield herself from the other crew members as she politely redirected her attention away from the male majority.

A male doctor motioned for them to follow and led them down the hall and into an elevator. Shivering, Kallen tucked herself into the back of the elevator and clutched to Rhys, her hands like ice. Andy and Jules kept their arms balled up against their chests as they shook. Axel appeared downright furious and remained simmering at just below boiling point.

After a walk down another uninviting hallway, they were deposited in a medical treatment room. Though separated by glass, Rhys was relieved to find Hodge, Terron, and Cantia.

"So, you really were shot," murmured Axel. Rhys turned to him. Axel nodded pointedly at the oozing hole in Rhys' abdomen. He hadn't realized the wound had reopened. "What about your head?"

"According to our records," said a medical student, entering the room, "Director Taiglar used advanced synthetic surgery methods to repair Falkrow's head trauma. She also…" The student paused briefly to listen to his AI and then continued. "She also cleared him of his previous biosynthetic corruption. Unfortunately, because the methods she used for the head trauma were so invasive, this left less biological energy to repair the abdomen wound. Don't worry. All internal organs were repaired as was the muscle. The blood you see now is the direct result of a superficial wound opening due to overexertion."

"Your name?" asked Rhys. The young man gazed at him, tilting his head. Figuring the student must have forgotten that Rhys was no longer connected to the Core, Rhys added, "I'm Rhys. This is Jules, Leo, and Kallen. The scowling man there is Axel."

Again, there was a suspiciously long pause before the medical student said in perfect Aabesh, "I am Forge Klick, a level three medical student." It was apparent Forge had been practicing speaking Aabesh for he was the only one, aside from Veran, who had spoken it without the help of the AI. "You are the child of Doctor Severiano Falkrow and Doctor Yadhira Bruaner."

"Yes."

Forge withdrew a scanner from a nearby shelf and turned to Axel. "According to Logos, you are recovering from a shoulder injury. Is that correct?" Axel remained silent. Forge approached Axel, scanned his body, and then nodded. "I can fix that. Who repaired your shoulder?"

"He did," said Axel, nodding to Rhys.

Forge leaned forward to examine the scabbing wound. "Logos also indicates that you have an injury to your lower leg."

"I'm fine," repeated Axel.

"Lie back," instructed Forge, setting the scanner aside. Axel glanced at Rhys before settling on the gurney. The medical station located on the back wall sprang to life and a small portion of it carrying numerous tools, scanners, and screens slid out. Axel darted from the bed.

Startled, Forge watched at Axel in alarm. With a sigh, Rhys pushed the soldier back to the gurney. "You're fine. He's controlling the unit."

"I swear, Rhys. When we get out of here…" Axel grumbled. Uncomfortably, the soldier lay back once more and allowed Forge to work on him. Rhys turned to watch over his crew. Andy and Jules were treated for dehydration though, in truth, neither probably needed medical attention. Forge completed his work on Axel and indicated that everyone could dress in the standard-issue uniforms on the counters except Rhys.

Rhys glanced enviously at the others who were already clothed and then went to the gurney.

After sterilizing all of the equipment, Forge withdrew the handheld scanner and studied Rhys' body. "You've… seen a lot of trauma," he murmured in Nefegian.

Rhys stared at the ceiling. "A lot has happened."

"Aside from Veran, who worked on you?"

"My sister," replied Rhys. "And a friend."

"Well, there is internal scar tissue. No matter whether you had AI support in your recuperation."

"I'm fine with that," said Rhys. Forge checked his vitals before placing his palm on Rhys' forehead. Unfamiliar with the gesture, Rhys asked, "What are you doing?"

Forge didn't answer immediately so Rhys pulled his hand away. "I'm reading your brain waves," the medical student explained. Rhys frowned. Had they always been able to perform such an intricate test simply by touch? Alina had never been able to do that.

"Are all medical students given access to such skills?" murmured Rhys.

Forge withdrew his hand. "No. I'm Doctor Taiglar's understudy. That's why I'm in here with you." He thought for a moment. "You need to rest."

"I'm aware of that," replied Rhys.

"No. Your elevated brain wave activity indicates that you are under enormous stress."

"Again, I'm aware."

Forge gazed at Rhys. "Our bodies are nearly perfect. We are immune to all disease and can heal at rates these others will never be able to achieve, but you are an exception. True, you are still immune to disease, however, since you no longer have an AI, your ability to heal has been greatly reduced. If you keep putting your body through the levels of stress that you are, you will succumb to your injuries." Rhys gazed at the ceiling. "Do you understand?"

"Yes."

Forge straightened himself. "Veran, of course, is aware of the situation. I am making all of your medical information available in the Core for medical staff."

"Great."

Forge began working to reseal Rhys' wound. Although he could sense the others watching, Rhys refused to look at them. Veran entered the room just as Forge completed the resealing and examination. Rhys saw her converse silently with her understudy before turning her attention to him.

"How's Hodge?" he asked, sitting up. Forge presented Rhys with a uniform of gray and white.

"The surgery went well," said Veran in Aabesh. Her choice of language was no doubt for the benefit of the others. "He should recover fully in the next twenty-two hours. Until then, I've kept him sedated to allow his body to rest."

"And Cantia?" asked Leo.

"She's also fine. She's going to be sore for a while longer but no lasting damage was done. We were able to repair her fractures, but she's going to be in some pain when she wakes." Veran watched as Rhys rolled the sleeves of the uniform. Veran switched to Nefegian. "Please don't take what Forge has said to you lightly. I know how you are."

"You don't know how I am," Rhys countered.

"What can be done for him?" Leo suddenly asked in Nefegian. Veran gazed at him in surprise and then tilted her head as she attempted to dissect his dialect.

"He can only help himself," replied Veran. "He needs rest more than anything."

Leo relayed all of the information to Kallen, Jules, and Axel. Rhys stood, finished dressing, retrieved Ethos from Leo, and started for the door.

18
DIVIDE

"WHERE ARE YOU GOING?" ASKED Axel.

"To speak with Doctor Falkrow," Rhys replied. "I want to know why they decided to rescue us." Sensing the group stop, Rhys paused in step. Leo had intentionally halted the others. "What?"

"You go do that," said Leo. "We'll check on Hodge. I'm sure having the rest of us around will make him and Cantia and Terron feel better."

Rhys regarded Leo before flatly saying, "Fine." Without another word he continued down the hallway.

"Can I speak with you now?" asked Ethos the moment they were out of earshot.

Rhys glanced into each of the rooms as they passed. The usual silence and sense of duty imposed upon Caelestis seemed to have been disrupted. Instead of diligently working, the residents of Neo-Colony Two spoke softly to one another without the use of their AIs. He even overhead a few speaking Aabesh.

"Back at the Brechin camp," said Ethos from Rhys' pocket, "I felt something."

"Like what?" grumbled Rhys.

"I felt as though something was calling to me."

"Something or someone?"

"Mmmm, something. I don't believe it was a human."

"A machine?"

"It's possible."

Rhys paused at the intersection of several hallways and looked down each. With the colony no longer connected to the rest of its segments, he had no idea where headquarters was. Two middle-aged women emerged from one of the hallways and froze before Rhys, their blue eyes lingering first on the shaved spot along his temples and then his face.

"I'm looking for Doctor Falkrow or Commander Purjey," said Rhys in Nefegian.

The two women side-stepped him. "Go that way," one said, pointing down the hallway to Rhys' right. She swiftly turned in step and hurried along with her companion.

Why was everyone acting so weird? Well... weirder.

"Rhys, I have to insist that we go back to the Brechin camp," Ethos continued as Rhys strode down the hall.

"That's the plan," replied Rhys. "We're missing Kashim and Otto." He frowned. "Who knows if our ship is even still afloat."

"Good," sighed Ethos.

Four more residents dressed in the green uniforms of engineers appeared down the hall. Rhys recognized each of them; they were colleagues, men with whom he had once shared the same title. Though they fidgeted upon his approach, the group continued toward Rhys, their eyes locked down the hall. Because there were four of them, Rhys paused to allow them to pass. Only one of the silver-haired men dared to look at him.

Rhys was sure he appeared odd now; compared to the others, he towered over them by several centimeters. His chest was broader, shoulders larger, and jaw line stronger. He didn't fit in with his people anymore, nor did he blend in with the people of Earth. He truly was a halfling.

After asking for directions once more, he finally came upon a large door that whizzed open to reveal several older members of the colony as well as his father and Commander Purjey. Aware that he was not properly dressed—he could no longer button the standard uniform shirt across his chest and he was barefoot—Rhys entered and allowed the door to close behind him.

"I apologize for the intrusion," he said, passing an eye over the half a dozen men and women. "You have my sincerest gratitude for saving the lives of my crew. We were in an impossible situation and are thankful for your support." He paused for a moment to meet each person's gaze. "However, I am led to believe that you had ulterior motives for rescuing us. Logically, it is not in your interest to intervene in Earth's conflicts. So, I must ask, why did you launch a rescue mission to save a group of people you have never before met, who hail from another solar system, and who are physiologically different than yourselves?"

"Why did you?" asked the old woman seated at the end of the table. Her white hair, which had lost its gloss due to old age, was pulled back in a tight bun, and her thinning face, though slightly wrinkled, was stern.

Taken aback by the response, Rhys glanced at the others. "Because they are my crew. They're my responsibility."

The woman nodded. "And you are our responsibility."

An emotional ploy? It had to be. There was no way the answer could be so simple. "Last time I was here, I was put on trial for a crime I did not commit." Rhys glanced at his father. "Do I stand before you as a citizen of Caelestis or as a criminal?"

"Neither," replied the ancient man seated in the middle of the table. He was one of the few Rhys had ever seen on Caelestis over the age of a hundred sixty years old.

"Caelestis is no longer my home," said Rhys, guessing what the elder was trying to say. "I am no longer a citizen."

"Very well. You are no longer a citizen," mumbled the old man, leaning on the table.

Rhys fell silent. Why hadn't his father or the commander spoken yet?

"Rhys Falkrow," said the old woman at the end of the table. "What you say is true. Intervening in Earth's conflicts could be detrimental to Neo-Colony Two, however, we are willing to risk that."

"Why?"

The old woman looked at Commander Purjey who leaned forward and motioned to the three-dimensional projection screen inserted in the table. A detailed and very clear image of Rhys appeared. It was of him sitting beside a fire with Kallen's head in his lap. Gauging from the point of view, Rhys knew he was reviewing Veran's memories. In the hologram, he spoke to Veran numerous times and then glanced down at Kallen fondly. He didn't realize his face softened so much when he looked at her.

The image shifted to display him leaning over Reza to measure the old man's vitals. It showed him administering help and disseminating orders; it showed him murmuring to Kallen and then smiling at Hodge. The constantly shifting images alternated rapidly, each showcasing with astounding detail the expressions on his face, the myriad of emotions that crossed his crew, the way they interacted with one another in confined spaces, the subtle looks his crew passed one another, the language they used. All of it was so refined, so perfect. When had communication with his crew become so beautiful? Had it always been so?

As the parade of images continued in the space above the table, the old woman spoke. "You are no longer a citizen of Caelestis nor of Neo-Colony Two; therefore, your trial does not fall under our jurisdiction."

"But you do not belong to Earth either," continued the ancient man across from him. "I theorize that you never will."

"I agree," Rhys replied.

"Henceforth, you will act as ambassador between our people and the Earthlings." The old man stood. "It is evident that there is much to study here. Undoubtedly, it will take years before we have the power to reconvene in space with the other segments. Consequently, we will be spending as much time as possible advancing the human race from here on Earth. Humans are the ultimate species, Rhys Falkrow. We have the power to adapt instantaneously to our environments. We have the ability to think and create. Our time here on Earth will not be in vain." The old man gazed at Rhys. "Do you accept this proposition?"

Rhys glanced at his father and at the commander. "Only if they do."

"Doctor Falkrow is allowed on this council because his daughter was chosen to become the next commander. He does not have the power to veto our decisions," the woman explained.

Rhys nodded to Commander Purjey. "And what about him?"

"He will acquiesce if we ask him to."

"What are you expecting from me should I assume the role of ambassador?"

"As ambassador, you would be required to relinquish all memories and information to the Core so that Caelestis citizens could study the results."

Rhys pursed his lips. "I'm sorry then. I must decline."

"How is this different than what you have shown Director Taiglar?" Commander Purjey asked.

"What I showed Veran was purely for her use. If she wanted to share with you my memories, then so be it. But at the time, I gave her those memories so she could better understand the world around her and function in it, a gift I was not granted."

"Why would you not want to share that knowledge with others?" asked the old woman. "It would allow our people to assimilate to Earth's cultures faster."

"Is that it? That's the only stipulation?" asked Rhys.

"Yes."

Rhys was silent for a long moment before turning for the door. "I would like to speak with my crew about this."

"What are your plans now? Director Taiglar has stated within the system that your health is in decline."

"I'm going after the rest of my crew," replied Rhys. "Because they're my responsibility." He left the room.

After asking for directions once more, he finally found the rest of his crew in a communal room, sipping on water, and quietly visiting. Everyone fell silent when Rhys entered. The only person who was still unconscious was Hodge who lay on a cot on the far side of the room. To his surprise, Veran was also present.

"Well?" asked Axel, leaning against one of the bunks.

Rhys closed the door behind him. "They... want me to act as an ambassador."

"Between who?" Kallen pushed a cup of water into his hands.

"Them and Earth."

"What did you say?" asked Andy.

"I said that I wanted to talk with you." Rhys sipped the lukewarm water and looked at Cantia who was curled up in one of the bunks, her eyes set on the far wall. Leo, who had been perched on the edge of her bed, smiled grimly to let him know she was fine.

"What's the catch?" Andy prompted.

Rhys downed the remainder of his drink. "I have to hand over my memories and all of the information I gather from this point forward."

"Why have they changed their minds?" growled Axel. "Last time, we couldn't get you out of here without a fight. Now, they're letting us just walk out?"

Rhys glanced at Veran. "I suppose I have you to thank in some way. But... "I'm no longer a Caelestis citizen." It hadn't bothered him when they had said it, but now he felt a twinge of pain.

"Is... that what they said?" asked Leo. Rhys nodded. "That's... cruel."

"It's the only way Rhys wouldn't be forced to stand trial for Alina's death," clarified Veran who peered around Axel. "If he's not a citizen, he can't be put to trial. That's colony law."

Rhys sighed and rubbed his head. He was exhausted. "Let's move on. We have another task at hand—retrieving Kashim and finding Otto."

"We should wait," asserted Axel.

"Kashim has..." Rhys blinked to keep his eyes open. He felt light-headed. "Kashim has no idea that we're..." He leaned against the wall and held his head. "I don't..." He could feel his mind slipping. Weakly, he looked at his crew. All eyes were on him. Was he hallucinating?

"Kallen, Andy," directed Veran.

Rhys looked at the Director of Medicine. She didn't seem upset or perturbed by his sudden and inexplicable weakness. In fact, no one did.

"You… drugged me?" he murmured, his legs shaking under him. He couldn't keep his eyes focused on anyone anymore; the room spun. His hearing dimmed, and his body drooped. He managed a few steps toward the door before his knees buckled. Arms caught him.

"I'm sorry," whispered Kallen into his ear. Rhys tried to look at her, to focus on her face, but he could no longer comprehend the world around him. Limply, he melted into unconsciousness.

19
THE DAMAGE

"YOU SHOULD HAVE KNOWN THIS was going to happen," chided Alina primly.

Rhys tried to turn his head to his sister, but his body was a lead weight, heavy and completely immobile.

"You saw it in Leo's eyes." Alina chuckled. "I'm sure even Ethos knew."

He wanted to reply to her remarks but couldn't. Every part of him was non-functioning.

Alina lay beside him. He could feel her weight and warmth against his side. "Pathos and Logos engaged our internal trackers when we first arrived on Earth. Our beacons have been going since we left the colony." His sister shifted beside him and added, "Do you think Pathos and Logos knew segments of Caelestis had landed on Earth? I like to think our AIs were aware of the colony's presence here and simply chose not to tell us."

Rhys felt his sister's company fade. When she next spoke, it felt as though time had passed.

"You are an Ethos user now," she said, resting on the edge of his bed. Rhys still could not see her though he could feel her weight. "You have in your hands the power of the past. Ethos is your partner now. Use it."

Rhys forced strength into his neck and turned to gaze at his sister. To his great disappointment, there was no one there.

He slid his arm over the bed's edge to double-check and then rolled upright. His head lolled to the side; he couldn't force his eyes open.

"Lie back down," came a small female voice.

"Alina…" he murmured, slumping back into the bed. "Tell Alina… I need to… talk…"

"Go back to sleep."

Rhys slipped back into a coma.

How long was he asleep? Why wasn't he waking up? Aside from his conversation with Alina, he didn't dream. His sleep was blank, white. There was nothing. Into infinity he slept, his body motionless, his mind void. At first, it was pleasurable. His body thirsted for sleep. Eventually though, he began to grow restless. He needed to be moving; he needed to be doing.

Wake up, he demanded of himself repeatedly. *Move.*

When not even a finger twitched, he succumbed once more to sleep. Again, time passed.

When he next tried to wake, his body shifted and his fingers pulled at the bedding around him. "Wake…up…" he murmured through his parched lips. "Wake up." He heard medical equipment move around him as he forced himself to roll onto his side. Slowly—finally—his eyes opened.

He expected to be in a medical room. Instead, he found himself in one of the bunks in the communal living quarters. On his wrist was a vitals sensor; an IV was pinched in the crook of his left arm. In a stupor, he allowed his eyes to shift about. Leo, Kashim, Axel, and Andy sat at a small table on the other side of the room, speaking lowly. Jules and Terron were asleep in separate bunks. Where were the others?

With a deep breath, Rhys rose in his bed and waited for his weight to settle on his body. After a moment, he realized he had a Foley catheter inserted in him. As discreetly as possible, he drew out the catheter underneath the sheet, closed it off, and then proceeded to take out his IV.

"Hey," greeted Leo, nodding to Rhys.

"How are you feeling?" Andy asked.

Rhys rubbed his head. He felt lethargic. "Fine," he grumbled. Leo left to retrieve water. "How… long was I asleep?"

"Three days," replied Kashim.

He fell still, contemplated that amount of time, and then looked at his crew. "What?"

"The drugs were for two," Leo explained, rejoining them with water. He passed the cup to Rhys who inhaled it. "Everything after that was you."

"I-I've been asleep for three days?"

They nodded.

Rhys sighed and slid to the edge of the bed. Andy stopped him. "Actually, you're not supposed to stand for the first hour after you wake. Veran's orders."

Rhys hung his legs off the bed and gazed at them in distress. "Three days?"

"Go get Veran," murmured Axel.

"She's… probably already on her way…" Rhys muttered. He was irritated and confused. When a thought occurred to him, he looked at Kashim. "Why are you here?"

Kashim gave a gruff chuckle. "Where would you prefer I be?"

Rhys glowered. "I'm disoriented and confused. What happened? How did you get here? Where is everyone else?"

"Everyone is fine," assured Leo. "Well… almost fine."

"It's nice to see you again, Rhys," hummed Veran, entering the room; Forge the medical student trailed behind her. "Pathos notified me you were awake. How do you feel?"

"Irritated," Rhys grumbled.

Veran pushed through the crew members and glanced at the small computer propped beside his bed. "Remnants of the drug are still in your system as well as the process inhibitors, so it's only to be expected," she said. "Let's get a tablet in you and see if that helps."

"I want answers." Rhys nodded to Kashim. "How is he here?"

Veran placed her hand on Rhys' forehead and stared at him for a long moment. She nodded and then began speaking in Nefegian. "Although the brain scan indicates that you are emotionally distressed, you are otherwise physically fit. The three days of recuperation have allowed your body the time it needed to focus its energy on healing. That, coupled with the nano-infusers I gave you two days ago, has brought your composite health to a sustainable and appropriate level."

"Great."

Veran glanced at Axel, a very un-Caelestis behavior, before saying, "Your crew decided unanimously to drug you. They were concerned about your health and, therefore, your ability to lead. It was for your benefit that they made the difficult decision."

Rhys looked at Leo. "It was your idea though, wasn't it?"

Leo sighed. "You're one person. Trust in others for a change."

"You drugged me."

Leo pushed Kashim forward. "And we retrieved him and Otto."

Leo had won; his crew had won. After a moment, Rhys held his hand out to Kashim. "Glad to see you. What about Otto?" He looked between his crew members, noting their grave faces. "Where's Otto?"

"He's being kept in a separate room," said Leo, "for his own safety."

"Why? What's wrong? What happened?"

Kashim's voice was small. "They got to him. He's lucky to be alive."

"You tended to him, right?" asked Rhys, worry gnawing at his gut. "He's fine now?"

Veran nodded hesitantly. "Physically, yes. He's fine."

"I want to see him." Rhys started to stand, but Veran stopped him.

"Wait an hour. Let's flush the drugs from your system," the director said.

Rhys begrudgingly sat back on his bed. "What about Hodge? Cantia?"

"Hodge is well. He, Kallen, and Cantia have been with Otto since midday," Veran replied, standing. She motioned to Forge who handed Rhys a packet of water as well as a tablet. Rhys downed both and was then escorted to a bathroom.

Forge helped him bathe despite his growing steadiness and returned him to the communal living quarters. When Rhys asked after Otto, the med student simply explained that he was not permitted to discuss the boy's status without Veran present. Rhys knew that was impossible as the director was always in communication with her staff, but he accepted the young man's response anyway. Once dressed in ill-fitting clothes, Rhys turned his attention to Veran who had been speaking familiarly with Axel, her head tilted toward him and eyes bright. When... had this happened?

"Take me to Otto," he said, interrupting their private conversation. The soft expression on Veran's face was replaced with a stoic one, and she nodded. With the exception of Jules and Terron, everyone followed her.

"When he was brought to my care," said Veran, striding down the hall, "he was in the worst shape I've ever seen a human be in. Multiple fractures and contusions to his legs and arms, two severe head injuries, burn wounds to his neck, chest, back, and shoulders, as well as—"

"Enough," interrupted Rhys, grinding his jaws. He should have gotten there sooner.

Veran stopped the group outside a door. Kashim placed a heavy hand on Rhys' shoulder. "Harden yourself," he advised. Rhys glanced at Leo and Andy who had stopped several paces back with the obvious intent of not entering.

Veran gazed at him. "I too will wait here."

Rhys stepped before the door, and it whizzed open. Hodge sat just inside, his arms folded over his chest and gaze set on the far wall. When Rhys stepped into the room, his friend stood and fondly hugged him. Hodge didn't say anything; the grim expression on his face was enough. He moved aside to reveal Kallen and Cantia sitting on the floor with Otto.

Rhys immediately took notice of the boy's bare scalp. Where there had been a perfectly designed assortment of intricate tattoo markings to indicate he was of the Pantarak faith, there was now only misshapen markings and uneven lines. Patches of bare skin healing from trauma mixed with the irregular designs to create an unpleasant illusion across his scalp. Despite the significant damage to his scalp, the teen appeared otherwise physically healthy. As expected, Veran had done a remarkable job.

Rhys approached, glancing at Kallen and Cantia. While they continued to sketch using a three-dimensional projection screen, Otto stared blankly at the white floor beneath him. His eyes didn't move; he blinked once every twenty seconds or so. He simply sat, oblivious to Kallen speaking to him or Cantia's hand on his arm.

The girls smiled in relief at Rhys. But, realizing that he was there for Otto, they remained silent. "Hey, Otto," murmured Rhys.

For the first time since he had entered the room, Rhys saw Otto stiffen. Though he kept his head down, the change in the boy was considerable. Rhys glanced at the others standing in the doorway and then knelt beside Otto.

"How are you feeling—"

Otto flung himself at Rhys, fists flailing. Caught off guard, Rhys toppled onto his back. Twice Otto's fists snagged Rhys' face before he began defending himself.

"Don't!" ordered Rhys, seeing Hodge and Kashim move.

Otto continued to slam his fists into Rhys' arms. When it became obvious his hits weren't connecting, Otto moved down to Rhys' chest and hammered there. Face stinging, Rhys grabbed Otto's left hand and then his right to stop the attack. Otto struggled for a moment before collapsing atop Rhys, sobbing and heaving. Rhys lay back to stare at the ceiling, his hands still clenched around Otto's wrists.

"I'm sorry, Otto," Rhys murmured. His heart hurt. He could have stopped it; he could have gotten there sooner. He should have stayed behind at the Brechin camp. "I'm sorry."

Chest growing wet with Otto's tears and mucus, Rhys released the boy and sat up. Otto wrapped his arms around Rhys and continued to sob.

For several long minutes, Rhys sat with Otto. He couldn't bear to tell the teen to calm himself. He was sure much more had happened to him psychologically than physically. Veran could repair the physical injuries; mending the psychological damage was a different story.

Eventually, Otto's weight against Rhys deepened and his crying faded. Resting on his hands, Rhys craned his neck to find the boy asleep. He took a deep breath and looked at the others who had gathered in the doorway. A mixture of expressions colored their faces. Cantia had her arms around Leo and was crying silently while Veran held the hem of Axel's shirt. It was Kallen who stepped from the group and joined Rhys. She kissed his forehead and then caressed Otto's bare scalp.

"He was raped," she murmured, kneeling beside them. "And tortured." She stroked Otto's face. "For leaving the Pantarak faith. He was barely alive when we found him." Rhys felt his eyes sting as he gazed down at Otto's ugly head.

"I should have...."

"Stop," whispered Kallen. "You cannot save every person in this world."

"Why did... you drug me?"

"We left for the Brechin camp shortly after you went to sleep," replied Kallen. "It was part of the deal. We did everything you would have done. We found Kashim, and we found Otto. Veran came with us as did her lead medical student. There was literally nothing you could have done that would have changed the operation." Kallen sat beside him. "He will heal." She met Rhys' eyes, and he knew she spoke truth. "It will take time, and he will never forget it, but... he'll heal."

"What will you do?" asked Veran from the doorway. For the first time while in Neo-Colony Two, she seemed unsure. Of course, she had never before seen someone in mental turmoil. How would she know what could be done? "He does not have an AI. We cannot force memory loss."

Kallen ran a ginger hand along Otto's head, her eyes soft and sympathetic. "Memory loss isn't the answer. Being surrounded by family is the solution." She motioned to Cantia who detangled herself from Leo and joined them. Kallen took the girl's hand. "Can you do this?"

"Do what?" asked Leo, leaving the group.

Kallen sat back and looked at him. "Vinz was my sheath. When I was raw and untrusting, he took me in. Cantia will do the same for Otto."

"Kallen..." murmured Leo, glancing at Cantia. "She's too young for something like that."

"I'm not," replied Cantia thickly. "I'm thirteen. I can do it."

Leo looked between Rhys and Kallen. "I'd… like to discuss this in private." He motioned to Hodge who joined them and lifted Otto from Rhys.

After Rhys wiped himself clean and stood, Kallen folded herself into his arms and kissed him. He patted her bottom fondly before looking to the others still in the doorway. "Could we have a moment?"

With Otto asleep in the bunk on the far side of the room and the others gone, Leo advanced on Kallen. "You can't ask her to do this. She is a *child*. She's younger than him."

Kallen glanced at Cantia who was perched on the edge of Otto's bed. "She's already seen more than her share of evil in the world."

"Kallen, you are asking a *thirteen-year-old* to become an emotional crutch for someone who was raped and tortured. Think about Cantia's wellbeing."

"She saw Otto when we brought him in. She saw what her people did to him," Kallen countered. "She will not ever forget. That is her job."

"Rhys, say something."

Rhys regarded Leo. "Otto needs a sheath, someone he can give himself to and trust unconditionally. But you're right. Cantia is too young."

"Thank you," Leo breathed.

"I don't want Cantia involved at such a young age." Rhys thought for a moment and looked between Kallen and Leo. "Thirteen is a young age, right?"

Kallen shook her head while Leo nodded vigorously.

"Otto was raped. This is going to open his recuperation to sexual issues," Leo continued, softer. "You can't force Cantia into a position like that when she is so young."

"That's precisely why it *must* be done," argued Kallen. "His frame of mind is so fragile right now; he just needs someone to be with him and to protect him from himself. Cantia is closest in age and has a reason to act as his sheath."

"A reason?" asked Leo.

Kallen's face grew grim. "Your people did this to him. It wasn't the Paducah refugees. It was your soldiers. Brechin's soldiers."

"Then let me or Terron be his crutch."

Kallen shook her head. "It must be Cantia."

"Kallen…" Leo ran an anxious hand through his hair. "She's thirteen. She doesn't know what to do or how to help him."

"And you do?"

"The emotional and psychological damage done will eventually have to be addressed. Cantia is not old enough to understand and comprehend that kind of pain. What is she supposed to do? Can this not be a, eh, family endeavor?"

"It doesn't work like that," said Kallen. "It will help, but his trust has been shattered. He needs someone to be vulnerable to."

"Then I'll do it," said Rhys. "I'll take care of Otto." Leo thought for a moment before nodding; Kallen, however, didn't seem sure. "He's my responsibility. I'll take care of him."

"I can hear everything you are saying," remarked Cantia from Otto's bunk. She stood and joined them. "Rhys and I will split the responsibility."

"Cantia," murmured Leo.

"No arguments," she swiftly replied. Her blood-shot eyes were determined. "I'll take care of him and when I can't... Rhys will."

Rhys nodded. "Let's move him to the communal quarters once he wakes."

"Is that wise?" asked Leo. "He attacked you."

"That was a one-time event."

"And if it isn't?" murmured Kallen.

"We'll deal with it then." Rhys gazed at Otto. "He's going to be out of action for a while. Did you see anything while you were there?"

"No. We found Kashim perched in a tree," said Kallen. "He had managed to escape detection after killing three officers. But a bullet got his leg. And... we found Otto in a secluded tent west of the camp. No one was around." Kallen's face darkened. "They probably thought he was dead."

"You mentioned a deal earlier?" said Rhys.

Kallen looked to Leo. "We made a deal with your people, well... with Veran. If she helped us rescue Kashim and Otto, we would allow her to drug you. According to Veran, the colony now has a vested interest in you."

"I bet they do," Rhys replied. He glanced at Otto once more in thought. "Are you staying here?" He motioned to Cantia who nodded and returned to Otto's bedside. With Leo and Kallen, Rhys left the room.

The rest of his crew and Veran, who had been patiently standing outside, straightened themselves.

"What now?" asked Andy. Kallen and Leo joined the others, leaving Rhys to stand alone before everyone.

"What state was New Arbroath in when you were last there? Do you know?"

Andy looked at Kashim and shrugged. "We don't know. Our only ventures were to the west of town."

Rhys looked to Axel. "What do you think?"

"The refugees from Paducah will have succumbed to the Brechin forces by now, especially with New Arbroath unwilling to trade or lend help," Axel reasoned. "For the moment, I would say both are lost."

"A stalemate for us then," said Rhys, glancing at Forge as he joined Veran. The medical student spoke silently with her before smiling at Rhys. Rhys didn't respond in kind. Instead, he sighed. "I need time to think. I don't have any answers right now."

And with that, the crew meandered back to their communal living quarters. Rhys didn't miss the subtle looks Veran passed Axel before she turned to walk with Forge in the opposite direction. Only Kallen remained. Rhys leaned against the wall and gazed at the floor.

She joined him so their shoulders were touching. "What are you thinking?" she asked in Elali.

He took her hand. "I don't know."

"Are you hurting somewhere?"

"No, I just don't know what to do," he replied, bringing her hand to his lips and kissing it. Kallen dragged his hand toward her abdomen and placed it there. "It's too early to feel anything, right?"

She nodded and then smiled fondly at him, prompting him to kiss her lips gently. It felt like it had been days since he had held her, had touched her.

He pulled her into his form, bending her into the curve of his body, suddenly hungry not for sex but for physical intimacy. His inner being thirsted for respite from the outside world, for a quiet time to collect himself and reweave the frayed threads of his identity.

Kallen kissed his neck. "Can… we go somewhere?"

With her hand in his, Rhys strode down the hallway toward the makeshift hangar. They passed several Neo-Colony Two residents who glanced stoically at them. When Rhys pulled Kallen into the hangar, two engineers looked up from their work. Rhys recognized both.

He slowed to a halt. "Beso, Temur," he acknowledged. He didn't know Temur, the middle-aged engineer, well as he was a different class of engineer, but Beso he was familiar with. Temur had his hair trimmed short in obvious distaste for Earth's gravity while Beso's pale locks had grown to his ears since the colony's descent. Although physically both appeared similarly, Beso's youthful face had more character than Temur's. His eyes were softer.

Neither said anything though their eyes shifted to Kallen. Rhys motioned. "Uh, this is Kallen."

Beso, the engineer who had days earlier been the only one to meet Rhys' gaze in the hallway, glanced at Temur who was obviously speaking via AI. After a moment, the two approached Rhys and Kallen. Beso gazed at Kallen, his azure eyes probing, before looking at Rhys. "Are you going to become the ambassador?"

"I haven't decided yet," Rhys replied. He felt Kallen shy under Temur's intense scrutiny. "It's good to see you again, Temur."

Temur's stoic gaze didn't leave Kallen. "Why does her skin glisten?" he asked. "It's not natural."

"It's a biological adaptation," explained Rhys. "She and the others have a second skin that prevents water and nutrient loss."

"Her skin, hair, and eyes are unpleasant to look at it," said Temur. Rhys was thankful they spoke in Interstellar Nefegian, not for Kallen's sake, but for theirs. Kallen was not a forgiving person.

"Then you don't have to look at them," Rhys retorted, careful that his tone didn't reflect his words. Temur glanced at Rhys and then walked away.

"That was unnecessarily spiteful," remarked Beso.

"Residents are starting to break free and form individuality," Rhys mused. "Some of you seem at home with my crew's presence while others can't tolerate us."

Beso tried to smile but the action appeared forced. "It is because the colony is dividing. There are many who believe that they must adapt and, therefore, habitually review the information of Earth's cultures. Others like Temur don't want anything to do with the outside world."

Seeing Kallen's questioning look, Rhys translated what Beso had just said into Elali. Afterward, she stepped forward and held out her left hand to Beso. "A pleasure to meet you, Beso." Beso glanced at Rhys for guidance.

Smiling, Rhys touched Beso's left arm and motioned for him to mimic her. Kallen gripped his hand and bowed her head as was customary. "A... pleasure to meet you, Kallen," said Beso, stiffly copying her motions. Kallen giggled and looked at Rhys, amused. "What is wrong?"

Kallen released Beso's hand and stepped back into Rhys. "You look like Rhys when he first came to Earth."

"Uh..." Beso thought for a moment and then continued in Aabesh, "Can I touch your skin?" Kallen held out her arm, and Beso ran hesitant fingers over her olive skin. "It's slick but intriguing. It helps maintain water retention?" Kallen nodded. Beso's hand traveled the distance between them and his fingers touched Kallen's hair. "Strange," he murmured, running locks of her raven hair through his hand.

When his other hand lifted to touch her face, Rhys gently intercepted. He knew what was happening. The information Veran had shared with the colony had memories of him touching Kallen fondly. Considering it to be the cultural norm, Beso had begun to do the same thing.

"Intimate touching between sexes is reserved for mates," explained Rhys in Nefegian. "It is not acceptable to do so with someone you are not familiar with."

"I understand," replied Beso. He smiled once more, this time more naturally. "Is this more appropriate?" he asked Rhys in Nefegian.

Rhys hid his humor. "Yes."

Beso's smile faded, and he tilted his head as Rhys and Alina had done while their AIs spoke to them. "My apologies. I'm needed elsewhere. It was a pleasure to meet you, Kallen." Beso strode from the hangar.

Rhys watched his colleague leave before leading Kallen to one of the many maintenance units.

"What are you doing?" murmured Kallen in Elali.

"You wanted complete privacy," Rhys replied, opening the side door. Kallen stepped into the unit, and Rhys closed the door behind them, immersing them in dim shadows. He moved to the cockpit to ensure the communication locks were on and then looked back at her.

"The other man seemed upset," said Kallen, sitting on the floor of the unit. Rhys joined her. "Was he mad at me?"

"I don't think he knew he was mad, but he was." Rhys rested his head against the cold unit wall. "He didn't like the way you looked. It seems that for the first time in Caelestis history, its citizens are breaking apart to form individual groups. There's been a splitting of ideology."

Kallen leaned against him. "That's unheard of, right?"

"Right."

They sat in silence. Finally, Kallen whispered despairingly, "What are we going to do about Otto?"

"I thought we decided."

Kallen looked at Rhys. "He will eventually have to come to terms with his sexuality. Leo doesn't understand that. That's why I want Cantia with him."

"Cantia is too young to engage in sexual intercourse, right?"

Kallen frowned. "She is, but if she's going to be Otto's sheath, that's something that will come with the territory. He's not that much older than her."

"He just turned sixteen," replied Rhys. "Alina was sixteen when she and Hodge became active."

"Age really isn't the problem here." Kallen shook her head. "He will have to face what's been done to him. He needs someone he can rely on emotionally and… sex is a big part of that."

Looking to change subjects, Rhys glanced at her abdomen. "How are you?"

"Exhausted. But I'm always exhausted, so not much has changed," chuckled Kallen.

"It might become difficult to eat soon," said Rhys, rubbing her stomach. "Because of nausea."

"Eh, I know. But so far, nothing." Kallen rested her hand atop his. "Do you want a girl or a boy?"

"I don't care," replied Rhys.

Kallen sighed. "I want a boy."

"Why?"

"So he doesn't ever have to go through what I did."

"He'll have a hard life," murmured Rhys.

"Not if we change everything first," said Kallen. She leaned into him and kissed his cheek. "That's what humans do. They work to change the world so their children can live better than they did."

Rhys tilted her face to his. "I like that."

"I thought you would." She kissed his lips. Their initially chaste kiss deepened until Rhys climbed atop her and pulled her blouse over her head. Kallen stripped him of his shirt and then moved to his beltline.

Rhys fell still and gazed down at her. In the hangar light filtering through the cockpit windscreen, Kallen smiled at him. He sighed and rested on his elbows over her. "Everything seems out of my control. I've lost the ship, my board, New Arbroath, Paducah, Otto." He laid his forehead on hers. "I don't know what to do. I wish Vinz was here."

"You're not alone. You have everyone here with you."

"Yeah, but I haven't the faintest idea of what we should be doing now."

Kallen pulled him down so his face was on her chest. Stroking his hair, she said, "Maybe we need to leave the area. Take *Themis* and just sail. Forget the refugees, New Arbroath, everything."

"I don't want that," Rhys muttered despondently into her breast.

"Then we go back to the Brechin camp and slaughter all of the soldiers."

"I don't want that either."

"They deserve it," replied Kallen. She traced the empty receptors along his temple with a finger. "We could stay here."

Rhys didn't reply immediately. It was true. They could stay at Neo-Colony Two. The colony had the resources and supplies to take care of them and could provide excellent protection. Their walls were virtually impenetrable.

"No," Rhys whispered.

Kallen chuckled. "I didn't think so." Her mirth faded. "I wonder what's happening overseas. What about Firekli and Bathsgate? What about the other territories under the Pantarak empire? Do you think word of New Arbroath and Paducah has spread?"

"I would be interested to find that out."

Kallen gripped the hair along his head and pulled his face to hers. Their eyes met. "We don't expect a miracle from you. We never have. You usually just surprise us. Whatever you choose, whatever you decide, we'll follow you." She kissed his lips. "You're the Overseer."

Rhys sighed, letting his body relax atop hers. "You're sure?"

Kallen bit his bottom lip gently and smiled. Rhys slid his hand between them and pulled at her waistband.

20

CARELESSNESS

IT WAS WELL PAST MIDNIGHT according to Ethos when they finally emerged from the maintenance unit and made their way back to the communal living quarters. The hangar was empty though the lights remained on.

Nearly everyone was asleep save Andy, Axel, and Hodge. Cantia and Otto shared a bed on the far side of the room beneath Terron's bunk.

"Where have you two been?" asked Hodge as they entered the room.

"Walking," replied Rhys.

"Is it very windy outside?" his friend teased. "Or does your hair naturally have that just-had-sex look?" Rhys flattened his locks while Kallen scowled. "Seriously though, where did you go? Every room is under surveillance."

"He grew up here," grinned Kallen. "He knows places."

"Have you eaten?" asked Rhys.

"If you mean those pill-things, yes," replied Hodge. He frowned with a heavy sigh and slumped at the table. "It's not as good as Kallen's cooking though. Or Alina's…"

Pretending he didn't hear the last part, Rhys chose a bunk nearby and flopped into it. Warily, he rolled his head back to look at the small computer stationed at the top of his bed which allowed for connection to the Core. Absent-mindedly he touched the receptors at his temple and then relaxed. Kallen kissed him in passing and climbed into the bunk above him.

"Kallen…" moaned Hodge from the table. "I want food."

"You're fine," Kallen replied.

Hodge whined dramatically before Axel and Andy continued their quiet conversation. Rhys drew a long breath, rolled over, and went to sleep.

A strong vibration along his leg woke him a mere two hours later. Drowsily, he withdrew Ethos from his pants pocket and laid the AI next to him. "What?" he murmured in Nefegian.

"I need to go, Rhys," replied Ethos.

"Go where?"

"Back to the Brechin camp," the AI replied.

Rhys stretched his neck and gazed at the bunk overhead. "Is something still calling to you?"

"I had thought to ask Kallen to take me when they went to retrieve Kashim and Otto, but I didn't want to endanger her should conflict arise."

"Thank you," Rhys groaned. He sat up and gazed about the dark room. Everyone was asleep. "So, what do you want to do?"

"Take me there."

"Ethos... now?" whispered Rhys.

"Rhys, I *feel* that I'm being called. Please, do this for me."

Rhys swung out of the bed. "You're sure?"

"Very sure."

"Do you know where they put our weapons and clothes? I need boots." He left the room via the automatic door.

"They're in storage near the hangar," replied Ethos.

Shirtless, Rhys strode down the hallway. He passed only two residents, both of which glanced at his bare chest before shying away. He found their clean clothes, boots, and weapons. After dressing and rolling his sleeves, he gathered a short rifle, a pistol, and his resonance cutters and headed for the hangar.

Cautiously, he peered into the enormous room. As he expected, several engineers were at work. He singled out a maintenance unit that had an unhindered line-of-sight to the hangar door and, with confidence, strode to the craft. A handful of engineers paused in their work, but knowing that he was not a citizen and that perhaps he was on business for the council, they ignored him. Rhys swung himself into the maintenance unit and started to shut the side hatch door.

"Where are you going?" asked a voice. Rhys whirled around to find Forge, Veran's medical student, standing just outside the unit. "Were you authorized to take this unit?" How he had managed to sneak up, Rhys didn't know.

"I have something I need to do," Rhys replied. "I'll be back before dawn."

Forge considered and then said, "I'm coming too."

"What? No." Rhys blocked the hatch door. "You'll only get in the way."

"Since when has any Caelestis citizen ever been anything other than useful?" countered Forge. Rhys saw the young man tilt his head as his AI communicated with someone.

"Stop," ordered Rhys. Forge looked at him in surprise. "Whoever you're talking to, stop."

"You no longer have your AI. How did you know?"

"Body language," replied Rhys. "And the high-pitched whining."

The sound of footsteps echoed through the unit as another joined them. It was Beso. Forge glanced at the engineer before saying, "I was speaking to Beso. He also wants to come."

"Rhys..." Ethos murmured plaintively from the innards of his pocket.

Rhys stepped aside and allowed the two to board. As the hatch closed, he stopped Forge from climbing into the cockpit. "I've got this." Solemnly, he regarded the two young men. "I'm in command here. Whatever I say goes. I don't care if it defies logic. If I tell you to do something, you do it. Understand?"

Beso and Forge nodded in unison. With a sigh, Rhys clambered into the cockpit; Beso joined him in the copilot's seat. Rhys expertly ran through the pre-launch checklist and then started the engines. As if he had never left the colony, his hands moved familiarly over the numerous buttons and switches along the cockpit paneling.

"Engines: nominal. Engaging thrusters. Rotating 95 degrees," relayed Rhys to his copilot. "Rotation complete. All systems nominal."

"Hangar door, opening," said Beso. "Course: clear."

"Launching." Rhys maneuvered the maintenance unit from the hangar and over the trees in the clearing. "Ethos, plot a course for the Brechin camp."

"Course already set," replied Ethos.

Rhys pulled the AI from his pocket and set it on the paneling before him. A three-dimensional map of the area appeared above Ethos.

"Heading, south-by-southwest. At optimal speeds, arrival time is estimated to be 02:41," said Ethos. "Accelerate to two hundred eighty kilometers per hour," instructed Ethos, "and hold."

"Rhys..." murmured Beso uncomfortably.

"Can we trust this AI unit?" asked Forge, leaning into the cockpit. "It's irrational."

"We can trust it more than Pathos or Logos," replied Rhys, watching the instruments.

Beso gingerly sat back. "What kind is it?"

Rhys gave the AI to the engineer. "Ethos."

Surprised, Beso studied the AI before passing it to Forge. "Where did you find it?" asked Forge.

"Otto found it in some ruins south of here." Rhys adjusted their flight path and reclined in his seat. "Nine minutes."

Forge returned Ethos and peered into the cockpit. "What are you doing? Why are you going back to the Brechin camp?"

Rhys waved Ethos at them before setting the unit on the paneling once more. "It told me to."

Beso's face fell. "Without explanation?"

"I'm being called there," replied Ethos. "Something is calling to me."

"Your AI is malfunctioning, Falkrow," said Beso.

Rhys folded his arms, allowing the automated piloting system to take control. "It's not."

"AIs aren't supposed to *feel* anything," explained Forge.

"I am aware," replied Rhys. "But Ethos has not once led me astray. I trust it."

"Have you attempted to adjust its settings?" Forge continued.

"It's a learning AI. It adjusts to its user's preferences."

"Rhys," interrupted Ethos. "I'm locked onto the signal. We're four minutes out."

"What do you plan on doing?" asked Beso. Rhys motioned for him to take the controls and then climbed out of the cockpit. He adjusted the bulletproof vest on his torso and tucked Ethos into the top. "Falkrow?"

"I don't know yet," replied Rhys.

"Take Klick with you," said Beso.

Rhys checked that his short rifle had a round loaded in the chamber. "No. Both of you are staying here."

"But I've already downloaded close-quarter combat skills," replied Forge. Rhys thought he sounded disappointed, but he knew that couldn't possibly be true. Disappointment was something a Pathos-user understood.

A thought crossed his mind, and he peered at Forge in interest. "You're a Pathos-user, aren't you?"

Forge regarded Rhys, suddenly dubious. "Why?"

Taking that as a confirmation, Rhys glanced over his shoulder. "Beso, you have a Logos?"

"Yes. How could you tell?"

Rhys checked his pistol and returned it to the holster at his hip. "It's easy," he murmured. "You've downloaded close-quarter combat techniques?" Forge nodded. "Holds, take-downs, throws?" Forge nodded once more, his eyes wide with excitement.

"Beso?"

"I'll stay with the unit," the young man quickly replied.

Rhys turned to Forge. "Your size is going to be your strength and your weakness. The men we will come across are like those on my crew—large, muscled, and unflagging in their beliefs. They will try to hurt you, maim you, kill you. You must understand that."

Forge's determination wavered. "Kill?"

"Many humans on Earth have no reservations about killing." Rhys held Forge's gaze. "Do you understand, Forge?" Forge anxiously nodded. "Good." After a moment, Rhys withdrew the pistol at his hip and passed it to the med student. "This is a gun. It will kill anyone you shoot."

The medical student's response was immediate. "Yes, I know." He took the gun, expertly checked it, and then looked at Rhys. "I know because of you and Doctor Taiglar."

Rhys glanced out the cockpit. The maintenance unit was slowing. "You're lucky. Alina and I learned everything by trial and error." He moved to the side hatch and prepared to deploy. "Here." Though he had planned to use the headscarf for himself, he felt Forge needed it more. After all, the young man was far paler than Rhys now. The medical student took the piece of cloth awkwardly and looked at him for guidance. Rhys wrapped it about Forge's head and tied it taut to keep his silver hair hidden. "You and I will stand out in the darkness. Hide your skin when you can."

"Forge, take my shirt," said Beso, maneuvering in the cockpit chair so he could pull his long-sleeve, dark green blouse over his head. Forge slipped into the shirt.

"We'll be back," hummed Rhys once the unit touched down. He flung the hatch door open and leapt onto the muddy ground. It was raining. Why was it always raining? Forge landed beside him, and together they knelt in the mud. "Which way, Ethos?"

"Shift ten degrees to your left. You're half a kilometer from the camp," the AI replied.

Rhys gathered mud, haphazardly smeared some on his hands, face, and neck, and looked out at the forest. Though he knew the mission was dangerous, he couldn't help but feel free once more. The smell of nature, rain, and mud was invigorating; the sound of the raindrops on the surrounding vegetation was a relief from the silence of the colony.

Rifle tucked against his body, Rhys discerned a path and started down it. Every few steps, he paused, listened, and looked. He wished he had remembered night-vision goggles, but that was hindsight. He would have to cope as humans had for the past million years.

It wasn't long before light began to filter through the trees. Clinging to the shadows and vegetation, they crept toward the Brechin camp. When they got closer, Rhys lowered himself into the mud and crawled his way through the low-level, sopping vegetation. Slightly elevated from the rest of the landscape, he peered through the brush at the camp.

"Where is it?" he murmured to Ethos.

"I believe it is on a person," replied Ethos. Rhys tilted his head downward to hear the AI. "It's been moving for the past several hours. I couldn't detect its movement earlier because we were too far away, but now it's apparent."

"What does it look like?"

"I don't know."

"Where is it in the camp?"

"Do you see the airship with the unit number 0-0-1? It's off to your right."

Rhys searched the numerous airships in the camp before finding the corresponding unit number. "There?"

"Yes."

Rhys looked over his shoulder at Forge who was also prone on the earth and then back out at the camp. "You have to give me more information, Ethos. This is going to be quick. I have to know what I'm looking for or what I need to do."

"I told you; I don't know. Just get to Unit 001."

Rhys hissed quietly in frustration, made sure none of the posted sentries were nearby, and then crawled on his hands and knees toward the west end of the camp. Numerous times they were forced to stop and cover themselves as a soldier passed. Though it was the middle of the night and pouring rain, the Brechin forces were on alert, possibly because of the recent jail-break Rhys' crew had carried out.

It took nearly forty-five minutes to reach the other side of the camp despite the mere sixty meters or so they actually had to cross. By the time Rhys finally lowered himself back into the mud just outside the flood light of Unit 001's perimeter, his arm and stomach muscles were burning. He couldn't imagine how Forge was handling the situation.

"It's still there," murmured Ethos as Rhys rested his head on a muddy arm.

Rhys nodded, caught his breath, and then motioned to Forge. The medical student, panting, crawled next to Rhys and lay down in the mud. "It's in there," whispered Rhys, nodding to Unit 001.

"There is someone in there," replied Forge. He lowered his head as a sentry passed.

Rhys glanced at the sentry who was surveying the forest several meters from them and then studied Unit 001. It looked like any of the other covered airships except larger. It was entirely possible that the craft itself could house others within it. Perhaps it held sunboards?

He rested his head once more on his arm and looked at Forge. "I'm moving in. Watch my back." He saw Forge ready his pistol. Rhys shook his head. "No guns. Not yet. The sound will alert the rest of the camp. Combat and physical force only." He looked behind them and motioned to a large tree a few meters back. "Get back there and ready yourself."

Forge nodded and, despite the fear in his eyes, confidently crawled to the tree. The moment he saw the med student straighten himself in the shadows, Rhys shifted his focus to Unit 001.

Like the other airships, the unit was propped on retractable stilts to keep its fans out of the mud. If he could make it under the airship, then it was possible he could crawl on his belly to the aft hatch and enter.

"Ethos?"

"Wait one moment," murmured the AI as it scanned the area and analyzed the movements of the sentries. Rhys pulled his feet under him in preparation; his boots slid in the mud. "Now. Go now."

Rhys scrambled from the mud and bolted for the airship. Spending nearly an hour and a half crawling around in the mud had left his muscles stiff. It was an effort to run and maintain quiet footsteps. Using his momentum, he hit the ground just beside the airship and slid underneath the unit. Mud and grit sprang up into his eyes as he shoved himself underneath the craft.

"Clear," whispered Ethos. Breathing hard, Rhys rolled onto his back, rested his short rifle on his chest, and began to wipe the grit from his eyes. Every part of him was covered in mud and soil. Eyes watering from the constant rubbing, he blinked about in the darkness and then, with some difficulty, rotated onto his stomach to begin the process of crawling to the aft hatch.

Though it was a tight fit—neither Kashim nor Hodge could have made it—Rhys wriggled constantly, shifting his weight between his hips and elbows. Twice, he clunked his head on a low-hanging pipe or piece of metal. When he finally reached the back of the airship, he laid his face on his arm and took a moment to catch his breath.

Ethos vibrated underneath Rhys' bulletproof vest, and Rhys tilted his head down to hear the AI. "The aft hatch," Ethos murmured, "is directly above you. Once you crawl out, there will be four steps into the airship. There is still a body in the ship, but only the one." Rhys took a deep breath in preparation. "Wait for my mark." He crawled to the shadow line where the floodlights on the other side of the unit shone brightly. "Wait..." Ethos murmured. A pair of boots passed before the unit. He listened as the sentry continued, the sound of his footsteps fading into the rain. "You have time. Go."

Rhys wriggled out from under the airship, rolled onto his feet, and sprang onto the metal stairs. The automated door at the top whirred open. Eager to get out of sight, Rhys darted in. The door closed behind him.

Though he stood with his short rifle at the ready, he was not prepared for the sight that greeted him.

He had been right.

Unit 001 was a holding craft—for a jet.

Confused and in awe, he stared at the rear of the small fighter craft. The jet did not appear like anything he had seen on Earth. On the contrary, it was as if it had recently descended from orbit.

To Rhys' trained eyes, the unit was space-capable. Not only did it boast a carbon-fiber body, reinforced wings, and various thermal shields, but engines, of which there were four, along the back. Glancing deeper into the cabin of Unit 001 to make sure its inhabitant had not yet heard his approach, Rhys continued to study the spacecraft.

The cockpit glass, which showcased a one hundred eighty-degree visual field, was also designed using thermal-resistant glass. The word "Anemone" was painted in black along the craft's steel-colored starboard flank. Though the word was in Interstellar Nefegian, Rhys could hardly pronounce it much less understand its meaning. He knelt and searched *Anemone's* underbelly for manufacturer information and details. He didn't find what he was looking for, but he did discover the numerous plasma armaments that crowded the spacecraft's belly. He was certain others were stored in its hull.

Rhys sat back on his heels in thought. This was used for battle, meaning that it had to have been developed before the downfall of Omega

Technologies, the same company that created Ethos. After Omega Technologies was decommissioned, the production of weaponized spacecraft was effectively halted. If what he speculated was true, this unit was well over two hundred years old, probably more. Yet, here it was, in near perfect condition.

Rhys cautiously moved to the front. Just beyond the jet, he found a single occupied bunk. Rifle raised, he crept toward the bed and its sleeping inhabitant. With the light filtering in through the cockpit glass at the front of the airship, he could make out a covered body.

Ethos vibrated to attract Rhys' attention. A dim light erupted from the eyeglass at the top of Ethos' unit to form a misty arrow which pointed at the small table bolted to the floor at the end of the occupied bed. Rifle still directed at the mystery occupant, Rhys shuffled over. The ethereal arrow Ethos had formed shifted to show Rhys text. **OPEN THE DRAWER.**

With another glance at the still figure in the bed, Rhys unlatched the drawer and extended it, using his fingers to muffle the sound of the metal sliding along its grooves.

Forcing himself to breathe slowly, he peered into the drawer. All that was there was a square, black disc no bigger than an egg. Ethos shone text before Rhys' face once more. **GET IT. GO.**

Rhys stuffed the disc deep into his pocket and closed the drawer. The bed's occupant stirred, moving the blankets around him. Rhys froze as silver hair cascaded away from the man's face to reveal his identity.

Trembling, Rhys raised his rifle. His hands were cold and clammy; his heart raced.

Before him lay Gealdir, one of the three Brechin-appointed "white gods" whom he had met months ago at a tribunal conference in Brechin.

RHYS, COME ON, projected Ethos. **NO TIME.**

Knowing the AI was right, Rhys lowered his rifle. He wanted to wake Gealdir at gunpoint and demand answers. He and the other two "white gods," Etion and Rullena, were directly responsible for the fiasco in Brechin. They were responsible for Vinz and Alina's deaths and for everything that had happened that awful night and the days to follow.

RHYS, urged Ethos.

"I'm coming back for you," Rhys muttered, turning on heel. In the shadows of the airship, he strode to the aft hatch.

WAIT, Ethos projected. Rhys strained his ears to hear outside but could only discern the dull roar of the rain. **GO.**

He stepped before the automated door. When it opened, he crept outside and down the stairs. A three-dimensional arrow created by Ethos pointed him into the shadows on the other side of Unit 001. He knelt under one of the enormous fans for a long moment before darting into the merciless light of the flood lamps.

Just as he stepped into the shadows of the forest, he slid to a halt before a Brechin soldier. The man, who was adjusting his pants' fly, startled and then lunged. Rhys swung his rifle onto his shoulder, redirected the man's incoming hands with a powerful thrust, and kneed him. The soldier fumbled slightly, but it was Rhys who doubled over in pain. Instead of striking the man's leg, he had aimed too high and slammed his knee into the soldier's armor.

Uninjured, the man snarled his hands in Rhys' shirt, lifted him clear off the earth, and threw him. A gasp erupted from Rhys' throat as the air was knocked from his lungs. Audibly wheezing, he grabbed for his rifle, but the soldier stomped the weapon into the mud. Still struggling for air, Rhys rotated his hips and swung his uninjured leg at the man. This time he connected with his intended target—the soldier's knee.

The man toppled to the ground with a cry. Rhys snatched his muddy rifle from the ground, whirled on his legs, and fired two shots. The soldier crumpled. Wheezing, Rhys scrambled to his feet and limped into the shadows.

"Quickly," Ethos urged.

"Forge," murmured Rhys, heavily favoring his injured right leg. It hurt too much to stand upright. "Forge." The med student materialized from the shadows, his eyes wide and hands trembling. "Notify Beso. We're leaving."

"Rhys, run," urged Ethos.

Rhys placed weight on his injured knee and stifled a scream. Whimpering, he clenched his shaking fists and attempted to analyze the situation rationally. His knee was broken. He had definitely fractured it. "Forge," he said, motioning to the medical student. Rhys maneuvered Forge to his side and leaned against him. "Go, go."

With the weight taken off his knee, Rhys limped deeper into the forest. Behind them, an alarm began wailing in the Brechin camp. Rhys could feel Forge's entire body quivering.

"Stay focused," said Rhys. "Ethos?"

"Twenty-eight meters," reported the AI. "Twelve soldiers approaching from our rear."

"Shit…" Rhys snarled as crippling pain shot up his leg. Wildly, he glanced over his shoulder at the soldiers entering the tree line. There was no way they were going to make it to the maintenance unit. Rhys released Forge and shoved him. "Go. Get to the unit." Forge stumbled in the underbrush before looking back at him. "Go!"

Several shots reverberated over the roar of the rain. Instinctively, Rhys dropped to the ground. His knee folded under him, and he melted onto the earth, moaning. When he looked up, Forge was gone.

Clenching his jaws, he grabbed his injured leg and dragged it out from under him. Once it was extended, he lay back in the mud and wheezed. He was going to die. He was going to die because he had carelessly attacked without first checking his target. His death was his own fault. He could blame no one else for his carelessness and inexperience.

"Three soldiers… approaching directly behind you," whispered Ethos. Rhys yanked his rifle to his chest and listened. Were those footsteps? Or was that the rain? "Six meters."

Using the tree, Rhys hauled himself upright so he stood on one leg. Calming his mind and body, he clamped his hands around his rifle.

Suddenly, a series of shouts echoed through the forest followed by loud thuds. There was a brief intermission of gunfire and then silence.

"Nine soldiers remaining," reported Ethos. "Maintenance craft is coming in for a landing." As the AI said it, the trees around Rhys began to flail and a muffled roar similar in decibel to the sound of a heavy rainstorm descended upon him. Rhys leaned against the tree for support and squinted through the wind. Though he couldn't discern the maintenance unit, he could hear it and feel it. Recognizing the depowering of the engines, he glanced out at the remaining soldiers, who seemed to be fighting a phantom, and then lurched toward the maintenance unit.

Beso appeared as the side hatch opened. He grabbed Rhys' arm with more force than Rhys thought the man was capable of and whipped him into the unit. Beso peered out at the forest and then ducked back into the cockpit. Momentarily, Forge flew through the hatch door. It closed and the maintenance craft sprang into the air.

Sprawled out on the floor of the unit, Rhys cried out as liftoff jarred his injured knee. Sensing Forge beside him, he rolled his head back and looked at the medical student. The young man had his face buried in his hands; his shoulders heaved as he tried to steady his breathing. His knuckles and elbows had blood on them.

For several long minutes, they sat in silence. When his heart finally began to calm, Rhys struggled to sit and examine his knee. Though his pants' leg seemed intact, it was soaked black with blood and mud. Wincing, he drew the material up to reveal a large, gaping incision where the edge of the soldier's armor had cut into his knee. He could see bone. He took several breaths to steady his trembling hands and gingerly touched the areas around his knee to determine the extent of the damage. Just his fingertips grazing the skin caused him to hiss in agony.

"Was it worth it, Ethos?" he growled.

"That has yet to be determined," came the AI's muffled response.

Rhys looked at Forge who had his knees folded to his chest and face pressed there. Like Forge, Beso also remained quiet. No doubt the man was shaken. Rhys gazed at his injured knee. He should have just grabbed Hodge and Kashim. Ethos' urgent prodding and pushing had made him quick to take action. In hindsight, Hodge, Kashim, Axel, and Jules would have been the ideal team. But he hadn't wanted to include them for fear of them being killed or horribly injured. Better it be just him than his crew. He hoped everyone was still asleep.

Several minutes later, with dexterous hands, Beso maneuvered the maintenance unit into the hangar of Neo-Colony Two. Forge stood without a word, opened the hatch door, and hopped out. Though Rhys wasn't entirely sure, he thought he saw a large red and purple welt along the left side of Forge's face. Beso clambered out of the cockpit and stoically regarded Rhys who was still seated on the floor. Like Alina, he was unreadable. Rhys could determine no emotion from his eyes or facial expression. After a moment, he left.

Rhys struggled to his feet and, limping horribly, made it to the hatch door. It took minutes to simply get down the three steps. Panting, he leaned against the maintenance unit and surveyed his leg once more. In the fluorescent light of the hangar, it looked horrendous. With his bloody pants leg now rolled up to his thigh, he could see that his knee was purple, green, and varying shades of red and pink. The gash over his kneecap bled sluggishly.

He searched the hangar for the water hoses they had used to clean off but found none. They were probably in storage. Realizing that he was alone and would have to care for himself, Rhys gingerly tried putting weight on his knee once more. He took a tentative step before crumpling onto the floor.

Noise on the far side of the hangar caught his attention, and he looked up to find Forge returning with Veran and a stretcher. Mercifully, no one else was with them. Veran motioned for Forge to retrieve something, and the medical student hurried into one of the storage centers. He returned with a rolling hose dolly.

"What happened?" asked Veran, stopping before Rhys. She didn't sound angry, only concerned. The gurney, which obediently followed her, fell still at her side.

"My knee," replied Rhys.

"I can see that." Veran leaned in to study his injury with a scanner. "You've fractured your patella." She straightened herself. Her normally distant eyes were hard and colored in a shade of emotion he couldn't identify. "Now, what happened?"

"I hit a soldier's armor on accident," Rhys muttered.

"And why is my medical student boasting a purple and black face?" she replied angrily.

"He saved my life."

Forge, who joined them with the water hoses, kept his gaze tilted downward.

"Rhys, if you want to endanger yourself and your crew members, then by all means, please do so. But I ask that you keep my subordinates out of your Earthly affairs. I know how reckless you are. I've seen it firsthand."

Instead of arguing with her, Rhys bowed his head. "My apologies. It won't happen again." He truly was sorry. He should have known better than to take people as inexperienced as Forge and Beso into the field. Even with the right training and skill downloads, experience was key.

Veran's harsh gaze did not soften. "Strip."

Rhys unbuckled his vest and did as he was told. Forge sprayed him down before Veran knelt beside him and cut his pants away. Nude, Rhys glared straight ahead. He had more nicks, cuts, scrapes, and bruises than he remembered getting.

Veran dried his arms and legs and then motioned for him to get on the automated gurney. Rhys sat back on the stretcher, defeated. "Where are your crew members?" Veran asked. She started across the hangar; the gurney and Forge followed.

"They don't know." Rhys glanced down at Ethos and the disc which were clenched tightly in his hand and then folded his arm over his eyes.

Veran escorted him to one of the numerous medical rooms and began working on his knee. Forge stood nearby; he did not say anything or offer his assistance. Nearly an hour later, the doctor motioned for the AI-controlled machines around her to back away. She looked to Rhys. "Everything is healed, however, you cannot walk on it for the next twelve hours. Is that understood? The repairs I've made must be allowed to set."

Rhys glanced at his knee. It was wrapped neatly with white gauze and bandages. Forge placed new clothes at the end of the stretcher and left the room.

"Unfortunately, we don't have anything that can be used to support your weight," explained Veran, folding her arms. "Normally, it wouldn't be a problem, what with us being in zero gravity but..."

"That's fine," murmured Rhys, sliding the shirt over his head. Veran checked the machines around her and then slipped from the room. With some difficulty, Rhys dragged on a new pair of gray slacks, gingerly pulling the pants leg over his newly mended knee.

As he lay back on the stretcher, Ethos murmured, "Can I have the disc now? I've been *really* patient."

"Ah, yes. What do you want me to do with it?"

"Insert it," replied Ethos. The paneling along Ethos' bottom rim glided aside to revealing a thin opening.

"Are... you sure?" Rhys studied the disc. "What if it's corrupt or protected? It could destroy you."

"No, it's mine," the AI promptly assured.

"I know it's yours but you can't just put things—"

"No, it *belongs* to me," corrected Ethos.

Cautiously, Rhys slid the disc into the bottom of Ethos and the compartment closed. Ethos' unit began humming loudly, something Rhys had not heard before. "Hey... Ethos." When the AI didn't respond, worry blossomed in Rhys. "Ethos."

"Hold on!" After another ten minutes or so, Rhys inquired after the AI's wellbeing once more. "Not yet," Ethos sighed.

"How long?" asked Rhys.

"I don't know. Go to bed."

Rhys closed his eyes. "Lights off," he murmured in Nefegian. The lights in the room turned off, and Rhys was immersed in complete darkness.

21
THE REAL PROBLEM

"WAIT. AXEL, PLEASE WAIT."

"Move."

Rhys stirred as the voices outside his room permeated the door. He woke just as the lights snapped on and Hodge and Axel barged in. Slow with drowsiness, he was unable to defend himself as Hodge jerked him from the stretcher.

"Stop!" Veran blurted.

Hodge's fist connected with Rhys' left cheekbone, causing Rhys to reel in his bed. Angrily, his friend grabbed a fistful of his hair and pinned him to the mattress. "Did you have fun last night?" Hodge seethed. Rhys squinted at him. The vision in his left eye was starry. "Huh?" Hodge shook him. Though Rhys knew his friend wasn't using his full force, it still hurt. "Why do you think… that you can just go and do whatever you want?" Hodge's face was but a few centimeters from Rhys'. "Huh? Because you're Overseer? Because you're *Rhys Falkrow?*" His friend's grip on Rhys' hair tightened. "You don't have your computer-thing anymore. You are just like the rest of us."

"I know that!" bellowed Rhys, breaking Hodge's grip. "I *gawan* know that!"

"Then act like it," Hodge hissed. He shoved Rhys against the gurney and then withdrew. "I hate how you are sometimes." His friend stalked from the room.

"Next time you do some bullshit like that, we're going to take turns beating you," snarled Axel. He spat on the floor and followed Hodge out.

Only Veran remained. Rhys rubbed his cheek where Hodge had cuffed him and started to get out of bed.

"Stop," ordered Veran. "It hasn't been twelve hours." Frustrated, Rhys flopped back onto the gurney. Veran glanced at the doorway and then joined him. "Can you... explain to me why he hit you? Is it customary on Earth?"

The sudden meekness in her voice made Rhys feel tired. "No. It's not customary. He's angry because he's worried."

"He hit you because he's worried?" Veran tilted her head. "That seems counterintuitive."

"Can you leave me alone, please?"

Veran did a cursory examination of his knee and started for the door. Her path was immediately barred by Kallen, Leo, Andy, and Kashim as they entered. It seemed the crew had split up to find him that morning. Axel and Hodge had been the first to learn of his whereabouts from Forge.

"How are you feeling?" Kallen's voice was flat as she approached him. Rhys edged away from her, but Kallen snatched the collar of his shirt. "You..." Just like Hodge, she shoved him back onto the gurney and glowered at him. "Don't do that again."

"What was the point of going back there?" asked Andy, the most level-headed of his crew. It was the first anyone had said of the actual mission.

Rhys fondled Ethos. "I needed to retrieve something." He showed them the AI. "A disc. Ethos has been reading it for the past few hours." Rhys looked at the AI. "But it hasn't said anything."

"What kind of disc?" asked Leo, his rage deflating.

"I don't know." Rhys paused to collect his thoughts. "I found it with Gealdir at the camp."

"Gealdir?" asked Kallen with a frown.

"One of the three white gods," explained Leo in surprise.

Rhys nodded. "He was one of the ones who indirectly led to Vinz and Alina's deaths... as well as all that followed." He sighed, frustrated. "I could... have killed him. I should have."

"What was he doing with it?"

Bewildered, Rhys shrugged. "He must know it's important. Why else would he have it on his person? I don't know. Maybe he needs it to pilot the spacecraft?"

"You found a spacecraft?" asked Veran from the doorway.

"It's well over two centuries old. I don't know if you know the corporation—Omega Technologies?" Veran nodded. "Although I didn't find a manufacturer's seal, I'm certain it belongs to that company."

"And you're sure it's space-capable?"

"It appeared trans-atmospheric to me."

"Where was it?" prompted Kashim.

"It was in a covered airship," replied Rhys. "Unit 001. That's where Gealdir was as well." He waved Ethos. "That's where the disc was too."

"Excuse me," murmured Veran, slipping from the room. Undoubtedly, she was going to report all that she had just heard to the council. Rhys didn't care.

"Were the other two there?" asked Leo. "Rullena and Etion?"

"No. I didn't see any signs of them."

"They must still be in Brechin," the noble mused. "I don't understand why they would split their power. The three are much stronger when they are together, when seen together. Their influence carries more weight."

"And you've met them before?" asked Kallen.

"Alina, Vinz, and I met them at the tribunal meeting last year." Rhys thought. "They… had some very outlandish opinions about themselves and wanted Alina to join them. They've been completely brainwashed by the higher-ups in Brechin."

"So, they don't understand what they're doing," clarified Andy.

"No. They understand. We debated about the outcome of humanity. They were completely aware and coherent of everything that was happening, but to them… They believe they are gods. They believe in a unified human race."

"Why is that bad?" asked Kallen. "I don't understand."

"Unified through subjugation," Rhys clarified. "They explained to us in great detail why the Pantarak Empire was necessary and how subjugation of every town, port, and people would lead to a unified human race."

Leo sighed. "I can ask my father if he knows anything, but it'll take time for my encrypted letters to reach him. He and my oldest brother have been in Bathsgate in hiding. I don't know where my mother is."

"What I want to know," began Rhys thoughtfully, "is what's going on outside of New Arbroath and Paducah. Word has to have spread. I mean, we started a rebellion in Paducah—on accident—and Brechin knew within two weeks."

"We still don't have a course of action," countered Kashim after a moment of silence.

"What is there to do?" Kallen asked. "We don't have our ship, we don't have weapons or sunboards…"

"I… might be able to offer some guidance," interrupted Ethos.

Rhys swung his legs off the gurney and laid Ethos on his lap. "Go."

"Uh… Brechin isn't your problem. The Pantaraks aren't the problem," said Ethos.

"They're the entire reason why this region is in complete disarray," argued Kallen. "They're the cause of everything."

Ethos fell silent, prompting Rhys to look at his crew members questioningly. "Two-hundred fifty-three years ago, there was a battle," the AI finally said, "between a group of people on Earth and Osiris, an artificial intelligence located on the lunar surface."

"There's… an AI on the moon?" murmured Rhys,

"Yes. Osiris. The AI was named after an ancient god which was believed to have ruled at humanity's inception. Osiris was not only the god of death, but of resurrection. He represented the transition from life to death and death to life."

"What is Osiris' purpose?" asked Rhys. "Why is there an AI on the moon?"

Ethos' response was immediate. "To control humanity."

The medical room fell deathly silent.

Ethos continued. "At the time of the great exodus from Earth, it was believed the planet was doomed. Humans had inadvertently disrupted the magnetic fields of Earth, causing a chain reaction of apocalyptic events. Earth was doomed. It could no longer support human life. Now, obviously, we know that wasn't entirely true since we currently have populations of humanity scattered across the planet. If the planet had ever become totally uninhabitable, all life would have been disappeared. Those who could left Earth. The colonies and space ports on the moon's surface at the time were destroyed, utterly obliterated by war between rivaling factions. The point is," continued Ethos, "the people who once dwelled on the moon left behind an artificial intelligence system which they named Osiris. Its purpose was to monitor Earth for signs of change and possible rehabilitation. That was over two thousand years ago."

"What about the AI controlling humanity?" Rhys prompted.

"Wait," instructed Ethos patiently. "There's more at play here because the AI that was tasked with overseeing Earth began to learn."

"What's the significance of that?" asked Andy, gauging Rhys' reaction.

"Osiris began to evolve. It observed, but it also experimented. That is why Earth is divided into thirty-seven quadrants," replied Ethos. "Each quadrant is its own experiment."

Kashim chuckled darkly. "That's ridiculous."

"*How* though?" asked Leo. "How would an AI be able to hold experiments without its subjects' knowledge?"

"There are no AIs left on Earth that know the planet has been separated," explained Ethos. "In order for an AI to know of Osiris, it had to have been present before or during the exodus. This is why the current models of Pathos nor Logos know nothing of Osiris nor of its boundaries set on Earth. They were created off-planet."

"You were created off-planet as well," mused Rhys.

"I was." Ethos paused as if in thought before continuing. "But my user was brilliant. Not only was he an astrophysicist and engineer, but he became a well-known humanitarian and diplomat here on Earth."

"Well-known..." Rhys glanced at his crew. "Was your user Ramsen Amadorri?"

"Even today his name endures, I see," said Ethos. The AI's voice sounded almost warm. "Yes. My previous user was Ramsen Amadorri." Kallen covered her mouth in shock while Andy and Leo exchanged emotion-loaded looks.

Rhys nodded, a stupid smile on his face. It was all coming together. He knew there had to be more to Vinz's ancestor than The Hallowed *Magris*. His name was too well-known and far-reaching. "His descendent, Vinz Amadorri, was our Overseer," said Rhys. "He built *Themis*."

"Is that so?" Ethos sounded warmed by the knowledge. "Ramsen was extraordinary to say the least. I've incorporated many of his vocal tones and fluctuations into my speech."

"He was from Mereena in the Hyperes Solar System, right?"

"Correct. He crashed-landed with several others in the area that is now known as Brechin. Despite my user's brilliance, it was years before he finally turned his eyes upward and began to study the moon. What he found there both frightened and excited him. Over several months of research and observation, he finally concluded that there were human structures on the moon. He began to make preparations to go into orbit."

Rhys felt his stomach leap. "The trans-atmospheric jet." He glanced at his crew. They were having a much more difficult time connecting the pieces than he was.

"The trans-atmo jets, which we had been shuttling before the crash, were to be used to reach the lunar surface, but..." Ethos imitated a sigh.

"Osiris learned of what Ramsen was planning. It had all of Ramsen's colleagues and workers—even his wife—turn against him. He fled the Brechin area and set out for the outskirts of the Pantarak Empire where he continued his research and created plans to destroy Osiris. He worked for nine years in a laboratory outside of Paducah. He wanted to return to Brechin to try to launch for orbit but... that was nearly impossible. Already, there had been several attempts on his life by soldiers, mercenaries, and assassins."

Rhys' grip on Ethos tightened, and he looked at the others. Ramsen had been tailed by soldiers and mercenaries because he had caused an upset in the balance of the experiment.

"Rhys?" asked Kallen.

"Osiris... is after me," Rhys breathed.

"No," Leo balked. "You infiltrated Brechin and killed the high priest. All of us have warrants out for our arrests."

"But only one of us... has ever been targeted for death," clarified Kashim. "They've only ever sought to kill Rhys, even when they could easily have killed us."

"How? I don't understand." Leo leaned against a nearby machine. "How is an AI on the *gawan* moon controlling people?"

"Osiris does not control people in the sense that it takes over their minds and free will," said Ethos. "It works through the hearts of men. It works through religion, politics, and economics."

"But there has to be a point of contact, right?" asked Andy.

"The three white gods," offered Leo. "Etion, Rullena, and Gealdir."

Rhys lay back and rested his arm over his eyes. "That's why the high priest, Michael, was killed. He had been acting as mediator to Osiris, but after Michael rescued those three, Osiris no longer needed him. That's why... Michael had a bomb inside of him. To keep him silent. If we took him hostage, Osiris needed a way to kill him to keep information from leaking."

"So Michael just ate a bomb of his own accord?" asked Kashim.

"If an omniscient, noncorporeal entity told him to do so, then yeah," replied Rhys. "The AI no longer needed Michael. He was disposable. Osiris had three new vessels with which to lead the Pantarak Empire."

"Ramsen knew Osiris was intentionally trying to rid the quadrant of him," continued Ethos. "On the day of Ramsen's death, one of Ramsen's former colleagues from Mereena entered the laboratory and attempted to wipe my memory per Osiris' orders. I am a learning AI, however, therefore—"

"Information cannot be erased, merely blocked," completed Rhys.

"Correct. A number of blocks were placed in my core to stop anyone else from learning of Osiris, and the upgrade, which Ramsen had been working on for nearly two years, was taken to the capital for safekeeping. Ramsen was murdered and his laboratory destroyed. I was buried in rubble until Otto happened upon me and my new life, so to speak, began."

For a long moment, Rhys lay in silence. When he was calm once more, he sat up. "Does Osiris know where I am right now?"

"Osiris is observing all of Earth. The AI cannot make change immediately. Even if it knew where you were, there is very little it could do instantly."

"But if it looked hard enough, it could find me, couldn't it?" mused Rhys.

"Yes. Fortunately, the AI relies exclusively on humans to carry out its deeds, so action takes time," Ethos explained.

"Before Ramsen was killed, what did he plan to do?" asked Andy. "He carried out research for years in preparation for it. What was his plan?"

"Attack Osiris on the moon and disable it. Ramsen carried out a minor hacking attack on the orbiting satellites, but Osiris was too strong. It nearly destroyed my operating system. It was shortly after that attack that Osiris learned of Ramsen's plans and turned his colleagues against him. That was when he fled Brechin and he began working on the upgrade."

"So, what can you do now that you have the upgrade?" asked Rhys.

"I can resist coded and encrypted attacks by Osiris. Also, most of the blocks around my memories have been removed which allows me to access the information Ramsen was working on."

Rhys fidgeted. He wanted to stand. "I need… to talk to the council."

"Why?" asked Kashim.

"Because this is bigger than all of us."

"Do you really want to involve them?" grumbled Leo.

"You'll endanger anyone who learns of it," Kallen added.

Rhys nodded. "Then who should we tell?"

"No one," asserted Andy.

Rhys sighed. "None of you understand the gravity of the situation."

"We understand that you already have a target on your back," said Kashim. "Do you want your people to also be pursued by Osiris?"

Osiris wasn't going to be stopped by mere Earthlings. Osiris was a creation of his people; it would take his people to destroy it. "I'm going to tell you now—I disagree with all of you," he said, looking between Kallen, Leo, Andy, and Kashim. "Osiris belongs to us. *We* have to be the ones who stop it. We need Neo-Colony Two."

Andy and Kashim exchanged looks while Leo gazed at the floor in thought. It was Kallen who finally spoke. "Rhys… you're leaving us behind. Again."

Rhys' voice was low. "Is that what you think I'm doing?"

"You've left us behind at every turn," asserted Leo. "Why would this be different?"

Rhys looked at Andy. "What would you do? As First Mate, what would you do?" When Andy didn't respond, Rhys shifted his gaze to Kashim. "And you? What would you do?" Frustrated, Rhys slipped from his bed and, balancing on his uninjured leg, said, "How can any of you contradict what I'm saying when you haven't the faintest idea what needs to be done? Stop second-guessing everything that I do or decide. I am Overseer. If you don't like that, then leave. Go back to New Arbroath and work for Joss." Once more, Andy and Kashim exchanged looks. "If you're not leaving, then help me to the council room."

There was a moment of stillness before Leo approached and slipped his shoulder under Rhys' arm. Kallen grabbed Ethos, stuffed the AI into Rhys' pocket, and slid herself under Rhys' other arm. Without another word, they helped him hobble from the room.

22
MOVING FORWARD

RHYS WATCHED VERAN, COMMANDER PURJEY, and the two senior council members as they spoke in silence. Though it had taken less than a minute to share with Veran via the adaptor all that Ethos had told him, the council and Veran had been in silent discussion for nearly fifteen minutes. While the body language of the council was subtle, accustomed to such unremarkable cues, Rhys could decipher the General response. No doubt, Osiris was a threat to Neo-Colony Two.

The door behind Rhys opened to admit *Themis'* entire crew. Even Otto was with them. Rhys leaned heavily on Leo to turn. "What are you doing?" he asked in Aabesh.

"Whatever you're planning, we're coming with you," Andy affirmed. "We've come this far. A computer on the moon… is nothing." Rhys couldn't help but chuckle at the vast understatement. Andy separated himself from the others, joined Rhys at his side, and looked at the council. "What have you decided?"

"This man is…" prompted the elder woman at the end of the table.

"First Mate," answered Veran with a tilt of her head. "He is Rhys Falkrow's next-in-command."

Rhys glanced at Andy and then looked at the council. Commander Walton Purjey sat back in his chair and studied Rhys. "What are you willing to do?"

Before Rhys could respond, Andy answered, "Why don't you tell us what you want from him, and we'll decide."

"Very well," said Walton. He conversed with the others in silence before continuing in Nefegian, "Osiris poses an absolute risk to the advancement of the human race which, as you know intimately, is the goal of Neo-Colony Two as well as Caelestis' other segments here on Earth. Nothing must hinder the progression and development of mankind. Therefore, Osiris must be disabled or destroyed. It has forgone its purpose and usefulness." The commander of Neo-Colony Two stood and folded his arms behind his back. "Therefore, we ask for your help and guidance."

Rhys gravely agreed.

"According to Ethos, there is an underground facility in the city of Brechin, is that correct?"

"Yes, but Ethos is not certain as to what the facility contains."

"Nonsense," interrupted Ethos. "Where there is one trans-atmospheric jet, there are others."

"Falkrow," said the old man seated directly across from Rhys. Rhys forced himself to balance so he could stand straight before the council head. "Do you accept the responsibility of ambassador to Earth and the conditions with which it comes?"

Decision made, Rhys nodded. "I do."

As Commander Purjey spoke via AI with the others, Rhys glanced at Veran whose solemn gaze was set on the table. Although Rhys had an educated guess as to what the plan was, he hoped he was wrong. The darkening expression on Veran's face, however, told him that he was on point.

Walton nodded to conclude the silent conversation and then looked at Rhys. As he opened his mouth to speak, Rhys stopped him. "Commander, might I ask that… whatever it is that you have to say, you say it in Aabesh?"

Commander Purjey glanced at Rhys' crew and then began. Though he spoke in Nefegian, his AI, Logos, translated aloud his words. "Falkrow, Neo-Colony Two asks this of you. Destroy Osiris."

"It's a… joke, right?" asked Hodge. He joined Rhys and Andy. "Osiris is on the moon. The *moon*."

"We are well aware of Osiris' location. Falkrow's task remains the same," replied Walton.

Hodge gaped. "Are… you going to give him… tools or weapons or anything?"

"No," provided Rhys, holding the Council members' gazes. "They aren't."

"What? Why?" asked Andy.

"They charge me with this responsibility because... I'm not a citizen of Caelestis anymore. Any other resident would not be permitted to do what needs to be done."

"You're sending him out weaponless?" barked Hodge, motioning with his arms. "How is he supposed to even make it into Brechin without so much as a *gawan* ship? Why are you people—"

"Hodge," interrupted Rhys. Simmering, his friend fell silent. "I accept the task and will attempt to complete it as best I can." He thought for a moment and then asked, "Will the information I've shared with you concerning Osiris be released into the Core?"

"Yes," replied Walton. "It was added as we spoke."

Rhys glanced at Veran and then limped to the door. Though he could put some weight on his knee, it still ached fiercely.

Once in the hallway and out-of-sight from the council, Rhys leaned heavily against the wall and rubbed his leg. It was still too early to walk on it, but he needed the council to see him exit alone, unhindered by injuries or their prejudice. Aware of his crew's eyes, he looked up at them. "Don't be angry at them."

"Rhys, they're taking from you without giving anything in return," replied Andy. "You don't have the tools, the weapons..."

"I have the people." Knee stiff, he straightened himself.

"We spoke among ourselves, and we swore that whatever happened, we would follow you, but..." Andy frowned.

"Do you remember when Alina and I first arrived on Earth?" He looked at Kallen. "When we were in the town square and Joss tortured that Pantarak man?" He looked at Hodge and Kashim. "Or when we first entered Paducah? Each time, we were pushed to the limit of our comprehension. Humanity no longer made any sense." He gestured toward the closed door. "That is what they are going through but on a much broader scale. They are still living as a secluded colony in the depths of space. What they've seen of Earth through my memories, through Veran's, and now Beso and Forge's... I'm sure it's been quite a shock."

"But without conscience, how can they ask you to do something like this?" asked Kallen. "Don't they ca—"

"The death of the one for the good of the many," interrupted Rhys. "Better for one person to be sacrificed than to allow an entire society be destroyed." The looks of incredulousness and confusion on the faces of his crew members would have been amusing had the situation been less dire. Instead, Rhys nodded. "It takes time, but you'll learn to live by it."

"I... don't want to live by that code," Hodge grumbled.

"Me either," said Leo.

Rhys motioned to Kallen; he leaned against her and started down the hall. "Don't have a choice," he said.

Exhausted from the drama and the lasting effects of his injury, Rhys lay down in his bunk. Otto and Cantia, who had been silent the entire time, returned to the three-dimensional screen with which they had been entertaining themselves while the others gathered around the small table at the front of the room.

Rhys laid his arm over his face and listened.

"How do we know they're just not scared?" asked Hodge, slinging himself into a chair and throwing his feet onto the table. "They're making Rhys do it because they know he'll oblige."

"You're not serious about taking the mission, are you?" asked Leo from the across the room.

"Yes," grumbled Rhys.

"It's *on the moon*," shouted Hodge.

"I know." Rhys sighed. "That's why we need to get to Brechin."

"What about New Arbroath and the Pantarak refugees?" Leo leaned on the table. "Are we just going to leave them behind?"

"We don't have much of a choice," replied Kashim.

"How are we going to get there?" Kallen seated herself cross-legged on the cold floor and looked up at the others. "We're... stuck here."

"Mmm, that's not entirely true," replied Rhys, rolling in his bunk to look at the others. "You forget, I'm a pilot."

"Your people just told us they're not lending any type of support," said Andy. "How do you figure we'll be allowed an aircraft?"

Rhys smirked. Hodge broke into maniacal laughter while Andy smiled and nodded.

"Watch what you say until we leave Neo-Colony Two. If you speak Elali, use it. Otherwise, keep important conversations at a minimal." He shifted to Elali. "We leave after midnight tonight. I need some time to recuperate." Knowing Kallen was the only one in the room who spoke the language, he added, "Use the written language. They don't have the key to the written language yet, though I'm sure they could figure it out if they got a copy of it to study."

He heard her move to her feet. Rhys glanced back as she leaned over the table and began to draw out invisible words with her fingers. The rest of the crew gathered around her and began a silent discussion. Kashim and Jules, the largest of the group, intentionally stood shoulder to shoulder to block the camera's view.

With a deep breath, Rhys rolled toward the wall and slept.

It was past midday when he finally woke. After lying in bed motionless for another ten minutes, he swung his legs onto the floor and examined his knee. When he pushed on it and only a dull pain resonated, he sighed in relief.

Ruffling his hair into place, he blinked about the room and then stood. He was the only one there. Where was everyone? The halls were silent as usual save the distant hum of the generators. The lack of sound and smell squeezed him and made the walls around him seem just a bit narrower. "Ethos?"

"Yes?" came Ethos' muffled voice.

"Where are the others?"

"Outside," replied Ethos. "The hangar is open if you would like to join them."

Rhys hobbled down the hallway to the hangar. He expected to find the engineering staff hard at work flitting from one maintenance unit to the next; instead, he found the department gathered along the open hangar entrance. As Rhys leaned against a crate to catch his breath, Kallen and Hodge broke through the line of silver-haired residents and started across the hangar, talking and laughing. Hodge's eyes settled on Rhys, and he smiled.

"We were just coming to get you," his friend said. "Hungry?"

Rhys glanced at Kallen. "No. We had the food tablets just two days ago."

Hodge turned his back to Rhys and knelt. "Get on."

"No," replied Rhys.

Hodge frowned. "I'm hungry and everything is almost ready. You are standing between me and food. The faster I get you to the food, the quicker I get to eat." With a sigh, Rhys clambered onto Hodge's back. His friend maneuvered his arms around Rhys' injured knee and stood with a soft groan. "You're getting heavy." He shifted Rhys to gain balance and then started back across the hangar at a lope.

Rhys clung to Hodge's neck and grimaced as his friend jarred his knee. "Easy..."

"Sorry." Hodge carried him beyond the line of engineers out into the shockingly brilliant sunlight. Despite feeling as though he had just stepped into an oven, Rhys took a deep breath and closed his eyes. "I felt the same way," murmured Hodge. Another few paces, and they entered the shade of the neighboring trees. Hodge deposited Rhys before his crew which was circled around a small fire pit.

"Hey," greeted Leo. Rhys shambled over to a rock and sat. A soft, warm breeze played across his face, and the scent of nature and of earth swept through his body. Relief overcame him. So easily had he reverted to existing within the confines of the colony. It was simple to remain indoors and not busy oneself with the matters of the outside world. When he finally looked at his crew, he found everyone watching him. To his surprise, Veran was also present and seated close to Axel.

"Please," groaned Hodge, breaking the silence. He stepped around Rhys. "I need food!" His friend snatched a baked fish from the impressively large pile of cooked meat near the fire, withdrew the green spice Kallen had inserted into the fish's belly, and ripped into it like a beast. Taking that as their cue, conversation started up again, and the collection of seafood was quickly passed out.

Despite having consumed a food tablet nearly two days prior, Rhys couldn't wait to taste real food again. Though the variety of fish had been cooked using a spice plant they had found nearby, the meal had very little taste; but he didn't mind. He smiled as Hodge shredded the fish carcass.

"You people keep your stupid pills," Hodge muttered as he tore at the meat. "I love eating too much."

Hearing quiet talking, Rhys glanced at Veran and Axel. "It's fine," Axel whispered, pushing the fish she was holding to her mouth. "Eat." Veran sniffed the filet and scrunched her nose.

"It tastes better than it smells," said Rhys in Nefegian. Veran solidified her confidence and bit into the fish gingerly. When she drew away with nothing but a thin layer of skin, Axel sighed, pulled the morsel from her mouth, and then bit into his fish. He pulled meat from his mouth and passed it to her.

Smiling, Rhys threw Kallen a fond look. She touched his head lovingly and then jerked a strip of filet from the bone of her fish. "Who did the fishing?" he asked.

"We all did," replied Leo.

"With what?"

Kashim nodded to a pile of folded tarps. "We were told they couldn't be destroyed, so we asked to borrow them. Took around two hours to make the catch."

"I've missed food," murmured Cantia.

Rhys motioned over his shoulder. "You're aware we have an audience?"

At least half the crew shrugged. "They haven't said anything," said Andy, throwing a set of bones into the fire pit. "They don't bother us; we won't bother them."

Rhys wiped the sweat on his forehead and took a deep breath. He had missed the things that made him human—sweating, eating, laughing.

Hodge leaned toward Cantia and moved the slack jaw of his fish to mimic speech. "Cantia," he cooed in a high-pitched voice, "won't you kiss me?"

Cantia squealed and shied behind Otto. "Stop!"

"Why don't you like my kind more?" continued Hodge, waggling the fish's stiff tail at her. "I'm so tasty. I just need a kiss."

"Stop. I don't like that." Cantia pushed Otto before her. "Make him stop."

"It's a fish," muttered Otto, his face folded in bewilderment. "The same you've been eating."

"I don't like looking at them though," Cantia whimpered.

"Come on, Cantia," growled Hodge, moving the fish as though it was swimming in the air. When a flake of flesh started to fall off the fish's flank, Hodge tore at it, stuffed the piece into his mouth, and then returned to Rhys' side.

"It's not bad, right?" asked Axel as Veran tentatively nibbled at a filet. She shook her head, but Rhys could tell from her expression that she was lying. "This isn't a real meal. You don't have to force yourself."

Veran leaned toward him and murmured into his shoulder. A slight expression of amusement passed over Axel's face—the first Rhys had seen from the man—before he nodded.

"The fish are the same in this area as our own waters," said Kashim to Jules and Andy. While they discussed the aquatic life, Cantia explained to Otto in plaintive detail why she didn't like to look at fish. Terron and Leo murmured in Nefegian. Rhys was sure they were discussing their family as both seemed intent not to be bothered by outside conversation.

Rhys finally looked at Hodge who was reclining on his hands beside him. His friend met his gaze and smiled knowingly. Peace and togetherness. They had needed this.

"Thank you," Rhys said. The conversation died, and everyone looked at him. "I'm here because of you. Thank you."

Hodge nudged his uninjured leg fondly while the others smiled.

"Ehh…" Otto conscientiously glanced at the others before setting his eyes on Rhys. "Cantia and I are leaving."

Rhys hid his disappointment. "Why is that?"

Otto bit his lip before saying, "I… can't forgive you for leaving me behind."

"Otto, we didn't have—"

Rhys silenced Hodge with a simple gesture. "I understand. Where will you go?"

Otto glanced at Cantia who was staring at the smoldering fire. "We… don't know."

"May I make a suggestion?" Rhys asked. Otto looked at him in mild surprise. Obviously, he had thought Rhys was going to put up more of a fight. "Stay here at Neo-Colony Two. You would be safe. The both of you."

"Could we?" murmured Otto.

Veran tilted her head and then nodded. "The colony agrees. It would be acceptable for you two to stay."

Rhys shifted to Interstellar Nefegian. "Please inform the proper people of his psychological and emotional needs."

"I'll personally tend to him," replied Veran.

Rhys glanced at Axel. He had been sure Veran was going to try to stay with Axel, but perhaps he was wrong. "You will be welcomed here for as long as need be," said Rhys. Otto, eyes turned downward, nodded. "Otto." The teen looked at him. "You and Cantia will always be a part of our crew, just, your paths are departing from ours." Rhys grinned. "They'll converge again."

Otto nodded but didn't say anything else.

"I'll see what I can do to help from here," said Cantia, gazing at Rhys.

"You're sure?" asked Hodge.

Cantia clasped Otto's hand firmly. "I'm very sure."

Rhys peered at Leo who wore a frown. "Leo?"

"Is there any way… you could postpone your departure?" Leo asked Otto. "If we return to our ships—assuming our ships are still in New Arbroath—we will need every pair of hands we have to make it to Brechin." Leo's reasoning was sound. He was right. They were going to be undermanned once more.

"I… don't ever want to step foot on that ship again," murmured Otto.

Leo opened his mouth to argue, but Rhys stopped him with a pointed look. "That's fine," Rhys said. "Stay here. I'm sure Veran will find both of you work within the colony."

Otto bowed his head to hide his eyes which had grown moist. "Thank you."

23
ANNOUNCEMENT

FOR THE NEXT TWO HOURS, they lounged in the shade of the trees and joked raucously among themselves. When the conversation turned solemn, Hodge or Leo redirected everyone's attention. The afternoon before their departure for New Arbroath was going to be a happy one. Though Rhys wanted to discuss their plans, Veran's presence coupled with Hodge and Leo's efforts kept him from doing so.

Sprawled out in the shade, Rhys watched his crew with a fond heart—but none more so than Kallen as she played a chance game with Hodge and Leo. It had been such a long time since he had seen her smile and laugh. Their lives had been clouded with such misery that he had almost forgotten her beauty and the way with which she brought everyone together. Undoubtedly, Hodge was the jester of the crew, but Kallen was the thread that bound them together. When there was trouble, her presence softened angry hearts; when there were disagreements, she was the voice of reason.

Vinz may have picked her from the docks in New Arbroath and trained her out of sympathy, but he had kept her for other reasons. Despite her mechanical expertise and willingness to do anything the men of the crew did, she was still a woman. She saw the world differently, she perceived problems in a different light.

Hodge made a smug comment, causing Kallen to laugh and then smack his arm. When she sat back, she absent-mindedly placed her hand on her abdomen and continued to talk. Rhys saw a strange expression pass over Terron's face. Though it was the first time Rhys had seen Kallen do it, the action itself was natural. Terron seemed to understand the significance of the gesture and looked at Rhys, questioningly.

Realizing that Kallen was eventually going to start showing her pregnancy, he grinned and nodded. Terron's face dropped first into surprise before a wide smile burst through his shock.

"What?" asked Hodge. "What's that look for?" Terron tried to recover, but it was too late. Hodge leaned back on his hands to look at Rhys. "What?"

Rhys nodded to Kallen. "Go on."

Everyone fell silent, and all eyes turned to her. "Eh…" She blushed some. "I'm pregnant."

"What?" Hodge leapt at her. Rhys' friend tangled himself around Kallen and rubbed his scruffy face against hers. "Ohhh Kallen!"

"Really?" asked Kashim looked between them.

"Yes," replied Rhys. Cantia flitted to Kallen and took her hand while Hodge continued to dote on her. Terron strode over to Rhys and took his arm firmly, laughing; Leo was by his side. Kashim, who also congratulated Rhys with a rough, enveloping handshake, was followed by Axel.

"Congratulations," murmured the former soldier. Though he wasn't smiling like the others, the softness in his voice was noticeable. Otto joined the others to bid well wishes to Kallen, leaving Veran alone.

Rhys pulled himself up, balanced on his good leg, and looked at the Director of Medicine who seemed caught off guard by the sudden news. Though she, of course, had known since their arrival at Neo-Colony Two, the crew's reaction to the news was bewildering. For a long moment, she tilted her head and watched as Hodge, Cantia, and Terron took turns touching Kallen's still flat abdomen.

Axel returned to his seat beside Veran and nudged her. She glanced at him before her eyes met Rhys'. "Congratulations," she offered in Nefegian.

The group remained around the smoldering fire pit late into the afternoon. Twice, they wandered down to the sandy and rock-encrusted beach, played in the water, and swam before returning to lounge in the afternoon shade.

"Let's check your knee," said Veran. Rhys, who had spent his time at the beach gently working his recuperating leg in the water, followed her toward the hangar. The engineers, who had long since lost interest in the activities of the Earthlings, were scattered about working in silence.

With a slight limp, Rhys trailed behind Veran through the colony hallways into an open medical room. Though his legs and feet were coated in a mild layer of sand and dirt, Veran didn't seem to mind. She motioned for him to lie on a gurney and began preparing a scanner.

"Your limp has become less noticeable." She turned to him and held the three-dimensional scanner over his knee. Together, they studied the healing wound. "I set the fracture and repaired the bone yesterday. Despite no longer having an AI, your body is still capable of using biosynthetic materials to repair and heal itself."

"So it would seem," replied Rhys. He studied the three-dimensional image for a while longer. "How long do you estimate before I can run and fight?"

"Those are two very different things," Veran asserted. "You'll be able to run perhaps by tomorrow, but using your knee in combat... I wouldn't recommend doing that for another few days. Although the bone is repaired, it's fragile. Anything could fracture it again during this period." She set the scanner aside and looked at him. "Why? Are you planning to do both?"

Rhys swung off the gurney. "No, but it's been my experience that when you're down, when you can no longer get up, that's when the worst happens." He stood, assessed his balance, and then looked at Veran, "Thank you for all your help. I don't suppose you'll be coming with us?"

A shadow of doubt passed over Veran's face. "I had considered it, but I'm the Director of Medicine for the entire colony."

"And... Axel?"

Veran looked at him in surprise.

Rhys smiled. "I had just thought that you would be coming with us because of Axel. You two seem close."

"Is... it so obvious?" she whispered. Rhys couldn't help but chuckle at the sudden worry in her voice. "What?"

"When was the last time you connected to the Core?" he whispered.

Veran glanced at the open door and then said, "Two days. Tonight, will be the third."

"Ah." Rhys nodded. "I thought I noticed a change."

"Actually, I'm not the only one. Forge and Beso haven't connected to the Core either."

"Do you know why?" asked Rhys.

"I suspect it has to do with you," the doctor replied. "You should ask them yourself. I... don't feel like it's my place to know what's going on in their minds anymore."

Rhys nodded and started for the door. A thought occurred to him, and he looked back at Veran. "You should be aware, the Core controls hormonal levels for all its residents. If you haven't been connecting to the Core, there's a good chance you'll start menstruating soon."

"How do you know that?"

Rhys smiled grimly. "Alina." He waved to her and limped down the hallway. Once back in the hangar, he paused in the entryway to watch as the multitude of engineers went about their work. What they had to upkeep since the colony was no longer in space, Rhys didn't know, but it seemed Commander Purjey was not having them sit idle.

Spotting Beso three maintenance units down, he made his way to the engineer. "Hey," he greeted in Aabesh. Beso, who had been staring blankly at the open electrical panel of the maintenance unit, glanced at Rhys. "Recalculating the required lift and drag for Earth's atmosphere?"

"Yes," replied the engineer, returning his gaze to the unit.

"I heard you don't connect to the Core anymore." Beso turned on him swiftly, his eyes searching the immediate area from prying ears. "No one's around. I already checked," assured Rhys.

Beso studied him. "Who told you?"

Rhys leaned against the maintenance unit. "Forge hasn't either."

The stiff expression on Beso's face changed. "He hasn't?"

Rhys shook his head. Forge was from a different department; he was Veran's responsibility. Beso belonged to the engineering department. There was no way for him to know about Forge's Core activities. "You're not alone."

Beso considered him, his blue eyes searching Rhys. What he was thinking, Rhys had no way of knowing. He had to assume, because Beso was a Logos-user, his thought processes were similar to Alina's. If he followed that line of speculation, that would mean Beso was contemplating a course of action—and Rhys knew what it was.

"Think about it," Rhys bid him under his breath.

"About what?" replied Beso just as softly.

"You know."

Beso crossed the hangar without another look. Rhys watched his colleague and then made to return to the outdoor festivities.

"Rhys Falkrow."

Attempting to keep disdain from his face, Rhys turned to meet his father. Dressed in the pale-yellow blouse of leadership, Doctor Falkrow didn't appear threatening, but Rhys knew better. "What?" Though he had managed to keep his face void of emotion, he couldn't control the spite in his voice.

"May I have a word with you?"

Doctor Falkrow motioned, and Rhys followed him to the other side of the maintenance units where they were hidden from the rest of the hangar. "What do you want?"

Doctor Falkrow smiled ruefully. "I wanted to speak with you about Alina." His father reached through the distance between them and laid a hand on Rhys' shoulder.

Rhys very nearly jerked away. Never on Neo-Colony Two or Caelestis did anyone touch another; it was socially taboo. But some distant voice in him wondered if his father was perhaps trying to make amends. The light smile painted on Doctor Falkrow's face transformed to a murderous glower.

Before Rhys could pull away, a mighty shock resonated through his body, seizing his muscles. His mind dimmed and flitted the line between waking and unconsciousness. Distantly, he felt his body collapse in a pile. A sharp pain blossomed like a bloody flower along the back of his head where his skull connected with the hangar floor. It took his entire being to force air into his lungs.

Suddenly, a distant siren began screaming and Ethos' voice wailed something he couldn't comprehend.

Momentarily, Rhys blacked out. How long he was unconscious, he didn't know. What had happened during that time, he didn't know. It was as if the world had left him behind.

When he stirred and willed his eyes to open, he found a most peculiar scene playing out before him. Kallen, Otto, and Cantia were around him, their fierce gazes fixed elsewhere. Veran sat cradling his head. Moaning, Rhys sat up and blinked. His crew and half a dozen colony engineers, including Beso, stood protectively before him. He could hear Hodge and Leo yelling, but bodies blocked his view.

"Hey," murmured Kallen.

Confused, Rhys looked back at her. "What happened?"

Kallen nodded to the barrier of people before him. "Your father attacked you."

"Ah," was all Rhys managed. He glanced at the crimson blouse Veran held in her hand. She had taken Otto's clothes to stem the bloody wound. Gingerly, he touched the side of his head. Though it seemed the bleeding had stopped, it was tender and raw. Stiffly, he moved to his knees and, with Kallen's help, brought his feet under him.

The sudden scuffling of a fight breaking out sent adrenaline skittering through Rhys' body, clearing his cloudy head. He pushed Kallen and Veran away and staggered through the group of people. The engineers stepped aside, their eyes flitting to the crimson hair matted on the side of his head. When Rhys reached Andy, he grabbed hold of his First Mate for balance and looked on at the fight.

He didn't expect to find Caelestis citizens in the mix, yet there they were, seven of them including his father, fighting with Hodge, Leo, Kashim, Jules, Axel, and Terron. Despite their slim physiques and lack of muscles, the combat downloads of the residents of Neo-Colony Two were keeping his crew from gaining the upper hand.

While Hodge and Leo grappled, fought, and rolled on the floor with Doctor Falkrow and two of his subordinates, the others fought one-on-one.

Rhys glanced at Andy who had remained out of the fight, no doubt to act as a backup or to defend Kallen, Veran, Otto, and Cantia. Andy was tracking the brawls, silently determining if he needed to lend assistance or step in. Only when Terron hit the floor hard and didn't get back up did Andy leave Rhys' side and dart into the melee.

Rhys had no desire to fight. It was ridiculous. They needed to combine their strengths to defeat Brechin and Osiris.

Hodge expertly rolled one of Doctor Falkrow's subordinates with a grappling move, sending the older man tumbling toward Rhys. Before the man could spring back to his feet, Rhys grabbed his shirt collar and jerked him back to the ground. "Enough!" he shouted in Aabesh. He repeated himself in Nefegian.

Kashim and Andy stopped what they were doing and went to Terron who was least skilled in combat. Hodge, Jules, Axel, and Leo however continued.

"Don't you move," Rhys ordered his father's subordinate. To his surprise, the older man sat back on his hands and fell motionless. Rhys stepped around him and approached Hodge who had his leg curled around Doctor Falkrow in a grappling move and was struggling to snatch the doctor's arm to finish the hold. The way his father flagged, Rhys knew that the shock he had delivered prior to the fight had left him weak.

Leo crossed Rhys' path trying to escape his pursuing attackers. Rhys seized Leo's arm and jerked him aside, causing him to stumble out of the fray.

"Enough!" Rhys shouted once more. He motioned to Kashim who turned to intercept Jules. Andy managed to grab hold of Axel and drag him away from the fight. "Hodge!" barked Rhys. Hodge, who had finally captured the doctor's arm, rolled, and pressed Doctor Falkrow into the cold floor. Panting and mop of hair askew, Hodge peered up at Rhys. "Enough. Let him go."

"He just tried to kill you," snapped Hodge. His lip bled sluggishly, and he had scrapes and bruises on his face. Rhys' friend held his gaze for a long moment and then, groaning in disappointment, released Doctor Falkrow. Hodge pushed himself to his feet and pointed at Rhys' father. "You just stay down."

Rhys' ragged crew gathered around him, wheezing and nursing injuries. While the doctor's subordinates remained on the floor, Rhys' father struggled to stand.

"I don't care if you're from Earth, if you're from Caelestis, if you're brown, white, purple, or green," said Rhys. "We have more important things to do than to quarrel amongst ourselves! There is an AI on the moon controlling Earth. Does that not bother anyone?" Though the question was meant primarily for his father and his subordinates, Rhys looked at his crew to make it seem as though he were speaking to everyone. "Again and again, we've seen what hatred can do. Just because we don't agree on ideas doesn't mean we can't work together." Rhys turned to his father. "You either support our mission or you shut up. I'm tired of your accusatory and ignorant comments." He looked at the doctor's subordinates and switched to Nefegian. "If you're going to disconnect from the Core, learn to think for yourselves. Don't blindly follow orders. Why do you think that just because Doctor Falkrow holds a superior title that his thoughts are more important? You're your own people. Have some dignity, damn it."

Doctor Falkrow straightened himself and glared at Rhys.

"Get out of here. I'm tired of looking at your face," muttered Rhys. He switched to Aabesh so his crew could understand him. "Know that next time, I won't stop Hodge or any of the others from doing more damage."

Quivering with anger, Doctor Falkrow whirled unsteadily on his heel and strode from the hangar. His subordinates trailed after him.

"You should have let me have him," Hodge muttered.

Though Rhys was inclined to agree, he shook his head. "We have other things to do." With a sigh, he turned to the Neo-Colony Two engineers who stood silently nearby.

Hodge gingerly touched his busted lip. "They were already pulling the doctor off of you when we got here."

Rhys looked his colleagues over before his gaze rested on Beso. "Thank you."

Without acknowledging his gratitude, Beso walked away; the others followed. An argument breaking out on Caelestis was unheard of, much less a physical fight. He couldn't believe his father had managed to persuade others to follow him. He couldn't believe his engineering colleagues had thought to intervene.

"What's wrong with them?" asked Axel.

"They've never seen a fight before," replied Rhys. "How else should they react?"

24
MIDNIGHT EXPEDITION HOME

"RHYS," WHISPERED ETHOS. IT WAS nearing midnight.

"Hmm?" Rhys rolled over and peered across the room at the other bunks. Despite the darkness, he could clearly make out members of his crew sitting up in bed.

In Elali, Ethos said in an almost indiscernible murmur, "I have brought your board to Neo-Colony Two. It's outside."

Rhys swung his legs out of bed and stretched his knee. When he felt no pain, he stood and motioned to the others. Once everyone was ready, he walked to the door, opened it, and checked the hallway. "Quick to move," he murmured over his shoulder. "Get to the hangar."

He stepped aside to allow his crew to pass. After Leo and Terron, the last in their line, jogged by, Rhys looked back into the dark room. Cantia and Otto stood near the bunks, hands intertwined.

"We'll be back," said Rhys.

"We'll be waiting," Cantia replied with a smile.

Rhys caught up with the others just inside the hangar door. Beso, Forge, and another engineer stood nearby. Rhys didn't ask questions when he saw them; he didn't need to. Instead, he started across the hangar. "Which one?"

Beso fell into step with him. "That one."

With practiced ease, Rhys stepped into the unit through the hatch and climbed over the seats into the cockpit; Beso clambered in after him. While they prepped the maintenance unit for launch, Rhys' crew and new members piled in behind them. Once the side hatch was closed, Andy said, "Clear."

"Roger," replied Rhys. He switched to Nefegian. "Opening hangar door."

"Hangar, door open," said Beso a moment later.

"Rhys, your board," called Ethos.

Rhys motioned over his shoulder. "Hodge, the door." He heard his friend reopen the hatch. A moment later, they pulled the board into the maintenance unit. "Ethos, shut it off."

"Hatch closed," reported Kashim.

"Main thrusters, online. Secondary thrusters, online." Rhys passed his hands expertly over an array of illuminated switches and buttons. "All systems nominal."

"Engaging thrusters."

The maintenance unit began to hum.

"Rotating twenty-eight degrees to starboard," said Rhys, shifting the unit to face the hangar entrance. "Course set. Preparing to launch."

Beso leaned forward, examined the digital gauges, and then announced, "All clear. Launch."

"Launching."

Rhys nudged the accelerator forward until the unit moved at a steady clip through the hangar.

"Incoming message from control," said Beso suddenly. "They're ordering the unit to be returned to its station." Rhys pushed the accelerator harder. "They're going to override the maintenance unit AI."

"Stop them," ordered Rhys.

Beso sat back in his seat and closed his eyes to better focus.

"What's wrong?" came Hodge's voice from behind the cockpit.

"Rhys, they're closing the hangar door," Beso reported.

"Override the hangar AI," snapped Rhys. Jaws clenched, he slammed the accelerator forward, causing the unit to shudder and then roar.

"Got it!" exclaimed Beso, opening his eyes and flinging his hands back onto the cockpit controls.

The moment they left the light of the hangar, Rhys pulled back on the accelerator and goosed the thrusters so the maintenance unit leapt lithely into the nighttime sky.

"Setting course." Beso checked the instruments to his right.

Rhys withdrew Ethos from his pocket. "Where was the board before you brought it here?"

"In the Brechin camp," replied Ethos.

"Do you have any idea where *Themis* and *Grisle* are?"

"I can run a scan of the area, but it will have to be done once we're closer," replied Ethos.

"The moment we cross back into our quadrant, start searching for the ships. Beso, anything on radar?"

"No, nothing."

"Ethos, estimated time of arrival?"

"In nine minutes," replied Ethos.

Rhys took a calming breath, engaged the autopilot, and relaxed. Everyone in the unit fell silent.

The next chapter was beginning. Whatever awaited them, whatever was to become of them, they were going to find out. The real battle started now.

"What's your name?" asked Rhys over his shoulder.

The second engineer, a middle-aged man of perhaps forty-five with a sharp nose, replied, "Zain Alatheia." He had a deeper voice than Rhys expected. "Department of Engineering. I was the Deputy Director of Propulsion and Nuclear Sciences."

"In Aabesh," said Hodge.

Zain repeated himself in the native tongue.

Hodge scoffed. "And you? I've seen you in the medical rooms before."

"Forge Klick," replied Forge. Hodge laughed. "What?"

"Hodge, don't," Kallen half-heartedly admonished.

"You do medicine, Flick?" asked Hodge.

"Flick?" Rhys could hear the confusion in Forge's voice.

"Hodge, leave him alone," groaned Andy. "This is stressful enough."

There was movement and suddenly Hodge's face peered between the cockpit seats. Rhys glanced at him as he studied the instruments, gauges, and switches. His friend screwed his eyes in an attempt to see out the cockpit glass and then looked at Rhys. "How do you know where we're going? What if we run into something?"

"We're not going to run into anything," Beso stoically assured.

"How do you *know*? You can't see out."

"The instruments." Rhys motioned to the glowing digital instruments and maps. "We're fine."

"So… who's flying this thing?" queried Leo, joining Hodge.

"We both are," replied Rhys. "But I'm relying heavily on Beso because his Logos has nearly full control of the unit." Hodge nodded and sat back.

"Rhys, four minutes," said Ethos. "We've crossed into Quadrant Six."

"Anything?"

"Our ships aren't in New Arbroath," replied the AI. "That much is certain. Also, the Brechin navy has arrived."

"But our ships aren't there?"

"Correct."

"Beso, Forge, Zain—open all AI scanners and sensors. Search for two seafaring ships within a fifteen-kilometer radius."

"Over seventeen points of contact have been found," reported Beso. "Can you be more specific?"

"Two minutes forty seconds until arrival," Ethos chimed.

Not for the first time, Rhys thought to himself that everything would be so much easier if he had Pathos. Growling, he murmured, "Engaging colloid shield."

Beso ran his hand over several switches. "Colloid shield coverage at seventy percent and increasing."

"Decelerating," announced Rhys. As he slowed the unit to ninety kilometers per hour, he beckoned Ethos to project a radar map of the area. Holding the AI before his face, he studied the topographical three-dimensional map and its occupants. "Kashim, Andy, Axel." All three peered into the cockpit. Rhys pointed to the layout of New Arbroath. "We're approaching from the northeast, here. This is the bay area and New Arbroath." He motioned to the fifteen or so tiny red dots glowing along the coast.

"Brechin naval ships," Axel asserted. "They're using a specialized formation that allows for control of the area's land and water. See? They've cut off all routes to the fishing waters along the northeastern and eastern coasts."

"Decelerating to fifty kilometers per hour," murmured Beso. "Colloid shield holding at ninety-nine percent."

"What does the Brechin military do with captured ships?" asked Rhys.

Axel shrugged. "It depends. Sometimes they scavenge and then scuttle them. Sometimes they commandeer them."

"Ethos, is there any way to identify *Themis*?" asked Andy.

"Not in the mess that's currently before New Arbroath. I just know that our ships are not where we left them," the AI replied.

Rhys studied the glowing map for a long moment before saying, "Ethos, can you zoom out? Can we get a wider view?"

The map hovering above Ethos shifted to reveal two ships farther out at sea. Rhys looked back at his crew. "You think that's them?" Andy mused.

"Let's go look." He showed Beso, and his colleague set a new course. Out of politeness, Rhys asked Beso, "You have this?" Of course, Beso nodded. Rhys expertly climbed over the high cockpit chairs. "Weapons armed. We're taking our ships back." Hodge passed the resonance cutters; Leo gave him a short rifle. "Kallen, Terron, stay behind. Forge, Zain, provide air support."

"Why only them?" asked Kallen.

"Can you see in the dark?" Rhys expelled the magazine in his short rifle, took count of his ammunition, and then looked at his crew in the dim light. "The radar equipment on *Themis*, although updated, is not sophisticated enough to track this unit. Fight smart."

"How are we getting down to the ships?" asked Leo.

"This unit hovers." Rhys motioned to Axel. "Divide the teams."

"Hodge, Kashim, and I will descend first." Axel thought, looking about the cramped cabin. "Rhys, Leo, and Jules will follow. If anything happens, Andy, Zain, Flick, and Terron will follow."

"What about me?" asked Kallen hotly.

"Eh…" Axel glanced at Rhys. "Stay with the pilot-guy."

"I'll follow with Andy if need be," she replied.

"Am I being called 'Flick' now?" Forge interjected.

"On approach," reported Beso from the cockpit. "Fifteen meters."

"Nineteen liretems," Rhys quickly translated. Kashim, Hodge, and Axel moved to the side hatch. "Ethos, confirm that it's *Themis* and *Grisle*."

There was a momentary pause before Ethos replied, "Confirmed."

The side hatch of the maintenance unit slid open to reveal choppy waters and a sky lit by a half-moon. "Preparing for alignment." Axel leaned out. "Aligned!" called Beso. "Descending. Hovering altitude, one and a half meters. Ready for deployment."

Axel dropped into the darkness. Rhys heard him land. Kashim and Hodge also disappeared. Rhys moved into the open doorway and looked outside. Never before had he felt so much relief from seeing *Themis*. In silence, he watched as Hodge, Kashim, and Axel spread themselves across the deck so they weren't grouped together.

"That marks fifteen seconds," said Beso. Rhys glanced at Leo and Jules on either side of him and then leapt from the maintenance unit. Though a twinge of pain rattled his recently healed knee upon landing, it remained steady. Rifle at the ready, Rhys planted himself near the central mast and knelt on the deck. Jules and Leo positioned themselves farther along the stern.

246

Axel crawled atop the bridge, checked the area there, and then scanned the ladder and staircase outside the bridge below. After a moment, he motioned to them. Kashim slid down the ladder; Hodge followed.

As Axel moved to join them, Rhys darted across the deck and took up watch atop the bridge. He peered down at the platform just outside the bridge door. Hodge, Kashim, and Axel motioned to one another before Axel slowly entered.

"Don't move! Don't move!" Axel immediately shouted. Rhys startled as the silence was shattered. Quickly, he slid down the ladder, twisted his body so he remained outside of the doorway, and readied his rifle. "Get on the ground."

"Wait, wait," rasped Hodge. "Wait, Axel."

Rhys looked into *Themis'* bridge to find Patrin, the medical assistant from Maliyansa, at the helm, his hands held in the air and eyes wide with fright. "Patrin?" asked Rhys.

Upon spotting a familiar face, Patrin wheezed audibly in relief. He signed Rhys' name in obvious elation.

"Who else is on the ship?" Rhys looked about the bridge. His heart hurt with joy. It smelled of old mold, water, and freedom—just as it always had.

Patrin signed Kahleela's name, one of only a handful of words Rhys had learned while working with the young man.

As if signing her name magically called her, Leela entered the bridge, a rifle shoved into her shoulder. The moment she saw Rhys, the ferocity in her gaze left her and she nearly dropped her weapon. "Oh!" she cried, flinging her arms around him as if he were her son. "Oh, child. You scared me!"

Rhys clapped her shoulder. "What are you doing here?"

"The Brechin forces were going to take your ships. We snuck them out," replied Leela. She looked at the others. "Is this everyone?"

"No." Rhys withdrew from her embrace. "Hodge, come with me. Axel, secure the ship. Kashim, contact *Grisle* and find out who's there." He and Hodge climbed the ladder back to the upper deck where the others waited. "Forge, contact Beso. Tell him to analyze the width of the unit to determine if he can land on *Themis'* stern." As Forge, Zain, and Beso worked to land the maintenance unit, Rhys updated the others.

After some discussion and extensive maneuvering, Beso ended up landing on *Grisle* which had a wider deck unhindered by double masts. Over the radio, Rhys explained to Reza and, to his dismay, Tessa who

Beso was, his background, and what all he had accomplished since their reunion. Knowing Reza would have everything under control, Rhys set down the radio in relief.

While Andy took the helm—he was all too delighted to be back home—Rhys met with his crew in the galley. He couldn't help but pause in the doorway. Instead of the normal five or six members, he now had ten pairs of eyes gazing at him.

"Uh, Patrin and Khaleela," he said. Introductions were in order. "This is Forge and Zain. Both are from my colony. At their own peril, they have decided to join us. Forge—Leela and Patrin both do medicine, like you." Forge attempted an awkward smile.

"It's a pleasure to meet you Zain. Forge." Leela offered her hand to Forge who was nearest. Forge glanced at Rhys for guidance before taking Leela's hand. She was the first ebony-skinned human he had ever met. Of course, he was put off by her appearance.

"There are ten people here," said Rhys. "We have to split us evenly between the two ships. Who's going over to *Grisle*?"

"Not me!" Hodge sang.

"Not Hodge," confirmed Rhys, smiling. "Those people are… Terron, Jules, Zain, Reza, Beso, Khaleela, and Patrin."

"And… Tessa?" asked Kashim. "What do you want to do about her?"

"I'm going to be having a conversation with her in the morning," replied Rhys. He looked to Jules and Terron. "Until then, keep her in check."

Terron motioned to Rhys. "Am I still… qualified to be Overseer?"

Rhys' response was immediate. "Yes. You may have Zain and Beso with you, but that doesn't mean they know how to lead." Terron nodded. Rhys had read his mind. "Use them as you would me." Leo nudged his brother playfully.

25
THEMIS AS USUAL

RHYS WOKE SHORTLY AFTER DAWN and stared up at the ceiling of his cabin. He breathed in the familiar scent and looked at Kallen who was sprawled out beside him in a breastband and shorts. He touched her bare abdomen gingerly and kissed her cheek before clambering out of bed. Dressed in nothing but a pair of cutoffs, he staggered down the hallway to the bridge, glancing in the crew's cabin as he passed.

Forge, Axel, and Leo still slept. Rhys gazed at Forge, a small smile on his face. On the colony, Caelestis residents slept motionlessly on their backs all night so as to remain connected to the Core. Released from such constraints, Forge lay haphazardly across his bed, an arm and a leg dangling from his low-level bunk and his body contorted.

"Hey," said Hodge, meandering from the galley. From the way he swaggered, Rhys knew he had been eating. "All quiet?" He threw a chilled fruit to Rhys who caught it in midair.

"As far as I know."

"Come to the upper deck with me?"

"Yeah. Andy on the bridge?"

"I'm going to relieve him here in a while. Kashim's on the stern fishing."

Together, they went to the bridge, spoke briefly with the First Mate, and then climbed the ladder to the upper deck. As Rhys attempted to break the skin of the frozen fruit, they ambled across the deck to where Kashim sat with a fishing rod. He had already caught nearly a dozen fish which were laid out in the shade of the second mast.

Hodge leaned against the deck railing and looked out at the sea. Kashim glanced at Rhys before saying, "Heard from Terron a while ago. Everyone over there is fine. There were some problems with Beso and Zain sleeping, but he convinced them they were safe."

Having finally broken the frozen skin, Rhys tore into the flesh of the pink fruit in his hand. "Good."

"Did you know they would be coming with us?"

"I wasn't certain, but I saw the signs," Rhys replied.

"We're going to have to train them like we did you," Hodge muttered.

"It's a long way to Brechin."

"Speaking of which," said Kashim, "we're not going straight there, are we?"

"No, we'll be stopping at Firekli to resupply." Rhys licked the pit of the fruit and then tossed it overboard. "We wouldn't make it to Brechin."

"So that means we're..." Hodge thought for a moment. "We're almost five weeks out from Firekli."

Rhys sighed. "Yeah."

"I checked inventory earlier," said Kashim. "Hence the reason why I'm fishing. Half of us onboard must eat a substantial meal daily."

Rhys considered Kashim's calculations and frowned. "Four? It's me, Forge, and Leo. Who's the fourth?"

"Kallen," said Hodge. "It's not absolutely necessary for her to eat daily, but it wouldn't hurt. Besides, once she's further along, she's going to start getting really hungry." The tenderness in his voice made Rhys smile. "You just *had* to have sex..."

Rhys reached over Kashim's head and punched his friend's shoulder.

"In all seriousness though," said Kashim, "she's a liability now, Rhys."

"She can still work," Rhys countered.

Hodge shook his head. "Having a pregnant woman around changes a man. It messes with your head." Hodge sighed. "I've felt it, and I'm not even the *gawan* father."

"We've all felt it." Kashim reeled his line in and cast it once more. "She isn't showing yet, so the feeling isn't as strong, but having a pregnant woman onboard is not going to end well. Men act weird around pregnant women."

They were right, of course. Rhys had purposefully avoided thinking of the baby. It was easy right now because Kallen wasn't showing. He just had to pretend she was fine and that nothing had changed. But he wouldn't be able to do that for forever. Eventually, she was going to show and there would be no avoiding the fact that a pregnant woman was waddling around the engine room. "I can't just dump her in Firekli," muttered Rhys.

"The safest place for her is with us," said Kashim. "We have the means to transport her elsewhere with that maintenance unit of yours, but to where?"

"Neo-Colony Two?" Hodge offered.

Rhys grinned. "She would fight us so hard." Both Kashim and Hodge made sounds of agreement.

After a long moment of silence, Hodge chuckled. Rhys looked at him questioningly. "The idea of a small you wandering around the ship," his friend explained.

Deciding that it had been a while since he had last beaten Hodge in a good-natured grappling match, Rhys stepped around Kashim, grabbed Hodge's arm and tried to force him to step back so he could then trip him. Hodge hip-checked Rhys and tangled a foot around Rhys' ankle; they crashed into a pile.

"Take it farther up deck," Kashim chided over the scuffle. "You'll scare the fish away."

Hodge slipped from Rhys' grip and jogged toward the main mast. Rhys chased him, grabbing his friend's clothes to slow him. Hodge slid out of his shirt, caught Rhys' wrist, and tried to pin him in a hold. Laughing, Rhys twisted his arm and kicked the back of Hodge's knee, sending him to the deck. Hodge cursed loudly, snatched Rhys' leg, and rotated his body, swinging his legs.

Rhys started to move from the hold, but Hodge stopped him. "Wait, wait, wait," his friend wheezed, "Hold on. I want to try this." The smile on Hodge's face dimmed as he focused on the placement of his legs.

"Uh, other foot here," said Rhys, pointing to Hodge's left leg.

"Here?" Hodge wrapped his left leg around the side of Rhys' right leg.

"Yeah, yeah." Sensing his friend was about to pull a fast one, Rhys withdrew his trapped limb and flung himself onto Hodge.

"Oh, you piece of… *gawanhu*," muttered Hodge as Rhys pinned him to the deck. "I was… practicing."

"I'm not here to practice," Rhys growled, struggling to fold Hodge's arm behind his back. His friend jerked his captured limb free—he was still vastly stronger than Rhys—and rolled. In a continuous wave of movement, they wrestled across the deck, each trying to wrap the other in a painful hold. Although Rhys had at his disposal a complete arsenal of fighting techniques, he still couldn't best Hodge in grappling.

"Hey!" shouted Kashim. Rhys flopped onto his back as Hodge squatted atop him and pretended to choke him. "You're scaring the fish off! Do it later!"

Hodge's shoulders went slack in disappointment. "But it's the morning! We always wrestle in the morning."

"Do it later!" Kashim snapped.

Hodge rolled off Rhys and lay beside him. Panting, they gazed up at the solar-paneled sails. After a moment, Hodge said, "I'm sure... a lot of those panels are going to need replacement soon. We haven't been here to tend to them."

"That's so kind of you to volunteer," chuckled Rhys. He sat up, wiped the sweat from his forehead, and added, "Actually, we need to be teaching Forge."

Hodge's face lit up. "Can I teach him fighting and sunboarding and stuff?"

"He already knows how to fight."

Hodge scoffed.

Rhys pulled his legs to him and rubbed his recuperating knee. It ached from their grappling match. "He saved my life when we were in the Brechin camp. When I messed up my knee, he downed four or five soldiers."

"He killed them?"

"No, I'm sure he wouldn't have done something like that even if he was terrified."

"Ehhh, it sounds like he has the guts, but *I'll* be the judge of that."

"I get the feeling he, Beso, and Zain are going to be more apt at adapting than Alina and I were."

"Why do you say that?"

"They've all downloaded my memories, or at least the ones I gave the council. They have some idea of what to expect, how to react, and what to do. Alina and I came in blind. They have a dramatic advantage."

Hodge nudged Rhys fondly. "You did all the hard work for them."

Eventually, Hodge went to the bridge to relieve Andy from his night shift, leaving Rhys with Kashim. Knowing they needed to get the catches cleaned and into the freezer, Rhys began butchering the fish along the starboard stern. A throng of other marine predators swarmed the ship, leading to Kashim successfully catching another two dozen variously sized fish.

Together, they spent the next two hours butchering fish and laying them out to dry. Leo joined them about an hour in and, sitting in the shade of the sails, wrote in his notebook. Axel, Leo explained, was in the galley cleaning guns and taking inventory; Forge was still asleep, Andy had gone to bed, and Kallen was in the engine room.

Heart light, Rhys and Kashim continued to work. After a while, Rhys took those they had cleaned into the galley, leaving Kashim to wash off the deck.

Standing in front of the freezer, Rhys ponder how to best fit all of the fish into the crammed space. Forge shuffled in, his nose wrinkled. "You eat these?"

"They are cooked first, but yeah," said Rhys. He smiled at the medical student's ragged hair. "Sleep well?"

"Uh, yes. I saw pictures."

"When was the last time you connected to the Core?" asked Rhys.

"The night before we went to the Brechin camp."

Rhys nodded. "Dreams. You're disconnected from the Core now, so your brain has to have some way to process the information you've seen consciously and subconsciously that day."

"Dreams. Do you have them?"

"Most nights." He neglected to mention the nightmares that frequented his sleep.

Leo appeared in the doorway. "Hodge is asking for you on the bridge."

"Can you figure a way to fit all of this in the freezer?" Rhys motioned to the crate of fish. "I'll be right back." He prowled onto the bridge. "What?" he growled good-naturedly at Hodge.

Hodge tossed him a radio. "Reza wants to speak with you."

Rhys brought the radio to his mouth. "Hey, Reza."

"Rhys, it's good to hear your voice," came the crackled reply.

"Same here. What's going on?"

"I was looking at that unit from the colony and was wondering what you wanted to do with it."

Rhys leaned on the forward paneling and peered out the bridge. "We definitely can't keep it on *Grisle's* deck."

"My thoughts exactly."

Hodge nudged Rhys with his boot. "Take it apart."

Rhys reviewed the mechanics of the unit, the parts that they could use, and its energy supply. "Have Beso and Zain take it apart."

There was a long pause from Reza before he said, "Are you sure? They've told me that unit could easily make it to Brechin."

"So why haven't we used it?" asked Hodge.

"It has no weapons," Rhys replied.

"So?"

"Hello?" crackled Reza's voice through the radio.

"Just a moment, Reza." Rhys laid the radio on the forward paneling. "We cannot fit the *entire* crew in there."

"We wouldn't fit the *entire* crew in there. Some of us would have to stay behind... like Kallen."

Rhys pursed his lips. Hodge had a point. Of course, the idea had crossed his mind once or twice, but he had dismissed it. His crew needed time to recuperate, just like his knee. They were worn, stressed, and on the brink of snapping. Weeks at sea away from corrupt judges, filthy slums, and Brechin forces could heal them and revive their spirits. Jumping into the fire again would break them.

Hodge reached between them, snatched the radio, and cued the microphone. "Tear it apart. We'll use the pieces to modify the ships."

"Rhys, do you approve?" asked Reza.

Hodge smiled at Rhys and tossed him the radio. With a sigh, Rhys replied, "Yes. Get Beso and Zain on it. Tell them to save as much as they can."

"Over and out." The radio quieted.

Rhys frowned at Hodge who was reclining comfortably. "I know that look on your face and... you're right," his friend said, smug smile fading. "We're not soldiers."

"Except Axel," replied Rhys.

Hodge shrugged. "He'll be fine. Besides, we need to train the guppies if they're going to be of any use."

"This will also give us time in Firekli to gather intelligence," Rhys added. "We've been distanced from the rest of the region. I'm sure there's more going on. When do you get off from your shift?"

"Sometime midafternoon. Why?"

"Need to start training our guppies."

Rhys spent the rest of the morning clambering about the main mast with Kallen and Kashim withdrawing burnt-out or damaged solar panels. With his third sling filled, Rhys moved to the shade of the sails and began splitting the piles based on their damage. Kallen eventually went inside to cook lunch.

Shortly after midday, Rhys, Forge, and Leo were called into the galley to eat. Rhys didn't miss Hodge peering sadly from the bridge after them. "What do you think?" asked Kallen, leaning against the counter as he entered. Already Leo and Forge were seated at the first table; Axel sat at the second table, a notebook in hand and rounds of ammunition before him.

"Smells good," murmured Rhys.

Kallen smiled and glanced at Forge. "Explain to him what cooking is. I've tried, but he is still worried."

"You can't explain it."

Kallen quickly filled a bowl of stew and handed it to Rhys. Judging from the texture of the meat, Kallen had cooked the spare flanks of the stored jerabo and added what sauces and vegetables were left in the supply. Rhys placed the bowl before Forge and seated himself beside Leo.

Forge gave a tentative sniff and then swirled the bowl gently. "It's... an animal carcass?" he asked in Nefegian. While Leo laughed, Rhys translated for Kallen and Axel. Forge frowned, tilted his head in silent conversation, and then lifted the bowl to his lips. He sniffed once more and then sipped.

Rhys watched as something akin to a realization crossed Forge's face, and a wild hunger ignited in his eyes. The medical student took a deeper sip and swallowed. Kallen brought Rhys and Leo bowls before sitting down with her own. Within twenty seconds, she was back on her feet depositing more stew into Forge's bowl.

"Talk to me, Axel," said Rhys.

Axel stored his pen atop his ear and leaned on the table in thought. "We've done a surprisingly good job rationing rifle and handgun ammunition despite the expeditions we've made."

"But?"

"We weren't able to resupply with military-grade ammunition for *Themis* or *Grisle*, leaving us with less than thirty-two percent of our current reserves."

Rhys stood, retrieved more stew, and set the bowl before Kallen. Without waiting for a response, he seated himself across from Axel. "So where does that put us?"

Axel looked down at his calculations. "We have twenty-two double-shots, seven exploding shells, three expanding bar shots, and... three thousand rounds of ammunition for the gunners. Now, I've spoken to Terron, and he claims that *Grisle* has reserves. They're doing a count right now. As for our remaining weapons and tools..." Axel flipped the page. "Between *Grisle* and *Themis*, we have twelve bullet proof vests, not enough to cover everyone. We have a small collection of knives that are better suited for filleting fish. As for rifles and handguns... Just like the bulletproof vests, we've slowly been losing them. Whereas prior to New

Arbroath, according to Kashim, we had nineteen short rifles and ten handguns, we now have fourteen rifles and six handguns. Again, not everyone is covered with a backup weapon."

Rhys looked at Kallen. "How many sunboards do we have?"

She set her bowl down. "Three plus yours. JiJi gave us his board when we went to search for you."

"And *Grisle?*"

"*Grisle* has no boards," replied Kallen. "We have all of them."

"Pilots include… Hodge, Kashim, yourself, and Axel." Kallen motioned to Forge. "I'm sure we could teach him."

"Why can't we divide the boards between the two ships?" asked Axel, reclining in his chair.

"Because *Grisle's* deck is open. It doesn't have a protected cabin to launch sunboards from."

"No offense, but the forward hatch hardly counts as a protected cabin," Axel replied. "An aft hatch would have been a better design choice for this ship. Any time we want to launch sunboards, we have to slow to a complete halt, exposing ourselves to enemies."

"The design of the forward hatch was an addition," said Kallen defensively. "We didn't know the ship would be carrying sunboards. It was only after the frame was built and work was underway that Joss recommended we carry sunboards."

"Doesn't matter. It may be a protected cabin for the sunboarders, but it makes the rest of the ship a target."

Rhys studied the grain in the table, his mind piecing together an idea.

"Vinz worked with the materials he had," Kallen argued. "I wouldn't expect a soldier like yourself to understand."

"It's extremely likely that I've been around more ships than you have, incubator," snapped Axel.

"Enough," interrupted Rhys.

"You're thinking," said Leo who had silently been eating until then. "What?"

Rhys motioned for Axel's notebook and drawing utensil. He turned a new page and began sketching *Themis*. Kallen and Leo joined him; only Forge remained out of the circle. "What if we build a chute that connected to the forward hatch and came down alongside our port? The end of it would be retractable, making it easy to slide into the water. If we're attacked while underway, we can launch sunboards through the chute along the port side. This would give the pilots a quicker launching sequence *and* have them in a protected environment."

"Where are you going to get the materials to build such a thing?" muttered Axel.

Rhys smiled. "The maintenance unit." He leaned away from the group and yelled to Hodge up on the bridge.

"What?" his friend called.

"Bring a radio!"

Within minutes, Rhys had relayed the message not only to Terron but to Zain and Beso. While Kallen cleaned the galley, Rhys took Leo, Forge, and Axel to the forward hatch to determine the plan's plausibility.

The rest of the afternoon was spent sketching, measuring, and drawing. Despite Forge's background in medicine, the medical student was still vastly more apt at completing measurements, formulas, and pressure calculations than anyone else on the ship, including Rhys.

Without the help of Pathos, Rhys could no longer instantaneously calculate the angles and tension needed. Working alongside someone with an AI only reminded him that he had dropped on the intelligence scale the day he removed Pathos. He now understood how the crew must have felt all those months; he must have seemed like a genius. Of course, he was still capable of complex mathematics, but he had to work through the problems, whereas Forge simply provided an answer.

It wasn't until late in the evening that they left their plans, schematics, and calculations and filed into the galley to eat once more. Afterward, tired and disheartened by the comparisons he had been making between himself and Forge, Rhys retreated to his cabin. For a long while, he stared up at the ceiling before rolling over and gazing at Vinz's bookshelf.

No doubt Vinz had felt inadequate next to Rhys. Despite having constructed a seafaring vessel, handpicked a crew, and taken on a monster of a mission, Vinz had to have felt some spite toward Rhys for seemingly having all of the answers. With cognitive abilities outranking his own, how could he not have?

The door to Rhys' cabin slid open. Rhys sat up expecting Kallen but instead found Forge. Knocking was not customary on Caelestis; to Forge's limited understanding, why would it be here? "Can we speak?" he asked in Nefegian.

Rhys motioned to the chair at his desk. Forge closed the cabin door and took a seat. "What's wrong?"

Without so much as a moment's pause, Forge said, "I need your memories."

"Why?"

Something like uncertainty flickered across Forge's face. "I'm... not strong like you. I am uncomfortable all the time and uneasy. I don't know what is expected of me."

With a gentle smile, Rhys said, "You're acclimating to a different culture. It took Alina and I weeks."

"I don't understand the facial expressions or the looks you pass one another. I don't understand the body language and the word-play." Forge gazed at Rhys desperately. "Help me."

Rhys studied the medical student and then said, "Why did you come here? Why did you leave Neo-Colony Two? What changed that night in the Brechin camp?"

"You... changed me," supplied Forge. "I was frightened; I knew you were scared as well. The expression on your face was foreign, but I recognized it. Even so... you moved with purpose. In the face of danger, you acted." Forge shifted in the chair. "I saw your fear turn to desperate resolve. It was like an AI had taken control, dictating your every move, calculating your next step." Forge smiled. "Knowing you no longer have an AI, Pathos explained to me the phenomenon of human instinct."

Rhys rested on his hands. "It's powerful. You don't recognize it until everything is over. Instinct couples with adrenaline to prepare you to fight or run."

Forge slumped in the chair, and Rhys smiled. It was strange seeing a Caelestis citizen sit, much less slump. "I don't want to be a burden to you and your crew."

"You're not. We are short-handed, so your arrival is perfect," assured Rhys. Forge frowned, causing Rhys to change the subject. "Why do you have a Pathos AI?"

"Why?"

"Nearly ninety percent of all Caelestis citizens are Logos-users. Was there a specific reason as to why you were given a Pathos unit?"

"Just as Alina was being groomed to become commander of the colony, I was created to become Veran's eventual replacement as the Director of Medicine."

"Huh," murmured Rhys. "Interesting." He knew Veran was older than him, but to have an understudy already hand-chosen so early in her career indicated that she was perhaps older than she appeared. "How old is Veran?"

Forge allowed Pathos a moment of his time before saying, "She will be sixty-three years of age in four months."

"Sixty-three?" gasped Rhys. "Are you serious?"

"Yes…" replied Forge hesitantly.

Rhys laughed aloud and rested his elbows on his knees. "Sixty-three. *Gawan*. I should probably tell Axel."

"Why is this surprising news? I don't understand your reaction."

"Because I thought she was in her mid-thirties," replied Rhys. "I've grown accustomed to people aging here on Earth."

"The people here on Earth age differently?"

"How old are you?"

"Twenty-four."

"You are close to Hodge's age," said Rhys. "Do you look like him?" Forge shook his head. "You have yet to meet Reza, Kallen's grandfather. Reza is in his eighties. Let me know what you think when you see him." Forge cocked his head. Suddenly, his brows furrowed in confusion. "Did Beso or Zain just show you?" Forge nodded. "Here on Earth, the average life span is late-seventies."

"Then… everyone on your ship will die before you," Forge asserted.

Rhys pursed his lips. It wasn't the first time that idea had crossed his mind. "Yes. They will probably all die before me."

"That saddens you."

"It does, but it means that I have to treasure the time I have with them now. Right?" Rhys stood and stretched. "If you need information or want to ask questions, you can ask anyone on this ship. All of them, with the exception of Axel, were around Alina and I. Don't be ashamed."

Forge stood slowly. "What can I do to help?"

"Tomorrow morning, Hodge will start working with you."

"Working with me? What does that mean?"

"You'll see."

26
CREW DOWN

DESPITE BEING BACK ON THEMIS and lying by Kallen's side, Rhys still dreamed of Alina. Though it wasn't the first time that week he had dreamed of her, it was the first in a long while that he woke from in a sweat, his cheeks wet with tears. Slowly, so as not to wake Kallen, he slid over her, walked across the room, and stood against the wall, his forehead pressed against the cool wood.

When he could no longer hear his heart in his ears, he sat heavily at his desk and gazed at Kallen's sleeping form. He envied her. Though she too suffered from nightmares, it had been weeks since her last one. After sitting in silence for well over half an hour, he went to the bridge, checked on Andy, and then returned to bed.

The following morning, Hodge's booming voice from down the hall woke him. Growling, Rhys rolled over. Kallen wasn't there. "Hodge!" called Rhys as his friend continued to speak enthusiastically. Hodge snapped open the door of his cabin. "Too early…"

"Not for guppies," replied Hodge. "Don't you want to see what Flick can do?"

Dressed in only his pants, Rhys followed Hodge down the hall to the crew's quarters where Forge sat on his bunk with Leo and Axel on either side of him.

"What's wrong?" asked Rhys.

Hearing Rhys' voice, Forge leapt up. Before the medical student could reach Rhys, however, Hodge grappled him into a headlock and began dragging him down the hallway.

Leo sighed. "Should you really have given him to Hodge?"

"I think it's perfect," growled Axel with a dark smirk.

Together, they followed the two to the upper deck. Rhys checked on the bridge where Andy and Kashim stood, learned Kallen was in the engine room, and then joined the others upstairs. He found Forge backing away from Hodge while Leo and Axel looked on in amusement.

"Rhys!" begged Forge.

"Rhys can't save you, kid," Hodge declared with a wolfish grin.

Forge, whose eyes were wide, shifted his gaze to Rhys. Recognizing that Forge actually feared for his life, Rhys touched Hodge's arm. His friend, still smiling, relaxed. "If you are to remain on the ship, you, Zain, and Beso will need to be trained," explained Rhys. "This means strengthening you physically. Because none of us, not even myself, have seen you fight, we need to know what you can do."

"You know what I can do," replied Forge. "I was with you at the Brechin camp."

"But I didn't see you. At any rate, you can spar with Hodge or Axel," said Rhys.

"What if I don't want to spar with any of you?"

"Then you spar with all of us," Rhys retorted. Axel and Hodge moved to either side of him.

The expression on Forge's face changed from fright to resolve. "This is barbaric and uncivilized."

Rhys shrugged. "I didn't make you join. It was your decision. My advice—don't pick Axel."

Forge squared his shoulders, and his body became tense like a coiled spring. "Fine, I choose Hodge." In a sweeping movement, he swung his arms fluidly before him and settled into a fighting pose.

Recognizing the combat style, Rhys nudged Hodge. "His strikes will be quick if he can manage the speed. Be careful."

"Yeah, yeah," Hodge muttered, approaching Forge.

"Pathos," called Rhys.

"Yes, Rhys Falkrow?"

"This is a sparring match; it is not a life-or-death battle. It is for practice. You are not to shock Forge's opponent. You may shield your unit from damage. That is it. Do you agree upon these terms?"

"Permission is required from my user," Pathos replied.

Forge nodded. "That's fine."

Hodge regarded Forge. "I've seen Rhys fight. I know what you're capable of. But technique doesn't always win." Hodge rolled his shoulders and brought his slightly curved palms before him in preparation to strike or counter. After a calming breath, he slid toward Forge.

Rhys didn't expect the med student to win, but he also didn't trust Forge to hold back. This was the second confrontation the medical student had ever experienced. It was possible he could accidentally hurt Hodge. For that reason, Rhys remained ready, his balance shifted forward slightly in preparation to intercept a blow.

Not surprisingly, as was Rhys' own technique, Forge leapt forward to attack first. With surprising grace, he struck upward, side-swept his palm across Hodge's face, and then rotated his body to kick. Though the strike to his face was painful, Hodge took the blow and, reading Forge as he had read Rhys those many months ago, stepped back and blocked the subsequent kick with a powerful arm.

Forge twirled on the ball of his foot to keep his momentum going and struck with his elbow. When Hodge blocked that attack as well, the med student began barraging him with an array of palm strikes, knee jabs, and kicks.

Rhys watched, impressed. He hoped he looked half that remarkable and imposing while fighting. Forge's movements were fluid, his speed surprising given his lack of practice, and his focus intent. But he was weak. He had no muscle. While the combat style itself was meant to magnify strength, Forge seemed like nothing but a flailing insect against Hodge.

After nearly a full minute of executing sweeping attacks, strikes, and jabs, Forge backed away from Hodge, panting. Unwilling to give Forge a moment of rest, Hodge followed and, when the time was right, darted in.

They exchanged a few blows, but Forge was flagging. To Rhys' trained eyes, he saw Forge attempt to disable Hodge by using a pressure point, but Hodge trapped his arm under his shoulder and threw him.

The medical student rolled gracefully and sprang back to his feet. But Hodge was already there. In a single motion, Hodge snatched Forge's leading arm, locked it in a hold bar, and cranked down. Forge crumpled under the pain and collapsed on the deck where Hodge firmly pinned him.

"Match!" called Rhys.

Hodge rolled off Forge and knelt beside him. "Not bad, Flick," he panted. "You're weak like Rhys was though." Forge remained prone on the deck, wheezing. "Hey, you hurt?" Forge shook his head. Hodge clapped his shoulder warmly and stood.

Forge dragged his feet under him.

"Well?" asked Rhys.

Forge passed an appraising eye over Hodge and then asked, "Can we do it again?"

After speaking with Kashim and Andy for a while on the bridge, Rhys grabbed a small breakfast from the galley and joined Kallen in the engine room. While she worked on engine adjustments, he sat in the hallway and repaired solar panels. Once that chore was completed, he dragged Leo, Forge, and Axel into the forward hatch and continued measurements and calculations for the new launching chute.

Late in the afternoon, they took the dinghy over to *Grisle* where they were greeted enthusiastically by Leela. They examined the work Zain and Beso had done in deconstructing the maintenance unit and chatted with the rest of the crew.

"Tessa," beckoned Rhys upon spotting her peer into *Grisle's* galley. It was the first he had seen of her since New Arbroath. Tessa entered and stood before him. "Why are you here?"

Tessa glanced at Leela and Patrin before saying, "I didn't want Vinz's ship to be destroyed. It's the last thing I have of him."

"You realize that I am never going to let you on *my* ship ever again," Rhys replied.

"Rhys," cooed Leela, sensing the tension between them. "Tessa has been a big help. She prepped both ships for departure in the middle of the night and piloted *Grisle* out of New Arbroath."

Rhys went to Tessa and began patting her down. Though he knew she had no weapons or incriminating evidence on her, the action itself meant to be demeaning. Tessa withstood the search as *Grisle's* entire crew looked on. "Have you checked her cabin and belongings?" he asked over his shoulder.

"No," murmured Leela.

Rhys nodded to the hallway. "Jules." Jules disappeared from the galley. Rhys looked about for Terron. "Where's Terron?"

Leela frowned. "He said he was going to bed early. He didn't look as though he felt well."

Rhys shifted his gaze to Reza. "Tessa is not to be on the bridge alone. She is not to be near any radio equipment."

"Understood," the old man replied.

Rhys held Tessa's gaze. "I hope you know that you are not welcome here, but we are shorthanded. You will carry out your tasks to the best of your ability; you will do as Terron and Reza ask of you. Am I understood?"

"Yes, Overseer," Tessa agreed.

After discussing possible uses for the materials and equipment Beso and Zain had taken from the maintenance unit, Rhys, Forge, Axel, and Leo returned to *Themis* to eat. To Rhys' relief, the rest of the evening went without trouble. Kallen cooked a lean supper of fried fish, and everyone once again dispersed. Rhys checked the bridge before going to bed.

The following morning, he was awakened by a putrid smell, an odor so vile that he couldn't help but hide his face under the blankets. Cursing, he rolled out of bed, opened the cabin window, and went in search of the source.

Outside the safety of his cabin, the acrid stink was overpowering. It burned his nose. He shut the door to his quarters and jogged down the hallway. He found Kallen in the galley standing over the sink filling a bucket of water. "What's going on?"

"Both Leo and Axel are sick," Kallen replied.

The hostility in Rhys faded. "What... does that mean?"

"Both have been throwing up since early this morning. Leo is running a high fever; Axel's is mild."

Kallen drew the heavy bucket from the sink and set it on the floor. She began washing a set of cloths.

Rhys had spent the majority of the time in New Arbroath treating the injured. He could fix wounds; he couldn't dissipate illness or disease however. "Maybe... I should be handling them," he offered. At that moment, Forge pushed past Rhys with a pile of sodden clothes. Rhys switched to Nefegian. "How bad is it?"

As Forge set the pile down in the middle of the galley, he replied similarly, "I personally have no experience with illness, so it is difficult for me to determine, but according to our records and databases, it isn't bad." Forge looked at him. "I've asked Kashim and Andy to remain on the bridge or outside."

"What about Hodge?"

Forge frowned. "He has a mild fever."

Kallen started to return to the crew quarters, but Rhys stopped her with a firm grip. "Go take a bath. When you're done, go outside."

"I'm fine. I can take care of them. I have before," Kallen retorted.

In Elali, he murmured, "You can't afford to fall ill."

Kallen defiantly glared at him and then set down the bucket of water. "Fine, but you're taking my place." Rhys patted her on the bottom as she passed to go to the washroom.

"You should know," said Forge, "Terron and Reza have also become ill. Tessa is in a similar condition to Hodge. She's not doing well, but she's functioning."

"Are Beso and Zain caring for them?"

"I've shared with them information concerning human anatomy and basic care, but they're not comfortable."

Rhys lifted the bucket of water and clean cloths and went into the crew's quarters. "I told her to go get you," murmured Hodge, lying listlessly in his bunk. He was ghostly; his skin was coated in a fine layer of cold sweat. Rhys soaked a cloth, wrung it out, and placed it on Hodge's forehead. His friend sighed in relief and closed his eyes. "Where did all of this come from? I don't understand. Everyone was fine yesterday."

Rhys withdrew Ethos from his pocket and laid it on Hodge's chest. As Ethos examined Hodge, Rhys moved to Leo. Despite the foul stench of vomit and sickness, he was sure Forge was delighted to finally be using his expertise. The medical student had never before seen an ill human.

Hodge frowned and looked across at Axel and Leo. "I think… Leela and Patrin made us sick."

Rhys moved to Axel, wetted a cloth, and placed it on the soldier's forehead. "Why do you think that?"

"They were both working with the sick in New Arbroath," Hodge replied hoarsely.

Rhys looked at Forge who considered the likelihood. "Depending on the virus, it's entirely possible," the medical student said.

"Stop talking please," Axel muttered.

Rhys laid Ethos on Axel's chest, checked his vitals, and did what he could to make the soldier comfortable.

As Forge washed his hands in the galley, he said, "I'll keep an eye on everyone. All of us from Neo-Colony Two need to be careful not to contaminate those who have not been infected."

The next three days were trying for everyone. Though Andy, Kashim, and Kallen didn't fall ill, the lack of capable crew members put a drain on Rhys. He ended up taking Hodge's shifts on the bridge as his friend became sicker. Kashim, Andy, and Kallen spent hours on the upper deck doing laundry, repairing and fine-tuning equipment, fishing, and washing the deck.

News from *Grisle* wasn't good. While Tessa had fallen ill, by the fourth day, both she and Terron were starting to recover. Reza was making slow progress despite the constant attention and care provided by Zain and Leela who alternated shifts. Rhys talked Kallen out of going over to *Grisle* to be with her grandfather. He valued Reza, but he also didn't want Kallen to become ill.

Having nothing else to do in the days surrounding his crew's illness aside from his shifts on the bridge, Rhys began marking the port wall of the forward hatch. By the end of the week, with Forge's supervision and Ethos' calculations, Rhys made the first cuts into the forward hatch wall with the resonance cutters. To prevent any problems that might arise from rough seas, he worked through the night to weld precisely-measured pieces from the deconstructed maintenance unit to the gaping holes he made. The following day, he created a counter-balance beam that was hung off *Themis'* starboard to offset the weight of the new chute.

By the time everyone on *Themis* had recovered, Rhys and Forge had shifted the majority of the forward hatch's contents to the starboard side, replaced the port wall with the material from the maintenance unit, and begun the extension shaft. While Forge continued to monitor the crew's health, he also worked tirelessly alongside Rhys, welding and continuing their construction plans. In the meantime, Rhys balanced on crates and built a system along the ceiling that would allow them to maneuver and deposit sunboards into the chute.

"Rhys," said Andy, appearing in the doorway of the forward hatch late in the evening on the seventh day. Rhys looked down at him from his perch on the crates. Andy tossed a radio upward. "It's Terron." The solemn look on Andy's face did not encourage Rhys.

"Hey Terron," said Rhys, leaning back on the crates. "What's going on?"

"It's Reza."

Rhys glanced at Hodge and Forge who were also in the forward hatch. "How's he doing?"

"Not well. His fever hasn't broken. Beso and Leela have done what they can for him, but it's... not looking good," murmured Terron. "He's dehydrated and weak. He can't keep anything down."

Rhys held the radio between his legs and gazed at the floor. In soft Nefegian, he asked, "Is he near his death?"

Realizing that Rhys was using Nefegian for a reason, Terron responded in a similar manner. "I think so. Leela and Patrin also think so."

Rhys pursed his lips. "Should I send Kallen over?"

"It wouldn't be a bad idea," Terron gravely replied.

"Is there any chance he will recover? Any at all?"

"Hold on." There was a long pause as Terron must have relayed the message to those near him. "Leela doesn't think so. His age is playing a significant role in his inability to recover."

Rhys looked at Forge pleadingly. Although Rhys himself had all the medical knowledge Alina once possessed, he still hoped the med student could provide him new information. Forge tilted his head as he spoke with Zain and Beso before passing Rhys a grim look. "We've done everything possible. Without medical equipment or supplies, there's nothing that can be done to alleviate his pain or aid his immune system in the fight against the virus."

"Rhys, are you still there?" asked Terron.

"Yes…" Rhys replied slowly. "I'll send Kallen over shortly. Out."

It took but a few minutes to explain to Kallen what was going on and send her and Hodge in the dinghy to *Grisle*.

Once the forward hatch closed and *Themis* was once more underway, Rhys retreated to the galley where he sat heavily at a table and stared at the wall. He still hadn't given Reza the numerous manuals he had translated from Elali into Aabesh.

27
PATHOS USER

REZA DIED THE FOLLOWING AFTERNOON.

Despite wanting to be there to send the old man off, per Kallen's request, Rhys remained aboard *Themis* and waited for her and Hodge's return. The small ceremony aboard *Grisle* was at dusk. Kallen and Hodge returned shortly thereafter.

Rhys, Andy, Forge, and Kashim, who were working in unison to weld an especially large layer of metal along the chute's outer wall, paused as Hodge and Kallen surfed through the open hatch and skidded up the ramp.

Kallen looked emotionally drained and distant, as if her mind was elsewhere. Once the motor quieted, she climbed from the dinghy and slipped out the forward hatch. Hodge sat on the edge of the boat and grimly regarded them.

"How are the others?" asked Kashim after a long moment.

"Leela and Patrin are beside themselves with guilt. They think... they killed Reza." Hodge ran a tired hand through his wind-whipped hair and sighed. "I... don't know what to say to them... or to her." He nodded to the open doorway through which Kallen had just disappeared. "She hasn't spoken in hours." Hodge rubbed his eyes and motioned behind him. "I brought over some more materials. Beso said you needed them."

Rhys encouraged his team to finish their welding project. Afterward, he released them from their work while he went in search of Kallen.

Unsurprisingly, he found her sprawled on their bed, her arm over her wet face. She didn't move when he entered. He stripped out of his sweaty shirt and lay beside her, allowing his legs to dangle off the side of the bed.

Kallen's mouth contorted and she rolled into Rhys. Her body began shaking uncontrollably with grief and her breathing grew ragged until she was sobbing. Her hands clenched down on his arm in anguish as she heaved great sighs of tears and pain.

There was nothing that could be said to console her just as there had been nothing to be said after Alina's death. Rhys could only hold her and remind her that she was not alone.

When Kallen finally fell quiet and dropped into a deep sleep, he rolled her onto her side of the bed, covered her, and left the cabin. He paused momentarily in the doorway of his crew's quarters. A single lamp glowed next to Leo's bed; Kashim, Hodge, Axel, and Forge were all asleep. Leo looked up briefly from his writing before returning to his work.

"I thought you went to bed," said Andy, stretching over the back of his chair as Rhys entered the bridge.

"Not yet," replied Rhys. He passed a cursory glance over the paneling. "Everything quiet?"

Andy set his book down. "The seas have picked up a bit, but nothing else."

"Has Kashim gauged the weather?"

"He did earlier. Said there was nothing to worry about."

"How's Kallen?"

"Asleep."

Andy nodded. "It's been a long time since I've heard her cry so hard." He sighed. "Forge couldn't understand. Her crying distressed him." Rhys must have seemed uninterested because Andy frowned. "What's wrong?"

"Sorry. No, nothing is wrong. I'm just going to the upper deck for a while. I'll be down in an hour or so." Rhys slipped out the external bridge door, climbed the ladder, and strolled to the port side of the ship with his hands in his pockets. He let the cool evening air sweep his hair from his face, breathing deeply before looking up at the billions of twinkling stars. He cleared his throat and withdrew Ethos from his pocket. "Hey?" His voice was almost a murmur.

"Yeah?"

"Tell me more about Osiris and Ramsen's plan." Another pleasant breeze raked through his hair and buffeted the solar-paneled sails.

"What brought this up all of a sudden?"

"I want to know in detail what it was Ramsen was planning."

"Mmm, as you know, Ramsen and I attempted to hack into Osiris while we worked in Brechin. It was this attack that actually led to Ramsen being targeted. He fled Brechin and began working on a new way to fight Osiris."

Rhys lay down on the deck and stared up at the waxing moon. "And that was when he began upgrading your software?"

"Correct. But to attack Osiris, he needed to be in Brechin. The trans-atmospheric jets, his shuttle, a myriad of computers, and other means to access Osiris' global network were there."

"Global network. What do you mean?"

"As a part of Osiris' system, the AI has a collection of satellites that orbit the Earth. There are thirty-two total—twenty-four global positioning satellites and eight geosynchronous satellites. The GPS satellites monitor what's happening on Earth and the geosynchronous satellites relay that information to Osiris. Initially, Ramsen's plan was to physically attack a cluster of satellites to allow him safe passage to Osiris' lunar base. But the satellites—all of them—carry phasers to safeguard them from damage. So, we began prepping for a cyber-attack instead."

"A cyber-attack." Rhys mused on the idea.

"The plan was to hack into the satellites and use me to shut off their sensors." Ethos paused. "At the time, I thought the plan was plausible. We didn't have many options; Ramsen was growing desperate. Now, that I think about, I don't think such an attack would work."

"Why?"

"Shutting off a satellite's sensors would alert Osiris to trouble. The AI is intimately connected with the satellites. It would notice immediately if its sensors were destroyed or no longer processing data."

"Then don't disable the sensors."

"Right, but Osiris will still see us coming."

"Not if we make it appear as though we aren't there."

"I don't follow. The satellites can detect colloid shields, Rhys. It's not a new invention."

Rhys shook his head. "It's nothing like that. Instead of disabling the sensors, we hack the satellites and overload their capabilities using a DDoS attack."

"A distributed denial-of-service attack," said Ethos. "Flood the online resources of the satellites, thereby compromising their ability to monitor Earth's activities. That... might actually work. I can do that. I need to be in Brechin, but I can do that."

Rhys chuckled. "I have good ideas sometimes."

"I never thought you didn't."

The smile Rhys' face faded. Bypassing the satellites was just one of many obstacles they faced. They still had to make it to Firekli to resupply and then get to Brechin. They needed to infiltrate the capital, discover the underground base, determine if the jets Ethos seemed to think were there were actually functioning, and decide how they were going to launch a unit into space.

"One thing at a time," said Ethos, guessing where his mind had wandered.

Rhys laid an arm over his eyes. "Why did all of this have to happen?"

"All of what?"

"Since Alina and I boarded *Themis*, the ship and her crew have seen nothing but trouble. We bring with us strife."

"How is any of this your fault?"

"We're venturing into territories they don't understand. Kallen, Hodge, Kashim… None of them has experience in space. They can hardly comprehend how the magnetic board works. How could they understand the physics of launching a trans-atmospheric unit into orbit?"

"If you try to solve everything all at once, you'll become overwhelmed."

"If I had Pathos, I wouldn't feel this way."

"Wouldn't you?"

Rhys sighed. "I don't know. After I disconnected, everything changed. I didn't need an AI anymore. There was no need to solve intricate equations or understand astrophysics because it wasn't relevant. But now… I need that ability. If our path is leading us back to space, I need to adapt."

"I will tell you this because you are my user now," Ethos said. "The trans-atmospheric jets are equipped with AI support and neuro-link systems. You won't be alone going into space."

"I'm… both terrified and relieved to hear that," murmured Rhys.

"Like I said, one thing at a time."

The following morning, Rhys rose early and slipped to the forward hatch to continue work on the chute. While everyone else slept past dawn, he measured, cut, and welded. Already, they had sunk three days into construction and they were nearly sixty percent complete. Although the chute itself was coming along nicely, work still needed to be done on the ceiling frames that would allow safe movement of the sunboards to and from the ramp.

Additionally, because he wanted to install a second pulley system extended the ramp into the water, Rhys was having to re-imagine their launching sequence. No longer could they secure a sunboard by its keel using an underwater sheath since the chute was designed for launch while they were underway.

After midday, Rhys took the afternoon shift on the bridge and worked on minor gauge adjustments. Once he finished those, he sat and read one of Vinz' many books that Alina had once tried to share with him. When he grew weary of reading, he paced the bridge, organized the map rack, repaired a few solar panels, and stared out at the emerald sea. By the time it was dinner, he could hardly contain himself. It was not that he was hungry, but that he wanted to leave the bridge. He was too wound up and restless to remain motionless watching gauges.

Despite Reza's death, the entire crew gathered in good spirits in the galley and for the first time Rhys was allowed a glimpse of his team in one room. Standing in the doorway, he couldn't help but smile. While Hodge and Forge rough-housed beside the table, Leo moved to avoid being caught in the tangle. Near the back wall, Kashim and Axel discussed rifles. Andy stood at the stove helping Kallen.

"Ah, Rhys, you should have seen Flick today," Hodge chorused, shaking Forge before pointing to his own bruised face. "He got scared and nailed me!"

"I've apologized!" argued Forge, glancing at Rhys.

Plates of steamed fish were passed out and everyone took their seats. For the first several moments, no one said a word except Hodge who, as usual, groaned his delight and squirmed in his chair. Eventually, conversation broke out and Andy and Leo began talking about Leo's writing which he had continued despite no longer being affiliated with the capital. Forge shifted his attention to Axel and Kashim and listened intently as the two continued to speak about weapons. Rhys picked at his food and then looked up at Kallen and Hodge who were watching him, amused.

"What?" he asked.

"You're not eating," Hodge pointed out. "You always eat. Something's wrong."

Rhys shrugged and gazed at the others. "I'm content. That's all."

Hodge nodded to Forge. "He moves like you do. Quick, with purpose. But he's got noodle arms. Jules is trying to teach Zain and Beso. Beso is having a difficult time with the concept, but Zain is progressing quickly."

"I'm not surprised about Beso," said Rhys, pushing his food around. "He's always been reserved. If he decides something, you won't find out until the moment he acts. He was always one of the last to weigh in on a decision."

"You worked together, right?" asked Kallen.

"We did. He was two classes above me, so by the time I entered the department, he was well-adjusted. As for Zain, I know almost nothing about him. My department had very little to do with his and, even when we cooperated, it was only the higher-ups." Sensing Kallen's eyes on him, Rhys looked up at her. "What?"

"Does that seem like a long time ago for you?"

"Yes," replied Rhys. "It was a completely different world."

Tearing into a hunk of fish, Hodge said, "I can't imagine living in that place. It was too quiet."

"No one needed to speak," said Rhys. "Everything was done through AI."

"Still, no way. No sound, no smell. No food! I don't understand how you could have lived like that." Hodge savored the bite in his mouth.

"We didn't know anything else," said Rhys. The conversation at the table quieted. "Caelestis was all we knew. The people, the customs, the processes. How would we have known that we could live otherwise?"

"Flick, what has shocked you most since leaving Neo-Colony Two?" Hodge prompted.

Forge, whose thoughtful gaze had been set on Rhys, said, "Nonverbal communication, the movements and gestures each of you makes to one another. Rhys, what about you?"

Rhys sat back. "Music."

Forge tilted his head as he spoke with Zain and Beso. "Music."

"Ehh, I don't think he knows what that is," muttered Hodge.

"Music is the sound produced by voice or instrument that creates harmonies, forms, and emotional expression," recited Forge.

"So, he doesn't know," Hodge chuckled. He pointed to Rhys. "Can you play Kyo's piax yet?"

"Only a few tunes," murmured Rhys. "Kallen can show him."

"I understand what music is," Forge argued with a frown.

As Kallen sipped water to clear her throat, Rhys shook his head. "You don't know what music is."

Kallen sang a short note to find the pitch and then took a sharp breath.

When I was young, a boy did come
To the market one day.

The butcher's son, who had once won
My heart along the way.
He said unto me, "Let us flee
To the hills today."

Warm with love and adventure full of,
Did I follow him that eve.
Into the night, despite the cold's bite,
To his chest did I cleave.
For liretems I ran,
With this young man,
Until we finally did heave.

When I looked back,
I saw pitch black
From where I had come.
I could not believe
I had been so naïve
And so painfully dumb.

Seeing my worry
And my eyes blurry
With tears I refused to shed,
The man said unto me
"So you agree,
Please come with me instead."

Years have passed and though I've been asked,
I still am sure of my way,
When I was young, a boy did come
To the market on that day.

Rhys, who had had his eyes closed throughout the song's entirety, looked at Forge. The medical student sat in stunned silence, his gaze transfixed on Kallen. His eyes were glassy and face contorted in a mixture of confusion and pain.

"Very nice, Kallen," said Andy.

"Thank you," she murmured, glancing at Rhys.

"Hey," muttered Hodge, nudging Forge good-naturedly. "She's taken."

Ignoring Hodge, Forge whispered, "How did you do that?"

Chuckling, Rhys gripped Kallen's hand. "I had the same reaction." Kallen blushed and picked at her food.

Conversation filled the galley once more, but Forge remained distracted while he ate. Rhys was sure he had shared Kallen's short performance with Zain and Beso, but Forge never tilted his head in silent conversation or acted as though he were speaking.

When Forge's brows finally knitted together in distress, Rhys smiled. *There* it was. The same realization he had made so long ago. Despite being an advanced people, the human race of the Hyperes Solar System had long forgotten what it actually meant to be human. Music, literature, poetry, the ability to create art. Forge had reached the same conclusion.

"Don't dwell on it too much," Rhys advised between bites. "You'll never understand."

Forge stared at his empty plate. "But why? Why would…"

"There's no explanation that will satisfy your curiosity."

After dinner, Rhys helped Kallen clean the galley while Andy returned to the bridge with Kashim. Leo remained seated at the table to continue writing as Axel, Forge, and Hodge left for the crew cabin. Rhys was pleased to see Hodge begin another rough-housing session with Forge in the hallway. Despite the fact that the tomfoolery was obnoxious, it was an important part of assimilating into the ship's dynamics.

As Kallen washed dishes, Rhys stood by her and dried them. Running a towel over a plate, he asked, "How have you been feeling?"

"Tired," she replied somberly. She switched to Elali and continued. "I don't know if it's everything that's been going on or the baby, but I'm exhausted all the time. Once I lie down, I am instantly asleep."

Rhys leaned into her and kissed her head. "Is there anything I can do to help?"

"No, not really," she admitted.

Trying to draw attention from her pain, Rhys said, "Did you see Forge's face?"

Kallen chuckled. "It's not the first time I've seen that expression." Rhys nudged her fondly. "You really like music, don't you?"

"I wish I could play Kyo's piax better, but I have nothing to learn from except the memories I have of him playing and even then, I don't have Pathos to help replicate those patterns."

"You don't have to copy the patterns," chided Kallen. "He taught you chords and notes. That should be enough. You *feel* music."

After the galley was clean, Rhys went in search of Forge. He found the medical student reading in his bunk. "You can read now, huh?" asked Rhys.

Forge looked up and smiled. "Our records match Aabesh fairly well." He set his book on his lap. "Is that how you learned to read?"

"Alina and I both used our AIs to help with language acquisition." Rhys allowed the expression on his face to change to tell Forge he was shifting topics. "Can you have Pathos do a sweep of the horizon? I saw a light off the stern."

Forge looked away briefly as Pathos checked its radar. "It's a single ship. That's all I can tell."

"Is it moving?"

"It is, but not in our direction." Forge fidgeted. When he next spoke, it was in Nefegian. "Uh, thank you for showing me music."

Rhys responded in kind. "I knew you would like it."

"Why me?"

Rhys leaned in the doorway. "Because you're a Pathos-user. I figured Beso and Zain would have a difficult time understanding music. Alina always did."

"Ahh." Forge nodded. "I shared with them Kallen's music, and neither had much to say. I didn't understand how it elicited no reaction from them."

"I felt the same way with Alina. She was a solid wall of stoicism. It didn't matter how beautifully Kyo played or Kallen sang, she never exhibited any type of emotional response." Rhys sighed. "At first, it confused me, and then it frustrated me, and then… I just let it go. She would never be able to comprehend emotion-loaded, free-form concepts. It may be the same with you and Zain and Beso."

Forge met Rhys' gaze. "That's why you kept me on *Themis* instead of one of them."

"I was a Pathos-user; I know the stresses and frustrations you will face. Zain and Beso need to rely on one another to navigate this world. You can help them and offer information, but only they will be able to fully understand how each processes his daily experiences."

"Hodge told me I was acclimating quickly. I believe that has to do with your guidance and the information you offered the council before our departure from the colony. I can't imagine how difficult it must have been for you and Alina."

"Vinz and his crew found us the night we crash-landed. They saw our ship hit the atmosphere and followed us to our landing location. Kallen,

Hodge, and Kashim came for us. From that first day on, Alina and I were never alone. The Overseer at the time didn't much like us and ended up betraying us, but Hodge and Kallen were always, unwaveringly, by our sides."

Forge set his book aside. "Tell me more." Rhys perched at the end of his bed and retold his story once more.

28
SEA BATTLE

FOR THE NEXT SEVERAL DAYS, life on *Themis* continued without trouble. Despite the numerous small seasonal squalls that blew up overnight and dowsed the ship, very few problems actually arose. While Hodge continued to train Forge in the mornings, Rhys, Axel, and Kashim worked on the launch chute.

After four days of around-the-clock work, they finished the infrastructure. The following three days were then spent installing ceiling cranks and tracks as well as extension rods that would allow the entire chute to be manually extended into the water while underway. Determined to complete the project before arriving at Firekli, Rhys spent his entire waking time on perfecting the system. After nine days of solid work and countless trial runs, Rhys declared the chute open for use.

"Hodge!" called Rhys through the forward hatch's open doorway.

"What?" came the reply.

"You're launching."

There was a long pause before the sound of Hodge dancing down the hallway echoed through the floors. Rippling with energy and excitement, his friend flitted into the forward hatch. Forge trailed him, curious.

"You have to test the ramp before you can fly though."

"Fly?" murmured Forge.

As Hodge breathlessly explained to Forge about sunboards, Rhys asked through the pipe system for the others to join them in the hatch. Once everyone save Andy had gathered, Rhys paced for a moment and then looked at his crew. Hodge finally fell still, though Rhys could see his friend's eyes brimming with anticipation. It had been well over two weeks since any of them had surfed due to the construction. If all went well, he too would launch.,

"Is it done?" asked Kallen, examining the ceiling tracks.

Rhys smiled and began the briefing.

"Waaaoooo!" cried Hodge excitedly after Rhys' lengthy explanation of the chute's new processes and procedures. "Look at that!"

Rhys moved forward to study the chute's movement. It was constructed almost entirely of the various metals they had pulled from the Neo-Colony Two maintenance unit. Where the chute sloped considerably to meet the water, he had installed a series of wooden slats to prevent people from slipping when the floor became wet. With Forge's help, he had also mounted lights along the ceiling.

Everyone gathered at the mouth of the chute. Once Hodge's board hit the end of the tracks and descended to the chute floor, Kallen joined Rhys. "What now?" she asked.

Although the majority of the chute was metal, Rhys and Forge had spent quite a bit of time measuring the sunboards' widths, keels, and hull depths. Where they had originally used a sheath to secure the keel, the entire board as well as the tracks now fit into a padded slip. "The board is heavy enough," Rhys explained, "that once the chain releases it, it will slide into the water without hesitation."

"That means we have to erect and control the fin *and* engage the fan?" asked Hodge, his excitement turning into incredulousness.

"You can do it," Rhys assured him.

"I want to try," said Axel.

"No way," snarled Hodge, ripping off his boots and shirt. "I'm first." He approached his board perched in the slip, studying the fin. "So, you've already attached the fin. And… it's being held down by what?"

Kallen pointed to a latch Rhys had recently installed. "Open that once you hit the water and the fin will pop up like usual."

Hodge considered what he had to do and then looked at Rhys. "What about docking?"

"Same process, just reversed. You ramp up into the chute." Rhys kicked the bumper at the top of the padded ramp. "If you're going too fast, this will stop you. Kallen or whoever will connect the chain and engage the crank system. It'll go back up onto the tracks on the ceiling and return to its port in the forward hatch."

Hodge shrugged, looked at his board, and said, "Let's do it."

"Kashim, let Andy know we're beginning live tests."

Kashim separated from the group to relay the message. Hodge rolled his pants and tentatively climbed onto his board. Though the angle of the chute was no more than ten degrees, Hodge had to balance himself. Once he was set and had reviewed the plan, he motioned to Kallen.

Rhys pointed to the clip that still held Hodge's board to the launch chain. Kallen snapped it open and Hodge, along with his board, began sliding backward.

Poised expertly, Hodge looked over his shoulder at the encroaching water. The moment his board hit the water and cleared the chute, he released the fin. It snapped open with a loud *thwack*. He stepped on the fan trigger, and the sunboard roared to life. Effortlessly, he maneuvered out-of-sight.

"How do we launch the dinghy?" asked Kallen, balancing on the bumper.

"The priority of the chute was to enable quick launch of sunboards. If we're launching the dinghy, there's a good chance we're not in a dire situation. We'll just use the original launch ramp."

Hodge appeared momentarily and lined up with the chute. Rhys and Kallen positioned themselves alongside the padded slip. Knowing Hodge had turned the fan off once he had cleared *Themis'* wake, Rhys motioned for his friend to engage it and dock. Leaning against the fin, Hodge evaluated the ramp. The moment he turned the fan on, his board shot forward. Not wanting to overshoot the chute and make a chaotic entry, he cut it off and flung the fin backward. In a graceful motion, he and his board glided onto the ramp and touched the bumper. Kallen secured his board on the launching chain and locked his fin into place using the latch Rhys had installed.

Whooping, Hodge slid off the board and grabbed Rhys. Lifting him from the ground, his friend laughed. "You genius!" Rhys flailed momentarily. "I wish Vinz could see this!" Hodge set Rhys down. "He wouldn't know what to think."

"Everyone helped," said Rhys, glancing at the others.

"*Gawan,* I'm going out again," said Hodge.

"I'm going too," said Axel.

Rhys looked pleadingly at Kashim who sighed and motioned for him to go.

Late into the afternoon, Rhys, Hodge, and Axel patrolled the skies over *Themis,* riding the hot thermals, darting around each other, and chasing the clouds. They worked with Axel to teach him some of the coordinated strategies they used while in battle. Though they were unable to explain to him in great detail the maneuvers due to the fact that they could barely hear one another, Hodge and Rhys were able to shout to him the purpose of each formation. When they had sufficiently practiced, Hodge led them back to *Themis*.

By the time they docked, it was dinner time. Wind-whipped and sunburned, Rhys shuffled into the galley with Hodge and Axel. Kallen and Forge looked up from their work at the stove.

"Kallen…" moaned Hodge.

"It's almost ready," Kallen sighed, stirring a large pot thoroughly before returning to a pan.

Forge left Kallen's side and joined them at the table. "You're pink," he remarked, eyeing Rhys.

"He's right." Kallen leaned against the counter. "I wish you'd cover up when you go out. You burn easily."

"I'm getting tan," murmured Rhys, laying his head on the table. Despite being in top physical shape, his muscles quivered with fatigue. He hadn't been on a sunboard in weeks. His legs and shoulders felt like jelly while his abdomen remained permanently flexed.

As Hodge regaled Forge with their adventures, Rhys stared into the distance, letting his mind go blank. Sensing his fatigue, Kallen kept dinner conversation short. When he made to help her with the dishes, she pushed instead recruited Leo. For a long while, Rhys sat in a trance, gazing at the distant wall. Even after Hodge left for the forward hatch with Forge and Axel went to speak with Andy and Kashim, Rhys remained seated at the table.

"What's wrong?" asked Leo, drying a dish.

Whether it was his fatigue or the fact that finally, after two weeks, the enormity of the situation had finally caught up with him, Rhys didn't know. Perhaps it was the fact that he no longer had a project to keep his racing mind distracted from the inevitability of their situation.

"Rhys?"

Rhys snapped from his trance and stood. "Nothing. I'm fine."

Before he could get to the doorway, Leo stopped him. "You've been staring off for the past half hour. What's wrong?"

"I'm just tired."

Kallen joined them. "I've told you you're a bad liar."

"What we have before us… is daunting," said Rhys. Both Kallen and Leo looked at him in confusion, immediately confirming what he had been thinking—no one except Forge, Beso, and Zain understood what it was going to take to disengage Osiris. "You'll understand once we're there."

Leo nudged him. "Explain it to us."

Rhys sighed and moved back to the table.

"Daunting, what's daunting?" asked Kallen.

"Osiris," said Rhys. He withdrew Ethos from his pocket and set the AI on the table. Running a hand over his face, he murmured, "Show them, Ethos."

"Right-o." Ethos began projecting a three-dimensional image of Earth centimeters above its unit.

"This is Earth." Rhys pointed to the planet and then made a motion. Ethos zoomed out so they could see both Earth and the moon. "And the moon. And…" The image shifted and then began zooming in. A red pinpoint appeared on the moon's cratered surface. "Osiris' location. We have to get ourselves from Brechin to there." Rhys looked at Kallen and Leo. "See a problem?"

"Is it really that far?" asked Kallen.

"Depending on the unit we have at our disposal in Brechin, it could take anywhere from thirty-six hours to five days to get to the moon," said Rhys.

She sighed in relief. "Ah, that's not bad. See, it's not that far." Rhys gazed at her solemnly. "What?"

"There's a catch," concluded Leo.

Rhys nodded. "*Themis'* maximum speed is, give-or-take, fifty niks. The sunboards' top speeds max out at around seventy-five niks." Rhys paused to make swift, silent calculations. "To break Earth's atmosphere and reach orbit, we need a unit that will go roughly twenty-one thousand niks."

"That's not possible," Kallen immediately supplied.

Leo leaned on his elbow. "With what we have it's not possible, but I bet their technology can do it."

Rhys nodded. "Our technology can break through the atmosphere and reach orbit."

Kallen tilted her head. "Orbit?"

"Uh…" Rhys thought for a moment and then shrugged. "You don't need to know what that is. Just know that what we find in the underground base is what will determine whether we can launch for the moon."

"You found a trans-atmospheric unit at the Brechin camp outside New Arbroath though, right? Did you learn anything about it?" asked Leo.

"Not as much as I would have liked," replied Rhys. "Ethos?"

"The trans-atmospheric jets that should still be underground are capable of breaking through Earth's atmosphere," said Ethos, "however, that then makes finding fuel a problem. They're nuclear-powered but they still need fuel for propulsion."

"How do you know about the jets?" asked Kallen.

"They were Ramsen's."

"What?" asked Rhys. This was news to him.

"I thought I told you—Ramsen was a commercial pilot for Omega Technologies."

Rhys interrupted the AI. "I know that. Why were the jets his?"

"We were shuttling them to another colony when we were pulled into the wormhole. Our shuttle is still in the underground base," replied Ethos matter-of-factly. "It was a hubbub of activity while Ramsen and his associates were there."

"Protocols for long-distance shuttle journeys haven't changed that much in the past century. It's likely they have fuel reserves. Right?" mused Rhys.

"Mmm, yes," Ethos hummed.

"Does the fuel have stabilizers in it?"

"It should. It's part of emergency protocols."

Rhys hit the table excitedly with his fist and then leaned back in his chair.

"So... we're sending a bunch of people... to the moon?" asked Kallen, cautiously choosing her words.

"Not people," replied Ethos. "*Person.*"

"Did someone from Neo-Colony Two volunteer?" Kallen met Rhys' gaze, and the intrigue which had colored her face faded into a dark frown. "Rhys..."

"Let someone else go," Leo argued.

Rhys smiled grimly. "Can't."

"Rhys." Kallen's sharp tone made him flinch. "You are Overseer. You have a ship, crew, and a baby on the way."

"Wouldn't Forge or one of the others from Neo-Colony Two be better qualified?" Leo quickly offered. "They still have their AIs."

"That's precisely why it has to be Rhys," chirped Ethos. "Rhys no longer has his AI. The neuro-link system on the jets as well as the AI connections onboard would interfere with anyone wearing a biological AI."

"Then let one of... us... go." Leo seemed to see the problem even as he spoke.

Rhys chuckled.

"I could... do it," muttered Leo. "You could just walk me through everything."

"That's a noble offer, Leo, but that won't be possible," said Ethos. "Once the unit leaves the atmosphere, there will be no communications between it and the surface."

"Why?" Kallen appeared alarmed.

"We can't let Osiris intercept radio transmissions... Once I'm up there, I'll be by myself," said Rhys. He nodded to solidify the thought in his heart.

"That's not fair, Rhys," Kallen murmured. She stood and returned to washing the dishes.

It was well after midnight by the time Kallen came to bed. Rhys woke briefly as she slid in beside him. Though she was rigid and stiff against his beckoning arms, eventually she allowed herself to be molded to his form. Half-asleep, Rhys kissed her shoulder.

Forge woke him a mere three hours later.

"What's wrong?" asked Rhys, adrenaline sending his heart hammering.

"Pathos and Logos have detected ships on radar," Forge said.

"Have you told Andy?"

"No, just you."

Shirtless, Rhys strode down the hallway to the bridge with Forge behind him. "How many? How far out?"

"Two airships," replied Forge in Nefegian. "It looks like they're three and a half kilometers out."

"That's outside of the ship's radar. What's their trajectory?"

"They'll pass right over us."

Rhys entered the bridge to find Andy leaning over the table of maps. His First Mate looked up in surprise. "What's wrong?"

"Forge says there are two airships heading our way," said Rhys. Andy cursed, slid the maps back into their drawer, and looked at radar. "They're too far out right now, but they'll come range here in a few."

Andy cursed and leaned on the instrument paneling. "It was only a matter of time. What are—"

"Uh..." Forge's face became alarmed. In a panic, he reported in Nefegian, "Nine more ships have come into scanning range—seven seafaring, two more airships. All courses are set to intersect with ours."

"Shit." Rhys turned, yanked the pipe communicator from the ceiling, and began speaking. "All hands to battle stations. I repeat, all hands to battle stations. We have incoming enemy ships." He looked to Andy who immediately snatched the radio from the wall and began speaking with Terron on *Grisle*. "All sunboards prepare for launch. Kallen, get to the forward hatch." Rhys flung the pipe back into the ceiling. "Forge?"

The medical student was frozen, hands trembling. "Five more airships," he whispered, staring out the bridge glass. "Four more seafaring vessels."

"Andy, prepare the weapons." Rhys darted across the bridge and down the stairs. "Leo! Arm the ship!" he shouted as he passed the cabin. "Hodge, get up!" He met Kallen in the doorway of their cabin. "We're about to be destroyed," he muttered. Kallen looked at him fearfully. "Get to the forward hatch and get the sunboards ready." Kallen hurried down the hallway. Hodge, Kashim, and Axel followed her.

Rhys dressed quickly, laced his boots, and jogged to the forward hatch. Kallen might not have had the ability to understand astrophysics, but she was a quick study and had learned the new routine. When Rhys walked in, Kashim's board was already on the launch ramp and the chute door was open.

While Axel and Hodge finished buckling the bulletproof vests, Kashim slid a short rifle over his shoulder followed by their only sniper rifle on the ship.

"Dawn hasn't broken yet," said Rhys, watching them in the dim light of the hatch. "Be careful. Watch each other." He looked to Axel. "Sunboards are most protected just before the bow. If you need to recuperate or are injured, get to the bow of the ship and stay there." Axel nodded. Rhys gazed at them solemnly and then looked at Kallen who was visibly quivering. "I'm going to be honest. It looks bad."

"Define bad," murmured Axel.

"Nine airships, eleven seafaring," replied Rhys.

There was a moment of stunned silence before Hodge cursed under his breath and looked away, distressed. "It's not worth us going out," Axel asserted. Kallen joined their little group. "There's a bigger chance of one of us being shot down and lost at sea than us taking out those airships."

"We can't outrun the airships though," replied Kashim. "Our best bet is launching. That'll put more distance between *Themis* and the enemy."

"Us three against all of those ships?" Axel swung his rifle over his shoulder. "You're joking. They're coming with a purpose. We'll be like flies to them. Annoying insects. We'll be shot down at first glance. The airships have tracking gunners. Their computers trace points of contact."

"That's our job though," said Kashim sternly. "Our job is to defend *Themis* and to draw enemy fire away from her."

"I get that, but it doesn't make any sense us launching against this number of enemies." Axel looked to Rhys. "If anything, he should be launching. Not us. That board of his is much faster and can handle sharp evasive maneuvers, the kind that will be needed to avoid automated tracking."

"We're still at least twenty-four hours out of Firekli," mused Kashim. "There's no chance of us running."

"Airships are closing in," called Andy through the pipe communication system.

All eyes fell on Rhys.

Both Axel and Kashim were right. If they didn't launch, then *Themis* was at risk. If they did launch, there was a high likelihood they would be killed.

"Hodge, Axel, standby," Rhys finally said. "Kallen, raise the ramp. Kashim, to the bridge with me." He turned on heel and with Kashim trailing him, hurried upstairs.

"Incoming enemy airships," reported Andy as they entered. "The first wave is nearly here."

"Kashim." Rhys motioned to the weapons seat on the far side of the bridge where Leo sat. "Ready the gunners and cannons. I want the exploding shells loaded. Prep the double-shots next. Save the expanding bar shots for the ships that come within range. Set the gunners at intervals of five. Watch the ammunition usage. Andy, bring *Themis* to flank speed." Rhys retrieved the radio from the forward panel. "Terron, prepare to engage. We are not, at the moment, launching sunboards. I repeat, we are not launching sunboards. Over."

"Roger," came Terron's reply.

"Increasing *Themis'* speed to true flank speed."

"*Grisle's* flank speed is fifteen below *Themis'*," Terron reminded.

Rhys cursed. He had forgotten. Although the ship was better suited for long sea voyages, it was slower than *Themis*. "Adjust to full speed. *Grisle*, come up to flank speed. Maintain your position off starboard."

Radar was peppered with red dots varying in luminosity dependent upon their distance. More than twenty vessels in all. There was no way they were going to survive this.

"Enemy airships within firing range," reported Kashim.

"Open fire," Rhys commanded. Deep booms tore through the cabin as the cannons on either side of the bridge spewed explosions.

"Incoming gunfire," said Andy.

"Gunners, fire." Rhys turned to the pipe. "Kallen, get to the eng—"

"Take those two airships out!" Axel shouted, darting into the bridge. "They're going to pass over with bombs. Take them out."

Rhys whirled around. "Kashim, get to the sonic cannon. Axel go with him. Leo, take up weapons." As people moved in a flurry, Rhys leaned over the radar. His heart sank as more ships appeared from the southwest, eleven in total. "*Shit…*"

"Enemy Airship One has been hit," reported Leo, examining the screen before him. "Incoming gunfire."

A moment later, an enormous blast detonated just off *Themis'* stern, causing the ship to lurch in the water. Rhys grabbed his chair to keep from sliding across the bridge. Forge staggered into the back wall while Andy and Leo worked to stay upright at their stations. "Damage?" Rhys called.

"Miss!" called Leo. "Sonic cannon is prepped."

"We've been hit!" called Tessa through the radio suddenly. "*Grisle* is hit!"

"Leo, load the double-shots. We're going to rapid fire," said Rhys, yanking the handheld radio from the wall. "How bad, Tessa?"

There was a moment's pause before Tessa responded breathlessly. "Damage to the upper deck. We're still afloat, but Jules and Patrin are injured."

Grasping the radio, he looked over his shoulder at Forge who had retreated fearfully to the back wall of the bridge. In the dim light of the instruments, Rhys caught sight of Pathos' unit buried against Forge's temple. "Keep going, Tessa. We're right beside you," said Rhys. He set the radio down and started for the doorway. "Forge, with me. Andy, you're in command."

"Where are you going?"

"Out," said Rhys. He rushed down the stairs to his cabin; Forge stumbled along behind him.

"Rhys?" asked Forge, his voice pinched.

Rhys grabbed the plasma weapon from his desk and pushed it into Forge's hands. "You know what this is, right?"

Forge nodded. "I've never used one before though. It's only for engineers."

Rhys grabbed Forge's arm and began strapping it on. "You're the only one on this ship who can use it. Pathos, link up."

"Linking complete," reported Forge's AI.

"Wait… I'm not going out there."

"You're not going alone," said Rhys. "You're staying on the upper deck with Kashim and Axel. They'll help you. Kashim is familiar with the weapon. Just let Pathos control your aim."

Rhys turned on heel and started for the forward hatch.

"Rhys!" called Kallen, appearing in the doorway of the engine room.

"I'm going out!" he shouted back.

"Put a damn vest on!" she screamed.

Rhys stopped Forge at the bridge stairs and met the medical student's eyes. "We are outnumbered. We have our backs against the wall. Forge, this is a battle. If we don't kill them, they will kill us."

"I know but—"

"Aim for the airships. Be prepared for anything once you start firing. They don't know what plasma weapons are. They might run or they might strengthen their attacks. There's no way of knowing."

"Rhys… I…" Forge's hands trembled.

Rhys reached between them and gently touched Pathos' unit. Forge startled from the intimate touch but didn't withdraw. "Fear is good. It keeps us from doing harm to ourselves. It's our mind and body working together to warn us of danger. But fear does not stop a battle or protect loved ones. Courage does. Courage is taking action in the face of imminent danger or threat." Rhys ran his thumb over Forge's AI. "Combine the two, Forge. Use fear to sharpen your senses and courage to move you to action."

The medical student took a deep breath and nodded. Rhys patted his shoulder and then turned for the forward hatch. "Wait, what are you doing?"

"I'm going out. I'm counting on you." And with that, Rhys disappeared into the forward hatch. Moving swiftly, he withdrew his board from the lock he had installed on the wall. Once he turned it on, he began arming himself with steady hands. After fitting himself with a bulletproof vest and tucking Ethos in the collar of it, he laid a short rifle across his shoulder, slipped a handgun into the small of his back, and strapped on the resonance cutters.

"I'm launching," he said into the pipe on the far wall.

"Go!" shouted Andy.

"Someone come close the chute after me." Rhys pushed his board, which was hovering in the forward hatch, down the chute. After a calming breath, he opened the chute door and stepped onto his board. Ethos' projection of the magnetic waves glowed before his face. "Dimmer," instructed Rhys, edging out of the chute.

"Better?" asked Ethos.

"Yeah." Rhys grimaced as a roar passed overhead. He took another deep breath to calm his pounding heart and then mashed on the back of the board.

Like a missile, he went screaming out of the chute and soared over *Themis*. Though it was dark, he could vaguely make out Kashim and Axel on the deck. Where was Forge? Was he still inside?

A luminous blast of orange erupted from *Themis'* stern illuminating the entire area. An explosion shook the air far overhead as the plasma shot connected with its target. Rhys maneuvered around the sails and looked up at the enemy airship which was now tipped precariously in the air, brilliant amber flames pouring from its engines and hull.

Forge, a shadow on the stern, fired once more, causing the airship to quiver. A red glow started from within the craft and then bulged outward until the entire ship was awash in a conflagration and dropping from the sky.

The encroaching airships overhead seemed to pick up speed.

Punching his heel into the board, Rhys rose as a blur and ascended to meet the units. Another orange blast exploded from *Themis'* deck to bore deep into the foremost airship. Two more beams erupted on either side of Rhys but neither originated from *Themis*.

"From *Grisle*," reported Ethos, sensing Rhys' curiosity.

"The maintenance unit must have had supplies on it," wheezed Rhys, speeding toward the next airship. He would need to congratulate Beso and Zain later. No doubt Forge had been the one to give the order.

"Incoming fire," Ethos informed. Rhys pulled his board upward to protect himself and rushed into the deep blackness of the sky. Bullets pinged off the bottom of his board as he continued to evade detection. "They're tracking you!" called Ethos.

Rhys scanned the magnetic field projection, secured a path to one of the rear airships, and then dove, keeping his board between himself and the ships. Gunfire spilled around him, littering the sky. Rhys crouched to gain speed and withdrew the resonance cutters. Beso, Forge, and Zain might be on the offensive, but they weren't going to be enough.

The wind whistled in his ears as he descended. His lungs froze, his body tensed in anticipation. When he was within a few meters of the airship, he jerked his boots from the board's clasps and perched motionlessly. The moment he was within range, he threw the board over the top of the airship and leapt onto the soldiers in the open cockpit below.

The gunfire remained trained on his board, allowing him to land safely, roll, and engage the enemy.

With precise movements, Rhys wielded the resonance cutters. In four strikes, he killed the two pilots and the weapons coordinator seated nearby. Just as he withdrew his weapon from the last body, a fist connected with the side of his face. Rhys slammed into the bridge paneling, his head reeling. Hands snaked around his throat and began squeezing.

Rhys struggled against the soldier's iron grip, which not only had his throat but the arm that held the resonance cutters. Despite the months of training and surviving he had done, his strength still didn't compare.

The soldier bore down, his fingers gnarled around Rhys' neck. The searing pain was debilitating. His head hurt; his vision was going dark. Choking and running out of options, Rhys slammed a knee into the soldier's side. Though he felt the man flinch, his enemy's grip didn't lessen. Realizing that, although his right arm was being held captive, his left was not, Rhys pushed himself forward enough to slip his hand into the small of his back. With another knee jab, he was able to move the soldier a few centimeters upward so as to give himself room to withdraw his pistol.

Without looking, Rhys raised his gun and fired. Again and again and again he pulled the trigger, emptying the magazine into the man. The soldier slumped onto the deck, leaving rivulets of blood down Rhys' front. Wheezing and ears ringing horribly, Rhys stumbled to the edge of the ship and stepped off onto his board. Gunfire spilled around him. Trusting that Ethos would guide him, he knelt on the board and ascended into the deep blackness of the sky.

"Rhys, breathe," instructed Ethos as Rhys coughed and rasped. He couldn't get enough air. He felt as though he was about to pass out. Shakily, he sheathed the resonance cutters and cripped the edges of the board. "Slow breaths." He felt nauseous, as if the panic which had built in him during the struggle was trying to release itself through his squashed trachea. "You need to get back to the ship."

When he tried to respond, nothing emerged from his throat. Only a scratchy sound.

"Easy, rest a minute," Ethos said. Below, a myriad of explosions, deafening booms, and orange bursts of plasma decorated the sky. In a colorful array of beautiful lights, the battle continued.

Loudly wheezing, Rhys forced some strength into his legs and strapped himself into the board. When he was ready, he withdrew his resonance cutters once more. Despite the significant amount of adrenaline pumping through him, he felt weak.

"Your next target," murmured Ethos, projecting an arrow before his face. Rhys examined the magnetic field around him and then darted northward. "This airship is trying to approach *Themis* from her stern. Forge is busy dealing with others." Rhys crouched to gain speed and rushed through the sky. Everything below him passed as a multi-chromatic cloud. "Adjust angle of descent by twenty-four degrees," commanded Ethos. "We're going to come up along its stern." Rhys adjusted his positioning. "There are seven soldiers total on this airship. Get to the helm and disable the weapons. Same tactic as before." Rhys withdrew his feet from the board's clasps and readied himself. "Jump in four seconds. Two, one…"

Rhys leapt off the board, landed on the airship, and ran the cutters through a soldier's armor, killing him instantly. Using the soldier's body as a shield, he pushed forward against the gunfire. Gasping and rasping, he ripped his cutters through the soldier's body and plunged them into the next. Allowing his instincts and innate skill full control, Rhys tore through the second soldier, whirled on heel, and drove toward the next.

With a yell, the third man attempted to deflect the cutters with his rifle. Unaware the cutters could cut through anything, the man crumpled to the ground. Panting so hard his wheezes sounded like groans, Rhys leaned on his knees, keeping his gaze on the remaining soldiers. All four were gathered on the helm, gazing fearfully at him, short rifles raised. It was apparent even in the dim light of the firefight that the presence of a white god on their ship was alarming.

"Rhys," murmured Ethos as his board rejoined him. Rhys stepped behind his board to safeguard himself from attack. "Leave this area!" shouted Ethos to the soldiers, imitating Rhys' voice. "Retreat—"

The radio at the helm crackled to life. "All units retreat. I repeat, all units retreat. The Firekli Fleet is here."

Rhys peered out from behind his board at the soldiers. After a moment, they laid their weapons on the deck and raised their hands. "We wish to retreat," one of the soldiers announced.

Rhys rotated his board, sheathed his cutters, and held his short rifle in his arms. He stepped onto the board and made a motion. Ethos spoke for him. "Then go."

The soldiers turned and began slowing the airship. Once it was apparent the vessel was in full retreat in the opposite direction, Rhys left them and headed back.

By the time he made it to *Themis*, the Brechin forces were specks on the horizon. Wearily, he landed on the upper deck. Kashim, Axel, and

Forge met him as he stepped from his board. "You hurt?" called Kashim, running to him.

Rhys staggered off the board, landing on all fours. He must have appeared hellish covered in blood splatters, his silver hair wind-whipped. More importantly though, he could hardly breathe. Every gasp he pulled felt as though he were breathing against a thick pillow. He grasped at his chest, hands shaking hard.

Forge knelt beside him and tilted Rhys' chin upward. "Your neck."

"I'm..." Rhys coughed as the air squeezed through his injured trachea. He couldn't catch his breath.

"He was choked," reported Ethos from its place inside his vest.

After a few more desperate breaths, Rhys swallowed hard and looked at the others. Kashim and Axel were covered in a fine grit from the smoke and explosions. Forge appeared uninjured and more concerned about Rhys than himself.

"Why did they suddenly retreat?" asked Axel, looking about.

Rhys motioned to Ethos which explained, "They were ordered to retreat. Something about a resistance force making an appearance."

Axel jogged across the deck and scanned the horizon. "Those... aren't Brechin's ships? Then whose are they? Their numbers go on forever."

Kashim pulled Rhys to his feet, clapped him on the shoulder, and joined Axel at the ship railing. Rhys was glad he had not been the only one to think that Brechin had brought more than thirty vessels into battle. It appeared the line of ships spanning the horizon to the southeast didn't belong to the capital.

"Where's Rhys?" called Andy from the bridge's open external door.

"Here!" shouted Kashim.

"We have incoming radio transmissions."

Rhys glanced at his board and then followed Kashim down to the bridge. With his heartrate decreasing, he was finding it easier to breathe.

"...No choice but to open fire," crackled the radio. Panicked, Rhys motioned to Andy who threw the radio to him. "I repeat, identify your ship and port of origin or we have no choice but to open fire."

Rhys opened his mouth to respond. Nothing but a few scratchy sounds escaped his throat. Frantic, he withdrew Ethos and held the AI to the radio. "This is Rhys Falkrow, Overseer of *Themis*. Off our starboard is the ship, *Grisle*, currently under the command of Terron Damien. To whom am I speaking?" said Ethos, using Rhys' voice. Kashim, Leo, and Andy gathered in silence.

"Rhys Falkrow…" murmured the voice. "Damien…"

Rhys waited for a moment before prompting Ethos to ask the question once more.

"This is General Malau Yanamichin. Where is Vinz Amadorri? Over."

"He was killed several months ago. I have taken his place as Overseer," replied Ethos. Rhys nodded in approval of the AI's response.

"Very well. Overseer, where are your ships going?"

"Our course is set for Firekli," said Ethos. "As you and your forces currently stand between us and the trading port, I ask that you peacefully let us pass."

"No," replied the General. Rhys bristled and looked at the others on the bridge. "We will escort you."

29
PORT ENTRY

RHYS HELD ANDY'S GAZE BEFORE cuing the radio. "And why would you want to escort us?" asked Ethos. "How can we be certain that you are who you say you are?"

Andy touched Rhys' arm. In a hushed tone, he murmured, "Yanamichin is our contact in Firekli. He was a personal acquaintance of Vinz's."

"Does this sound like him?" asked Ethos, predicting Rhys' response.

Andy cocked his head in thought. "I can't be certain. I haven't spoken with him in over a year and even then, I wasn't well-acquainted with him. Kashim?"

"I know him. It sounds like Yanamichin."

Rhys passed Kashim the radio as Ethos said, "Ask him something only he would know."

Kashim held the radio to his mouth for a long moment and then said, "This is Kashim Vogland, Vinz's former proxy. Yanamichin, it's been a while. Over."

"Kashim," chuckled Yanamichin. He seemed in high spirits. "It's good to hear from you. You have a new Overseer, I hear."

"That's right."

"He's a bit of a celebrity in most ports."

"We weren't aware," replied Kashim. His voice grew serious. "Yana, remind me—how did you, Vinz, and I meet? I don't recall."

There was a long pause before Yanamichin's gruff voice permeated the radio static. "Met the two of you as you climbed from a battered dinghy in port. Vinz was all sorts of beat up. Over."

Kashim nodded; it was the correct answer. Rhys motioned for Andy to set *Themis* at cruising speed. "Thanks, Yana. We'd be happy to have your company."

"Very good. Lead the way, and we'll fall in around you. Over and out."

Kashim returned the radio. "It's him. There wasn't anyone else there on the docks that day because of the storms. He gave Vinz and me shelter after we escaped the slave ship."

Rhys gripped Ethos to help the AI better read his intentions. "Please tell *Grisle* that we're being escorted to port. Also, get me a status report on Jules and Patrin," Ethos commanded.

As Andy began to communicate with *Grisle*, Rhys teetered from the bridge to the galley. Forge, Axel, and Hodge, who had been standing on the stairs just outside the bridge, fell silent as he passed.

"I should examine you," said Forge in Nefegian.

Rhys waved his AI at Forge. "I'm fine," Ethos chirped in Rhys' stead. He looked up as the door to the engine room opened to reveal Kallen decorated in black smears.

Wiping her hands on her blouse, she gazed at Rhys. Her eyes widened and her brows knitted together in horror. "Rhys," she murmured, running to him. She made a cursory glance over his body to determine if the blood there was his before her eyes rested on his neck. "What happened?"

"He was choked," explained Ethos. "He will be fine. He just needs rest."

"You can't speak?" Kallen whispered.

Rhys opened his mouth to respond, but Ethos cut him off. "No, he cannot. It would be best if he did not speak for a while as his vocal cords are swollen from the assault."

"Assault?" Kallen leaned in to better examine his neck.

"Be prepared to launch for *Grisle*," said Ethos. "She was damaged during the fight."

Rhys attempted to push past Kallen, but she took his arm and led him into the galley where she began unbuckling his bulletproof vest. Once she threw his vest and shirt on the floor, she began wetting towels. Forge, Hodge, and Axel appeared in the doorway.

"What's going to happen now?" asked Axel as Kallen began wiping away blood from Rhys' neck and torso.

Straddling a chair, Hodge said, "At least they're on our side."

"We don't really know that," countered Ethos.

"You said the Brechin soldiers called them the Firekli Fleet?" Axel asked.

"Yes."

"That implies this conflict's been going on for a while now. If the battalion currently gathering around us has a name, they've had victories. The Brechin navy fled from them. That means something."

"Forge," murmured Kallen, stepping aside.

With gentle hands, Forge ran his fingers over Rhys' neck. "Swallow," he instructed in Nefegian. Rhys obeyed. "Speak to me."

Rhys opened his mouth to speak. The moment air passed through his vocal cords, he fell into fits of coughing and wheezing. When he tried to catch his breath, he wheezed loudly. Kallen noticeably turned away.

"Be still," said Forge, pressing his hand against Rhys' neck. "All of it is quite swollen. It will be several hours before you're able to speak again."

"Use Aabesh," Hodge complained.

Forge straightened himself. "His throat is severely swollen. It will be several hours before he can speak and even then, he will be hoarse."

"That's it? Nothing else is wrong?" asked Hodge. "He has purple marks all over him."

"Bruising. There's no permanent internal damage," replied Forge. "Drink water and don't talk. It's important to remain hydrated to decrease the swelling." The med student glanced at Kallen who stood at the sink. "He will be fine."

"Will he, Forge?" Kallen's voice was tinted with bitterness.

Forge glanced at Rhys in confusion and repeated himself, "He will." With a sigh, Hodge rose from his seat, took Forge by the arm, and escorted him from the galley. "Wait, Hodge. I don't... understand..." Axel followed.

"This isn't fair, Kallen," chided Ethos from its position on the table. "He can't argue back."

"Stay out of it," she snapped, whirling to glare at Rhys. "Why do you do this? Since the day I met you, you've been nothing but reckless."

Rhys gazed at her solemnly. He wanted to reply, he wanted to make her see that it was his responsibility.

As if she read his mind, Kallen approached him. "I know you think it's your duty, that you alone can protect this ship and everyone on it... and maybe that's true, but... *please* take into consideration what would happen if you were to be killed." She touched his chest. "I know what you did. I know that you killed more soldiers and that, like always, it was a life-or-death struggle. Sometimes I'm glad I'm not a fighter like you or Hodge because I wouldn't want to be there to see you like that." She grinned bitterly, sadly. "But maybe, if I were there, I could stop you."

"I've had this conversation with him numerous times," said Ethos. "I don't agree with his methods either, but I understand them. Sometimes you have to fight to protect the things in this world you love."

Rhys expected Kallen's response to be harsh. Instead, she sighed, "I know that. And… that's not what I'm talking about." She took Rhys' hand and placed it on her abdomen. "Please, if for no one else, then for me— stop being reckless. You're human. You no longer have Pathos to protect you. You are as human as we are."

Unable to argue, he nodded that he would try harder, even though he didn't mean it.

Once Kallen finished sufficiently scolding him and retrieved clean clothes, Rhys returned to his board, docked it, and then went to the bridge where he spent the majority of the morning monitoring the ships around them. Although Kashim had validated the General's identity, both Rhys and Andy remained on edge. Being surrounded by so many unknown ships was not a welcoming sight, especially having spent the past several weeks alone in open waters. Per Rhys' request, Andy stayed in constant contact with *Grisle*, speaking with Terron as many as five or six times an hour. *Grisle's* crew was also made anxious by the crowded waters.

Rhys skipped midday meal due to his sore throat and instead busied himself repairing solar panels in the shade of the sails on the upper deck. After lunch, Kallen and Hodge traveled to *Grisle* to examine the damage. When asked if he should join them to look in on Jules and Patrin, Forge assured everyone that both Zain and Beso had everything under control.

After a stormy but uneventful night, gray skies and breezy weather greeted *Themis* and *Grisle* as they Firekli came into view. Everyone gathered on the bridge.

Hoarse, Rhys addressed the crew. "We don't know what's happened while we were gone." He motioned to the numerous ships around them. "Keep your eyes open. Be aware of people watching us; take note of anyone who seems too interested or who is asking too many questions. We need to get in, make repairs, and get out. Depending on *Grisle's* repairs and how quickly we can resupply, I'm looking at a turnaround time of four days."

Hodge raised his hand. "We have no money."

Rhys snorted and Kashim huffed in amusement. An understatement.

Forge raised his hand as he had seen Hodge do. "Money is a medium of exchange such as coins or paper, right?"

"Correct," replied Rhys.

Forge tilted his head as he conversed with Zain and Beso. Rhys shared amused looks with the others, now fully understanding what they had tolerated with him and Alina. "Uh, would any of the materials or technology that we took from the maintenance unit be of value?"

Rhys looked to Kashim and Hodge for an answer; both nodded. "They'll sell for a high price in the black market off the docks," Kashim mused. Hodge nudged Forge, causing the medical student to smile shyly.

"Kashim, Kallen, and Beso will go to the black market once we arrive." Rhys nodded to Forge. "I'm leaving you, Zain, and Beso to determine what to sell. Don't give away something we can use in the future." Forge nodded and began to silently speak with his *Grisle* counterparts. "Once they get back, I'll take Forge and Hodge to purchase medical supplies. Axel, you and Leo look into ammunition."

"What happened to the medical supplies we had?" asked Andy.

"We left them in the forest outside of New Arbroath when we went to rescue everyone," said Rhys.

"Well, if we're ever around there again, we'll know where emergency medical supplies are," Hodge darkly joked.

Rhys peered out the bridge glass at the port slowly growing larger. Even from this distance, it was apparent Firekli was swamped with ships. Aside from the fleet gathered around them, commercial and private boats crowded the waters outside the port.

"This is General Yanamichin, *Themis* do you copy?" buzzed the radio.

Rhys glanced at Andy, retrieved the radio from the wall, and replied. "This is Rhys Falkrow. Go ahead, over."

"My ship alone will escort you into port. As you can see, the waters around here are busy. There's not much room for an entire fleet to dock. I am currently off your port flying the red banner. Please follow my lead. Over."

"Roger, will do," said Rhys. He held the radio at his waist and looked at Kashim. "You're sure about this?"

"Absolutely. He's a good man." There was no doubt in Kashim's voice.

"Once we're in port, Forge—you're not to be alone. Pass that message along to Zain and Beso. We haven't dyed your hair. All of you will stick out horribly. Please make sure that if you go out, your hair is covered."

"Is it dangerous?" Forge asked.

"Don't know," replied Hodge. "But you should cover your head anyway. You'll get sunburned."

"Also, all external doors are to remain locked. Andy will remain with the ship for the duration of our stay." Rhys thought. He opened his mouth to speak, but Forge interrupted him.

"Why do you place rules on Zain, Beso, and I but not on yourself? You will also *stick out*," remarked the medical student.

"For your protection," Kashim replied. "Rhys has been here long enough to understand the dangers he willingly places himself in. You three don't know what to look for."

"He'll be covered too," chuckled Hodge. "He may look tan next to you, but he still burns."

It took another two hours for them to reach the port city and be assigned slips at the docks.

"Uh…Rhys?" beckoned Andy.

Rhys, who had been speaking with Kashim, Axel, and Leo at the back of the bridge, turned. "Hm?" Andy pointed out the bridge glass at the swarms of people gathering on the docks. To see a sea of people jostling one another along the narrow wharves was somewhat unnerving. "Kashim, Hodge, Axel," he murmured. "Dock us."

As the three disappeared to the upper deck, Rhys took the radio from the wall and brought it to his mouth. "General Yanamichin, what is the meaning of this?" He hadn't meant to sound harsh, but he couldn't keep his alarm hidden. Rhys leaned on the paneling and gazed out at the dock hands as Kashim, Hodge, and Axel exchanged ropes with them.

"Word has spread that you are back in Firekli," crackled the radio.

Rhys looked at Andy and Leo in confusion; both shrugged. "Why would our arrival in Firekli have any significant meaning? Last time we were here, our ships were torn apart. It took us nearly two months to make repairs."

The radio was silent for so long that Rhys almost asked if Yanamichin was still present. Finally, he replied, "You don't know—Brechin attempted to take over Firekli and bring it under the Pantarak Empire three weeks ago."

"What?" hissed Andy.

"Everyone knows that Paducah fell, and they know about New Arbroath," Yanamichin continued. "Not all of those in Paducah fled for New Arbroath. Many are here." He paused and then said, "And everyone knows of the part that you and your crew played in the battle against the capital. They're here to support you."

Wide-eyed, Rhys glanced first at Andy and then at Leo and Forge.

"I know you and your crew have been through a lot over the past few months, so I understand your hesitancy, but please, rest assured, you are safe here." Yanamichin chuckled. "Firekli might be the safest port anywhere right now."

Rhys returned the radio to his mouth. "Thank you, General."

"How could so much have happened in such a short period of time?" whispered Andy, gazing out at the masses.

"Osiris," murmured Rhys. He wished Alina was here; he wished Vinz could see this. After all, they had been a part of it from the beginning. "I'm going out." He turned and started back down the hall to his cabin. Forge followed.

"I don't understand," said Forge in Nefegian. "What's going on? Why are all of those people out there? Are we in danger?"

Rhys snatched his short rifle, resonance cutters, and a long headscarf from his cabin. As he stood in the hallway arming himself, he said, "I don't know if we're in danger or not." Once the resonance cutters were strapped to his back, he wrapped the headscarf around his head. "Stay inside." Without another word, he strode down the hallway, retrieved Leo from the bridge, and stepped out.

The constant hum of hundreds of people waiting in anticipation quieted, leaving the docks deathly silent. Hodge, who was leaning on the outer platform, looked at Rhys.

"Brechin tried to take over Firekli," Rhys said under his breath.

"What?" muttered Hodge.

"Three weeks ago. That's what Yanamichin said." He glanced up at Kashim and Axel who were seated on top of the bridge.

Kashim smiled and then jumped down to the outer platform. "I want to go talk to Yanamichin," the wolfish man mused.

Rhys motioned to him. "Lead the way."

Kashim retrieved three short rifles from the bridge, distributed them to Hodge and Axel, and then started down the stairs to the docks. Anxious, Rhys took comfort in his crew's presence. The moment Kashim stepped onto the wooden planks, the people crowding there jostled against one another to form a pathway.

In hushed silence, they made their way along the docks to the slip left of *Themis* where Yanamichin's ship floated. Already, the so-called general was making his way to them. They met at the end of his dock, strangers sporting various skin tones clamoring silently to listen.

"Kashim," greeted Yanamichin, extending his great hand. Just like Kashim, Yanamichin was enormous with rippling muscles, a long curly, black beard, and a broad chest. His coarse, dark hair was pulled taut in a ponytail to reveal a white scar running horizontal across his forehead. Needless to say, he towered over Rhys.

Kashim greeted Yanamichin briefly before stepping aside so the General could see Rhys who stuck his hand out. "I'm Rhys Falkrow. A pleasure."

Seemingly taken aback by Rhys' size, Yanamichin chuckled and then swallowed Rhys' arm in his hand. "A pleasure, Rhys. I expected you to be taller, what with the stories and all."

Rhys ignored the comment, pulled away, and motioned to Hodge. "This is Hodge." He nodded to Axel. "And Axel." Both greeted Yanamichin with firm grips of the arm. "Thank you for your support out at sea."

"We thought you were some of our merchant ships being attacked," said Yanamichin. "But when we found no merchant or trader banners, we knew something was up." Yanamichin folded his hands on his hips. "You don't look like much, but that battle earlier tells me otherwise. Two ships survived a full assault by Brechin forces." The mirth on Yanamichin's face faded and his gaze settled on Rhys. "We heard what happened in Paducah… and New Arbroath."

"We were fighting a losing battle," Rhys explained. "But here…" He motioned to the people around them. "We just might win."

"Well, that's what we're going for!" shouted Yanamichin. "Right?"

The people around them cheered in agreement, causing Rhys to grin. He had been naïve to think that they could save Paducah or prevent the Brechin navy from taking over New Arbroath. They had not had the resources or the people to put up a substantial fight. The majority of Paducah had been destroyed upon their return, and New Arbroath had chosen the coward's way to peace by compromising with Brechin's military.

It seemed all of his failures had finally led him here.

30
FIREKLI AGAIN

HALF AN HOUR LATER, RHYS found himself in Yanamichin's office three blocks from the docks.

"Sorry about all of this," Yanamichin chuckled, leaning against his desk. The office in the back of the supply shop he ran was small and cramped with fat folders of paper, piles of registration documents, and a myriad of knick-knacks. Maps of the region covered the walls as well as color-coded moveable pins that indicated fleet status. "I reported that *Themis* and *Grisle* were en route, and… well, word got out." He regarded the group for a moment. "So, how did Vinz die?"

"The high priest in Brechin killed him." Kashim nodded to Rhys. "His sister was also killed."

"And so, you took over as *Themis'* Overseer?"

"Yes," replied Rhys.

Yanamichin sighed. "I've heard stories from the Paducah refugees and rumors, but I still don't understand why *he* became Overseer of *Themis*. He's so young."

"Vinz was young," Kashim countered.

"Not *this* young." Yanamichin laughed. "How old are you? Fifteen?"

"Nineteen," corrected Rhys.

The General nudged Kashim warmly. "Why didn't you take *Themis*? You've been on her longer than anyone except Vinz. She should have been yours."

Kashim gently stepped back. "Yana, I value your candor, but Rhys is our Overseer. Address him, not me."

The expression on Yanamichin's face changed to one of perplexed seriousness, and he looked back at Rhys who had been watching the discussion in silence. "My... apologies."

"Don't apologize," Rhys replied. "I'm aware that I'm young."

Yanamichin chuckled tensely. "If the stories I've heard hold any truth, I will admit in full honesty that it is not your age that unsettles me."

"We chose Rhys as our Overseer," Hodge said. "That alone should be reason enough to respect him."

"Yes, you're right." Yanamichin stood and gestured to the map on the wall behind them. "As you can see, our fleet maintains a perimeter around Firekli. Total, we are seventy-two ships strong."

Rhys studied the map. "All you have are seafaring vessels?"

"We've managed to capture two airships, but they aren't much use."

Rhys pointed to Axel. "He can help you get those running."

"Why him?" asked Yanamichin.

"He's a former Brechin soldier." Rhys pointed to Firekli's south. "Ships are patrolling the open waters, but what land defense do we have? There are trading roads leading south out of the port."

"We have half a dozen militia groups stationed from here... to here." Yanamichin marked the spots on the map with a thick finger.

"And about how many men make up a militia?" asked Rhys, not familiar with the word.

"It varies. Total, I would say we have... maybe five hundred men set up along the trading roads all the way out to the main thoroughfare... here." The General pointed to a spot on the topographical map where the varying elevation of the port gave way to a desert.

"Have you had any trouble there?" asked Kashim.

"No, not yet. Initially, Brechin presented Firekli with a proposal that would allow the peaceful assimilation of the port under the Pantarak Empire. Obviously, that didn't work, so they brought in airships."

Rhys leaned against the wall. "And?"

"They didn't think we were prepared to fight, but we were. Firekli has kept several militias for a number of years on the off-chance that something like this would happen. We launched sunboards and intercepted with armed ships."

"Casualties?"

"That first battle went on for two days... We lost four hundred seventy-eight people." Yanamichin smiled grimly. "But Brechin backed off. Since then, we've had skirmishes out at sea but nothing as bad as that."

"And they haven't tried attacking by land?" asked Rhys.

"Not yet. That would be a difficult endeavor. To bring foot soldiers along the trade routes south of the port would mean that they would need to travel through the desert. It sounds doable, but something of that magnitude doesn't work for foot soldiers."

"He's right," said Axel. "It's risky. Traversing the deserts would be doable via airship, but that still means you need supplies for hundreds of soldiers. Clothes, food, medicine, ammunition. Even by airship, it would take several days to cross the desert—and that's assuming they're coming from Bathsgate. A full deployment from Brechin over land is unwise."

Yanamichin pointed to Axel. "You got it."

"But that doesn't mean you can fully discredit the idea," argued Rhys.

"They're not. They have militias out there," Axel replied.

Rhys fell into thought. Taking into account the geographical complexities of the area, Axel and Yanamichin were right. No army would want to cross a desert and then fight. That was a death sentence. Still, something told him the forces along the southern border needed to be reinforced.

If Osiris was the one pulling strings amongst the Brechin high-ups and having a say in military action, there was a possibility the AI would forgo human rationale and force deployment of troops to the southern border. It didn't matter to the AI if human lives were lost. All of Earth was just an experiment and because Rhys, like Ramsen, was an outlier in Osiris' regional trials, it was likely the AI would begin to take drastic measures. Human lives were nothing; results were everything. Osiris would want to rid the experiment of him however it could—and that included destroying an entire city.

Unaccustomed to Rhys' sudden spells of thoughtful silence, Yanamichin fidgeted. "What's wrong?"

"You need to put more troops along the southern border," Rhys asserted. "I hope we won't need them, but with the way things are progressing, there's a very good chance Firekli's southern border will be attacked."

"Why do you think that? Explain it to me because I have scouting reports coming in every hour. I have spies tracking Brechin's movements." All anxiety disappeared from Yanamichin and the General, for the first time, spoke to Rhys with authority. "And every one of them indicates that Brechin is maintaining a safe distance from Firekli."

Aware that he was being challenged, Rhys replied calmly, "History has shown us again and again that when we least expect something, the worst happens. The Battle of Trilanes in 245 A.C.E., the Battle of Puglear in 333 A.C.E., the Siege of Wyan in 403 A.C.E. Every one of them ended similarly—no one expected an attack and the entire battle was lost. Whether it was due to geographical difficulties or faulty intelligence, it didn't matter. Preparation and readiness are vital to winning." Yanamichin held his gaze. "Fortify your southern defenses."

"I'll consider it," replied Yanamichin.

"Yana, if we could, I'd like to discuss resupplying," Kashim said, redirecting the conversation.

His dark eyes still on Rhys, Yanamichin nodded.

It was evening by the time Rhys, Kashim, Hodge, and Axel returned to the ship. Rhys was surprised to find Kallen and Leo missing. Andy reported that they had gone off with Beso to the black market two hours earlier to sell materials.

With Hodge to keep him company, Rhys threw together a small dinner and ate. "Was all that stuff you said earlier true?" asked Hodge. "I've never heard of any of those battles." Mouth full, Rhys shook his head. "*Gawan*, lying to the General."

Rhys swallowed. "It's Osiris."

His friend leaned on the table. "How do you figure?"

"According to Osiris, all of Earth is just a collection of experiments. Osiris wants to know how political, economic, and religious factors influence human societies. I already have a target on my back because I have been an instigator of trouble since I landed here. Fortunately, or unfortunately—depending on how you look at it—many have followed in my steps. This will lead to Osiris implementing larger measures to quell the disruptions in its regional experiment."

"Uh-huh…"

"This also means that Osiris will be more willing to disseminate orders that directly put human lives at risk. The AI doesn't care whether human lives are lost so long as its experiments continue. If it decides to, it will deploy troops south of Firekli, force them to cross the desert, and then fight to the bitter end. And if Firekli isn't prepared to take on that kind of threat, countless deaths will follow."

Hodge nudged him. "This is why you're the Overseer."

Kallen and Leo returned a few hours later, laughing and in good spirits. Rhys and Forge, who had been sitting on the bridge discussing Osiris, peered down the hallway as Leo got into a roughhousing match with Hodge.

"What's going on?" queried Rhys, amused.

Standing at the top of the stairs laughing, Kallen explained, "Leo's drunk."

Out of habit, Rhys turned his head in confusion. Drunk? Was he physically ill?

"Inebriated," supplied Forge in Nefegian. It was clear Pathos had just explained it to him. "Intoxicated."

"He hasn't really been one to drink," said Kallen, joining them. She had tears in her eyes from laughing so hard. "It took three mugs and he was gone."

At the bottom of the stairs, Hodge wrestled Leo to the floor and pinned him there. "You reek of alcohol," grinned Hodge. "Lightweight." Leo weakly struggled against Hodge between fits of laughter. "Why did you let him drink? Kallen, he's a noble."

"I didn't realize he had," chuckled Kallen. "He said he was thirsty and disappeared into a store. I found him twenty minutes later on his third mug."

"Ah, Overseer," Leo effused, craning his neck to see over Hodge's arm. "When… did you get here?"

"It took all of my effort to get him back to the ship," said Kallen. "He kept stopping to talk with people."

"Pathos, explain alcohol," said Rhys in Nefegian. Forge must have been wondering the same thing, because the medical student did not dismiss the request.

"Alcohol, a volatile and colorless liquid found in many manmade concoctions usually produced by fermenting fruits or grains. It can also be used as a fuel or solvent," replied Pathos. "It can vary in toxicity. Different alcohols may cause inebriation quicker than others."

Rhys started down the stairs to better study Leo but Kallen stopped him. "Here," she said, holding out a small cloth bag of cream-colored bills, the local currency. "We got more than enough for supplies and repairs. Everyone was eager to purchase the indestructible material Beso brought with us." Relieved, Rhys closed the bag and looked back at Leo. "Don't be angry with him."

"I'm not." Rhys chuckled as Leo flailed under Hodge. Briefly, the Brechin noble managed to wriggle his way from Hodge's arms but was quickly taken hostage again and forced back to the floor.

"Whatcha want me to do with him?" asked Hodge. Leo sighed as he gave up.

"Let him up so Rhys and Forge can see how a drunk person moves," bubbled Kallen.

Hodge rolled off of Leo and stepped away. "I'm... not an... e-e-experiment," huffed Leo, shuffling to his knees. He reached out to steady himself on the hallway wall but missed and collapsed back to his knees.

Kallen leaned on the railing laughing while Hodge offered to help him up. Begrudgingly, the Brechin noble accepted, and Hodge drew him to his feet. Once upright, Leo swayed, took a step forward, and then stumbled into the wall.

"How is this possible? You didn't drink that much," Hodge teased.

Leo thought that was funny and, grinning, pushed his hair from his face. Forge descended the stairs to regard Leo. "You... have really... pretty eyes," murmured the noble.

"Thank you," Forge replied. Swiftly, the medical student grabbed Leo's wrist and checked his pulse. He then took his temperature and analyzed any other vitals Pathos could measure.

All the while, Leo attempted to touch Forge's hair. "You should... push it this-this way," the noble lilted, ruffling Forge's hair to the left. Unaccustomed to the new parting, Forge's silver locks stood on end, causing Leo to fall into fits of giggles. When Forge turned to face the others, Rhys broke into laughter. Kallen cackled into his shoulder while Hodge leaned against the wall and howled. "It's... a-a good look for you!" said Leo.

Kashim stepped through the unlocked external door. "What's going on?" Axel and Andy were behind him. Kashim took one look at Forge and snickered.

"Leo's drunk," Kallen explained.

"And what happened to Forge?" asked Andy.

Forge frowned, flattened his hair, and started back up the stairs.

"Noooo," Leo wailed dramatically. "You messed up my work! Forge!" Hodge crumpled to the floor unable to contain his mirth. Rhys too found it hard to remain silent when his crew was in hysterics.

"Come on," said Andy, pushing past everyone and going to Leo. "Let's get some food in you." Leo touched Andy's shoulder-length hair and then leaned heavily against the ship's First Mate.

"Rhys, a word?" asked Kashim. Together, they entered the bridge, and Kashim closed the door behind them. All amusement fell from the Second Mate's face. "I spoke with Yanamichin. They're going to go ahead and bolster their forces along the southern border."

"Good."

Kashim sighed. "Yana is a good man. Please don't lie to him again."

Unsurprised Kashim had caught the lie, Rhys asked, "Does he know I made all of that up?"

"No," replied Kashim solemnly.

Rhys leaned against his chair. "I can't just explain to him that there's an artificial intelligence on the moon using Earth as its own research facility."

"What does Osiris have to do with adding more men to the border?"

Rhys quickly explained his logic to Kashim. "And Forge, Beso, and Zain all agree with this assessment."

"No, I don't guess you can share that just yet," said Kashim. "Fine, just… make your lies more believable. I knew they weren't real battles because I've studied all of Vinz's old books. Yanamichin may not be as well-read, but that doesn't mean he can't discern truth."

"I'll keep that in mind. How was your meeting with the port registrar?"

"Fine. Both *Themis* and *Grisle* are on the master list. No problems."

Although the bridge door was closed, Rhys lowered his voice. "Safety-wise, how are we looking?"

"The docks seem to be clear of riffraff. If it's any indication, Kallen managed to get Leo back to the ship without incident."

"That doesn't mean we should drop our guard," replied Rhys.

"I know."

Rhys slipped from the bridge. Suddenly somber, he bypassed the galley where Leo, Andy, Axel, and Hodge still laughed and went to his cabin. He closed the door behind him and flopped onto his bed. "Am I right?" he asked Ethos.

"Yep," replied the AI from the innards of his pocket. "I haven't spoken in the past several hours because I have had nothing else to add. Everything you've said concerning Osiris is absolutely correct."

"Oh… no. I meant… Am I right? I'm still a target?"

"I haven't spoken in the past several hours… because I have had nothing else to add," repeated Ethos. "Everything you've said concerning Osiris is correct."

The door to his cabin opened to admit Kallen. "Why are you sitting in the dark?"

Rhys sat up to turn on the lamp, but Kallen stopped him. With more force than usual, she climbed atop him and straddled his hips. She took his wrists playfully and trapped them above his head.

"What?" he whispered, bewildered by her sexually aggressive behavior. "What's wrong?"

"Nothing," she replied with a coy smile. "I just I'm you." Kallen leaned down and pressed her lips to his. Rhys struggled half-heartedly to free his hands, but Kallen kept his wrists trapped. "What are you going to do?" she whispered into his mouth. She kissed him for a long moment and then slid her lips down his chest. When she moved to his beltline, she released his hands to better undress him.

Rhys sat up, pulled her shirt over her head, and then drew her breastband downward. His lips followed her collarbone before kissing her mouth once more. Kallen balanced herself on his lap and drew his shirt over his head.

Suddenly, the door opened, spilling light into the cabin. "Rhys, have you considered—"

Forge stopped, his eyes falling on Kallen's bare chest.

"Forge, get out!" Rhys barked, throwing his shirt at the medical student. Forge whirled around and slammed the door. With a sigh, Rhys collapsed onto the bed. Kallen sat back, grinning. "I've told him countless times to knock."

She chuckled and kissed his cheek. "Doesn't look like the message got through."

"He's already sexually frustrated," said Rhys. "He didn't need that."

Kallen peered at him in surprise. "Really? How do you know?"

"Several days ago, he mentioned he felt strange around you. Pathos explained it to him as enamorment."

"But… it's not, is it?" Kallen murmured.

"No, it's not. He must use Pathos differently than I did, because Pathos always gave me direct, biological explanations for everything I felt." Rhys traced a line along Kallen's breast down to her hips. "Sexual attraction was sexual attraction, not enamorment."

Kallen propped herself on her elbow. "I thought all Pathos units were the same."

"They have the same function, but how each person utilizes the AI is different." Rhys ran his hands over her hips and belt, his eyes lingering on her breasts before slipping to her abdomen which appeared slightly swollen.

Grinding slightly against him, she ran a rough hand along his bristled jaw, touched the empty sockets along the side of his temple, and then combed her fingers through his hair. Rhys sighed at her touch and smell. Lowering herself, Kallen kissed him, smiling into his mouth.

31
MISS

THE FOLLOWING MORNING, RHYS SET off for the market with Forge and Hodge. Leo, Axel, and Kashim walked with them before going to the local munitions merchant. After spending more than they probably should have on medical supplies, Hodge led them to a small inn that served food on its veranda.

Though Rhys ripped his headscarf immediately to save himself from the heat, Forge kept his hair completely covered. The medical student finally understood why they had told him to wear a headscarf outside the ship. While Rhys was accustomed to the bold stares and hushed whispers, Forge was not. Even as the inn attendant waited on them, Forge kept his eyes down.

Rhys exchanged knowing glances with Hodge before discussing the port's history quietly. When their simple midday meals finally arrived, they ate in silence.

After lunch, they picked up a handful of other items specific crew members had asked for and headed back to the ship. He repaired burnt-out solar panels Kallen had pulled earlier that morning on the upper deck and then fell asleep under the sails.

He woke sometime later to the sound of footsteps on the upper deck. Squinting against the setting sun, Rhys looked to find Hodge. "Ready to go?" his friend asked.

"Go where?" mumbled Rhys, covering his eyes with the back of his arm.

"Everyone is going into town to take a break." Hodge nudged him with his boot. "Come on. You've been up here all afternoon."

Groaning, Rhys rolled onto his knees. He and Hodge gathered the repaired solar panels and returned them to their designated barrel in the forward hatch. Kallen and Andy met them in the hallway. "Leo and Forge went on ahead with the others," said Kallen.

"Kashim and Axel are staying with *Themis*," added Andy. "Leela, Patrin, and Zain are with *Grisle*."

Recognizing that the others were dressed in their less ratty clothes, Rhys hurried to his cabin to change into a pair of clean slacks and a blouse. He emerged rolling his long sleeves up to his elbows. Although he trusted Firekli, he strapped his resonance cutters between his shoulders; a pistol remained trapped against the small of his back. He was sure the others were also armed.

Gleefully, Hodge grabbed Andy and pushed the First Mate out the external ship door. "Grab a radio!" Kashim called from the bridge.

Despite the setting sun, it was still hot, and Rhys instantly began sweating. Hodge, on the other hand, seemed utterly beside himself with joy and jovially strolled down the cobblestone street, rocking Andy as he went.

Chuckling, Kallen fell into step beside Rhys and slipped her arm around his. "It's been a long time since I've seen him so happy," she mused. "You didn't know, but Hodge used to drink a lot." She nodded. "He was also a ladies' man. When we were in New Arbroath, he would visit the taverns in the evening and come home hours after midnight." Kallen's amused smile changed to a warm one. "He changed when he met you and Alina."

"I didn't know that," said Rhys, watching his dear friend speak enthusiastically with Andy. "So, tell me how you managed to con so much money from the locals at the black market."

While Kallen explained how Beso had used high-level vocabulary and jargon to encourage buyers to purchase the materials from the maintenance unit, they followed Hodge and Andy down several more streets. Just when Rhys began to wonder how far into town they were going, Hodge dragged everyone up the stairs of a tavern tucked at the end of an alleyway. Even from the street, Rhys could hear exuberant music and raucous laughter.

At the top of the staircase, Hodge slammed open the thick door and boomed, "Heyyy!" A chorus of voices welcomed them into the tavern.

Rhys ushered Kallen ahead of him out of politeness before following. Although the tavern itself was large and comprised of two floors, the crowd there made it seem half that size. People of varying backgrounds and trades gathered at chunky tables of polished wood throughout the room while tavern staff—three young women and a middle-aged man—supplied mugs and food to their patrons.

"Hodge!" called Leo from the far side of the tavern. Hodge flitted across the room, clapping strangers on the shoulder as he went.

Rhys was surprised to find Beso and Forge actively engaging in the festivities. While Beso spoke with Terron—Rhys had noticed they had grown close over the past several days—Forge bobbed his head in time with the jig that filled the tavern. Tessa, who had made it her priority to stay away from Rhys, sat near Terron and Beso, listening politely to their conversation. It wasn't until Rhys leaned in that he realized Terron and Beso were speaking in Nefegian and that Tessa was only pretending to follow the conversation for the sake of appearances.

"Hey hey!" called Hodge, tackling Forge and pushing Terron. "Could you appear any more conspicuous?"

Rhys had to chuckle; his friend was right. Normally, Terron and Leo would not have warranted a second look in Firekli, but sitting with Forge and Beso transformed them into beacons. Though the tavern seemed relaxed enough, Rhys didn't miss the subtle looks of curiosity its patrons threw their direction.

"We're here to help you blend in," said Hodge, taking Andy once more by the shoulders and maneuvering him between Terron and Beso. Kallen began laughing as the effect immediately changed the look of their table. Andy—tan and dark-haired—was the complete opposite of Terron and Beso. He appeared to be the minority at their table. Hodge seated himself beside Forge and waved to Kallen and Rhys.

"We were waiting for you," announced Terron, motioning to the nearest waitress. She nodded and disappeared into the back room.

"Ah, you didn't have to do that." Kallen leaned on the table. "Now, you know this is the first time any of them have had alcohol, Terron. I hope you didn't order something too strong."

"Just the cheapest they had," Terron replied.

Rhys couldn't help but laugh as Hodge, swaying with the music, began rocking Forge in time with the rhythm. Despite the roughness with which Hodge moved him, the medical student seemed to be thoroughly enjoying himself and soon they were swaying together.

Kallen leaned into Rhys and kissed his cheek. This was the first time they had all been out in a public location together like a normal group of friends and colleagues. Terron's face wasn't a solemn expression of stone, and Forge seemed to be enjoying the atmosphere. Andy, who had moved to escape Beso and Terron's conversation, gazed about the tavern in interest and tapped his finger on the table in time with the music.

When the waitress brought mugs of spirits and deposited them before each crew member, Hodge whooped in excitement. "Wait!" he ordered, before anyone could partake. "Newcomers first."

Rhys sniffed the beverage and drew away in disgust. The acidic smell burned his nose. He peered at Beso who was also sniffing the mug. His colleague tilted his head in consideration and then, in one motion, drank heavily from the mug. After the third gulp, he started coughing, splashing alcohol across his face and down the side of the mug.

"I'm *not* drinking that," Rhys asserted.

"Oh, come on." Hodge pushed a mug closer to the medical student. Forge wrinkled his nose. "Come on, Flick," he murmured, egging him on. "Drink it."

Forge stuck his tongue out and touched just the tip of it to the foamy liquid. He tasted it. He quivered in revulsion as he rolled his tongue around his mouth. "Don't do it. Don't do it, Rhys."

Rhys decidedly pushed the mug back to the middle of the table, causing Hodge to groan. "Come on, you two. Beso did it."

"It tastes… so bad," gagged Forge.

Hodge took a short sip before motioning to Beso. "No more?"

Beso, who was still trying to swallow the bad taste, shook his head. "Please, no more."

Kallen motioned to the waitress who seemed alarmed by Beso's reaction and requested water. Momentarily, cups were placed on the table, and both Forge and Beso drank deeply.

"Gravel bed," muttered Hodge. "All three of you."

"How can you even swallow that?" Forge asked.

Beso raised his hand in mock defeat. "It burned my throat." Terron clapped him on the shoulder and Andy laughed.

The music shifted and a string of chords Rhys knew well tinkled through the air. Smiling, he looked to Kallen who was nodding in recognition—"The Maiden's Call." It had been the first song he had heard on Earth, the first Kallen had ever sang to him.

"Why this song?" he asked as the piax player in the corner of the room began humming the chorus.

Kallen shrugged. "It's easy to remember and has a catchy melody."

Everyone at the table fell quiet. Even Hodge, who was determined to get every crew member drunk, watched the piax player finish the slow introduction and then break into percussion and rhythm.

The entire tavern began belting out the lyrics, Rhys included. The only people who remained quiet were Beso and Forge, neither of whom knew the song. In tempo with the musician's strumming, the tavern clapped and bobbed. Though Rhys much preferred Kallen's singing, the atmosphere was entertaining and warm. He found he couldn't keep a straight face when surrounded by so many who were having a wonderful time.

When the musician tore from the melody to allow for an instrumental break, his partner, a fiddle player, leapt into the scene and began enthusiastically playing variations of the song.

Rhys swiveled in his chair to look back at Forge and Beso. He expected Forge to be dancing in his seat and beaming; instead, the med student was leaning toward Beso, who was holding his head, a pained expression on his face. Realizing something was wrong, Rhys touched Kallen's arm. She followed his gaze and stood. Terron, who was already speaking with Beso, exchanged worried glances.

Just as Rhys rose from his chair, Forge fell still, his eyes widening. The med student flailed from his chair and slipped around the table, shoving a patron. Rhys and Kallen joined him. Around them, the music and exuberant singing continued.

"What? What?" asked Rhys as Terron moved aside.

Forge was already in the process of drawing Beso from his chair to the floor. "Something is wrong." Just as Beso settled on the sticky wood flooring, he rolled over and began vomiting brilliant crimson blood.

"Shit," muttered Rhys. Beso quivered violently as he continued to throw up. Terron turned on heel and disappeared into the tavern's crowd as Rhys kneeled beside Forge. "Isn't that enough, Logos?" Already a pool of bloody mucus and liquid was spreading under Beso.

"A foreign substance has been detected," provided Forge. Over the music, Rhys could hear Beso gasping loudly, a rasping choking sound.

"Rhys," shouted Ethos from the innards of Rhys' pocket. "He's been poisoned. Get the waitress."

"What?"

"Find the waitress!" Ethos ordered.

Rhys leapt up, scanning the tavern. When he could not find the woman who had served them, he sprinted into the back room. He ran headlong into one of the other waitresses. With an iron-like grasp, he clutched at the young lady. "Where is she? Our waitress?"

"Who? Which one?" the woman asked, panicked.

"She wore a blue blouse. Her hair was pinned up."

"She stepped out," the young woman replied. "Is... there a problem?"

"Where'd she go?"

The waitress pointed to the back door of the kitchen. Rhys gazed at it for a moment, torn between chasing after her and returning to Beso. The decision was made for him when the music in the tavern suddenly stopped and concerned murmurs arose. He dashed back into the main room where many of the tavern's patrons were looking on as Rhys' crew lifted Beso onto their table. Forge climbed atop a chair and knelt on the edge of the table.

Moving swiftly, the medical student ran his hands over Beso, checking his vitals. Though it appeared as though Beso had stopped vomiting, his breathing was labored. Wheezing audibly, he clutched at Forge. Kallen stood at his head and wiped his face, panicked.

"Go after the waitress," advised Ethos. "There's nothing more you can do here."

Rhys' voice was low. "He's not going to make it... is he?"

"Go find the waitress."

Fists clenched, he shifted his gaze to the ground. Was Beso' mug the only one poisoned? Why would they poison Beso? Had Hodge or Forge's drinks been tainted as well? Fearfully, Rhys looked at Hodge. His friend seemed fine; Forge too looked strong though it seemed the medical student wasn't feeling well.

Rhys moved across the room. He grabbed Hodge's arm and looked at Forge. "Both of you, go throw up, now." Without a question, Forge slid off the table and disappeared outside; Hodge followed. Rhys climbed atop the table and began examining Beso. "Talk to me, Logos," he murmured in their native tongue.

"Biological energy output is falling," replied Logos. "All vitals are weakening. Liver efficiency is at forty-two percent and dropping. Heart rate slowing to forty-nine beats per minute. The internal lining of the stomach is sloughing off."

Realizing he had nothing to combat poison, he gripped Beso's arm. Already pink foam seeped from the corners of his mouth. His eyes were bloodshot, and his skin had a blue-purple tint.

"What's wrong?" asked a tavern patron.

"He's been poisoned," replied Kallen. "Does anyone know of a remedy? Anyone?"

Many of the patrons looked amongst themselves before a hand shot out from the group. An old ebony-colored man Rhys had seen working on the docks the day prior stepped forward. "It depends on the poison," he explained.

Kallen ushered him to Beso. The old man examined Beso for a moment and then sighed. "It may be too late, but it can't hurt to try." He turned and motioned to the group he had been with. "I think it's monkshood. We need charcoal. Go to the kitchen and grab some." The old man nodded to another stranger. "Find something we can use to smash the charcoal."

Feeling Beso's grip on his arm tighten, Rhys looked down at his colleague. Beso was staring at the ceiling, his breathing becoming shallower by the minute. "Logos?"

There was a moment of silence before the AI spoke in their native tongue. "Why did I follow you?"

"Come on, Beso."

"Why did I ever leave Caelestis?" whispered Logos.

Rhys grabbed Beso's face and forced his fluttering eyes onto him. "Come on, stay awake." When Beso didn't respond, Rhys shook him. "Logos! You keep him alive!"

"Rhys, Rhys!" called Kallen, touching his arm. "Move."

Rhys leapt off the table as the old ebony-skinned man slid near Beso and pried open the engineer's mouth. He poured a charcoal-water mixture down his throat. "Swallow, boy," the man instructed. "Come on." Beso struggled for a moment before swallowing. The man gathered another spoonful of the concoction and spilled another and another into Beso's slightly-parted mouth. Afterward, the man nodded and looked to Rhys. "And now we wait."

"I don't... What does charcoal do?" asked Rhys. He understood trauma surgery, anatomy, biology, and medicinal interactions, but Rhys' knowledge was finite when it came to herbology and local treatments.

"Charcoal is used as a universal antidote," replied the old man. "It can absorb most toxins within one to two minutes. It's the only thing that might work in a situation like this, but it looks like he's ingested a lot." Hodge and Forge reappeared, their solemn gazes set on Beso. "You two poisoned too?"

Hodge shook his head. "I'm fine. He said he was feeling a little nauseous, but nothing else."

The old man held out the bowl of water and charcoal mixture. "Take a sip and swallow."

Forge obeyed before immediately returning to Beso whose quivering breaths were steadying.

"Rhys…" murmured Ethos. "Go."

"Take Andy, Tessa, Kallen," said Terron in Nefegian. Aside from Forge, he was the only other one who understood Ethos. "I'll take care of everything here."

Rhys started through the crowd toward the front door. "Andy, Kallen, Tessa."

"You're going to leave your friend there?" asked a man, stopping Rhys.

Rhys glanced at him. "I'm going to find the person who did it to him."

The tavern patron exchanged looks with his group members and then nodded. "We're going with you."

Before Rhys knew it, a swarm of people was following him out the tavern. Outside, he turned to the group. "We're looking for the waitress who was wearing a blue shirt. She had her hair pinned up."

"The girl with the freckles?" asked one of the patrons, a middle-aged woman who reminded him of Tessa. "She said her name was Wyma."

"Does anyone know her?"

"She's new to town. She's a refugee from Paducah," replied the woman.

Rhys thought. She didn't appear like the Pantarak women he had met in Paducah. "Spread out. Ask around. She can't have gone far. We need people searching the streets, the docks, and the area south of here." Groups formed, and everyone took off in different directions, leaving Rhys alone with Andy, Kallen, and Tessa. "Take Kallen. Head toward the docks. Tessa, you're with me."

Tessa frowned but didn't argue. Kallen threw Rhys a worried look before jogging after Andy down the darkening streets. "We should look east. I didn't see anyone go that direction," suggested Tessa, starting to cross the cobblestone street.

They searched the local roads for half an hour, asked passersby, and peeked into inns, taverns, and bars. Nothing. When lightning in the distance illuminated the low-hanging clouds, they gave up and started the walk back to the tavern. By the time they returned to the street their tavern was on, the storm clouds had drifted over the port and a light sprinkle had begun.

"Rhys!" Kallen's voice was distant. "Rhys!"

Rhys exchanged looks with Tessa and hurried down the street to find Kallen and Andy standing in the rain waiting for them. "Hey!" he called.

"They found her," breathed Kallen. "About ten minutes ago." Quickly, they led Rhys and Tessa toward the rear of the tavern. Even before they rounded the building, Rhys could hear the people gathering there. "Move," Kallen ordered, pushing a man. A path emerged through the crowd of citizens guiding Rhys and the others to the center. There, the young waitress who had served them their drinks, lay on the glistening cobblestones, her face turned downward to expose the back of her neck. Her hands were bound before her, and she had a large welt under her left eye.

"Found her trying to board a merchant ship destined for Bathsgate," said one of the men, hands on his hips.

Rhys planted himself beside her. Under the dim light of the tavern, he could see she was crying. She was frightened; her damp hair gave her the appearance of a weak, mousy girl half her actual age. "Have you questioned her?"

"Was waiting for you," replied the man.

The girl sobbed hard and then looked up at Rhys pleadingly. "Please," she cried. "Please."

"What were your orders?" asked Rhys.

"W-what?" she stammered.

"Who gave you the order to poison my crew?"

"I don't know what you're talking about."

Rhys knelt. "Why did you poison my crew?"

The waitress panted and then whimpered. "I didn't do anything. Please... Please don't hurt me. *Please.*" Her crying grew more hysterical. "I'm begging you. Please don't hurt me."

"Maybe it wasn't her," suggested a tavern patron from within the group.

"It wasn't!" the waitress cried, sitting up. Rhys leaned forward, snatched at the rope binding her wrists, and jerked her back to meet him.

"Rhys," hissed Kallen disapprovingly.

Her crying softened as her eyes met his. "Your antics won't work with me. Now, tell me, why were you ordered to poison my crew? Who gave the order?"

"Please, I don't know anything."

Rhys pursed his lips in frustration and then pushed her to the ground, pressing her face into the stones.

"Rhys, come on," said Kallen. "She said—"

Andy barred Kallen's approach. "Stop."

Holding the waitress to the ground, Rhys leaned into her. "You were careless," he murmured. The young woman's crying quieted. "Your squadron number is showing." Rhys sensed her body tense under him.

Before she could leap upward, he smashed a knee into her shoulder and pinned her hard to the cobblestone. He withdrew his resonance cutters, engaged them, and held them above her. "Now, why were you trying to poison my crew?" When she didn't speak, Rhys lowered the cutters near her skin so she could feel the heat exuded from them.

"I wasn't trying to!" she screeched as the heat from the tool began to blister her skin. Rhys pulled the cutters away from her face. "I wasn't trying to poison them. *You* were the target."

"But at least three mugs were poisoned," said one of the tavern's patrons. "Gard tested them."

Rhys thought and then said, "You didn't know which of us was Rhys Falkrow, did you?" The woman shook her head. "So, you put poison in all three and hoped for the best. Your only orders were to assassinate me?" Again, she nodded. She was far more compliant than Axel had ever been. "Are there others here in town?" The waitress didn't reply. "I'll take that as a 'yes.'"

Rhys released her, sheathed his cutters, and stepped over her. With a wary eye, the woman watched him.

"What do you want us to do with her?" asked a patron.

Rhys cuffed the woman's shoulder. "You see me? You can see my face?" The woman didn't reply, though her eyes were trained only on him. "*I* am Rhys Falkrow. I am one hundred fifty-five senmers. Silver hair, blue eyes." He pushed his hair away from the temple of his face to reveal the injector sockets. "I have these on the side of my head. Burn my image into your brain. Don't forget my face. Make sure everyone else knows what I look like." He nodded to one of the men. "Release her."

The response from the crowd was instantaneous. "What? Why?"

"Andy."

His First Mate untied her and helped her to her feet.

"Are you *mad*?" a tavern patron gasped.

"What are you doing?" asked another.

The waitress stood before Rhys, her shoulders squared and eyes set. Now that she wasn't sobbing and acting demurely, Rhys could clearly discern her as a soldier, as a woman with power and confidence. "Go," he said. "Tell your superiors and the men in your squadron who I am and what I look like. Don't miss next time." The woman glanced at Kallen and the others before turning and darting through the crowd. Not a single person tried to stop her.

Overhead, a dim streak of lightning flashed, thunder rolled, and it began to pour.

32
FRAYING

FOR A LONG WHILE, RHYS stood in the rain, allowing the coolness of the downpour to numb the emotions that threatened to consume him. While the crowd of vengeful tavern patrons moved inside, Kallen, Andy, and Tessa remained nearby.

He was still a target, still wanted by Brechin and by Osiris. How many times had he escaped death? How many times had he unknowingly put his own crew and others in danger? Now, not even those from Caelestis were safe.

"Where are you going?" asked Kallen as he turned toward the street. When he didn't answer, she added, "You need to come look after Beso."

"Beso is dead," Rhys replied. "He ingested too much poison."

"It's not safe," called Andy over the thunder of the rain. "You shouldn't be alone."

Rhys ignored his First Mate's warning and strode from the tavern's alleyway to the main street. He sensed Andy and Kallen fall into step behind him but didn't acknowledge them. In the dim light emanating from shop and house windows, Rhys trudged through the streets.

"Rhys," said Andy after several long minutes. "Kallen's getting cold. Let's get out of the rain."

"Go back to the ship," Rhys commanded.

Kallen caught his arm and pulled him to a stop. Her dark hair was plastered to her face and goosepimples decorated her chest and arms. Pleadingly, she gazed at him. "Don't be out here by yourself. Come on." Though he truly wanted to be left alone with his guilt and rage, he conceded and started the walk back to the ship. As they neared the docks, Andy turned back for the tavern to help sort out everything.

Axel greeted them at the bridge door. "What happened?" he asked, seeing the look on Rhys' face. Kashim, who was seated in the Overseer's chair, stood up in worry. Rhys passed Axel and started down the bridge. "Where's everyone else?"

"Beso was poisoned," Rhys heard Kallen murmur.

"Where are they?" asked Kashim, leaping up.

"The tavern, but they should be on their way back."

Rhys shuffled into the galley. Standing in the middle of the room, sopping wet, he listened to the waves against the ship's hull and the roar of the rain on the upper deck. He had thought the sounds were soothing, he had thought they would instill calmness in him. He was wrong.

In a sudden frenzy, he threw the chair nearest him across the galley and then kicked the table. With a snarl of unbridled rage, he grabbed a pot drying on the counter and hurled it across the room. It smashed into the wall and then clattered to the ground.

Panting, he glared at the dark porthole on the opposite side of the room. Lightning flashed and thunder rolled across the horizon. He wanted to do more; he wanted to scream and kick another chair or go sprinting off the docks and disappear into the desert. He wanted to hit something or-or—

When the tremors left his hands and his breathing slowed, he moved to the galley counter and leaned against it. "Ethos," he murmured.

"Yes?"

He continued in Nefegian. "How does Osiris control the regions?"

"What do you mean?" replied the AI.

"You said Osiris controls each quadrant on Earth by manipulating different facets of the region like economics, politics, religion… How?"

"Osiris has refined its ability to predict human behavior. It has thousands of years of information and data to support its theories and predictions. Consider a ripple in water. It starts small and then grows. Osiris controls many quadrants of Earth by utilizing this effect with dexterity and skill."

"But *how*?"

"For Quadrant Six, your quadrant, Osiris uses a computer to communicate with Brechin's clergymen. Remember, my information is dated though. It's entirely possible that computer or whatever form of communication being used in Brechin has evolved to something I'm not aware of."

"What about the other quadrants on Earth? Certainly not everyone has a computer or means to receive information from Osiris directly."

"True. This is where the ripple effect comes into play. Osiris is a masterful player. It has purposefully positioned regions with computers near quadrants without them. For instance, our quadrant, Quadrant Six, has a means to receive communication from Osiris. Perhaps the region to our far south does not. Undoubtedly, the chaos that is caused here in Quadrant Six influences the region to our south. Maybe it's even started war or strife there. We have no way of knowing because humans in this region have not successfully traded beyond Quadrant Six."

"Because Osiris has not allowed them the means to," Rhys confirmed.

"Right."

"So, the expansion of the Pantarak Empire is an order disseminated from Osiris?"

"Whose words are more holy than your own amongst the high priest and Brechin clergymen," Ethos clarified.

"And this communication device is in Brechin?"

"As far as I know. During Ramsen's time, it was a simple data computer made to receive commands like humanity's first attempt at the invention thousands of years ago. With the additional materials Brechin has collected over the past few centuries, however, it would not surprise me if the computer has evolved."

Rhys sighed. "I need to get out of here."

"That's not going to go over well with your crew."

"I'm killing people, Ethos. Everyone around me is in constant danger because I have a target on my back."

"Did not your crew already pledge their loyalty to you? We've already been through this—they decided they were going to stay by your side despite the risk."

"That's *their* decision, not mine," Rhys growled. Ethos fell quiet. Sensing the AI was being withholding, Rhys prompted it. "What?"

"I just think you should consider all of your options before you set off on your own."

"You know there is a strong possibility that the assassins will begin using my crew against me. They'll capture Kallen or Hodge or someone and use them against me."

"Yes… that is true," said Ethos. "They did that to Ramsen. Do you think your crew is so helpless though?"

"Why can't you just agree with me?" Rhys exhaled.

"Because that's not my purpose," Ethos snapped. "If you want to leave and go to Brechin alone, that's fine, but don't you *dare* disrespect your crew and leave without consulting them. I know you, Rhys Falkrow. If you had it your way, you'd leave in the middle of the night and not look back. You owe your crew, your family, more than that."

Scowling, Rhys moved across the galley and picked up the chair he had thrown. Ethos was always right, and he hated that.

There was a soft knock from the doorway and Rhys looked up to find Kallen holding towels. Quelling his frustration, he followed her to their cabin. She closed the door and began drying off. "What... was that all about?" she murmured, stripping out of her sopping shirt. "With Ethos?"

"Nothing," replied Rhys, ruffling the water from his hair. He pulled his wet shirt over his head, threw it to the floor, and began drying himself. Only then did he realize Kallen had stopped moving.

"I hate when you do that," she muttered.

"I haven't done anything."

"You rely on that stupid computer more than us," she said. "You've stopped talking to me—"

"Do *you* know about Osiris? Do you know how to best get to Brechin and infiltrate the underground base or how to find the computer Osiris is using to communicate with the high priest and clergymen?"

"No, but..."

"No one else has answers! Everything is on me, Kallen. Everything. There is *literally* nothing any of you can do without my guidance. The entire world is at stake here, and I'm the only damn one who can do anything about it. My own people have forsaken me. Even with Earth in jeopardy, they won't help. Why then should I rely on anyone else besides myself?"

"Because we're your family!" Kallen snarled. "And you're right— there's literally nothing we can do to destroy Osiris. I couldn't even tell you how to start. But by you withdrawing from us, relying only on yourself and that computer, it's like you're not even here."

"I haven't been here since Alina died," retorted Rhys.

"Get over it! Get over her, Rhys." Kallen's voice cracked. "She's not coming back; she's not ever coming back. You have to keep moving." She must have seen the look of hurt on his face because she added, "We all miss her. Hodge can't step foot into your old cabin because he sees her there. You're not the only one but..." Kallen swiped at her eyes but her tears fell anyway. "We need you, Rhys. You hold us together."

Rhys sat heavily on the floor so his wet pants wouldn't dampen their sheets, and rested his back against the bed. After a moment, Kallen, sniffing loudly, joined him. He wrapped a towel around her and then held her hand.

"I'm leaving," he said finally.

"No, you're not."

Rhys bowed his head in frustration. "Kallen, I'm endangering all of you. Always."

"We've been in danger since before you and Alina came along."

"This is different."

"You think that just because you and Alina showed up, the Pantaraks suddenly started attacking our ships in New Arbroath? Rhys, before we picked you two up, we were constantly being sent out by Joss to defend the town. Kashim's covered in scars and cuts; Hodge—I'm sure you've seen the scar along his hip. Old bullet wound injury."

"The Pantaraks aren't the enemy. They're a cover-up for the real evil," Rhys murmured.

"Then show us. Show everyone who the real enemy is. We can't... see it. We can hardly understand Osiris. If you want a region-wide rebellion to start—something far more powerful than what's currently happening—then the people *have* to know. And the only person who can tell them is you."

"They'll think I'm mad if I go spouting outlandish declarations like there's a computer on the moon controlling Earth." He scoffed. "Please. They would have me stoned or hanged, or whatever it is that they do to people here."

Kallen studied her hands. "What if you showed them?"

"I can't show them anything that ties to Osiris. That's the problem."

Kallen nudged his pocket. "Ethos."

"Let me ask—what did you think when you first heard Pathos and Logos speak? What went through your mind as you watched a piece of non-organic material engage in intelligent conversation, ask questions, and theorize?"

"Rhys, show a select group of higher-ups here in Firekli and push them to your side. You already have Yanamichin working with you."

"Hesitantly."

Kallen ignored him. "Get together Yanamichin and others and reveal to them what you know about Osiris. Use Ethos as a tool. It can already produce images and sounds, pictures and explanations."

"What happens if they think I'm mad?"

"Hodge and Kashim will be there with you."

Decompressing, Rhys leaned heavily against her. "I'm sorry. For everything."

"You're stressed."

Rhys pursed his lips to keep his mouth shut.

"What?" Kallen drew away to better gauge his expression. "Rhys, what?"

"No, you're right. I'm stressed."

"He lies," interrupted Ethos.

Rhys dug the AI out of his pocket and stuffed it under their mattress. Realizing Kallen was now suspicious and would need an explanation, Rhys buried his face in the bed. He could feel Kallen's eyes on him. Defeated, he withdrew Ethos from under the mattress and set the AI atop the sheets.

"Rhys?" Kallen's voice was small.

Pressing his face into the bed, Rhys motioned for Ethos to continue. "Kallen, should Rhys accept the mission at hand and launch into space, there is a possibility he will not be returning," explained the AI.

"Why wouldn't you be able to come back?" whispered Kallen.

"This mission is a high-risk assignment. Calculated, yes. But high-risk. The equipment he will be using, although trans-atmospheric, is old. Over two centuries old. Anything could go wrong. In addition, assuming our plans run smoothly and there are no equipment malfunctions, we... have no way to bring him home. We cannot help direct his angle of reentry into Earth's atmosphere because we don't have satellites or any method of communication aside from radio. Everything must be done manually aboard the unit."

"Get someone else to do it," said Kallen.

Rhys sighed. "Kallen..."

"No, get Forge to do it or Zain or... someone else."

"We've been over this."

"Then... get someone else. Please," begged Kallen. Her tears were coming fast. "Rhys, I don't want to lose you. I can't."

"I'm sorry," he said, standing. He gathered Ethos and his dry clothes and started for the door, fortifying his heart against Kallen's quiet cries. "It would probably be best... if you slept elsewhere from now on." Rhys closed the door behind him before he could see the hurt on Kallen's face.

Half an hour later, the rest of the crew returned carrying Beso's body. It was as Ethos had stated earlier—Beso was dead. He had ingested too much of the poison too quickly. Once Hodge, Andy, and Forge placed Beso's body in the forward hatch, they left for the galley, exhausted and stressed. Rhys remained behind perched atop a crate of supplies.

His colleague was pale, his white skin almost translucent. Rigor mortis had set in and Beso's body was stiff and cold. Someone had shut his eyes.

Rhys had never been attached to Beso. He was a colleague, someone with whom he had once worked. The engineer had always been aloof, quiet, and reserved. He had not been someone Rhys would naturally have singled out as a friend. Nevertheless, Beso was a Caelestis citizen, or rather, a member of Neo-Colony Two. He was one of Rhys' people. He was a life.

"You shouldn't have so adamantly declared your identity," said Forge in Nefegian. Rhys turned to look at the medical student who had stripped out of his wet shirt and now stood bare-chested in the forward hatch doorway. "You should have passed Beso off as yourself. You should have let Osiris think you had been killed."

Rhys sighed, his heart sinking—he *should* have done that. Another mistake made on his part that would haunt him.

Forge joined him, leaving behind a trail of wet footprints and droplets. "All of this was unexpected."

Rhys continued in Nefegian. "You're taking this unusually well."

Forge nodded. "He's dead. I couldn't do anything even though I'm a medical student." After a moment, he said, "So, what will happen to his body?"

"We'll take him out to sea," said Rhys. "Like we did with Lyruc, Kyo, and Alina."

"Is that customary?"

"It is for our ship." A sudden thought occurred to Rhys. "Have you communicated any of this to Neo-Colony Two?"

"No, but Zain has," replied Forge. "He's been in constant communication with Neo-Colony Two since we left."

"And you, Zain, and Beso always spoke to one another?"

"Should… we not have?" Forge murmured.

"No, I expected you to. Any response from the colony?"

"Not that I know of."

Rhys glanced at him. "I'll stay here for now."

"Why?" Forge's voice was small. It was obvious he was attempting not to offend Rhys.

"Go get some rest, Forge," murmured Rhys. Forge glanced at Beso's still body once more and then slipped out of the forward hatch. Rhys hopped off the crate onto the floor where he pulled his legs to his chest and rested his head on his arms. He would keep vigil for Beso just as he had for Alina.

33
THEY WHO COME AND GO

IT WAS NOT THE THUNDER or water lapping along the ship's hull that woke Rhys the following morning shortly before dawn, but the sound of feet atop the upper deck. Despite having sworn to himself he would stay awake, the weight of the day's events had finally caught up to him forcing him into a deep sleep. Now though, he sat up in the forward hatch and, blurry-eyed, gazed about in confusion. No one was on duty on the bridge because they were in port.

Rhys glanced at Beso, stood, and wearily shuffled from the forward hatch. Once in the hallway, he stood motionlessly and listened. Everyone on *Themis* was asleep, therefore, the heavy footsteps atop the vessel had to belong to other people. Port code indicated that non-crew members were not allowed to board another ship without permission, thus suppliers and cargo haulers in port were out of the question.

Jogging down the hall, Rhys peered into the crew's dark quarters. "Hey, get up. We have company," he alerted. He made sure he saw movement from Kashim and Andy before going to his cabin. He found Kallen wadded in a pile of blankets, deep asleep. Despite their quarrel the previous night, Rhys went to her and gently shook her awake.

"Hmm?"

"There are people on the upper deck. Arm yourself."

Kallen took a deep breath, sat up, and began dressing. As Rhys outfitted himself in a vest and his resonance cutters, she strapped a short rifle to her shoulder and placed a holstered pistol in her waistband.

Rhys met Hodge, Kashim, and Axel in the hallway. They too had been standing in silence, listening.

"What are they doing up there?" Hodge muttered, his wild hair pressed to the side from sleep. "They sound like a bunch of jerabo."

"They're not soldiers," asserted Axel. "Soldiers would be quieter."

Forge appeared in the doorway. "It's our people."

Everyone looked at him. "*Our* people?" asked Rhys. "As in Neo-Colony Two?" Forge nodded. "What do they want?"

"I don't know. They cut me off from all communication." The med student glanced at the others. "I think they're upset."

"Do they know what time it is?" sighed Hodge. "I'm tired."

If Forge seemed to think his people were upset, then there was a good chance something big was about to happen. Though the people of Caelestis operated using the ideology that everything should better or advance humanity, whomever they had sent to Firekli was not going to behave in such a fashion. They were out of their element, surrounded by unknown dangers and mysteries. They would be on edge, nervous.

"I'll go," Rhys concluded. "Forge, Hodge, come with me. Kashim, Axel, Leo, set up a defense at the ladder and lower platform."

"There's not really any defense that can protect against those weapons of yours," Andy remarked from inside the crew's quarters.

"Still, a show of force will hopefully persuade them to back down." Rhys started for the stairs; the others followed. He saw Kallen fall in behind Forge but didn't say anything.

The morning air was cool from the night's thunderstorm and the sky, though dark, was tinted purple from dawn's approach. Knowing he had to maintain peace no matter what, Rhys took a deep breath and climbed the ladder to the upper deck.

"Halt," came a command in Aabesh.

"It's me," he replied in Nefegian without pausing on the ladder. Rhys drew himself onto the deck. Although he could barely see the maintenance unit perched on *Themis*' stern, he had no trouble discerning the five Caelestis citizens from the dark background. Their silver hair, white skin, and pale clothes were like beacons. "I wasn't expecting you."

"We weren't expecting to make a trip out here either," replied a male voice.

Kallen, Forge, and Hodge joined Rhys in silence.

"I wish we were here under better circumstances."

Rhys recognized that voice. "Veran, to what do I owe the pleasure?"

There was a moment's pause before Veran said, "My apologies, Rhys. We've forgotten that you cannot see us."

"No matter," replied Rhys.

"Is there a particular reason why you have your crew hidden and armed?" asked another.

"It's a precaution." Rhys shifted; he felt Hodge fall into the space beside him. "What do you want?" He waited politely for them to speak via their AIs before asking again.

Finally, a body left the group and started across the deck. As she neared, Rhys realized it was Veran. "We're here concerning Beso's death," she said in Aabesh. The Director of Medicine stopped before Rhys. "We're also here for the information you've been collecting."

Rhys bristled but forced his face to remain expressionless. "I see."

Veran gently took his hand and placed a small device in his palm. Rhys closed his hand around it and pursed his lips; it was the adaptor. "As ambassador, you are bound by your oath to provide information to Neo-Colony Two."

"Wait, wait," said Kallen. She switched to Elali, a language Rhys' people did not know. "You don't have to do this. You said it yourself— they haven't done anything to help you. They've left you to deal with Osiris by yourself."

Rhys considered her. She was absolutely right. Truly, he didn't owe them anything. Except... Veran. He owed her his life. "Fine," he said. In Nefegian, he added, "For the advancement of the human race and for those on Caelestis."

He pushed his hair aside to reveal the injector sockets along his temple. Gently, he seated the adaptor and looked at Veran in the dim light. "We're taking all of it, Rhys," she said softly.

Swallowing, Rhys closed his eyes and prepared himself. Previously, he had had full control over what was viewed and shared. This wasn't going to be like last time.

Unexpectedly, Pathos' voice resonated within Rhys' head, startling him terribly. *All repaired synthetic synapses are functioning,* reported Veran's AI. *Synthetic systems, nominal. Preparing to initiate data collection and memory recall.*

Rhys felt Veran's hand grip his arm comfortingly. "Initiate," she said in Nefegian.

Initiating, replied her Pathos unit.

Physically, Rhys felt nothing. With the exception of his quickening heart, he remained motionless. Within his mind's eye, however, memories flooded him, swarming his senses.

Instances he had forced to the back of his mind; events that visited his nightmares; worries that frequented his thoughts; fights he had had with Kallen or Hodge; and conversations he had had with Ethos, Vinz,

Veran, and Leo clouded his mind. Sleepless nights of anxiety and joyful moments of music, sunboarding, and sex followed.

He saw quiet evenings sailing on a still sea, stargazing with Kallen on the upper deck, angrily yelling at Hodge, being shot in the head, falling overboard. Images of his failure in Paducah—deafening explosions, gunshots, yelling, death—engulfed him. Memories tasting of bitterness, hatred, rage, and confusion spilled over him. And then there was Alina.

Not for the first or last time, her slight figure danced forward. He saw her cooking in the galley, sleeping against Hodge, fighting viciously, tending to the sick and injured in New Arbroath, yelling at him, crying with him, playing games with Vinz. He saw her, all that she was.

It was as if the memories were being drawn from him like a well. The longer the duration of the connection, the deeper the memories. Soon, Rhys found himself and Alina trapped in the life pod attempting to escape. The event he had worked hard to forget was there in all its overwhelming terror; he had endeavored to forget the shock and crippling anxiety they had felt as the water climbed in their submerged coffin.

"Stop."

Rhys wavered on his feet before stumbling backward. Hodge bolstered him. "Hey," his friend murmured. Overwhelmed, Rhys gripped Hodge's arm to keep himself standing. He knew his cheeks were wet, but he could do nothing to stop that. All of his greatest fears, his most nightmarish memories had been dragged to the forefront of his mind and replayed clearly for him to see. "What did you do?" snapped Hodge.

"Memory extraction," replied Veran.

Rhys slid down Hodge until he was on the deck. Once there, he sat on his knees and took deep breaths. Too much. It was too much.

"You took his memories?" asked Kallen.

"No, duplicated them. Don't worry. His physical reaction is a response to the reviewing of every memory he possesses." Veran sighed. "Last time I was exposed to his memories, I wasn't prepared to handle so much emotional data. This time, however, we've created a system within the adaptor that will allow us to store the information and—"

The ringing sound of a slap resonated through the air. Rhys peered up at Kallen who stood before Veran. The Director of Medicine held her cheek. Even in the dim light of dawn, Rhys could see Kallen's hand still poised.

Panting, Kallen said, "He's *not* an experiment!"

Rhys half-expected Hodge or one of the others to stop her or intervene, but it became apparent that no one from *Themis* was going to come to Veran's rescue.

"I expected *you* of all the people here to understand that," added Kallen. "You've seen his life so far. He's showed you personally what he's gone through. And you're still not willing to *gawan* help him!" Shaking, Kallen pointed a vehement finger at Veran. "You touch him again, I'll *kill* you."

"Kallen, enough," called Kashim.

Kallen whirled on her heel and joined Rhys. "How do I eject it?" she asked in Elali. Rhys tilted his head toward her and she withdrew the adaptor. A weight lifted from Rhys; ashamedly, a whimper escaped his lips. Though the memories were still there, they were no longer being amplified. "Here," Kallen snarled, throwing the adaptor at Veran like a rock. The Director of Medicine caught it with ease and stashed it on her person. "Do you want to blame him for Beso's death while you're here?"

"Kallen," Kashim chided, joining them. Axel, Andy, and Leo also appeared on the upper deck. The whole crew was present.

"No, we're here to collect Beso's body," replied Veran. Kallen seemed to be distressing her.

"Andy, Axel—take them to the forward hatch," Rhys muttered, struggling to his feet.

As the three silver-haired citizens disappeared into the ship, Rhys worked to regain his composure. "I didn't mean for this to escalate," said Veran in Nefegian. Kallen, who stood before Rhys protectively, fidgeted. Though she didn't understand Veran's words, she understood the tone. "I know this is hard on you."

Rhys felt Hodge shift; his friend's presence comforted him. Seeing Kallen rise to his defense eased his heart.

In silence, they waited until the others returned carrying Beso's body between them. As the Neo-Colony Two citizens loaded Beso, Rhys and his crew watched. Of course, he had noticed Zain standing atop *Grisle* in the slip to their right.

"Rhys," said Veran, approaching him once the loading was complete. "We've heard from Zain what happened, however, we will review your memories and learn for ourselves before we declare blame."

"Great," murmured Rhys.

Veran glanced back at the maintenance unit; the other citizens were waiting for her. "I shouldn't be telling you this," she said softly in Aabesh, "but our sensors have picked up activity concerning Osiris."

"What kind of activity?"

"We've identified an increase in communicative transmissions between Osiris and this region, though we have been unable to decrypt them."

"Why wouldn't you be able to decrypt them?"

Veran peered over her shoulder once more and lowered her voice. "Personal AIs have no problem communicating, but the backup communication device we use within the maintenance unit immediately went offline when we crossed into the area." Veran shifted anxiously. "We haven't reviewed your memories yet, but have you any information that could help us better understand this change?"

"Osiris is trying to kill Rhys," supplied Hodge.

Rhys threw his friend a look, but Hodge didn't appear remorseful.

"It's trying to kill Rhys?" Veran looked between them. "Why do you think that?"

"I've been a target for several months now," Rhys explained. "That's why Beso was killed."

The look on Veran's face was one of disbelief and horror. "Are you sure?"

"Forge would have also been poisoned had he chosen to drink," Hodge added.

"That's an outlandish claim, Rhys," Veran scoffed.

"It's no claim," intervened Ethos. "It's the truth. It happened to my user over two centuries ago. Osiris doesn't approve of outliers in its experiments. Rhys has done an extraordinary job remaining alive."

"Thanks," muttered Rhys sarcastically.

"If that's the case, then there's a possibility that we might have to intervene," Veran mused. She tilted her head and then nodded. "I'm being summoned. We'll be in contact." She glanced at Kallen, who still glared at her, and then hurried to the maintenance unit. In complete silence, the unit lifted from *Themis'* stern and vanished.

34
SEPARATED

DAWN CAME QUICKLY. WHILE KALLEN and Leo worked to cook for both crews, Rhys called everyone to *Themis'* galley. Clothed in the aroma of warm food, everyone squeezed into the cabin or stood in the doorway. Once Kallen set the stew to simmer, she leaned against the galley counter.

Rhys glanced about. There were more of them than he thought. Not only did it seem that Jules was on the mend but so was Patrin. Though both were still bandaged, they didn't seem to be in any pain. Leela greeted Rhys warmly as she always did by hugging him and kissing his cheek before turning to Kallen and rubbing her abdomen. Tessa remained in the doorway where Axel and Kashim stood. Zain and Forge sat stoically at the tables, their backs against the wall. Only Rhys recognized their motionlessness for what it was—a silent conversation. While Hodge chatted with Andy, Terron visited with Leela.

Rhys cleared his throat and the crew settled. "For those of you unaware, Veran and a group of my people arrived earlier this morning to reclaim Beso's body. They left a short while ago for Neo-Colony Two." His gaze passed over the men and women around him. "From here on out… it's only going to get more dangerous. The tentative plan is to finish resupplying and head out for Brechin tomorrow morning. Those unwilling to proceed any further, please let me know by this afternoon. You will not be shamed or mocked. This is life or death we're talking about." He pursed his lips. "I'm going to be very blunt. In addition to the usual danger we will be facing, more assassination attempts like what happened in the tavern are likely. You endanger yourselves being with me. I do not expect answers at this moment. I only ask that you let me know before the end of the afternoon so we can compensate with proper resupplying and inventory."

"Rhys," beckoned Leela. "Why does this have to be you and these people? Why can't you leave this for someone else?"

"Because he's the only one who can do it," Kallen interjected.

Leela looked over her shoulder at Patrin before smiling grimly at Rhys. "My apologies, but I'm afraid this is as far as we go. We're... not meant for this. I thought perhaps you could use our medical assistance, but we haven't been of much use."

"You've been more than helpful," assured Terron warmly. "There's no way I could have cared for Jules and Patrin alone. Your service has been invaluable. Is there nothing I can say to persuade you stay?"

"We're not soldiers," Leela continued. "We never have been. Because of our field of expertise, we've just always been involved in battle."

Terron looked at Rhys for support. With a sad smile, Rhys said, "I can't say anything to dissuade them. This is a decision they must make themselves."

"Fine, I'll do it then," said Jules gruffly. He pushed through the doorway to be better seen. "You saved my life and Patrin's. You didn't save Reza, but you *gawan* tried. We need you and your expertise." He looked to Patrin. "Both of you."

"Let us think on it," Leela offered.

Kallen turned, stirred the pot on the stove, and said, "Breakfast is ready. We made enough for everyone. Let's eat."

Once everyone was served, he passed Kallen a large bowl and patted her butt. Hodge relinquished his chair to her as the rest were full.

Though the meal was quiet, it was not an uncomfortable silence. In fact, Rhys enjoyed it as much as he did their rowdy and boisterous dinners. He half-expected Hodge to make a scene to liven everyone up, but never did his friend crack a rousing joke or break into his infamous laughter.

Eventually, crew members returned to work. Kashim, Axel, and Leo needed to finish weapons and armaments procurements while Kallen wanted to head into town to purchase more meat for the freezer. Rhys needed to go through the medical supplies they had acquired and divide them between the two ships, but he couldn't finalize the division until he knew with certainty what Leela and Patrin decided.

Midafternoon found Rhys on the upper deck rechecking solar panels and ropes. Despite being soaked in sweat and under the sun, he enjoyed the work. It was mindless and kept his hands busy.

Just as he decided his satchel of tools was becoming too heavy and he began to climb down the central mast, Ethos, which had been tucked in his pants pocket as usual, spoke for the first time that day.

"There seems to be some activity on the southern side of Firekli."

Rhys balanced himself on one of the crossbeams and looked. His headscarf shaded his eyes. "What kind of activity?"

"Can't tell. Radio interference is bad. Besides, the southern end of town is just out of range of my sensors. Find Forge or Zain."

Rhys checked his footing before climbing down. Halfway down the mast, a series of booms like thunder rolled along the horizon followed by higher-pitched pops. Gunfire. All work on the docks came to a halt; every sailor, mechanic, overseer, and dock manager fell still.

Rhys hurried to the forward hatch to deposit his tools. He found the hatch door down and Kashim, Axel, and Leo listening. They had been finishing loading the new munitions.

"What was that?" asked Leo.

"Ethos says it's coming from the southern end of town," Rhys supplied.

"Let's hope Yanamichin deployed those extra forces like he said he would," Kashim said. "He was supposed to have—"

Another great wave of thunder echoed in the distance. They froze. Unlike the previous boom, this one didn't disappear. It grew and swelled.

Rhys' heart dropped as he realized they weren't hearing explosives. He leapt over the crate of munitions and dashed out the forward hatch onto the docks. Within seconds, the roar—which rose exponentially in decibel—climaxed, and an aircraft screamed by. He covered his ears with his hands and gaped up at the unit in horror. It wasn't an airship. Airships didn't move that fast. What he had just seen did not belong to Earth. It was *Anemone,* the trans-atmospheric jet he had discovered while in the Brechin camp outside New Arbroath.

"No!" he screamed, realizing the unit was heading south.

Heart in his throat, he looked at the others. The expression of horror and panic on his face must have been a new one because Leo backed fearfully into the depths of the forward hatch. Kashim's eyes were glued to Rhys, searching for answers. Axel seemed to be the only other one who understood the significance of what they had just witnessed.

"Ethos," Rhys said.

"It's what you think it is," replied the AI.

"Rhys," murmured Kashim. For the first time in his life, Rhys saw real fear on the man's bearded face. Never before had they seen an aircraft move at speeds like *Anemone* had just showcased. They didn't know or understand the horrible cruelty of humanity's innovations.

Rhys glanced back at the sky and explained, "It's a trans-atmospheric jet. It's old but because of its high level of technology, it's still functioning. At one point... it was used to defend colonies, spacecraft, and shuttles." He pursed his lips. "Its power... is meant for space."

"Where would they get something like that?" asked Axel.

Rhys leaned against a crate, feeling defeated. Was this the beginning of the end? Was mankind going to destroy itself once more?

"Rhys!" called Kallen, running along the docks, a pack on her back; Forge sprinted after her.

"Jet!" shouted Forge in Nefegian.

As Kallen entered the forward hatch, Rhys raced out to meet Forge. "How many? Is it just the one?"

"It's just the one," replied Forge in Nefegian. "It's the unit we saw in New Arbroath."

Rhys looked southward in hope of catching another glimpse of the unit, but the sky was empty. Forgetting himself, he began speaking rapidly in Nefegian. "What is it capable of? I saw its armaments back then, but I'm sure it has more. Does it have an AI onboard? What about the pilot? Is it him? Is it Gealdir?" Rhys looked at Forge to find the medical student staring at him. "What?"

"There is literally no defense against such a weapon," Forge asserted. "It's just as you've explained to me before... Our tools, weapons, and ships are overpowered here."

Rhys looked back at the others who were watching from the safety of the forward hatch. Brechin had just unleashed its ultimate weapon on the port. Sunboarders could do nothing. Normal bullets and weapons would have no effect on *Anemone*. "Only *our* weapons will work against it," he concluded. Forge nodded solemnly in agreement. "Axel, get everyone back to the ships. Kashim, contact Yanamichin and relay to him what we know. Leo—"

Together, Leo and Kallen approached Rhys, took his arms, and dragged him down the ramp back into the forward hatch. Kallen shoved him onto a crate. "And... you're sitting right here."

Leo fiercely motioned to Forge. "You too. Get over here." Meekly, the med student joined them.

"The both of you, stay here," Kallen demanded, "until everyone is back onboard and we know what we're up against."

Rhys knew she had recognized the expression on his face and the change of tone in his voice. He had slipped into Overseer-mode and begun disseminating orders that would ultimately throw his crew into danger. Frowning, Rhys slumped on the crate and glowered out at the afternoon sun. Axel rushed off the docks to find Hodge and Andy while Kashim hurriedly stashed ammunition.

"If we wanted," whispered Forge, "we could easily escape from here."

Kallen, who seemed to be in a no-nonsense kind of mood, tilted her head and furrowed her brows. "Was that a threat?" Forge shook his head quickly. "No, I didn't think so."

"Hey!" called Hodge. Rhys leaned forward to look out at the docks. Hodge, Andy, and Axel were running down the wharf. "Did you see that? Did you?" His friend leapt over the ramp and landed in the forward hatch. "Was that ours? I mean… is the colony helping?"

Rhys shook his head. "It's Brechin's."

The excitement in Hodge's shoulders melted and his face folded into worry. "But… all of the gunfire stopped after it passed overhead."

"Not ours," confirmed Rhys.

"Rhys, I advise that we prepare to launch," said Andy, entering. "The other ships are doing the same."

"But Brechin's navy is nearby," said Forge. "That's where *Anemone* just came from. It launched from an airship about eight kilometers north of Firekli."

Andy shrugged. "Either way, the other ships are preparing to leave port to form a defensive line. I recommend we also go."

Rhys nodded and stood. "Prepare *Themis* to launch. *Grisle* is to remain behind in port. Notify Terron. Close the forward hatch and load the guns." Rhys started for the bridge with Andy, Kallen, Hodge, and Forge on his heels. "Kallen, check the engine room. Make sure all minor repairs you've made in the past few days are satisfactory and that we are battle-ready." Kallen turned and jogged down the hall. "Forge, keep me updated on the navy's major movements. Warn us if there are any changes in their formations. Hodge, handle the dock ropes."

It was a mere two minutes before *Themis* pulled away from the docks and joined the line of ships leaving port. By the time they reached open water and joined the ranks, Yanamichin had already addressed all of the ships via radio and disseminated orders to each section.

As *Themis* prepared for battle, Rhys leaned on the bridge paneling and pulled a radio to his mouth. "Yanamichin, this is Rhys Falkrow. I wanted to talk to you about that unit from earlier. Over." Learning from Kashim that Yanamichin probably had half a dozen radio operators working under him, Rhys waited patiently for a response. The General's attention was being split between forty-plus ships.

"You have a plan?" asked Andy, standing at the ship's helm.

Rhys turned to answer him, but the radio in his hand interrupted him. "This is Yanamichin, over."

"You know normal munitions will not work against that unit. It's not from this planet. Don't waste time and effort trying to bring it down. Over." Rhys gazed out the bridge glass. For as far as the eye could see down both their port and starboard sides, there were ships—and still more were moving into position to create a defensive barrier around Firekli.

"I am aware of the unit's other-worldliness. We have means to take it down should it attack. Thus far, it has only done fly-bys. Over."

Rhys exchanged confused looks with Andy and Kashim. "What does he mean?" Both of his crew members shrugged. Hesitantly, he cued the radio and asked, "Do you have plasma weapons?" If Firekli had miraculously gotten its hands on a plasma weapon, the tides of war were about to shift.

"What's a plasma weapon?" came Yanamichin's reply.

Knowing he would have to simplify the explanation, Rhys said, "It's like a beam of light. It's very hot. It can destroy anything."

Andy shook his head. "There's no way…"

"Oh," replied Yanamichin. "Yes, we have that."

Rhys rested his forehead on the bridge paneling. After a moment, he nodded to himself and spoke into the radio. "I'll leave it to you then. Out."

"Do you believe him?" asked Andy of Kashim.

Kashim leaned back in his chair. "If he says he has plasma weapons, then he has them."

"No, do you think he understands what a plasma weapon is?" Andy clarified.

"I think so," replied Rhys. "There's nothing else in this region that could mimic a plasma weapon. He said he understood that *Anemone* was not of Earth. He knows more than he's letting on."

Rhys studied the radar map below him. Two lines were forming to shield Firekli's coastline from attack while farther out at sea a mass of enemy vessels and airships moved into offensive positions. *Themis*, which had been given orders to join the second defensive line, was near the mouth of the port with fifteen ships on either side of her.

Explosions resonated over the water, and clouds of thick, gray smoke enveloped Firekli's front line. Trusting that Yanamichin would inform the defensive line whether it needed to engage, Rhys remained watchful. The rest of the crew appeared on the bridge wanting to know what was happening.

Out at sea, Firekli's front line disappeared into a cloud of dense, black smoke.

"Was that an attack?" asked Hodge, leaning forward.

"Smokescreen," replied Kashim. "They're using it to shield their movements."

As he spoke, an eruption of missiles spewed from the clouds. Firekli was making its move first! Although Rhys didn't like to admit it, he felt empowered. They had, for as long as he had been on Earth, always been on the losing side, constantly taking damage, injury, and death. Now, it was Brechin's turn to pay.

In the distance, numerous explosions resounded; cannon fire followed. As the smoke cleared and blew off to the east, the battlefield was revealed in the orange light of the afternoon sun. Although the ships were in an all-out gunfight, the true battle was happening overhead in the azure sky where hundreds of sunboards weaved, dove, and whirled. Having never been on the ground while watching an aerial battle, Rhys gazed up in awe.

He struggled to follow the battle tactics and strategies the sunboarders used. Just like he, Hodge, and Kashim, Firekli's sunboarders had team strategies, many of which involved high-maneuverability tactics that relied on sunboarders' skills. Several times he saw pilots weave around one another to take the brunt of an attack for a comrade. While it was apparent the pilots were skilled, those belonging to Brechin were just as experienced and seemed to be better equipped.

"We're losing people," said Rhys after a moment, his eyes trained on the heavens.

"Brechin technology," explained Axel, unsurprised. "They have a steadier supply of stronger materials."

Hodge leapt forward as a Firekli pilot suddenly separated from his board and began plummeting toward the water. Arms flailing in an instinctual attempt to slow his descent, the pilot seemed to fall in slow-motion. "Get him!" shouted Hodge.

A sunboard swept from the sky, tilted forward, and dove after the pilot. Even from a distance, Rhys could see it was a woman from her long, black hair and slight frame.

"She's not going to make it," murmured Kashim, leaning forward in anticipation.

Meter by meter, the female pilot drew closer to her falling comrade who was trying to provide her with a free hand or arm. She must have realized there was no way she was going to be able to pull her comrade onto her board, because the pilot withdrew her outstretched hand and angled her board downward steeply.

"She's going to try to catch him," Hodge said. As he said it, the pilot accelerated past her falling target. "Pull up, pull up," Hodge breathed. Straining against the fin, the female pilot adjusted her board's angle. With her speed now equal to the terminal velocity of her comrade, she darted expertly under the male pilot. He hit the fin just hard enough to make it bulge. The pilot began descending.

"Forge!" shouted Rhys, spotting an incoming enemy sunboarder targeting the falling couple. Forge, who had been standing just behind Rhys, darted out of the bridge to the outer platform. "Come on, Forge…"

A burst of orange erupted from the side of the bridge as the med student fired on the enemy sunboarder with the plasma beam weapon. The Brechin sunboard disintegrated beneath its pilot, causing the soldier to topple through the air and smash into the sea.

"Andy, we're going to pick up those two," ordered Rhys. The First Mate throttled *Themis*. Both downed pilots were between Firekli's offensive and defensive lines; it didn't appear as though anyone else had noticed them. Rhys pushed the radio to his mouth. *"Themis* is breaking formation to retrieve downed pilots."

"Roger, go ahead," came a radio-reviewer's response.

"Kallen, prepare to receive them. Kashim, you and Forge watch our backs. Leo, inform Forge," said Rhys. He glanced out the bridge at the woman's sunboard which floundered in the space above the water. Its sail was damaged; the weight of two pilots was too much. Momentarily, the limping sunboard smashed into the water and its fin snapped.

"Bring them down our port," added Rhys. He glanced at the battle roaring overhead. Although they weren't protected from aerial attacks, at least the vanguard of ships would defend them from artillery.

Rhys descended into the forward hatch where Kallen had already opened the new, rear-facing launch ramp. Peering down the chute, Rhys caught sight of the crash and the female pilot struggling to keep her unconscious comrade above the water. Rhys didn't have to say anything. Hodge and Axel stripped out of their boots and shirts, ran down the ramp, and dove into the sea.

"Kallen, the new medical supplies," said Rhys, hurrying down the chute after them. There was a brief conversation between Hodge and the pilot before he maneuvered around her and unbuckled her bulletproof vest. In the meantime, Axel took control of her unconscious comrade, laid him on his back, and began stroking back to the chute. Hodge stripped the woman of her rifle and pulled her alongside him.

When they were close enough, Rhys leaned out from the chute, grabbed the unconscious man's arm and, with Axel's help, dragged him onto the ship. Once they moved him to the forward hatch, Rhys knelt beside him to examine him. He was young and lean like Hodge with brilliant golden hair. Rhys turned the young man's scalp to the left to study the bloody gash along the back of his head. He had probably struck the support bar of the sunboard upon landing on the fin.

"Gwin!" panted the female pilot, emerging from the chute with Hodge. "Is he alive?"

Rhys nodded and motioned to Kallen who held the medical pack. "He hit his head. Axel, tell Andy we're set. Withdraw. Have Kashim and Forge cover our retreat." Axel disappeared upstairs.

The young woman sat beside her comrade. "Are you a doctor? How bad is it?" she asked. Rhys glanced up and met her startling green eyes. "Are you or are you not a doctor?"

"Yes, he's a doctor," said Hodge. "Calm down."

Rhys withdrew Ethos from his pocket and set the AI on the man's chest and withdrew sutures, gauze, and bandages from the pack. As Ethos reported to him its findings in Nefegian, Rhys prepped his sewing materials. It was for this exact reason that he had installed a central light in the middle of the forward hatch.

"That was pretty nice flying," Hodge awkwardly said after a moment. "How long have you been flying?"

The young woman gave Hodge a cursory glance before saying, "I'm not interested."

Rhys focused on his work to keep from smiling; Kallen was not so successful hiding her obvious amusement. Hodge scowled and leaned against the wall.

It took but a few minutes before Rhys finishing suturing the man's head wound and tying bandages around it. Finally, he sat back and looked at the woman. "Are you hurt?"

"Just bruised," she replied. "The impact hurt."

Rhys raised the man's shirt, bared his knuckles, and rubbed hard against his patient's sternum, pressing bone-on-bone. Instantly, the man woke from the pain. "Easy," coaxed Rhys, pushing him back onto the floor. "You're safe."

"Hey," cooed the young woman.

The man, Gwin, looked at her for a long moment and then sighed in relief. "Sefora, you saved my *gawan* life."

Sefora took his hand and nodded. "I'm glad."

"Where are we?" Gwin looked at Hodge, Kallen, and then Rhys.

"You're safe," replied Rhys, folding the spare bandages and repacking the medical bag. "You're on the defensive line just outside port. What ship were you with?"

"We weren't with a ship. We launched from Firekli," replied Sefora, pulling her long black hair from its tie. As she spoke, she squeezed water from her tresses and swiftly braided it. "We're part of the aerial militia. Our forces were split between here and the southern border."

"Take it easy for a little while," said Rhys, watching Gwin sit up. "Don't do anything in a hurry."

"Rhys, we have enemy sunboards bearing down on us," called Kashim through the pipe system.

"Hodge, Kallen, be prepared to launch our units." Rhys stood, placed the medical pack on the crates, and started for the bridge.

"You're launching sunboards?" asked Sefora.

"Don't know yet." Rhys glanced at Hodge and then hurried to the bridge. "How many?" he asked as he entered.

"Forge is attracting too much attention," said Andy. "But we can't pull him in because he's protecting the ship."

"Ally ships are intercepting," said Kashim. "At this rate, the rear defensive line will turn offensive."

"Have any orders come in from command?" Rhys queried, standing over radar. The entire area was a complete mess. Where there had been two definitive lines of Firekli ships and organized batches of sunboards, there now were fragmented clusters of vessels grouped together withstanding enemy fire. "What's going on?" Rhys leaned on the bridge paneling. "This doesn't make sense."

"No orders from command," replied Andy. "The radios have been silent."

Rhys tilted his head in thought. "Silent... Ah! *Gawan!*" He went to the open bridge doorway and bellowed, "Forge! Get in here." Panting and wind-whipped, Forge appeared. Leo closed the door behind them. Rhys switched to Nefegian. "Veran said there had been increased radio interference this morning. Is it still there?"

"Radio interference?" Forge tilted his head just as Rhys had done. "It's still there. Actually, it's worse. There so much noise in the atmosphere that it's impossible for radio signals to get through."

"When did it increase? Does Pathos know?"

Forge nodded. "Twenty-nine minutes ago."

Rhys looked at the others. "Osiris is creating atmospheric noise to jam all radios. The fleet has no idea what to do because no one is in command."

"Who's Osiris?" came a voice from the back of the bridge. Rhys looked up as Sefora strode in. "Is he a Brechin noble like yourself?" She withdrew the handgun strapped to her hip and pointed it at Rhys and Forge. "You speak the nobles' language."

Forge glanced at Rhys. "The noble's language? It's our language."

Rhys' eyes slipped to Axel, who had been standing at the rear of the bridge silently watching. The soldier reached through the space between them and grabbed the woman's pistol, placing his thumb between the hammer and the pin so it couldn't fire. The woman jerked the handgun downward, spun, and struck Axel's shin with the heel of her right foot. Axel staggered a single step before wrenching his arm back and slugging her hard across the face. Sefora crumpled to the floor.

"Too much, Axel," Rhys murmured, returning his focus to the problem at hand.

"There has to be a way around the noise," said Andy. "How are the Brechin forces communicating with one another?"

Rubbing his knuckles, Axel joined them. "They use satellite radio. It has nothing do with radio waves; it can't be intercepted or interfered with."

"What does that mean?" asked Andy.

"Normal radio waves travel through the atmosphere based on line-of-sight or along the Earth's curvature," explained Forge. "They can also bounce off the ionosphere, one of the top layers of Earth's atmosphere, and be received at greater distances. Satellite radio doesn't use any of these; instead, it travels through Earth's atmosphere and taps into satellites orbiting Earth. If you have the technology to transmit and receive, there is very little that will interfere with the broadcasts because the signals are going straight up and then straight back down."

"So, we're the only ones being blocked," Kashim mused.

"It looks like Osiris is becoming more involved in our region," said Rhys. He paced a few lengths and then looked at Forge. "Where's Zain?"

"On *Grisle*."

"Tell him to take Terron and go to the command center in port."

Forge's face grew expressionless, and his eyes peered into the distance.

"If we can't communicate, Firekli will fall," said Rhys. He looked at the others. "Forge and Zain will be our radios."

"That means we're going to the front lines," Andy stated. The bridge fell silent as they looked at one another.

"It's done. They're on their way right now," said Forge.

"Good." Rhys withdrew Ethos and held it between him and Forge. "Pathos, Ethos. Make nice. We're going to need both of you for this to work."

"Pleased to make your acquaintance..." muttered Ethos.

"Mutual," Pathos grumbled.

"Hodge, Kallen—come here!" Rhys called. Both appeared and casually stepped over Sefora's limp body. "We're going to the frontline to act as a receiver and disseminator of orders. Axel, Hodge, and I will launch. The receivers will be me and Forge. I will pass orders to the sunboarders; Forge and *Themis* will disseminate orders to the fleet."

"You should give Ethos to Hodge," said Andy. "And you should return to port."

"He's right," said Kallen. "If you're the only one who can disable Osiris, you can't be here."

Realizing they were right, Rhys begrudgingly passed Ethos to Hodge and said, "Don't die."

"We'll be fine," his friend said. Rhys could hear the forced confidence in his voice.

"Kallen, help me get her downstairs." Rhys motioned to Sefora. Kallen hurried to his side and helped lift the woman from the floor. She groaned and tried to fight them, but Rhys gathered her in his arms and stood. He looked back at the others. "I'm counting on you."

"Go on," said Andy, returning his attention to the instruments.

"What happened?" gasped Gwin as Rhys entered the forward hatch carrying Sefora.

"She got in the way," Rhys replied. Kallen hurried past him and prepared to launch the dinghy. He set Sefora next to Gwin and began arming himself.

"Did you hit her?" snarled Gwin, trying to move to his feet.

"No, I didn't hit her." Rhys buckled his bulletproof vest, slung his resonance cutters and a short rifle over his shoulder, and slid a holstered pistol into the small of his back. "We're going ashore."

The ferociousness on Gwin's face faded some. "Why?"

344

"Both of you are injured and need to be away from battle."

"Rhys," called Kallen.

"Can you stand?" he asked, offering Gwin his hand. The man took Rhys' arm and pulled himself up. Grumbling, Sefora followed Rhys and Gwin down the chute and clambered into the waiting dingy.

Rhys turned to Kallen. "I'm needed here," she murmured in Elali.

"I know." He circled the dinghy and took her in his arms. "*Please*, take care of yourself." Kallen kissed the side of his head and then his lips before nodding. He withdrew from her until only their fingers were touching. Kallen pulled her hand from his and backed away from the ramp. Feeling as if he was leaving behind his entire world, Rhys hopped into the dinghy, settled himself at the fan, and then motioned that he was ready. Kallen pulled the release and, in a single motion, the dinghy slid into the water.

He started the fan, maneuvered away from *Themis*, and began motoring back to port. Occasionally, he looked over his shoulder at his ship in heartbreak. By the time they reached port a half hour later, *Themis* was no longer discernible; his ship appeared just as the multitude of others—a speck on the water. He docked the dinghy and climbed onto the wharf. Looking out at the battle set against a blood-orange backdrop, he couldn't help the feeling of despair swelling in his chest.

"So, who are you really?" asked Gwin, still seated in the dinghy. Sefora sat propped up against the edge of the dinghy, the left side of her face varying shades of purple, red, and pink. "There's more going on here than you're letting on."

"You should get back to command," suggested Rhys, his gaze set on the chaos out at sea.

"What about you?" asked Gwin.

"I'll stay here." Rhys inhaled as a short-lived gust of wind pulled at his hair and clothes.

Was this what it was going to feel like to leave behind everything he knew and launch into space? He was going to leave behind Kallen, and Hodge, his ship, his family, and rely solely on himself to pilot a unit into orbit and somehow miraculously destroy or otherwise disable Osiris? How was he supposed to make it back? Was... he supposed to make it back?

The thought alone made his heart throb painfully in his chest.

"Thank you for rescuing us," muttered Gwin, seeming to sense Rhys' change in mood.

"Yeah, but not really," Sefora groused.

Gwin left Sefora's side and approached Rhys, hand extended. "Gwin Ladley." Rhys took his arm. "And this is Sefora, my wife." Sefora, who had her arms crossed, looked at Rhys spitefully. "Thank you."

"We were happy to help," replied Rhys, forcing a smile.

"What's your name?"

"Rhys Falkrow." He withdrew his hand and turned back to the sea. "I hope you feel better. That was a nasty fall. I'm glad you weren't hurt more." So absorbed by worry and fear, it took a moment for Rhys to process the fact that Gwin had offered no reply. Expecting the husband and wife to be halfway down the docks, he glanced over his shoulder. Instead, he found Gwin and Sefora gazing wide-eyed at him. "What? What's wrong?"

"You're Rhys Falkrow?" asked Gwin. Rhys nodded. "And the ship we were on…"

"*Themis*," replied Rhys.

Sefora turned away from them and buried her face into her hands.

"What's wrong?" whispered Gwin.

"I pointed my gun at him," she muttered.

Gwin guffawed before looking at Rhys apologetically. "I'm so sorry."

"It's fine."

"Did you want us to show you where command is? Because we can do that," Gwin offered.

"No. I'm going to wait here," Rhys replied. "You two go ahead."

Gwin exchanged looks with Sefora before asking, "Why did you leave the ship? It wasn't really to be with us, was it?"

"No, but the truth is far more complicated than I care to explain."

"The woman on the ship," said Gwin, "she your wife?"

"Yes," replied Rhys.

"And she's going into battle without you."

"Yes."

"Are you sure you don't want us to take you to the command center?" asked Sefora.

"Two of my men are already there. My presence is not needed." Rhys forced yet another small smile on his face. "I'm fine here."

Despite Rhys insisting that they leave, both Gwin and Sefora remained on the docks. He was only thankful he had docked the dinghy farther inland giving him the space to wander to the end of the wharf to be alone. The couple didn't follow.

Rhys kept his eyes trained seaward until dusk. Only when he could no longer discern ships on the water did he finally resort to pacing. He searched for *Themis'* familiar silhouette against the backdrop of explosions.

Thoughts crowded his mind and he meticulously worked to reason through them. When panic clutched at his heart and threatened to stifle his breathing, he remembered the numerous times his crew had escaped danger. He assured himself tirelessly that they were fine, that they had a swarm of allied ships protecting them. After all, they were acting as the flagship. They would be defended.

When he wasn't worrying incessantly about his crew, he pondered his own fate and what his role in the grand scheme of everything was. If he was so vital, why was he just waiting? Why wasn't he fighting? Why wasn't he already in Brechin? Twice, he almost ran in search of a sunboard, but his own heart kept him rooted to the docks. He couldn't leave without knowing whether Kallen and his crew were safe. For the sake of his own sanity, he couldn't.

When his legs finally grew tired, Rhys lay on the docks and stared up at the stars. Thoughts of Osiris plagued his mind, effectively forcing him to shut his eyes. He must have dozed for a while because when he next became aware of the sky, the full moon had disappeared behind clouds and the stars were gone. In the distance, lightning illuminated the horizon. He would be glad when the wet season was over.

He sat up, stretched, and looked down the wharf. Gwin and Sefora were gone. They must have grown weary. Rhys scanned the sea for any signs of Firekli ships returning. Though the gunfire had died down, only a handful of ships had limped back to port; *Themis* was not among them. Rhys stood and began pacing the docks once more. He wished he at least had Ethos; he felt naked and alone.

Another half hour passed and battle once more broke out at sea in a flurry of explosions, gunfire, and distant blasts. As thunderstorms approached Firekli, it became impossible to differentiate between thunder and cannon fire. The warm winds gushing out from the encroaching storms tore at his hair and clothes and threw sea spray into his face. When the sea mist began to mingle with heavy rain, Rhys retreated to the open canopy of a dock shop. He was surprised to find Sefora and Gwin already waiting there for him.

Ruffling the water from his hair and shaking out his shirt, he murmured, "I thought you left."

"We wouldn't hear the end of it if we left you alone out here," said Gwin.

Rhys leaned against the shop's wall. "How's your head? Any pain?"

"It's been throbbing, but nothing too bad," Gwin replied. He motioned to Sefora. "The swelling has gone down in her face too."

"Glad to hear that," Rhys said hollowly.

Only the sound of pouring rain filled the silence between them. Lightning streaked overhead before thunder crashed over the docks like waves.

"So why did they kick you off the ship?" asked Sefora.

"Sefora," hissed Gwin. She shrugged.

"They didn't kick me off," said Rhys. "I chose to leave."

"Why?" Sefora prodded.

"You don't have to answer," said Gwin, throwing his wife a dirty look. Sefora didn't seem to care. "I know of a small inn nearby. Sailors normally rest there. We should get dried off."

"Go ahead," murmured Rhys, squinting against the lightning.

"They'll be fine," said Sefora. Though he knew she meant it to bring him comfort, her naturally monotone voice didn't convince him.

"I'm sorry," apologized Gwin. "Sefora has had a very long day."

"You two should go rest," Rhys offered. "Both of you are injured. I know how draining even minor pain can be."

"Is standing on the dock for the next five hours going to help your comrades?" asked Sefora. Rhys looked at her, taken aback. When Gwin tried to quiet her, she brushed him off. "Seriously. Is pacing the wharf going to help your comrades?"

"No."

"Would getting rest in preparation to take over for them when they return to port help them instead?" continued Sefora. Rhys considered her and then nodded in defeat. "Good, come on."

He glanced once more at the sea before following the couple down the cobblestone streets to their preferred inn. Despite it being the middle of the night, they were warmly welcomed in. As they pulled off their soaked clothes, the inn keeper lit a small fire in the hearth and brought out warm cups of broth to drink.

"I can only afford one room," said Gwin, sheepishly glancing at the inn keeper. The graying woman shrugged and motioned for them to follow her upstairs. Although Gwin and Sefora followed, Rhys did not. Instead, he stood in the common room and gazed about. He had not forgotten that he was a target, even if the entire port was in the midst of battle. He needed to know his escape routes.

"You coming?" called Sefora from the top of the stairs.

Rhys joined them upstairs and peered into the quaint room lit by a single lamp. The inn keeper bowed her head as he entered and then closed the door behind him.

Sefora threw a pillow at Rhys, startling him from his trance. Gwin hissed in disapproval but, as usual, Sefora didn't seem to care. "Sleep. You're tired," she instructed, unceremoniously toppling a pile of blankets onto the hardwood floor and flopping down in the middle of them.

At a loss, Rhys gathered blankets from the enormous pile on the far side of the room and created a rather uncomfortable-looking nest on the floor. Weapons in his hand, he stood at the window and gazed into the dark distance.

"It's hard to come down from a fighter's high," offered Gwin, perched on a narrow bed. "When you've been alert for so long, it's hard to relax."

"He hasn't been fighting," muttered Sefora. "Look, just lie down and you'll go to sleep. Seriously."

"I can't," said Rhys solemnly. "It's not safe here."

Sefora sighed and began retying her hair. "It's not safe anywhere."

Rhys looked at them. "No, for me." Both Sefora and Gwin sat up. "I have assassins after me. *Themis* is the only place I can sleep."

"We'll keep watch for you," said Gwin. "That's not a problem."

Rhys sat with his back against the wall, his short rifle and resonance cutters between his legs. He glanced at Gwin. "Is your head bothering you? I can re-bandage it but… I don't have any clean bandages."

"No, no. I'm fine. Please rest."

Rhys checked the magazine of his rifle once more to reassure himself, dragged a blanket around his shoulders, and felt his head loll to the side. Within seconds, he was asleep.

35
TRAUMA

THE VIOLENT QUIVERING OF THE window pane above his head startled Rhys from his sleep. He lurched to his knees, his hand already on the resonance cutters. A roar he knew all too well swelled in the distance, building indefinitely until it cracked overhead. Despite the deep darkness of the early morning hours, he knew what had just flown by.

He peered out the window at the weak lamppost lights glistening along the rain-streaked cobblestone street and then pressed his face against the pane to see if he could discern anything. The moment his eyes connected with the southern sky, a brilliant burst of glittering gold originating from the ground suddenly illuminated the low-hanging clouds.

"What was that?" whispered Sefora who knelt at the small window a few paces away. Gwin was still asleep.

Rhys gaped. A plasma cannon?

The golden beam engulfed half the port in an iridescent aura and revealed the numerous Brechin airships hanging in the skies to the south. The beam, though mercilessly bright, was short-lived and disappeared in shards of light, leaving Rhys' vision spotted. There was a moment of silence before an explosion erupted, and *Anemone* was illuminated in a ball of crackling orange flames and glowing embers.

"Oh my…" breathed Sefora.

Rhys rose to his feet. He couldn't believe it. Yanamichin had said they had plasma weapons, but… a cannon was something else! And to be able to hit a trans-atmospheric jet easily going Mach one or two… They had computers; humans couldn't calculate and track something moving that fast.

Heart in his throat, he watched as *Anemone* struggled to remain aloft, floundering in the air. Even from a distance, Rhys could discern the unit's thrusters and jets working frantically to maintain altitude and control. A dark speck suddenly erupted over the flaming inferno as the cockpit ejected. An airship appeared, snatched the pod from the air, parachute and all, and whirred away from the battlefield.

Rhys waited to hear gunfire, but none followed. In fact, as *Anemone* disappeared in a brilliant blaze, he saw a number of Brechin airships turn to withdraw.

"Is it over?" Sefora whispered.

He pulled away from the window. "No. They know we have a plasma cannon now. Brechin will stop at nothing to seize or destroy it."

"That's the power of the white gods," murmured Sefora, sitting against the wall.

Rhys looked at her, surprised. "You're Pantarak?"

"I thought my looks were enough to tell you that," replied Sefora.

"So then… you know who I am?"

"Everyone knows who you are." Sefora laid her head back and looked at him. "I didn't think you'd be so young though."

"How old do you think I look?"

Sefora shrugged. "Fifteen. I don't know."

Rhys frowned. "If you're so familiar with white gods, you would know that our looks are deceiving."

"I figured that much. You're an overseer and have a wife. You asked me how old I thought you looked, and I gave you an answer."

Rhys himself around his weapons under the window. Firekli had a plasma cannon. This was a game-changer. Undoubtedly, Brechin was going to go all out to gain control of the weapon.

"I see you plotting. What are you going to do?"

He considered her question and then sighed in defeat. "Nothing. There's nothing I can do right now except wait."

"Why do you need to wait for them?" asked Sefora. "You're a white god. You can do anything."

Rhys looked at her incredulously. It was unusual to find someone of such fervent faith in Firekli. "You really believe I'm a white god?"

Sefora nodded. "Your reputation and achievements precede you. I know what you tried to do for the people of Paducah. The entire Pantarak Empire knows."

"Brechin is Pantarak-controlled; they don't like that I've instigated rebellion."

"Brechin's people have a much different understanding of what you've done." Sefora touched the side of her face where Axel slugged her. "I'm sorry for implying that you were a noble. I deserved the punishment."

"Axel doesn't know the word 'restraint,'" replied Rhys. "He's a former Brechin soldier. He shouldn't have dealt with you so harshly."

"You have a Brechin soldier on your crew? How? Do you know what squadron he was with?" murmured Sefora.

"The fifth," replied Rhys. "He was the captain—" He stopped. "Do you hear that?"

Sefora listened. "No, what do you hear?"

What *was* he hearing? Rhys gazed about the room for a long moment before moving to his feet. "It's a... high-pitched tone..." He tilted his head in confusion. It didn't sound like anything in his environment. It sounded synthetic.

"I still don't hear anything," said Sefora, watching him curiously.

Rhys covered his ears to block out the sound, but it was still there. In fact, it seemed to be growing louder. He pushed his hair back from the injector sockets along his temple and tapped them, fooling himself to think that such an action would have any effect. "It's... getting louder," he murmured. Suddenly, the whining in his head began pulsing in a pattern.

Dot dash dot—dot dot dot dot—dash dot dash dash—dot dot dot. And then it faded momentarily before starting once more.

"I don't know what that means," he growled.

The pulsing tone grew louder and a new series of dots and dashes began to pound through his head. Rhys squinted against the harsh sound and turned in the room. Facing Sefora, the sound was muffled, as if the tone were coming from behind him. Quickly, he angled himself toward port; the whine blasted in full stereo in his head. "I've got to go," he said, jerking his still damp bulletproof vest from the floor and wrapping it about his torso.

Sefora woke Gwin, and they too dressed as Rhys flew down the inn staircase. The married couple followed him.

In the silence of the early morning, he stood in the middle of the cobblestone street and turned his head back and forth. When he determined with certainty that the sound was coming from the docks, he took off at a sprint. He could hear Sefora and Gwin behind him.

By the time the docks were in sight, Rhys could hardly see straight the pulsing was so loud. Gripping the side of his head, he staggered off the street and began searching the wharves.

He found a dark figure at the end of one of the docks. He couldn't discern the man's face or the details of his body; for all he knew, he was walking into an assassination attempt. Struggling to ignore the deafening high-pitched tone pounding his mind, Rhys brought his short rifle to the ready and approached the dock.

"Hey!" called Hodge wearily. "Stop, stop. It's me! It's me!"

The whining disappeared. Rhys breathed out in relief and lowered his weapon. "Hodge." He had never been so happy to see his friend. With Sefora on his heels, he jogged down the dock. Rhys' mirth was short-lived, however, as the particulars of Hodge's face and body came into view. He slowed to a halt just before his friend, his heart sinking.

Hodge had several old cuts along his forehead and cheeks cemented closed by crusty blood; his clothes were in rags. One of his pants legs was soaked through with blood. His hair, which was pulled back in a bun, was covered in dust and grime.

"The others?" Rhys inquired.

"*Themis* is still floating, but she's taken a lot of damage. Brechin's navy has retreated for the time being."

"Why are you here?"

"I came to get you," Hodge solemnly replied. He withdrew Ethos from his pocket. "Axel was downed. We can't find him." There was movement from the corner of his eye, and Rhys found his magnetic board rising above the docks to hover beside Hodge. "Forge passed out," Hodge continued. "Pathos knocked him out. He was delirious on his feet."

Rhys glanced at the water. "You rode the board here?"

"All of our sunboards damaged or out of energy."

"Is anyone else hurt? Anything critical?" Rhys went to his board and examined the scuff marks along its hull where bullets had ricocheted from previous battles.

"No, nothing serious. Minor injuries."

"And you?" asked Rhys, turning back to his friend.

Hodge looked down at his crimson pants leg and shrugged. "I fell and the shifting lever on the board snagged me. Kallen wrapped it but it's still bleeding."

"Sefora, look after him," instructed Rhys. "Take him back to the inn and do what you can."

"Gwin has some medical experience," Sefora offered. "He can help."

Hodge touched Rhys' shoulder. "Listen, Ethos marked Axel's last position, but you know how the sea is. Also, he went down in, what was at the time, enemy territory. Brechin has withdrawn farther out to sea leaving the location open, but no one is in any condition to go search for any length of time."

Rhys pushed the board to the dock so he could step onto it. "Was he injured?"

"Unknown," replied Hodge.

Rhys stepped into the clasps and locked his boots in place. He then slipped Ethos into the front of his vest. Once secure, a dimmed version of the numerical map illuminated before Rhys' face.

Hodge nodded. "Ethos knows where *Themis* is."

"Take care of him, you two," murmured Rhys. Sefora and Gwin nodded.

Rhys scanned the numerical readings of the magnetic field and then stomped on the back of the board, causing it to slingshot into the air. Wind whipping his hair, he looked down in time to see Hodge collapse on the docks and then sprawl out on the wood, his arm over his eyes. Sefora knelt beside him and began tearing off his pants leg.

"How bad is he?" asked Rhys.

"Worse than he was letting on," replied Ethos, projecting his altitude on the numerical map so Rhys could see in the darkness how far from the waterline he was. "He didn't fall. He was shot. Hodge was the only one well enough to come get you."

Rhys' heart settled in a panic. If Hodge was considered well off, what had happened to the others?

"I'm glad to be with you again," said Ethos. "You're my user. I don't have to work as hard to understand motives, speech, or actions." Sensing Rhys' fear, the AI continued. "The battle was successful. Brechin forces have withdrawn. We had casualties, but it's believed far less than what Brechin suffered. Your idea to use Forge, Zain, and myself as transmitters and receivers worked well, but minor adjustments had to be made in order to better disseminate orders to the other ships. Kallen had the brilliant idea to bring up an old flag system which corresponded to the orders being transmitted by command."

"Who's injured on *Themis*?"

"Everyone," replied Ethos. "In varying degrees. Kashim, Hodge, and Axel took the brunt of the attacks and managed to defend the ship well, but, as you now know, Axel was shot down. Kashim also took a bullet, but Kallen managed to pull it out. Forge eventually allowed Pathos full control of the situation and simply sat acting as a medium. He became delirious with fatigue and Pathos knocked him out about two hours ago. Kallen was in the engine room when *Themis* was struck by cannon fire. She slammed into the converter and gave herself a concussion. Leo was also injured in that blast, but his wounds aren't as serious, so he's been caring for everyone else. Andy is the only crew member who managed to escape completely unscathed, but he's managing the ship alone."

Rhys glanced back at the port which was a collection of tiny specks of light. "Did you see the plasma cannon?"

"It spiked on my radar. Likewise, Pathos and Logos sensed it. You saw it?"

"Firekli took down *Anemone*."

"So *that's* what happened," mused Ethos.

"Gealdir wasn't killed though."

"It's going to take a lot more than a single plasma cannon to kill the pilot. The trans-atmospheric jets have extra defense around the cockpit to defend pilots from direct attacks," the AI explained. "Ah, we're approaching Axel's last known appearance."

Below was nothing but black water. Rhys slowed the board to drift above the tame waves. "Any signs of life?" he asked, straining his eyes.

After a moment, Ethos reported, "No. Nothing. Only wreckage. And it doesn't even belong to one of our sunboards."

"What's the best way to find him?"

"I don't have as strong of sensors as Pathos or Logos. My radar can only read contacts within a kilometer depending on their size; all other sensors like heat and sound are dependent upon the environment. It's difficult for me to find objects at sea because the water saps the heat from the contact, making the heat signature too weak for me to read."

"But you *can* read heat signatures, like when we saved Leo and Cantia that one time? So I just need to cover as much sea as possible?"

"As much as I want a better way to do this, I can offer none," replied Ethos.

"Then we'll use a grid pattern. Mark our position, create a grid over the surrounding three kilometers, and give each sector an identifier."

Using Ethos as a guide, he began flying in circles in exact circumferences so as to cover each sector through which he passed. Slowly, his circles grew wider and wider until, after nearly twenty minutes, he extended the search to the adjacent four kilometers.

By the time the sky began lightening with the blush of dawn, Rhys was ready to give up. Either Axel had been rescued by someone else or he had drowned. There were no other options.

"Rhys, I found someone," Ethos said suddenly, causing Rhys to startle. the AI had not spoken in over an hour. "The location is on your screen."

He focused on the three-dimensional map and then looked out at the horizon. "That far?" Leaning into the wind, he skimmed along the waterline. Though he couldn't make out anything floating in the water, Ethos' map continued to show a blinking red beacon. Two kilometers? So far!

"There!" snapped Ethos, drawing a line of blinking lights along the map.

As Rhys neared the waypoint, wreckage and debris suddenly materialized in the water around him. Parts of sunboards, ships, engines, airships, and water craft littered the area. Ignoring the debris, he made for the body which was collapsed over a piece of broken sunboard. As he drew closer, he recognized Axel.

Rhys slammed his board to a halt over the soldier and lowered himself to the sea line. "Axel. Hey," he said, crouching. Axel didn't move. Ethos dissolved the translucent map and issued a beam of light, illuminating Axel. Rhys gaped in horror. Axe's left arm below the elbow was gone. "Shit, shit, shit," he muttered, pushing the magnetic board into the water.

He began trying to drag the soldier from the sea but found that Axel had tied himself to the board to keep from going under. With trembling hands, Rhys withdrew his resonance cutters, gripped Axel's good arm, and cut the strap the soldier had used to tether himself to the sunboard.

"Come on, Axel," growled Rhys, straining against his solid weight. "Come on." Panting, he dipped his shoulder under the man and lifted. When Axel started to slip off, Rhys jerked him upward, causing him to moan. Fresh blood from a wound along Axel's hip slithered over Rhys and mingled with the draining sea water. Knees quivering, Rhys balanced Axel over his back and shoulders. "Easy, Ethos," Rhys murmured, rotating the board and starting southward.

Several times Rhys thought he was going to drop Axel. The man was far larger than himself and built of pure muscle, making him nearly twice Rhys' weight. Straining, Rhys clutched at the soldier as best he could. When *Themis* finally came into view, Rhys was slick and crimson.

"Notify the others. Get the medical supplies ready in the galley," Rhys muttered.

"Already ahead of you."

Andy and Leo met Rhys on the upper deck. They didn't ask questions; they didn't seem surprised. As Rhys lowered the board to the deck, he said,

"Grab him, grab him. I'm going to drop him." Andy took the brunt of Axel's weight. Rhys stepped from his board, forced some steadiness into his legs, and then motioned to Andy and Leo. "Go." While they carried Axel to the galley, Rhys stripped from his bulletproof vest and blood-sodden slacks. Nude, he grabbed his weapons and Ethos and hurried across the deck.

As he entered the galley, he threw his weapons onto the floor, slid Ethos across the galley counter, and began washing the blood from his shoulders and arms. "Leo, get me some pants," he ordered. When he rinsed off what he could, he slipped into a pair of trousers, washed his hands well with soap, and then turned to Axel who was lying on the second galley table. Medical supplies were strewn out on the first table as well as bandages, cloths, and cleaning materials.

"Andy, wash your hands," Rhys instructed. "Leo, gather buckets of water." Using scissors to cut away the soldier's ragged shirt, he examined the wound along Axel's left side. It looked as though something had pierced him. As Leo deposited a bucket of clean water beside him, Rhys said, "Grab Ethos from the counter." Both Leo and Andy joined him at the table. "Lay it on his abdomen."

"No internal bleeding that I can detect," reported Ethos. "His vitals are weak though."

"He's lost a lot of blood." Rhys grabbed a handful of bandages and pressed them on Axel's side. He motioned to Andy. "Get on the other side and hold this." The First Mate slid behind the table and placed his hands over the bandages. Rhys withdrew and began unwinding the soaked shirt haphazardly wrapped along the nub of Axel's left arm. The soldier had used his rifle strap as a tourniquet and cinched it just below his elbow. "Good, Axel," Rhys murmured.

"What? What's wrong?" asked Andy worriedly.

"He put a tourniquet on himself." Rhys thought for a moment, studying the bloody nub. It appeared as though his forearm had been literally ripped from his body. Threads of tissue, muscle, and tendon hung limply from it. "When did he go down? How many hours ago?"

"Eh, I don't know..." murmured Andy, looking to Leo. "Before midnight."

Leo nodded. "Before midnight."

"More than seven hours," mused Rhys.

Axel groaned before taking a sharp intake of air. "I..."

"Easy," murmured Rhys.

Axel turned his head toward Rhys' voice but didn't open his eyes. "I... a tourniquet..."

"I see that," Rhys calmly replied. "When did you apply the tourniquet?" Rhys began gathering supplies. "When you went down?"

"No. Long time... after."

Rhys leaned over Axel and tapped his face. Axel's eyes cracked open. "Listen to me. The tourniquet is only barely holding. It was loosened during our flight back, and you're bleeding out. We don't have blood reserves here, and it'll take well over two hours to get back to port."

"Just..." Axel wheezed audibly. "Take it off."

"We don't have anything that will fully knock you out," said Rhys, glancing at the medical supplies on the adjacent table.

"Do it," moaned Axel.

Rhys exchanged dark looks with Leo and Andy before retrieving the strongest numbing agent they had. He no longer had the advanced medical supplies of Caelestis. While it could have been much worse and they could have purchased only topical medications, the intravenous anesthetic that they had managed to find in Firekli was not ideal.

Swiftly, he injected the anesthetic into Axel's shoulder and monitored him. When it was clear he wasn't going to experience any immediate ill effects, Rhys nodded. "Leo, hold his arm. It's going to take a few minutes for the anesthetic to kick in."

Leo gently took Axel's arm. Rhys showed him how far he wanted the limb to be held out. While they waited for the anesthetic to set in, Rhys worked on the abdominal injury.

Steadying himself, he pushed Andy's hands off the abdominal wound. With firm pressure, he blotted the extra blood and then withdrew the soiled bandages. Axel was lucky. There was no internal bleeding, meaning only the abdomen wall had been punctured. Rhys sterilized the area with a pungent concoction of liquids they had purchased from the local hospital. Fresh blood immediately began pooling.

"As I work, I need you to keep the area as dry as possible," murmured Rhys, glancing at Andy. "I'm going to close the abdominal wall using a layered closure. So, each layer will have to be manually sutured shut. This is going to take a while."

"Fine," Andy asserted.

"I'm going to close the first layer and then turn my attention back to the arm," explained Rhys. Leo nodded. "Here we go."

Although the abdominal surgery progressed well and without problems, Axel's arm was proving to be a challenge. Half an hour after administering the powerful anesthetic, Rhys tied another tourniquet around in preparation for surgery. Once he completed the first layer of the abdominal wound, he stepped back to regard Axel. Even in the semi-sanitized environment they had created in the galley, he couldn't risk using regular tools on the severed arm for fear of infecting it. But he did possess one tool that was incapable of carrying with it bacteria or disease.

Seeing the pained expression on his face, Leo spoke to him in Nefegian. "What? What's wrong?"

"I'm going to have to amputate above the tourniquet."

Leo's brows rose in worry. Axel was not under full anesthetic; as far as Rhys knew, general anesthetic was not even available in this world. After a moment, Leo nodded, glanced at Andy, and asked, "What do you want us to do?"

"Let me finish the abdomen. I have one more layer left. Administer another dose of the local anesthetic."

It took roughly fifteen minutes before Axel's abdomen was completely closed. After Rhys cut the outer sutures, he stepped back and, holding his bloody hands before him, gazed at his patient. This was going to hurt. This was going to trump any pain Axel had ever felt before. With a steadying breath, he maneuvered around Leo and peered down at Axel. "Hey, Axel. Axel."

When he didn't answer, Rhys motioned to Ethos for another vitals report. After learning that, despite the trauma, Axel's vitals were steady, he tried to wake the soldier once more, but he didn't move. Rhys' resolve solidified. If he was unconscious, now was the time to do it.

"Andy, the resonance cutters," said Rhys, moving back around Leo.

Andy grabbed the weapon from the floor and began viciously washing the handle in the sink. When he finished, he passed the cutters to Rhys.

"He's unconscious, but that doesn't mean he can't feel anything. I have no doubt this will wake him. Leo, lay the arm down and move to his legs. Andy, you're going to brace his chest and right arm." Rhys studied Axel's stump as they moved into position. "I'm going to cut..." He pointed to the point just above Axel's elbow. "Here. I'm going to cut inward slightly to create an extra flap of skin at the end so I can suture it back to itself. I will try to be quick." Both Andy and Leo nodded, hardening themselves.

Urging himself to view the surgery objectively, to understand the procedures as a medical professional and not as an Overseer or friend, Rhys engaged the resonance cutters. He reviewed what needed to be completed in his head. He envisioned the cut and Axel's immediate waking response; he saw the thin flap of skin he needed to leave. He could do it.

Rhys moved into position. With steady hands, he slid the cutters under Axel's arm and pinched the skin above the joint where he meant for the cutters to exit. Taking a deep breath, he gently moved his hand upward. As though he were slicing air, the cutters met no resistance. Just as a piercing screech tore from Axel's lips, Rhys maneuvered the cutters outward underneath the shallow lip of skin. His elbow joint dropped to the floor and a small amount of blood began seeping from the cut.

Screaming and writhing in pain, Axel bucked fiercely against Andy and Leo. His desperate cries of pain sent shivers through Rhys and made the hair on his neck stand up. Tears poured down the soldier's face and a raging sweat broke across his forehead, neck, and chest.

Rhys cleared his closing throat. "Hold him still."

With trembling hands, Andy forced Axel's injured arm back to the table. All the while, he spoke to Axel. "Hey, hey. You got this. Hold on."

Heaving great sobs, Axel tried to sit up, but Andy pushed him down. "Stop!" Axel screamed, his voice splintering.

Andy looked at Rhys for guidance. "Let me look," Rhys murmured, leaning in to examine the wound. When he found a freshly cut nub with a slab of skin hanging off, he nodded to himself. "It's good, it's good." Gently, he dabbed at the wound with cloth, causing Axel to flinch fiercely and pant in pain. Rhys studied the wad of muscle, tissue, tendons, veins, and ligaments in search of the arteries. When he located them, he leaned over Axel who was glaring up at the ceiling through free-flowing tears. "I need to cauterize the arteries and then suture the wound closed." Axel didn't response.

Rhys motioned for Andy and Leo to brace the soldier once more and then took the tip of the resonance cutters and touched the head of the arteries. Axel writhed, but Andy kept his injured arm still.

"There, there," announced Rhys, disengaging the cutters and throwing them to the floor. He went to Axel's head. "That's it. We're done. I just need to close it up. That's it."

Sobbing, Axel relaxed slightly under Andy's hands though he continued to shake violently.

"That's it. The worst is over," reassured Rhys. "Don't get up. You've lost a lot of blood." He administered another dose of the intravenous anesthetic before applying a local topical to dull the nerves. As Andy applied a cool cloth to the soldier's head, Rhys washed Axel's arm with sterilizing liquids and prepared the sutures.

"How… bad is it?" whispered Axel hoarsely as Rhys finished the ring of tightly-knit sutures along the nub.

Rhys wiped his forehead on his arm and looked tiredly at the soldier. "I've done exactly what the hospital would have done for you. The only thing they have that we don't is access to antibiotics and blood. We need to get you back to port and admitted. You don't have internal damage, but you've lost a substantial amount of blood.

Axel nodded shakily and closed his eyes. With a deep breath, Rhys rolled his neck and stretched his shoulders and arms. His feet ached from standing motionlessly for so long.

"Good job," Andy murmured.

Rhys pursed his lips. "Well, let's see what the hospital says."

For the next half hour, he and Leo sterilized medical tools, washed tables and cloths, and cleaned the floors while Andy stayed by Axel's side. Once everything, including Rhys himself, was void of blood, he, Leo, and Andy began the process of moving Axel to a bed.

With Axel's weight spread between them, they slid him from the table and shuffled out of the galley. Forge, who sat in the hallway, eyes transfixed on the opposite wall and fists balled in his shirt, didn't looked up as they passed into the crew's quarters.

"Easy," murmured Rhys as they set the soldier in his bed. Favoring his heavily bandaged shoulder, Kashim grimly watched them from his bunk. Once Axel was comfortable, Rhys checked his bandages again and then looked up at Kashim. "Do I need to examine you?"

Kashim shook his head. "No, go rest."

Rhys scoffed and left the room with Andy. His First Mate disappeared onto the bridge—no one had been there in over three hours—while Leo flopped onto his bed and laid an arm over his eyes.

Rhys stood in the hallway listening before turning his attention to Forge. "Hey," he murmured in Nefegian. Forge didn't move. Rhys held his hand out in an offer to help him up. When the medical student didn't make an effort, he pulled the med student to his feet and guided him to the upper deck.

It was midmorning and the sun was already high in the sky.

Rhys led Forge across the deck. He hadn't realized how strongly the galley had smelled of blood, sanitary fluids, and bandages. After a deep breath, Rhys looked at Forge.

The young man had the worn eyes of a soldier. His gaze was distant. "I will… never forget his screams," admitted Forge after a long moment. His words were so soft, they were almost carried off by the wind. Rhys nodded. "I don't think… I could have done that. I don't know… how you managed to stay focused without an AI to guide you."

"Because Axel's life depended on me staying focus," replied Rhys, studying the ships around them. "I've been in a few situations where myself or Alina have been the only people with medical knowledge present. You can't… think about how much pain they must be in; you can't let their emotions influence your own. You have to focus objectively and work without distraction." Rhys nodded. "But yes… I will remember his screams as well." He leaned on the deck railing.

Forge joined him. After several long minutes of silence broken by the lapping of the water on the hull, Forge said, "Neo-Colony Two is preparing to dispatch teams to the area."

Alarmed, Rhys looked at the medical student. "Why?"

"Because Zain and I have been feeding them data for the past two days concerning the conflict here."

"It has nothing to do with them though…"

"Does it?" Forge nodded toward port which was a speck on the horizon. "A plasma cannon took down a trans-atmospheric jet this morning. They have an AI or computer-guided plasma cannon at their disposal. What else do you think they have?" Forge sighed. "And now Osiris knows too."

"What are the teams from the colony planning?"

"To destroy the cannon." The contemplative look on Rhys' face must have caused some uncertainty in Forge, because the medical student shifted and asked, "Why?"

"I have to make a difficult decision soon. Do I wait for my ship to be repaired and my crew healed before setting out for Brechin? Or do I go ahead and leave them behind?" His throat closed around his words. He couldn't share with Forge the grave reality that if he left them behind, that was it. He would probably never see them again.

"I can't make that decision for you," said Forge.

Rhys composed himself. "If I decide to leave for Brechin, will Neo-Colony Two take me there? The journey by ship is nearly two weeks. By one of our units, it would be a few hours."

"It's… a possibility. I will pass the idea along."

The medical student turned to leave, but Rhys stopped him. "If I left for Brechin, you and Zain would be coming with me. There's no debate. You understand that?"

"It was our intent from the beginning."

"Thank you."

36
A DIPLOMATIC SOLUTION

IT WAS NEAR NOON WHEN they finally reached port. Upon their arrival, volunteers poured onto the wharf to help dock the ship. Rhys sent word to the doctors patrolling the docks and quickly turned Axel over to them. He tried to persuade Kashim to go with them, but the large man declined and remained on the bridge with his shoulder tightly bandaged.

Once Axel was in the care of Firekli's doctors and *Themis* was locked, everyone went to bed—except Rhys. Though exhausted, he needed to find Hodge. Dressed in pants, a long-sleeve shirt with rolled sleeves, boots, and a headscarf, Rhys strode down the wharf into town. Guessing Hodge was at the inn Sefora and Gwin had taken him to, he made for the establishment. He found Hodge draped across a couch in the common area, his leg heavily bandaged. His friend didn't seem to notice Rhys as he continued to fidget and tap his fingers on his knee.

"Would you *stop*?" came Sefora's voice from a cushioned chair whose back was to Rhys. "You're driving me crazy."

Hodge snarled at her and sat up. "I can't just sit here!"

"Then come on," chimed Rhys, joining them.

"*Gawan!*" declared Hodge, leaping up to balance on his good leg. "Did you find Axel?" Rhys nodded. Hodge sat with a sigh of relief. "Is he hurt? What happened?"

Rhys pursed his lips. "He lost his left arm from the elbow down and had a deep wound to his abdomen." Hodge gaped. "Surgery took about three hours. He was conscious for most of it. He's being admitted to the hospital as we speak."

Hodge's voice was small. "Will he make it?"

"If I did everything right, yes," Rhys replied. "But he lost a lot of blood. I'm hoping the hospital in Firekli has access to antibiotics."

Hodge nodded. "How's everyone else?"

"Resting. I've come to retrieve you."

Hodge stood and limped over to Rhys.

"What about me?" asked Sefora.

"What about you? You belong to Firekli." Hodge nudged Rhys toward the door.

"Thank you for taking care of him," called Rhys before supporting Hodge out of the inn.

Upon their approach to *Themis'* dock, Rhys stopped Hodge. "Hey, can I talk with you?"

Hodge limped to a nearby crate and leaned against it. "Yeah."

Rhys swallowed. "I'm going to be leaving for Brechin soon."

"How soon?"

"Tomorrow."

"Fine."

"Hodge, don't do that," Rhys murmured. "Please."

"No, it's fine."

Rhys glanced at a dock hand as the man passed before saying in a low tone, "Firekli took out a trans-atmospheric jet this morning with a plasma cannon. Osiris now knows Firekli has high-tech weaponry. Things are about to get worse." Hodge purposefully redirected his attention to the water. "*Themis* is in dire need of repairs and nearly the entire crew is injured. I don't know what else to do." Rhys' throat closed around his words. Sensing Hodge's gaze on him, he turned away ashamedly. "I need your help."

"I know," Hodge grumbled.

Rhys took a deep breath to compose himself.

"Can we talk later? I... need sleep."

"Yeah."

Hodge waited for Rhys to help him up, and together they returned to *Themis* in an uncomfortable silence.

It was late afternoon when Rhys woke. While his crew slept, he sat on the bridge, a radio nearby and Ethos in his hand. Though he knew he was short on rest, he was anxious. His mind raced and his body felt feverish.

"I don't think Neo-Colony Two should destroy the plasma cannon," Ethos murmured.

"I don't either," replied Rhys.

"It leaves Firekli open to attack after they leave. Up until now, Firekli has kept the plasma cannon hidden and has only used it in self-defense. It acts as a deterrent."

"I agree. But my people don't see it as that. It's a relic of the ages when we still engaged in warfare. It's a weapon and, therefore, should be destroyed. In their minds, it doesn't advance the human race."

"So, your people had no weapons on Caelestis?"

"None that were used for that purpose. The resonance cutters were originally created to be used in a zero-gravity vacuum environment to cut material. The plasma armament that I had was meant for the same purpose. Weapons like guns and rifles mean nothing to them because they've never seen them. They meant nothing to Alina and I when we first got here. You saw when we were in the colony. Axel pointed his rifle at them, and they just stared. But they understand plasma weapons. They understand the power and destruction of a plasma cannon."

"So what will you do?"

"Try to reason with them."

"And if they don't listen?"

"Then I'll fight them for it."

"And once you're done fighting them, you'll politely ask that they take you to Brechin?"

Rhys rolled his head back. "I don't knowwww…"

Ethos made a sound similar to a thoughtful hum and said, "Rhys, you know you won't be fully alone going to face Osiris, right? Forge and Zain will be with you and anyone else from Neo-Colony Two."

"Will they all crowd in the cockpit with me during take-off?"

"Well… no. But I'll be with you."

"No offense, Ethos, but that does not encourage me."

"Why not?" The AI sounded taken aback. "If I were Pathos, you wouldn't have a second thought."

"You're wrong… because Pathos would be so aligned with me that it wouldn't let me go."

"I'm not making you do this, Rhys."

"I don't have a lot of options here," Rhys snapped. "Either I attempt to disable Osiris or I stay here and avoid assassination attempts for the rest of my life and watch the entire region fall into chaos."

"Neither of those are appealing options," muttered Ethos. "You know, once we get to Brechin and I can discern the conditions of the remaining jets, I can determine the amount of actual risk you're taking."

"In other words, if I'm going to blow up on take-off."

"Well… yes. But not just that. I can tell you what you have at your disposal and whether you'll be able to make reentry."

"*Shit*, I don't want to do this," moaned Rhys, folding his arms around his legs and burying his head in his knees. "I don't want this. I don't want it." He felt his eyes sting. "I don't want to leave everyone. I just started living. This isn't fair."

To the AI's credit, Ethos remained silent.

About an hour later, Andy tiredly shuffled onto the bridge. He must have seen the state Rhys was in because he didn't ask questions nor did he offer any words of encouragement. He simply sat at the helm, propped his feet on the paneling, and stared out the bridge glass.

As the sun started to disappear below the horizon, Andy shifted in his chair and asked, "Do you want to go check on Axel with me?"

Rhys, who had been staring blankly at the far wall, nodded and rose stiffly from the floor. Andy went to speak with Kashim and returned with Kallen.

Rhys started out the external door, avoiding her gaze. It was too painful to look at her. Of course, he was glad she was feeling better—her concussion hadn't been serious—but he would rather have journeyed to the hospital alone with Andy. His First Mate had always treasured silence and, at the moment, that's what he needed.

Rhys stumbled down the stairs and started down the docks flanked by Andy and Kallen. Only when he reached the final slips did he slow to a stop because he didn't know where the hospital was. Without a word, Andy passed him and started up the cobblestone road.

He expected Kallen to try to talk with him or to start conversation, but it seemed she, like Andy, recognized the mood Rhys was in. Instead, she kept distance and walked with her eyes fixed forward.

It was nearly a half hour walk to the hospital. Once there, they disarmed, checked in with the head physician, and then wound through the numerous hallways to the critical ward where Axel was being kept. They found the soldier in a small room resting under the brilliant light of a surgery lamp as a nurse rewrapped his wounds.

"Hey…" murmured Axel as they entered his room.

"We came to check on you," said Andy warmly.

The nurse glanced up briefly before doing a double-take, her eyes resting on Rhys. Quickly, she finished bandaging Axel, bowed to Rhys, and hurried out.

Rhys moved to Axel's bedside and examined the setup which he was connected to. It seemed they were feeding him a myriad of medications intravenously. It had been a smart move to pass him to the hospital.

"How are you feeling?" asked Kallen, perching at the foot of the bed.

Axel cleared his throat. "Groggy."

"The painkillers will do that to you," replied Andy.

Rhys gently touched the bag of fluid hanging from the bed post. "Did they give you a prognosis?"

"If no infection happens…" Axel blinked in an attempt to clear his head. "Then I should be fine."

"Good."

"What happened?" asked Kallen. "Hodge said he saw you fall but was in the middle of a battle and couldn't get to you."

"My sunboard took a… barrage of bullets and it went down." Axel drew a deep breath. "My arm got caught on the shift… lever and… ripped off." He looked at Rhys. "Is anyone else hurt?"

"Kashim took a bullet to the shoulder, Hodge to the thigh. Neither are too serious," replied Andy. "Kallen sustained a concussion."

Axel chuckled dryly. "*Gawan*, we're pretty beat up." The faint smile on his face faded, and his eyes fell on Rhys. "Did you see it?"

"What?" murmured Rhys.

"The bright light."

Rhys nodded.

"You know… what that means, right?"

"Yes."

Axel laid his head back. He took a long, steadying breath. "You don't have time now." Axel's eyes closed. "I'm sorry… I can't… stay awake for much longer."

"That's fine," said Andy. "We just wanted to come check on you. We'll let you know of our plans."

Axel nodded. Rhys turned to leave, but the soldier made a sound. "Quickly, Rhys," Axel murmured. "In the next few hours… Brechin…"

"Yeah, I know. Leave it to me." Rhys strode from the room.

Andy and Kallen caught up with him in the front lobby as he reclaimed his resonance cutters and the handgun he usually carried. He sensed their eyes on him, but neither said anything.

Once they were well along their way, Andy asked, "What was he talking about? What bright light?"

Kallen moved in front of Rhys and looked at him expectedly. "Rhys, we have a right to know."

"Just… give me a minute," murmured Rhys. He couldn't think with them talking.

Ethos seemed to be following his train of thought because from the folds of Rhys' pocket, the AI said in Nefegian, "Our current position is not far from the cannon's location."

"There's no point in me going there," mused Rhys. "Neo-Colony Two needs to redirect their attention."

"Firekli knows Brechin is coming," replied Ethos. "So, for now, your opponent is your own people."

Kallen moved into his field of vision. "What do you need from us? What do you want to do?"

In an attempt to help Rhys, Ethos began speaking. "Firekli has in its possession a plasma cannon. Last night, it took down a trans-atmospheric jet. Forge notified Rhys that Neo-Colony Two residents are en route to destroy the cannon. In addition, it is likely Brechin will be coming for the weapon as soon as they can rally."

"I'll get in touch with Yanamichin," said Andy. "We'll make sure Firekli is prepared."

"Hold on, hold on," murmured Rhys. His First Mate, who had begun to jog off, stopped. Rhys paced the street. The most immediate threat was his own people. They could come in without being spotted by radar, infiltrate the warehouse the cannon was being kept in, and disappear into the night. "Ethos, what did you use yesterday to attract my attention?"

"Despite no longer being integrated with an AI, you have residual biosynthetic materials that allow you to sense AI or robotic-produced frequencies. This is also the reason why you can hear a high-pitched whining when the people of Caelestis use their own AIs to communicate near you."

Rhys shook his head and paced the lamp-lit street under Kallen and Andy's gazes. "Can they hear it? Could you use that to direct them elsewhere?"

"Probably not. Their AIs offer natural protection against such frequencies."

Rhys looked at Kallen. "Go back to *Themis* and prepare to intercept the Caelestis citizens should they show up. Go."

"What are you planning?" asked Kallen. "I want to know if I need to worry."

"Diplomatic talks," explained Rhys. Satisfied with his answer, Kallen jogged off into the darkness.

"She's healing from a concussion you know," Andy muttered. "You could have sent me."

Rhys looked at his First Mate. "No, because you're taking me to Yanamichin. Where are he and the other generals right now?"

"Probably at headquarters. It's about a ten-minute walk from here."

Rhys motioned to Andy who turned and led him down a perpendicular street. As they walked, Rhys spoke to Ethos in Nefegian. "Contact both Forge and Zain. I want to be notified when Neo-Colony Two enters Firekli airspace. Also, ask that they get into contact with whoever is heading the mission and indicate that the port is wanting to instigate diplomatic talks with them."

"Why would they believe that when Firekli has no idea they even exist?"

"Because I'm about to explain everything to Yanamichin and the other generals. Caelestis citizens would not turn down a chance to discuss logic, politics, and ethics."

"It's not your best plan, but we're running out of options right now," replied Ethos.

Rhys and Andy exited the winding cobblestone streets and alleyways and appeared before a large, five-story gray brick-and-mortar building decorated with flood lamps, armed guards, and a tall metal fence.

"This is Firekli's primary government building," explained Andy, walking along the black, iron-rod fence. "Because the port doesn't have an actual military, it uses militias—volunteer soldiers and officers from the community. They always meet here."

"Conspicuous," murmured Rhys, studying the enormous building. He had been unable to see it before because the rolling hills of the port's shops, homes, and markets blocked it entirely from the docks. Rhys was sure the building was a beacon from the air.

They stopped outside an enormous metal gate guarded by four armed citizens. "We need to speak with General Yanamichin," said Andy. "This is Rhys Falkrow, Overseer of *Themis*."

The gate opened, and Rhys and Andy were admitted into the government building grounds. They ascended a plain staircase and were motioned through a single open door.

"Please disarm here," explained one of Firekli's militiamen.

Rhys withdrew his pistol and holster and set both on the table, but he didn't make any movement to unsheathe his resonance cutters.

"The sword too," said the militiaman.

"It's not a sword," explained Rhys, withdrawing it so that they could see. "It's just for appearance, see? No blade."

The militiamen exchanged looks, said it was fine that he kept his tool, and then led them from the foyer. The interior of the government building was modest and austere with few wall decorations, little furniture, and bare wooden floors. Though other militiamen and government officials in pristine suits hurried from room to room carrying piles of papers, radios, and folders, there was a sense of organization and calm. No one appeared panicked, alarmed, or otherwise concerned.

"This way," instructed their escort, leading Andy and Rhys down a separate hallway. At the end of the corridor, the militiaman opened a door to reveal a well-lit, polished staircase descending deep underground. At the bottom, the militiaman stepped aside and motioned for them to continue alone.

Rhys and Andy left the confines of the enclosed staircase and moved into an enormous underground room that stretched into the distance. Though the room itself was cavernous, it was lit with white lights that hung from the vaulted ceiling. A dozen or so two-meter-long boards were strewn throughout the room and decorated with red, blue, and green pins and flags. Desks and large conference tables spotted the area; numerous radio systems, cords, and headsets were piled atop desks along the back wall; four flat screens hung on another wall. Men and women dressed in a variety of crisp outfits leaned over desks, spoke with one another, and listened to short-wave radios which appeared to be back online.

Rhys exchanged looks with Andy, who seemed just as impressed, before moving through the room. "Excuse me," he said, stopping a middle-aged man folded over a nearby desk. "I'm looking for General Yanamichin." Without looking up, the man pointed across the room before scribbling at a document.

As Rhys and Andy moved across the room, they began to draw attention. Unlike the others there who were well-known and appeared as if they belonged, Rhys and Andy were foreigners. Luckily, Yanamichin materialized from the innards of a group of officers and waved to them. "Ah! Overseer."

Andy by his side, Rhys moved across the room with purpose.

"Didn't think I'd ever see you again," said the General. He was in remarkably good spirits. Rhys glanced at the other militiamen and officers who had been with Yanamichin. None of them had ever seen or met Rhys. Undoubtedly, his stunning silver hair and brilliant blue gaze were eye-catching if not alarming. "I can't believe you and your crew! The battle at sea could have turned out much different had you not been there."

Rhys smiled grimly. "Actually, General, I need to speak with you on a matter of grave importance."

"Now's not a very good time, Overseer," said Yanamichin, motioning to one of the men around him. "We're in the middle of discussing defense fortification."

The smile on Rhys' face faded. "It's urgent. I need you and the other officers' attention."

Yanamichin flipped through a folder of papers one of his subordinates had handed him and then nodded. "Fine. Five minutes."

"I need you and the other officers or high-ranking government officials," clarified Rhys.

"You're not going to get them. Everyone is busy," Yanamichin replied, pointing to an error on one of the documents.

Rhys squared himself before Yanamichin. "It's about the plasma cannon." Yanamichin looked up from his work; the circle of officers and militiamen around him fell silent. "There is another part to this situation that you are not aware of. I'm here to discuss that."

"Give me ten minutes," said Yanamichin. "It's going to take that if not longer to get the others down here."

"Fine." Rhys moved away from the group, pretending not to notice the suspicious gazes throughout the room. "Any word from Pathos yet?"

"Both Forge and Zain are in communication with the Neo-Colony Two units en route," whispered Ethos. "You were correct in your assessment. They are open to diplomatic conversation."

"What are you planning?" Andy asked, turning his back to the room so the others couldn't see his lips move.

"My people will come here and discuss the plasma cannon. Hopefully, we can work out some sort of agreement."

Andy folded his arms. "Are you planning to leave us after that?" Rhys glanced at his First Mate. Andy nodded. "Thought that was the case."

It was another fifteen minutes before the other officers were downstairs. All other administrative employees and nonessential militiamen were ordered out of the bunker; the doors were locked. As t Firekli officers gathered at the largest of the conference tables, Yanamichin seated himself near the front where Rhys stood, and motioned to him. "You have our attention."

In total, Yanamichin had asked at least twenty-five officers and government officials to be present. When the chairs around the conference table were all occupied, the remaining stood, arms folded, near the back.

"I'm Rhys Falkrow, Overseer of *Themis*." He considered how to begin and then said, "And… I'm not from Earth." There were quiet murmurs. "I'm not from this planet. I was born on a colony in space." He pushed back his hair to reveal the injector sockets alongside his head. "I am not from here. You may be familiar with Zain who was acting as a medium last night during the battle. His silver hair has been dyed black to draw less attention, but he is also from my colony." He withdrew Ethos and set the AI on the table. "Now, the problem. Ethos, display a map of the region." The AI began projecting a three-dimensional map of Firekli and its coasts overhead. Rhys felt everyone in the room lean forward in interest. "Your enemy is Brechin. For years, it has been Brechin."

"What's your point?" asked one of the older men standing near the back. It was obvious he was impatient.

Rhys pursed his lips in preparation for what was to be the most outlandish claim of his presentation. "Thousands of years ago, before humanity's mass exodus, mankind built a computer to watch over Earth."

"I'm done," said the old man, turning to leave. He and three others started out of the room.

Rhys thought to stop them, but decided against it. He needed people here of their own accord. They needed to be free to believe him or not. "This computer was left on the moon where, for thousands of years, it has observed Earth. It's called Osiris. And it's controlling Brechin."

Sharp conversation broke out between the government officials and officers. Looks of disgust, disapproval, and disbelief painted their faces. Only Yanamichin remained silent, his eyes set on Rhys.

"Osiris is behind Brechin's sudden movements to overtake Firekli," continued Rhys. "It is behind the entire Pantarak Empire."

"That's a bold statement," Yanamichin murmured, reclining in his chair. "What do you suggest we do about this computer?"

"The plasma cannon," said Rhys. "You used it. Osiris now knows you have it." The concern on his face must have been more than he had meant to show because Yanamichin nodded and motioned for quiet. "The computer is smart. It learns. Its number-one priority now is to destroy Firekli."

"Why?" asked another man.

"Because over thousands of years, Osiris has been conducting experiments across the planet. The plasma cannon and the influence it allows you to wield will disrupt this quadrant's experiment."

"Again, what do you suggest we do about, eh, Osiris?" asked Yanamichin.

"*You* won't have to deal with Osiris. I will."

"But… didn't you say it was on the moon?" asked another.

Rhys motioned that he would come back to the question and said, "There is another faction here that none of you is aware of. Myself and my sister crash-landed on Earth over a year ago. I only just found out recently that, due to a disaster in space, segments of my colony also ended up on this planet." Rhys looked at Yanamichin. "They're on their way here. Now… Because you used the plasma cannon."

Yanamichin leaned forward on the table. "Because we used this 'plasma' cannon, a computer and people from your colony are now targeting Firekli? Why are your people on the way here?"

"Because the plasma cannon is ours," replied Rhys. "We created it."

"They're not taking it from us!" chorused a woman from the rear of the room. "It's our last defense."

"I agree!" called Rhys. "I agree, which is why I'm here. Zain and another one of my colleagues have been in communication with the others. They are willing to meet with you to discuss a diplomatic solution."

To his surprise, silence followed.

"We suggest," said Andy, stepping forward, "that you take this rare opportunity to gain a strong and technologically-advanced ally."

"Very well," said Yanamichin. "We'll meet with them, but we are unwilling to forfeit the cannon."

"Ethos, what's the status of the units?" asked Rhys in Nefegian.

"They've just arrived in port," replied Ethos similarly.

"Direct them here. *Not* everyone, only representatives."

"Veran is one of the representatives."

Rhys nodded and looked at the room of government officials and officers. "My people have just arrived in port. I've told Zain to direct them to this government building."

"But… nothing has come up on radar," said a man near a computer in the back.

"And nothing will," replied Rhys. "It's as my First Mate says—this is an opportunity for you to gain a strong ally."

"They're on their way here?" asked Yanamichin, standing. Rhys nodded. "How long will it take?"

"About two minutes," replied Rhys.

"Then let us go meet these people from space." Yanamichin threw Rhys an indecipherable look and then led the others to the bunker staircase.

By the time everyone was gathered on the front lawn of the government building, a maintenance unit had materialized from the darkness and landed silently. Only the grass around them rustled. Rhys pushed through the gawking officials and hurried to the craft. The door opened, and Veran stepped out.

The slight expression of worry on her face lessened when her eyes found Rhys. "Veran," he greeted.

"Oh, I'm glad to see you," Veran said. Noticing her nervousness, he touched her arm. Veran turned to the others emerging from the maintenance unit. To Rhys' great surprise, Cantia stepped around one of the silver-haired men and smiled mischievously.

"What are *you* doing here?" he asked. Cantia chuckled and hugged him. She looked as though she had lost some weight and her eyes appeared older. Her striking blond hair was neatly tucked in a bun at the back of her head. She wore the light-blue blouse and pale pants of a government official on Caelestis.

"I'm an ambassador, like you," replied Cantia. Saying the words aloud must have affected her, because the smile on Cantia's face faded. She moved to Veran's side, glanced at the woman, and then looked at Rhys to indicate they were ready.

Relieved that he was dealing with individuals who were accustomed to Earth's culture, Rhys led Veran and Cantia across the lawn to the group of government officials and militiamen officers. "General Yanamichin, may I present Cantia Sorex. Like me, she is an ambassador for Neo-Colony Two." Rhys motioned to Veran. "This is Veran Taiglar, Director of Medicine at Neo-Colony Two."

While Cantia bobbed her head politely, Veran stared at the group.

"It's a pleasure to meet you," said Yanamichin, holding out his left hand to Cantia. She took it and bowed her head. The General turned to Veran but did not offer a handshake. Veran glanced at Rhys and then offered her left hand as was custom. Pleasantly surprised, Yanamichin took it. "Should we retire to the bunker to discuss matters more candidly?"

Feeling Veran's gaze on him, Rhys nodded to show her that it was fine. Veran accepted, and the entire group started back inside. Rhys glanced over his shoulder at the maintenance unit and the Caelestis citizens standing guard.

It took a few minutes before everyone was once again seated at the conference table. With Cantia and Veran on either side of him, Rhys spoke. "Representatives from Neo-Colony Two wish to speak with government officials of Firekli concerning the possession and use of the plasma cannon." Politely, he stepped aside to give Cantia and Veran the floor.

With unbridled confidence, Cantia began addressing the room. "As ambassador to Neo-Colony Two, I respectfully ask that Firekli dismantle its OT-403 plasma cannon and surrender its core to Neo-Colony Two. Per Caelestis Code Ninety-Two, Chapter Four, Paragraphs Twelve through Nineteen, all tools designed or used for inflicting bodily harm, damage, or destruction shall be surrendered to the Caelestis government and obliterated."

Having the vantage point that he did, Rhys was unsurprised to see the displeased expressions on the faces of Firekli's government officials.

"We are attempting a diplomatic solution," Yanamichin graciously replied, "therefore, I would like to inquire further concerning your reasons for our weapon's surrender."

Cantia looked to Veran. Hesitantly, the director spoke. "Our history has taught us that all of mankind's suffering has been caused by weapons. Earth's own destruction and the primary cause for the mass exodus was because humanity nearly destroyed itself using weapons. Armaments such as plasma weapons are not meant to be used in Earth's atmosphere. They are, like many of our tools, mercilessly overpowered. In the wrong hands, they could cause mass destruction not unlike that which befell our ancestors."

Though Veran's mastery of the Aabesh language was impressive, Rhys could still hear her accent.

"May I suggest that you and your people look at the situation from a different angle?" asked Yanamichin, folding his hands on the table. "Consider that your colony is under attack. Your people are in danger of being completely obliterated by an enemy who outnumbers you three-to-one and whose technology supersedes even yours. What do you do?"

Veran tilted her head. To the unknowing, it appeared as though she was thinking. Every person on *Themis* had made Rhys and Alina question Caelestis' idealistic points of view. He and Alina had both found their answers. Would Veran and the others from Neo-Colony Two follow?

For an uncomfortable amount of time, Veran stood in silence as she spoke with the others from the colony through her AI. Recognizing that those from Earth were becoming anxious, Rhys stepped in. "Please give her a moment longer," he said. "In our culture, these kinds of questions are never pondered; therefore, we do not have answers readily available."

"Ambassador Taiglar," said Yanamichin kindly. "What would you do?" Veran looked at him startled that he had used her name. "You personally, what would you do?"

"My opinion does not reflect the consensus of the colony and is therefore invalid," replied Veran. "Colony consensus indicates that should all defenses be compromised and options be exhausted, evacuation of the colony is paramount."

"And what if you can't escape?" probed Yanamichin. "What if as you escaped, the enemy shot you down and killed you and your families?"

Veran tilted her head once to the left and then to the right. "Such an enemy is not present here on Earth."

"Ambassador Taiglar, hypothetically," corrected Yanamichin. "What would you do?"

Veran looked at Rhys. He knew the thousands of memories he had transferred to the Core were vying for prominence within her. He knew what the answer was and she knew what the answer was, but it was the colony's decision. "I personally would fight," Veran finally replied. Rhys nodded and looked out at the others.

"Precisely," said Yanamichin, standing. "The situation I have just described to you is our current dilemma here in Firekli. We were forced to use the plasma cannon because Brechin, the capital of this region, was utilizing an advanced aircraft to carry out covert attacks."

"A trans-atmospheric jet," clarified Rhys in Nefegian. Veran nodded.

"We are in the midst of a battle that will determine the fate of our people and this region. Should this port be defeated, Brechin will slaughter its people, replace the republican government with a religious oligarchy, and strip its citizens of their rights. The region will crumble because trade will fail, and freedom as we know it will disappear." Yanamichin stopped before Veran and Cantia. "The plasma cannon, as you call it, has been a part of our military defenses for years. It was found well over a century ago and kept in secret to safeguard it and its guidance computer from Brechin. It is considered Firekli's last line of defense."

"Understood," Veran replied.

Yanamichin looked at her in mild surprise.

"The colony agrees that you are allowed to defend yourself. If, however, it is determined that the weapon's power is being abused—"

"And who determines that?" interrupted an officer.

"We have perfect faith Firekli's leadership will use the weapon with discretion," said Rhys, heading off the confrontation.

"We will continue to monitor its output," Veran concluded.

Yanamichin, and many of the officers, leveled wary even angry looks at her.

"Will the colony be willing to offer any other support," muttered Rhys in Nefegian as he turned away.

"What did you say?" asked Yanamichin.

Rhys pursed his lips. "I asked her if Neo-Colony Two would be willing to offer any other support in regard to Firekli's defenses."

All eyes moved back to Veran, who stared at the back wall, her head tilted slightly. Finally, someone asked, "What's wrong with her?"

Rhys sighed. "Please do not take her silence as a sign of being rude. She's speaking with the rest of the colony right now. The, uh, AI attached at her temple allows her to communicate with others. Please give her a moment."

Veran opened her mouth to speak, her brows furrowed, but then remained silent.

"And where's yours?" asked Yanamichin, nodding toward Rhys.

"Gave it up months ago—"

"There is some division within the colony regarding additional support for Firekli," Veran finally said. "Please allow us time to further discuss a possible alliance. Warfare is a foreign concept to us. I ask for your patience and understanding as my people step into this new reality."

Yanamichin stood. "It is evident we could learn much from your people. We will keep an open line of communication ready for you." He held out his hand, and Veran took it.

Rhys exchanged looks with Andy who appeared just as relieved before repossessing the room's attention. "Thank you for hearing our concerns," he said.

Yanamichin chuckled. "I suspect you and your people aren't going to be the only ones having to adjust to this new reality." Yanamichin glanced between Rhys and Veran. "As for Osiris, the computer you mentioned, what are your plans?"

"We have a tentative plan to travel to Brechin," said Rhys.

"What's in Brechin? I thought you said this computer was on the moon?"

"It is… but we have inside information indicating that there is a base carrying advanced technology like the jet you saw the other night."

Yanamichin nodded thoughtfully as he usually did, his eyes set on the back wall. Finally, he looked at Rhys. "I'm leaving Osiris to you and your crew. We have more than enough to deal with here."

"That's fine. I wasn't looking for your support in that endeavor," replied Rhys. He glanced at Cantia and Veran to subtly indicate it was time to go.

"Thank you for your time," said Cantia, bobbing her head.

"I hope we meet again, young lady," Yanamichin said. He nodded to Veran and then turned and began speaking lowly with the officers around him.

In silence, Rhys led Cantia, Veran, and Andy from the bunker. Once outside, Veran stopped him. "You are prepared to leave for the city of Brechin soon?" she asked.

Rhys glanced at Andy and then nodded. "The longer I sit here doing nothing, the more time Osiris is allowed to formulate strategies."

Veran nodded. "We will take you to Brechin, but we recommend that you not go alone."

"Forge and Zain are accompanying me."

Veran shook her head. "You need more than them. You need your people. I know how you are, Rhys Falkrow. I know how you act and how you think. You will need soldiers, people accustomed to fighting. Not us."

"My entire crew is hurt," he said.

"I have Forge and another medical staff member currently working on Hodge and Kashim," said Veran. "Kallen is doing better and Leo has just finished his own medical evaluation." Seeing the look on his face, Veran sighed softly. "Forge told me you were in dire need of medical assistance."

"Axel," murmured Andy.

Veran shuddered, a most un-Caelestis-like behavior. "Forge shared with me all that he saw during Axel's surgery. Your methods are not conventional, Rhys."

"They are when I don't have any medical equipment. Axel is currently at the hospital." He motioned west. "It's about a ten-minute walk from here."

"We will take the unit," said Veran. "Once I work on him, we'll bring him back to the ship."

The trip to the hospital was brief. Once the maintenance unit landed outside the building, Rhys leapt out and helped Veran, who carried a backpack.

378

"Make it quick," warned Andy from the open hatch door. "Hospitals are not normally open to the public after dark."

With Veran in tow, Rhys strode through the hospital doors, passed the empty front desk, down to Axel's room. He expected to be stopped, but the few doctors on shift never appeared. Only two nurses saw them.

Rhys opened the door to Axel's room and slipped in; Veran followed. Unsurprisingly, Axel was unconscious, no doubt as a result of the medications he had received. Rhys stepped aside for Veran and closed the door behind her.

The Director of Medicine hesitantly approached Axel's bed, her eyes studying his ragged body. She set her backpack on the floor and rested on the edge of the bed. Normally, Rhys would not have noticed such a natural movement, but it was Veran sitting beside Axel, not Kallen. He watched as Veran ran her fingers down the length of his stubbly face and then rested the palm of her hand on his forehead to analyze his brain waves. When she was satisfied with the results, she pulled the bandages away from his abdomen to inspect the wound there.

In the dim light of the bedside table lamp, Rhys saw her gently run her fingers over the sutures there. "Clean and precise," Veran murmured. She looked up at Rhys. "It's good work given the material you had." She turned and began carefully digging through her backpack. She withdrew a small syringe attached to an injector, touched Axel's side gingerly, and then pressed the injector near the site of his wound. "If you followed the emergency procedures like I think you did," Veran murmured, "then this should encourage cellular regrowth in the abdomen and complete the work."

"Is there any danger of it interacting with the medications he's already been given?" asked Rhys, moving to the end of Axel's bed.

Veran shook her head, replaced the syringe, and began undressing Axel's arm bandages. Her face was knotted in a mixture of worry, pain, and tenderness. Once the bandages were clear of his stump, she simply stared at his amputated arm.

"Do we have anything that can be used as a substitute for a human limb?" Rhys murmured.

"There are some trial medications that will essentially force growth of muscles, tendons, ligaments, and bones, but it will be a tedious and painful process. And I'm not willing to carry that out here or on your ship."

"What can you do now?"

"Inject the same serum at the site of the wound and allow it to heal." She withdrew another vial from the backpack, loaded it in the injector, and inserted it just above the nub's end.

"How long will the healing process take for his abdomen and arm?"

Veran shrugged. "Thirty minutes, maybe." She touched his abdomen. "How many layers were cut through?"

"Four," replied Rhys.

"Combined with the sutures, his abdomen wound should be halfway healed by now. It works from the inside-out. As for his arm, it would be best if he was awake so he can tell us what he's feeling. I don't have all my equipment here, otherwise I would be able to determine the amount of pain he is in."

"Axel," said Rhys. He nudged Axel's foot and said his name again.

"You don't have to wake him," said Veran.

Seeing Axel stir, Rhys tapped his foot again and called to him. The soldier groggily opened his eyes. "Hey, come on. Wake up." Axel struggled to keep his eyes open, but they sporadically rolled back into his head and fluttered closed.

To Rhys' surprise, Veran leaned closer to Axel and touched his face. "Hey, wake up," she murmured. "Open your eyes. Keep them open."

Axel made a sound, but his eyes remained closed. "Ver... n..."

"I need you to focus," said Veran. "Can you focus?"

A single-toned sigh that sounded somewhat confirmatory slipped from Axel's throat.

Veran touched the shoulder of his injured arm. "Can you feel this?" She tapped his shoulder with her finger. Again, he sighed in confirmation. Veran moved her hand down to his arm and tapped there. "Can you feel this?" Pain flickered across Axel's face, and she stopped. "I've given you some medication that will promote cell growth so the pain should be subsiding."

Axel breathed deeply and tried to open his eyes, but they appeared insufferably heavy. "Why?" he managed to mumble.

"Why did I give you the medication?" asked Veran.

"Why are you here?" clarified Rhys, following Axel's train of thought.

"Because you need to heal." Veran touched his face and gazed at him tenderly.

Rhys had previously seen how attracted to Axel she was and just how protective he was of her. Though Axel didn't know Veran was twice his age, did it really matter? Her life span would far outreach his. Even if he wanted children, there was time for her despite her being in her sixties.

In Nefegian, Veran spoke to Rhys. "How can we best get him out of here?"

"Get him to walk on his own. If need be, I can carry him, but it's going to be a long trip to the front door. He's twice my weight."

Veran touched Axel's nub once more and asked, "Does it hurt now?"

"No," Axel muttered.

Veran touched his abdomen. "How bad does this hurt?"

He shook his head.

"We'll give it a few more minutes and then go from there," explained Veran, turning to stand. Axel weakly reached across the bed with his good arm and touched her leg. Veran fell still and looked at Rhys in mild confusion.

In Nefegian, Rhys murmured, "He doesn't want you to leave."

"I'm not leaving. I'm right here."

Rhys shook his head. "He doesn't want you to move from his side. You're a comfort." Veran relaxed and looked at Axel warmly. "In situations like these, it is acceptable to hold his hand, if you want to do so. It is natural to be worried about people you care for."

Veran took Axel's hand, glanced shyly at Rhys, and said in Aabesh, "Try to wake up. We need you to be able to walk."

"Why?" Axel murmured, forcing his eyes open.

"We're moving you back to the ship. Once we have everything organized, you're going to Neo-Colony Two. The sooner the better, right?" said Rhys. Axel moaned softly. "Would you rather be here in a hospital in Firekli or under Veran's care?"

Axel took a deep breath. He released Veran's hand and rubbed his eyes. "I want out..."

"We can move slowly," said Veran, watching him. "There's no rush."

Axel laid his head back and looked at her, his eyes bloodshot and moist. The expression of adoration and softness on his face as he looked at Veran was disconcerting to Rhys who had only ever seen him as a soldier. Axel cleared his throat and said, "I'm... glad to see you."

It took a few minutes before Axel was sitting up and consciously moving his injured arm. The medications Veran administered had finally gone into effect, giving him greater mobility and less pain.

Rhys helped Axel dress in a pair of hospital-issued pants before nodding for Veran to lead the way. With the soldier leaning heavily on Rhys, they shuffled from the room and down the corridor.

"What... are you doing?" asked a nurse, emerging from a patient's room.

"I'm feeling better, thanks," said Axel before Rhys could reply. "I'm going home."

"But… you haven't been cleared to leave yet," the nurse replied. Her gaze settled on Veran and she fell silent.

Rhys rebalanced Axel and continued down the hallway. Andy and one of the other Neo-Colony Two citizens helped Axel into the maintenance unit before Veran and Rhys followed.

Once the unit was in the air, Rhys studied Axel who was lying on the floor, panting. The advanced medications were helping, but that didn't mean his body wasn't weak with exhaustion. Veran knelt by his head and listened as silent conversation poured through her AI.

"How's Otto," Rhys asked. As the maintenance unit banked, Cantia leaned into him.

"He's doing much better," she replied. "He came with us. He stayed behind on *Themis* to look at the ship's engine." Cantia nodded. "It was a smart move to keep him at Neo-Colony Two."

Their conversation was short as it took but a minute or two to reach the harbor. After the unit touched down along the docks, Rhys helped Axel out and guided him to *Themis*. Forge and Leo met them halfway there.

"Leo!" shouted Cantia. She crashed into Leo and hugged him tightly.

"Cantia?" stammered Leo in confusion. "What are you doing here?"

Cantia buried her face into his shirt. "I'm an ambassador."

"I thought only Otto came." Leo looked at Rhys and then at Axel. Holding Cantia to him, he asked, "How you are doing, Axel?"

"I want to sit down," Axel growled, resting more of his weight on Rhys.

"Help me," Rhys murmured. Andy came to Rhys' aid, and together they guided the soldier onto *Themis* and deposited him in the crew's quarters. Veran followed and sat at his bedside while everyone else gathered in the galley.

Rhys was delighted to find Kashim and Hodge up and moving about. Although both were still bandaged, they looked livelier and stronger. Kallen also appeared more alert as she spoke with Otto near the back of the room.

Rhys shouldn't have been surprised to find the silver base of an AI pressed snuggly against Otto's temple. Although it was not possible for him to be biologically integrated with an AI, it was feasible that he be matched with an external one that could read brain wave activity and biological impulses, much like Ethos. The boy looked calmer and surer of himself. The AI must have been given to him to help him recuperate.

"He's had it for a couple weeks now," said Cantia, noticing Rhys' gaze. "Veran offered it to him as a trial. He took it without a single thought and has been doing better each day." Cantia smiled. "He sleeps without problems now."

Rhys wrapped an arm around Cantia fondly and then pushed her into the crowded galley. Aside from his own people, the crew from *Grisle* was also present. Jules, Leela, Patrin, and Tessa all stood warily in the corner of the galley, their eyes on the Neo-Colony Two residents who were still tending to others. Terron, on the other hand, was in deep conversation with Zain and another Neo-Colony Two citizen.

Rhys felt a hand on his shoulder. Veran nodded to him and followed her to the end of the hallway. "What do you want to do, Rhys?" she asked in Nefegian.

"Get to Brechin. Osiris will want Firekli's plasma cannon destroyed. Brechin reinforcements will be on their way and another battle will start."

Veran studied him. "Assuming Ethos is correct and the base in Brechin harbors trans-atmospheric jets, will you launch?"

"Yes."

"There is a high risk, depending upon what we have at our disposal in the capital, that we will be unable to track you once you're in orbit. We will not be able to conduct a guided atmospheric reentry… if you can reenter the atmosphere at all."

"Yes."

Veran's face became stoic. "Who do you want to accompany you to Brechin? It is the colony's wish that your team is comprised primarily of your own people as they are accustomed to the physical force that will be necessary to infiltrate the base."

"Hodge, Forge, Kashim, Leo, and Zain."

"Six total. Will that be enough?" asked Veran.

"If we have too many, it will no longer be a covert operation," Rhys explained.

Veran tilted her head and nodded. "Forge and Zain have agreed to go with you. We will leave at dawn to give your people time to rest."

"Thank you, Veran."

Veran's solemn blue eyes fixed on his face. "When I first received your memories, I didn't know what to do because I couldn't understand the emotions that resided within them. Over time though, myself and the other Pathos-users in the colony have been able to discern the collection of emotions. Fear, anger, wonder, lust, horror, elation…" She smiled. "But there was one emotional element that took some time to process."

Veran glanced down the hallway as Kallen emerged from the galley obviously searching for Rhys. When she spotted them, her face darkened in concern.

"Courage, Rhys," said Veran, her face softening. "Strength in the face of pain or fear. There was never a need for Caelestis citizens to know courage because we were never threatened, we were never in pain or knew fear. Rhys. You have always had within you extraordinary courage."

Speechless, Rhys just gazed at her. He couldn't believe that one of the most motivational and heart-touching compliments he had ever received had just come from a citizen of Caelestis.

"Please know," continued Veran, "that if something should happen and you are unable to reenter the atmosphere, I will personally see to Kallen's wellbeing."

Rhys pursed his lips to keep the sound of his heart breaking from leaking out. He nodded and motioned for Veran to rejoin the others. He knew her words were meant to strengthen and comfort him, but it just made the realization of what he was about to do even more difficult.

"I'll be there in a minute," he called after Veran. He slipped into his cabin and shut the door.

The moment complete darkness surrounded him, his fear broke through and threatened to engulf him completely. Sinking to the floor, he fought to keep back his tears, but the stress was too much. The fear was too much. Panic gripped his heart and wormed its way up his throat. Silently, so as not to concern anyone else, Rhys cried. In great heaves, he melted onto the floor and gripped at his clothes.

For minutes that stretched into infinity, he lay on the cool wood of his cabin, allowing waves of fear and heartache to roll over him like the sea's swells. Again and again, he was beat by his own spirit. Like relentless wind, his anger, resentment, fear, and despair smashed into him. Numerous times he dried his face and took deep breaths to collect himself only to have his composure snap instantly. Tears came and his chest shook from the deep hopelessness lodged within it.

After telling himself over and over that he needed to go speak to his crew, the tears finally stopped. Lying in the middle of his cabin, he stared at the ceiling. His face was hot, and he could hear his heartbeat in his ears.

"Tell me…" he whispered thickly. "Tell me it has to be done."

From the innards of his pants pocket, Ethos murmured, "It has to be done. Someone has to do it, otherwise Osiris will continue to dominate Earth as it has done for generations."

"Tell me… *I* have to do it."

"*You* have to do it, Rhys," said Ethos. "There is no one else. You have both the training and knowledge. You are not hindered by an AI. You are the only one who can do it. To release Earth from Osiris' control, to stop Brechin's encroachment—you are the one. Veran can't do it, neither can Forge or Zain. Leo, Andy, Hodge… none of them can do it. Alina couldn't do it either. It has to be you."

Rhys took a deep, steadying breath and then sat up. "You're sure?"

"Have courage, Rhys," said Ethos. "Have faith in all that you stand for."

37
KALLEN

AFTER COLLECTING HIMSELF AND MAKING sure his face was no longer heated, Rhys left the confines of his cabin and joined the others in the galley. He was relieved no one seemed concerned about his sudden disappearance and that conversation had continued without him.

Standing in the doorway, he gazed at his crew until everyone fell silent in anticipation.

Once all eyes were on him, he gave a small smile. "I'm leaving for Brechin at dawn. Neo-Colony Two is willing to provide transportation, but I need a team to go with me." He paused for a moment. "Hodge, Leo, Kashim, Forge, and Zain." The smile on his face faded. "I am not asking." He lowered his voice. "I am commanding. Come with me."

"What about the rest of us?" asked Terron.

"You'll stay here in Firekli with the ships." Rhys kept his eyes from Kallen. "Complete repairs and do as you would normally. Veran and Forge will see to it that everyone is healed or tended to before we leave." He gazed at his crew. "This is our last gamble." There were solemn nods of agreement around the room. "Everyone get some rest."

As Terron passed, he said, "We'll see you off in the morning."

Rhys glanced at Jules and Tessa as they followed Terron from the galley. He didn't expect many words from them. Although they claimed loyalty to the cause, technically they belonged to Terron. While Rhys had been busy taking care of *Themis* and his crew, Terron had been doing the same.

Leela, who had been fidgeting near the rear of the galley, finally approached Rhys. "We'll see you at dawn," the ebony woman murmured, pulling him into a deep embrace. She kissed the side of his head fondly, rubbed his arms, and then slipped from the galley with Patrin at her side.

With only his crew remaining, Rhys leaned against the wall. "Forge, how is everyone?"

"I've tended to each of them," Forge tiredly replied. "Kashim's shoulder should be nearly healed; Hodge's leg will take a bit more time. But, as you know, even if they're healed, their bodies will be tired and weakened from the strain."

"I'm not limping anymore," supplied Hodge who was perched on the galley counter.

Rhys gazed wearily at his friend and then peered over his shoulder across the hall. "Veran?"

"Hm?"

"When are you leaving?"

"As soon as you tell me to." She appeared in the doorway. "We have two maintenance units. One will return to Neo-Colony Two and the other will take you to Brechin."

"And you're taking Axel?"

Veran nodded.

"Eh… I want to come too," came a soft voice. Rhys looked at Otto who sat at one of the tables. Cantia stood behind him, her hands on his shoulders. "I've given it some thought, and I want to help."

Rhys' gaze flickered upward to Cantia who smiled. If anyone knew Otto's current mental status, it was her. "There will probably be combat," said Rhys. "With our team already in recuperation, I can't have any stragglers."

"I won't be a burden," Otto asserted. "Besides, I can help. I work in propulsion and nuclear sciences."

Rhys couldn't help the surprise on his face. "That's impressive, Otto."

Cantia nudged Otto fondly. "He's there every waking moment. Even the technicians are impressed with how quickly he's advanced."

"Can you shoot a gun?" asked Hodge. "Can you kill?"

"I've killed men in my dreams for the past several weeks." The murder in Otto's eyes and conviction in his voice made Rhys recoil in discomfort. "I'll be fine."

Kashim cleared his throat and then nodded to Kallen who had been silently leaning against the table, her gaze set on the floor.

"Leo, Andy—would you help Axel to the upper deck?" asked Rhys. Both nodded and filtered into the hallway.

"Rhys," said Veran. She continued in Nefegian. "Keep my boys safe."

Rhys glanced at his crew. Who did she mean?

"Otto and Forge," she clarified, sensing his confusion. She smiled. "Actually, Forge is... my biological son. Of course, I never gave him my surname." Veran gazed at Otto over Rhys' shoulder. "And Otto... He is mine now."

"You know I can't make that promise," Rhys murmured. "I can't make any promises."

"Take care," murmured Veran. She gave a small smile and then followed Leo, Andy, and Axel out of the ship.

Without looking back in the galley, Rhys called, "Kallen?" He waited for her to join him and then led her to their dark quarters. After switching on the desk lamp, he watched her. Kallen closed the cabin door, her eyes on the floor. For a long moment, neither said anything.

What *could* he say to her? There was literally nothing that could be said that didn't sound like he was saying goodbye. At dawn, he and the others would leave her and the ship behind—and he probably wasn't coming back.

Rhys swallowed hard. He had been purposefully distancing himself from her. Of everyone, she was going to be the most difficult to leave behind. She had been the first to speak with him, to meet him and Alina. She had been there since the beginning. She was the cornerstone of so many of his memories on Earth.

"Promise me..." murmured Kallen. Rhys finally looked at her. Her cheeks were wet. "Promise me you'll come back."

Rhys breathed out in despair. "I can't."

"Just promise me." Her voice cracked.

"I can't."

"I don't care!" she snapped, quivering. "Lie to me." Stifling sobs, she gazed at him. "Lie to me, Rhys. Lie." A cry escaped her, and she covered her mouth. Taking a deep breath, she said, "Lie to me... or I won't be able to keep going. Give me something. Anything."

"Kallen." Rhys' voice trembled. "I don't want to do this. I'm making the hardest decision of my life." He approached her and took her hands in his, rubbing his thumbs over the back of her palms. "I can't make you any promises. I can't give you false hope."

"Rhys..." she murmured, sinking to the floor. "Please."

"Rhys?" interjected Ethos softly. "Could I have a moment? To speak?" Rhys withdrew Ethos from his pocket and slipped the AI into Kallen's hand. "Although it is true that the prospect of Rhys returning is not a hopeful one, that does not mean it isn't impossible. At the moment, we are treating the situation as a worst-case scenario. Unfortunately, we won't know until we're in Brechin and can ascertain the condition of the equipment in the underground base."

"Then let me go with you," whispered Kallen. Before he opened his mouth, she added, "I'm pregnant, not disabled. Forget the baby. *You're* more important. What you're trying to do is more important." She stood. "*Please.*"

Rhys wavered.

"I can use a gun. I know some combat. I can kill," asserted Kallen, wiping her tears. "I won't slow us down any more than Hodge will limping around like he is." The fire in her eyes was back.

"It's possible we could use her mechanic skills," offered Ethos.

"You're sure?"

"I am yours, and you are mine," she replied. "Don't leave me behind."

"Fine," he said. He squeezed her hand. "But listen to me." Her deep brown eyes glistened in the lamplight. "Once we're there, I... have to focus on what I have to do. I can't keep myself... emotionally tied to everyone or I won't be able to go through with it."

"Of course, you can," she replied with the smile he had fallen in love with. "You're doing it *for* us. Hodge and Andy, Kashim, Leo, Cantia and Otto... For me." She touched his face. "You have always been a beacon for us, all of us." She chuckled wetly. "Why do you think we've followed you this far? You started as a blank slate, as nothing. Look at what you have. Look at how blessed you are, Rhys. You have a family; you have a home. Do you know how many people would sacrifice all of that for the greater good of the world? To fight for the right thing, to fight for freedom?" Tears slipped down her face as she shook her head. "Very few." Voice trembling, she added, "You are rare, Rhys Falkrow. That is why we follow you and why everyone here wants to be by your side during this fight. Including me. We've supported you, followed you for this long... Why should we stop now?"

Rhys swallowed the knot in his throat. "Come with me then."

Kallen leaned in and rested her forehead against his in intimate silence.

38
INFILTRATION

A DEEP AND FAMILIAR ROAR woke Rhys from his sleep. A jet. "Shit." He rolled out of bed, hit the floor, and grabbed his boots. Kallen sat up in their nest of blankets. He could see her wide eyes in the dim light coming through the cabin window.

Shirtless, Rhys grabbed his resonance cutters and a short rifle and jogged from the room. Kashim and Andy met him in the hallway; Hodge was right behind them.

They climbed to the upper deck where the remaining maintenance unit was perched. Veran and the others had left hours prior. Though the unit was locked, it was still visible. Swinging his rifle over his shoulder, Rhys sprinted to the craft, unlocked the hatch, and flung himself into the cockpit. Within seconds, he had engaged the colloid shield.

Heart racing, he sat crossways along the pilot's seat and glared out the wind screen. A moment later, the trans-atmospheric jet screamed by again, heading south. Rhys leaned forward to watch. As the sound of the jet faded into the distance, a spectacular array of orange and golden lights blossomed along the port's southern border; fiery explosions followed in its wake.

"It's time to go," said Ethos.

Resting his head on the wall next to the pilot's seat, he nodded. Brilliant beams of glittering light illuminated the sky once more and blasts rocked the port city.

"It's time, Rhys!" Ethos called over the resounding booms.

Trembling in anger and horror, Rhys clambered out of the cockpit and leapt from the unit, leaving the colloid shield engaged. He hung his rifle on the ajar hatch door and headed back to the bridge.

"We're leaving!" he shouted, entering the ship. "Let's go." He hurried down the hallway to his quarters and began dressing. Kallen, who had already pulled on pants, a dark shirt, and handgun holsters, silently stuffed a shirt or two into a spare pack and then ran from the room to the galley.

Rhys met Hodge and Kashim in the hallway and began laying out weapons along the hallway wall. As Hodge checked the rifles, Rhys took stock of their ammunition. Kashim and Andy disappeared onto the bridge. Forge and Zain, who had slept over in preparation for the morning's departure, stood in the doorway of the crew's quarters and watched. Just as Rhys finished counting spare magazines, cases of ammunition, and rifles, Kallen deposited the medical pack and another bag in the hallway.

"Zain, Forge." Rhys handed each a rifle. "Forge, show him how to use it." He slung his cutters onto his back and began distributing rifles. "Hodge, take the medical pack and get to the upper deck. Otto, go with Hodge. Kallen, lower the launch ramp and make sure my board is turned on. Afterward, get upstairs. Leo, help her." All disappeared. "Ethos, get my board into the maintenance unit. Forge, Zain—the colloid shield is engaged. Zain, you pilot. I'll co-pilot." The two Neo-Colony Two citizens hurried from the ship, leaving only Rhys, Kashim, and Andy.

Worriedly, Rhys looked at the top of the stairs where Andy leaned on the railing. His First Mate smiled and nodded. "I'll be fine. Go. *Grisle* is nearby."

Rhys and Kashim climbed the stairs and stopped before Andy. He wanted to say goodbye or somehow bid his First Mate good luck, but both sounded too final.

"Come back," said Andy, holding out his hand.

"Leave the ship if you need to," Rhys said, taking his First Mate's arm. "You're the only one here. Just leave it—"

Andy shook his head. "Then where will everyone live when they get back?" Rhys opened his mouth to object, but Andy stopped him. "Go. I've got everything here." He clapped Rhys on the back. "I'll tell Cantia and Terron and the others."

Rhys nodded, slipped from Andy's grip, and then motioned to Kashim who hurried from the ship and disappeared into the brisk morning air. Rhys turned to leave but stopped.

The emptiness of the hallway, the familiarity of the ship's smell, the sound of the water lapping at the ship's hull. He gazed down the vacant hallway of his ship, his heart throbbing painfully. Despite the mass chaos outside, all he could hear was silence. His ship. His home was here.

Realizing he was wasting time, he glanced at Andy who, as always, seemed to understand him just a little bit more. With a bittersweet smile, Andy motioned for him to hurry.

Without another look, Rhys hurried to the maintenance unit. Panting, he looked over his shoulder at Firekli which was aflame and quickly being devoured by smoke. It would be a miracle if *Themis* or *Grisle* survived.

Grabbing the rifle he had hung on the maintenance unit's side door, he leapt in. Forge closed the hatch as Rhys clambered into the co-pilot's seat. "We're all here?" asked Rhys without looking back.

"Yes," came the chorused response.

"Zain, lets go," Rhys said, his hands flying familiarly over the numerous switches and levers on the instrument panel. He switched to Nefegian and continued. "Rotate ninety-two degrees, set heading east-by-northeast. Ethos, provide coordinates for Brechin."

The unit jumped from *Themis'* stern, leaving Rhys' stomach along the water's edge, and then rotated eastward. "Pre-flight cursory checklist, complete," reported Zain stoically. "All systems, nominal. Course set."

Rhys glanced at the navigational instrument before him. "Course confirmed. Launching." He rolled the accelerators forward while noting the various instruments before him—the altimeter, altitude indicator, trajectory reader, vertical velocity dial, and the airspeed gauge.

Silence engulfed the unit, and Rhys laid his head back in the chair. Everything had happened so quickly; he hadn't had time to speak with Terron. He hadn't even been able to see the destruction of Firekli. He hadn't been able to mentally prepare.

A brilliant beam of sunlight suddenly broke over the horizon as they met the sunrise, causing Rhys to squint momentarily before Logos auto-tinted the windscreen.

This was it.

Realizing no one had said anything since take off, Rhys looked over his shoulder at the others. He found Kallen, Leo, and Otto perched atop his board while Hodge, Kashim, and Forge sat legs folded on the floor, packs and weapons around them. "Everyone fine?" he asked.

There were grave nods.

Rhys sat back. "I'm counting on you," he said in Nefegian to his co-pilot.

"I know," replied Zain.

The first hour of the journey was a sullen one. No one spoke. Though Rhys and Zain often exchanged instrument information as was standard Caelestis protocol, no one else said anything. Eventually though, Rhys heard Kallen murmur something and there were low grumbles of agreement.

Momentarily, her face appeared between the two cockpit chairs. "Hungry?"

"Oh." Rhys glanced at Zain and nodded.

Kallen handed them two strips of smoked jerabo meat. "I have tea too," she said, returning to the cargo hold.

While they had been preparing weapons and ammunition and bulletproof vests, Kallen had been in the galley gathering food, packing water, tea, and a variety of snacks to keep stomachs happy. Hearing Hodge moan in contentment, Rhys smiled and ate the humble breakfast.

It was shortly thereafter that a quiet alarm from the unit's radar alerted them of activity far below. Rhys glanced down at the endless field of emerald water and then at radar.

"What is it?" called Hodge from the back.

"We're at the Golden Corridor," replied Rhys, glancing out once more. Far below, plumes of smoke decorated the space above the sea and great orange and ruby flames spilled from ships. Who was winning—Brechin airships or the Aabesh navy—was indeterminable.

Hodge suddenly appeared and peered out the windscreen. "Brechin's fighting a two-front war?"

"Possibly three-front," said Leo. "I received word from my brother two days ago. Brechin's currently fighting Firekli, the Aabesh navy, and Maliyansa."

"Who does the Aabesh navy belong to?" asked Forge in confusion.

"It runs itself," Leo explained. "It's comprised of people from all over the region and funded primarily by Firekli and Maliyansa. Its only mission is to stand guard at the Golden Corridor to ensure that Brechin can't deploy its entire arsenal. It wouldn't surprise me if we lose the Golden Corridor soon though."

"At this rate, there won't be anything to go home to," Kallen solemnly remarked.

"Not if we can stop it." Rhys withdrew Ethos and set the AI on the instrument paneling. "Where exactly do you believe the base to be?"

"Sooo, I'm not entirely sure," chuckled Ethos in mock embarrassment. "The knowledge I have is from over two centuries ago. I call it a base, but really I mean Ramsen's shuttle. I know they have it, I just don't know its exact location. The jets were in our shuttle. And, although they're nuclear powered, they still require fuel. And that blend of special fuel can only be found in one place. Now, it's possible the fuel cells were transported alongside the jets long ago and Ramsen's shuttle destroyed, but that doesn't explain how the jets are launching."

"Why?" asked Rhys.

"Unless Brechin has built a magnetic catapult, launching the jets is a difficult task. Ramsen's shuttle was made primarily for transportation, but because it was necessary for pilots to launch from it in dire situations, it needed to have onboard a magnetic catapult. I suspect Brechin is using Ramsen's ship catapult."

"If they don't have the, eh, catapult, what's happens?" asked Leo.

"The units can still launch, but it eats into fuel and energy reserves. Vertical launches are achievable, but it's much more efficient to use a catapult."

"Would they really care though?" Rhys leaned on his elbow. "We know of only three people who are capable of piloting the units. If their only task is to set fire to the world, why would they care about fuel efficiency?"

"Because there is a limited amount," replied Ethos, "which is why, let's hope, that they haven't been going on reconnaissance missions around the world. Blasting your ass into orbit is going to require an exorbitant amount of fuel."

There was a moment of silence before Kashim asked, "What happens… if there isn't enough fuel?"

It was Rhys who responded. "We'll figure that out when we get there."

"Eh… so… how are you proposing we locate this shuttle?" asked Hodge. "We were just in Brechin last year and nearly destroyed the entire temple. People have not likely forgotten our faces."

"Eh…" started Leo.

Rhys leaned around the cockpit seat and looked at the noble.

"My brother and father are in Brechin. Or, they should be," Leo murmured. "My father would know where something that special would be hidden."

"They left Bathsgate?" asked Kallen, concerned.

"They left about two weeks ago and returned to Brechin. They didn't say why. I don't know if they were found out or if they went back of their own accord… I mean, they could be in prison. The letter I just received in Firekli was written about three weeks ago. So, technically, if all went well, they should be back in Brechin."

"You think your father was reinstated to the council?" asked Rhys.

Leo shrugged. "I have no idea. They don't ever share important information like that because the letter might be intercepted."

"So, them helping us is a slight possibility depending upon their situation," said Kallen.

"If we can find them," added Kashim. "If they were arrested, then we won't be connecting with them any time soon."

"They've been very careful," assured Leo. "They wouldn't be arrested…"

"Assume we can't find them," mused Rhys. "Is there any way we can locate where the jets are being kept?"

"*If* they're using Ramsen's shuttle, I can get us there," said Ethos.

"When will you know?"

"When we enter the airspace around Brechin," the AI replied.

Rhys glanced down at the remaining distance. They had another forty minutes or so. Folding his arms across his chest, he settled himself in to wait.

"Oh, I forgot to tell Andy to keep an eye on the converter," Kallen said suddenly. She sighed. "Oops."

"He'll figure it out when he starts sweating on the bridge," replied Hodge.

"But if he's out at sea—"

"He won't leave port," interrupted Rhys. "Even if the others from *Grisle* join him, he won't go out to sea."

"He's right," said Kashim. "Andy doesn't have his usual crew. He has no one he can rely upon."

"Someone should have stayed with him," Hodge muttered.

"Don't look at me," snapped Kallen. "You should have stayed."

"Hey, he's got Cantia… even if she *can* sleep through a typhoon," said Otto softly. "He's not completely alone."

"You've been awfully quiet since last night," said Hodge. Rhys turned in his chair to see his friend kick Otto's boot. "What's going through your mind right now? You've got a computer-thing now. How's that working out?"

"I'm fine," said Otto.

There was a painful moment of silence as everyone waited for Otto to provide more information, but it never came.

"Heyyyy." Hodge kicked Otto's boot again.

"I'm fine," he murmured. "Seriously."

"Kashim, it's true," said Forge. "Otto is doing well. Pathos has not indicated that he is in any type of emotional distress."

"See?" growled Otto. "I'm fine." He gently touched the AI alongside his temple. "Pathos helps me. I don't expect... any of you to understand that but... I'm fine."

"Hey, just making sure you're on level footing before we trust you with guarding our backs," said Hodge, stretching out along the wall.

"You don't have to worry about me."

Hodge grunted and lay down. "Good, because I'm not—"

A single alert from radar followed by two wailing sirens interrupted Hodge.

"Enemy units approaching," reported Zain in Nefegian. "Eight kilometers out."

Rhys moved to turn the sirens off but stopped. What was that other sound? It wasn't a siren; it sounded like a pulsing hum. What was it? After a moment, he pulled back and looked at Zain in confusion.

It was Ethos.

Zain switched off the alarms, dumping the ship into silence. With the instrument panel and radar now quiet, Rhys could hear it. Ethos was laughing. It was low and intermittent as if Ethos had just heard some dirty gossip. When another siren began pulsing rhythmically overhead, Ethos burst into cackling fits of manic laughter.

Rhys motioned for Zain to turn off the alarm and then asked, "What's going on, Ethos?"

The AI mimicked trying to catch its breath before breaking into another fit of gleeful screeches.

"Enemy airships along the horizon," reported Zain.

"Is it broken?" asked Leo.

Ethos' laughter died. When the AI spoke, it sounded smug. "I'm back. After two centuries, I'm back. I'm home." He sighed in pleasure. "Ramsen's shuttle is in Brechin."

"How do you know?" asked Kallen, peering into the cockpit.

"I'll let you in on a little secret," chuckled Ethos. "Ramsen's shuttle was mine. I was the AI in control of it. And now that we're near it, I can communicate with it." The mirth in Ethos' voice faded and the AI fell solemn. "Brechin has been using the shuttle's radar and tracking systems to monitor enemy forces, including ourselves."

"Wait, so those airships know we're coming?" asked Hodge.

"They do," said Ethos. "Visually, they will be unable to see this unit, however, if they are in contact with whoever is operating the shuttle's radar, they can open fire in our general direction. But... I will take care of that, right now." Ethos sighed. "I wish they had asked me before so rudely barging into my domain. I'm shutting everything down on the shuttle's bridge."

"Good, Ethos," cooed Rhys, disengaging the autopilot feature.

"Gain some altitude and put distance between you and the airships," instructed the AI. After a moment, it added, "I've shut the bridge down, but they still know our heading, speed, and altitude."

After a moment, Rhys glanced over his shoulder. "Everyone sit down." He pulled on the yoke to increase their altitude. Airships were relatively fast compared to the technology of the region, but there was no way they would be able to reach the higher altitudes the maintenance unit could.

"Three thousand meters and rising," reported Zain.

"Enemy airships are not giving chase," reported Ethos. "We're in the clear."

Rhys relaxed at the controls. "You're sure?"

"Don't question the Great Ethos!" boomed Ethos. The AI seemed exceptionally pleased with itself.

Rhys leaned forward over the instruments to study Brechin which was coming into view on the horizon. From a height of almost four thousand meters, the capital didn't appear as impressive as Rhys remembered. It was smaller and its suburbs not nearly as far-reaching as he recalled.

"Ramsen's shuttle is near the main temple," said Ethos. "Morons."

Rhys pulled back on the throttle. "How are we going to get there?"

"They've been using the magnetic catapult. Once we're close enough, I'll open the catapult hatch. You'll have to look for it because I'm guessing its hidden."

It took but a few minutes before they arrived at the city's port and began circling Brechin's massive temple. Spitefully, Rhys glowered out at the structure, murder and rage swelling in his heart. Evidence of the previous year's events was nonexistent. The glass window panes he destroyed near the top floors had been replaced; the bullet smears along the entrance were gone. He was sure the interior was just as spotless. It pissed him off.

The tone in Ethos' voice changed and the AI spoke in Aabesh, "Focus, Rhys."

Rhys took a steadying breath and, despite the rage within him, returned his attention to the AI.

"I'm preparing to open the catapult hatch. I've passed Zain the coordinates of the shuttle's location," said Ethos. As Zain maneuvered the maintenance unit east of the temple, Ethos made a confirmatory sound. "You're directly above it. I'm opening the catapult. Watch for it."

Both Rhys and Zain rose in their chairs and began searching the dizzying array of streets, alleyways, and roads.

"There!" Zain pointed to an inclined cobblestone street that was shuddering and rising from the earth. Rhys grabbed the throttle and pushed the maintenance unit closer until they were just above the street.

"It's on hinges?" asked Hodge, peering into the cockpit. "Look at it. They just put the *gawan* street on hinges."

"Not hinges," murmured Rhys, studying the entryway. "Hydraulics. They've kept the shuttle underground to allow pilots to sortie."

"Stop gaping at it. Let's go," Ethos demanded.

Rhys pushed on the yoke, rolling Hodge down the length of the cabin, and whipped the unit along the cobblestone street. In a single movement, he adjusted the thrusters, maneuvered the craft into the hatch opening, and throttled down the brilliantly illuminated catapult launch ramp.

"Ease up," instructed Ethos. "In about seventy meters, the ramp is going to come to an abrupt halt." Rhys could sense the rest of his crew pressing in around the cockpit to see. "Good, slower. Keep the colloid shield engaged. See the platform there at the bottom just before the blast wall? Set the unit onto it, and I'll transfer us from the catapult into the hangar."

The maintenance unit came to rest on the enormous platform at the bottom of the catapult. After a breath's moment, the platform began moving downward, drawing the unit into the shuttle's enormous belly.

"Welcome to *Apex*," Ethos proudly announced. Illuminated by brilliant white lights, the platform sank into the floor, leaving the maintenance unit free to taxi in the ship's hangar.

Rhys expected Ramsen's shuttle to be large in order to transport jets and other war units, but *large* was an understatement. Before them spread a space seven times the length of *Themis*. Lit by stark white lights, the hangar was cavernous, boasting a ceiling twice the height of *Themis'* primary mast and walls that extended into the infinite.

Ten or so empty slots where jets and other war machines were to be anchored for maintenance lined the hangar on either side. Each slip had two tool chests bolted to the wall and a variety of mobile devices locked to the floor to be used for en-route repairs and maintenance. Of the numerous slips in the hangar, only the two nearest the rear wall were occupied with jets similar to *Anemone*.

"The shuttle was a transport craft. The magnetic catapult, which is atop the shuttle, can extend double the ship's length, making it long enough to acclimate to any type of launching situation," Ethos pointed out. "It has a large cargo hold to carry supplies, fuel, and parts, two crew quarters, an officer's quarters, a galley, pilot and astronaut preparatory room, and control room. Nearly ninety percent of the ship is comprised of storage."

Though surprised at the upkeep of the shuttle, Rhys was not stunned like the others by its grandeur. His people had built it. Of course, it was impressive. "Ethos, the bridge—where is it?" he asked.

"The shuttle has a bridge *and* control room. Both are equipped with radar, but only the control room has the ability to operate the catapult and launch units," Ethos replied. "The control room is at the end of the hangar. See the far wall? It's difficult to discern; it's covered in one-way glass so the control room can better see the hangar."

"And they use cameras to follow the launch process?" concluded Zain stoically. He too seemed unfazed by *Apex's* vastness.

"Correct," Ethos promptly replied.

"So, eh, what's the plan here?" asked Hodge. "I don't see anyone."

"That's because whoever's in command is in the control room," offered Forge from the rear of the unit.

Rhys sat back in his chair. "I want to keep the colloid shield active, but if we leave it engaged for too long, it'll sap the unit's power."

"Clear the area, secure the control room, and then disengage it," said Kashim. "If we're going to move, let's move."

Rhys exchanged looks with Zain before saying, "Hold on. I'm going to move us farther in." Using only the thrusters to manipulate the unit's altitude and direction, he maneuvered the maintenance unit into the hangar before setting it down in one of the empty slips. At least with the wall on one side, they would be shielded from attack and have a defensive position.

As he shut down the engines, Rhys said, "Arm up." In Nefegian, he added, "Zain, I want you to stay with the ship. I need your expertise if we're going to launch a counterattack using a jet." Rhys clambered over the cockpit chairs. "Can't have you getting killed, not when we've come this far. Forge, same for you. You're medical personnel. If any of us in injured, you're in command."

"Right," replied Forge with more determination than usual.

Rhys adjusted his bulletproof vest, slung his resonance cutters over his back, and checked his holstered pistol. Afterward, he ran a cursory glance over his short rifle and prepped the ammunition cases for rapid reload by sliding them near the hatch door and opening the boxes. "Kashim, set us up."

Kashim passed Forge a short rifle. "You're to provide cover fire if need be, otherwise wait here. Don't put yourself in danger." Forge checked the rifle and sat on Rhys' magnetic board. "Hodge and I will act as vanguard; Leo and Rhys will be backup. Kallen and Otto, stay hidden but be prepared to guard the unit. If it is attacked or we lose it, that's it. This unit is our only way out of Brechin." Kashim ran a final check over himself and then looked at Hodge. "Don't push yourself. We may be healed, but our bodies are still weak."

Hodge leaned against the inner unit wall. "Right."

"Hey, Ethos, how do we get into the control room?" asked Kashim.

"Look out the cockpit for a moment," instructed Ethos. Kashim and Rhys obeyed. "So, the rear wall is mostly one-way glass, right? There is an automated door just to the left of that wall in the far corner of the hangar. You might not be able to see it from here, but trust me—it's there. Once you enter, the control room will be on your immediate right."

"Logos indicates there are six bodies currently in the control room," said Zain.

Kashim turned to start the operation, but Rhys stopped him. "Ethos, are there any AI-controlled weapons or defense devices in the hangar or the control room?"

"I've disengaged all of them," replied Ethos.

"And the door leaving the hangar will just open?" Hodge asked warily.

"Correct. This is my ship, remember? Now that I'm aboard, I control everything." The AI cackled softly. "*Everything.*"

"Opening the hatch door," said Rhys, slipping Ethos into his pocket. The side hatch of the maintenance unit opened, allowing the faint scent of cold, sterile metal to waft in. Kashim listened and then stepped into the hangar; Hodge followed. Because Rhys had intentionally positioned the maintenance unit's hatch door away from the rest of the hangar, his entire crew now had cover and protection.

Rhys and Leo moved to the hatch door and watched as Kashim and Hodge crept to the unit's tail, listened, and then motioned to one another.

There was silence between them before Kashim darted out. Hodge disappeared as well.

Though Rhys expected their entry to have drawn attention, it didn't appear as though their presence had been detected. Perhaps it was because, to the control room, it appeared as though the catapult ramp had opened and closed by itself. If Rhys' guess was correct, the control room, although made of one-way glass, was soundproof. It had to be in order to be next to the hangar and the catapult. Therefore, not even the hissing of the technologically superior thrusters of the maintenance unit could have been heard.

Leo settled beside Rhys and followed his gaze. "This is too surreal."

Rhys glanced over his shoulder at Kallen and Otto who were standing in the open hatch. Unlike Otto, who appeared like a war-battered veteran, Kallen's eyes were wide and, though it was obvious she was trying to cover the fear on her face, from the way she held herself, Rhys knew otherwise. She had done operations like this before. In fact, she, Hodge, and Kashim had been the first to locate him and Alina in enemy territory when they first arrived.

Up until now, the base in Brechin had been a distant, fantastical place where they would eventually set up a counterattack against Osiris. It had always been in the future, ever-looming but distant. Now though, here they stood. They were there, and reality was hitting Kallen hard.

"Let's go," whispered Leo, nudging Rhys. Without waiting for a response, the Brechin noble moved out from the safety of their cover and jogged across the hangar to the nearest jet; Rhys followed, his eyes darting warily toward the one-way glass on the far wall. Once perched under the jet, Rhys looked for Hodge and Kashim. He found them crouching near the hangar door.

Hodge motioned to Rhys.

"Do it, Ethos," Rhys murmured.

"Yosh-a!" chortled Ethos. The door leading from the hangar whizzed open. Kashim slipped in, and Hodge disappeared after him. Rhys and Leo filled their positions near the door.

"On the floor!" bellowed Kashim. "Now! Hands on your heads, get on the floor!" The sound of a brief scuffle, followed by a few gunshots, exploded from the control room. Leo started to charge in after them, but Rhys grabbed his pants leg and jerked him back.

"Don't move," Hodge ordered. A pause and then, "Ehhhhh... Rhys?"

Rhys cautiously moved through the hallway and into the control room. There, he found Kashim and Hodge standing over six people. Five of the hostages were nobles. The sixth captive, however, had short-clipped silver hair and ghostly pale skin. "Rullena…" Rhys said, lowering his rifle.

Unlike the others who were prone on the floor, Rullena was strapped to the wall of the control room, her arms bound behind her by the elbows. Her hair, which used to be glossy, was dull and great purple bags darkened her eyes, giving her face a hollowed look. She still wore the gray robes of a white god, but they appeared old and ragged. From under the hem, Rhys could discern her bare feet which were blue in color from the chill that pervaded the ship.

"Rhys… Falkrow…" Rullena whispered, looking up at him, her great blue eyes just as brilliant as his.

Rifle trained on the nobles, Kashim asked, "You know this woman?"

Rhys stared at Rullena. "She's one of the three so-called white gods. She, Etion, and Gealdir work for the high priest. The last time I saw them was in the tribunal meeting when Alina was taken prisoner."

"So… not friends?" clarified Hodge.

Rhys passed a cursory glance over the other control room captives. "Where are Etion and Gealdir?"

"Etion's dead," Rullena replied.

"And Gealdir?"

She nodded to the wall of glowing screens, controls, and radar maps. "Firekli."

Rhys scanned the monitors before his eyes fell on the cockpit camera of the jet. While Gealdir wore a helmet, his face was completely visible. His eyes darted from his instruments to the space around him and narrowed in determination; his mouth was set in a sickening smirk. "Ethos, if we escort these people out of the shuttle," Rhys asked in Elali, "can you guarantee they won't be able to reenter?"

"Yes," asserted Ethos.

Rhys brandished his rifle. "Everyone, to your knees. Keep your hands on the top of your head."

"We're moving them?" asked Hodge.

"We're getting them off the shuttle." Rhys glanced at Rullena. "Stay put." He knew she couldn't technically move; the order was more to dictate to Hodge and Kashim his intentions. "Leo, get in here. Kashim, take the others. Ethos, where's the nearest exit?"

Rullena's eyes grew, if possible, larger. "Ethos?"

"Go down the hallway. There will be an external door at the end," instructed Ethos. The AI switched to Elali. "Once I've locked everything down, they won't be getting back in."

"Even with the proper tools?" probed Rhys, pointing his rifle at one of the male nobles.

Ethos' response was solemn. "I can defend against an external assault, if need be."

Once the other nobles had been locked out of the ship, Rhys sighed in relief and returned to Rullena. "What happened? Why are you bound?"

She jerked her head toward the screen. "Gealdir."

"What happened to Etion?"

"Gealdir killed him," she replied.

Rhys gazed at her in surprise. A Caelestis citizen murdering another? That didn't make any sense, especially since Gealdir, Etion, and Rullena had been rescued and escalated to the lofty title of gods together.

"After you killed Michael, Gealdir became the high priest."

Rhys slung his rifle over his shoulder. "We didn't kill Michael. Michael killed himself."

"Oh... We heard..." Questioning her own words, Rullena gazed in defeat at the floor.

"He grew power-hungry and killed Etion for not obeying?" Rhys concluded. Rullena nodded. "And what about you?"

"After Gealdir became the high priest, he and Etion quarreled constantly. When Gealdir ordered Etion to become a pilot, Etion adamantly declined. He and I... both felt that using war machines was not right, especially as Caelestis citizens..." Rullena looked at Rhys. "Gealdir killed him because he wouldn't pilot those war machines." She wiped her tear-streaked cheek on her shoulder. "I didn't have the previous knowledge needed to pilot a war machine, but I know how to do everything else in the control room."

Rhys glanced at the others who had rejoined them. "So, he imprisoned you in the shuttle?"

"Any time he's on a mission, I'm in the control room disseminating orders and monitoring his flight and combat."

"Leo, would you let the others know we've cleared the ship?" asked Rhys. "And get Forge in here. He needs to look at her."

"What are you wanting to do with her?" asked Kashim, leaning against the rear wall. "You're obviously not going to kill her."

Rullena peered fearfully at Rhys. "Kill me? Why? Why would you want to kill me?"

"Because your high priest murdered Alina," snarled Hodge. "And it was because *you three* wouldn't stand up against him."

"Alina's dead?" Rullena whispered. She moved on her knees toward Rhys but was jerked to a halt by her restraints. "Alina's dead?"

"Michael killed her a few days after that tribunal meeting," explained Rhys. He looked up as Forge came running in with a small bag hung over his shoulder. Kallen and Otto followed. "You, Etion, and Gealdir have been on my to-kill list since then."

Forge knelt before Rullena and slid his medical pack onto the floor. Rullena startled. "You!" she gasped.

Forge tilted his head in confusion before processing who sat before him. "Clare Budeaux, you're..."

"Why are you here?" Rullena murmured.

"Because you're hurt," replied Forge.

Rhys looked between them. "Wait, you know who this is?"

Forge sat on his heels. "She worked in Colony Control and Biofeedback. She was with the department in charge of monitoring the Core."

"Why are you *here*?" shrieked Rullena.

Rhys sat in the chair nearest Rullena and leaned on his knees. "Caelestis didn't make it. Segments of the colony landed here on Earth."

Rullena began crying loud, unashamed sobs. "I want to go home. Please, take me home!"

"Forge, tend to her." Rhys turned to study the monitors. There were several screens dedicated to Gealdir's unit, including a hull camera which revealed the trail of destruction that his unit left in its wake. "How long can he be in flight? How long before Gealdir has to come back to resupply?"

"A couple of days. There's an airship that carries fuel reserves specifically for *Jasmine*." Rullena watched Forge monitor her vitals before saying, "His goal was to completely annihilate Firekli."

Both Hodge and Kashim made disapproving sounds, and Kallen leaned heavily in the doorway. Rhys sat back in his chair and gazed up at the monitors. "And why is Gealdir attacking Firekli? Did someone tell him to?"

Again, Rullena didn't respond. Rhys began to rephrase the question, but Leo interrupted him. "She knows. Just look at her."

"I don't know," Rullena muttered.

Rhys sighed and looked at Hodge. "I see what you mean now. We are horrible liars." His friend gave a knowing shrug. "So, Rullena, how long have you known about Osiris?"

Rullena's mouth fell open before she admitted, "Since we were rescued from the escape pod. He is the divine word. He knows and sees all."

"And how does Osiris communicate with you?"

"Why?" she asked.

"Answer the question," Hodge grunted.

Rullena drew away from Forge and, with determination, avoided Hodge's gaze.

"No matter," said Hodge quickly. "We'll just—"

"No," interrupted Rhys, leaving his chair to kneel before Rullena. "Osiris isn't a god. You have to know that. Osiris is an AI, Rullena. An AI on the moon."

The woman blinked at him, agape.

"You have to understand the magnitude of what Osiris is doing. It's controlling Earth. All of it." Rhys released her bindings. "All of Earth is one petri dish broken into quadrants. You, Gealdir, Etion, Michael, the royal family heads. All of you are just part of the religious, oligarchical system implemented by an AI. Because of you—because of *all* of you— thousands of people, *humans*, have been slaughtered. In your name, they have been slaughtered. You have brought war to this region. *You* did this."

Rullena took a slow, deep breath. "There's a computer at the top of the temple that disseminates orders." She wiped her face on her shoulder. "It also updates clergy on enemy movements and provides suggested methods to quell uprisings. I think it's an AI, but it's old. Older than this ship or anything we've found. Gealdir never let me anywhere near it though."

"Yeah, I bet not." Rhys stood with a sigh. "We have our work cut out for us. Let's get started."

"What? What are you going to do?" asked Rullena.

"I don't know," he replied, regarding the monitors. "Save the world, I guess."

39
HARBINGER OF CHANGE

AFTER BRIEFLY EXAMINING THE REMAINING two units in the hangar, Rhys turned Zain, Forge, and Otto onto the jets to gain a better understanding of their capabilities. Following Ethos' instructions, he took Kallen and Hodge to the shuttle's cargo hold farther down the hall. Leo and Kashim remained in the control room.

"And you're sure no one is going to reenter the ship?" asked Hodge warily.

"Yes," Ethos replied. "*Apex* is completely under my control."

"Does that mean you could fly it?"

"*Apex's* fuel reserves are at sixteen percent, hardly enough to go any distance with a ship this size," the AI explained. "By the time we made it into the air, we would already be well below ten percent."

"Why is it so low on fuel?" Hodge paused in the doorway of an open room which appeared to be a communal bunk before jogging to catch up.

"Like Rhys here, we also slipped into the beta-wormhole and ended up inside Earth's gravitational pull. We spent most of our fuel trying to keep from burning up upon reentry."

"Wait? What?" Kallen pulled Rhys to a halt. "I don't understand. What does that mean?"

"Use layman's terms, Ethos," reminded Rhys, studying a map on the wall.

"Earth has gravity, correct? Gravity is the force that attracts things to a body that has mass. So, gravity is keeping you from flying off this planet at this very moment. Well, Earth's gravitational field is very, very strong. Not as strong as other forces in the universe, but strong enough. Rhys, please withdraw me." Rhys obeyed, and Ethos began projecting an image of Earth above its unit. "Now, when a meteor, a rock from space, enters the gravitational pull of Earth—see the circle around Earth? That's where the gravitational field begins. When a meteor enters the gravitational pull of Earth, it is automatically drawn toward Earth's core because of…"

"Gravity," concluded Hodge.

"Correct. Earth's atmosphere though extends higher than you can possibly imagine. Because this allows an object, or in this case, a space rock, the time to accelerate and increase its speed exponentially, the object begins to heat."

"And that's why it glows?" asked Hodge.

"It becomes so hot that, depending on the rock's mass and materials, it might dissolve from the heat."

"As in it disappears?" Kallen murmured.

"Correct," replied Ethos. "The same principles apply to any object entering Earth's atmosphere. The speed an object accelerates to upon reentry creates so much heat, that many times the objects will just dissolve."

Kallen pursed her lips. "But this ship made it here, right?"

Rhys was following her train of thought. "Yes, this ship made it here." He continued down the hall. "It has a thermal protection system to guard against heat."

"Did you know about this? About gravity?" Kallen stopped him once more. "This theory applies to you too, right?"

"Of course, he knows about it," said Hodge.

"Can you… If you go up there…" Kallen cast about for words. "If you go up there, can you come back down?"

"That's what the others are trying to figure out right now," replied Rhys. Hiding the fear in his heart, he led them to an enormous doorway which Ethos promptly opened.

"What are we looking for exactly?" asked Hodge, standing in the doorway and staring into the dark room. Despite being closed for nearly two centuries, the air smelled fresh.

Rhys slipped between Kallen and Hodge. From the sound of his footsteps shuffling along the floor, he could tell the cargo hold was cavernous, far larger than the hangar. "Ethos?"

"Here you go," replied the AI. Nothing happened. "Uhhh… Oh. There's a loose circuit."

"Great," murmured Rhys, withdrawing his resonance cutters. He engaged them, illuminating a radius of two meters in neon blue light. "There's nothing here."

"I've checked the cargo log. There should be fuel cells in…"

Rhys pointed the resonance cutters.

"No…"

He pointed a different direction.

"No. No…" chirped Ethos. "Yes, there. That direction."

Rhys walked several paces and then stopped. "Uh… Ethos?" He held out the AI to show it the numerous oblong boxes spread evenly before them. In perfect rows, the boxes extended far into the darkness.

"Those aren't mine," Ethos asserted in confusion. "People must have put them here."

Rhys started to move forward, but Kallen caught his arm. In the hue of the resonance cutters, he could see both her eyes and Hodge's wide. There was something here they understood, but he didn't. "Those are coffins," Kallen whispered.

"What's a coffin?" asked Rhys in similar fashion.

"They hold the dead," replied Hodge.

Rhys pulled his arm from Kallen's grip and edged toward the nearest coffin. Though constructed primarily of metal, traces of wood lined the lids and the edges. Looking over the coffin, he found to his surprise a small glass window built into the lid. His heart starting to hammer, he glanced back at Kallen and Hodge before bringing the resonance cutters close to the milky glass. A man's pale face with staring blue-gray eyes and white hair reflected back at him.

Startled, Rhys jerked away and took a few steps to his left. His leg hit another coffin, and he whirled around to find another silver-haired individual with wide, blue-gray eyes and silver hair. "They're…" He stumbled back to Kallen and Hodge. "They're my people. They're mine."

"It's a graveyard," murmured Hodge, gripping Rhys' arm.

"Why are they here?" Rhys whispered.

"I wish to speculate," said Ethos softly. "While Ramsen was still alive and in Brechin, many of the shuttle's crew members were killed. We never knew what happened to their bodies, but it is very possible that, to keep outsiders from asking questions, they began storing bodies down here."

"But only Rhys' people," said Kallen.

"Correct. If the believers were to ever see a white god's dead body, they would then question the faith. Therefore, if there were no traditional death ceremonies and no one ever saw what happened to the bodies, the population would continue to believe them alive."

"But… there are so many." Hodge left Rhys' side and approached another coffin. "Were there this many in your crew?"

"No, but there were others here before us and, of course, after us."

"There have to be at least a hundred coffins here," said Kallen, staying close to Rhys. Though her voice was a mere whisper, it could be heard across the cargo hold.

"We aren't here for the coffins," Ethos urged. "We're here for the fuel cells. Get going."

Rhys motioned to Hodge. Together, they began weaving through the labyrinth of coffins toward the rear of the cargo hold. When the back wall finally came into view, he asked, "What am I looking for, Ethos?"

"Those," replied the AI when the cutters' blue aura illuminated dozens of pallets of cylinders. Marked with Interstellar Nefegian warnings, the cylinders of fuel stood as tall as Hodge and were strapped to metal pallets which were bolted to the floor.

"How many of those… do we need to bring to the hangar?" muttered Hodge.

"All of them," replied Ethos.

"I don't understand much about how your technology works, but I'm pretty sure neither of those jets can hold that much fuel," said Hodge.

"No, they can't. But the equipment we're going to be attaching to Rhys' unit can. Rhys, a maintenance bot is thirty-four paces to your right. Turn it on, and I can help you."

Rhys jogged along the pallets of fuel cells until he found the bot—a spherical, rotating AI unit atop four independently operating legs with interchangeable feet and wheels.

"Hurry back please," called Hodge. "We're… in the dark over here… with dead bodies."

Rhys knelt beside the bot and turned it on. The orb, which made up the center of its mass, spun first to the left and then to the right to calibrate. "Got it, Ethos?" asked Rhys, standing.

"Yup," replied Ethos. The bot bounced slightly as the AI spoke and rolled along behind Rhys as he jogged back to Kallen and Hodge. "I'm going to unlock the pallets, and we can start transporting them to the hangar."

"Ehh… What about the coffins?" Kallen asked.

Ethos growled. "Make a path for the pallets."

Holding the resonance cutters overhead, Rhys helped Kallen start sliding the coffins aside. Though Hodge managed to move one casket at a time with little difficulty, Rhys and Kallen had to work together to make the coffins skid noisily across the floor. For a good ten minutes, they worked to clear a path from the rear wall to the cargo hold door. Eventually, Rhys passed the resonance cutters to Kallen so he could use both hands to strain against the heavy caskets. When they finished, all three found themselves covered in a fine sweat and panting.

Cackling, Ethos sang, "Here we go."

Rhys looked up from his place at the entrance of the cargo hold to find the shuttle's bot effortlessly towing a pallet of fuel cells down the coffin-lined pathway they had created. Holding the pallet handle with one of its legs, the bot powered along with its remaining three. Though Caelestis didn't use bots during his lifetime, Rhys knew throughout history the units had been important to the functionality of the colony.

"Ethos," said Rhys as the bot rolled out the cargo hold. "Did every crew member of this shuttle have an AI or was it only Ramsen?"

"It was only Ramsen," Ethos asserted.

Rhys, Kallen, and Hodge followed the bot and its load into the hallway and watched as it zipped down the corridor to the hangar. "AIs weren't for everyone?"

"No," replied Ethos. "Ramsen was a captain and a highly respected transportation specialist."

"And you controlled this entire ship and the bots inside it?"

"Correct." There was a moment of silence before Ethos asked, "Are you impressed?"

"I wish I had known you were such a powerhouse."

"A powerhouse?" laughed Hodge.

Rhys nodded and motioned to the ship. "Pathos, Logos—neither of them could control something of this size. The pinnacle of technology during my lifetime was the complete integration of machine and man. To me, AIs were always an integral part of human survival. Even so, the AIs Caelestis and Neo-Colony Two use today are nothing compared to the amount of power AIs had throughout history."

"Thank you, Rhys," said Ethos. The AI sounded sincere.

"Wait, wait," said Kallen. "The way you've talked about Pathos and Logos all this time has been like you've known the other breeds since the beginning, but Rhys just said they wouldn't be able to do what you do."

"No, I meant, the Pathos and Logos units that I know today," corrected Rhys, sheathing his cutters and starting down the hallway.

"Pathos, Logos, and Ethos were all created at the same time, however, the Ethos model quickly grew out of favor because humans didn't want a robot telling them what was morally right. They didn't trust an AI to make difficult decisions in morally ambiguous situations. So, Ethos was forgotten and only the foundational layers of Logos and Pathos proceeded throughout our history."

"Poor Ethos," murmured Kallen.

Rhys thought to remind her that the AI didn't have emotions but stopped himself. With all that he and Ethos had been through, perhaps it really had learned that which makes humans human—emotions.

"Thank you, Rhys," said Ethos in Nefegian.

Knowing the AI had probably just synched with the electrical signals in his brain and picked up on what he was thinking, Rhys scoffed. Once in the hangar, he called, "Well?" to the others.

While Otto knelt under the unit nearest them studying the myriad of plasma weapons, Zain had his glossy gaze set in the distance as he completed calculations in his head. Only Forge, who was perched near the unit's cockpit, acknowledged their return. "Is Ethos controlling the bot?"

Rhys nodded and approached the unit labeled *Heather*. "What's wrong with the other one?"

"Fuel cells and lasers have been stripped," replied Forge, moving to the wing. "*Heather* is the only one remotely space-ready."

"Zain, Forge, Rhys," said Ethos. Rhys withdrew the AI from his pocket once more. "Once you've determined whether this unit is flight-capable, we're going to start taking apart *Clover's* thrusters and attaching them to *Heather*."

"That's not going to be enough to get him into orbit," said Zain. "He still needs a rocket engine."

"Which is why while you three are taking *Clover* apart, Hodge, Kallen, Kashim, Leo, and I are going to see what we can do about creating a makeshift rocket engine."

"I don't like it when you throw around that word—makeshift,'" muttered Rhys.

"It's not *makeshift* exactly," replied Ethos. "We have the fuel, now we just need to find a rocket engine of which this shuttle has three. You are standing on them." The AI laughed. "They're directly below the hangar."

"Rocket engines for… the shuttle or a jet?" asked Forge.

"Jet," clarified Ethos. "Of course, a jet. We don't have the manpower to strap a *shuttle* rocket engine onto a jet. Are you crazy?" The AI sighed in a very human-like way. "Questions? Comments?"

Zain woke from his trance, exchanged looks with Forge, and then said, "We've been informed that Firekli has used the plasma cannon again."

"Well, four more times," corrected Forge.

"And? The result?" prompted Rhys.

"Its aim was the Brechin fleet, but half of its port was in the direct line of fire," explained Forge.

"Let's get to work." Rhys passed Ethos to Kallen and rolled his sleeves. "Ethos, once the bot is done delivering the fuel cells, leave it here so we can use it."

"Right-o," replied Ethos. "Let's go, others."

As Hodge and Kallen went to the control room to gather Kashim and Leo, Rhys stalked around *Heather's* tail and examined the engines there. They needed to hurry, but the work ahead of them was undoubtedly going to take hours. To ensure the mission would be a success, that meant checking, double-checking, and triple-checking connections, fuses, the nuclear reactor, fuel cell injectors, and anything else that could possibly fail.

Rhys bowed under the jet's hull to join the boy. "What do you have, Otto?"

Otto, who had his torso shoved into *Heather's* belly, murmured something and then kneeled. "I want Zain to check what I've found, but it looks like you have an array of weapons here including plasma lasers and laser pins. And I think a cannon, but I don't know what it is or what it does," replied Otto.

"Not going to work," Zain provided from atop the jet. "Even if *Heather* is equipped with plasma cannon, you'll never be able to penetrate Osiris' shields."

"You're sure?" asked Otto.

Rhys cocked his head. "How do you know Osiris has shields?"

"It's logic," replied Forge, sliding off the wing and joining them under the belly of the jet. "If our people put that AI up there, we also must have safeguarded it with shields strong enough to withstand centuries of solar flares and debris. If the shields can withstand thousands of years of raw solar flares, it can withstand a plasma cannon with no problem."

Rhys frowned. "So, the only option I have is to go to the lunar base and disable it manually."

"Correct. Another problem you're going to encounter," continued Zain, "are the orbiting satellites."

"Ethos and I are going to take care of those once Hodge returns," replied Rhys.

"What is your definition of *take care of?*" Zain slid off the wing and peered under the belly of the unit. "You can't approach them without being spotted. Osiris will instantly know of your presence, perhaps even the moment you launch."

"Ethos' memory was scrambled and sealed off by Ramsen's colleagues." Rhys looked pointedly at Forge. "That's why we went to the Brechin camp outside of New Arbroath that one night. Ethos has that information again."

"And what does that allow it to do?" asked Forge.

"If I remember correctly, Ethos said it can now resist coded and encrypted attacks facilitated by Osiris."

"That doesn't explain what it is the two of you plan to do," Zain said.

Once Rhys explained their plan to take down the satellites using a DDoS attack, he looked at Zain for commentary.

Zain shook his head. "It's simple but seems like it will be effective."

"So, it's up to Ethos to create the attack?" concluded Otto.

"Right." Rhys looked at the other jet. "We still have several hours of work left to finish however."

"Let's do it then," said Forge.

Within thirty minutes, they had dismantled *Clover's* thrusters and, using Ethos' bot, laid the heavy machinery on the floor behind *Heather*. Dismantling the four thrusters was the easy part; attaching them to Rhys' unit was the real challenge. Though *Heather* had the ports for spare thrusters, wiring them was tedious.

About an hour into the process, the group was startled from their work when the lights in the hangar switched to crimson and an alarm began wailing. Knowing he couldn't move or else Zain would lose the wires he was working with, Rhys warily looked about the hangar.

Suddenly, a section of the hangar floor began parting and from deep within the belly of *Apex* a rumbling swelled. Like a giant rising from the depths of the sea, a fifteen-meter silver and black rocket engine ascended from the hangar floor.

"Got it," murmured Zain, snarling a hand around the wire Rhys offered.

Riding on the engine's lift directly below the rocket was the rest of his team. "Does this work?" called Hodge, motioning to the monstrosity. Rhys, Otto, Zain, and Forge left *Heather* and approached the enormous unit. Hodge stepped from the moving platform as it leveled off with the hangar floor and jogged to Rhys. "There're two more down there."

"One will be enough," assured Ethos.

"Uh… Ethos…" Rhys approached the rocket engine. "Will this fit on the catapult and in the chute?"

"Yes, of… course… Mmmmm. No, it won't." Ethos growled in mimicked due process. "No, it won't fit if we're underground. Well, why didn't you think of this sooner, Rhys?"

"*Me?* It's your shuttle."

"One moment, one moment," mused Ethos. "Let me think." Everyone stood in silence while the AI mumbled to itself in Nefegian. Rhys exchanged looks with Zain and Forge. All three of them knew what Ethos was trying to calculate—the maximum angle of the catapult chute and its width versus its length. To launch a rocket engine would take more than the seventy meters or so the catapult had to offer. "Well, damn it," Ethos concluded. "We need a new plan."

"Launch the shuttle," suggested Otto.

Forge's response was immediate. "Not enough fuel."

"Just need to stay in the air long enough to launch him and the rocket, right?" Otto looked between Rhys, Zain, and Forge for confirmation. "Right?"

The boy *was* right, but what would happen after they launched? And what would happen after they ran out of fuel? They would crash-land in the middle of enemy territory.

"That *could* work," said Ethos.

"The launch alone will kill people, Ethos," Rhys said.

"Mmm, not if we clear the area beforehand."

"Could we use some of the fuel cells from the cargo hold to load up the shuttle?" asked Kallen. "If what you said earlier is true, we won't make it out to sea before crashing."

"We can use whatever is left once we fuel Rhys' unit and the rocket engine. Just a warning though, there isn't going to be much left." Using the bot parked beside Otto as a makeshift body, the AI maneuvered the robot between the group and pointed across the hangar with one of its four mobile appendages. "See those pallets? All of those pallets are going to Rhys. If we're lucky, we'll have maybe two pallets left. The fuel cells weren't meant to fuel a transport shuttle or even a rocket engine. They were meant for the exclusive use of the jets."

"If we launch in this thing in the middle of Brechin," said Leo, "we'll kill hundreds. Can we clear the surrounding area?"

"*Apex* has an external siren. We can use that," Ethos mused. The bot pacing zoomed under the belly of *Heather*. It examined the remaining thrusters lying on the floor. "Get those attached. Leave the shuttle launch to me."

"Even if we launch the entire shuttle, will we be able to get the rocket engine outside?" asked Leo. "It doesn't matter if we're underground or not; the rocket engine is wider than the catapult."

"It does matter," said Ethos. "The catapult can expand to accommodate the rocket engines, but it has to have the room. Whoever built this tomb only took into consideration the launch of jets; they didn't foresee the shuttle itself ever launching again."

Rhys raised his hand. "Next question. Can the catapult withstand the heat and pressure of a full-throttle burn?"

"Yes. The catapult is magnetic, meaning that it can withstand the heat and pressure of a full-throttle burn *and* assist in the launch. Again, leave the catapult and shuttle launch to me. You four, complete the work on *Heather*. Hodge, you and Kashim take the bot and go back to the cargo hold. There should be explosives on the far side of the hold."

"But it's dark… and there are bodies down there," muttered Hodge. Rhys slid the resonance cutters off his back and passed the sheath to his friend.

"The bot will show you where they are. Get going," instructed Ethos. The little robot spun in place and rolled out of the hangar; Hodge and Kashim jogged after it. "Leo and Kallen, I need you two to help me on the bridge. Also, Rhys… I'm going to need Rullena's help."

Rhys had been waiting for the AI to bring up their hostage. Of everyone there, she had spent the most time on the shuttle and knew the control room. "Fine."

"You're sure?" asked Kallen.

Rhys went to the nearest tool chest and searched for a moment before withdrawing wire and a pair of wire cutters. He nodded to Kallen and Leo, and together they headed to the control room. Rullena looked up when they walked in but otherwise didn't move. "We need your help," said Rhys, moving toward her.

Rullena scooted away. "I don't want to."

He knelt behind her and cut through the cords that bound her to the wall. "You don't have a choice." Rullena pulled her arms free and rubbed her elbows and wrists. He held his hand out to her. When she hesitated, Rhys said her name. Begrudgingly, Rullena slid her hand into his and pulled herself up.

"What do you need help with?" she asked.

"Ethos is going to take you, Kallen, and Leo to the bridge," he explained. He slid the wire cutters into his back pocket and brandished the length of wire he had cut.

Rullena backed away. "I thought you needed my help."

"We do. But I don't want you doing anything that you'll regret. We're going to bind your hands for your safety."

Rullena gaped at him and then looked between Kallen and Leo. "Just do it, Rullena," said Kallen, her tone icy.

When Rullena didn't move, Rhys sighed, took her arm, and pulled her wrists forward. Using the wire, he bound her hands together and pushed her to Leo. "She's your responsibility." Leo caught Rullena who flinched.

"Cooperate," said Leo. "You'll be fine so long as you cooperate. We need your help."

"Watch her," said Rhys in Elali. "Watch what she says and what she does while you're on the bridge. Don't let her near any of the instruments." Kallen nodded.

"Ready?" asked Ethos. "Let's go."

Leo exchanged looks with Rhys and then guided Rullena from the control room, leaving Kallen and Rhys alone briefly. "I hate this," murmured Kallen in Elali.

Rhys reached through the distance between them and reeled her into his arms. In silence, he rested his forehead against hers and just breathed her in.

"Kallen?" called Leo from down the hallway.

Kallen cleared her throat. "Coming." She started to pull away, but Rhys held her still.

"I'll do everything in my power to come home," he whispered. "I swear it." Kallen turned into him and gripped his shirt. "Kallen, I promise. I'll try everything I can." He kissed her forehead and enveloped her in a deep embrace.

"Kallen?" Leo peered back into the control room with Rullena. Upon spotting them, he gave a small apology and disappeared into the hallway.

Rhys kissed Kallen's lips before he released her and watched as she wiped the tears from her face. No one else could know she had been crying. Stoic expression cemented on her face, she strode from the control room.

Rhys glanced over his shoulder at the monitors featuring Gealdir, his unit's operating status, and the numerous cameras perched atop his unit.

If he didn't kill Gealdir, he needed to make sure someone else did. That sounded like a job for Hodge and Kashim—if they survived this.

The next two hours went by in a flurry of activity. Not only had his team managed to attach the additional thrusters to *Heather*, but they had also run four remote start-up tests with no problems. Though Hodge and Kashim returned to the hangar, Leo, Kallen, and Rullena never reappeared. By the time midday rolled around, Rhys was anxious.

"Do you want us to go look for them?" asked Hodge who had been lying on the hangar floor near the rocket engine's platform.

"If they were in trouble, Ethos would let us know," replied Rhys, wiping grime from his hands.

"What's next?" asked Otto.

"Rhys needs to familiarize himself with the cockpit and then suit up," said Zain, staring at an electronic handheld. Though they had just come across the handheld the previous hour, Zain had been using it nonstop to track their progress along the long checklist of unit preparations. Of course, Zain and Forge didn't need the device, but it was useful for Rhys and Otto to communicate to one another what had been done.

"Oh yeah!" whooped Hodge. "I want to see."

As his friend strolled across the hangar to the unit, Rhys climbed the ladder along the port wing and balanced himself on the cockpit rim. Because Zain had been the one running all of the tests from the cockpit, this was the first Rhys had seen of what he would be flying.

Like *Anemone*, which he had found outside of New Arbroath, this unit too boasted a one hundred eighty-degree visual field and thermal-resistant glass. He had expected the cockpit to appear similarly to that of the maintenance unit from Neo-Colony Two; what he found was a control panel void of any buttons, levers, and throttles. The only sliver of paneling situated at the front of the cockpit had a handful of small switches. There were no instruments, no monitors, nothing.

Aside from the nearly empty dashboard, there was a single seat whose skeletal-like structure boasted armrests garnished with spheres where the pilot's hands would rest. Along the spine of the chair, a small, silver box glistened. Cautiously, Rhys peered into the bottom of the cockpit. Where there should have been pedals or some sort of gears, there was empty space.

He must have stood staring for a long time because eventually Hodge clambered up the ladder and joined him. "Ehhh... how do you fly it?" his friend asked.

Rhys shook his head. "I... don't know. There's... literally nothing."

"Eh, Zain?" Hodge called.

"Familiarize yourself with the cockpit and then get suited up," repeated Zain from beneath the unit.

Rhys stepped into the cockpit and stood between the chair and the paneling. He looked around in confusion before shrugging at Hodge.

Zain appeared on the wing. "Whereas in our time and space we have AI-integrated humans that control machines, these units are machines controlled in tandem by human and AI. Therefore, you will be piloting the unit with your body. So, I will repeat myself once more—familiarize yourself with the cockpit and then suit up."

"I need the suit," concluded Rhys, leaning down to examine the silver box along the back of the chair. Zain nodded. "It connects through here."

"And the hands and chest," added Zain. "Your hands will control the majority of the unit's movements. From what I understand, the gloves you will be wearing have highly sensitive sensors in the fingertips."

"*That's* what Ethos meant." Rhys touched the chair and then looked at the paneling. "I'm the only one... because I know how to fly and... I don't have the interference of a bio-integrated AI."

"Correct."

Rhys considered the idea and then slowly sat on the chair. Though it appeared stiff, the seat itself was conducive to comfort and made him feel well-balanced. "The instruments?" he asked over his shoulder.

"All will be projected along the glass. I speculate that the glass within your helmet will also have interactive properties." Zain studied the glowing handheld and then looked at Rhys. "Ready?"

Rhys glanced about the cockpit once more and then clambered out with Hodge's help. Together, they followed Zain across the hangar. Kashim, who had taken to napping inside the maintenance unit, glanced at them as they passed. Otto and Forge remained behind to continue the long checklist.

"Ethos pointed out the pilots' briefing room a couple of hours ago," said Zain, striding down the hallway. To Rhys' surprise, Zain stopped at a door adjacent to the control room. It whizzed open to admit them.

Three rows of lockers and several benches crowded the cabin. At the back of the room was a translucent screen upon which maps and mission materials could be projected. There were also toilets, showers, and sinks.

Rhys went to the nearest locker and opened it. Inside hung a long silver and black suit as well as a helmet. He rubbed the material between his fingers. It was surprisingly thin for something to be worn in a vacuum.

"It's made of a mixture of materials."

Rhys turned to find Kallen, Rullena, and Leo. Ethos had been the one to speak.

"To be precise, it's comprised of spandex, nylon-tricot, mylar, and Dacron," continued Ethos. "And, that size is going to be too large for you. Move over one aisle. Locker 177-180."

"Where have you been?" asked Rhys, following Ethos' instructions. He was relieved to see both Kallen and Leo.

The look on Rhys' face must have been obvious because Leo gently pushed Rullena into the locker room. "She was a big help, just like Ethos thought."

"What was she a big help with?" asked Hodge.

Leo started to explain but fumbled for an explanation and looked to Rullena.

"We instigated a DDoS attack—with no problems," said Rullena.

"It took a bit more energy than I was prepared for," said Ethos. "Osiris has bolstered its defenses in the last two centuries."

"Were you detected?" Rhys prompted.

"No. Not that I could discern," the AI replied. It sighed. "I'm going to take a little break. Let me know if you need me."

"AIs don't need to rest," said Hodge.

"This one does," Ethos countered.

"Rhys, we don't have a lot of time." Zain motioned for him to get moving.

As Rhys went down the next aisle, Leo asked, "How long will this entire mission take?"

"It will take Rhys about eight minutes to leave Earth's atmosphere but another…" Zain thought. "But another forty-nine hours to reach the moon."

"It won't be exactly forty-nine hours," muttered Rhys, opening the locker Ethos had indicated. "We haven't done those calculations yet."

"I just did them," replied Zain.

Rhys gazed at the suit hanging within the locker and then withdrew the helmet. Studying it, he said, "And you're sure… about Osiris' shields?"

Zain knew what he was doing, knew what he was looking for. He remained silent.

"So… we're looking at a complete lunar mission," Rhys concluded.

Zain watched him. "That's… correct."

Rhys fell still, anger and fear welling inside him. This was turning into an unavoidable suicide mission. There was no way they had the materials or technology to pull off something on such a grand scale. Some part of him had hoped he would be able to destroy Osiris and its base with a well-placed cannon blast. But… He drew a steadying breath. He wouldn't be coming back from this. "Can I have a minute?" he quavered.

Kallen started for him. "Rhys."

"Just…" He controlled his anger. "Give me a minute." He heard Hodge direct everyone out of the locker room. The door closed behind them, leaving Rhys in complete silence.

Heavily, he leaned against the lockers and glared at the floor through moist eyes. He could run. He could turn and walk out of the shuttle. He could go back to Firekli, pick up *Themis*, and never look back.

Why was this his problem? Why was any of this his problem? Why had he taken on the responsibility of ensuring the region's safety? Why had he thought this was an even remotely plausible solution? Why not just destroy the temple or the computer? Why not just destroy Brechin?

Run, just run. Go. Run.

He slid down the locker and buried his face in his knees. He couldn't run; this was his responsibility. He and Alina had agreed upon that; they had agreed that it was their duty to guide the next generation of humans.

It wasn't about surviving. It was about thriving and living. Being human meant suffering, rejoicing, fighting, and hoping. It meant being selfless; it meant risking life to protect loved ones. It meant being supportive; it meant sacrifice; it meant courage.

Therefore, it was his turn.

Even if he failed, even if the rocket engine exploded upon launch or the thrusters failed midway through the atmosphere, he needed to try. For the future, for the thousands of generations of humans that would be born unto Earth, he had to try.

He couldn't be selfish and think of the people he might lose; he couldn't think of the possibility that he himself might die. He needed to try so everyone could see what it meant to have courage and what it meant to sacrifice in the name of peace.

Caelestis and the numerous other colonies in the Hyperes Solar System represented the apex of humanity; they were the culmination of all of mankind's struggles.

It was as Rullena, Etion, and Gealdir had once told him the previous year—human and territorial conquest had been the cornerstone of mankind since the dawn of civilization. Invasion, subjugation, and assimilation have been the keys to the creation of a future as history has shown.

Rhys would prove history wrong.

Humanity surely had bricks of incursion, suppression, and conquest at its base, but its foundation was comprised of more than that.

He would show the world.

He would lay a level of bricks along humanity's groundwork and give the humans of Earth something they once had thousands and thousands of years ago—choice and freewill.

Rhys wiped his eyes and with a deep breath stood. He might not succeed but he would be a harbinger of change.

40
RENEWED ALLY

AFTER CLEARING THE DEPTHS OF the locker and laying its contents on the nearby bench, Rhys studied the components of his suit. He was familiar with space suits as some colleagues in the engineering department on Caelestis wore them while working outside the colony, but he had never been required to don one.

It was strange. All of the space suits Caelestis owned were bulky and difficult to move in. They had consisted of several pieces, including gloves and boots and cumbersome oxygen kits. What lay before him, however, was the complete opposite.

The suit and its inner lining draping over the bench appeared sleek, thin, and flexible. Due to the slickness of its material, the steel-gray inner lining of the suit sliding off the bench. Rhys jerked his shirt off and drew the inner lining before his face for inspection. Though he didn't recognize the material, he knew its purpose—to cool and ventilate. Pulling away the double zipper he peered into the suit. He noticed a small coil of slender tubing covered in sterile plastic. Frowning, for he knew what it was by its location in the suit, he followed the tube to a pouch on the thigh.

Groaning, he let the suit go slack and rolled his head back in annoyance. It was a catheter. There was no way to relieve himself once in the suit, but the idea of having a coil of tubing snaked up into him was not an appealing one.

After visiting the toilet to relieve himself, he stripped from his clothes and stood nude before the suit. Clenching his jaws in silent resolve, he opened the inner lining, stepped into it, and began drawing it up his body. As the cool material wicked away his body heat, chills spread down his spine and the hair on his arms stood on end. After glowering down at the catheter, Rhys removed the sterilizing cover, inserted the coil, and inflated the small bulb along the tube to prevent it from slipping out. After the urge to relieve himself again passed, he continued to pull the inner lining up his chest.

Chilled, he straightened the long sleeves and pressed the double zipper against his chest to form the suit to his body. Once in place—slightly off-center of his chest—he zipped it up, allowing only the material around his throat to remain open. With gentle hands, he took the collar and folded it, fastening it to a clasp on the side of his neck.

He walked a few paces in the inner lining, frowning. It was tight, very tight. Although he could move well with it on, every muscle, every curve, every angle of his body was emphasized. Picking at the lining's edges, he returned to the suit itself. Though his feet were covered by the lining, his wrists and hands were not. Briefly, he ran a finger over the suit, taking in its fine craftsmanship before peering into it.

Despite its sleek appearance, it had some heft which was reassuring. It appeared thin, but he had to trust that his ancestors understood the need for protection from the elements of space—radiation, heat, and cold. He sat on the bench, opened the suit, and slid in his left leg. Once his foot was secured in the boot, he moved to his right leg. Where the suit met the urine collection pack trapped alongside his right thigh, there was a nozzle, presumably to release fluid should the pack become too full. Ensuring that the urine collection pack was aligned with the external nozzle, he continued pulling the suit up along his body.

Realizing that once he had the suit on, he would have less dexterity, he paused with the suit folded around his waist and turned to examine the helmet. Nearly three-quarters of the helmet was made of a polycarbonate plastic dusted in gold, resulting in a one hundred eighty-degree field of vision. Rhys ran a ginger hand around the interior of the helmet and, finding nothing suspicious, brought it closer to inspect the seal which would attach to his suit. Encouraged by the helmet's soundness and relative heft, he set it down and returned to dressing.

Sliding his shoulder into the suit, he watched as his hand moved down the sleeve into the attached glove. At the tips of the glove, he met a rough patch of material. Curious, he slipped his other arm into the suit and began adjusting the suit's torso to his form. He pulled at the collar before snapping it into place.

Rhys looked down at himself. The suit didn't appear to fit correctly. It was baggy around his crotch and armpits and the collar was loose. He searched for some sort of hint before locating a large flat button along his hip. Warily, he pushed it; the air within vented, causing the suit to cinch down on his body. The spare room that had been at his armpits disappeared and the baggy material around his crotch tightened. The rough surfaces in his gloves, which he had thought were only at his fingertips, now pressed uncomfortably against his palms.

Though the majority of the suit was white, a thick, black line ran down the back and over his right shoulder, stopping short just of his chest. "Omega Technologies" was printed in small characters along his left arm.

Seeing himself in uniform, in gear outside of that which he had known for the past year of his life, instilled resolve in him. Courage solidified in his heart, and his gut hardened.

Spotting a small pack of pills hanging at the top of the locker door, Rhys leaned forward to examine the baggie. According to the directions, the purpose of the pills was to break up solids and turn them to liquids, thus eliminating the need to defecate for up to five days or one hundred twenty-five hours. He hurriedly took one. That was one biological function he didn't want to have to deal with while in zero gravity.

After reviewing his equipment and glancing at himself in the mirror, he grabbed his open helmet and strode from the locker room.

Clutching at his newly reformed resolve, he stepped before the hangar door. It whizzed open, and he walked in. Hodge and Kallen, who were seated against the maintenance unit talking, glanced up at him. Ignoring their alarmed stares, he walked into the hangar. "Zain," he called.

"What?" replied Zain from atop *Heather*.

Hodge leapt up and ran to Rhys. "Look at you," he murmured, circling Rhys.

In his friend's gaze, Rhys found fear and worry. In an attempt to calm Hodge, Rhys punched his shoulder fondly. "Hey, I didn't bring you along to slack." Switching to Nefegian, he continued to *Heather,* ignoring Kallen's anxious eyes. "Have you finished the calculations?"

"Almost," replied Zain who leaned against the cockpit and vigorously tapped his glowing handheld. "I finished the calculations, but they need to be on this so your unit can access them." Zain looked up at Rhys, nodded, and continued working. "Our people knew how to prepare for anything. The bulky suits we used on Caelestis were nothing like what you have on now."

Forge and Otto, who had been working together to adjust a thruster, finally pulled away from their work. Forge seemed unsurprised, but the look on Otto's face was one of instant fascination. Quickly, the boy crawled out from under the jet and joined Rhys.

As Otto touched Rhys' suit and examined him, Forge said, "We've already filled the secondary oxygen tanks behind the cockpit seat. We have your primary air here." He motioned to a small pile of supplies just beyond the jet. Rhys noticed among them was a survival pack like the one he and Alina had used upon their arrival on Earth. Seeing his gaze, Forge continued. "Since arriving on Earth, all of the maintenance units are equipped with survival packs. We've given you ours. We're going to put spare clothes in the smaller bag there. You have your primary air tanks as well as a rifle, handgun, and resonance cutters."

"What are these ports for?" asked Otto from behind Rhys.

Rhys motioned to Forge, who circled him and, after a brief conversation with Zain, said, "How you're going to connect to the jet."

"Hey," called Ethos from within Hodge's pocket. "Take me out." Hodge joined them and held out the AI. "You're not done dressing."

Rhys glanced at the others before saying in Nefegian, "I took care of the catheter."

"No, no. Everything with the suit is fine. You missed pieces."

"What pieces? This is all that was in the locker."

"Mmm, no. Take Forge; you'll need help. You're missing the tracers."

Sighing, Rhys passed his helmet to Otto and started back across the hangar with Forge by his side.

"What's going on?" asked Leo who appeared in the hangar doorway with Rullena behind him. He stared at Rhys before silently stepping aside. Rhys expected Hodge to follow, but his friend returned to Kallen and instead stood at a distance.

"You're upsetting them," said Forge as they walked down the hall.

Rhys entered the pilots' briefing room and returned to his open locker. Sure enough, at the top of the locker where the helmet had been there sat a small box. He drew out the box and carefully opened the lid. Inside, he found four slivers of thin metal as well as a small tube of what appeared to be applicator gel. "Electroencephalogram tracers," he read, taking one of the pieces from the box and running his fingers along it.

"Ethos just sent the information to Pathos," said Forge. "Sit down. I'll do it."

Rhys perched on the bench next to his clothes and passed the box to Forge. While the medical student worked to unscrew the tube of applicator gel, Rhys folded his clothes and gathered his boots. By the time he was finished, Forge had laid out the slivers of metal on the bench and lined the first one with the gel. With ginger fingers, the med student drew the tracer into his hands and approached Rhys.

"The first two adhere to your temples. The other two go along the back of your head between the occipital lobe and cerebellum," Forge explained. Leaning in, he placed the first tracer along his right temple and firmly pressed on it. As he lubricated the second one, he added, "These won't come off without the unbinding agent. I'll put it in your pack just in case."

"Hey," murmured Rhys lowly. "Can I ask you… for a favor?"

Forge paused in his work. "Yes."

"If I don't make it back… will you make sure Kallen delivers the baby safely?"

Forge gently laid the second tracer close to the empty receptors along Rhys' left temple. "I thought it was already understood that I would do that."

"Just…" He met Forge's gaze. "Make sure others know how to help when the time comes. Teach Hodge and Leo; tell them what to do. I don't want you being the only one who has the knowledge."

"I will," replied Forge.

"And you'll watch over the others as well? I mean, their health?"

Forge nodded, prepping the third.

"So… Was it worth it?"

"Was what worth it?"

"Was it worth leaving Neo-Colony Two?"

Forge scoffed, something Rhys had yet to see him do. "Of course. I've experienced more in the past few weeks than my entire life." The slight smile on his face faded. "I miss the peace of Caelestis and the commonality of the colony, but… it's much more interesting here. Everything is brighter, more colorful."

"How does Zain feel?"

"Similarly, but he doesn't show it." Forge smiled at Rhys. "I'll make him work on that."

Rhys nodded. "Listen, Forge. It's our responsibili —"

"I know," Forge interrupted. He motioned to Rhys. "Lean your head down." Rhys tucked his chin into the collar of his suit, and Forge began pushing the hair along the back of his neck upward. "I know we have a responsibility to Earth and its people."

Rhys chuckled grimly. "True, but that's not what I was going to say." Forge turned to collect the last tracer. "I was going to say, it's our responsibility to lead and protect, but… promise you'll find someone to love."

Forge tilted his head in confusion. "Love?"

"Intensely like," Rhys explained. "Someone you're very fond of."

"Ah…" Forge smiled. "Like you and Kallen?" Rhys nodded. "I promise. I'll look."

"Don't look," said Rhys. "Feel."

"Ah, right. I'll feel."

"And please, eventually tell Axel how old Veran is." He couldn't help but chuckle at what he imagined the look on Axel's face would be. "There's nothing wrong with her age, just make sure he knows."

Forge tipped Rhys' head down again and applied the final tracer. "From what I've gathered from Ethos, these tracers and those within your gloves link up to the unit's onboard AI. These are what allow you to control *Heather*." He pressed the tracer firmly onto Rhys' scalp and then drew away.

"Can you solidify the final plans here for me?" asked Rhys, still gazing at the floor. "I know you, Zain, and Ethos have been in constant contact. Can you let me in on what we're doing?"

Forge sat beside him. "We're going to run some tests right now to ensure compatibility between yourself and *Heather*. Afterward, we're going to begin preparations to launch *Apex*. Because Ethos is masterminding this entire operation, Zain and I will be divided between *Apex* to handle the launch of your unit and the rocket engine."

"I want you working with me," said Rhys. "I want Zain watching over *Apex*."

"To keep the others safe," concluded Forge. Rhys nodded. "Fine, I can do that. Once *Apex* launches, we're going to try to get outside of port to launch you and the rocket engine. According to Ethos, the catapult, when given enough room, can expand to nearly four times its standard width." Rhys saw the look on Forge's face change. "Although the catapult can expand and adjust, it lacks a point for vertical liftoff, meaning that, in order for you to launch from the catapult, *Apex* will have to be titled at a minimum of forty-five degrees."

"Given the fuel reserves the shuttle has, that may or may not be possible," mused Rhys.

"Correct."

"Has Ethos provided an estimated time for how long *Apex* might remain airborne?"

"No, not yet. It will only be able to provide that once the shuttle has launched as it cannot with certainty discern how much fuel will be used upon the initial launch."

"Because it's been resting for over two centuries." Rhys sighed. "And the backup plan?"

Forge remained silent.

"There is no backup plan." Rhys stood and rolled his neck to familiarize himself with the weight of the tracers along the back of his head. Grabbing his clothes and boots, they left the locker room.

"Rullena," called Forge, peering into the control room. Rullena, who sat at a station with her hands still bound, looked up from her conversation with Leo. "We're going to start tests for *Heather*. Once Rhys is in the cockpit, we'll clear the hangar. Be prepared for emergency actions should something go wrong."

Rhys gazed at the monitors overhead for a moment. Gealdir's cockpit was empty. He was obviously on break while his unit was resupplied. Frowning, Rhys leaned in the doorway.

"I know that look," said Leo. "You don't have the fuel to make it to Firekli and back."

"Who's going to stop Gealdir? These units have more than enough power to destroy a city."

"Leave Gealdir to us. We'll figure something out—"

A sudden beep emitted from the station where Rullena sat. Alarmed, she looked to Rhys and said, "It's an outside communication being passed through the bridge to the control room."

Rhys stalked across the control room, leaned on the paneling, and acquired the transmission.

"This is Sal Damien, former Minister of Education in Brechin. To whom am I speaking?"

Leo nearly fell out of his chair. Though Rhys was certainly thrilled to hear Sal's voice, he hesitated. Why was Leo's father contacting *Apex*? How did he know about the shuttle?

"Who is it?" asked Forge.

"Leo's father," replied Rhys, straightening himself. He thought for a moment, glancing at Leo who was shivering in apprehension. Rhys knew Leo had been deathly worried for his family since their departure from Brechin all those months ago, but they needed to play it safe. If Sal and Leo's brother, Sean, had been caught, then this could be a trap. Clearing his throat, Rhys replied, "We are a group of resistance fighters who have need of this ship. Why is the former Minister of Education contacting us?"

Leo returned to his chair to gaze worriedly at the radio.

"We're here to help you," came Sal's reply.

"See?" gasped Leo.

Rhys motioned to his friend for silence before saying, "What could a former royal family head do to help us?"

"My eldest son and I have been snooping around the capital. We know about your ship, and we know about a *second* ship."

Wide-eyed, Rhys looked at Leo who shrugged. Not wanting to play into their hands if it was a trap, he calmly said, "We've already set our plan in motion. Why would we need a second ship?"

"Because according to the readings I'm receiving from your ship, you're low on fuel," replied Sal.

Rhys cursed and leaned on the paneling again. "Your readings are incorrect. We don't need fuel."

Leo motioned his displeasure to Rhys. "What are you doing? We need *gawan* fuel."

Rhys waved to Leo and cued the radio once more. "Minister?" When there was no answer, he turned to Rullena. "Where would they be that they can receive readings from this ship's bridge?"

Rullena shook her head in complete bewilderment. "I honestly don't know. The only way to contact this control room is from the bridge or a radio within the temple."

"Rhys," moaned Leo. "Come on. We're going to lose them."

"Calm down," replied Rhys, though he too was worried he had scared off Sal and Sean.

"Well, that's a real shame," Sal finally said. "We brought this ship all the way from Bathsgate."

"They have the ship," groaned Leo, folding over the paneling.

"We're interested," Rhys said into the radio.

"I thought so," replied Sal, "because I'm calling you from the bridge of *Lucille*."

Rhys looked over his shoulder. "Forge, get Ethos in here. Now." As Forge hurried off to the hangar, Rhys spoke to Sal. "You're speaking with an expert on white god technology. What type of ship is *Lucille* and what are its specs?"

Sal's response was immediate. "We are unwilling to share that information. We will, however, be happy to speak with you face-to-face."

A quiet beep alerted Rhys to the small call-box that had flickered onto the screen. He touched the screen.

The monitor overhead flickered on and Sal appeared. Rhys half-expected the former Minister of Education to appear haggard and worn from constantly being on the run. To his great surprise, however, Sal seemed to be at the peak of health. His golden hair was pulled back in a sleek horsetail and his skin flawlessly clean.

The hard expression on Sal's face morphed as he saw Rhys. His brows rose in surprise and a smile cracked across his face. "Rhys?"

"Hi, Sal," replied Rhys.

Leo leapt onto Rhys excitedly. "Father!"

Sal rose from his chair. "Leo!"

Suddenly, another flaxen-haired person lurched into the frame. "Leo?"

"Sean!" cried Leo, melting into Rhys. "You're safe." His throat was thick. "I was so worried."

"How did you end up… Why are you…" Sean breathed heavily to contain his excitement and relief before looking at his father.

Beaming, Sal cleared his throat. "Well, this changes *everything*."

"Do you really have a ship?" asked Rhys.

"Of course," replied Sal. "How do you think we're calling you?"

"Where are you right now?"

"Just outside of Brechin's suburbs. We have a… what was it called? A calliloid shield on. That's why we haven't been found."

"We have so many questions," bubbled Leo.

"Gauging by your appearance, Rhys, it would seem you're preparing for a journey." Sal leaned on the paneling. "Let us help you with that."

"Here," said Forge, reappearing with Ethos. Rhys took the AI.

"You have new friends," Sal said with interest.

"I have confirmed that they are on *Lucille*," interjected Ethos. "Their ship is roughly sixteen kilometers east of us."

Rhys tried to peer behind Sal. "What kind of ship is it?"

Ethos chuckled. "A supply shuttle belonging to Omega Technologies."

Rhys gaped at the monitor as Sal smiled proudly. "How did you… Where was it? How did you find it?"

"Long story short, once in Bathsgate, we heard rumors from contacts that a white gods' ship was being held in secret. It took a few weeks, but we found out where it was and commandeered it," explained Sal.

"Took a few days just to figure out how to operate it," added Sean. "But once we were inside, no one could get in. So, it became ours."

"We knew all of you were fighting on the front lines," said Sal. "We wanted to help any way we could and taking a supply ship from the Brechin military seemed like the best way to go about that."

Rhys playfully shoved Leo, who was grinning ear-to-ear, and then nodded. "Ethos will provide you with a detailed explanation of our plans. Forgive me. I must cut our reunion short. I have testing to do. Rullena, Leo, and Ethos will inform you of what is to come."

"It's good to see you, Rhys," said Sal fondly. "You look well, if not a little tired."

"Same to you." Rhys passed Ethos to Leo and followed Forge into the hangar.

41
ETHEREAL BLUE

KALLEN, HODGE, KASHIM, ZAIN, AND Otto stood waiting next to *Heather*. Upon seeing Rhys, all conversation quieted. Otto hurried forward and handed Rhys his helmet.

Studying his digital handheld, Zain said, "Logos has set your launch time for one hour and fifty-four minutes from now. The launch time is flexible but only by a few minutes. Once you're connected with *Heather*, Ethos will share with you the more detailed portions of the plan." He finally looked up from his handheld. "Questions?"

"No," Rhys mumbled.

"Put your helmet on. Do not engage oxygen flow," instructed Zain, motioning to Rhys.

Rhys slid his helmet on and connected it to his suit. Otto guided his hands to the clasps on either side of his neck. Once finished, Rhys stepped onto the mechanized ladder which folded out from the port wing and ascended to the cockpit. Distantly, he heard Zain tell everyone to retreat to the control room.

"It's you and me," declared Ethos. The AI's voice was inside his helmet. "The sensors in your gloves allow you to interact with machines and computers, that includes me." Rhys stepped into the cockpit and seated himself in the cockpit chair. "Do you see the slot directly to your left? Put me in there."

"You're sure?" whispered Rhys.

"Hey, as long as you have me, there's nothing we can't do," assured Ethos.

Rhys swallowed and obeyed. The AI disappeared into the paneling. The cockpit chair slid forward; *Heather* began humming. A harness layered in shimmering metal slithered over his shoulders and down his chest. Heart hammering, Rhys remained motionless.

"Right, let's get started," said Ethos, its voice in his ear. "Control Room, are you ready?"

"Roger," replied Zain. "Test number one will be to perform basic ignition operations. Ensure that all instruments are functioning and that power flow is stable. Copy?"

"Roger," said Rhys, his throat tight.

There was a momentary pause before Ethos began speaking. "Listen to me, Rhys. The system that each of these units is equipped with is humanity's first attempt to integrate man and machine. Forget your independence. Remember who you were when you had Pathos. Remember how it felt to be connected with a high-functioning computer, to have your questions answered instantly, to have whatever knowledge you wanted before your eyes. *Heather* will become an extension of yourself, and you and I will be bound."

Rhys nodded.

"Remember," chided Ethos. "Remember how it felt."

"Yeah," he murmured.

"Ignition," replied Ethos.

A jolt like a bullet to the center of his back thwacked into him, tearing a gasp from him. What felt like tiny, hot needles entered that spot along his back. He reared upward, the restraints keeping him bound to the chair. A whimper escaped his throat.

"Steady…" Ethos encouraged. "You're being connected to *Heather.* Easy, Rhys."

Panting, Rhys tried to keep his body from trembling, but the sudden pain along his back had spiked his adrenaline. A tingling sensation not unlike what happened when his limbs fell asleep began pricking his hands.

"Don't move," instructed Ethos. "Easy. Deep breaths."

The paneling before him illuminated in a hue of blue, and instruments he knew well materialized along an interactive, holographic board. The cockpit glass surrounding him became crowded with a variety of indicators, warnings, crosshairs, analysis tools, and measurements. A radar screen morphed along the paneling to Rhys' right while a holographic sphere which he recognized as a Unit Positioning Orb appeared above it. Realizing he understood and knew how to read and operate every instrument, Rhys relaxed.

"*Heather's* cockpit is tailored to each pilot. Your knowledge is reflected on the surrounding paneling. This is why the pilot needs to understand flight and has experience operating units in space."

"*Heather*, all systems are operational," remarked Zain in Rhys' ear. "When you're ready, you may begin your tests."

Ethos chuckled. "I had forgotten how complex humans are. I've got *a lot* of information on you now."

"Great," Rhys muttered, scanning the glowing instruments and gauges. It was as Zain had said. All systems were operational; fuel levels were at maximum; the nuclear core hummed flawlessly.

Pleased, Rhys decided to test the thrusters. The roar around him grew, and *Heather* began quivering.

"*Heather,* you have not been authorized to test thrusters," said Zain calmly.

"Sorry, sorry!" Rhys quavered, starting to reach toward the paneling.

"Stop," ordered Ethos. Rhys froze. "Put your hand back down." Rhys obeyed. "Control Room, AI is overriding pilot's command."

"Roger," replied Zain.

The bellowing of the engines died, and Rhys took a deep breath. "Sorry."

"I haven't given you full control yet," said Ethos. "Now, listen to me when I say this—don't take your hands off the readers. You touching the paneling isn't going to do anything. Your commands are delivered via biofeedback through the sensors in your hands and the tracers. Don't absentmindedly think that to pull back on the throttle, you should do it manually. It doesn't work like that. Got it?"

"Yes."

"Why did the thrusters engage?" queried Ethos.

"Because I told them to."

"How?"

"I thought it."

"You must control everything you think. I can, of course, act as a filter and safeguard you to a certain extent, but be cognizant of thoughts that can directly influence *Heather.*"

"Right."

"Control Room, we will now test the thrusters," said Ethos.

"All systems are still operational. Your test is a go," replied Zain.

Rhys glanced at the instruments around him and then at the small holographic diagram of his unit being displayed just above his head. *Thrusters one through four, engage at five percent,* he thought.

The roar around him grew, and the diagram above his head illuminated the two thrusters just under the unit's nose and the two at his stern.

Disengage. Thrusters four through eight, engage at five percent, he continued.

The unit lowered to the floor before slowly rising once more as the thrusters they had stolen from *Clover* engaged. Rhys gazed upward at the unit diagram. The moment he began thinking about the wiring within the thrusters, the diagram zoomed in on the port rear thruster to reveal a chart that mimicked what he, Forge, Otto, and Zain had been working on. Everything looked to be in order. He analyzed the other seven thrusters before reviewing the gauges and instruments before him.

As he set the unit back on the hangar floor, Zain said, "*Heather,* disengage your engines and come to idle."

Rhys obeyed, and the unit fell still.

"Uh, Ethos?" asked Forge.

"Yes, Forge?"

"I want all of Rhys' vitals accessible to the control room for monitoring. Is that possible?"

There was a momentary pause before Ethos asked, "Do you see them now?"

"Yes, thank you. Please ensure that his vitals are available for monitoring at all times."

"Once we reach orbit, that will not be possible; however, I will do what I can until then," replied Ethos.

"Rhys, I have a few adjustments to make to the thrusters. I want to do another ignition test. Turn off the system and disengage from *Heather,*" said Zain.

"Roger," replied Rhys. He gave the glowing paneling a cursory glance before issuing the order to disengage. A thud rocked his body as the system disconnected from him. *Heather* quieted, and the blue ambience of the cockpit faded. When everything fell silent, Rhys took a steadying breath and laid back his head.

Zain and Forge appeared before his unit. While Zain moved under the jet's belly, Forge activated the mechanized ladder and made his way to the cockpit. Ethos opened the cockpit glass, and Rhys stood.

"How are you feeling?" asked Forge.

"I think I'm fine," said Rhys. He didn't feel any ill-effects from his connection to *Heather*, but he definitely felt something akin to loss. It was profoundly familiar.

"Even now, you still remember what it's like to be separated from an AI," Ethos chimed inside his helmet.

"It's not something you forget," replied Rhys.

"Your vitals were all strong. Your brain waves indicated nervousness and apprehension and, of course, your heart rate was high. Otherwise, you seem like the perfect pilot candidate." Forge nudged him familiarly as Rhys and Hodge often did to one another.

Rhys leaned on the edge of the cockpit and looked toward the control room. "How is everyone?"

"Anxious, like you. We've changed the target feeds from Gealdir to you so we can follow everything that happens both inside and outside the cockpit." Forge nodded. He must have sensed what Rhys was wanting to ask. "Kallen hasn't said much. Hodge has been sitting in the corner, silently watching."

Rhys thought. "Do you think either of them would want to do radio communications with me?"

Forge glanced at Zain. "I honestly... don't feel that's a good idea." Rhys took notice of the medical student's word choice—*feel*. "The others aren't... They're out of their element. They're in an unfamiliar environment and you're—"

Forge fell silent. Rhys smiled grimly. "I've become a stranger once more." Looking to change the subject, he asked, "I see the rocket engine there has an attachment along its dorsal."

"Once you feel secure in your control of *Heather*, we'll have you move your unit to the rocket engine and attach it there." Forge looked down as Zain spoke via AI. "We have time for two more tests. Make them count."

"Right."

Forge slid off the port wing with a comforting smile. Rhys touched the blank paneling beside him. "Ethos, once we approach lunar orbit, what's the plan on getting to the moon's surface?"

"We'll leave the rocket engine in orbit and descend in *Heather*."

"You know precisely where Osiris is being kept?"

"I do, in fact," replied the AI.

"Can you get us into the facility?"

"Yes."

"Could an AI alone do what I'm planning to do?"

"Nice try, but no. It's got to be a manual override."

"What can I expect inside the lunar facility?"

"Uhhh..." Ethos chuckled. "You and I will be surprised, how about that? Don't let that frighten you though. Seriously. Think about it. If Osiris and its base are man-made, why would the men who left it there make it impervious to other humans, especially if they thought Earth was doomed? They would have wanted to make it as simple as possible so future humans could perhaps use the base to contact others—assuming they were advanced enough to make a lunar landing. Osiris was put there by humans *for* humans. Even if Osiris no longer perceives itself in such regard, it has had no way to increase its external defenses. It has no access to resources or materials."

"And you have all the necessary calculations to navigate us successfully to the moon, land at the facility, disable it, and get us back?" murmured Rhys.

"Yes. Zain made all the calculations and loaded them a while ago. If everything goes according to plan, it will take eight and half minutes to leave Earth's atmosphere and forty-nine hours and six minutes to reach lunar orbit. We'll be in lunar orbit for twenty-four minutes before we pass the base. We'll descend and complete the mission. Sound good?"

"Yeah," murmured Rhys.

"I thought you'd be happier. We have a solid plan now."

"Doesn't mean I'm excited about it though."

Zain hit the belly of the jet. "We're ready, Rhys. Give us a minute to return to the control room."

"Right." Rhys watched as Forge and Zain exited the hangar. It was oddly comforting knowing that people from his colony had his back. It eased his restlessness to think that Zain was in complete command of *Heather's* maintenance, repairs, and preparations.

It wasn't until Ethos prompted him that he seated himself once more in the cockpit and the glass closed around him. "Ready?" asked Ethos. Rhys nodded. For the control room's benefit, Ethos said, "Ignition."

That same painful jolt in his back cracked along his spine, wrenching him upward briefly. Panting, he bowed his head and glared at the floor while *Heather* roared to life around him. The cockpit was doused in a blue hue as the numerous gauges and instruments, graphs and diagrams appeared on the paneling and cockpit glass once more.

"Very good," murmured Ethos. "Staying calm, staying focused."

Rhys straightened himself and scanned the instruments.

"*Heather*, go ahead and test your thrusters again," came Zain's voice from the speaker in Rhys' ear.

For the next half hour or so, Rhys worked to follow Zain's instructions, eventually maneuvering *Heather* atop the rocket. Using *Heather's* hull cameras, he aligned himself with the rocket engine's clasps and docking conduits. When a diagram on the cockpit glass indicated that he was aligned, he gingerly set the jet atop the rocket engine.

His unit connected, and the clasps along the rocket engine locked *Heather* to it. Conduits intertwined between his unit and the rocket engine before several mechanisms within *Heather's* hull clicked. When all clasps and unit attachments were connected, he fixed his gaze on the wall on the far side of the hangar. Throughout it all, Ethos provided precise counsel and guidance, the AI's voice a constant stream of knowledge and steadfastness.

"We're going to—" Zain's voice cut out.

Rhys glanced at his instruments in an attempt to figure out what it was Zain was studying but found nothing noteworthy. After waiting a moment, Rhys prompted Zain. "Control Room, is something wrong?"

It was Ethos that replied. "Brechin forces are surrounding the ship." The AI sounded preoccupied, as though its attention was focused more on *Apex* than on *Heather*.

"Help them," Rhys instructed.

Ethos sighed. "Launch time for *Apex* might have just been bumped up. I'm going to guide the others. Don't move."

Once again left in silence, Rhys peered up at the ceiling of the hangar looming nearby and listened. After a moment, he realized that *Heather's* cameras remained under his control and so asked for the aft camera so he could better see the hangar door. From his vantage point, he could discern no activity.

His desire to know what was going on outside *Apex* was strong and the worry brewing in his gut made him nauseous. Although he was sitting in a war machine, once again, he was helpless. He could literally do nothing to assist his crew.

With a soft sigh, he peered about the cockpit. All the provisions they had prepared were packed tightly behind the cockpit seat. His primary oxygen tank was attached to the back of the chair; his secondary oxygen tanks, basic life support, and reserve oxygen unit were tucked against his survival pack. Rhys also found a handgun holstered to the outside of his secondary oxygen tanks, a short rifle cinched atop the survival pack, and his resonance cutters within grasping range. Packed beneath his survival gear was his magnetic board.

Truly, he had everything he needed for the mission. All that was left was connecting *Heather* to the rocket engine, running a pre-flight checklist, and then launching. It sounded simple but with hundreds of factors playing a part in the mission, would they be able to pull it off?

"Control Room, can you give me an update?" prompted Rhys after sitting in silence for a few minutes.

"Hold on, Rhys," came Forge's voice. Though it wasn't the response he wanted, it comforted him to know that at least someone was still listening.

Another few minutes passed during which red strobes in the hangar began whirring to alert hangar personnel of an external threat. Anxiously, Rhys shifted in his seat and scanned his instruments for the hundredth time.

Suddenly, from deep within the cavernous shuttle, a low rumble began building. The hangar floor tremored violently.

The thunderous rumble rose in decibel until it broke into a high-pitched shriek. The entire hangar quivered. The scream of *Apex's* ancient engines swelled, and Rhys felt the bottom fall out of his stomach. The station where they had been working on *Heather* shifted and loose tools rolled toward the back of the hangar.

"Rhys," breathed Forge. "*Apex* has launched. We are escaping port to meet up with *Lucille* for refueling. In thirty seconds, we'll be stable. Let's run the pre-launch checklist."

With a single thought, the camera on his starboard wing flickered on to reveal Ethos' bot furiously working at a command panel far below. "This is so dumb," Rhys murmured anxiously. The rocket engine was meant for a jet, but that had been over two centuries ago. Any number of things could go wrong.

By the time he and Forge finished the checklist, Rhys was a simmering mess of nervousness.

"All systems are a go," interrupted Forge.

Rhys swallowed. "What happens if something goes wrong?"

"Then Ethos will walk you through recovery."

Rhys nodded shakily. His time was drawing near. "Can you tell me what's going on outside?"

"Brechin forces were trying to break into the ship. It became a problem when they started succeeding. Ethos engaged the blast doors to prevent further insurgence, but we needed to take off." Forge sighed. "Everything is fine. Rullena and Zain are on the bridge with Kashim, Otto, and Leo."

"Where're Kallen and Hodge?" asked Rhys.

There was a long pause before Forge said, "They're right here, Rhys."

"Listen up!" boomed Ethos into Rhys' ear. The AI's voice was strained. "*Heather's* launch sequence will begin in three minutes. We're moving you to the catapult."

"Wait. Now?" quavered Rhys, looking up at the cockpit camera. He knew the control room could see him. "Now? Are we done refueling and everything? Where're Sal and Sean?"

"Everything is fine," replied Forge with more authority than Rhys was accustomed to hearing from the medical student. Forge switched to Interstellar Nefegian and continued. "Control to Bridge. Opening hangar doors."

The bridge's reply came instantly. "Roger, preparing *Heather* and rocket engine for catapult launch," said Rullena in Nefegian.

As conversation between Forge and the bridge continued, Rhys looked upward at the doors opening along the hangar's ceiling. The lift began rising from the floor. Slowly, *Heather* and the rocket engine were swallowed by the catapult chamber as the lift positioned the entire unit for launch. Settled like a bullet in a rifle chamber, Rhys saw the narrow catapult widen and stretch to accommodate its oversized load. Azure sky appeared at the end of the runway.

"Hey, hey, hey..." murmured Ethos comfortingly. "Calm down. Easy."

Until that moment, Rhys had been unaware of his rasping breathing and trembling body; his hands and feet were icy. As the rocket engine settled against the blast shield and connected to the catapult, a *thunk* reverberated.

Panting, Rhys leaned into his harness and stared at the floor. "I can't do it," he whispered. "I can't do this." Panic climbed up his throat while his heart hammered painfully against his chest. "I can't do this. I want out. Ethos, I want out."

"Come on, Rhys," said the AI. "Deep breaths."

So much could go wrong. It was a suicide mission. He could easily die within ten seconds of launch. What waited for him outside *Apex* was death.

"I can't do this," Rhys wheezed, clinging to the seat's armrests. "I can't do this."

"Stop saying that!" snapped Kallen into his helmet. Her voice tore through his hysteria and held his core still. "Stop saying you can't do this. You can. You're the only one. Let's go, Rhys!" Though her voice quivered, her words gripped him. "You've got this."

"Don't…" Hodge cleared his throat. "Don't worry about us. Zain and Rullena are going to take care of everything. Ethos already taught them about the ship. We'll be fine."

Still breathing heavily, Rhys leaned back in his chair. "What's the ship's plans once I launch?"

"Head to Firekli," said Hodge. "We've got the fuel now. We'll take out Firekli's plasma cannon, deal with Gealdir, and then go to Neo-Colony Two. Sound good?" Rhys nodded. "You do you, Rhys," his friend concluded.

"We will be unable to communicate with you once you leave Earth's atmosphere. Ethos will take care of you," explained Forge.

Again, Rhys nodded.

"Start the launching sequence," interrupted Zain from the bridge. "Control Room, you're in command."

"Here we go," Ethos murmured.

"Catapult connection, secured. Assistant catapult conduits one through four, secured," began Forge in Nefegian. "Opening all catapult vents; engaging catapult fans." A distant winding up followed by a deep hum engulfed Rhys as the catapult's hundreds of fans powered up. "Catapult vents, open," Forge continued. "Fans at seventy percent and rising. Starting remote ignition of rocket engine. In five, four, three, two, one. Ignition."

Rhys felt *Heather* shudder, and he was jarred into his harness. Adrenaline pumping through his body, he felt unbearably nauseous.

"Control Room to Bridge. *Heather* and rocket engine are prepared for launch. Initiate pre-planned launch procedures."

"Bridge confirms. Initiating pre-planned launch procedures," replied Zain. "All personnel, prepare for pitch bow angle sixty. I repeat, all personnel, prepare for pitch bow angle sixty." Even over the dull roar of the rocket engine's idling, Rhys could hear *Apex's* screaming engines as the bow of the shuttle began tipping upward, slowly tilting the dorsal catapult vertical.

Having nowhere else to look, he watched as the pink and orange clouds of the setting sun at the end of the catapult were replaced with a vast sky of endless purple and navy. By the time *Apex* stopped moving, Rhys was lying on his back, gripping the handles at the end of his armrests.

"Pitch bow angle sixty, achieved. Control Room, you are clear for launch," said Zain.

"Remote launch of *Heather* and rocket engine in fifteen seconds," confirmed Forge solemnly.

The roar around Rhys increased tenfold, and his entire body began vibrating horribly. Wheezing, he prepared himself for the g-forces that would hit him during launch. He scanned the instruments around him to check for abnormalities. When he found none, he fixed his gaze once more on the abyss above him.

"Ten seconds," announced Forge.

As the medical student began counting down, Rhys glanced up at the cockpit camera, knowing Kallen and Hodge were watching him. He wanted to lie to them and tell them that he would come home, but he couldn't promise that. He couldn't even promise that he would make it out of Earth's atmosphere. He just, more than anything, wanted them to know how much he loved them. All of them.

"Come back to us, Rhys," said Kallen over Forge's countdown.

Rhys nodded.

"Two... one... Full remote ignition. Catapult launching."

Rhys felt the entire rocket engine quake as the catapult whipped the rocket forward in a single slingshot motion. The orange glow of the rocket's flames, which had begun to fill the catapult chute, disappeared, and he was slung into the sky. The cockpit glass around him darkened to a black, impenetrable shield.

"Engines at ninety percent." Forge's voice was still strong. "All systems, nominal. *Heather* and rocket engine have launched. We have full lift off."

"Ethos?" Rhys could barely form the AI's name on his lips. Shuddering, he clung to his chair and gazed up at the numerous gauges before him.

"I'm here," asserted Ethos. "I had to disconnect from *Apex*. We're no longer in range. All systems, nominal. Look at your instruments." Rhys did as he was told. "Reducing rocket engine to sixty percent to lessen the effects of breaking the sound barrier." Rhys couldn't hear a difference in the roar around him. His mind was thoughtless, his body was both hyperaware and numb. "We're going to throttle up in thirty seconds."

Rhys glanced once more at his instruments. Already, he was five and a half kilometers up and one kilometer downrange of the launch site. Speed: one thousand two hundred seven kilometers per hour.

"Go to throttle up," instructed Ethos.

Rhys increased the rocket engine speed, did a sweep of his instruments, and then sat in silence.

"We're one minute thirty-nine seconds into the flight," Ethos reported after a moment. "Thirty-five kilometers in altitude, thirty kilometers downrange. Speed: four thousand two hundred kilometers per hour. Main engine nozzles, setting course for the projected flight plan. Speed: five thousand one hundred fifty kilometers per hour. Main engines, nominal."

Rhys closed his eyes. He needed to forget Earth.

"We've got this, Rhys," said Ethos. "Look." A map showing their trajectory leaving the atmosphere appeared on the cockpit glass. "Once we're clear of the atmosphere and have left Earth's orbit, you can rest." Rhys nodded. "We've passed the point of negative return."

"Roger," replied Rhys.

"The flash evaporator system has been activated," continued Ethos. "Four minutes, thirty-five seconds into the flight. We're halfway to orbit."

Rhys glanced at his instruments again.

Altitude: one hundred five kilometers.

Distance: three hundred kilometers downrange of launch site.

Speed: eight thousand forty-six kilometers per hour.

He looked away briefly to study a diagram of the rocket engine. When he next saw his speed, the unit had reached over eleven thousand kilometers per hour.

"Once we're in space, the cockpit glass will automatically adjust," Ethos continued. "Use the cameras if you need to look out." Rhys considered the AI's suggestion but decided against it. He didn't want to see what was going on. He didn't need any more confirmation that he was leaving home.

For what seemed like an eternity, he meditated on the roar of the rocket engine around him. Ethos had encouraged him to remember what it was like to be one with an AI, not to better his piloting skills but to prepare him for being alone in space once again. He had been born on a colony in the stark expanse of black. He had been in and out of zero gravity all his life. He was returning to what he knew best.

"Eight minutes, ten seconds into the flight," reported Ethos. "Altitude: seven hundred kilometers. We're leaving Earth's thermosphere. Entering the exosphere. Making slight adjustments to our course." There was a momentary pause before Ethos added, "Course corrected and set. Reducing main engines to twenty percent."

This time, Rhys heard a noticeable difference in the decibel of the roar around him, and he breathed deeply. Letting his shoulders go slack, he bowed his head. He was exhausted.

For several seconds, there was nothing but silence. He remained staring down at the floor, weary with fatigue. The adrenaline that had been pumping through him earlier was gone; now, he was drained.

"Rhys, we're in space," said Ethos.

Rhys looked up to find the cockpit glass transparent once again. Billions of iridescent stars glittered on a backdrop of solid black. Directly before him was the moon. Wanting to see Earth, Rhys brought up the rear camera. His breath caught in his chest, and he gaped. He expected to see a planet; he didn't expect to see the cradle of humanity illuminated in a glow of ethereal blue.

How could something so perfect exist?

"I like this feeling I'm getting from you," cooed Ethos warmly.

With unwavering eyes, Rhys continued to study the image. Kallen, Hodge, everyone on *Apex*, Sal and Sean, Brechin, New Arbroath, Firekli, Neo-Colony Two—everything was so insignificant. So meaningless… or meaningful. He couldn't decide.

The magnitude of it all was too much. Of course, he and Alina had explained to the others how insignificant they were in the grand scheme of things. He himself had tried to teach Leo astronomy. Humans were insignificant; they were irrelevant to the universe. If or how they survived was only pertinent to the species, not to the infinite stars and galaxies.

"I'm going to make it home," said Rhys after a moment.

Ethos chuckled. "I didn't expect anything else. At our current speed, we will arrive on the light side of the moon in forty-six hours. You should get some rest. I will take care of things for a while."

Rhys rested his head on the headrest but kept his gaze on the field of stars. After a few minutes of complete silence, he started to feel his eyes grow heavy. After checking his instruments and oxygen once more, he relaxed and went to sleep.

42
CONVERSATIONS WITH A FRIEND

THE FAMILIAR SENSATION OF WEIGHTLESSNESS. The feeling of his hair floating over his forehead as he fidgeted in waking sleep.

With a deep inhale, Rhys opened his eyes to find the windscreen immersed in darkness. Only a dim map at the bottom of the cockpit glass showed his location. The holographic instruments were turned off; the cockpit glass, which had been transparent, was now opaque as it had been during launch.

Clearing his throat, he composed himself. "Ethos?"

"Yes?"

Rhys released the restraints on his wrists and rolled his neck. "Why is everything dark?"

"To conserve energy."

"Can… you at least let me see out?"

The cockpit became transparent, and the moon filled the entire viewing area. "How long was I asleep?" murmured Rhys, checking the map below.

"About nineteen hours," replied Ethos. Rhys blanched. "It seems all of this has been difficult on your body. You still have another twenty-six and a half hours to go before we hit lunar orbit. You need to drink. You're mildly dehydrated."

"Can I lift my hands?"

"Yeah, I've got everything."

Rhys stretched and began fishing out the survival pack. When he finally managed to withdraw the cumbersome bag from its restraints, he left it floating before him as he searched it contents.

"Nostalgia," murmured Ethos.

Rhys popped a food tablet into his mouth, grabbed a packet of water, and gently pushed the pack over his head. "Why do you say that?"

"Because that's how you feel right now. It's an interesting sensation. It's like... warm sadness."

Rhys took a long drink from the water packet—he *was* dehydrated—and said, "So... when you left with my unit, Zain and the others were put in command of *Apex*?"

"I passed all the information I could to Zain and Forge so they could manually fly the ship. I don't like my descendants Pathos and Logos, but they're quick learners."

Rhys thought. "You were controlling everything on that ship?"

"And the ship itself. Yes."

Rhys nodded. "Compared to you, Logos and Pathos are nothing."

"Aww," hummed Ethos. "But to be honest, Pathos and Logos were at one point just as strong and capable. Over time though, that changed. Humans no longer wanted Ethos-model AIs. I became a thing of the past, and Logos and Pathos slowly became more compact and intimate until they became bio-integrated. It's not a bad thing. It's what mankind wanted."

"For the record, I think it was a mistake." Rhys fidgeted with his water packet. "I suppose that's indicative of a race of beings whose free will was squashed though."

"If you could return to Caelestis, to the way things once were, would you?"

Rhys' response was immediate. "No."

"I already knew the answer to that, but why?"

"Because then I would never have met Kallen or Hodge or any of the others. I would never have understood what friendship was or family or what it meant to make difficult decisions in times of crisis. No way. I would never go back."

"If you could take your crew back with you, would you do it?"

Rhys considered the proposition and then shook his head. "No. I wouldn't want to do that to them."

"Otto seems to have adjusted well."

"Otto needed to be in an environment devoid of any familiarity to cope with his trauma." Rhys sighed. "He's one of my biggest regrets. I should have done more to find him at the Brechin camp. Really, I should never have asked him to sail with us."

"He needed a home," replied Ethos.

"He could have found it somewhere else."

"Could he? Because from what I understand, the boy was an absolute mess when you picked him up. Finding a home had not been working out for him."

"I still wish I had never brought him aboard. Living on the streets in Firekli would have been better than the fate that awaited him at the hands of Brechin's soldiers."

"You know, Ramsen and I used to talk like this all the time. We would spend hours evaluating morally ambiguous situations and philosophizing." Ethos chuckled. "To be honest, the conversations I had with him have helped me better understand you. You may live centuries apart, but humans have always wondered the same things, faced the same ethical dilemmas. You're not the first to have regrets, nor will you be the last."

Rhys gazed out at the moon. "Thank you, Ethos."

"For what?"

"For being my partner." He sipped at the water packet and then let it drift near him. "You gave me purpose when... I was lost. You kept me grounded and reminded me who I am."

"Well... I don't know that I did all that..." murmured Ethos.

"You did," replied Rhys. "I've come to depend upon you as much if not more so than Pathos."

"How is that?"

Rhys gazed out at the black abyss. "I used Pathos as a crutch. Anything I didn't know or understand, Pathos told me. I was never without answers. Since we separated though, I've learned the importance of solving problems myself. I've learned to depend upon myself and my knowledge rather than the help of an AI."

"And how do I play into this?"

"You're like another human." Rhys didn't expect those words, yet there they were. "You provide guidance and suggestions, recommendations on courses of action, but you don't always know the answers. You call me out when I've done wrong and encourage me when I'm weak." He chuckled as understanding colored his thoughts. "You're not just a partner; you're a friend."

For a long minute, there was nothing but the sound of *Heather* that filled the silence between them, allowing Rhys the chance to ponder on why he had said something so absurd. An artificial intelligence unit, a friend? It was laughable.

"Thanks, Rhys," Ethos finally said. "I've... never been called a friend before."

Picking up on the shift in the AI's tone, Rhys asked with some hesitancy, "Do you really feel emotion? Or are you mimicking it?"

Ethos chortled. "Both. I'm a learning AI, remember? Over time, I pick up emotions and learn how to reuse them in given situations. Do you remember my first activation with you and Leo?"

"Yes."

"Do you remember how... sporadic and illogical I was at the time? I hadn't interacted with another human in hundreds of years. So, when I woke, how was I supposed to act?"

"But you've relearned."

"No, not relearned. *Learned*," corrected Ethos. "Ramsen and I were close, but he was the only human who ever used me. No other humans interacted with me, not even while we were aboard *Apex*. So, to suddenly be thrown into a situation where I had a primary user but I was being utilized and depended upon by numerous people was a learning experience. To be honest, my coordinating *Apex*'s launch, *Heather's* preparations, and your crew's training was a culmination of the months of knowledge I gained from being with you. I knew who was best suited for what; I knew what needed to be taught and what needed to be skipped. I was multitasking and interacting with several people at once."

"You were experiencing leadership," concluded Rhys.

"Ah... That's what that was. Leadership." Ethos chuckled. "I like it. I like guiding others." A hint of mischievousness entered his voice. "And I liked bossing around Pathos and Logos."

Rhys laughed whole-heartedly and curled a leg to his chest. "Did they complain much?"

"No, in fact, they were quite open to being led."

The smile on Rhys' face faded, and he gazed at his instruments. "Tell me honestly, will I be able to go home?"

"I don't know," replied Ethos. "Don't give me that face. Seriously, I don't know. It will depend upon what we find at the lunar facility."

Lowly, Rhys asked, "Hey, Ethos?"

"Yeah?"

"If... I can't make it home... will you kill me... before I suffer?"

"If it comes down to that, yes. I will help you find a way. It is my sincerest hope though, that we don't reach that point." Ethos moved away from the grave topic. "Now, if my information is correct, the lunar facility is protected but not impenetrable. You are right, of course, in thinking the plasma cannon would not be effective against it. Osiris has been shielding itself from solar flares for thousands of years."

Rhys touched the water packet floating in front of him to make it spin. "Right. We have to manually shut it down."

"Yep."

"Can you show me what you think the lunar facility looks like?"

"Unfortunately, no. I only have coordinates. Once we're closer to the moon, perhaps we can use cameras, but until then, we're flying blind."

"Do you have any reserves about completely destroying the facility?"

"Yes," replied Ethos.

"And those are?"

"The satellites. We've bypassed them thanks to the DDoS attack, but if we destroy Osiris, I worry they will drop their payloads. Therefore, it would be best if we can manually override Osiris' system to gain control of the satellites *before* disabling the AI."

Rhys sighed. "And how do we do that?"

"With me."

"You can do all of that?"

"Of course. Your job is to get me there."

"Right." Rhys stretched his shoulders before snatching his water packet from midair and sipping from it. "Uh, should I be worried about emptying the catheter bag?"

"No, *Heather* takes care of that for you. I thought you would have noticed by now."

Rhys glanced down at the external valve of his suit to find it perfectly aligned to a clasp on the chair. A black tube ran alongside the cockpit chair into the floor. "Huh…" He stretched once more before surveying the instruments. "So, is *Heather* equipped with its own AI system?"

"Yes, but because you inserted me, I have taken over as the primary AI." Ethos sounded as though it was grinning. "Why? Dissatisfied with my company?"

"Just curious. Can both be running at the same time?"

"No."

"So, the unit is named *Heather*, but what about the AI? Does the AI have a model type like you?"

"The AIs installed into units, bots, and the like are different from model types like Pathos, Logos, and Ethos. While we are learning AIs, those in other units are not."

"So, technically speaking, even without you, I could still fly *Heather*?"

"Of course," replied Ethos. "*Heather's* AI, however, is meant to act as *support* to the pilot. You could still pilot the unit because you're a pilot and you know how to fly, but you wouldn't have a backup. Since we left *Apex,*

I've acted as a filter to keep your system commands in order. Without me, whatever commands you give will be carried out by *Heather's* AI promptly without consideration or hesitancy."

"How can I prevent unwanted orders from being disseminated to the AI?"

"A calm and clear mind. Treat the unit as an extension of yourself."

"That's easier said than done when your adrenaline is up."

"It used to take pilots months to clearly and concisely dictate to their units what it was they wanted. New pilots who had not been taught the basics of flight were especially prone to mistakes."

"How am I doing compared to them?"

"If you had asked me in the hangar back on Earth, I would have laughed, but you pulled together once we launched. You know how to fly and understand the physics behind it. It's just a matter of focus for you. I've known worse pilots."

"Thanks…" Rhys gazed at the moon looming ahead and then glanced at the small map glowing on the cockpit glass to his left. They still had almost a full twenty-four hours of travel remaining until lunar orbit.

"Would you like to listen to music, Rhys? I have a collection stored in my memory from when Ramsen was traveling throughout the region. I collected quite a bit from festivals and taverns."

Heart soaring, Rhys couldn't help but lean forward in his chair in delight. "I want to hear! Start from the beginning."

The cockpit was suddenly filled with the jubilant sound of a stringed instrument Rhys recognized instantly, a piax. Grinning, he sat back and listened as the player rolled through a tumult of notes before moving into the slower chorus. In the background, Rhys could hear the murmur of people talking or the shuffling of plates.

"I think this was in a tavern in Maliyansa," said Ethos.

Rhys closed his eyes and listened.

43
OSIRIS OF THE MOON

"RHYS? HEY."

Rhys stirred from his sleep once more. After listening to music for nearly seven hours and discussing Ramsen's writings and journeys, he had drifted back to sleep.

"Rhys, wake up."

"I'm up," he mumbled. He was met by the blue glow of the instrument panel.

"There have been some minor pressure glitches in the rocket engine, but I've managed to fix them. Unfortunately, these pressure changes imply a larger problem."

"It's with the rocket engine, not with *Heather* though, right?"

"Right… The rocket engine uses two types of fuel which, when mixed, explodes causing thrust. I've received a single line of code indicating a leak in one of the valves. It's not something that can be repaired quickly, but it should hold long enough for our mission."

Although all his instruments and gauges indicated there were no problems, he trusted Ethos. If the AI said a problem was inevitable, then it was truth. "Keep me updated on any fluctuations."

With sixteen hours left, there was more than enough time for things to go wrong.

"Ethos, bring up *Heather's* manual." The cockpit glass darkened and an enormous wall of scrolling text materialized in a blue hue. Taking a deep breath, Rhys began studying the manual.

In the following nine hours, the pressure in the rocket engine climbed on four separate occasions, prompting Ethos to override errors and manually command the rocket engine to release the pressure. When Rhys asked if it was something that *Heather's* AI could do, Ethos encouraged Rhys to stay focused on familiarizing himself with *Heather's* specs.

By the time they reached the outskirts of lunar orbit, Rhys was weary. Despite having slept over half the trip, he was tense and stressed.

"Bring it up," Rhys ordered. An image of the lunar facility appeared on the cockpit glass. From afar, it looked like nothing more than a pale-colored warehouse, but as they entered lunar orbit and *Heather's* cameras were able to gain a better view, the grainy image cleared. "Well?"

"The flight plan is to be in lunar orbit for twenty-eight minutes. Since we had to leave early, our time in orbit has been extended slightly."

"Does it know we're here?" asked Rhys, studying the moon's barren, crater-pocked surface.

"We're the first object that's purposefully entered lunar orbit in thousands of years. It knows we're here." Ethos paused and then added, "Pressure in the rocket engine is forty-two percent above normal. I'll take care of it. We're twenty-seven minutes until drop."

"We need to time this perfectly. If we're gone for too long, the rocket engine will cease to function properly. Show me the flight route."

Lines, coordinates, altitudes, and times appeared on the cockpit glass. "At the moment, pressure sensors indicate that without manual release, the rocket engine will go critical in thirty-four minutes."

Rhys bit his lip. "Then we have less than thirty minutes to enter the facility, do what needs to be done, return to *Heather*, and meet back up with the rocket engine?"

"Right..."

"But the rocket engine will still be in orbit. Orbit around the moon takes about... two hours..." Rhys murmured. "If we cut the time in the facility short though, we can chase the rocket engine and reattach before it's out of reach. That way we don't have to wait for it to travel around the moon. That leaves us, what? About nineteen minutes to get in and out?"

"Yeah."

Rhys rolled his head back and groaned. "Shit."

"Yeah, not our best plan," agreed Ethos.

"So, we either complete the mission in under twenty minutes or go over the time limit and watch the rocket engine explode."

"Now, *Heather* can chase the rocket engine, but you're going to waste fuel doing that."

"Is the nineteen-minute mark the point at which we cannot reach it at all?"

"The nineteen-minute mark is the point at which we will, for certain, reach the rocket engine and have time to release the pressure. Between twenty and twenty-four minutes, we can chase the rocket engine, but at that time the rocket engine might go critical and explode, putting your unit in danger."

Rhys studied the flight plan and time estimates and then motioned for the cockpit glass to show the lunar facility once more. "Maybe we can do nineteen minutes. If absolutely everything is ready and there aren't any glitches, maybe we can pull it off." He checked his primary oxygen tank. He had only used oxygen during launch. Since then, he had had the glass on his helmet retracted and utilized the system within *Heather* to breathe.

"When you stand, your oxygen tank pack will detach from the chair and rise with you to affix across your back," explained Ethos. "The harness you are currently wearing keeps you strapped into the chair, but once you stand, it breaks away to support your tank. Grab your secondary oxygen pack and attach it to the bottom of your primary. The moon's gravity is eighty-three percent less than Earth's. You've been weightless for the past two days. Don't forget to adjust your movements accordingly."

Rhys untied his short rifle and let it drift beside him as he searched for spare ammunition. Once he had another four magazines hanging around him, he snatched the resonance cutters from their netting and laced the strap across his chest.

"Twenty-two minutes, twenty-four seconds until drop," said Ethos.

Sensing time accelerating, he began storing the spare magazines in the thigh and hip pockets of his suit. By the time he finished testing the connections within his helmet, he was layered in a fine sweat.

"Six minutes, forty seconds," Ethos announced.

Rhys laid his hands on the chair's armrests and began calming himself. He was ready. He had done everything in his power to make his descent and retreat from the cockpit as smooth as possible. Before he closed the visor on his helmet, he shook the sweat from his hairline so water droplets danced into the space around him.

"Ninety seconds."

Rhys nodded and continued to focus on his breathing.

"Sixty seconds."

The flight to the moon had been both infinite and short. Already—and yet, too soon—he was there.

"Thirty seconds. Releasing rocket engine pressure in preparation for departure," said Ethos.

Rhys watched the pressure gauge to his left, which read thirty-tree percent higher than normal, drop to nominal levels.

"Fifteen seconds…"

Rhys raised his visor once more, shook the sweat from his face, and then closed it.

"Ten, nine, eight…"

He could hear his breathing.

"Four, three, two, one. Detach."

The nose of *Heather* dipped as it pulled away from the rocket engine and angled toward the moon's surface. The distant rumble Rhys had grown accustomed to faded, and he was enwrapped in complete silence.

"Main engines idling," said Ethos. "Thrusters on standby. Descent engine will power on in twenty seconds."

Rhys kept his eyes turned down at the instruments and gauges. Ethos had already been slowing them upon their approach to the moon, but dropping from orbit was going to take work.

"Prepare to fire descent engines in ten seconds," instructed the AI. Rhys pressed his fingertips into the biting underbelly of his gloves. "Fire descent engines."

Heather rattled ominously as the lowest-mounted engine on the unit swiveled downward and began spewing retrograde thrust.

"Slow it down, Rhys," Ethos ordered over the roar. "I'll watch fuel consumption."

No sooner had he thought it than *Heather's* thrusters were hissing in unison.

"Estimated time to moon's surface: one hundred ten seconds. All systems, nominal. Easy, Rhys."

Time inched by. The countdown Ethos continuously announced couldn't conclude fast enough. Rhys felt as though he were falling for minutes, hours. He was sure the descent to the moon's surface was the longest leg of the journey. Briefly, his gaze flickered to the abyss of space, his eyes fixing on the farthest star he could discern. While lying on the upper deck of *Themis*, he had felt the stars unreachable; yet here he was surrounded by their eternally cold beauty.

Suddenly, before he realized it, *Heather* had touched down on the pock-marked surface, blowing dust and sand into the air and rolling small rocks across the ground. Panting, Rhys stared at the vast wasteland of nothingness as Ethos disengaged the engines and thrusters and began shutting down his unit.

"Let's go, let's go," the AI chorused, noticing Rhys was unmoving.

Snapping from his trance, Rhys stood shakily, pulling at the oxygen pack behind his chair. With ease, the tank emerged and settled across his back. He gathered the secondary oxygen pack, clasped it to the bottom of his primary and then looped his short rifle over his shoulder. After giving the cockpit a cursory glance, he ejected Ethos and stuffed the AI into the tight pocket along his hip.

Rhys opened the cockpit and, with some difficulty, clambered onto *Heather's* wing. He knew their time was limited, but how could a place so stark and devoid of life be so breathtakingly beautiful? Looking over his shoulder, he set his eyes on Earth, the blue sphere hanging in an abyss of black.

"Not that way…" murmured Ethos. "Turn your head. Turn it, turn it. There. That direction. The lunar facility is just over that small ridge."

Rhys leapt from the starboard wing and landed clumsily on his knees in the dust. Adjusting his movements to the new gravity, he pulled his feet beneath him and started bouncing with less grace than he had hoped across the rocky terrain. A few awkward paces took him up the slight ridge to his east where he overlooked a vast expanse of the lunar surface.

He pushed off hard and drifted down the gradual slope toward the facility. At the foot of the ridge, he paused to study the building. They had been right, of course. The lunar facility, though warehouse-shaped, was covered in pale plating to block electrostatic discharges and protect against solar flares. Every inch of the building was cloaked in unique hexagonal plates to safeguard against space's multitude of dangers and harmful elements. Aside from its exceptional covering, the facility had another oddity—it had no door that he could discern.

After prompting from Ethos, Rhys started alongside the base in search of an opening. Halfway alongside the building, movement ahead distracted him, causing him to slow to a stop.

"Ethos?" he murmured as three bots rolled out from a small door hidden in the dusty ground. Rhys swung his short rifle before him defensively and took a few steps back.

"Hold on, hold on," replied Ethos, obviously occupied.

The three bots were clunky, square-shaped, and utilized continuous tracks to roll along the uneven lunar surface. Their bodies, though painted primarily gray, had stripes of neon yellow and orange running the length of their carriages.

"Easy, easy. Hold on," Ethos instructed. "There!"

The bots fell still. "What did you do?"

"Just deactivated them for a short while. Also, after rummaging around in their codes, I've found that there is no door into the facility."

Rhys looked at the hole in the ground from which the bots had emerged. "Does that lead inside?"

"It does," replied Ethos. "We're on the same page."

"Why isn't there a door? Humans built it."

"It was sealed to keep the AI protected."

Warily, Rhys bounced past the bots and kicked the sealed door in the ground with his boot. "How far down does it go?"

"Just a meter or so beneath the ground, but because of its size, it will take some time for you to make it down there and back out. It's an option, but not a good one."

Rhys glanced back at the small warehouse before looking down at his resonance cutters. "Why can't I just cut a hole into the wall?"

"Let's find out," replied Ethos. "When you get to the outer wall, place my unit against it so I can try to determine if there's anything on the other side that will be damaged."

Rhys bypassed the bots and approached the base. When he was next to the wall, he withdrew Ethos and pressed the AI against the pale plating. "Anything?" asked Rhys after a moment.

"I can't get any readings. It's too heavily shielded."

Rhys returned Ethos to his belt, slung his rifle over his shoulder, and withdrew his resonance cutters. "It's about time these were used the way they were meant to be." He engaged the cutters and tentatively touched the tip to the wall. At first, he was met with surprising resistance, but as he pushed harder, the cutters sank into the plating.

"Cut something big enough for you to pass through."

Rhys worked to create a hole large enough to accommodate his body and oxygen packs. By the time he completed the chore, he was out of breath and had wasted nearly four minutes of precious time.

"Put me through first," instructed Ethos. Rhys withdrew the AI and shoved it into the hole. Just when he was about to pull the AI out, Ethos said, "Come on, let's go."

Using the resonance cutters for light, Rhys crawled through the hole. He was not surprised to find the entire facility pitch black. AIs didn't need light; why waste the energy?

"Here," murmured Ethos. A light atop Rhys' helmet flickered on. Pleasantly surprised, he looked around. Though the light was feeble, it was enough. They had been calling Osiris' home a "facility" because of its relative impenetrability, but really, it was just a large room cluttered with supplies, tools, and crates.

Along one wall were multiple tool chests, repair kits, and spare parts for bots, some of which appeared quite worn. To his left, he found numerous crates labeled in a language he didn't know. In the middle of the vast room was an extensive table crowded with electrical equipment, radios, odd devices Rhys had never before seen, metal conduits, and two badly worn monitors. Cautiously, he approached the messy length of table.

This was Osiris? This single, slightly lopsided table of junk was Osiris, the all-powerful AI controlling and manipulating every society on Earth?

"Don't be fooled," growled Ethos, sensing Rhys' confusion and disbelief.

He glanced about to make sure he hadn't missed something and stepped before the table. The room was completely silent. The only sound in his ears was that of his own breathing.

"Rhys, the monitors," Ethos murmured.

He redirected his attention to the monitors on his left. While one was dark and cracked, the other glowed dimly. He reached for the screen, but Ethos stopped him with a quiet warning. Momentarily, numerous lines of speech in various languages and characters began scrolling down the screen. Rhys first saw the greeting in Aabesh and then in Interstellar Nefegian.

Welcome. To continue, please choose a language.

"Choose whichever you want," said Ethos, "but if I tell you to stop, do so immediately."

Rhys pressed the line of text written in Nefegian. The screen blackened and remained that way for several tense moments.

"It's old," Ethos offered. "Give it a moment."

Slowly, the screen began glowing a shimmering blue that grew in intensity as the monitor warmed. White text in Nefegian scrolled down the page, and Rhys leaned in to read it.

OSIRIS Artificial Intelligence Global Monitoring System.
Model: Legacy, c. 10mo3140.

The purpose of the OSIRIS Artificial Intelligence Global Monitoring System is to monitor the third planet of the Solar System, Earth, for indications of life and inhabitability. In the event that life is observed and homo sapiens can once again flourish on the planet, this artificial intelligence has been programmed to hinder, stall, or otherwise disrupt all efforts made to destroy humanity anew. All endeavors to explore, diversify, and trade globally are deemed harbingers of change and will not be tolerated.

This artificial intelligence has access to humanity's collective written history until Earth's mass exodus. Because this artificial intelligence has absolute knowledge concerning the history of the human race, it has been programmed to operate as it sees fit to prevent global conquest and the reinstitution of warfare amongst humans. This artificial intelligence is allowed to communicate with the race homo sapiens to deter harmful or life-threatening behavior. Additionally, it has been provided weaponry to stop all detrimental human activity should the need arise.

All geologic upheavals, anomalies, and disasters will be observed and recorded for posterity, however, this artificial intelligence will not interfere with or warn of such catastrophes as it is not responsible for humans' abilities to cope with natural disasters.

WARNING: In the event that this artificial intelligence unit is disconnected, harmed, or fails and the backup system does not engage, its satellites will cease functioning until each can be manually rebooted.

Beneath the introduction was a list of specifications describing Osiris as well as a log of its orbiting satellites, their current locations, and the repairs each satellite needed.

"What do you want to do?" Rhys touched the bottom of the screen to scroll through the lengthy wall of text.

"You're not taking this seriously."

"It's difficult to believe that this run-down piece of crap is what has been causing all the problems on Earth."

"If we had the time, I would allow you to read the hundreds of rules and regulations that were set forth by humanity that Osiris must follow, but as it is, we don't. Osiris has learned over these thousands of years what works and what doesn't." Ethos thought and then added, "Manually rebooting all of Earth's satellites is not an option right now."

"But we can't let them fail either," replied Rhys. "Brechin is the only one I know of using the satellites to communicate, but it's entirely possible that other civilizations out there are using them as well. A complete breakdown of the satellites could be catastrophic in its own way." Rhys gazed at the screen. "We can't leave Osiris active…"

"Replace it," suggested Ethos matter-of-factly.

"So, its replacement can, in a few thousand years, manipulate Earth again?"

"Humanity has solved hundreds of thousands of problems throughout its history, Rhys. It can solve that problem when or if it arises, just like what you're doing."

Rhys sighed. The AI was right. "Replace Osiris with what? What AI is powerful… enough…" He felt his chest tighten. "You, Ethos?"

"I did tell you I was the key here," the AI replied.

"Yeah… but how am I going to get back to Earth without you?"

"You'll find a way. Remember, you're not the worst pilot I've met."

"And you're sure you can substitute?"

"I have ten times the power Osiris has now." As though the AI was smiling, Ethos said warmly, "Ramsen knew what he was doing."

"Where are we on time?" asked Rhys.

"Twelve minutes, twenty-two seconds until you need to launch."

"Fine, what do I need to do?"

"Go around the table to the backside of the AI and remove the rear panel." As Ethos rattled off instructions, Rhys obeyed. "You're going to find a series of conduits. Follow the largest conduit to the core of the unit. *Don't* bump anything. Got it?"

"Yeah," muttered Rhys, holding his breath to keep his arms steady. "I've got it."

"The conduit you have your hand on should have two cords inside it."

"I… can't tell."

"You just have to trust me. Both of those cords are plugged into Osiris' main core. We are going to disconnect only *one* of them. Only one, Rhys."

"Does it matter which?" Rhys replied.

"Yes."

"Shit…"

"You need to detach Cord 2904 and draw it out here so you can connect it to me."

Rhys tilted his helmet left and then right in an attempt to squeeze in more light to better see the head of the conduit, but it was to no avail. Frowning and sweating profusely, Rhys groaned. "Give me a hint, Ethos. Do they feel different? Are they different colors?"

"Slide me in there," commanded Ethos. With his free hand, Rhys pushed the AI into the crevice below the conduits. Ethos flashed light into the area and began projecting a three-dimensional image of what it saw into the space outside the rear panel. "Can you see that?"

Rhys studied the image, wiggling a finger slightly to better discern what he was looking at. "Yeah, yeah… hold on." Watching the projected image of his hand and the head of the conduit, he manipulated the small cords winding out until he held one between his two fingers. "This one?"

"Yes," replied Ethos.

"You're sure?"

"Yes!"

Rhys withdrew Ethos, held the AI at his side, and gently pulled the cord attached to Osiris out of the core. There was a moment of mild resistance, but with a slight tug, he freed the cable from its ancient hold.

"Plug me in," Ethos ordered urgently. The side panel on Ethos opened to reveal numerous ports.

Rhys matched the cord to one of Ethos' ports and jammed the clip into the AI. "What now?" Ethos didn't reply. Assuming the AI was preoccupied, he waited patiently before asking again.

"Hold on," Ethos murmured. "I'm overriding Osiris' controls and rerouting them to my core. Once the majority of those are mine, then you can disconnect the other cord and give it to me. One minute." Rhys left Ethos on the table and began fishing through the jungle of conduits for the remaining cable. The moment his fingers touched it, Ethos said, "Do it. I'm ready."

Rhys yanked the second cord from Osiris' core, pulled it gently through the forest of conduits, and jammed it into Ethos. He wanted to ask after the AI's wellbeing like a human, but he refrained. Ethos was an artificial intelligence. In silence, he regarded the AI. How much time did he have left? Seven minutes, maybe?

Suddenly, the bots Ethos had hacked rolled through a little door in the floor and lined up beside the table.

"You're clear, Rhys," said Ethos in his helmet.

"You can still communicate with me?"

"I've been using *Heather's* comm system to communicate with you since you suited up. I can stay with you for a while longer. Your job is finished here."

Rhys threw a cursory glance of the table. "You're sure?" He felt like he was leaving behind a friend.

"Yeah. I got this."

Hurriedly, Rhys bounced around the table and took wide strides across the room to the hole he had created. "Do... I need to fix this?"

"No. The bots can fix it."

With care, Rhys stepped through the gaping hole in the side of the facility, glanced at the black abyss overhead, and then looked back at the lone, lopsided table with the one good monitor still glowing. His heart hurt, much like it had when he had bid farewell to Pathos. He was leaving behind a piece of himself.

"Rhys—"

"I know," interrupted Rhys, turning. "Running low on time." He leapt across the dusty, rock-encrusted earth back to the slight ridge from which he had come. By the time he had hopped his way up to the crest of the hill, he was audibly wheezing. Going up the ridge took more energy and time than coming down it.

Pumping his legs hard, he sprang across the barren wasteland to *Heather*. He waited for the ladder to descend along the port wing and then awkwardly climbed it. By the time he was back in the cockpit, he was shaking horribly from the effort and adrenaline.

"Calm mind. Calm mind," he chided himself.

Rhys lowered himself into the cockpit chair, taking care to maneuver his oxygen pack over the back of the seat. *Heather's* cockpit closed, and the pod pressurized. He pushed himself into the back of the chair. "*Heather*, ignition." The hard and painful *thunk* in the middle of his back knocked air from his tired lungs.

"Ignition," murmured an unfamiliar female voice within the cockpit.

Rhys gasped for air, laid his shaking hands on the arms of the cockpit chair, and forced his mind to focus. The cockpit was doused in a familiar blue hue and began quivering with the activation of the engines

"Pilot Number 011," cooed the soft female voice that was *Heather's* AI, "All systems are nominal. Pre-flight checklist, complete."

Before Rhys was ready, *Heather* leapt into the air, thrusters lifting the unit twenty-four meters within a few seconds. "Easy, easy," Rhys murmured to himself, glancing over his instruments and gauges. "*Heather*, locate the rocket engine and set course."

"Locating rocket engine model number SX000451449. Confirmed. Setting course."

A map with detailed coordinates materialized on the cockpit glass. Clenching his jaws, Rhys urged *Heather* upward. "Make adjustments as I go," he ordered, watching the instruments before him.

"Pilot, another one thousand sixty-nine kilometers per hour is needed to enter lunar orbit," hummed *Heather*.

Rhys gripped his chair and gave the conscience order to increase thrust by the needed amount. If he thought descending to the moon's surface took forever, the journey back into orbit was the opposite. Within seconds, he was kilometers above the surface and in full view of the rocket engine he had left spinning perfectly in lunar orbit.

He had barely thought it before *Heather* shot toward the rocket engine. When warning alarms erupted in the cockpit, Rhys wildly decelerated. He was in command, not the AI, not Ethos. *Heather's* AI could help him by offering warnings and suggestions, but it was up to him to perform them. Aiming the thrusters forward, Rhys decelerated, hard; the entire jet trembled from the effort. If he overshot the rocket engine, another few precious minutes would be wasted trying to match up to it once more.

"Come on..." he murmured. "Come on."

"Thirty meters until sync," reported *Heather*. "Twenty, seventeen, fifteen, eleven, ten... Five meters until sync."

Rhys redirected the thrusters to adjust to the rocket engine's velocity, his eyes set not on the spinning engine outside his craft, but on the myriad of gauges and instruments indicating his speed, angle, and pitch.

"Pilot, you're synchronized with rocket engine model number SX000451449. Calculating rotational speed. Rocket engine's rotational speed: fourteen revolutions per minute."

Using the cameras on his hull and starboard wing, Rhys began inching *Heather* closer to the rocket engine.

"Pilot, in fifteen seconds, engage docking arms."

Rhys' eyes bounced between the camera angles on the cockpit glass and the instruments below.

"Pilot..." There was a moment's pause before *Heather* said, "Dock."

Rhys released the docking unit and watched, heart pounding, as the clasps caught those on the rocket engine and snapped closed. Instantly, *Heather* entered the rocket's rotational spin. Ignoring the disorienting sensation, he ordered the secondary docking units to attach and the conduits to connect. When the conduits attached to *Heather*, readings of the rocket engine's status poured in and warning sirens began pulsing. The pressure within the rocket engine was at ninety-two percent.

"*Heather*, release the pressure," Rhys ordered, his eyes on the pressure gauge. He watched the three-dimensional needle in the gauge and willed it to lower. Instead, it crept upward. "*Heather*, release the pressure of the rocket engine. Now!" he screamed, his voice shaking.

"This AI does not have access to rocket engine model number SX000451449 as it is not considered a part of this unit," replied *Heather*.

"What? Can't you find a way around it?" asked Rhys, bringing up a map of the current trajectory of their orbit. He had managed to catch up to the rocket engine, but the unit was preparing to enter the dark side of the moon. He would use lunar orbit to slingshot himself back to Earth. "*Heather*, find a way around it."

"Pilot, this AI does not have access to rocket engine model number SX000451449 as it is not considered a part of this unit."

"You've said that already!" he snarled. It didn't make sense. What had changed? He had controlled the rocket engine's speed and thrust on the journey to the moon with no problems. He had merely to think the speed, and the rocket engine had obeyed. "Why don't you have access to the rocket engine? I don't understand!"

"Rocket engine model number SX000451449 is not considered a part of this unit and is therefore outside of this AI's jurisdiction."

"But it's attached! We've docked! I can see the gauges."

Ethos' voice suddenly broke through the chaos. "Rhys. *Heather* can only engage and disengage the rocket's main engines. Nothing more. It is as the AI says—the rocket engine is not considered a part or even an extension of the unit. *Heather* has no other control over it."

"But... the pressure..." Rhys gazed despairingly at the gauge; it read ninety-four percent. "Why is this any different than our journey to... the... moon." Rhys' sentence faded as a dark thought occurred to him. "Ethos."

"Yes, Rhys?"

"You knew this would happen?"

"Yes," Ethos replied solemnly.

"You knew... I wouldn't be able to release the pressure?"

"Yes. I figured it out the moment the problem was reported. In truth, I was never able to release the pressure. I only adjusted the gauges on the screen so it looked like I was maintaining the rocket's pressure levels. It's been beyond our control since the beginning."

Rhys relaxed. "You knew... that I wouldn't be able to get home?"

"Yes." Ethos sighed. "The sacrifice of one for many, Rhys. Had you known, you wouldn't have completed the mission. You *needed* to complete your mission."

"But... you could have warned me. Or something!" Rhys' voice cracked as panic and utter despair broke through his courage. "You could have said something!"

"I'm sorry."

"Ethos..." The AI's name was the only word left on Rhys' lips.

"Rhys," said Ethos calmly. "You need to make a decision."

He knew immediately what the AI was implying—stay with the rocket engine and be caught in the explosion or return to the lunar surface and die.

"No," seethed Rhys, his adrenaline spiking in complete and utter defiance. "No!" He glanced at the map and then at the pressure gauge—ninety-six percent. "Fuck this. I'm..." He began giving rapid orders to *Heather*. The unit shook, and the glowing light of the rocket engine igniting filled his cockpit. As the cockpit glass dimmed to block out the brilliant glow, Rhys muttered, "I'm going home."

44
REENTRY

HE HEARD NO DISPUTE FROM Ethos nor a negative response from *Heather's* AI. Working fast, Rhys began manipulating the course map before him, examining *Heather's* trajectory and at what point he needed to add speed to break free of the moon's gravity. Lines of calculations and formulas began zooming down the screen as *Heather's* AI recorded Rhys' struggle to remember the laws of astrophysics he had learned so long ago. All the information and knowledge he had acquired on Caelestis from years prior was suddenly his only tool for success. Jumbled formulas only Pathos had ever used swam to the forefront of his brain.

Feverishly, he inserted variables and numbers, worked through layers of math, struggled to remember the value of letters, and retraced his steps numerous times. Faster and faster… and faster and faster his mind moved, adrenaline narrowing his focus to a sharp point.

In less than two minutes, the entire cockpit screen was nothing but numbers, formulas, coordinates, thermodynamics, and quantum mechanics.

"Execute," he breathed, overlaying the course map atop his calculations. Worriedly, he shifted his gaze to the instruments and watched as *Heather's* speed increased. He had ninety seconds left in lunar orbit but after studying the rocket engine's pressure gauge, he wasn't sure he would make it. He just needed a boost, just a moment of exponential thrust to shoot him from orbit.

"Pilot, fifty seconds until acceleration," answered *Heather* calmly.

Rhys glanced once more at the pressure gauge—ninety-eight percent.

Like so many times on this journey, time distorted. It unraveled around Rhys in tendrils of anxiety and fear. It slowed to nothingness and merged with the spiraling black abyss until suddenly the moment arrived.

"Acceleration in five, four, three, two, one," chorused *Heather*.

Rhys punched the rocket engine with his mind, jerking forward in an unconscious effort. The altimeter ceased to function as *Heather* whipped out of lunar orbit; the cacophony of sirens which he had silenced earlier began wailing all at once.

"Speed: twenty-one thousand five hundred kilometers per hour and increasing," *Heather* reported.

"Disengage and detach!" Rhys screamed. Immediate confirmation that the rocket engine had stopped was displayed overhead. "Detach, detach!" The docking unit couldn't disconnect quick enough. Before the conduits had fully retracted into *Heather*, Rhys slammed his unit's throttle to maximum to put distance between himself and the rocket engine which were synchronized in flight.

Unfortunately, that wasn't enough.

Heather jerked and then lunged downward, throwing Rhys into his harness. A brilliant orange and amber explosion erupted around him. The sound of metal peeling and screeching radiated through the cockpit as an ominous and fierce rattling hummed beneath Rhys' feet. *Heather* bucked and rolled, jarring him so that his head whipped back and then to the side. The chair beneath him quaked, and the three-dimensional images of the instrument paneling on the cockpit glass flickered sporadically.

Another force at *Heather's* back hurled Rhys once more into his harness and then whipped him back like a slingshot, effectively knocking him unconscious.

The syncopated whine of one of numerous alarms slowly brought him back to reality. For a long moment, he struggled to open his eyes. His body hurt all over, and his neck ached fiercely.

Words tried to escape his lips but remained caught in his throat. He coughed, licked his dry lips, and murmured, "*Heather?*"

"Pilot has regained consciousness. Transferring control," replied the unit's AI.

The myriad of alarms and warnings quieted. Resisting the temptation to remove his hands from the chair for fear of interfering with *Heather's* biofeedback functions, Rhys forced some composure into his body. He grimaced as his neck muscles flexed and pain roared through his head. "Status... report," he wheezed.

A large and detailed map of *Heather* materialized on the cockpit glass. Blocks of red and black indicating damage or non-functionality heavily colored the diagram. "Pilot, forty-eight percent of the unit has incurred damage, seven percent of that has ceased functioning," *Heather* reported. "Damage to engines one and two is significant."

"Show me our course map."

The diagram of *Heather* minimized to the corner of the cockpit and the course map he had created emerged. He groaned as he found his unit currently spinning about fourteen degrees off his planned flight path. He studied *Heather's* diagram once more to discern how bad the damage was to his engines and thrusters. He was disappointed to find that of his eight thrusters, the two rear ones were no longer functioning and three others were damaged. As *Heather's* AI had indicated, engines one and two had damage but appeared minimally operational; engine three was unharmed.

"*Heather*, status of thermal shield?" asked Rhys unable to determine the answer from the diagram alone.

"Thermal shield is down to sixty-two percent," replied the AI.

"The nose of the unit is untouched though?"

"Correct."

Wincing as he unintentionally pulled his neck, he thought. With *Heather's* heat shields functioning at only sixty-two percent, living through reentry wasn't assured.

"*Heather*, begin adjustments to realign with the planned flight path."

"Pilot instruction is needed to realign with set course," replied *Heather*.

Annoyed by the AI's helplessness, he glanced at the numerous instruments indicating flaws and anomalies within the system and, with clenched jaws, activated the starboard thrusters. It took but a few seconds before a red warning was displayed on the cockpit glass and a high-pitched alarm began chirping. Two of his damaged thrusters were overheating.

"Come on!" he snarled, urging all the starboard thrusters to accelerate. He couldn't afford to miss his flight path.

"Pilot, thruster five has ceased functioning. Thruster four will reach critical in twelve seconds," reported *Heather*. "Detaching thruster four."

Rhys acknowledged the action and continued to push the remaining two starboard thrusters, hard. As he realigned with the plotted route, he relaxed. He steadied the unit with the port thrusters before falling still, his eyes set forward. Wishing to see the damage for himself, he cleared the cockpit glass of diagrams and maps and peered out at the star-littered field of black. Earth loomed brilliantly before him.

For several long moments, he stared at the planet, his mind blank. He was weary and could no longer contemplate the concepts of life and death. All that remained was the instinctive will to survive, a deep and nagging urge to overcome.

Footage of the numerous cameras positioned along *Heather* popped up along the cockpit screen showcasing raw, curled metal, pock-marked wings, a tattered tail, and scorched thrusters. A timer appeared at the bottom of the screen—thirty-six hours until he reached Earth's orbit. It seemed this journey was nothing but long periods of waiting coupled with short bursts of potentially fatal mishaps and trials.

Sighing, Rhys closed his eyes. He would need to rest before his inevitable death upon reentry.

Over the next twenty-four hours, he managed some sleep though without Ethos' watchful eye, he felt less comfortable doing so. He woke intermittently to check on gauges and instruments and to ensure *Heather* was still on course. While the laws of physics would eventually work against him, for the moment, the momentum he had gained from the rocket engine's final burst—and in some regard, the ensuing explosion—was enough to propel him home. What little fuel he had left he would use to slow his descent into Earth's atmosphere.

During his waking time, he stared at the ethereal blue planet and mused with spite over the dilemma in which Ethos had put him. The AI had *known* he would be unable to release the pressure on the rocket engine, yet Ethos had kept the information to itself.

Of course, it had been the right thing to do. Had Rhys known there was no way to release the pressure, he wouldn't have descended to the lunar surface and left the rocket alone.

The sacrifice of one for many.

Rhys understood the concept and he was sure, that if he survived reentry, in time he would come to terms with Ethos' decision to keep him in the dark about his fate, but for the moment, he was bitterly angry and hurt.

Ethos had been his closest confidant. Since Alina's death, no one had guided him so intimately as the AI had. No other person had offered resistance when he suggested dangerous plans. Ethos had been the only one to discuss philosophy with him and to be his constant companion. Even Kallen and Hodge didn't possess the knowledge and critical thinking skills to do that. Rhys had put all his faith in the AI, and Ethos had intentionally led him to a doomed fate.

He wasn't dead—yet—but that stroke of luck had been contrived by his own quick thinking. Had he simply accepted what Ethos had provided, he would have returned to the lunar surface to live out his remaining hours of life before killing himself.

The AI had promised, in the event of failure, it would offer Rhys a method to kill himself, but still, Rhys couldn't help but feel betrayed. He could have done everything quicker; he could have disconnected Osiris faster. He could have spared himself a few minutes to return to the rocket engine, realize that he couldn't release the pressure, and then use that spare time to distance himself from the attachment. As it was though, he had returned to the rocket engine too late and had had only minutes to calculate a trajectory to Earth using the moon's orbit and implement it.

When the timer at the bottom of his cockpit screen showed his arrival time into Earth's orbit to be just under twelve hours, he began the process of calculating deceleration increments which he implemented over the next few hours. In the meantime, he mentally prepared himself for reentry.

The greatest trial of his life was about to unfold. With unwavering focus, he reviewed *Heather's* specs and unit manual, ran simulations in his head, and considered various methods to decelerate should the engines— which, given the state of *Heather*, was entirely possible.

With four hours left until atmospheric reentry, he began dreading. He cycled between periods of overwhelming panic and grave resolve, crying and stone-faced determination. He pondered why this particular event frightened him so when he had come close to and perhaps even experienced death before.

Countless times he had been in danger and horrifically injured. When it came to defending *Themis* and his crew, he didn't stop to think. He listened to his gut and instinct. But now... The hours of sitting in silence with nothing but thoughts of his inevitable death to keep him company were torture. In gory detail, he imagined his final moments and the pain that would accompany them.

Fighting was different; he had faith in his skills and in those of his crew members. Here, he was a pound of flesh stuffed in a metal craft. He had no control of the situation. He had no control over his fate. His survival upon reentry was predicated upon *Heather's* ability to withstand the heat.

Not soon enough and yet all at once, it was time. After notifying *Heather*, he left the confines of his seat and worked to pull the auxiliary oxygen mask over his shoulder from the life support kit. He cinched down the netting that kept his supplies in check, made sure he had a pistol within arm's distance, and reviewed the hundreds of strategies he had prepared.

No sooner had he settled back into his chair than he was notified that his primary oxygen tank was low on oxygen. Rhys switched to his secondary tanks. A warning appeared on the cockpit glass indicating that the oxygen in the secondary tanks was nonexistent. What had happened? Forge and Otto had checked his backup canisters before launch.

Searching the tank, he found the nozzle damaged. The explosion had jarred the canister, causing it to spew a steady stream of its contents into the cockpit.

After turning off his primary oxygen, he opened his visor and began preparing the auxiliary life support mask. Although the cockpit was pressurized and had oxygen, reentry was going to be a trial. In the event *Heather* faltered, he wanted to know he had a constant supply of air.

Rhys wiped his sweat-soaked face with the tip of his glove, pushed his soaked hair back, and slipped the oxygen mask over his face and around his helmet. He took a few cautious breaths to determine if the oxygen tasted strange and then snugged the straps down.

With Earth taking up most of his cockpit screen, he darkened the glass so he could focus on his instruments. As the speed of his unit began increasing in response to the Earth's gravitational pull, he turned inward for a moment of peace.

"Rhys."

A scratchy voice emerged from the radio.

"Rhys do you copy, over?"

Glaring murderously at the paneling before him, Rhys replied. "What do *you* want?"

Ethos sighed. "Don't be like that. Once you left lunar orbit, I couldn't contact you anymore. It took me a while to organize Earth's satellites."

"What do you want?" growled Rhys over the rising roar in the cockpit.

"I've prepared help," Ethos replied. The AI's voice was garbled and difficult to hear, but Rhys understood.

As *Heather* began trembling, Rhys shouted, "What kind of help?"

"You have to make it through reentry."

"That was the plan." He glanced at his instruments. *Heather* was heating.

"Disengage the AI," ordered Ethos.

Rhys was jarred in his chair as a sheet of metal on his starboard wing buckled. "What?"

"Disengage *Heather's* AI. Manually pilot the unit," Ethos replied quickly. "The AI is going to follow certain protocols upon reentry, leaving you with little to no control."

Rhys frowned. He didn't want to trust Ethos. "You're not trying to kill me, are you?"

"No! Do it!"

Remembering the manual override system he had read about in *Heather's* manual, he gave the command. "*Heather,* disengage all AI support systems."

"This artificial intelligence unit has been ordered to disengage all support systems and to transition the pilot to manual flight mode. Please confirm," replied *Heather.*

"Confirm," Rhys panted.

"Manual flight, confirmed. Disengaging all support systems and transitioning the pilot to manual flight."

The cockpit was dunked into complete blackness. Controlling his fear, he listened as his unit whined and moaned. There was a suppressed *thunk* followed by movement within the cockpit. Rhys' face was suddenly illuminated by a menagerie of variously colored tangible gauges. The paneling, which had been the interface platform for the three-dimensional gauges, was now open to reveal glowing instruments coming online.

The armrests below his hands slid downward as his chair moved forward. A stick rose from the floor and slipped between his legs while pedals fitted to the bottoms of his boots to act as toe brakes. A long arm extended from the instrument paneling to provide a throttle, speed brakes, and access to the unit's flaps.

The cockpit glass regained its full transparency to reveal nothing but Earth's brilliant azure aura; a handful of diagrams and a heads-up display indicating angle of descent and altitude illuminated on the glass screen. Vivid yellow handles labeled EJECTION rose on either side of Rhys' cockpit chair and secured themselves at his knees.

Rhys glanced over the newly formed cockpit before firmly taking hold of the stick with his right hand and resting his left arm along the throttle and speed brakes.

"Transition complete. Relinquishing control of unit in five seconds," chimed *Heather's* AI. "Five, four, three, two, one."

Heather bucked. The various vibrations and quaking the AI had been suppressing shook Rhys, jarring him into his harness. Hands moving swiftly, he began making adjustments and assessing the craft. Despite the sudden onslaught of movement and shuddering, *he* was in control.

He could sense Earth's pull on *Heather*, and the air on the unit's shivering wings.

He could feel the tension on the stick and the minute adjustments he made to compensate.

An ominous howl began wailing along his starboard wing as the metal there shifted and reared against the increasing heat and wind.

"Rhys, the whole world is watching you," said Ethos.

Sirens wailed rhythmically around him. He ran his hand over a number of switches to force some stability into *Heather* before wheezing, "What?"

"All of Earth is watching your reentry. No matter where you land, someone will find you. I've trained all the satellites on you. Anyone on Earth who has a monitor or screen can see your unit right now."

Rhys tightened his grip on the stick, which was pulling hard to the right, and muttered, "Thanks, now everyone... can watch me die."

"No, you're going to make it," the AI asserted.

Gritting his teeth, Rhys left the speed brakes and put both hands on the stick, which was becoming increasingly resistant to his command. He glanced at the gauge indicating the temperature of the cockpit and of the unit itself. *Heather* had begun atmospheric reentry with only sixty-two percent of her thermal shielding functional. Judging by the steadily increasing level of heat in the cockpit and *Heather's* engines, the unit was losing its thermal plates fast. Already the temperature in the cockpit had reached thirty-two degrees Celsius.

Sweating, Rhys worked the toe brakes, shifted his hand back to the flaps and speed brakes, and then regained his grip on the stick. Every movement, every minute command, resulted in *Heather* quaking violently.

"Ethos," Rhys groaned. He strained against the stick before panting, "I think... I'm getting ready to lose my starboard wing. The thrusters were damaged during... Aghhh, the explosion."

"You've calculated that your angle of descent is correct?" asked Ethos quickly.

"Yeah!" Rhys scanned his gauges once more and let out a soft cry of fear as he spotted the dangerously high temperature of the engines. "Come on, come on..."

Using his right knee to help support the stick, he risked moving his left hand back to the speed brakes. The moment he touched the lever, *Heather* dipped nose-first. A cacophony of warnings and alarms began singing over the roar. Thrown against his harness, he struggled to keep his grip on the stick.

"Correct your angle!" screamed Ethos. "You're too deep!"

"I… can't…" wheezed Rhys. The temperature in the cockpit was now just over forty degrees. Sweat ran down his face in rivers; his hair stuck to his forehead and neck.

"Pull up!" Rhys had never heard Ethos sound so panicked. "Rhys! Pull up!"

Clamping down on the stick, Rhys jerked it toward his navel. *Heather* moaned loudly but steadied. His instruments reported that he had returned to his proper angle of descent, but that moment of tearing through the atmosphere unprotected by the hull's thermal plating was going to cost him. No sooner had he thought it than a heart-wrenching screech from his starboard struck terror into his heart. Metal on metal grinded and squealed as the front of his starboard wing peeled back on itself.

"I'm losing my wing!" Rhys cried, panic clawing at his gut. "Ethos, the starboard wing."

"Hold on!" Ethos' voice crackled. "Hold on, Rhys. Hold on!"

Rhys glanced at his altimeter—seventy-three kilometers and falling. All of *Heather* shook. The temperature in the cockpit swelled to fifty-one degrees. Refusing to leave the stick, Rhys let the stinging sweat slide into his eyes.

"Come on, Rhys," Ethos encouraged. "Just a bit longer. Push it."

Despite every muscle in his body screaming in protest, he kept an iron-like grip on the stick. The aching joints in his fingers and the burning in his wrists couldn't deter him. The pain in his neck that radiated down his back though agonizing couldn't persuade him to relinquish the stick.

"In ten seconds," crackled Ethos' voice, "throw everything. Do whatever you can to slow down."

Rhys nodded frantically.

"Got it?"

"Yeah, yeah!" shouted Rhys.

A moment passed before Ethos screamed, "Now! Rhys, now!"

Trusting inherently in Ethos, though he shouldn't have, he throttled the toe and speed brakes to their maximum efficiency; he deployed the flaps and engaged all the thrusters.

"Slower!" commanded Ethos.

Rhys slammed the landing gear down and, having already rotated the nozzle on one of his remaining engines to fire retrograde thrust, fired his remaining fuel reserves.

"Is that everything?" asked Ethos.

"Yeah," breathed Rhys.

"Hold on, hold on…"

Rhys glanced at his altimeter once more—thirty-eight kilometers. Just as a slight, almost indiscernible smile crept over his face, there was a loud and sudden *thwack!* From the corner of his eye, he saw the starboard wing snap and disappear behind his unit. *Heather* whipped downward and began spiraling at a steep angle.

Fighting to regain some stability, Rhys jerked on the stick but it was no longer responsive.

"Rhys, eject!" commanded Ethos. "Eject the cockpit. *Heather's* frame won't make it."

Rhys ignored the AI, continuing his fight to straighten the unit. If he used his momentum to force stability into *Heather*, then, in the final moments, he could glide to Earth.

"Rhys, eject! Eject!" Ethos sounded more like a synthetic siren. "Eject, eject!" The AI's voice seemed mechanical, screeching, rhythmic.

Seconds, minutes, hours—there was no way to tell how long he fought with *Heather*. He couldn't release the stick, he couldn't relinquish what little control he had over the unit. It was this infinitesimal amount of power that could potentially save his life; he was certain. If he could just force stability into *Heather*, if he could just make it low enough into the atmosphere then he could coast.

When Ethos next spoke, the AI's voice was low and calm. "Rhys. If you want to survive, eject your cockpit."

"I can… I can do this!" he gasped.

"*Heather* is falling apart around you."

Wheezing audibly, Rhys glanced at the ejection handles on either side of his chair.

"Eject the cockpit. You're low enough in the atmosphere now. That's what we were waiting for—for you to be at a lower altitude." Ethos paused for a moment. "Eject, Rhys."

Still fighting the stick, he glanced at the ejection handles once more. "You're… sure?"

"Do it. Now."

Rhys released the stick, snatched at the ejection handles, and jerked them upward. There was a loud bang, and an explosive force erupted under him. Before his ears could start ringing, the g-forces knocked him out.

45
FROM ONE TO THE NEXT

WHEN RHYS REGAINED CONSCIOUSNESS, HE wasn't sure if he was dead or alive. The cockpit was an impenetrable shield of black, a sensory deprivation capsule where no light or sound entered. The distant humming of *Heather* which had surrounded him for the past one hundred hours was nonexistent. Silence blanketed him, stifling his breath and squeezing his heart. Briefly, he thought he was back in space, but the constant rolling and dipping of his cockpit coupled with the ineffable sensation of perfect gravity reassured him that he was on Earth—or a purgatory-like Earth. In the complete and utter blackness, he could not discern up from down, he could not explain why he was constantly rolling in a nauseating, non-formulaic manner.

Moaning, Rhys gripped his chair to keep his arms locked downward. His neck hurt—he was sure he had torn something—and his back ached. Despite the harness' secure hug, every movement of the cockpit forced him to grimace or groan in pain.

"E-ethos…" Rhys murmured. His voice was thin and scratchy. He cleared his throat and tried once more. "Ethos?"

There was no response.

"*Heather*?" called Rhys.

"Yes, pilot," *Heather's* AI replied promptly.

Relief spilled over Rhys' face. "Where am I? What's…" Rhys paused as the cockpit somersaulted violently to the left. "Where am I?"

"After separating from *Heather's* frame, the cockpit landed at the following coordinates."

While *Heather* rattled off a string of numbers that meant nothing to Rhys, he struggled to force clarity into his mind. "So... I'm on Earth?"

"Yes, you are on Earth," concluded *Heather*.

Rhys wheezed as a particularly terrible roll jarred him in his seat. "How far... from the launch site am I?"

Heather paused and then said, "You landed twenty-two thousand five hundred fifty-three kilometers west of the previous launch site."

"What?" whispered Rhys. He was literally on the other side of Earth from Quadrant Six. "*Heather*, you're sure?"

"Affirmative," replied the AI.

His cockpit rolled fiercely before correcting itself. It was then that Rhys figured out where he was. "The ocean..." As if to confirm his suspicion, his cockpit rose and then dove in a flurry of rolls.

To his surprise, laughter bubbled up through Rhys' throat and escaped his lips. Though the pain in his neck and back told him that it was best to sit still, he couldn't help the sudden glee and elation he felt. He was on Earth. It didn't matter where on Earth he was, it didn't even matter that he was currently in a capsule rolling around in the middle of the ocean—he was home! It was far better to die here surrounded by an overwhelming abundance of life than in the cold and lonely embrace of space.

"*Heather*," Rhys called. "Do we have radio contact?"

"No," replied *Heather*. "Much of the cockpit was damaged after separation from the main frame. The nuclear reactor dropped into the sea thirteen kilometers from here. All instruments and gauges were short-circuited during reentry due to the extreme heat."

Rhys laid his head back and gritted his teeth as the cockpit passed over a swell. "Is there... no way to contact *Apex*?"

"An emergency signal is being produced, but due to this cockpit's current location, it is unlikely that contact will be made soon."

Unaccustomed to having an AI so blatantly and stoically share with him bad news—he really disliked *Heather*—Rhys resolved himself to spending the next few hours on the watery and hellish ride.

By the time the seas settled, Rhys was beyond relieved. Finally able to release his harness without the risk of knocking himself out, he cautiously moved from his chair. Fierce pain reverberated down his neck and back. Every muscle along his spine burned. The joints in his fingers were stiff, and the tendons at his elbows remained painfully taut.

Resting at the edge of his seat, he worked his weak fingers before gingerly undoing the clasps of his suit at his throat. After testing the extent of movement his neck would allow, he slipped from his space suit. When the weight was off his torso, he rolled his tight shoulders. After several long moments of methodically working out his fingers, arms, and shoulders, he unzipped the internal lining and unceremoniously dragged it down to his waist, leaving him bare-chested and out of breath from the effort.

Moaning, he sat back in his chair and stretched out his legs, taking care not to move his neck. Mentally and physically exhausted, he stared at the darkened cockpit screen.

It took but a few minutes before he was jerking the interior lining of his suit back on. It was cold, uncomfortably cold. He had to be at a different latitude.

With his space suit hanging around his waist, he stiffly opened the cockpit. A sharp and bitter wind tore into him, shocking the air from his lungs. Never in his life had he experienced such fierce cold. He stood on the cockpit seat and gazed out at the dark, gray sea. There was nothing for kilometers. Just roiling dark water and eternally solemn clouds.

After marveling at the extreme difference in temperatures, he retreated to his cockpit and closed the hatch. Pulling his space suit back on to regain the warmth he had lost, he sat.

Over the next few hours, the temperature in the cockpit dropped. No longer powered by the nuclear reactor, the pod was succumbing to its environment. By midday, Rhys had pulled the spare clothes from his pack and begun wrapping his exposed skin. He would like to have moved around to warm up, but the tight space in the cockpit barely permitted him to stand much less perform exercises.

He managed to sleep for a few hours late into the afternoon but eventually woke, cold and miserable. Despite Ethos' promise that someone would come pick him up, not a single ship was on the horizon. Realizing that he might have to do some engineering to the cockpit capsule to encourage directional movement, he began evaluating the supplies and materials he had at his disposal.

The close of the day found him once again staring blankly at the cockpit screen, idea-less and without any means to propel himself. The irony of his circumstances did not pass him. The fact that he was in a state-of-the-art war machine that had no means to propel itself when detached from its frame—at least in Earth's gravity—was not encouraging.

Resting his feet on the instrument panel, he pulled his emergency pack beside the cockpit chair and began going through its contents out of boredom. As he took apart his pistol and examined it, he attempted conversation with *Heather*. The AI was as talkative as Andy and had the comprehension of a young human. Because it was not a learning system, words outside of its vocabulary remained a mystery even after Rhys explained them. *Heather* only knew commands, vocabulary, and jargon related to the piloting of its unit. Eventually, he gave up and sat in silence.

A few hours later just after he had begun dozing, *Heather* woke him with a soft beep proceeding its report. "Airborne contact, twelve degrees off port."

Rhys turned—painfully—in his chair and grabbed his resonance cutters, the short rifle, and his pistol. With some difficulty, he wrapped the holstered pistol around his waist and then strapped the resonance cutters over his back. The short rifle he rested on his lap. He would wait until the unit arrived before opening the cockpit. It was impervious to most threats which would give him time to evaluate his possible rescuers.

The airborne unit *Heather* had spoken of arrived. Though he couldn't see the craft, *Heather* constantly reported its location. When the AI confirmed the unknown unit was atop the cockpit capsule, Rhys fell motionless and listened. There were no roaring engines, there were no indistinguishable voices—there was nothing. He wanted so badly to know who had arrived but didn't dare open the hatch for fear of being killed. Not all humans could be trusted; he had learned that long ago.

Two loud clunks on either side of the cockpit were followed by the irrefutable sensation of being lifted. As *Heather's* cockpit was pulled from the rolling of the sea, Rhys leaned toward the hatch. When the swinging of his cockpit capsule grew rather uncomfortable, he finally risked a peek. Cracking the door open, he glanced upward. A smile pulled at his lips as he recognized the hull of a Caelestis maintenance unit.

Unwilling to face the bitter cold and fierce wind, he retreated into the capsule and mused on his situation. He had been picked up by his own people. So, it was true—Caelestis had crashed. Pieces of the colony had managed to find their way all over Earth. He wasn't being rescued by Earth natives nor by people he actually knew, but this was good enough. These people were of his home colony. They spoke the same language and had the same cultural values. Of course, they had seen Ethos' broadcast; they had even picked up on his rescue beacon. They could help him get back home.

When it became apparent this was not a short trip, Rhys settled back in the cockpit chair and allowed himself to doze. Nearly two hours later, the patterned rocking of his capsule came to a sudden halt, causing him to wake. Realizing that, though he had stopped rocking, he still hung in midair, Rhys cautiously peered out the cockpit.

He expected to see a segment of Caelestis neatly tucked away on an island or along a deserted forest line. What he found was a fortress surrounded by impenetrable walls of metal which were illuminated by searching spotlights. Though he could discern a large fragment of Caelestis from the metal encampment, he found the majority of the fortress comprised of carved stones and rocks neatly layered to create towers and other buildings. The fortress was set in the middle of a barren land decorated with scrub, dry grass, and rocks. In the distance loomed purple mountains.

Realizing that perhaps he was not with the people he thought, he braved the cold to watch their descent into the protection of the metal walls.

The maintenance unit set his cockpit outside a large, spiraling tower and released the clamps which had secured the capsule to its hull before landing nearby. Lights flooded the area in a golden radiance. From his vantage point behind the cracked cockpit hatch, he saw the pilots of the maintenance unit leap out into the cold. At first, he was pleased to find silver hair, but his relief was short-lived.

Though they were certainly Caelestis citizens, their chests and shoulders broader. They were clothed in the skins and furs of animals and had plasma weapons strapped to their arms. As one of them turned to motion to another, Rhys spotted a pair of resonance cutters hanging from his waist. These people moved with intimidating confidence and assuredness; they carried with them grit that Rhys normally recognized as a characteristic belonging to Earthlings. Attached to their temples were AIs.

Summoning the courage he had left, he brought his short rifle before him and pushed open the cockpit hatch. The half a dozen or so Caelestis citizens speaking silently to one another fell still, their brilliant blue eyes on him.

Unwilling to trust them just yet, Rhys kept his short rifle at the ready and his gaze unwavering. Clearing his throat, he shouted into the wind, "I'm Rhys Falkrow. Where am I?"

"Neo-Colony Nine," replied one of the men in clear Interstellar Nefegian. Rhys was surprised by the coarseness of his voice. The man who answered left the group of his colleagues and approached the capsule. "We weren't sure you were alive after watching your unit explode."

"You're... from Caelestis, right?" asked Rhys, looking around.

"Yeah."

The man's casual reply puzzled Rhys. It was such an un-Caelestis-like response. "Uh, permission to enter Neo-Colony Nine?" He glanced at the others. "You rescued me, so…"

"Yeah, that's fine." The man ruffled his hair and sighed tiredly. "We've been on shift for the past fifty-six hours, so we're going to rest. You should do the same."

"Why is that?" asked Rhys.

"Because tomorrow, the fighting continues." The man motioned to the others, and together they walked off.

"Wait… What?" shouted Rhys.

Realizing no one was going to help him, he grabbed his survival pack and worked to heave it over the rim of the cockpit onto the frozen ground. The moment he lifted it, however, a crippling pain radiated from his neck deep into his spine. He collapsed onto the floor of the cockpit, panting. Was he dying? The pain was profound; he could hardly lift his arms.

After taking a moment to regain his composure, he forced his feet under him and, using his knees, hoisted the survival pack up to the edge of the cockpit rim. He pushed it over and stood gasping in pain. In disbelief, he looked about. Not a single person was present. Those who had rescued him had gone inside; he was once again alone.

His ears and nose burning from the cold, he looked back at his magnetic board which was secured along the innards of the cockpit. He would come back for it. There was no way in his current condition he would be able to use it.

With a small sigh, Rhys began the task of clambering out. No longer attached to *Heather's* frame, he couldn't just step out onto the wing. Instead, he perched himself on the cockpit's rim and then jumped two meters to the frozen ground. He meant to land with grace but instead collapsed to his knees and smashed his nose on the frosty earth.

He rubbed his face fiercely, but could do nothing to quell the fierce agony along his spine. Moaning, he rolled onto his back and stared up at the gray clouds streaking across the dark sky.

"You hurt?" came a voice from his right.

Rhys meant to look at the speaker but found he no longer had any movement in his neck. He said, "Yes, I'm hurt. I've been hurt for the past seventy-six hours." He expected an answer, but none came. After a long and awkward moment of silence, he said, "Hello?" Silence. Sighing, he pushed his elbows under him and struggled to bring himself to an upright position. He could hardly feel his nose, ears, and cheeks; he feared moving his neck or doing much anything else. It seemed his exploits in space had not gone unnoticed by his body.

"Sorry. Our senior medical staff are preoccupied right now. It looks like you get me."

Rhys regarded the boy who had spoken. He was young, perhaps eleven or so, and had large, blue eyes; his body was slight. His long silver hair was tied in a horsetail and blew behind him in the wind. He too was clothed in animal skins and fur-lined boots.

"Can you help me?"

The boy held out both hands. With some difficulty, Rhys pulled himself up before doubling over in pain. "Let's get inside," said the boy, collecting Rhys' pack. "I'm not supposed to be out right now."

As the boy strode off toward a metal door in the side of the stone tower, Rhys hobbled after him. The door slid open, and Rhys was enveloped in the protection of the stone walls. Though it was still cold, the wind was gone, and he could feel the blood rushing back to his cheeks and nose.

"This way," chirped the boy, crossing the barren stone floor and entering Caelestis' segment through yet another automated door. At least the hallways were the same; Rhys reveled in their familiarity. "Here." The boy stopped a few meters in, opened a door, and motioned to him

Rhys stopped in the doorway. Four other boys and two girls of the same age sat perched in their bunks, solemn eyes on him. "Hi…" he murmured. He was accustomed to Caelestis citizens' blank stares, but the looks in these children's eyes were grave. The expressions on their faces were grim, as if they had undergone months of trials and tests.

The boy deposited Rhys' pack on the floor and began stripping from his animal cloaks. "We can tend to you for now until someone from medical is available."

"Why are they busy? Where are they?" asked Rhys.

The boy, who was now shirtless, shrugged. "Tending to the wounded. It's been a hard day."

Rhys sighed and started across the room to a bare bunk. He sat on the bed carefully and looked at the others. They no longer seemed interested in him. Already, two had returned to bed while the others continued to speak silently. By the looks on their faces, he suspected they were not talking about him.

Rhys began pulling at his space suit but winced visibly.

"Uh… I was training in medical," came a small voice. "Before we got here, I was training to enter the medical department." The speaker, one of the girls, approached Rhys and gazed at him. "Do you need help?"

"Just get me out of this suit and analyze my neck. I can prescribe treatment for myself once I know what's wrong."

The girl began pulling away Rhys' space suit. Once it hung at his waist, she worked at the internal lining. He noted her calloused palms as she brushed his skin; hers were not the hands of a Caelestis citizen.

"I'm going to touch your neck now," she murmured. Rhys gave his approval, and the girl set her chilled hands on either side of his neck. "You might have a few torn muscles…"

"That's what I thought," replied Rhys. He had already diagnosed himself and taken painkillers in the cockpit. The best course of treatment was rest and inflammation reducers. "Could you bring me my pack?"

When he had his survival pack and the clothes bag his crew had packed for him, he dressed. After administering another anti-inflammatory injection, he pulled his shirt on and breathed in its familiar scent. When it came to removing the lower half of his suit and the catheter, he asked the girl to turn away. She returned to her bunk without question.

"We saw your unit explode," said the boy who had escorted Rhys inside. "Everyone was sure you died."

"Well, I didn't," replied Rhys, gazing at the boy. "Say, can you explain to me what's going on? You said all the medical staff are preoccupied with the wounded? You're at war?"

The boy shrugged and seated himself at the table in the middle of the room where two of his cabin mates watched. "We've been fighting the locals since we arrived. They weren't pleased to see us." The boy's nonchalant attitude disappeared as he said lowly, "It's never going to end."

"Yes, it will." Rhys arranged his weapons within arm's reach along the bunk's interior wall. The two other boys seated at the table scoffed. He gazed at them and then said, "Let me tell you a story."

It was nearly dawn when Rhys finished explaining about Osiris and his mission to the moon to the cabin of eager-eyed children.

"So… your home is on the other side of Earth?" asked Connel, the boy who had first reached out to Rhys. "Is that why you're so much darker than us?"

"Right," replied Rhys.

Connel exchanged looks with the others before saying, "It's… probably going to be a while before you get back there."

"Can't… I just take one of the maintenance units? I was an engineer. I can fly anything." Rhys looked between Connel and another of the boys who had been particularly talkative. He still didn't know the child's name.

Connel, who sat on the floor, leaned back on his hands. "We only have the one unit that picked you up."

"What else do you use for transportation?" asked Rhys, distraught.

"Nothing," replied Connel.

"There's… no solar-powered technology here?"

Connel and the others shook their heads. "From what I understand, we were one of the less lucky segments. We were given unequal resources before detachment from Caelestis."

"And we landed in this shithole," added another. He sounded bitter. "Others landed in better places."

"Why haven't any of the other colony fragments come to your aid?" asked Rhys.

"Because we're small," replied Connel. "And we don't have vital divisions." He nodded to Rhys. "What segment does your region have?"

"Neo-Colony Two."

Every person in the room sighed in jealousy, despair.

"But all of this should change now that Osiris is no longer in power," assured Rhys. He felt he needed to provide some encouragement to these children, even if he felt none.

"War is a slow process," said one of the girls.

"It's been going on since we got here," said Connel. "Each day we think it will end, but it doesn't. They come up with new tactics and new weapons."

"How are they getting the weapons? From whom?" Rhys thought. "What kind of weapons are they? Do they look like these?" he asked, pointing to the short rifle behind him.

"Some of them do," replied one of the boys.

"They have bombs and missiles," added Connel. "We've reinforced the old castle remnants here with our own materials, but their weapons still do damage."

Rhys motioned to the door. "What's your population here?"

"Uh…" Connel looked at the others.

It was one of the girls who spoke. "When we first came here, we were two thousand four hundred strong."

Rhys looked between Connel and the girl. "And what is it now?"

"I think eighteen hundred, but I could be wrong." The girl smiled. "We're children here. None of the adults tell us much because…" Her smile faded. "Here on Earth, we can't do much."

"We're not strong enough or tall enough," added one of the boys sourly.

"At least on Caelestis we had class and lessons," said Connel. "Here we just hang out all day and sometimes help the adults when there's an attack. Mostly, they just tell us to stay out of the way."

Realizing that was a good place to stop, Rhys motioned to them. "I need to sleep, as do all of you. Keep what I've told you between just us for now. I need to figure out my next course of action."

There were solemn nods before everyone returned to their bunks. After a few minutes, Connel turned out the lights. Rhys lay in his bed and stared into the darkness. The room was completely silent, making the thoughts in Rhys' head loud and intrusive.

Was it possible that his time in Quadrant Six was over and the next chapter of his life had begun? Was that it? Just like that, every relationship he had built over the past year and a half was gone? Was he meant to be here at Neo-Colony Nine? Was he going to grow to love this land and then, in a year's time, be forced to leave it?

Tears gathering in his eyes, he worked to calm his mind. He needed to think rationally, he needed to think logically.

What would Alina, bold and decisive, advise?

What would Andy, always knowing, softly recommend?

What would Kashim or Axel, strategic and logical, suggest?

What would Leo theorize, speculate?

What would Hodge begrudgingly tell him to do?

What would Kallen whisper encouragingly to him?

Holding tightly to the heartache swelling in his chest, Rhys finally managed to fall into a restless sleep.

Only an hour or two passed before a deep rumble rose outside Neo-Colony Nine. Thinking it was the wind, he forced his heavy eyes to close once more. No sooner had he done so than a terrible and ear-splitting boom like that of a crack of thunder shook the colony. So loud was it that Rhys thought something had just crashed through the rear wall of the bunk.

Months of training and sudden exercises in survival rolled him from his bed, pistol in hand. Kneeling on the floor, he gazed about in the darkness and listened. Outside Neo-Colony Nine, he could hear gunshots and the undeniable boom of cannons.

Taking a few calming breaths to quell his nerves and the aching pain in his neck, he sat back against his bunk.

The red emergency lights within the cabin flickered on. He looked at the other beds and was surprised to find all of Caelestis' children piled into two bunks sitting silently, watching him. Connel appeared grim as did two others, but the rest were stricken with fear. Their eyes were wide and cheeks flushed and tear-streaked.

"Do you know what's going on?" asked Rhys, dragging his survival pack to his side. The pain in his neck was crippling.

"We're under attack," replied Connel.

"I got that much." Rhys administered another anti-inflammatory injection. Though the time between the doses was short, he sensed he was going to need the extra pain-killer.

"Like I said earlier, they don't tell us anything," Connel gravely concluded. "We're expected to stay out of the way."

Rhys rolled to his knees, winced, and pushed his feet under him. "Certainly they would have told you whether—"

An alarm within the colony began wailing, and he froze. This warning was different than the others he had heard. It moved rhythmically between two pitches before transitioning into a series of yelps. Footsteps pounding at the end of the hallway were followed by gunfire and yelling.

Adrenaline pumping through him again, he snatched his resonance cutters from his bed, threw them over his shoulder, holstered his pistol, and prepared his short rifle. He glanced back at the children. Connel and another boy stood from their bunks, brandishing two forearm-mounted plasma weapons while the others crowded together on the bed.

Rhys understood now. That particular siren meant intruders had infiltrated Neo-Colony Nine. "Connel, you. Get over here," commanded Rhys, motioning to the door. The two boys jumped to action. Rhys stationed Connel on one side of the door and then shoved the table in the middle of the room upright on its side. He motioned for the other boy to position himself behind it.

Rhys placed himself beside Connel and listened. There was still gunfire, but it sounded as though it was moving down another corridor away from their cabin. For several long moments, they remained silent and still. Just as he thought to check the outer hallway, the door to the cabin opened and an enormous, burly man brandishing a rifle cautiously stepped in.

Not knowing who this person was or if he was danger, Rhys decided to speak out. "Don't move."

The man swung his rifle. So close was he that Rhys was able to push the man's weapon downward with his forearm before firing two shots into his attacker. As the man collapsed to his knees, Rhys jerked the rifle from his opponent's grip and tossed it behind him to Connel. Thinking quickly, he looped his own rifle over his shoulder, grabbed the man's arm in an arm bar just as Hodge had taught him long ago, and—with some difficulty—dragged the intruder into the room.

"Weapons up," ordered Rhys, releasing the man and hurrying back to the open door. As Connel and the other boy trained their plasma arms on the enemy, Rhys peered into the hallway to make sure the gunfire had not been heard. Seeing no one else, he closed the door and turned to the enemy.

The man was as large as Kashim if not broader. Brilliant blond hair covered the man's head while an impressive golden beard covered the lower half of his face. He too wore animal skins, but his garb was of superior quality and make than those of Neo-Colony Nine and was interlaced with fabric.

"Who are you?" asked Rhys in Nefegian. He had to start somewhere. When the man just glared up at the floor, Rhys asked again in Aabesh. Again, no response. Somewhat doubtful that his final language would be much help, he said in Elali, "Who are you?" To his utter and complete surprise, the man looked up at him. "You know that one, huh?"

The man spat at Rhys' feet before curling around his abdomen. Already his blood seeped onto the floor.

Rhys motioned for Connel to step back and then knelt beside the man. "You will tell me who you are, or I will let you bleed out. I'm a doctor; I can save your life. But if you do not start giving me answers, I will let you die right now."

"It would be an honor to die at the hands of the enemy," growled the man.

Groaning, Rhys gazed at the man. The stubbornness was all too familiar. "Come on, *kalul*." Rhys silently thanked Kallen for teaching him old Elali slang. "Do you really want to die, alone..." Rhys motioned to the children. "This room is full of children. Should your comrades find your body, they will say, 'Ah, he was killed by children.'"

The man glared up at him, but Rhys thought he saw some softness enter his gaze.

"I am a doctor. I can save your life. Can you really blame me for shooting you though? Come on, *kalul*. They're children. Look at how frightened they are." Rhys nodded to the girls sitting on the bed at the back of the room. "Give me some answers? I'm new here and don't know what's going on."

The man's light eyes narrowed. "You're new? What does that mean?"

"I'm not from here. Can't you tell by the fact that I speak your language? My wife speaks your language. That's how I know it."

"I will… talk with you… but only if you tend to me first."

Rhys shook his head. "You know that's not fair. Once I save your life, then you will just betray me. I know how it works."

"No, *you* will betray *me*," snarled the man. "You silver-haired rats are good at that."

Trying to keep up a positive façade, Rhys nodded. "See, *kalu*? Already I know more now. These people here are not very trustworthy and have betrayed you in the past, yes?" The man gazed at him uncertainly. Switching languages, Rhys asked over his shoulder, "What did you do when you first got here? He says you betrayed them."

Connel shook his head. "I don't know. A lot of things happened when we first got here."

Rhys returned to Elali. "The boy says he doesn't know what you speak of, but that doesn't mean they didn't betray your trust. He's a child, after all."

"You don't… have one of those metal things on your head," said the blond-haired man.

Rhys pushed his hair away from the receptors. "I used to, but I got rid of it. Listen, I just want to know what's going on. I don't want to kill any of your men. And I don't want to kill you."

"Coward," the man muttered.

"Wanting to save a life is cowardly?" Rhys shrugged. "I suppose if you've been taught from birth that your life is meaningless and that upon your death you'll triumphantly be reunited with your fallen brethren among the stars, dying isn't such a bad thing." He glanced at the man. "But for those of us who do not believe in such a thing, life here and now is what matters. Life is for certain."

The door to the cabin slid open suddenly to reveal three silver-haired men from Neo-Colony Nine. Rhys leapt up and barred their entry into the room.

"Move," ordered one of the men. "He's one of them."

"No, this has to stop. I'll deal with him," Rhys demanded.

"He is their *leader*!" came the snapped response.

"Oh…" Rhys glanced at the man who was watching the conversation with disgust. "Post sentries at the door then. I want to question him."

"No, he will die for what his people have done."

"Enough!" barked Rhys. "Did you ever stop to think that maybe *you're* in the wrong here and not them? I have no idea what's going on, but why can't you just stop and talk? You have the technology at your fingertips. Talk to him." One of the men raised his plasma firearm. "Stop!" Rhys knocked his arm downward and twisted it into a hold. "Just... stop." He met the citizen's blazing blue gaze. "Talk for a minute."

Rhys felt a hand touch his shoulder. A split second later, a roar of electricity coursed through his body, knocking his knees out from under him. He crumpled to the floor, muscles taut and unresponsive. Barely conscious and vision swimming, he willed himself to move, but his body remained motionless.

A handful of gunshots echoed in the hallway. Before Rhys could comprehend what had happened, the Neo-Colony Nine men standing in the doorway collapsed, dead, a pile in the doorway.

"Enough," the blond-haired man ordered in Elali. Struggling to move, Rhys managed to look up at the four burly men who appeared in the doorway, rifles bared. "Get me up."

With some feeling returning to his body, Rhys fought to roll onto his elbows and knees. When he felt the barrel of a rifle touch his head, he froze, eyes glued to the floor.

"He's coming with us. Grab him," asserted the blond-haired man as his subordinates dragged him to his feet.

Rough hands like those of Kashim's snatched the back of Rhys' shirt and jerked him backward. "Give me a second!" Rhys snarled in Elali. "I've been shocked."

The newcomers, obviously startled by his ability to speak their language, fell still. Rhys took a deep breath and pulled his feet under him. He wavered there for a moment before looking at the silver-haired bodies in a crimson pool.

"Grab him," ordered the leader. "Let's go."

Hands once again began pulling him, but Rhys rooted himself to the ground. "My pack. At least let me get my pack."

One of the burly men dragged Rhys over his fallen people. "Come on."

"If you want me to save his life, you will let me get my damn pack!" snarled Rhys.

The men looked between themselves before motioning for him to retrieve the bag. Wobbly, Rhys staggered over to his pack and lifted it. As he turned, he caught Connel's eyes. "Not everything is what it seems," he murmured to Connel. "Keep searching for answers."

Connel, who had tears in his eyes, retreated to the rear of the room where the other children cowered.

Before Rhys could make it over the bodies in the doorway, one of the men wrenched him into the hallway and yanked his short rifle from him. He was unceremoniously escorted down the hallway and out into the howling wind of the frigid morning.

Wearing only pants and a shirt, Rhys felt the air in his lungs freeze. His feet burned and every tendril of heat in his body was ripped viciously from his skin. He resisted leaving the stone-encrusted doorway and backed into the shelter of the tower. There was a momentary struggle before he was overpowered and pushed headlong into the wind. Feeling as if he were dying, Rhys folded his arms into himself and tucked his head against the cold.

Unnoticing of his condition, the men around him urged him onward with constant prodding until after a few meters, he was met by a strange vehicle. Settled upon spiral-shaped wheels was a carriage which showcased a glass screen and a sloping, aerodynamic frame. Atop the carriage were two oddly-shaped sails, three or four meters in length, straining against the wind. Rhys only had a moment to consider the vehicle before he was lifted clear from the ground and tossed into the carriage. He somersaulted once before lying on the bare, carpeted floor, wheezing. At least the vehicle offered respite from the cold.

The wounded leader piled in next followed by his subordinates who shut the door and motioned to the pilot of the unit. As the leader lay on the floor of the carriage, Rhys gathered himself in the corner and watched.

"Fix me," the leader huffed, drawing Rhys' attention from the launch of the vehicle—not that he could see out anyway.

Shivering violently, Rhys dragged his pack across the floor and knelt beside the leader. With shaking hands, he withdrew spare clothes and threw those over his head quickly. The relatively thin, long-sleeved blouses weren't much, but they were better than nothing. Rubbing his hands between his legs to warm them, he began organizing the medical equipment beside the pack. He expected the ride to wherever they were going to be a rough one. If the vehicle was wind-powered as Rhys suspected, the torrential gales would rock the vehicle like an angry sea tossing a ship. As he considered his options, however, he realized he had noticed little movement from the vehicle other than simple acceleration. It was quiet.

Once organized, Rhys turned to the leader, met his gaze briefly, and then began pulling his clothes away from his abdomen. "Light," he murmured in Elali. To his surprise, an overhead light flickered on. Studying the leader's wounds, he thought through his options. The first shot had just grazed the man's side leaving a nick of skin raw and bleeding. The second, however, had been a direct hit to his abdomen. After withdrawing another small light from the pack, Rhys investigated the depth of the wound.

"Are you sure he's a doctor?" whispered one of the men.

"Yes, I am," replied Rhys without looking up. After prodding at the man's gut and pushing on his organs, he discerned that, miraculously, none of the organs had been damaged. "Nothing is punctured," he concluded, sitting up and cleaning his hands on a sterilizing wipe. "It looks like both bullets entered and exited which is good. You'll only need maybe five or six stitches along your side. The bullet hole will just take a bandage." He retrieved cleaning supplies from his pack and began sterilizing the wounds.

"Manus Robasdan," offered the leader. Rhys glanced at him but continued to work. "What's your name?"

"Rhys Falkrow."

"The savior of the world?"

Rhys looked up in humor but, upon seeing the utter seriousness on the men's faces, fell still. "Why do you think that?"

"We received a radio transmission the other day from a mysterious source concerning a 'Rhys Falkrow,'" explained Manus.

Rhys continued to work. "And what did it say?"

"That you saved all of mankind from a fate worse than anything Earth has ever known," replied one of the other men.

Ethos had always had a flair for the dramatic. Rhys finished cleaning the main abdominal wound and began bandaging it.

"Are you that Rhys Falkrow?" asked Manus.

Rhys gently applied the bandages and nodded. "That's me." To his surprise, smiles broke over the men's faces as they looked between themselves. They appeared to be genuinely thrilled. "Can... any of you tell me what's going between your people and Neo-Colony Nine?"

"Is that what it's called?" asked one of the men.

"It was a segment from a space colony that crashed here on Earth." Realizing that perhaps, like the Pantaraks and those in his home region, he would need to explain the concept of space, Rhys added, "Uh, space is the dark sky overhead that holds the stars—"

"We know what space is," Manus interrupted. "We're not savages like those people on the colony." The utter confusion and bewilderment Rhys felt must have been evident by the expression on his face because Manus continued. "We may be dressed in furs, but we're not uncivilized. The animals around here are some of the heartiest beasts on the planet. Their skins are perfect for protection against the cold weather. Those white-haired space rats are the true barbarians."

Rhys sat back and gazed between Manus and his men. What had he stumbled into?

46
BUREFELL

By THE TIME RHYS FINISHED Manus' sutures, the vehicle had stopped. Everyone waited for him to complete his work before opening the side door to allow icy wind to sweep through the carriage. Rhys, who had been cleaning up, cowered against the cold. He would much rather be sweating through multiple sets of clothes than fighting the frozen tundra. Once everyone, including Manus, was out of the carriage, a man returned with heavy clothing as well as boots.

With the doors closed to protect against the wind, Rhys examined the clothes he had been given—an oversized, green tunic lined with fur, fur-lined pants, water-resistant boots, and an enormous coat with a furry hood. By the time he finished dressing, he was no longer cold. In fact, he was sweating from the effort of getting dressed. When he stepped from the vehicle pack, slung over his shoulders and resonance cutters in hand, the cold wind cooled him, and he finally found a happy medium.

In the early morning light emanating from the low-hanging, gray clouds, he found himself standing in the middle of a city. Before him were paved roads, colorful low-profile buildings with interesting architecture, and women and children draped in winter trappings greeting fathers and husbands. It appeared they had ended their journey in the military section of the city for there were numerous warehouses, artillery similar to cannons perched in rows under shelters, and men who had just returned from the attack on Neo-Colony Nine standing about in the cold talking.

Beyond the military buildings were, Rhys assumed, homes built into the side of rolling, bare hills. Shops and other government buildings distinguished by their elevated architecture and eye-catching colors lined the paved roads into the distance.

"Falkrow. This way," called one of the men who had been traveling with him.

Rhys followed him through the crowds of men into one of the nearby buildings which, he discovered, was a prison. Frowning, Rhys stopped in the doorway. "Why am I here?"

The man eagerly motioned for him. Rhys crept down the aisle of iron cells. Though a few were occupied with locals, most of the cells were, to his relief, empty. At the end of the aisle, he met up with the man who stood before a barred chamber, his hands folded behind his back. Rhys followed the man's gaze to find a silver-haired individual sitting cross-legged on the cold, stone floor. Though Rhys was happy to see that he at least wore fur clothes, the middle-aged Caelestis man had an iron chain locked around his ankle. His hair was long and grungy, and his face mildly gaunt. He refused to look up at them.

"He is our first and only captive from the colony," explained the man beside Rhys. He did not sound boastful, only matter-of-fact. "When the colony first arrived, we were willing to provide aid. Survival in such a harsh environment is based on teamwork and resources. We started to trade with them to help, but they wanted more. Although we didn't speak the same language, it was apparent they wanted to control all the resources and to dictate who received what." The man looked at Rhys. "That's not how it works here." He nodded to the prisoner in the cell. "He was their leader. We captured him about two months ago. Ever since, there's been nonstop fighting."

"Why did you attack the colony this morning?" asked Rhys.

"The colony attacked us the other day, killing several people including children. The chief is trying to discern how many people are in the colony to determine the likelihood of complete annihilation."

Rhys remained silent. He was in no place to judge these people. He did not know what they had gone through the past several months. One thing was for certain though—Neo-Colony Nine was at fault.

Despondently, he looked at the man in the cell who still wore his AI. "So, how much of what he says is true?" Rhys asked in Nefegian. The man looked at him with wide, panicked eyes. "He says you Caelestis survivors have been trying to gain control over the trade routes and resources in the area."

"What are you doing here?" asked the man. "You're supposed to be back at the colony."

"I was captured," replied Rhys. "Look, is what he said true?"

"You shouldn't have left the colony," the man said ominously.

"Why?"

"Because they will come for you. They will kill for you just as they did for me."

"I understand that…"

The imprisoned Caelestis man shook his head. "I've tried to persuade them to stop, but they won't listen. Now that you've been captured, they'll kill everyone in their path. They will come for *you*."

"Explain to me what you mean. Why have the people of Caelestis gone mad?"

"The Core has been corrupted."

Rhys looked at him incredulously. "They're… still connecting to it?"

The man nodded. "Nightly. Several months ago, a list of instructions was passed through the Core and disseminated to the citizens. Since then…" The man swallowed visibly. "Everything has been wrong."

"Osiris," concluded Rhys. "And you don't know where the instructions came from?"

"We thought it was from one of our other segments. Was it not?"

Rhys sighed. "No, it was from an AI."

"I've been unable to connect to the Core for several weeks," the man continued. "Even now, what they do is incomprehensible. I can't understand their motives or why they've collectively begun acting as they have."

"Except the children," said Rhys.

"What?"

"The children haven't been connecting to the Core. At least, not the ones I found." Rhys pushed back his hood and ruffled his hair. "Let me see what I can do. This isn't going to be easy. The data within the Core has been tampered with."

"What's going on?" asked the man.

Rhys motioned to him. "Where is Manus? We need to talk."

After much debate with Manus' advisors and men posted at the doorway of the chief's home, Rhys was refused entry. Standing with his back against the howling wind, he looked at Daidh, the man who had been tasked with escorting him. Daidh, a bearded and burly individual like most of the men in the region, shrugged and suggested that they retire for the day.

Not denying his own exhaustion, Rhys followed Daidh to the man's house buried in a hillside and gratefully retreated from the cold. The moment Daidh stepped foot into his home, a blond-haired, green-eyed little boy waddled in from the adjacent room, crashed into the man's shins, and wrapped his small arms around the man's furs.

Laughing, Daidh lifted the child and moved aside so Rhys could enter and close the door. The aroma of food was strong; the warmth of the home was sincere.

"This is Faolan," said Daidh, presenting his son to Rhys.

Rhys leaned forward and smiled at the boy. "Hi, Faolan. It's a pleasure to meet you." The boy, who had been laughing just moments ago, fell silent upon seeing the color of Rhys' hair. Pretending not to notice, Rhys set his pack down and began shedding his clothes.

"Is that you?" came a lilting voice from the next room. As Rhys pulled his tunic over his head, he heard footsteps enter the small foyer. "I was wondering when you'd finally get off shift. I wish they wouldn't keep you so long."

Rhys slung his tunic over his shoulder and ruffled his hair into place before looking at Daidh's wife who had her arms wrapped around him. Over Daidh's shoulder, her gaze fell on Rhys and the warm smile on her face shifted into a horrified expression.

"Daidh!" the petite woman gasped, staggering away.

"Liosa, please. Easy," coaxed Daidh, stepping before Rhys. "It's not what it looks like."

"He's one of *them*!" she snarled, shoving Faolan into the next room and standing defensively in the doorway. Liosa, being the first woman Rhys had seen up close in the new city, was quite a surprise. Though petit, she was fierce with brilliant blue eyes and long, orange hair the color of a sunset.

"Liosa, please…" Daidh cooed. "He's fine."

"Mother, what's going on?" came a new voice.

Rhys looked up to find two teenagers—a boy and a girl—standing in the doorway both as copper-haired as their mother. The boy, who was perhaps Otto's age, thrust his sister protectively behind him and assumed a combative stance. Rhys chuckled nervously and said, "I suppose my appearance *is* somewhat alarming." Realizing that he spoke their language, the family fell still.

"As I was saying," continued Daidh, "he's fine. Liosa, you know that radio broadcast we received a day or two ago? It was about him."

Daidh's wife gazed at Rhys and then relaxed some. "So… you can speak our language?"

Rhys slid his hands into his pants pockets to appear less threatening. "My wife speaks your language. She taught me."

Daidh smiled and gave Liosa an expectant look. With a sigh, Liosa turned and collected Faolan before disappearing into the next room. Daidh sighed in relief and motioned for his other two children to approach. "This is Seoc. He'll be turning seventeen this month. And my daughter, Nia, who is nineteen."

"Pleased to meet you," said Rhys awkwardly. The hostile look in Seoc's blue eyes was disconcerting. "I'm Rhys Falkrow."

"Ah," said Nia.

Rhys glanced at Daidh to try to find the resemblance in their faces. While Nia didn't look at all like her father, she was the spitting image of her mother with glowing pale skin, long copper hair, and vibrant blue eyes. Small, tan freckles decorated her cheeks and nose and gathered around her shoulders and collarbone where her long-sleeved dress parted. Ashamedly, Rhys found her highly attractive.

"Don't get cozy," muttered Seoc. The eldest son, though of average height, was lean; his long-sleeved tunic neatly outlined his solid build and muscled chest. His crop of wind-whipped copper hair shaded hazel eyes and furrowed brows. "You're one of them. One wrong step and I'll take you down."

"That's likely to be impossible," said Daidh. Seoc scoffed and disappeared into the next room. "I'm sorry for his behavior."

"Don't be. I would expect nothing less," replied Rhys, glancing at Nia once more.

"You two go wash up," called Liosa. "Both of you reek."

"You'll be staying with us for a while. We were one of the only households with a spare bed."

"Hey!" shouted Seoc, reappearing in the doorway. "He is *not* sleeping in my bedroom!"

"Yes, he is," snapped Daidh. "Deal with it." Seoc kicked the doorway and retreated. "Come on."

After a quick bath, during which Rhys learned about wells inside the earth, he dried off and dressed in clothes that belonged to Seoc as, height-wise, they were well-matched. Clothed in pants, a long-sleeved blouse, a vest, and socks, Rhys left the confines of the washroom and shuffled down the hallway, peering into each room. He very much liked the narrow feel of the house; It reminded him of *Themis*.

Hearing hushed conversation from the front room, he slowed to listen.

"He's not going to do anything." That was Daidh.

"You don't know that. He's one of them," replied Liosa. "Please, Daidh… for your family. He could kill them in their sleep."

"The radio said he was the savior of Earth. How are we supposed to just disregard something like that?"

"What if it was a trap set by those rats?" asked Seoc. "What? I'm serious. It's possible."

"The transmission came from outside our network," said Daidh. "Come on. He saved the chief's life."

"Why do you trust him so readily? You know nothing about him. Please. Talk to Manus," Liosa urged.

"And say what?" whispered Daidh. "Sorry your Minister of Defense got scared? Liosa, you know Manus would never accept that."

"Why isn't he staying with Manus?" asked Seoc.

"You call him 'the chief,'" scolded Daidh.

Seoc sighed. "Why isn't he staying with *the chief*?"

Rhys leaned against the wall in the hallway and stared at the floor. He understood the position in which he had placed the family. He hadn't asked to be kidnapped, but truthfully, he hadn't resisted either. He had been all too curious to learn about the region's situation.

"You know eavesdropping is frowned upon here."

Rhys startled, slamming into the wall, as Nia joined him in the hallway. "I…" He cleared his throat and tried to regain his composure. "I didn't mean to." He glanced back toward the common room. "I've put your family in a strange predicament."

"Nonsense. It's my father's fault, not yours." Nia smiled sweetly and walked past him, leaving behind the faint scent of a floral perfume. "Are you hungry?"

Rhys followed. Daidh motioned him into the dining room and bid him to sit with the family around a small table. In silence, Nia and Liosa served food in bowls. Not recognizing the meat—or anything in the dish—Rhys watched the others as they ate.

"What's wrong?" asked Daidh.

"Uh…" Rhys looked to Liosa. "Is this *liiman*?"

"What's that?" asked Liosa. It was obvious she was doing her best to hide her disgust for his presence at her table.

"An animal… from the sea," murmured Rhys, realizing how ungrateful he must sound.

"No, it's not from the sea," Liosa replied.

"What's wrong with animals from the sea?" asked Nia curiously.

"I can't eat *liiman*," said Rhys, picking up a spoon. "I'm allergic apparently."

"I'll remember that," muttered Liosa. Rhys saw the disapproving look Daidh passed his wife.

The first few minutes of dinner were painfully quiet with only the clatter of utensils on bowls. The atmosphere combined with the food which rivaled Kallen's culinary skills depressed Rhys greatly and made his heart ache. The look on his face must have reflected his sudden dip in mood because Nia said, "Do you feel ill, Rhys?"

"Eh... no. I'm fine," he replied. It took him a moment to realize he had responded in Aabesh. Recognizing his mistake, he corrected himself and stood from the table. "If you don't mind... I'm going to go lie down."

"Are you sure you're not ill?" asked Daidh. The concern in Daidh's voice pressed upon Rhys how valuable he was.

"No, just very weary." Rhys shuffled from the dining room. He no longer cared if he was being rude or breaking some sort of cultural protocol. He just wanted to be alone.

In the cockpit of *Heather*, he had wanted nothing but to be back with humans, but now... Too much had happened already. Once in Seoc's room, he leaned against the wall at the foot of his bed and slid to the floor. Head in his arms, he listened to himself breathe and worked to ease the heartbreak in his chest that threatened to swallow him.

When he grew drowsy, he flopped onto his designated freshly-made bed and fell asleep. Unsurprisingly, he dreamed of Kallen and Hodge and of his home in Quadrant Six. He woke to a profound pain in his heart that physically hurt and made him feel ill. Wiping silent tears on his arm, he sat up and gazed about. Though he was certain he had lay down to rest shortly after midday, the window across the room was dark. Had he truly slept the entire afternoon?

He ruffled his hair into place and then shuffled into the hallway. He ran into Seoc who recoiled in disgust. "What time is it?" Rhys murmured.

"Midafternoon," replied Seoc, sidestepping him. "Why?"

Rhys peered into the common room where Daidh sat reading a book by lamplight. In the dining room, Nia leaned over a large map on the table and typed on a handheld device. The windows on the front of the house showcased twilight skies. "Why... is it dark right now?" he asked, entering the room. "Is this normal?"

Daidh glanced up from his book, amused. "During winter it is. We only get about four hours of sunlight during the winter. It's different where you're from?"

Rhys crossed the room and peered outside. Though the sky was dark, a thin line of light stretched along the horizon. Straightening himself, he thought. According to Ethos, despite the Earth's recent geographic upheaval, areas around the Earth's equator were typically warmer. Latitudes near the poles, despite having shifted over the past thousands of years, were still cold. Already, he was piecing together his location in relation to Quadrant Six.

"Rhys, is something wrong?" Nia stood in the doorway of the dining room. "You have a very solemn look on your face."

"Eh, sorry. No. I was just thinking." He glanced briefly at her afraid of what meeting her bewitching gaze would do to him. Instead, he redirected his attention to Daidh. "I'm sorry for disappearing earlier."

Daidh folded his book on his knee and shrugged. "It's obvious you're exhausted. Even before you excused yourself, you looked drained."

"Do you feel any better?" asked Nia.

"Yes, thank you. Has there been any word from Manus? I would like to speak with him. I could look at his wounds too."

Daidh continued reading his book. "No, only that he's resting. I've heard you did a good job tending to him though."

Frowning, Rhys glanced back outside. The quicker he spoke with Manus and helped solve the problems at hand, the faster he could begin working on returning home. How long had it been since he last saw Kallen? Or Hodge and Andy? Over a week? Maybe more?

"Am I allowed outside?" asked Rhys.

"You are, but I must escort you," replied Daidh. "Was there somewhere you wanted to go?"

Realizing that other than needing to speak with Manus, there was no where he needed visit, Rhys shook his head. Daidh continued reading, and Nia hesitantly returned to her maps and handheld device. Though Rhys should have been curious, he kept his attention focused.

Over the next few hours, he paced the house, lay in his bed, inventoried his pack's contents, checked his pistol, and stared blankly into the fire. By the time it was supper, he was beside himself with anxiety. Being cooped inside the house despite its warmth was a death sentence. The more he dwelled on it, the more he was compelled to action.

"What's your problem?" asked Seoc, watching Rhys pace between the hallway and common room. "Why can't you just be still?"

Rhys glanced apologetically at the boy and stopped in the middle of the room.

"You've been pacing all afternoon," added Daidh who had been dozing on the couch. "What's wrong?"

"I just…" Rhys sighed. "I need to speak with Manus. Please. Is there any way I can speak with him?"

"I can check, but you must know that it's going to be a while before you're needed."

"What?"

Daidh stroked his beard back into place and leaned on his knees. "Change doesn't come quickly. The conflict between Burefell and your people won't be solved in one meeting."

"Let me just speak with Manus. I can give him the information he needs, and I'll be on my way."

"You can't go back to the colony," said Seoc casually. "We'll have to kill you before that."

"Seoc," scolded Daidh. Seoc shrugged. "We're not going to kill you. But he's right. You can't go back to the colony. I'll give Manus a call and try to find out when he can meet with you. How is that?"

"Why did the chief even bother taking him?" asked Seoc. "He's done nothing but eat our food and sleep."

"Get!" shouted Daidh, pointing Seoc out of the room. The boy threw a glare over his shoulder and disappeared into the hallway.

"He's right though," murmured Rhys. "Why *did* Manus take me? Just because I could save his life?"

Daidh stood and stretched. "He must have seen something in you. I can't begin to know what goes on in the chief's head."

"Right…" Rhys glanced once more out the darkened window. Was this how Axel had felt after Rhys had taken him captive? Restless, anxious, helpless?

Dinner at the table was an awkward affair. While Nia and Daidh spoke of the maps she had been looking at, Liosa busied herself with cleaning dishes. Seoc picked at the food on his plate and threw hateful looks at Rhys.

Once the uncomfortable meal was over, Rhys retreated to the common room and stared into the fire. About an hour later, Daidh called to him. "Come on, we're going to the market to pick up a few items before the stores close."

Realizing he had nothing else to do, Rhys collected his winter clothes, resonance cutters, and pistol from the bedroom. With Daidh and Seoc, he dressed in the common room. Though he was sure Daidh knew he had a pistol, Rhys took measures to hide the weapon under his long tunic and jacket. Because he was too bulky for the resonance cutters to fit over his back, he buckled the tool along his waist for quick access. Rhys saw Seoc eye the weapon briefly, but the boy didn't say anything.

"Take care," chirped Nia from the dining room.

Stepping from the hillside cottage took Rhys' breath away. In the short amount of time he had spent indoors, he had forgotten the ferocity of the wind and its bitterly cold qualities. Pulling the hem of his tunic up around his face, he followed Daidh and Seoc along the main road back into the town. As the father and son spoke between themselves, Rhys studied the homes and buildings around him.

They certainly weren't glamorous like Brechin's architecture, but they had a certain quaintness about them that reminded him that these people had a wealth of resources at their hands. The buildings, though low to the ground to stand against the harsh winds, were beautifully carved from stone and painted in a variety of bold colors like reds, oranges, and turquoises, showcasing slanting roofs and spires to defend against lightning. The land surrounding Burefell was comprised of bare, rolling hills. If the sun ever rose again, Rhys was certain the mountains he had spotted from Neo-Colony Nine were just over the next ridge.

Once in town, Daidh led them to a butcher where he purchased meat from a list Liosa had provided. Afterward, they visited a grains store and then an herbs and spices shop. Rhys quickly learned to keep his hood over his hair. Pale skin and blue eyes were a cultural norm, but the addition of silver hair presented a problem.

On their way back to Daidh's home, Rhys fell in step behind Daidh and his son and contemplated escape routes. Once they entered the home, he stripped out of his winter gear, helped Daidh carry in the supplies, and then went to bed. He heard Seoc come to bed sometime later but didn't pay much attention to the time.

He didn't sleep long. Since space, his sleep cycle had been sporadic. That, coupled with his anxiety and general restlessness, prompted him to rise and go to the common room where a low fire burned in the hearth.

He sat before the flames and gazed at the embers glowing there. He wondered what Kallen and Hodge were doing. Were they worried? Had Ethos managed to communicate to them that he was alive? What about Firekli and Brechin? Had the fighting stopped? Had Brechin retreated? What about Neo-Colony Two?

Rubbing his aching neck, Rhys pondered on the fate of Quadrant Six. After an hour or so, he began feeling drowsy and so leaned against a nearby chair. Never without a weapon, he rested his resonance cutters on his lap and dozed.

The next thing he knew, Daidh was waking him. "We've got work to do. Get up."

Rhys glanced around the dimly lit room to find the rest of the family assembling with weapons. Rhys moved to his knees but crumpled as the pain in his neck and back flared.

"What's wrong?" asked Daidh.

"Can you get my pack?" Rhys murmured. He tried moving once more, but the motion made his entire body quiver from the effort. Daidh reappeared with his supplies, and Rhys withdrew a pain killer and injected it into the back of his shoulder. He remained motionless until the pain began subsiding. "I'm fine, I'm fine." Rolling to his feet, he stood. "What's wrong?"

"You sure you're fine?" asked Nia.

"An old injury," he murmured.

"Enemy forces have been spotted heading this way."

Rhys' first instinct was to check Ethos, but remembering that he was without an AI, he sighed quietly. "From where? The colony?" Daidh nodded. "How many?"

"Not sure yet."

Rhys hurried into the bedroom and retrieved his pistol. Wrapping its belt around his waist, he returned to the common room and began dressing in his winter clothes. He was surprised to find Seoc and Liosa both wearing rapiers on their hips while Nia and Daidh had weapons resembling rifles.

Motioning to Nia, Daidh opened the door and disappeared outside. Seoc and Liosa moved farther into the home and turned out the lamps. Somewhat confused by the family's battle strategy, Rhys hesitantly followed Daidh and Nia into the cold night.

The door to the house closed behind him and everything within went dark. Rhys watched as Nia murmured to her father and then stepped on something in the ground. A lever snapped up from the frozen earth, and Nia jerked it upward to reveal a trapdoor. With practiced ease, she sat and then disappeared into the ground. Daidh motioned for Rhys to follow.

Trusting fully in his captors, Rhys mimicked Nia and stepped through the trapdoor. Just inside there was a shallow ledge where he placed his feet before taking another step and descending to the floor below.

It took a few moments for him to realize that he was not in a hidden room but a tunnel which stretched in either direction along the city's main roads. Tying back her long copper hair, Nia watched as Daidh closed the trapdoor. Dim light bulbs overhead faintly illuminated the tunnel, casting deep shadows between their lengthy intervals.

"Where are we going?" Rhys whispered.

Daidh motioned toward town and took off in great strides. Nia and Rhys jogged to keep up with the giant man. Though it was apparent all of the homes in the area had access to the tunnel, they came across no one else. Either the others had already gone ahead or they were barricading their homes. Rhys didn't dare ask Daidh. The man's demeanor had changed drastically in the past few minutes and once more he had become the hardened and unapproachable man Rhys had met in Neo-Colony Nine.

In silence, they walked for half a kilometer before Daidh motioned for them to stop. Crouching at an intersection in the tunnel, he peered around the corner and then nodded to indicate it was safe to continue. Nia withdrew a device and worked on it in mid-step. Twice more did Daidh pause at an intersection in the underground corridor, look cautiously around the corner, and then signal that it was safe to continue. Glancing at the screen of Nia's handheld device, Rhys finally comprehended what they were doing.

The device was in communication with others in the area which tracked the enemy's movements and to determine safe routes using the underground tunnels. Nia was User Number One. She was the one who had to first determine if the tunnels were safe before the other citizens could begin to utilize the underground route.

For nearly two kilometers this continued until Daidh stopped them once more. Judging from his body language, the large man had heard something. Rhys fell still and listened. He could hear footsteps coming down the tunnel to their right.

Daidh pushed back Nia and readied his rifle. There was a moment of silence before Rhys heard clothes shuffling—and a high-pitched whining. Realizing that he was the only one capable of hearing the whining as it was a result of the remnants of his AI connection, he slid out of his enormous coat and let it fall to the floor. With a gentle hand, he took Nia's arm and pushed her farther behind him. He approached Daidh and touched the man's shoulder. When Daidh looked back at him, Rhys motioned for him to step back. Hesitantly, Daidh obeyed.

Caelestis citizens were present. How had they gotten there? Rhys leaned into the corner, his hand on his resonance cutters. He swallowed the apprehension building in his throat and said in Nefegian, "You're not welcome here. Go back to the colony."

There was a moment of silence before a voice called, "You know why we're here."

Refraining from the urge to retort, Rhys crouched. "Are you aware the Core has been tampered with?" There was a long moment of silence. "You realize that everything you've been doing for the past few months has been dictated to you by an AI on the moon, right? That was my whole mission while in space—to disable that AI so Earth could live the way it was meant to."

"We've been told, by that same entity, that you are not to be harmed under any condition," came the low response. Judging by the voice, the speaker was approaching the corner. "But if you resist us, we will use force."

"Stop connecting to the Core," warned Rhys, his muscles tightening under him like a spring. "Things might start making sense if you do."

The speaker stopped just around the corner. "Come. Let's handle this as citizens of Caelestis."

Rhys backed away from the intersecting tunnel. If he replied now, he would give away his location. Undoubtedly though, their AIs had already detected their heat signatures. Rhys glanced back at Daidh and Nia who both had rifles raised. "Don't shoot," he murmured in Elali. "Please." Neither of them moved; the resolve in their gazes remained unwavering. "Fine!" he said in Nefegian, straightening himself. He raised his hands and stepped into the intersecting tunnel.

He found four Caelestis citizens clothed in skins and armed with plasma weapons. Now that he was properly facing men from Neo-Colony Nine, he could see the vast difference in physique between them and those from Neo-Colony Two where Veran and his father were. These men were larger and more broad-shouldered, equaling Rhys both in height and weight. Despite connecting to the Core nightly, it seemed that living in such a stressful and harsh environment had caused the citizens to adapt to survive. Their faces were haggard, sharp, like they'd not had a decent meal in weeks.

"Disarm him," murmured one of the men.

Realizing this was going to be one of the only chances he had to escape, Rhys waited for the Caelestis citizens to approach him. The moment his resonance cutters were touched, he slammed his arms downward to push the hands away and then spun on his heel. His boot connected with someone's face. Before his first opponent staggered into the wall, two more lunged forward.

Dancing back to avoid being shocked, Rhys evaluated the situation. If the first man remained down, then perhaps he could take on the other three—but it was going to be a difficult fight. With sweeping arm motions, he blocked the incoming flurry of expert punches before unfurling a kick to his primary opponent. As his second adversary doubled over, the third man attacked.

In matched strength and skill, Rhys and his third opponent exchanged blows, kicks, and punches. Realizing that he needed to use tactics people from the colony didn't know, he took a direct kick to the gut to bring the man's foot into his control. Trapping his opponent's leg to his side, Rhys jerked it sideways, effectively rotating it so the man's knee was now parallel to the floor. With a powerful palm strike, he snapped his adversary's knee and rolled him onto the floor.

"Stop!" came a voice.

Panting, Rhys looked up to find the first man he had kicked and the fourth who had abstained from fighting pointing their plasma weapons at Daidh and Nia. Both Daidh and his daughter had been forced to deposit their arms onto the floor.

"You're making a mistake," growled Rhys in Nefegian. "What you're doing, what all of you are doing, is wrong." Seeing his second opponent approach him, hand outstretched, Rhys withdrew his resonance cutters and engaged them. Everyone fell still.

"You want to get home, right?" asked the man who had not joined the fray. "We can help."

Suspicious, Rhys remained poised. "What do you mean? How?"

"Neo-Colony Seven is a twelve-hour flight from here. They have the means to get you home."

Rhys glanced at Daidh and Nia who were watching darkly. Though they didn't know what was being said, it was obvious by Rhys' reaction that something of great importance had been offered. "What happens if I come with you? What do you want from me?" Rhys asked. "How do I know you won't kill me?"

"Because the Core told us not to," came the nonchalant response. "As for what we want... You know where their leader is. Take us to him, and we will see to it that you get to Neo-Colony Seven."

"No. I'm not helping you kill these people."

"We don't want to kill them, just their leader."

"That amounts to the same thing," Rhys snarled.

"You want to return home to Neo-Colony Two, right? Show us where their leader is, and we'll you take to the nearest colony. We know they—"

In a flurry of movement, Nia jerked a small rapier from within her jacket and swung forward, ducking underneath her captor. With impressive speed, she tore into her opponent's gut and, whirling on the ball of her foot, sliced through the arm which carried the plasma weapon.

A split-moment after Nia began her assault, Daidh pushed his opponent's firearm away, withdrew a secondary pistol from within his robes, and fired. In the time span of four seconds, both had maimed or killed their captors. Without pausing to breathe, Daidh turned and in single shots, killed the other two. Side by side, Daidh and Nia squared up with Rhys.

"What did they say to you?" Daidh demanded.

Rhys gazed down at his dead brothers. He wasn't fond of them; he felt no connection to them. But they were lost lives. Their deaths could have been avoided. He had even planned to tend to the man whose leg he had broken.

"Rhys," barked Daidh, pointing his pistol. "What did they say to you?"

"That they could get me home," Rhys murmured. "That I could go home." He looked at Daidh. "If I told them where the chief was, I could go home."

"What did you say?"

"No…" Rhys stared despondently into the darkness. "I said 'no.'"

"You realize your wavering just now has put me in a bad position," said Daidh. "I've been ordered to give you free range so long as I escorted you because Manus trusted you."

"I know."

Rhys heard Daidh holster his pistol. "Hand over your weapons."

"You know I don't need my weapons to kill you," Rhys muttered.

"Fine, keep your arms. If I see you so much as reach for them though, I'll put a bullet in your back."

Rhys sheathed his resonance cutters. "It didn't have to end this way."

The ground above suddenly quivered and a deep rumble ensued. Nia whipped out her handheld. "Fighting has begun along the western edge of town."

"Let's go," said Daidh. He stepped over the bodies and grabbed Rhys roughly around the arm, yanking him upward. "You are not to leave my side. Got it?"

Rhys didn't resist. "Yeah."

Nia threw Rhys his jacket and started at a jog down the main tunnel. For more than a kilometer, they ran until Nia climbed a set of steep, narrow stairs and pushed on a trapdoor with her shoulder. She climbed out; Rhys and Daidh followed.

"There you are," wheezed a familiar voice. Rhys turned to find Manus clothed in nothing but an open fur-lined jacket, bandages, and pants. The chief looked them over and seeing blood asked, "What happened?"

"We were intercepted," replied Daidh. "But everything is taken care of. What's the situation?"

Manus pulled Daidh away and began speaking lowly. Rhys glanced at Nia, who was studying her handheld, and then looked at the enormous room they had entered. It appeared to be a temple for within the cavernous room were numerous rows of pews and a dais centered at the front. Windowless walls painted with colorful abstract art soared upward to form a beautiful dome overhead.

"Rhys," called Manus. "Walk with me."

Rhys followed Manus through a door at the rear of the temple into a preparatory room. The moment the door closed, the chief turned on Rhys. "You want to go home? Figure out how to solve this conflict."

"No pressure," Rhys mumbled sarcastically.

"I'm serious. If that's your only motivation, then we will make it happen. But right now, we have a war going on."

"Why didn't you just leave me with the children in Neo-Colony Nine? I was already aware something big was going on. I wasn't going to join the colony in their battle."

Manus nodded thoughtfully. "I was right."

"About what?"

"Your character." Manus gingerly handled his beard. "The inhabitants of your colony recognize themselves as a superior race; unfortunately, we do not. They want to control everything. We're not willing to let that happen."

"They can't help it. Everything has always been controlled for them by the colony government." Rhys glanced about the room. "I'm guessing they feel that everyone on Earth should be controlled too." He sighed. "Look, I don't know how to solve the problem. I don't even fully understand what the problem is. Besides, you're going to need more than one person to dissolve the animosity here. One person won't be enough."

Chuckling, Manus dug deep into his coat pocket and withdrew a handheld device like the one Nia carried. "That's not what I've heard," he said.

"Hi, Rhys," came a heartbreakingly familiar voice.

In that moment, Rhys forgave; he forgave all. "Hey… Ethos," he whispered, his voice trembling. Never had he been so thrilled to hear the voice of an AI, much less one that, several days ago, had betrayed him. "Hey. It's good to hear you."

"Haven't been back for more than a week and already you're causing trouble," chirped Ethos.

Not caring that Manus saw his relief, Rhys gave a wet laugh. "Ethos. My calculations… were wrong. I was off by several degrees."

"Rhys, you hand-calculated your trajectory without the aid of a computer," chuckled Ethos. "Not many people could do that."

Rhys finally looked at Manus who was smiling. "Eh, how did you… How are we talking right now?"

"It took a while, but I tracked down *Heather's* beacon. From there, I found Neo-Colony Nine and gathered the information they use to monitor their citizens' whereabouts. It's the same tracking technology they used to find you when you were shot," explained Ethos. "I found a terminal capable of receiving satellite radio and here I am. I know, I'm a genius."

Rhys wiped his eyes. "Yes, you are. Kallen and the others?"

"They're fine. They know you're alive and are currently trying to find a way back home."

"I'm sorry to interrupt," said Manus, "but I need to know…" He held out his hand. "Will you come fight with us?" Rhys gazed at Manus' handheld. "Your friend here has told me about some of your conquests. I'm sure we could find a use for you."

"Will… I be able to get home?" Rhys murmured. The question was meant more for Ethos, but he was willing to accept an answer from Manus.

To his relief, it was the AI who replied, "One thing at a time, right?"

"Yeah." Roughly, Rhys took Manus' arm and shook it.

"Welcome to Burefell," said Manus, releasing Rhys' hand and pushing the device into Rhys' palm. "I think this should belong to you." The chief of Burefell clapped Rhys on the shoulder and started for the door. "Let's go. We've got work to do."

Rhys smiled at the handheld, stuffed it into his pocket, and followed Manus back into the temple.

EPILOGUE
1 YEAR, 18 MONTHS, 19 DAYS LATER

THE EVENING AIR WAS WARM and the breeze along the bow of the ship pleasant. Overhead, purple-tinted clouds decorated the golden sky as the sun slipped below the horizon. Leaning on the railing, Rhys breathed deeply and gazed out at the sunset.

"It's so disgustingly hot," came a voice from behind him.

He glanced over his shoulder, allowing the wind to whip his raven horsetail around him. The look of revulsion on Seoc's face warmed Rhys' heart. "It's only going to get hotter," he replied, amused.

"How can you stand it?" Seoc joined him and leaned on the railing. The boy had grown over the past year; already he was taller than Rhys. His untidy crop of copper hair stood out brilliantly against his pale skin, emphasizing his luminous blue eyes. Pushing nineteen, he was leaving his awkward teenage stage and blossoming into a lean adult. "So... does any of this look familiar?"

Rhys chuckled. "No. It's water. Where's Arian?"

Seoc groaned. "The woman is insatiable. All she wants is sex. I'm only one man."

Rhys shrugged. "You're the one who wanted to bring her."

Seoc kicked Rhys' pants leg playfully. "She brought herself. If you recall, I tried to get her to stay back in Morwen. But nooooo."

"Just so I understand—you're complaining because you're getting *too* much sex?"

Seoc closed his mouth, thought, and then nodded. "Yeah, I take all of that back. Sorry."

"That's what I thought." Rhys touched his still healing shoulder and winced as pain reverberated down to his elbow.

"Do you want Connel to look at it again?" murmured Seoc.

"No."

"Don't let it get worse. I know how you are."

"Yeah, yeah." Sensing Seoc's gaze on him, Rhys looked at his friend. "What?"

"Does it ever hurt?"

"What? My shoulder?"

"No, your…" Seoc motioned to the dull scar that stretched from the middle of Rhys' forehead between his eyes to his left cheek. "Does it hurt?"

Rhys shrugged. "Sometimes it aches, but it's healed for the most part."

"What do you think your family will say when they see it?"

Rhys thought. He wasn't sure. It had been nearly two years since he last saw Kallen or Hodge or any of the others from *Themis*. Though he had strong memories of them, their faces had become distant and their voices quiet. "I don't know."

"Hey, it's time for dinner!" called Connel from the open cabin door across the deck. "The others are already eating. If you don't hurry, there won't be anything left."

"Shit," muttered Seoc. Together, they raced to the galley, hoping the merchants hadn't eaten everything already.

Just as Rhys had predicted, the following week grew hotter until once again he found himself sweating while doing nothing. The merchants they were traveling with eventually sought Rhys' guidance to make sure they weren't sailing into some sort of hell. The forty or so crew members of the enormous merchant ship—including Connel and Seoc—began complaining regularly, and soon, the topic of the day everyday was if the thermometer measuring the temperature outside the ship was going to reach a new record. While Rhys also felt the pressures of the heat, he reminded himself that this was nothing compared to the sauna he used to work in while on *Themis*.

During his free time onboard, Rhys taught the ship's fair-skinned crew how to make headscarves, how much water to drink, and how to cool off. Daily swimming expeditions into the tepid sea provided much-needed breaks from the heat and every evening after dinner, large portions of the crew could be found on the lower rear deck lounging in the water gathered there.

Connel, who had thrown himself at Rhys' mercy during the conflict between Burefell and Neo-Colony Nine, had blossomed like Seoc. Despite being only fifteen, the boy was naturally out-going and personable. His intelligent eyes, though sharp, were perpetually full of warmth which encouraged Rhys to confide in him often. The merchant crew also adored Connel. Rhys always found Connel tailing someone onboard or listening to instruction from other crew members. The boy enjoyed learning just as Rhys did and thrived in the environment.

While Seoc spent most of his days with his lady friend, Arian, whom he had met in the last port, he found time to carry out chores aboard the vessel. Daidh had instilled in him discipline and shared in the workload. Unlike Connel, who thirsted for knowledge and experience, Seoc was content with who he was and his skills. Already, Daidh's son had been by Rhys' side for over a year. Though he was not as personable as Connel, Rhys heavily relied on him.

When it came to conflict, Connel tended to avoid it, choosing instead to collaborate behind-the-scenes; Seoc, on the other hand, could be found in the middle of the fray beside Rhys. Thanks to the training Daidh had given his son long ago, Seoc was a natural fighter and teammate. He could take a hit and keep going which hinted more at his stubbornness than his strength. When Seoc's obstinacy strained the dynamics between him and Rhys, Connel stepped in and patched up the relationship. In return, Seoc and Rhys watched over Connel and safeguarded what innocence he had left. Though they had once been enemies, both Connel and Seoc enjoyed each other's company and, when Rhys wasn't around, could be found hanging out, talking lowly of their frigid home.

As for Rhys, much had changed over the past year and a half. Not only had he acquired some new injuries and scars from the constant battles he had taken part in, but he had undergone new life experiences as well. He was now fluent in four languages—Interstellar Nefegian, Elali, Aabesh, and Panganese—and had served as a representative and translator for three different nations during his travels. He had learned what it meant to order men to their deaths in combat and of the guilt and grief that accompanied that kind of power.

He had learned farming techniques and merchant skills and even created the first prototype solar panels for a city. He had picked up the flute and now carried it with him in his travels for when he lacked entertainment. Not only had he seen an extraordinary array of plants and wildlife, but he had met many different people from a variety of backgrounds and cultures. It was because of his encounters that he wore such tokens as a large beaded bracelet and a hair a tie made of a special leather; it was also because of these encounters that he knew he needed to keep up the habit of dying his hair until he was back in familiar waters. Never was his now shoulder-length hair a shade lighter than dark gray.

Rhys had also experienced what it was like to be with another woman and learned that not all women were like Kallen.

He had never thought anything of the sort would happen, not when he was surrounded by conflict and determined to find a way home, yet he had found himself in bed with the copper-haired Nia on numerous occasions. No one knew, not even Seoc, Nia's brother. It had been Rhys and Nia's secret made in a time of stress and desperation. Seoc and Connel didn't know and neither would Kallen. His relationship with Nia was over. It had never been anything more than two humans seeking comfort with one another and, even though Rhys sometimes wondered what she was up to, more often, he thought of holding Kallen in his arms once more.

He no longer had anything to remind him of home. All his supplies, clothes, and weapons had been lost or destroyed. About seven months into his journey, he lost his magnetic board after a stray plasma blast from Neo-Colony Six disintegrated it. A month after that, Seoc broke the handheld Manus had given Rhys by sitting on it, making communication with Ethos no longer possible. He had long ago discarded his clothes as they were unfit for the climate. The survival pack he had carried for a few months after leaving Burefell was left behind when a small city they had been staying in was forced to evacuate due to an all-consuming fire.

The only memento of his previous life that Rhys carried was his resonance cutters. Never were the resonance cutters out of his sight. Even as he moved about on the merchant ship, he wore the weapon. The cutters remained in his hand or close to his body at night.

By the time another week had passed, both Seoc and Connel were ready to disembark. Seoc had cabin fever and refused to spend daylight in his cabin despite Arian's purring pleas. While Connel remained as pleasant as ever, Rhys saw a shift in his desire to learn, and soon, the boy was listlessly carrying out chores. Rhys was sure it was the heat.

The merchants whom he had promised wealth and prominence— they were discovering a new trade route after all—grew restless and aggravated with one another and bickered constantly. Knowing the crew was a strong one, for he had seen them in action while in cooler weather, Rhys could only conclude it was the heat. The men and women aboard had sailed together for years. This new climate was not sitting well with them.

Rhys, on the other hand, felt at home. It took a few days for his body to re-acclimate to the hot and humid weather, but once it did, he found the heat strangely comforting. It was the old and familiar. Noticing his willingness to work out in the sun, many of the ship's crew members ended up requesting that he take their outdoor jobs. Rhys bartered with them and shared his new-found wealth with Connel and Seoc.

After weeks of sailing from port to colony to port, Rhys knew they were getting close. Undoubtedly, they were back in Quadrant Six. His innate sense of direction told him that. The weather, the color of the sea, the wind, the plant and animal life—all of it added up. Every day, he calculated their position and relevance to where he thought Firekli was. Though he didn't have exact coordinates, he had used his own people to point him in the direction of Neo-Colony Two. From there, he had calculated Firekli's general location.

As he repaired the instrument paneling on the bridge of the ship one morning, a call suddenly rose from outside. Not thinking anything of it, he remained lying on his back underneath the bridge paneling, wires tangled around his hands. In a matter of a minute, reports came to the bridge that land had been spotted. Hurriedly, Rhys finished his reparations and, with the Overseer of the ship, surveyed the land through a spyglass. The outline and general geographic characteristics appeared familiar even from a distance, but how trustworthy was his mental map? It had been almost two years since he had last been in the area.

Over the next three hours, he continuously studied the land and paced the deck outside the bridge. He couldn't help the excitement, nervousness, and apprehension swelling within him.

All of that came crumbling down, however, when airships deployed from the port and made for the merchant ship. Hurrying back to the bridge, Rhys pushed the radio engineer aside and began speaking in Aabesh, a language he had not used since he was last in Quadrant Six. The words came slowly, and his mind struggled to utter their pronunciations.

"We are a merchant vessel seeking trade in the port of Firekli," he managed to say. He cringed at how stiff he sounded. He hadn't realized how out of practice he was with the language.

In a flurry of words, a reply came back. Rhys stood motionlessly, trying to remember vocabulary and how to properly form a grammatically correct sentence. When he could not discern the entire response, he asked, "Who is the port authority? Is Yanamichin there?" There was no response. Rhys reviewed the structure of his question and then nodded. He had said it correctly. Why weren't they responding?

"What's wrong?" asked the merchant ship's overseer.

Rhys shrugged. "They aren't answering my question."

"Should… we prepare for an attack?"

"No, no… Hold on. If we show hostility, they'll meet us likewise." He leaned on the paneling and gazed out at the airship hovering overhead. He couldn't see who was aboard it. If it was Brechin soldiers, they were done for. That thought sparked an idea, and Rhys queued the radio once more. This time he spoke fluently in Nefegian. "We are a merchant vessel seeking trade in the port of Firekli. Who is the port authority? Is Yanamichin present? Over."

"We do not speak the nobles' language," came the reply in Aabesh. "Please wait."

Rhys sighed. He was both relieved and troubled. It seemed Brechin had not taken over Firekli; Aabesh was still the primary language of the port. That meant trouble for Rhys because he was the only one onboard who could speak Aabesh—and his language skills were wanting. "Slow us down," Rhys ordered the Overseer. "I think they're trying to reach the port authority. They've asked that we wait."

The ship's overseer slowed the vessel until they had just enough speed to fight the current.

"This is Malau Yanamichin," came the General's voice. Rhys couldn't help hide the smile on his face. "I am the port authority. To whom am I speaking?"

Rhys puzzled through the translation before answering. "Yanamichin, this is Rhys Falkrow."

Laughter burst through the radio. "Rhys? It's about time, boy! Where have you been?"

Rhys considered the sentence. "On… the… eh… world. No, on the other side of the world." So as not to cause suspicion, Rhys added, "I have not… spoken Aabesh in many months. Eh, so my skills are rustic. Eh, sorry. Rusty. My skills are rusty."

"Get into port, boy. We'll talk then," came the reply.

"Thank you. Over." Rhys set the radio down and breathed in relief. He was flustered with excitement and the urge to communicate intelligibly.

"Everything set?" asked the Overseer.

Rhys nodded. "It's good. Head into port."

As the Overseer gave the orders, Rhys retreated to the back of the bridge where Seoc and Connel stood. "That's what they speak here?" asked Seoc.

Rhys leaned against the wall. "I'm unbelievably out of practice."

"But… you can still speak it, right?" Connel prompted.

"Yeah, it's just going to take a few days for my proficiency to get back to where it was."

There was silence between them before Connel said, "You're not going to leave us once we get to port, are you?"

"I can't. I promised the merchants I would act as their translator until it was time for them to leave." Seeing the looks on Seoc and Connel's faces, Rhys smiled. "No, I'm not leaving you. To be honest… I don't know where anyone is. They could all be in another port or out at sea. I have no way of knowing." Rhys nodded to Connel. "You need to pick up Aabesh. It's a descendant of Altaic languages. Use those records to build a basic understanding of the language."

"And what about me?" asked Seoc.

"There are a few Elali speakers in the region, but the language is dying out here. I'll teach you."

Seoc looked out the bridge with a frown. "What happens if they don't like us?"

"Firekli is a mixing port. People from all over gather here. You're not going to stand out. You'll be fine so long as you remain polite." Rhys motioned to them. "Come on, let's go clean up."

After a nerve-wracking hour to port, the enormous merchant ship finally docked. Rhys, Seoc, and Connel disembarked before a crowd of onlookers and escorted the Overseer and his subordinates to meet Yanamichin. The port authority greeted them at the end of the dock with three armed militiamen. Rhys stepped before the Overseer and gazed at Yanamichin. He remembered the man being much larger and foreboding. Perhaps being in the presence of so many larger individuals for so long had skewed his view of Yanamichin.

The port authority also seemed puzzled by Rhys' appearance. Yanamichin studied him, searching his face. Realizing that perhaps he did appear different, Rhys held out his arm. "Hey, it's good to see you again."

Yanamichin took his arm and gave a small bow over their hands. His eyes never left Rhys. "Are you…" Yanamichin seemed thoroughly confused. "I don't really know who I'm looking at."

Rhys smiled. "A lot has happened since I was last here. Do we have…" His grin faded as he realized he couldn't remember the correct word to complete his sentence. "Do we have… eh, the right? No, ah! Permission!" Rhys laughed. "Do we have permission to dock here?"

Yanamichin laughed. "It *has* been a while, hasn't it? Of course."

Rhys introduced the Overseer to Yanamichin and then Seoc and Connel. While Seoc put on a strong front and mimicked Rhys' greeting,

Connel remained soft-spoken and reserved. After introductions, Rhys translated for the merchant Overseer and Yanamichin as they worked to determine the proper course of action for establishing trade. By the end of the lengthy conversation, Rhys found his comfort with Aabesh returning.

Yanamichin eventually requested that they follow him to his office to register. After Rhys advised him on port etiquette, the merchant Overseer relayed to his crew what they should and shouldn't do. They then followed Yanamichin to the main port office. Everything was just as Rhys remembered it—the roads, the docks, the buildings, even Yanamichin's crowded office.

For nearly an hour, Rhys translated paperwork for the ship's overseer and worked as an intermediary between him and Yanamichin. After a while, Connel and Seoc left the stuffy office to wait outside. Once Yanamichin and the merchant Overseer came to a legal agreement concerning what they were eligible to trade, they shook.

Mentally exhausted from straining to remember Aabesh, Rhys left Yanamichin's office. He found Connel and Seoc speaking with, to his utter delight, Kashim. The rugged man looked exactly the same save his now neatly trimmed beard. Heart in his throat, Rhys watched as Connel worked to formulate sentences and stumbled over words. Kashim nodded in complete understanding and offered supplemental vocabulary when Connel faltered.

"Hey," murmured Rhys, approaching them.

"Help me," Connel pled softly.

Kashim, who had had his back to Rhys, turned and froze. For the first time in his life, Rhys saw a wide smile break over Kashim's face. The man's eyebrows lifted in surprise, and he laughed aloud as he grabbed Rhys' hand and jerked him into a hug. "Hey, hey. When did you get here? Were you on that merchant ship?"

Rhys clapped Kashim's enormous back and pulled away. "We just got in a few hours ago."

Kashim smacked Rhys' arm fondly. "Look at you. You're so… different."

"Yeah. Since…" Rhys stumbled over his words. "Since when did, eh, you cut your beard?"

Amused by his stiff response, Kashim stroked his beard. "Since I've been working with Yanamichin here in the port. I started about ten months ago."

Not knowing what else to say, Rhys turned to Seoc and Connel and, in Elali, said, "This is Kashim. He was my Second Mate." Rhys switched back to Aabesh. "Kashim, this is Seoc Penry and Connel Eztia. Seoc is from a city called Burefell, and Connel is from Neo-Colony Nine."

"It's a pleasure to meet you," said Kashim.

"Likewise," replied Connel. Seoc nodded despite not having understood what was being said.

"Rhys," called the merchant Overseer, leaving Yanamichin's office. "We have to go have these notarized, right?"

"Right," replied Rhys. He smiled at Kashim. "Is anyone else here?"

"Kallen, Hodge, and Andy are all in town. Otto and Cantia are still at Neo-Colony Two. Leo and Terron are back in Brechin with their father. I don't know where Jules is. Let's see—Tessa is in New Arbroath and Leela and Patrin, I believe, went back to Maliyansa." Rhys glanced at the merchant Overseer. He knew he was promised to the Overseer for the next several days. "Go on. I'll find the others and let them know."

"Thanks." Rhys smiled at Kashim and then followed the merchant Overseer from the port authority office.

The afternoon passed in a whirl for Rhys. So busy was he tending to the merchant Overseer and admonishing the ship's crew for breaking port protocols that he didn't notice the setting sun until he found it too dark to read. Perched on a set of crates on the dock, Rhys stretched.

"Can we please eat?" groaned Seoc, resting against a nearby crate. "I'm dying."

"I think the galleyman is cooking," offered Connel.

"Noooooo." Seoc leapt to his feet and looked about. "We've been on that wretched ship for weeks. Can we please find some real food?"

Rhys squinted at the documents. It was becoming impossible to read the Overseer's contract. A strong but pleasant gust of wind swept through the port pulling Rhys' horsetail over his shoulder. He took a deep breath and nodded. "Yeah, fine. Let's go eat. Connel, go tell the Overseer we'll be off-ship for a while."

Connel, who had been lying flat on the dock, rolled to his feet, and with grace, climbed the stairs to the ship's main deck.

As Rhys folded the Overseer's contract into his pants pocket, he asked, "Where's Arian? I haven't seen her since we docked."

Seoc leaned on the crate, chuckling. "She left."

"She... left? How? When?"

"Shortly after we got back to the docks, she left. Said goodbye to me and disappeared into the city." Seoc grinned. "Don't give me that look. You knew there was nothing to it but sex."

Rhys slid off the crate and straightened his clothes. "I did. To be honest, I'm more worried about Arian. She doesn't speak anything but Elali."

Seoc shrugged. "She's a free spirit. She's meant to wander."

Connel reappeared momentarily, and together they started down the lamp-lit cobblestone street toward town. They stopped at the port authority office once more to give Rhys a chance to find Kashim, but no one seemed to know where he was. Rhys, Seoc, and Connel took their time wandering Firekli's streets.

After paying for dinner at a local eatery with the money they had exchanged earlier in the day, Rhys led Seoc and Connel deeper into town. Though he hoped at every intersection that he would run into a familiar face, he never did. As the evening passed, Seoc, wanting to drink, encouraged Rhys to find a tavern. The first one they came upon, they entered.

As Connel eagerly ate a sweet cake, Rhys and Seoc sipped on local alcohol and listened to the duet playing music in the corner.

"You look restless," Seoc remarked.

Rhys tossed back the rest of his drink and rested his chin on his hand. "I thought that when I finally got here, I would feel like I'm back at home." He frowned. "I just feel like a stranger."

"I'm sure that'll change once you're reunited with everyone," encouraged Connel. "Do you want this?" He held up a piece of fruit. "I don't like it."

"Wait, I wanna try," said Seoc, intercepting Rhys' hand.

"You're not going to like it," Rhys chided, remembering the first time he had eaten that particular fruit.

Seoc took a bite; his face folded in on itself. Quickly, he chewed and swallowed. "It's so bitter!"

Rhys took the remaining half and calmly ate it. Looking about the tavern, he sighed. "Ready to go back to the ship?"

Seoc must have sensed his despondency because he finished his drink and stood. Connel stuffed the final bite of his cake into his mouth and hurried to dig out money from his pocket. Rhys thanked the owner before they started back to the docks.

"Everything will turn out fine," assured Connel, nudging Rhys. Rhys flinched as the pain in his shoulder flared. "Ah, sorry. Sorry. I forgot. Maybe I should look at it once we're onboard."

"Yeah," murmured Rhys. He saw Connel exchange looks with Seoc. "I'm fine. Seriously. It's been several weeks now. It's just going to take time."

In silence, they walked down the street. Every so often, Connel stopped to look at a store front window or study an intricate piece of woodwork. The boy encouraged Rhys to explain to him what it was he was looking at; not wanting to dampen his thirst to learn, Rhys patiently provided explanations. Eventually, Connel skipped ahead to better examine the presentation inside a clothing store window leaving Rhys alone with Seoc.

"What happens if you don't find them?" asked Seoc.

"Then we move on," Rhys replied.

"You don't want to stay here?"

"Not if they aren't here."

"Connel told me your friend in the port authority office says others are in town."

Rhys frowned. "Why haven't they come to the docks yet then? We've been down there all afternoon."

"Oh…" Seoc nudged Rhys fondly. "Everything will work out. Hey, please start teaching me Aabesh. At least, give me some words so I can function."

Despite himself, Rhys chuckled. "It's been fun watching you struggle though." Seoc tripped Rhys in mid-step. "Fine."

"Just easy words like 'please' and 'thank you.' Where? What? Who? When? You know, easy stuff."

For the remainder of their journey, Rhys taught Seoc Aabeshian vocabulary which greatly livened the mood as Seoc was *horrible* at the language. Even Connel, who had been using Pathos that day to learn the language, laughed at Seoc's butchered attempts. By the time they reached the wharves, Connel and Seoc were play-fighting one another.

"It's about damn time," came a voice down the pier.

Rhys froze; Seoc and Connel stopped their rough-housing. There, standing in the light of a single lamp on the docks, were Hodge and Kashim.

"Where have you been? We've been waiting for hours," chided Hodge, approaching Rhys. Seoc stiffened by Rhys' side, discerning the situation based solely on Hodge's tone.

"Hey, hey," murmured Rhys, touching Seoc's arm as he passed. "Sorry, I wasn't... eh... expecting guests."

Hodge burst into laughter and grabbed Rhys roughly around the shoulders.

"Ah, ah, wait! Hodge," said Rhys as his friend hugged him tightly. Rhys pushed on him hard. "I'm hurt, I'm hurt."

Hodge pulled away and looked him over. "Shit, what happened to you?" he laughed. "What happened here?" He traced the scar on Rhys' face. "Which shoulder's hurt?"

"The left one."

Hodge clapped Rhys on his right shoulder, beaming. "You have... no idea how good it is to see you." Rhys gripped Hodge's arms. "Do I look different?"

Rhys couldn't help but nod. Whereas Kashim had not changed, Hodge looked like a different person. His once-wild hair was trimmed neatly and parted on the side and his face was clean-shaven. Though he still had the same build as before, he wore nice clothes—pants, a long-sleeved blouse, and a vest. "What... do you do? Why are you dressed like that?" Rhys finally asked, amused.

"I started my own courier company." Hodge laughed. "I had to do something to support Kallen."

"Kallen, where is she?" asked Rhys.

Hodge's smile faded. "It's come as a surprise that you're back in town. It's going to take her a little bit to come around."

"Oh..."

"But," said Hodge, "you'll be glad to know that she and the baby are fine."

"What is it?"

"A boy," replied Hodge. "His name is Ronan." Rhys laughed, his heart aching. "He's just over a year old."

"Ronan," said Rhys, trying the name out.

"Ronan Falkrow. Don't worry. Kallen will come around. It's been hard on her with you not being here." Hodge looked back at Kashim. "Right?" The wolfish man nodded.

"Eh." Switching back to Elali, Rhys motioned to Seoc and Connel. "This is Hodge. He's a sunboarder and now, apparently, owns his own courier company here in port." He slipped back into Aabesh. "This is Seoc Penry and Connel Eztia. Seoc is from a city called Burefell, and Connel is from Neo-Colony Nine."

Hodge shook their hands, exchanged greetings, and then asked, "So, you're staying on the ship?"

"We don't really have anywhere else to go," replied Rhys.

"What did he ask?" said Seoc.

"Whether we were staying on the ship."

"Please tell me he has a spare room," Seoc breathed. "I don't want to go back on that damned ship."

Smiling, Rhys glanced at Hodge who had been watching the conversation in interest. "You wouldn't happen to have a spare room, would you?"

"Hehe, see here's the problem. I live with Kallen, the baby, and Forge and his girl. We—"

"Wait, Forge has a girl?" interrupted Rhys excitedly.

Hodge looked back at Kashim. "You didn't tell him?"

Kashim shrugged. "I forgot."

"Yeah, Forge met a girl about six months ago." Hodge chuckled warmly. "It's been fun watching him change. She's been putting him through the ringer, but they're doing good." It took a moment for Rhys to translate what Hodge had said but already his friend had caught him. "What's going on? You're acting strange."

"Eh." Rhys glanced at Seoc and Connel. "I haven't spoken Aabesh since I was... last in Brechin."

"Ahhh, I see." Hodge nodded. "Well, let me talk to Kallen when I get home. I'm sure she'll still be awake. Do I need to find you a doctor?"

Rhys gestured to the teen. "No, Connel can take care of me."

"Get some rest." Hodge handled the side of Rhys' face with familiar fondness. "We'll see you in the morning." Kashim ruffled Rhys' hair as he passed and followed Hodge back into town.

"I like him... I think," Seoc admitted.

That wasn't the Hodge Rhys had yearned to see for months. That person calmly strolling down the docks was a different man. Why?

"Is something wrong?"

"No." Rhys turned for the ship. "Come on."

The following morning, he rose before dawn and stood out on the rear deck overlooking the open waters. He watched as fishing boats trolled out to sea and dock workers began their shifts. The breeze was already warm; it was going to be another hot day.

He had had a restless night. His mind worked feverishly to remember Aabesh, forcing him to periodically murmur aloud phrases to test how they felt on his tongue. He thought of Hodge and Kashim and wondered what Kallen was thinking. He tried to picture Ronan in his head, but he found that, even with having seen hundreds of children over the past two years, he could imagine nothing. Would Kallen still love him? What if she was angry with him for being gone so long?

Rhys began pacing the deck, stopping briefly to look out at the sea. All this time he had dreamed of being back in Firekli, of being where he thought home was. But everything had changed.

Eventually, he returned indoors to prepare for another long day of translating. Because he had been softly reprimanded for not appearing more well kept the day prior to better represent the merchant Overseer, Rhys dressed in the best clothes he owned—a pair of slacks, a long-sleeved blouse whose sleeves he rolled to his elbows, a vest, and an emerald sash which he borrowed from the ship's First Mate—and waited for the Overseer on the bridge. Seoc and Connel were not needed, so Rhys did not wake them.

When the merchant Overseer and three other officers appeared, Rhys led them off the ship into town to meet with Yanamichin once more. He was supposed to be directing the merchants to the market, but Rhys no longer remembered where the open market was.

When they arrived at the port authority office, Rhys found a middle-aged female secretary at the front desk in the common room. After explaining what they were there for, she provided a small map and drew for him a route to the open market. He thanked her and, after briefly looking for Kashim in the other open offices, led the merchant and the crew members to the market.

Walking ahead of the group listening to them chatter in Panganese, Rhys felt miserably alone. Of course, he understood what they were saying, but because he was not a part of the crew, his opinions didn't matter nor did his input. He was their guide; whatever they wanted, he provided. That had been the agreement.

At the entrance of the market, Rhys pulled the group together. Though their appearances wouldn't stand out, their language and nonverbal cues would. He described appropriate and acceptable behavior. He gave them hints as to how they should bargain and to whom they should give attention or money. When he felt he had exhausted the subject, he stepped aside and motioned for the Overseer to take the lead. They weren't there to purchase anything yet; their mission was to scope out the goods and commerce. Rhys fell into step beside the Overseer so he could best act as interpreter.

For the next hour, they wandered up and down the numerous aisles of goods, produce, cargo, merchandise, and commodities. Rhys found his ability to translate faster than the day prior.

As the heat of the morning swelled in intensity, he pulled out a headscarf and wrapped it about his head and neck to defend against the sun. He suggested the others do the same, but only two listened. They would learn soon enough how much sunburn hurt.

Around midday, the group settled inside a small bakery and ate lunch. As the Overseer eagerly spoke with his subordinates, Rhys remained separated at another table. Their business matters were of no importance to him. He merely needed to act as their translator and guide.

Resting on his elbows, he watched the baker and his two daughters work in the next room to prepare a batch of bread and variety of sweet cakes. When he grew weary of watching their happy faces, he shifted his gaze to the cup of tea before him.

What would he do if it turned out that he was no longer wanted? He had told Seoc and Connel they would continue traveling, but to where?

For nearly two years, this had been his destination; this had been his goal. Perhaps he was meant to wander for the rest of his life. Maybe he was supposed to write a compilation of his travels and publish it to the world as Ramsen had.

Rhys dipped the tip of his finger into his tea and watched as the ripples spilled outward toward the cup's edges. He and Ethos had always said 'one thing at a time,' but he no longer had *one thing* to do.

When the door to the bakery opened, he didn't look up. He remained gazing glumly at his tea.

"Rhys, could we get your opinion here?" asked the merchant Overseer.

"Yeah." Rhys stood and crossed the narrow aisle to join them. Just as he was about to pull a chair out, he stopped. He could feel someone's gaze on him. He looked at the patron standing at the baker's counter.

Kallen.

Rhys stared at her, eyes wide and heart pounding. He had thought she was the most beautiful woman he had ever seen when he first arrived on Earth, and he still thought so. Her once short, raven hair was pulled into a bun on the side of her head, revealing the piercing at the top of her ear. No longer did she wear a crop top and grease-smeared cutoffs, but a blue, short-sleeved dress and slippers. She looked older, more mature and feminine. Her face was thinner and her cheekbones sharper than he remembered. She was a full woman. Despite all the changes though, her eyes were the same—intelligent, warm, and inquisitive.

"Rhys," called the merchant Overseer.

"One moment," Rhys murmured in Panganese. He approached Kallen who moved only to breathe. Her eyes darted from his gaze down his body and back in an obvious attempt to understand the changes he too had undergone.

Rhys stopped before her unsure of what he should do. She had intentionally avoided seeing him, which meant she had reservations about them as a couple. Unwilling to touch her without knowing for certain, he smiled nervously. "Hi."

"Hi," Kallen breathed. Her eyes searched his before focusing on the scar running down the middle of his face. Slowly, she reached through the distance and touched his cheek. Though relishing her familiar touch, he remained unmoving, still unsure of her intentions. She caressed his jaw and then moved her hand to his forehead where the scar began. "What happened?" she whispered.

"Long story," he replied.

Kallen slid her other hand to his jaw and rubbed her thumb there. After a moment, she said in a quivering voice, "Where have you been? I've missed you."

"I've missed you."

Kallen wrapped her arms around his neck and buried her head into his chest. "I've missed you. Rhys, *I've missed you.*"

Rhys folded his arms around her and kissed the side of her head. "I know," he murmured. "I'm sorry." A sob escaped Kallen's throat, and she clung to him tighter. "I'm sorry. I'm so sorry."

As if a floodgate opened, tears of relief flowed down her face in great streams. Desperately, she clung to his clothes, her fingers knotting into his sides. Rhys hungrily grasped at her body and held her to him, burying his face into her neck. She smelled faintly of sweat and of the soap they always bought when in port.

Kallen turned and kissed his neck numerous times before Rhys met her there and pressed his mouth hard to hers. He couldn't keep the kiss going for long though because he was smiling so much. Gasping and crying, Kallen pressed her forehead to his. "I've missed you," she whispered.

Rhys swallowed her in his arms once more, pressing his face into her neck. "Kallen," he whispered, heart throbbing from the overwhelming relief and happiness that consumed him.

After a moment, Rhys drew away. Eyebrows upturned and teary eyes squinted in heart-pounding delight, Kallen's eyes didn't leave his face. Rhys wiped his own unexpected tears on his shoulder, motioned for her to stay put, and then turned to the merchant and his crew who had watched the spectacle in silence.

In Panganese, Rhys said, "Would you mind if we took a break from our work here? I can meet again with you later this afternoon, of course. Would that fit your plans?"

The merchant glanced at Kallen and then at his crew. "It's too damn hot anyway. Please come by the bridge sometime this afternoon. I believe we have enough information to get started." Rhys withdrew the map the secretary had given him and presented it to the merchant Overseer. He hastily explained how to return to the docks.

"Go, I've got it," urged the Overseer, stuffing the map into his front pocket.

"I'll be back at the ship before sunset," Rhys assured him.

"Please do. We're helpless without you." The Overseer glanced once more at Kallen and then waved them off with a knowing look.

Rhys motioned to Kallen who followed him from the bakery back into the heat of the day. "Are those the people you traveled with?" she asked, falling into step beside him.

"Yeah," replied Rhys. He could hardly compute Aabesh at the moment. He was so flustered; his brain had shut off. Stopping her in the middle of the street, he said in Elali, "Can we speak in Elali? I'm having a hard time with Aabesh."

Kallen glanced down the street. "That's fine."

Rhys didn't miss the change in the expression on her face. "Is there somewhere we can talk?"

She led him down the street and over three alleys before pointing to a small herb shop. Once they were seated in the shade of the store's front porch, they ordered tea—and then sat in silence. How was Rhys supposed to convey two years' worth of history in a conversation? They had not been a couple since he left for the moon.

"I see you're still dying your hair," Kallen remarked, folding a leg under her. She corrected herself when she remembered that he wanted to speak only in Elali.

"Yeah, it turns out my people are not well-liked around the world," replied Rhys. "Both Connel and I dye our hair to keep eyes off of us."

"Who's Connel?"

"A friend from Neo-Colony Nine. I'm sure you'll meet him."

An awkward silence ensued as each worked to come up with a conversation topic.

"You look older," Rhys pointed out. Kallen frowned. "I mean, in a good way. In a good way."

Kallen shrugged. "You do too. Your shoulders are wider and chest harder. I think maybe you've grown, but I can't tell without you standing beside..." Her sentence faded.

"Where's Ronan?" prompted Rhys.

"With Forge and Emmi," replied Kallen. "Forge doesn't have to work today."

"I heard he works at the hospital. How is that going for him?"

"He's made great strides in bettering the local health system. He's their top surgeon and is regularly called on in the middle of the night for trauma care." Kallen smiled down at her tea. "Everyone adores him."

"And Hodge runs a courier business now, right?"

"Eh, right."

Ignoring her uncomfortable response, Rhys continued. "And Andy? What does he do?"

"He actually works with the city's government to coordinate military efforts."

"There's still fighting?"

"Not any more. For a while there, Brechin was desperate to get a hold of Firekli, but after *Apex* and *Lucille* began hanging out in port, they backed off. Some skirmishes will break out along the southern border or out at sea periodically, but for the most point, Sal is doing a really good job keeping Brechin in check."

"Sal?"

"He's prime minister of Brechin," chuckled Kallen. "All three of his sons hold positions in his cabinet, including Leo."

Rhys nodded, impressed. "I'm sure that takeover didn't go easily."

"It wasn't a takeover," Kallen corrected. "After discussing his plans with the remaining family heads, Sal was elected into office, and the oligarchy was dissolved."

"Damn," murmured Rhys, smiling. "It worked."

"I don't know what Sean does, but I think Terron now oversees the department of education and Leo is head of foreign affairs since he has the most experience traveling and working with other people."

"And Otto and Cantia?"

"They're still at Neo-Colony Two, but they visit often. The colony has created a new wing to house those who still want to be a part of the colony but who want to live by the rules of the land, not by colonial government. Or something like that. Otto is well-respected there. And with Cantia's help, the colony has opened itself to trade, particularly with Firekli."

"What about Axel?"

"Axel lives in Brechin…" Kallen smiled. "With Veran and their daughter."

Rhys leaned on the table in surprise. "Their daughter? How old is she?"

Kallen laughed. "About three months old."

"Wow… And how's Axel's arm?"

"Good. A few months after the accident, Veran was able to create a functioning prosthetic for him at the colony. It's quite remarkable. But yeah, Axel is doing well. Actually, I'm supposed to notify him if you ever showed up."

"And Zain?"

"He went back to Neo-Colony Two. I don't know what he's up to."

"What happened to Gealdir?"

"Sal and Sean destroyed his unit and killed him using *Lucille*."

Rhys lowered his voice and gazed at Kallen. "And… how's Ronan?"

The smile on Kallen's face faded once more, and she fidgeted with her cup. "Listen, Rhys… A lot has happened since you've been gone."

"I know you live with Hodge… and Forge and his girl."

Kallen nodded.

Rhys glanced out at the street and, fiddling with the beaded bracelet on his wrist, asked, "Is there more going on between you two than…" He didn't have to finish his sentence before Kallen nodded again. Rhys pursed his lips and continued to fidget with his bracelet.

That explained why Hodge had been acting so strangely the night prior. It also explained why Kallen had resisted immediately meeting with Rhys.

He wasn't surprised. He wasn't even sure he was upset. He had been gone for nearly two years with no certainty that he would ever return. In the meantime, Kallen had gone through her pregnancy, given birth, and begun raising a child. Hodge had been her rock. Before Rhys, he had been her pillar of support. It only made sense that after Rhys, he would return to the position. And raising a child… How was Rhys supposed to fit back into the relationship?

"I gave up hoping you would ever come back," whispered Kallen. "We stopped getting reports from Ethos. For all I knew, you were dead."

Rhys nodded. "I understand."

Kallen reached across the table and touched his hand. "Listen, Hodge has always told me that he would move aside should you come home. Rhys, I want to make this work."

"I'm just… sorry I ever left," he murmured.

Kallen clenched his hand. "Hodge has always known that he was a stand-in. He needed a place to live, and I needed someone to help me. That's why Forge and Emmi live with us. None of us had money after the war. But with multiple separate incomes, we could keep a household and live comfortably."

"You say Hodge has known he was a stand-in, but does he actually feel that way?" said Rhys. He smiled kindly. "You know how soft he actually is."

"He knows," assured Kallen, despite the tears spilling down her cheeks. She wiped them and held his hand. "He knows. He came home last night after seeing you and reiterated to me again the agreement we had made."

"Kallen…"

"Hodge was there for me when I needed him. He's brought money in, taken care of Ronan and myself. He's been the emotional support I've needed."

Rhys thought, his gaze set on the table. "Do me a favor. Go home and talk to him again. Because… no matter how this ends, the dynamics of our friendship will never be the same."

"Rhys."

"Truly. I'm not angry." He tightened his grip on her hand and looked at her. "I'm not. He's done exactly what I asked him to do before I left. I'm not angry. So, take some time tonight and talk with him again. Come up with what you two want."

"Rhys," said Kallen, hurt.

Rhys insisted. "Listen. I have no right to disrupt the lives you've built. If you decide you want to keep things as they are, that's fine. I will respect it." Kallen gazed at him, her lips trembling. Rhys tried to give her a reassuring smile. "Give it a day or two and talk it over."

Kallen nodded and withdrew her hand. "I'm sorry."

Rhys sat back in his chair and looked out at the crowds of shoppers milling about the open market. "I've missed the warm weather. It's nice breaking into a sweat not doing anything." Kallen gave a soft albeit a wet chuckle. "You know, I always thought that if I could just make it back here, I would feel at home and my journey would be over. But… I'm a stranger in a familiar land."

"Don't say that," Kallen scolded quietly.

"Everything has changed." No longer feeling up to the task of creating conversation, he stood and straightened his clothes. "I hope you don't mind. I'm going to try to find the merchants I was with. I promised I would meet back up with them. I'm their translator."

"Eh, yeah. That's fine." Kallen stood as well and gazed forlornly at him. "I'll see you soon, right?"

"Yeah." Rhys wrapped his scarf about his head and stepped out into the sunlight once more. He gave a small wave to Kallen and hurried back into the market.

Head turned down against the sun, he strode down several streets until he found a deserted alley between two shops. Pulling himself into the shade, Rhys leaned against one of the walls and took a deep breath to keep at bay the tears that had been building. That didn't work though. Slowly, he sank to the ground, folded his knees to himself, and cried silently. No one noticed him; no one even looked his way. The crowds went on about their shopping.

When the shadows on the streets grew long, Rhys finally stood, dusted himself off, and wearily wandered back to the docks.

Wearing a stoic face, he met with the merchant Overseer and reviewed the man's plans to initiate trade. Rhys advised him to make a few corrections but, in the end, agreed upon the purchase prices the Overseer had set. Afterward, Rhys changed from his nice clothes and went to the rear deck where several of the crew members played games. Not wanting to be around loud, raucous people, he visited the forward deck. Just as he lay down, Seoc and Connel appeared.

"We didn't think you'd come back," admitted Seoc.

"We thought you left us," Connel added.

"Sorry," Rhys muttered.

"What's wrong? Did something happen?" Connel seated himself beside Rhys and looked out at the wharves.

Rhys folded his arms around his legs. "Kallen… is with my best friend."

Seoc grimaced and exchanged looks with Connel. "The… man we met last night?"

Rhys nodded and watched as a small group of dock workers carried a crate to the next pier.

"Are you sure?" asked Connel softly.

"I'm sure."

Seoc sat across from Rhys and stretched his legs. "You had to have known that was a possibility."

"Seoc," scolded Connel.

"No, he's right." Rhys fidgeted. "He's right. I mean, before I left, I told Hodge to take care of her. And… he's done that. He's provided for her and taken care of… Yeah, I knew it could happen."

There was a long moment of silence before Seoc asked, "So what now?"

"If things don't change… we can either return with the merchant's crew when they leave or… head in another direction." Rhys didn't care which they chose. He didn't care about anything anymore.

"Hey, whatever happens," said Seoc, "we'll be there."

Rhys looked out at the docks laced in the deepening shadows of dusk. Perhaps it was time he began contemplating a life abroad.

Determined to get his mind off those in Firekli, Seoc forced Rhys to continue teaching him Aabesh. Late into the evening, Rhys instructed his friend in the language while Connel listened raptly. Eventually though the weariness and stress of the day caught up with them, and together they retired to their small cabin.

Rhys knew he talked throughout the night before Seoc ever said anything the following morning. His sleep had been restless, and the only thing on his mind was Kallen and Hodge. Knowing the merchant and his crew were going to be late risers as the stress of being in a new nation was heavy on them, he urged Connel and Seoc up and, after dressing, led them into town for breakfast.

Rhys was grateful for Connel's infinite energy and light heart. The boy's kind words, innocence, and curiosity saved Rhys from plummeting into the depths of despair. Now that Connel was getting the hang of Aabesh, he stopped to speak with everyone and ask questions. When they finally found a small shop selling bakery items and tea, they went in and sat at one of the few tables available. Connel immediately struck up a conversation with the waitress.

"Why can't you just be a foreigner like me?" growled Seoc, obviously jealous of the boy's ability to now speak the language.

"These people are so interesting," chirped Connel, leaning on the table and looking about at the other customers. "Don't you think? It's very quiet. The atmosphere is pleasant and warm." Connel nodded to Rhys. "I see why you like it here."

Rhys chuckled softly and sipped his tea before saying, "It wasn't always like this. Last time I was here, the city was in complete disarray and on the verge of being overtaken by the capital. I'm surprised they've managed to rebuild in such a short period of time."

"We haven't been here for long," said Seoc, "but I get the sense that, of the numerous ports we've been in, this is a relatively safe one. You know how riffraff normally hang out around the docks."

"Eh, I can't say right now. For all we know, it could be like Odiene, remember?" murmured Rhys. Both Connel and Seoc nodded in agreement. "Just keep your eyes open. I've warned the Overseer about the possibility of people becoming too interested in the new ship. We have technology they don't and commodities that would sell for a good price on the black market here in town. The only thing possibly keeping an attack at bay is the fact that the crew is so large." Looking to change the subject, Rhys motioned to Seoc. "Have you sent word to your family recently?"

Seoc leaned on the table. "The last time I had the chance was back in Odiene, but we were run out of there so fast, I didn't."

"I'm sure we can find a way. If things don't work out here, we could always head to the capital. I know for a fact that they have satellite radio capability. I'm sure we could get word out there." Rhys sipped his tea. "Besides, that'll give me time to meet with others."

"So... is that the plan?" Connel asked.

"Yeah, I think so," replied Rhys. "I'll finish up my work with the Overseer and then find a ship to take us to Brechin. Sound good?"

Connel and Seoc nodded cautiously as if agreeing with Rhys would cause trouble. "You're sure?" murmured Seoc.

"Yeah."

And that was the end of that conversation.

By the time they began the journey back to the docks, the sun was low in the sky and already the heat of the day was swelling. "I'm dying," moaned Seoc. "This is so miserable."

"I agree," Connel whined. It seemed the sun was sapping the energy from him. "Is it going to be this hot—"

A shout from the docks caught their attention, and all three looked up at the chaos unfolding aboard the merchant ship. In unison, they bolted down the street and along the wharves to their dock where a melee of fighting and yelling had erupted.

Before they reached the ship, one of ship's crew members met them at the end of the dock, wheezing. "There's about twenty or so of them."

Seoc stormed down the dock, copper hair thrown back by the wind. Rhys pushed Connel into the crew member's arms. "Watch him," he ordered, streaking after Seoc.

In mid-step along the docks, Seoc launched himself into one of the locals who was fighting with a merchant sailor. Realizing that this was a scuffle and nothing serious, Rhys shouted to Seoc, "Break them up!" as he hurried aboard. He was glad to find the bridge door locked. Quickly, he leapt over the railing and landed on the middle deck where several other skirmishes had broken out. "What the..."

Rhys grabbed the nearest sailor, heaved against his weight, and ripped him out of the fight. "Knock it off!" Rhys shouted first in Panganese and then in Aabesh. Although most of the sailors, recognizing Rhys' voice, immediately withdrew from their individual snits with the locals, a handful were forced to continue to fight. "Enough!" Rhys roared in Aabesh, sliding between them and blocking a punch from a local. Once he had full control of the man's arm, he leveraged the local over his shoulder and threw him to the deck.

Everyone fell still. Panting and injured shoulder throbbing, Rhys glowered about. "If you are not a part of this crew, get the hell off the ship!" he ordered in Aabesh. "Now!"

"They were trying to forcefully enter," a merchant explained breathlessly in Panganese.

"Yeah, I got that," replied Rhys angrily. The pain in his shoulder was making his temper flare. "All crew members, over there, now!" He pointed to the opposite side of the deck, and the crew slowly shuffled to obey. The locals, however, didn't move. Shifting back to Aabesh, Rhys approached the group of ruffians who were just as bruised and bleeding as the crew. "Do you realize how bad this makes Firekli look?" he snarled. "You are the reason why international trade is so limited. People like *you*. Port after port, riffraff like you make merchants' lives so damn difficult! Now, get the hell off this ship before I call the port authority."

There was a moment when Rhys thought no one would obey before the locals began shuffling off the middle deck and down the stairs. Gripping his injured shoulder, he turned on the merchants and started in on them in Panganese. "You are representatives of your country. If you cannot defend yourselves against shit like this, as I've told you for weeks on end now, how are you supposed to defend your merchandise? If those men had been serious, there would be dead bodies on the deck right now."

"That is *enough*!" barked the Overseer, appearing outside the bridge deck. "All of you, get back inside. Rhys, come talk with me."

Angry and in pain, Rhys stormed up the stairs to the bridge and entered. The moment the door closed behind him, the Overseer began speaking.

"Do you understand that this isn't your ship?"

"Yes," replied Rhys.

"Do you understand that perhaps there was a reason I left my men to quarrel with the locals?"

Rhys gazed at the Overseer in confusion. "No?"

"Rhys, I agreed to carry you and your companions under the pretense that you would not interfere with the commerce and business of my ship."

"But... I haven't. You and your men are a representation—"

"I heard you and while I fully agree, we must eventually show that we're willing to fight for our goods."

"That would make more sense if your crew actually knew how to fight," Rhys countered. "Leaving them to quarrel with locals because you want to show how well they can defend themselves..." He motioned to the deck behind him. "Were we watching the same fight? It was like children squabbling."

"Even still," replied the Overseer, folding his hands behind his back. "I've tolerated your insubordination for the length of the journey because we were out at sea and needed guidance. We are in port now. Therefore, I want you and your friends to clear your cabin and get off the ship. Register with the port authority where I can find you in the event I need a translator per our agreement."

Rhys glared at the man. "Is that all, Overseer?"

"That is all."

Holding his shoulder, Rhys left the bridge and descended to the docks. Seoc met him at the bottom of the staircase. "What happened?"

"We're being kicked off the ship. You and Connel gather our things. I've... messed up my damn shoulder again." Rhys leaned on a crate with a grimace.

"Connel!" called Seoc down the docks. There was a moment's pause before Seoc beckoned, "Eh... Rhys?"

Rhys looked up to find Connel standing at the end of the dock with Hodge and Kallen by his side. Making sure the ruffians from the skirmish were well away from the docks, Rhys straightened himself. Seoc moved into place beside Rhys. "Is that... your woman?" he murmured.

Rhys gazed morosely at Hodge and Kallen. He was entering an all-time low in his life. The last thing he wanted to see was Kallen and Hodge standing before him together.

Realizing that he was hurt, Connel left the two and jogged down the dock to Rhys. "I told you not to overextend it," the boy scolded, placing his hands on Rhys' shoulder. Rhys flinched visibly but kept his eyes on Hodge and Kallen. He saw them exchange looks before starting down the dock. "Let me go get our medical supplies."

"Go ahead and get everything," Rhys replied. "The Overseer wants us off his ship. Now." Rhys nodded to Seoc. "Go help him."

Seoc, whose gaze was on Kallen, nodded and followed Connel up the stairs to the deck. Holding his shoulder, Rhys met Hodge and Kallen.

"Still getting into trouble," said Hodge fondly.

Rhys scoffed. "Not for a lack of trying."

"I suppose that's true," replied Kallen uncomfortably. His anger and distress were palpable. She fidgeted and looked to Hodge for guidance.

"What happened up there?" asked Hodge. "We could hear you yelling all the way into town. Your voice is unmistakable—"

"Look, just say what you've got to say," Rhys interrupted. "I've got other things to deal with right now." He grimaced as the pain in his shoulder flared and rippled down his back. Wheezing, he sat back against the crate and gripped his shoulder. After a moment of deep breaths, he looked at Hodge and Kallen. He dreaded what was about to happen and yet, he wanted to get it over with.

Kallen touched Hodge in a silent gesture of encouragement before stepping forward and wrapping an arm around Rhys. "Come home," she murmured. "Your home is here with us. Come home." Kallen pulled away, kissed his cheek, and gazed at him tearfully. "We want you to stay here."

"Kallen's always been yours," added Hodge with a sad smile. "I always knew you would be back one day. I never forgot it because I've never known anyone quite as determined as you." Hodge held out his hand.

Rhys looked between them. "You're sure?" All the anger in him began seeping out. "Because... I will just keep going. We were planning to go to Brechin to contact Burefell. It's not any trouble. I don't want to mess up... I-I don't have any right to be..."

Hodge gently pulled loose Rhys' grip from his injured shoulder and forced their hands to meet. "Your home is wherever we are. And right now, it's here. You're home."

Relief gathered in Rhys' eyes causing Kallen to kiss him and once more embrace him. With his good arm, Rhys gripped Hodge's hand tightly.

"So… we're staying, right?" asked Seoc. Rhys pulled from Kallen's embrace and looked at Seoc and Connel standing on the staircase with their packs. Though they had been unable to understand the conversation, it was obvious what had happened. Seoc shrugged. "I was getting tired of traveling anyway. I love getting into mischief with you, but I would like very much not to have to worry about being killed in my sleep, ya know?"

Connel leapt down the stairs and bounded over to Rhys. Beaming, the boy looked at Kallen. "I'm Connel." He took Kallen's hand enthusiastically and pumped it a few times.

"Easy," chided Seoc, walking down the stairs. "Don't know what was just said between them." Connel frowned as Seoc set Rhys' pack beside them.

Kallen turned to Seoc and held out her hand. In clear Elali, she said, "I'm Kallen Falkrow. Thank you for taking care of Rhys. He can be a handful."

Seoc glanced at Rhys before taking her hand. "You don't know the half of it."

Hodge lifted Rhys' pack. "Let's get home. I skipped breakfast to come get you… and you know how much I hate skipping meals."

The walk back into town was a surreal one. Just paces ahead of him Connel and Hodge spoke excitedly about food in Aabesh. Walking alongside Rhys, Kallen and Seoc discussed the local economy. The family he had made upon first arriving on Earth was merging with the friends he had made abroad; his worlds were colliding. Never would he have thought while arguing with Seoc in Burefell that one day the young man would be one of his closest friends. Never would he have thought that Seoc would be casually talking with Kallen as if they had known each other for months.

It was a robust half hour before Hodge turned down a quiet street and stopped before a narrow, two-story gray brick home decorated with large windows and a covered veranda. "This is it," he announced proudly, climbing the few steps to the front door. Kallen followed him, picking up a wood-carved toy on the steps as she did. Rhys gazed up at the home forlornly.

"You sure you're fine with this?" Seoc asked, leaning into Rhys.

"Yeah, it's… just not what I was expecting," murmured Rhys.

From within the house, Rhys heard a young woman's voice. "Ah, Hodge. Can you hold him? He's driving me crazy."

Realizing that he was about to meet his son, Rhys climbed the stairs and stood in the doorway. Normally, he would have taken in his surroundings, noting cleanliness or the smell of the place, but none of that seemed to process with him. The only thing that mattered was the wriggling toddler attempting to hurl himself from Hodge's strong arms.

Rhys could feel Kallen's gaze as she watched his reaction.

"Come on," growled Hodge, fighting with the child. "Why are you so..."

"Hodge," Kallen said. "Put him down."

Hodge set the toddler on the floor. The babe fell on his knees, picked himself up, and wobbled over to Kallen. Gripping her pants, he looked up unsteadily at Rhys. Though his skin was pale and his cheeks pink, the mess of hair atop his head was dark brown. His eyes were a shocking blue.

Kallen knelt beside the boy, smoothed his hair, and pointed to Rhys. "Do you know who this is, Ronan?" The toddler buried his head into Kallen's shoulder, prompting her to untangle him. "Ronan, look. Do you know who this is?"

Putting a hand in his mouth, Ronan gazed at Rhys before turning back into Kallen's chest. Rhys crouched so he was on the same level as Ronan. He wanted to say something, anything, but his voice was caught in his throat.

With more force, Kallen pulled Ronan from her bosom and gave him a small push. On wobbly feet, Ronan stood before Rhys, a hand in his mouth and eyes darting between the strangers who lingered in the doorway.

"Hi," Rhys murmured unsure of what else to say.

"Speak to him in Elali," encouraged Kallen.

Feeling awkward, Rhys reached between them and took Ronan's free hand. "Hi, Ronan. How are you doing today?"

The boy turned and waddled back to Kallen. He fell into her arms, and she repositioned him so he was looking at Rhys. "Do you know who that is? That's your dad. Dad." Ignoring Kallen, Ronan extracted himself from her arms and waddled across the room past Hodge to his toys. Chuckling, Kallen stood. "Don't worry. He's shy with everyone."

Rhys stood, and Seoc hit his back. "You didn't tell us you had a kid."

"Didn't I?" mused Rhys. He was certain he had mentioned it before. Eyes on Ronan, he smiled. He could see how the toddler was a handful.

"Rhys, this is Emmi," said Hodge, motioning to the buxom, blond-haired young woman crossing the room. She was unbelievably attractive. Silently, Rhys congratulated Forge.

"I've heard a lot about you," said Emmi, bobbing her head in greeting.

"It's nice to meet you. This is Seoc and Connel," replied Rhys. "Friends of mine."

"A pleasure," Emmi hummed.

"Who is she with?" whispered Seoc as the young woman turned to watch Ronan.

Rhys nudged him. "She's taken, stud. Calm down." Seeing the knowing in Kallen and Hodge's eyes, Rhys couldn't help but smile.

"Yeah…" agreed Hodge with a sly smile. "Forge got *that*."

"Where is he?"

"At the hospital," replied Emmi, sitting beside Ronan. "He got called in about an hour ago."

"Please, come in," urged Kallen, motioning to Seoc and Connel. "Are you hungry?"

"No, we just ate," replied Connel. He glanced at Rhys and then at Kallen. "Can… I play with the baby?"

"Go, sit," urged Hodge, pushing Connel toward the common area. Connel happily flung himself onto the floor and studied Ronan as Emmi shared Ronan's favorite toys with him.

Hodge leaned in the doorway of the next room. "It'll take time," he said. He must have seen the expression on Rhys' face. "His world is small. Only recently did he start caring about anyone but Kallen. You're a stranger. You smell weird and sound weird." He smiled. "Don't worry. He'll come to you in time."

Kallen fixed her shirt and looked to Seoc. "Would you help me in the kitchen?" she asked in Elali.

Seoc set his pack down, and with a glance at Rhys, followed Kallen into the next room, leaving Rhys and Hodge standing alone. They watched Connel and Emmi attempt to persuade Ronan to take a toy, but he was fixated on the item in his hand.

"You'll learn too," said Hodge. He looked at Rhys with a warm smile. "I've had the advantage of going through Kallen's pregnancy and birth. You never got to see her when she was enormous, but being around a pregnant woman does something to a man. It's awkward now because you don't feel connected to him, right?"

Despite the nearly two years they had been apart, Hodge could still read his thoughts. Smiling, Rhys nudged Hodge. "Yeah."

Hodge nodded in understanding. "He'll grow on you. For a while, I was helpless. I couldn't do anything. All he wanted was to sleep and eat and the only one who can feed him is Kallen. So, I was really just taking care of her." Rhys nodded, subconsciously touching his shoulder. "So, what happened? How did you mess up your shoulder?"

"I broke it a few weeks ago."

"Fighting?"

"I was fighting, but the fight itself didn't break it. I was pushed out of a moving vehicle. The fall broke it."

"Shit, Rhys…" mused Hodge. "And your face?"

"I pinned an assassin after he attempted to kill the city's chief. He had a hidden blade along his arm. When I looked away, he popped it through his sleeve. I turned, and he got me down the middle of my face." Rhys nodded. "And I had just lost my medical pack… so, I had to treat it without much help. Hence the horrible scar."

"It's not horrible," Hodge laughed. "It makes you look dignified. You've been through a lot, haven't you?" His smile faded, and he looked at the floor. "We didn't think you made it."

"When?"

"When you came back from space."

Connel look up from his antics with Ronan.

"When you reentered the atmosphere, your cockpit camera went live. Everyone on *Apex* saw and heard your conversations. Ethos told us not to say anything, not to interrupt you." Hodge nodded. "You ejected a split-second before your unit disintegrated. The cockpit camera went dead, and all communication between your craft and our ship was lost. We thought you had been killed…" Hodge sighed heavily. "That was… some day."

"But Ethos contacted you later, right?" asked Rhys, watching Ronan.

"A couple of days later. It said that you had been picked up. A day after that, Ethos told us that it had managed to track you down and contact you." Hodge gently clapped Rhys on the back. "It's good to see your face."

After breakfast was served, Hodge bid everyone a quick farewell and hurried off to his work. While Kallen showed Seoc her shop behind the house, Rhys and Connel watched Emmi bathe Ronan. An hour later, the front door opened and Forge appeared.

Sitting in the common room talking softly with the others so as not to wake Ronan from his nap, Rhys looked up at the medical student. He was shocked by how much Forge had grown both in height and width. He was taller and had a broader chest; his jaw line was stronger. His matte silver hair was swept neatly across his forehead revealing his Pathos unit.

Forge stared at the newcomers, confused, as he closed the front door and walked into the room. "Uh, hello…" he murmured, looking to Kallen and Emmi for an explanation. It was obvious he did not recognize Rhys.

Seeing Forge's AI, Connel leapt up and approached the medical student. "Neo-Colony Two?" asked Connel in Nefegian.

"Yes. And you're Nine. How did you get all the way here? Why are you here?" asked Forge. Rhys was amused to hear that Forge's voice had deepened as well.

Connel turned and looked at Rhys who, taking that as his cue, stood and approached Forge. "Hey, Forge."

Recognition colored Forge's gaze, and his mouth gaped. "Rhys," he breathed.

"You know who I am now?" Rhys chuckled.

"I just..." Forge laughed. "I just... didn't expect..." He looked at Kallen and pointed at Rhys; she nodded in mutual excitement. "Rhys!" Forge went for a hug, but Rhys stopped him.

"Sorry, my shoulder is messed up." Rhys took Forge's hand instead and smiled enthusiastically. "It's so good to see you. I've heard you've made quite a name for yourself."

Forge began speaking rapidly in Nefegian. "I'm the senior surgeon at the hospital. They offered me a different title that is, I think, a promotion, but I decided to decline because I'm already being called to the hospital on my off-days. I didn't want more work. I haven't wanted more work since I met Emmi."

Rhys glanced knowingly at the others and, in Nefegian, said, "Good job, Forge. Where did you find her?"

"She's a waitress at a tavern," Forge happily replied.

Rhys struggled to keep the smile on his face. "Oh, that's... nice."

"Actually, it really is. She can stay home and help take care of Ronan while Kallen does repairs out back. And Hodge never gets home until the evenings. Emmi works at night, so it's perfect," said Forge. Seeing the merit in the argument and how happy Forge was, Rhys clapped him on the shoulder. "I took your advice."

"I see that," replied Rhys. "I'm glad."

After introductions, the rest of the afternoon was spent watching Ronan play and talking about all that had changed. With some prompting, Rhys finally pulled from Kallen that *Themis* had been destroyed while resting in port and *Grisle* had been damaged beyond repair. Andy had suffered some wounds from the attack but had managed to dive overboard to escape death.

Kallen showed Rhys, Seoc, and Connel the rest of the house, including all the bedrooms, of which there were four. Of course, Rhys noticed Hodge's clothes, bedding, and belongings stacked neatly in the middle of an empty room. Seoc asked if Hodge was leaving, but Kallen denied it. Rhys knew why his belongings were there. Upon talking the night prior and deciding how they wanted to proceed, Hodge had cleared his belongings from her room and moved down the hall.

Though Hodge pretended it was fine, Rhys knew it was going to take time before their relationship was healed. His friend might have always known that Rhys would eventually make it back, but that didn't change the fact that he had become intimate with Kallen and taken on role of caregiver and father in Rhys' absence.

Hodge returned that evening shortly after Emmi left for work and flopped on the floor next to Ronan who began crawling on him. Rhys frowned. He had been working all afternoon to get Ronan to trust him. Without so much as a thought, his child simply climbed atop Hodge and began playing with his clothes. "I'm so tired," moaned Hodge.

"You run a courier service, right?" asked Rhys.

"Well, not for long. I lost two sunboarders today. One quit and the other twisted his knee. That just leaves Sefora and Gwin." Hodge looked at Rhys. "Want to make money and fly around and deliver stuff?"

"Ask again in a few weeks," Rhys replied. "I can't hardly lift my arm." He glanced at Seoc and Connel, a thought forming in his head. When he looked back at Hodge, his friend was sitting up, smiling. As usual, they were thinking the same thing. "Say, Seoc, Connel—you want to learn something new?"

"Like what?" asked Seoc from a pile of pillows.

"Sunboarding," replied Rhys using the Aabesh word.

Seoc looked at him. "What?"

"Forge, show Connel," instructed Rhys. Quickly, he explained to Seoc what sunboarding was.

Seoc's eyes lit up, and he nodded enthusiastically. "Yes, please," said Seoc to Hodge.

Connel kicked Seoc's pants' leg. "Forge showed me. It looks like fun."

"We'll have to train you," said Hodge. Rhys translated this to Seoc who shrugged. "Then, it's agreed?" Connel and Seoc nodded. Happily, Hodge hit the floor and then shook their hands. "We'll begin tomor—"

A polite knock on the front door interrupted the conversation. Looking between them, Rhys stood and opened the door to reveal Andy, Kashim, Otto, Cantia, and—to Rhys' horror—his father. Stunned, Rhys just stared at them. The surprise must have been mutual, because for a split second, no one said anything.

"I told you," said Kashim, settling a bet he had obviously started with the others.

"Who is it?" asked Hodge, leaning around Rhys to peer into the dark.

Rhys stepped aside. "It's… everyone."

Tearfully, Cantia threw herself at Rhys, causing him to stumble back into the room. He flinched but resisted the urge to push her off his injured shoulder. It was Forge who drew the girl off Rhys, murmuring in Nefegian that he was hurt.

"Oh, sorry!" she breathed, eyes red. She had grown. No longer was she a flat stick; she had small breasts and a slight curve to her hips. Her face was fuller and her cheek bones higher. She wore Caelestis-issued pants under a short pale-yellow dress. "We didn't recognize you. Look at you!"

As Forge drew her away, Otto stepped in and shook Rhys' hand. His eyes were solemn but a small smile played on his mouth. His hair was neatly trimmed to his head revealing the Pathos unit attached his temple. Although he had not muscled up in the way Forge had, he had still grown; it was evident that he was his own man now. "Hey, Rhys."

Rhys clapped him on the shoulder. "Hey, Otto. How are you?"

"It's good to see you."

"Yeah, weren't sure you'd ever get back," mused Andy, leaning in the doorway. Otto stepped aside so that Rhys could hug his First Mate. "You look like you've been through a lot since we last saw you."

"That's an… eh…" Rhys fought to remember the word. "Understatement. That's an understatement."

Andy chuckled and turned to Kashim and Rhys' father standing on the veranda. "Kallen—you want to explain this one?" he called over his shoulder.

With Ronan on her hip, Kallen crossed the room and stood beside Rhys. Realizing that he must have been having a hard time remembering Aabesh because of the flurry of emotions and activity, Kallen spoke in Elali. "So, that day you were coming back down to Earth… we were at Neo-Colony Two. The entire colony watched you come back to Earth."

Rhys looked at Hodge. "I thought only you watched the cockpit camera." Realizing that he had spoken in Elali, he corrected himself and reiterated his response in Aabesh.

"Eh, no. That's the thing—all Neo-Colony Two saw your reentry," said Hodge, joining everyone.

"At any rate," continued Kallen, "I suppose there's been some change in attitude toward you. And… since then, your father has visited when Otto and Cantia come." She smiled. "He's actually quite fond of his grandson."

Rhys looked back at Doctor Falkrow before asking in confusion and disbelief, "What?"

Doctor Falkrow, dressed in his usual Caelestis-issued uniform, approached Rhys, his eyes flitting between Rhys and Ronan. "It would not behoove the human race to ignore the brave efforts of one man. We knew when you started atmospheric reentry that we had made a grave mistake in not supporting you and your endeavors. We should have realized that your efforts were not to spite us but to support the human race. After that, I couldn't help but feel that I had lost something very important." He nodded to Ronan. "And then I remembered that I have a *grandchild*—that's the name Kallen taught me."

"Thanks," muttered Rhys.

"This isn't going to be a problem, is it?" asked Kallen, motioning between them.

"No," replied Rhys the same moment his father did.

"Good." Kallen pushed Ronan into Rhys' arms and then motioned for everyone to come in. "I'm cooking. Dinner will be ready in about an hour."

Feeling his arm give under the toddler's weight, Rhys turned and passed him to Forge. Holding his shoulder, he sighed in pain.

"Let's look at that," said Forge.

While Kallen, Severiano, and Andy cooked, Forge led Rhys into the common room and helped him take off his shirt. "You're covered in scars," murmured Forge, sitting beside Rhys.

"I lost my medical pack a while ago," Rhys explained once again.

"Damn, Rhys…" said Hodge, leaning in. "Your entire shoulder is purple and green. No wonder you can't do anything."

"The bruising is normal," said Forge, gently placing his hands on either side of Rhys' shoulder. After a moment, he said, "Your fracture was set correctly, but you've overextended the muscle."

"Probably did that this morning," said Rhys. He tried to ignore the wide stares of his crewmates.

By the time Forge wrapped his shoulder and helped him back into his shirt, it was dinner time. Because the dining area was not meant to house eleven people, half the group sat while the others stood. In another testament to Kallen's cooking, lively conversation started up around the comfort of good food. Rhys listened aptly to each person, struggling only slightly to keep up. For Seoc's sake, Kallen spoke exclusively in Elali.

It was near the end of the meal while Connel was explaining the conditions of Neo-Colony Nine, when he stopped in midsentence and looked at Forge. Conversation at the table grew quiet. For a long moment, Forge, Connel, Otto, and Doctor Falkrow peered at one another in confusion.

What?" asked Hodge.

Forge motioned for him to wait.

Once the silent conversation was finished, Connel turned to Rhys and spoke in Nefegian. "That was Ethos." He glanced at Forge. "It just reported to all of the colonies that scouting units have been detected entering the Solar System."

"What? What is it?" asked Hodge.

Connel started to translate but grew too slow in the process. Forge finished reiterating the message to the others.

"What does that mean?" asked Andy, leaning on the table.

"Ethos doesn't think the scouts belong to another colony. They appear quite advanced," replied Forge.

Rhys thought, remembering all that he had encountered over the past year and a half. "Scouting units…" He looked at his father. "Is it possible they know segments of Caelestis went down on Earth?"

"They're scouting Earth as a potential habitat," concluded Forge.

"Did Ethos say anything else?"

Forge, Otto, and Connel shook their heads. "We should head back to the colony," said Severiano, standing. "We can gather more information there." Otto and Cantia followed suit.

Dinner was over. As Andy began picking up plates, Doctor Falkrow bid goodbye to Kallen and then to Ronan. Rhys watched as his father, who had once shocked him unconscious, smiled and cooed to Ronan.

"Don't look so gloomy," said Cantia in Nefegian, hugging Rhys from behind. "We'll let you know if we learn anything."

Rhys patted her hand and watched as the three departed. Feeling at a loss, he glanced at Connel and Seoc. Though the others, including Kallen, saw that something was wrong, only Connel and Seoc recognized the expression on Rhys' face.

"One thing at a time, right?" asked Connel in Panganese. "You don't have any information and have no means to contact Ethos. Sit back and be patient."

Rhys nodded and retreated to the common room. A few minutes later, Hodge carried Ronan in and deposited him on the floor in front of his toys. Rhys, whose eyes were set on the distant wall, didn't register his friend's worried gaze.

He needed to be doing something. Ethos had contacted the people it had because it knew they could relay the message to Rhys. Ethos was asking for guidance. A new threat was encroaching upon them, and there was literally nothing Rhys could do.

Feeling a sudden weight on his leg, Rhys startled and looked at Ronan who was struggling to climb onto pillows. He passed a furtive glance to Hodge and then gently pulled the toddler into his lap. As if Rhys weren't there, the baby continued to fidget with the toy in his hands.

"Hodge?" called Kallen from the next room.

Smiling, Hodge stood and joined her and the others, leaving Rhys alone with Ronan. Uncomfortably, Rhys waited for someone to relieve him of the child, but no one came. After a moment, the toddler turned in Rhys' lap to show off his toy.

"I see," replied Rhys in Elali. Ronan rotated before Rhys and leaned his head against his chest all the while fiddling with his wood-carved plaything. An enormous yawn escaped Ronan, and Rhys felt the toddler's body slacken. Whether it was instinct, Rhys didn't know, but he wrapped his arms around his son and pulled the toddler's body close to his. Stomach full, Ronan pressed his face against Rhys' chest and started dozing.

At that moment, all other worries faded from Rhys' mind. Concern for the future disappeared like a heavy fog lifting. The weight of his past vanished. At that moment, all that mattered was Ronan and the ineffable desire to protect and care for him swelling inside Rhys.

Mystified, Rhys tried to think of the countless worries that had, up until a few moments ago, plagued his mind. Not even a shadow of them appeared. Gripping Ronan, he took a deep breath and closed his eyes. He was holding *his* child, the human whose DNA he shared half. This clumsy toddler was his; Ronan was his and Kallen's.

Rhys didn't mean to fall asleep, but his son's warmth coupled with the events of the day weighed heavily on him. For the first time in a long while, he slept soundly.

Sometime later, a soft hand on his face woke him. For a split moment, he forgot where he was and startled before Kallen. She smiled in mild amusement and then looked at Ronan who was snuggled against him. "Let's go to bed."

"I'm… fine here," said Rhys, looking at Seoc and Connel who had been given piles of blankets and pillows nearby. Everyone else was gone. How long had he slept?

Kallen extracted Ronan from Rhys' arms and motioned for Rhys to follow her upstairs. Groggily, Rhys stood, and with another glance at Seoc and Connel, followed her. The doors to Forge's room and Hodge's newly assigned room were closed indicating that everyone was in bed.

Rhys hesitantly followed Kallen into her bedroom where she set Ronan in a cradle. Standing in the doorway, he watched as she pulled the toddler's day clothes off, cleaned his diaper, and dressed him for bed. All the while, Ronan remained asleep.

When she was done, she looked at Rhys. For several long moments, they stared at one another in the dim lamp light. "You don't have to be here if you don't want," she finally murmured. "I know this is hard on you."

Rhys entered and closed the door behind him. This was the first time they had been alone since their conversation at the tea shop. "It's just strange," he whispered. "I don't... really remember how to be in a relationship." He gazed at her apologetically.

Kallen crossed the room and stood before him. "If it's what you want, it'll happen. It might take some time to relearn how to, but it'll happen." She smiled at him. "Do you want to try?"

Rhys struggled internally, remembering that his best friend had been kicked out of his room and now slept down the hall. "Are you sure?" he whispered. "Kallen..." He glanced at Ronan. "I can't just..."

Kallen slid her hands around his waist and leaned into him. "I'm fine. Hodge is fine." She kissed his chest before lifting the hem of his shirt from his waistline. Where her fingers touched, his skin caught fire. Gently, she helped him from his shirt, taking care not to pull his bandaged shoulder. Once he stood before her bare-chested, Kallen stared. He knew he was covered in an assortment of scars. Her fingers flowed down his chest, tracing scars and old injuries with a delicate touch before placing a light kiss on them as if to heal them.

When she finally straightened herself, she leaned in and kissed his nose. She caressed the scar running down the middle of his face and then kissed his cheek where it ended. For a breath's moment, she remained motionless, her lips hovering. To Rhys' surprise, he realized that she had to stand on her tiptoes to be even with him, something she had never had to do.

He wrapped a hand around her waist and pulled her closer. Their lips touched. The previous day he had simply been overjoyed to see her and too preoccupied to relish her kiss. But now, fire blossomed between them rocking Rhys to his core. A desperate hunger that he had not felt in nearly two years roared to life. His grip on Kallen tightened, and he pulled her hard against him. Gasping, Kallen wrapped her arms around his face and neck and yielded to him, opening her mouth wider to deepen the kiss.

Stumbling slightly, Rhys bore her to the bed and climbed atop her, spreading her legs with his waist. He kissed her hard, tangling his hands in her hair before pulling away to gaze down at her. Panting, Kallen stared up at him, her skin glistening in the lamplight.

And suddenly he remembered doing this before.

He remembered straddling her for the first time in the crew's quarters aboard *Themis* and gazing down at her beautiful face in the dim light of a yellow lamp. He remembered the excitement he had felt and the yearning that swelled within him.

Smiling, he rested his forehead against hers and cradled her head.

"See? I told you you'd remember," she whispered, kissing his cheek. Rhys nodded. "Welcome home."

The Adventure Continues in…

RONAN OF SPACE

The Falkrow Narratives
Book III

Ronan Falkrow, son of the famed "Savior of Earth" Rhys Falkrow, has never really known his father—or cared to learn. At seventeen years old, Ronan is more concerned about maintaining his freedom and making a name for himself. Whether that's a good or bad name, he doesn't care.

But when Ronan and the rest of his family are suddenly swept out of Firekli per his father's instructions, the teen is thrown headlong into a foreign world of autonomous machines, silver-haired humans, and technology far beyond the scope of his imagination. And yet, the most upsetting new adjustment to his young life is not the sudden upheaval of his home, but the appearance of the Alphas, an advanced humanoid species threatening to sap Earth of its resources.

With his father's crew in danger and the world falling apart around him, Ronan must find his own path and walk outside his father's extraordinary shadow.

ACKNOWLEDGMENTS

Since the release of my first book, I've had a number of people randomly jump into various supporting roles and I'd like to recognize them for their enduring encouragement and wisdom.

To Wendy Lawson who talked me through the several medical-related procedures found throughout the book and provided in-depth information concerning treatments, alternative methods for care, and how to properly use tourniquets. Thank you, Wendy.

To Michael Smith who unknowingly uplifted me when doubt clouded my way and whose own passion for writing and storytelling encouraged me to push forward. Thank you, Mike.

To my husband, Dakota, for reading this book in its rawest form and meticulously picking it apart. Thank you, Husband.

ABOUT THE AUTHOR

Kara has been writing creatively since the young age of thirteen. It has always been her dream to become a prominent, young-adult author. Despite having written numerous manuscripts over the years, it wasn't until 2013 that Kara published her first novel, *The Empress' Consul.*

Kara graduated from the University of Arkansas in 2012 with an M.A. in Communication specializing in Intercultural Communication and ESL Education.

Kara lives in Arkansas with her husband, four furry children, and toddler. In her free time, she enjoys playing piano, hiking, playing video games with her husband, volunteering at the nearest library, and working on her next novel.

www.ingramcontent.com/pod-product-compliance
Lightning Source LLC
Chambersburg PA
CBHW020821030726
47496CB00001B/34